PRAISE FOR Clementine ™

"WALDEN'S KNACK FOR CHARACTER DEVELOPMENT AND UNIQUE PERSPECTIVE RESULT IN A TALE PERFECT FOR DIEHARD FANS OF THE WALKING DEAD, AS WELL AS NEWCOMERS."
-LIBRARY JOURNAL (Starred Review)

"TILLIE WALDEN IS THE FUTURE. HER BOLDLY AUTHENTIC VOICE BRINGS NEW HEIGHTS TO THE WORLD OF THE WALKING DEAD. I COULDN'T BE MORE PROUD OF WHAT SHE'S DOING WITH THIS SERIES."
-ROBERT KIRKMAN (THE WALKING DEAD, INVINCIBLE)

"TILLIE WALDEN IS ONE OF THE MOST EXTRAORDINARY ARTISTS WORKING TODAY, AND HER STORYTELLING TALENT SHINES ON EVERY PAGE OF THIS TENSE, HEARTBREAKING, AND EPIC THRILLER. CLEMENTINE WILL HAVE YOU TURNING PAGES LATE INTO THE NIGHT, HEART IN YOUR THROAT, DESPERATELY URGING THE CHARACTERS TO SURVIVE. AN INCREDIBLE WORK."
-MARIE LU (#1 New York Times bestselling author of Skyhunter)

"WITH CLEMENTINE, BELOVED CARTOONIST TILLIE WALDEN BLOWS OPEN THE WALKING DEAD UNIVERSE WITH A STORY FULL OF BLOSSOMING RELATIONSHIPS IN THE SHADOW OF WINTERY DEATH. IT'S OMINOUS AND MAGICAL AND WILL HAVE YOU CRAVING MORE WHEN THE FINAL PAGE TURNS."
-CHIP ZDARSKY (Daredevil, Batman)

"TILLIE PAINTS THE GRIM WITH THE LUSH, THE DARK WITH THE SOARING. GRITTY AND RAW, CLEMENTINE IS A BEATING HEART."
-NGOZI UKAZU (Check, Please!)

"TILLIE WALDEN'S CLEMENTINE IS GORGEOUS AND GUTTING. EVEN AS A NEWCOMER TO THE UNIVERSE OF THE WALKING DEAD, I FOUND WALDEN'S WORK TO BE A COMPLETE AND CAPTIVATING EXPERIENCE. I COULDN'T PUT IT DOWN "
-TRUNG LE NGUYEN (T

"CLEMENTINE BRINGS ITS OWN DISTINCT VOICE, STYLE, AND SENSIBILITY TO THE WALKING DEAD UNIVERSE, WHICH IS QUITE A FEAT ON ITS OWN. ON TOP OF THAT, IT'S AN EXQUISITELY DRAWN STORY ABOUT HOW TO SURVIVE TRAUMA AND FIND STRENGTH IN OURSELVES AND OTHERS."

-KELLY SUE DeCONNICK (*Captain Marvel*)

"CLEMENTINE IS AN ARRESTING EXPLORATION OF TRAUMA, COMMUNITY, AND HOPE, DEVASTATINGLY RENDERED IN TILLIE WALDEN'S SIGNATURE STYLE. A TRIUMPH OF THE ZOMBIE GENRE."

-SHANNON WATTERS (*Lumberjanes*)

"TILLIE WALDEN'S BITTERSWEET, CHARACTER-DRIVEN ZOMBIE STORY ABOUT THE TRAVELS OF CLEMENTINE IN THE WALKING DEAD UNIVERSE IS INTROSPECTIVE, HAUNTING, AND GORGEOUSLY DRAWN."

-KRISTEN GUDSNUK (*Making Friends*)

"THIS IS A FANTASTICALLY GRITTY, COMING-OF-AGE TALE STARRING MY ABSOLUTE FAVORITE HEROINE FROM THE WALKING DEAD SERIES. THE STARK VISUALS AND HEAVY ATMOSPHERE DRAW YOU IN AND MAKE YOU FEEL AS IF YOU ARE A PART OF THE STRUGGLE, FIGHTING AND SURVIVING ALONGSIDE CLEMENTINE AS SHE OVERCOMES LOSS AND FINDS NEW HOPE ON HER JOURNEY."

-MICHELLE FUS (AVA'S DEMON)

"A TOUCHING, COMING-OF-AGE STORY OF HOPE IN THE DARKEST TIMES."

-MAIRGHREAD SCOTT (SEA SERPENT'S HEIR)

"DESPITE STEELING MYSELF FOR TILLIE WALDEN'S ZOMBIE APOCALYPSE, I WAS FULL OF EQUAL PARTS DREAD AND HOPE ON EVERY SINGLE PAGE -- I COULDN'T PUT CLEMENTINE DOWN UNTIL I'D SEEN HER TERSE, POIGNANT JOURNEY THROUGH."

-IRMA KNIVIILA (EVERYDAY HERO MACHINE BOY)

"A POIGNANT WALKING DEAD COMING-OF-AGE STORY, TOLD THROUGH THE EYES OF ONE THE MOST LAYERED AND COMPLEX CHARACTERS IN THE SERIES. SIMULTANEOUSLY BRUTAL AND TENDER."

-TRI VUONG (EVERYDAY HERO MACHINE BOY, LEGO® NINJAGO®: GARMADON)

"TILLIE WALDEN'S CLEMENTINE ASKS A DIFFICULT QUESTION: CAN HONEST, TRUE INNOCENCE SURVIVE THE END OF THE WORLD? A HARD AND REWARDING READ. JUST AMAZING."

-PABLO TUNICA (SEA SERPENT'S HEIR)

Clementine

SKYBOUND
COMET

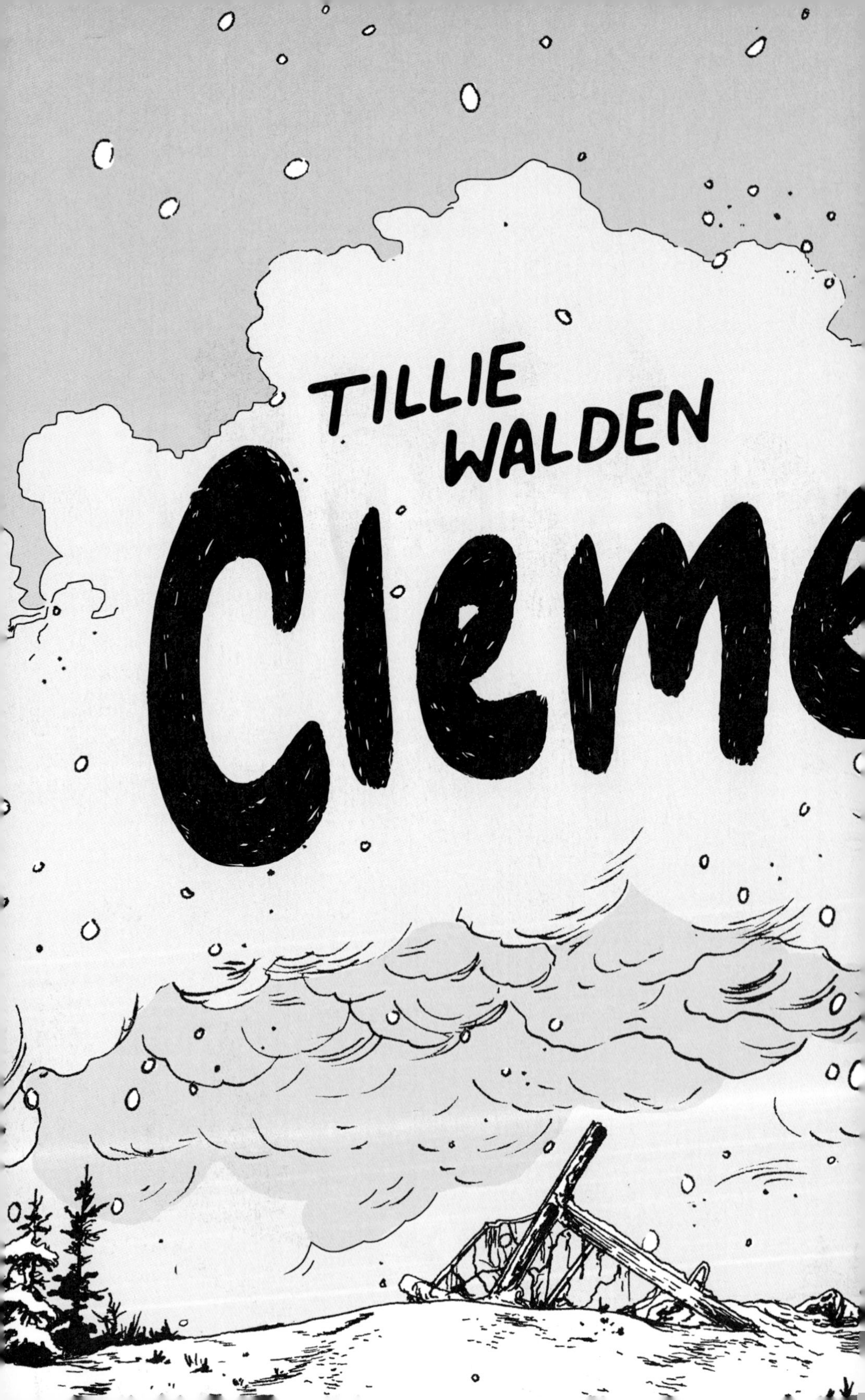
TILLIE
WALDEN
Cleme

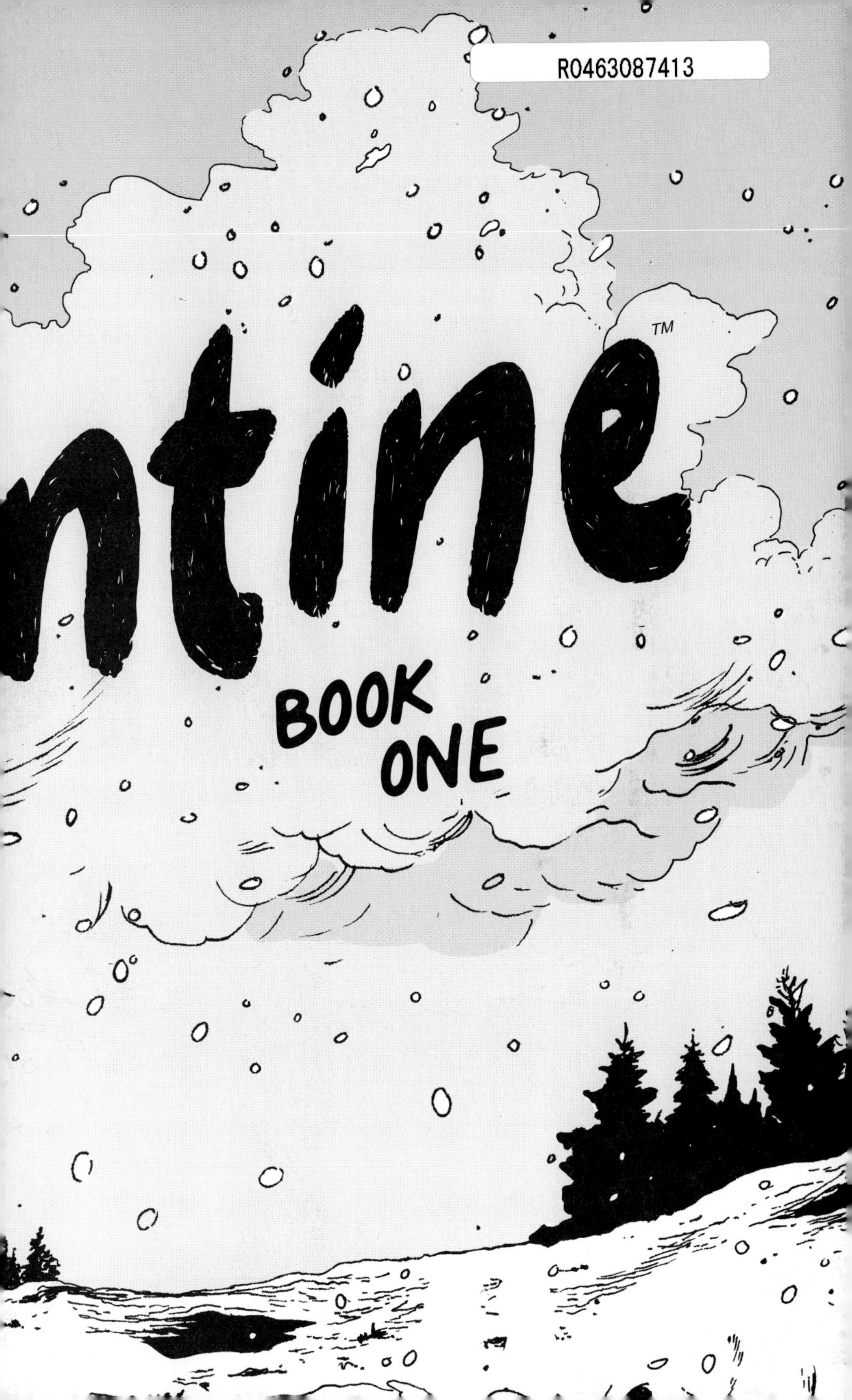

ntine™
BOOK ONE

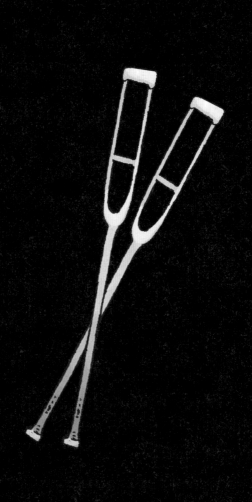

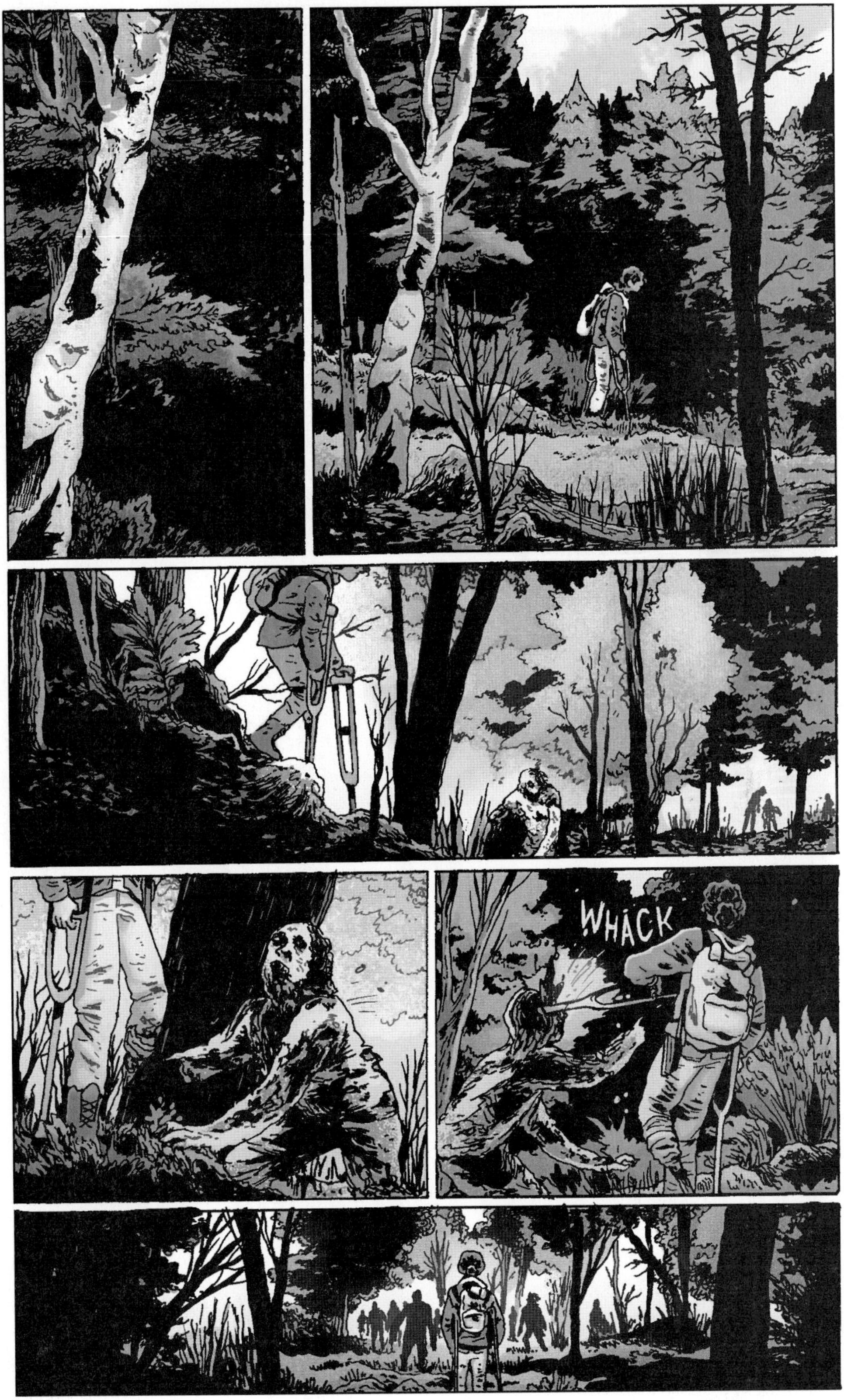
WHACK

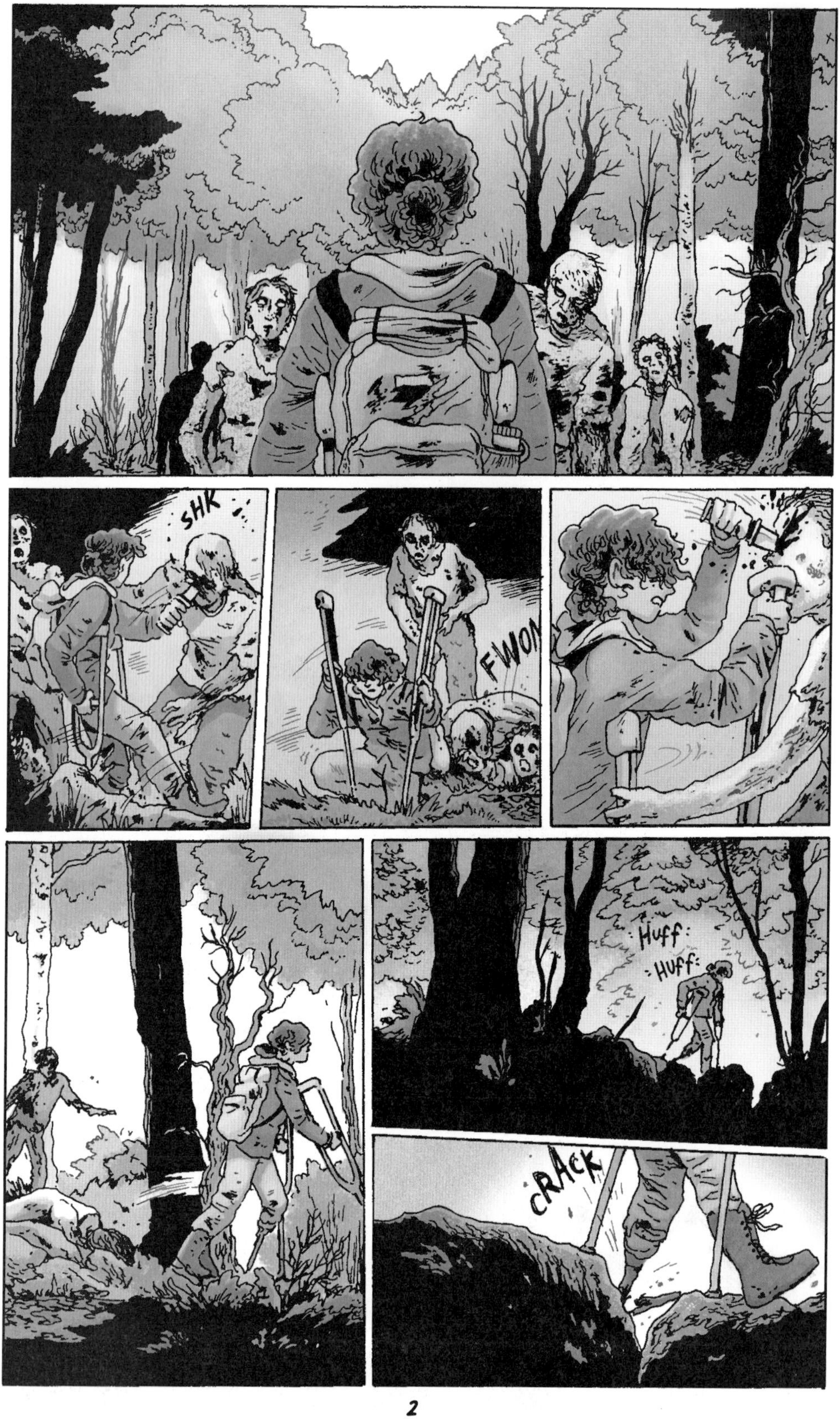
SHK
FWOM
HUFF
HUFF
CRACK

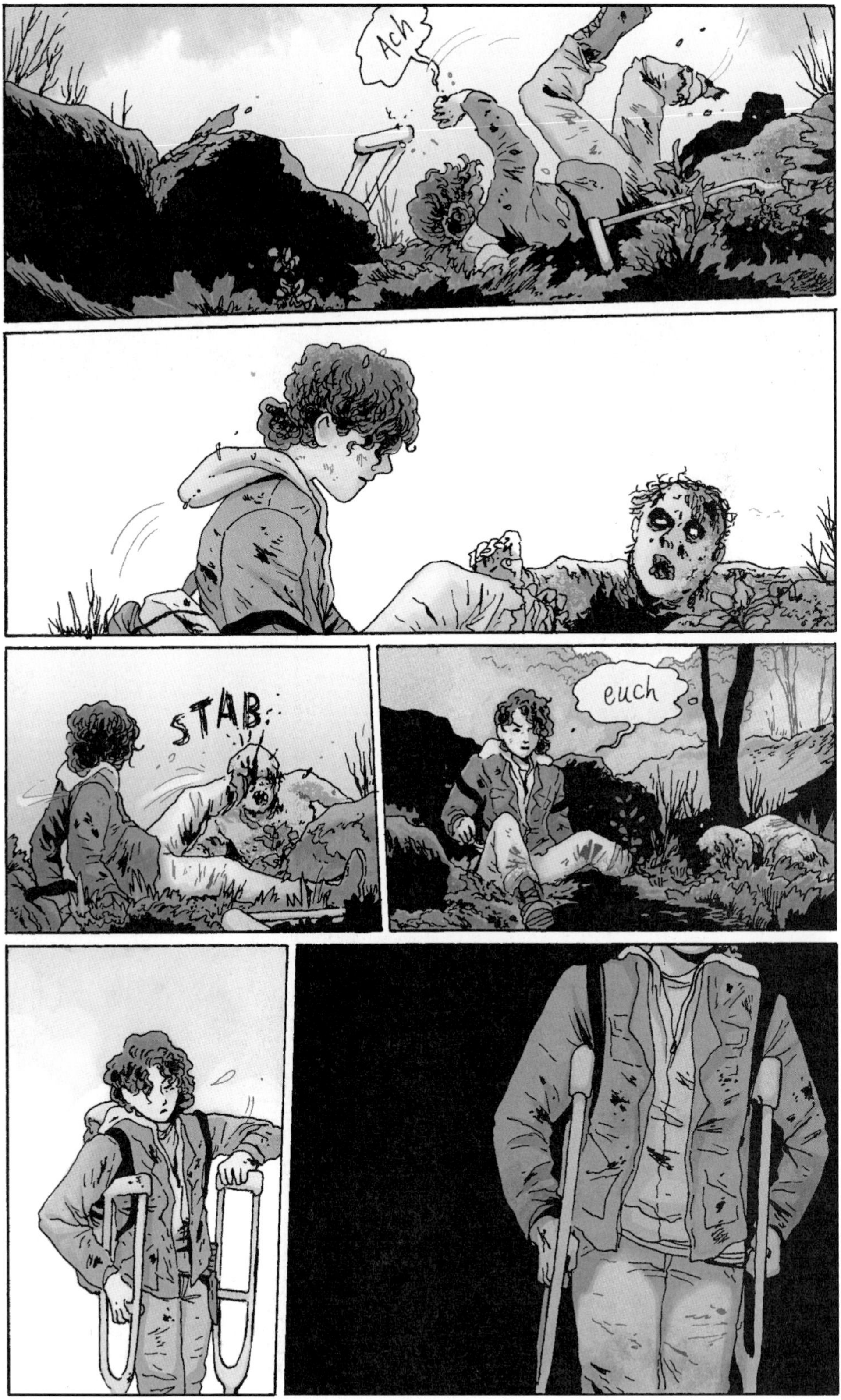
Ach
STAB
euch

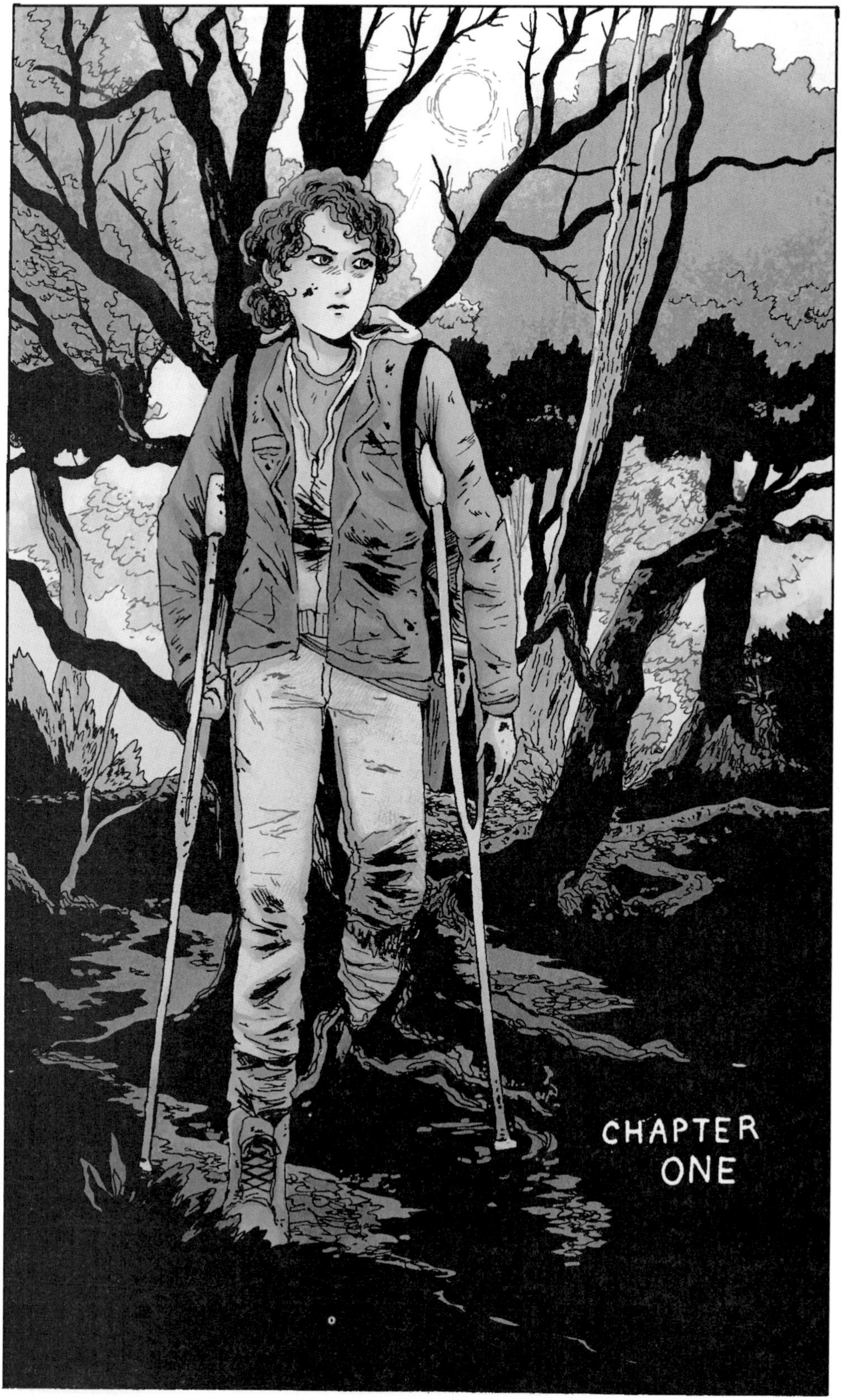
CHAPTER
ONE

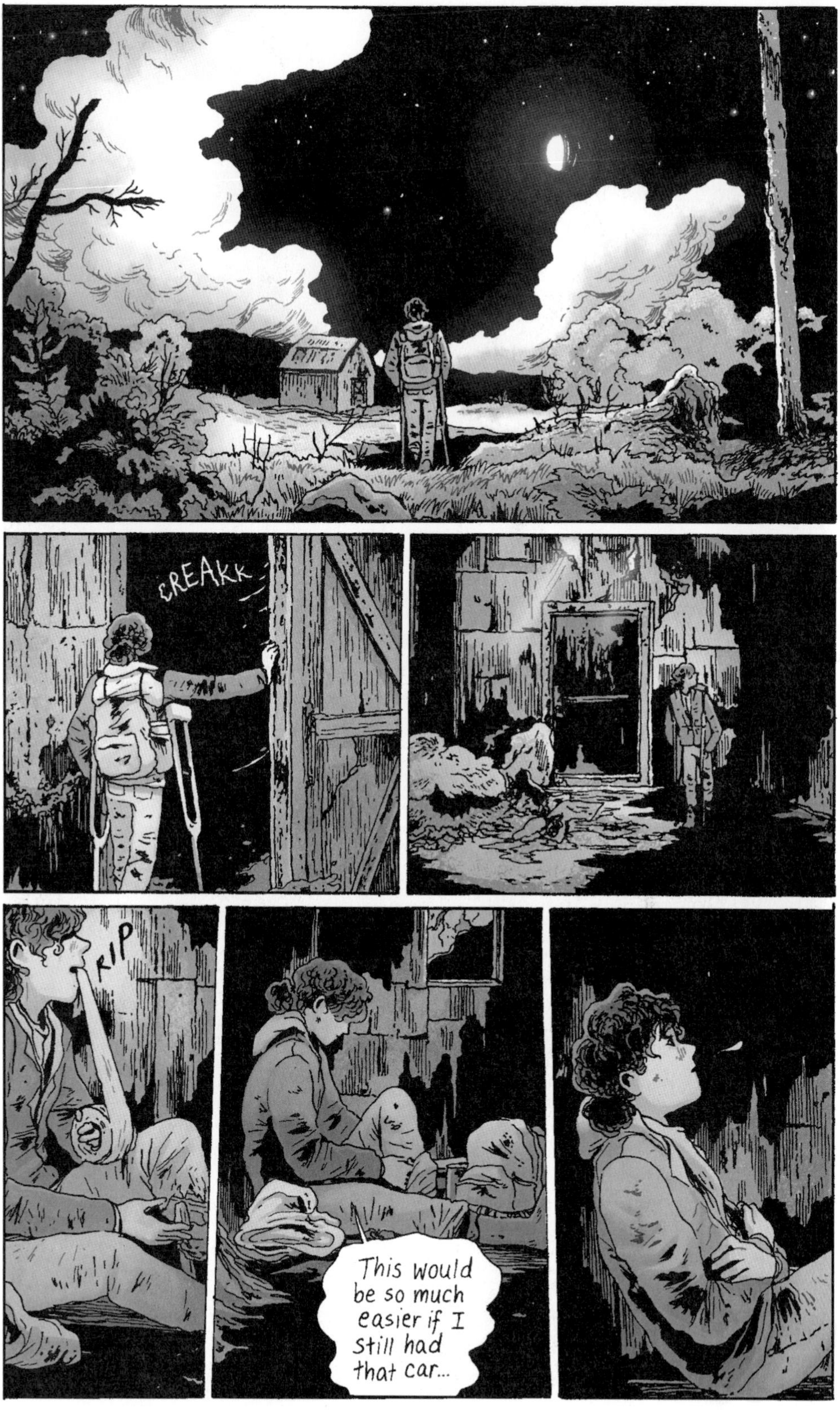
CREAKK
RIP
This would be so much easier if I still had that car...

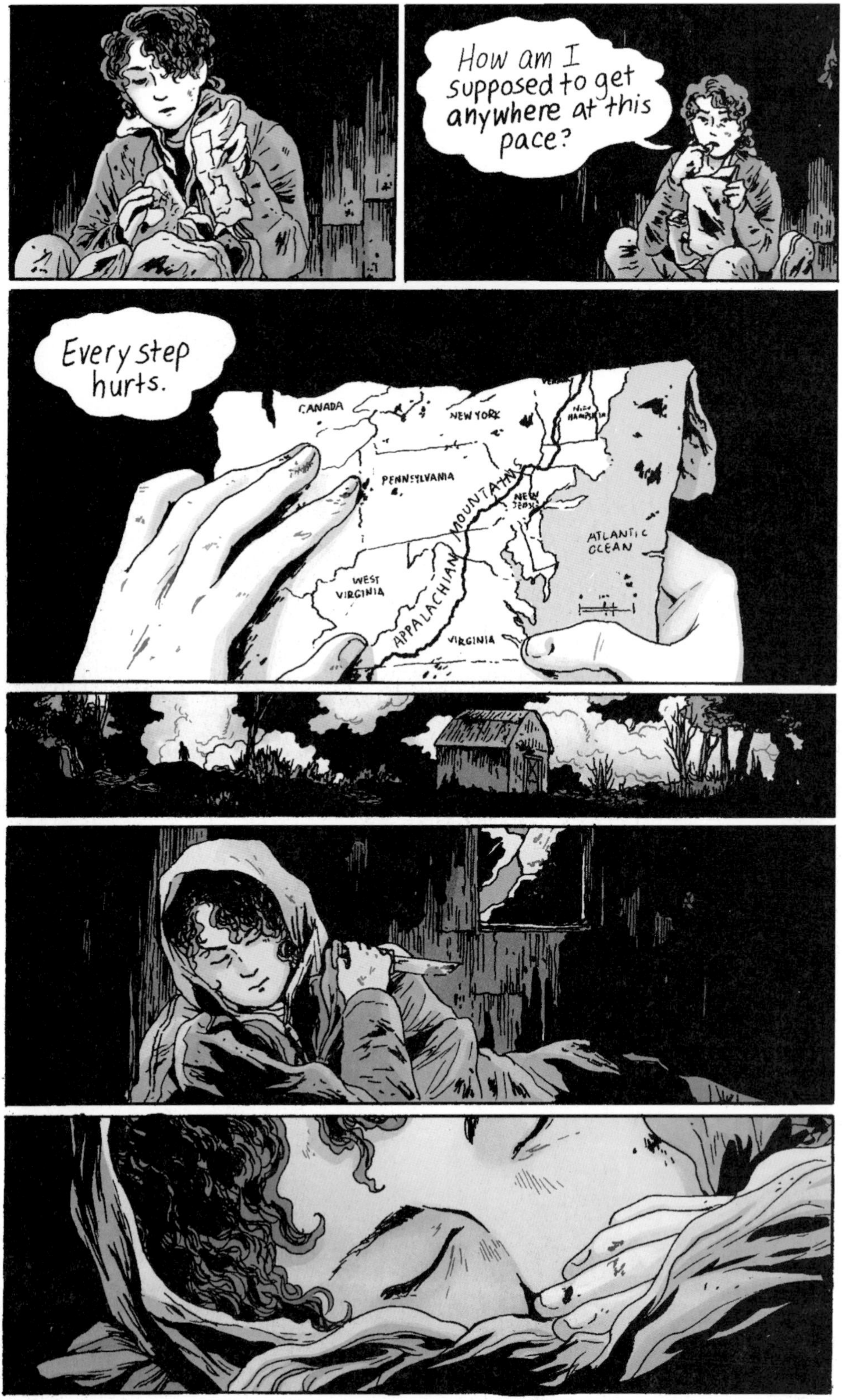
How am I supposed to get anywhere at this pace?
Every step hurts.
CANADA
NEW YORK
PENNSYLVANIA
APPALACHIAN MOUNTAINS
ATLANTIC OCEAN
WEST VIRGINIA
VIRGINIA

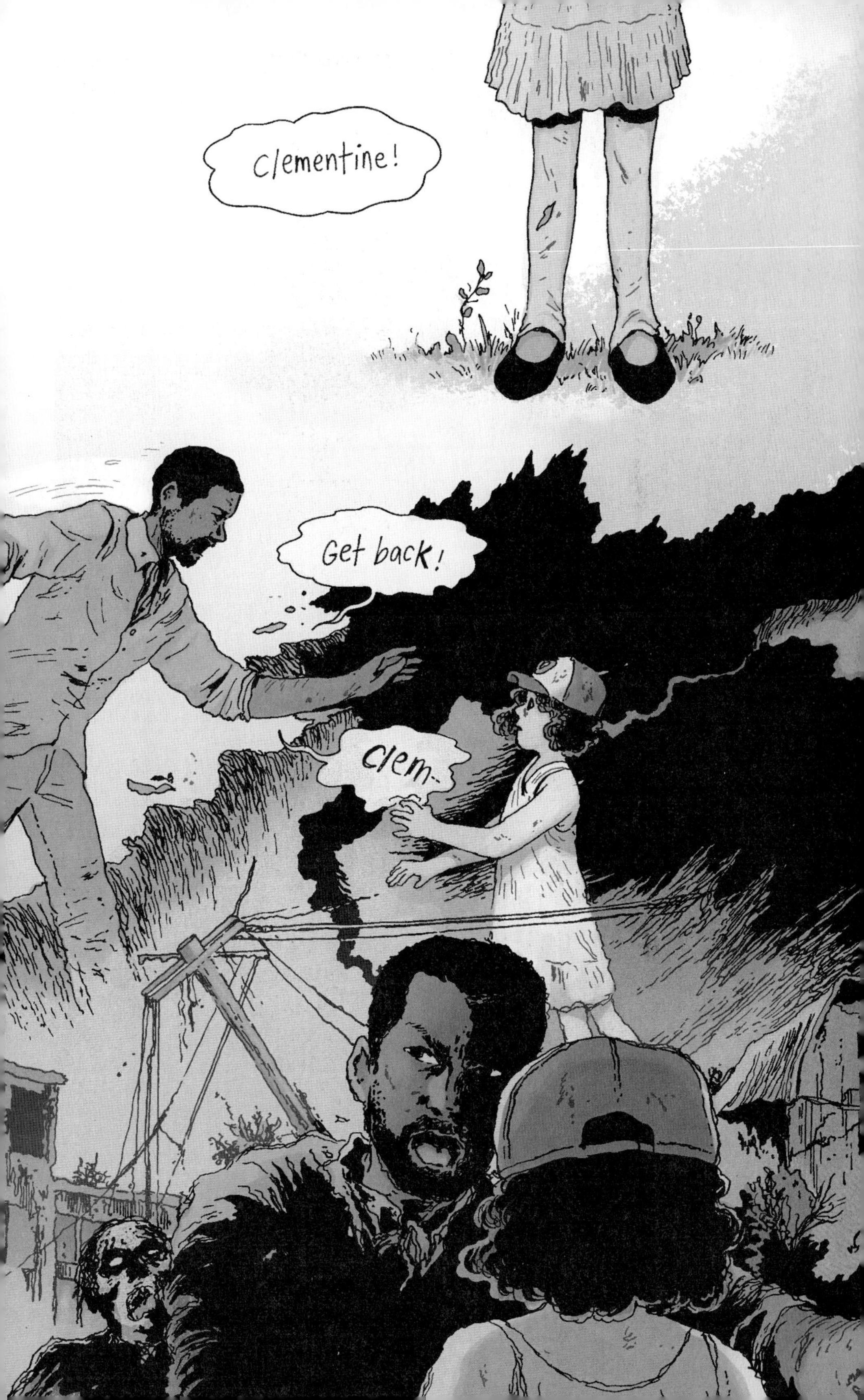
Clementine!
Get back!
Clem-

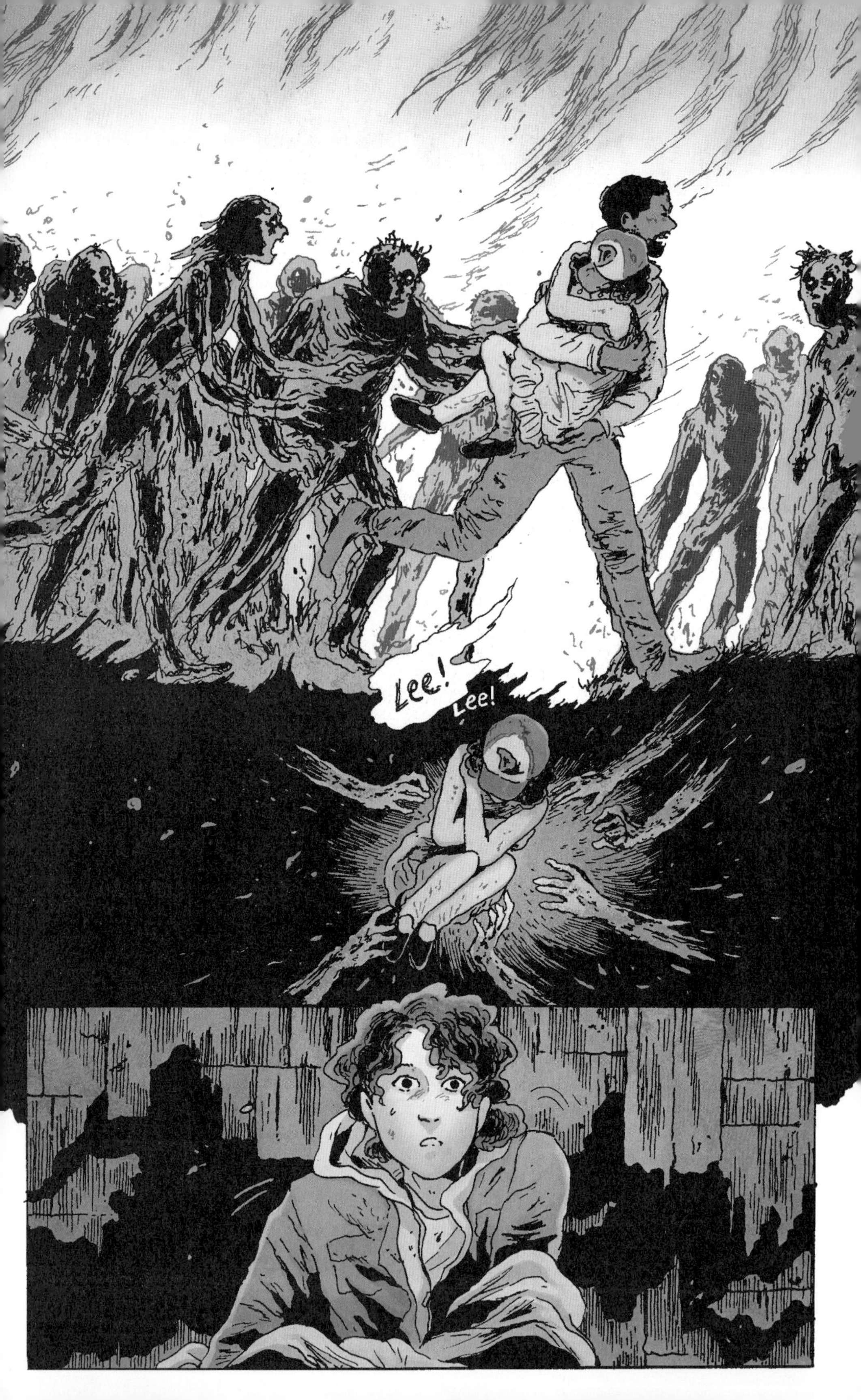
Lee!
Lee!

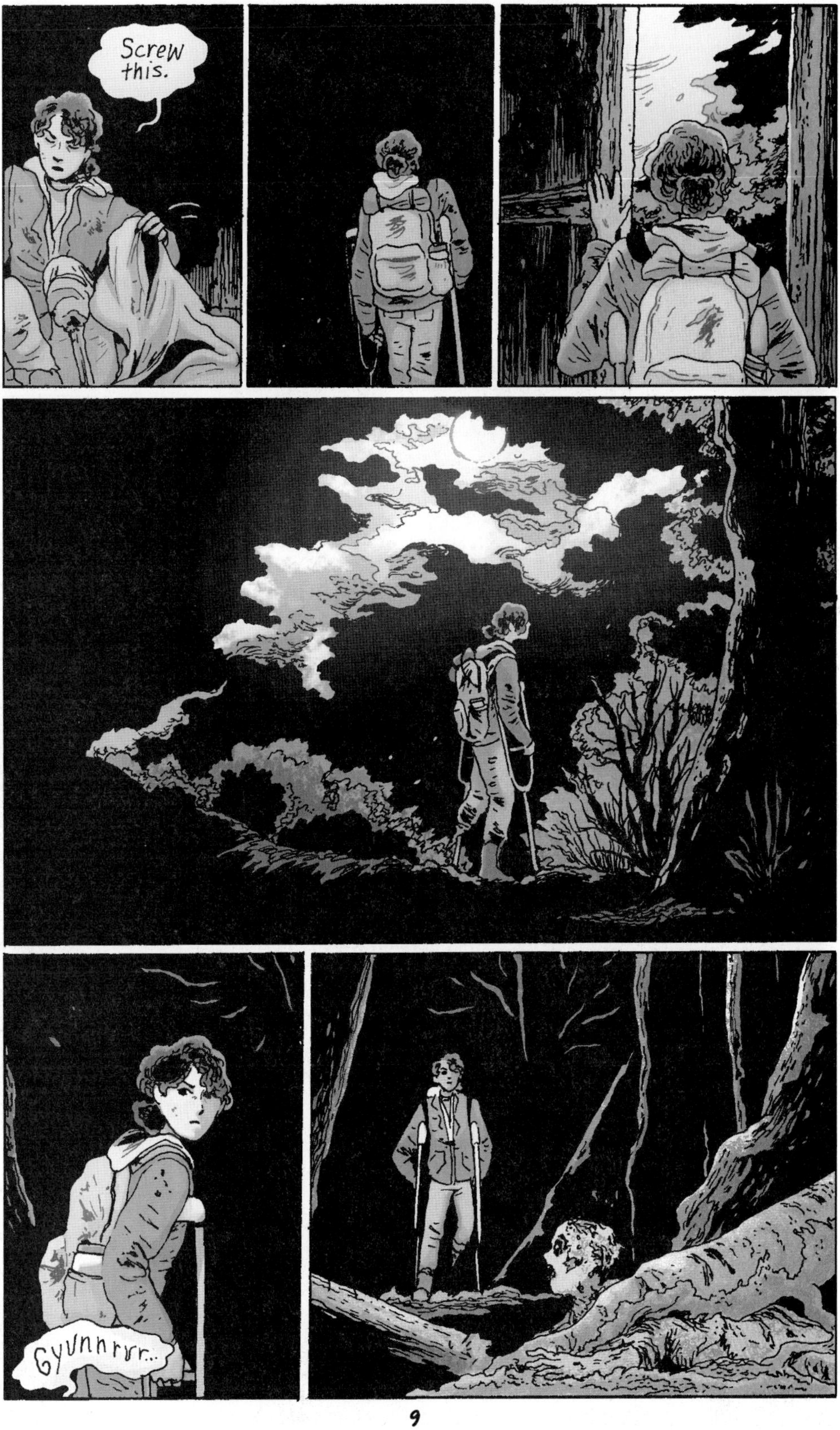
Screw this.
Gyunnrrr...

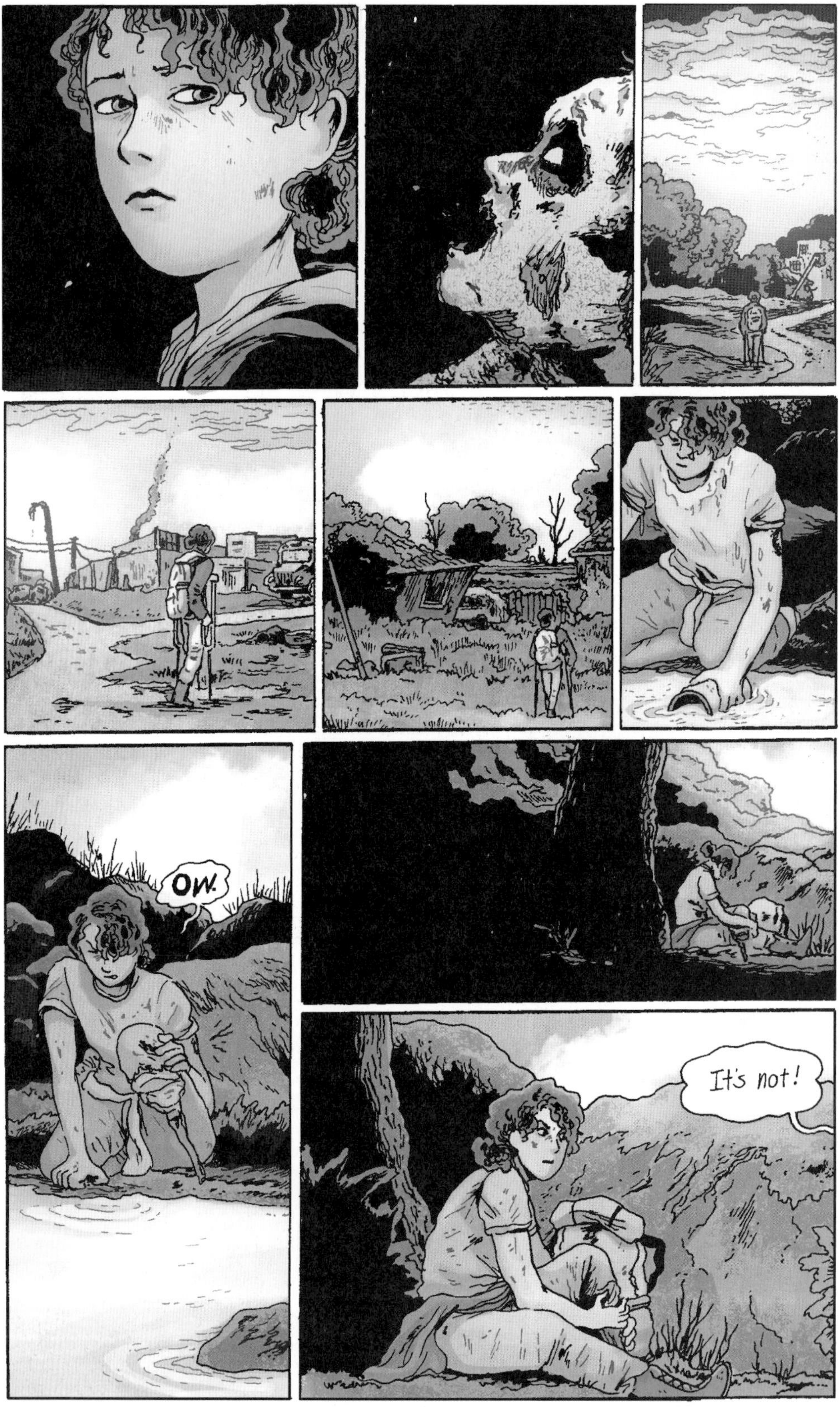
OW.
It's not!

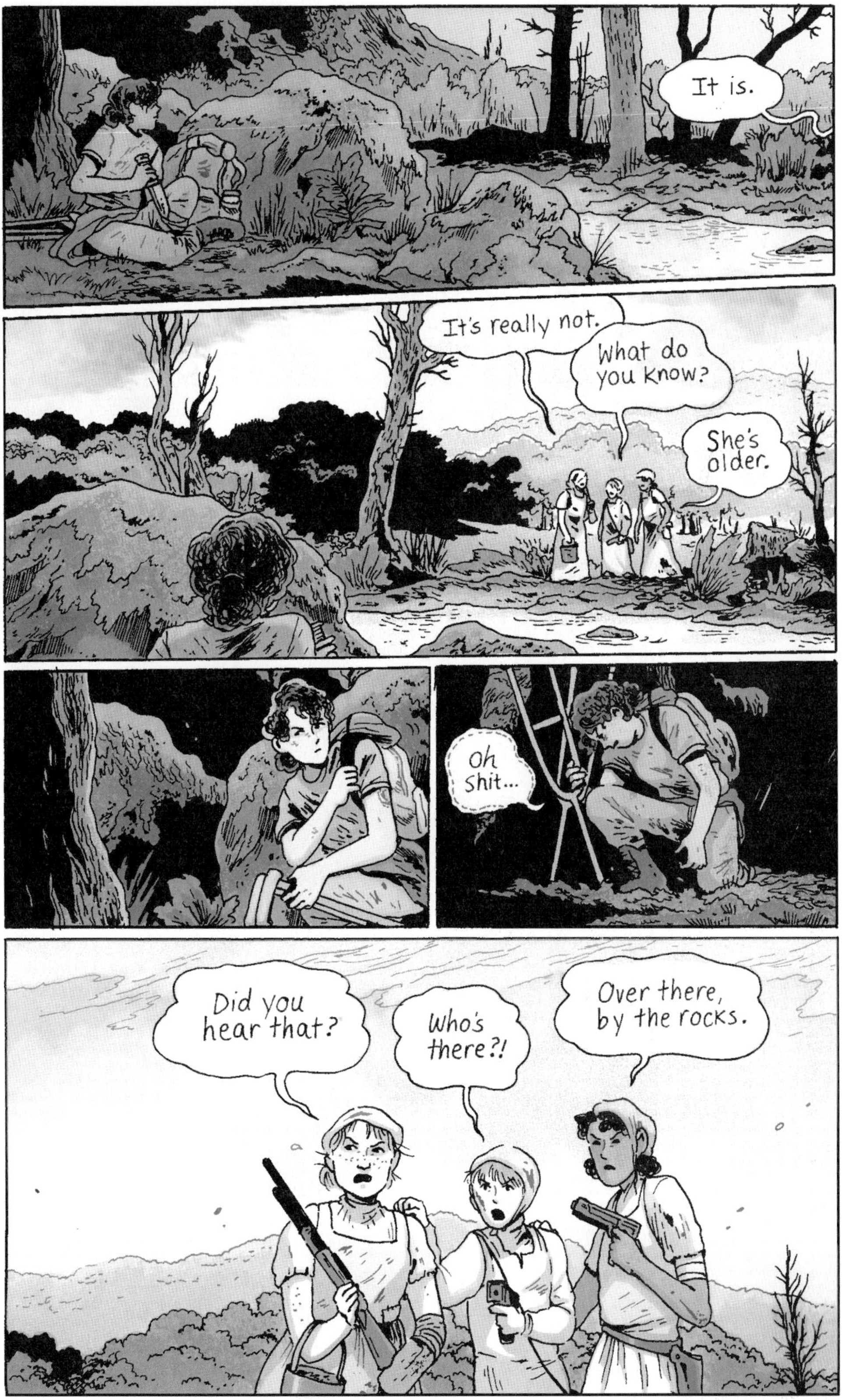
It is.
It's really not.
What do you know?
She's older.
Oh shit...
Did you hear that?
Who's there?!
Over there, by the rocks.

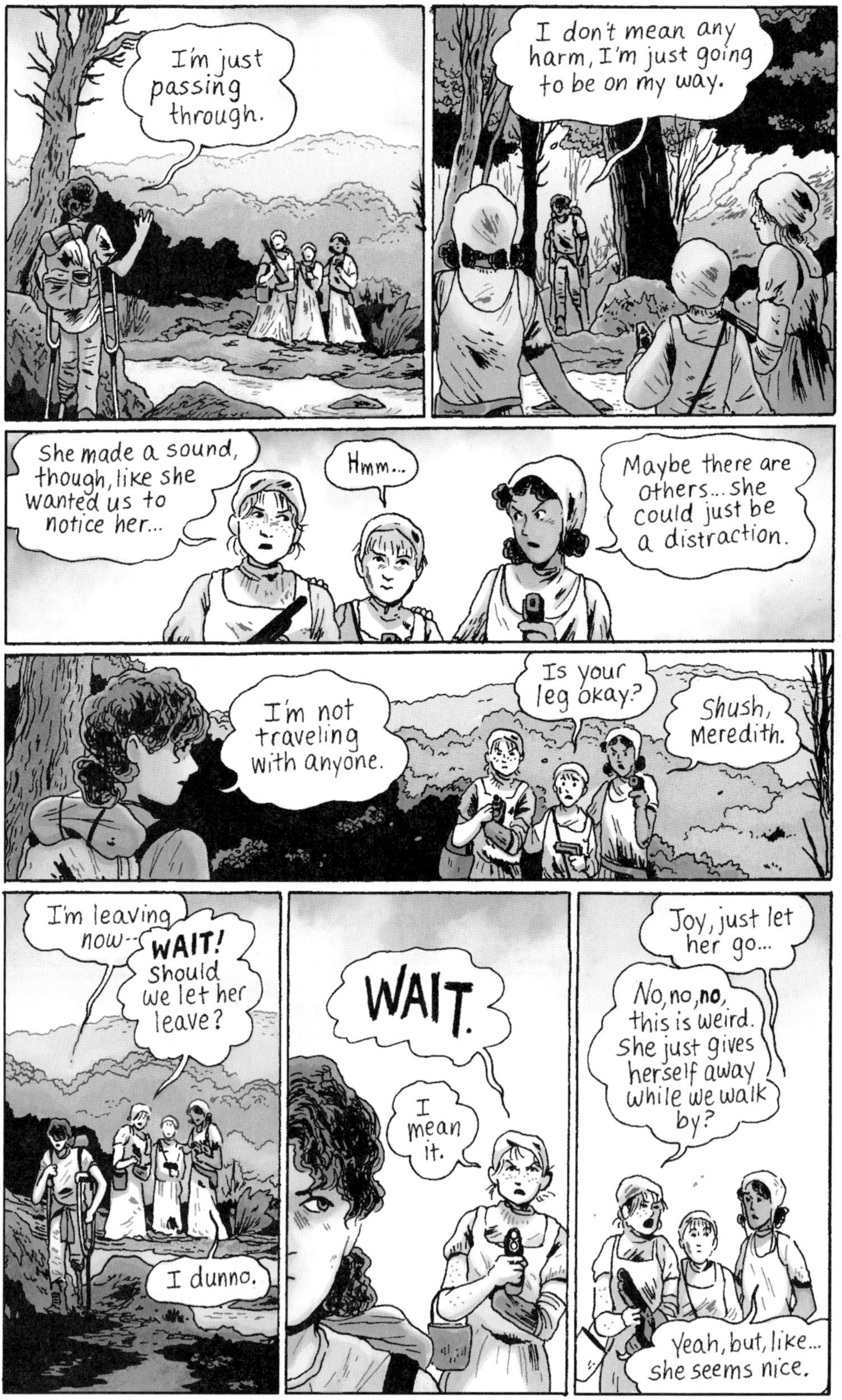
I'm just passing through.
I don't mean any harm, I'm just going to be on my way.
She made a sound, though, like she wanted us to notice her...
Hmm...
Maybe there are others... she could just be a distraction.
I'm not traveling with anyone.
Is your leg okay?
Shush, Meredith.
I'm leaving now--
WAIT! Should we let her leave?
I dunno.
WAIT.
I mean it.
Joy, just let her go...
No, no, no, this is weird. She just gives herself away while we walk by?
Yeah, but, like... she seems nice.

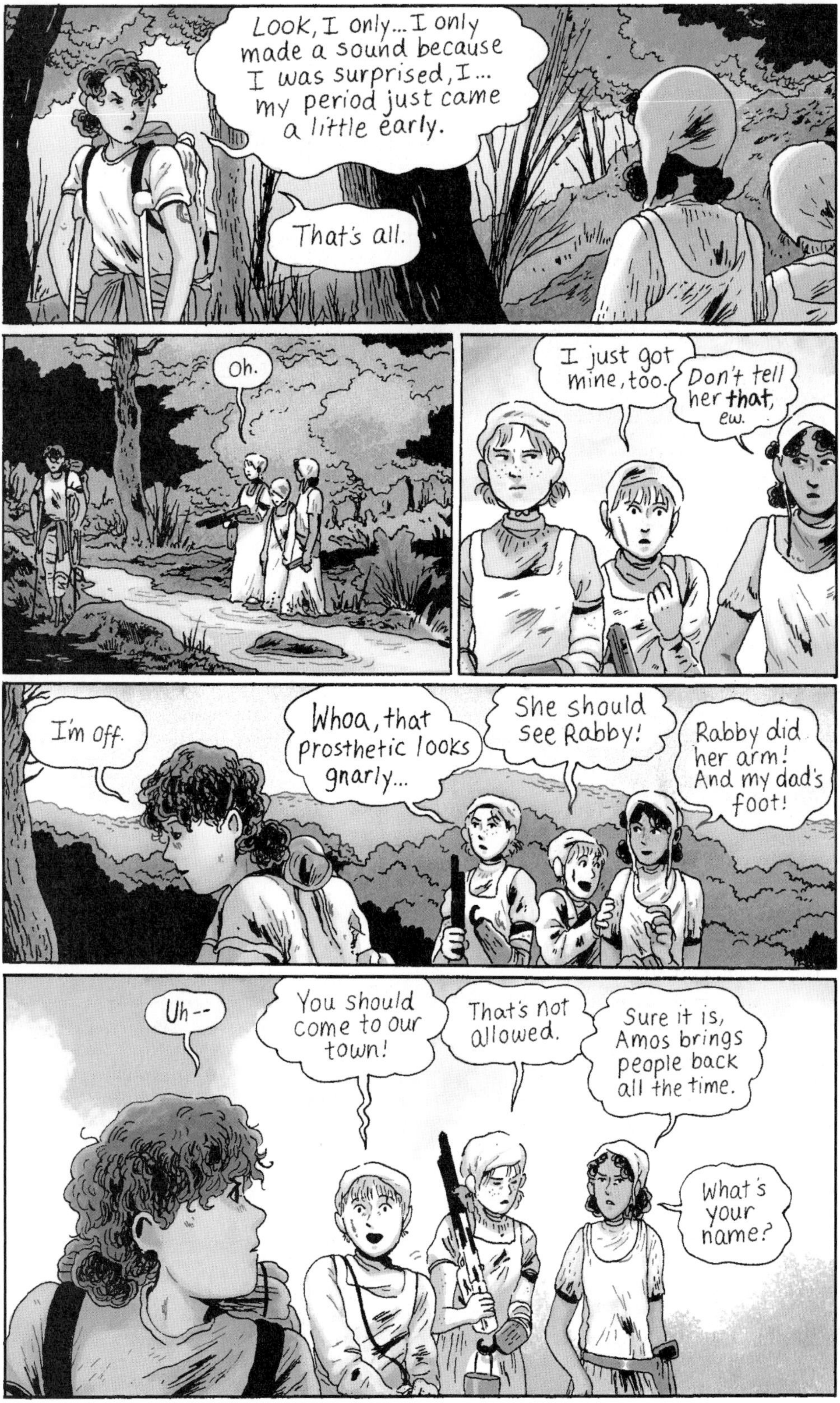
LOOK, I only... I only made a sound because I was surprised, I... my period just came a little early.
That's all.
Oh.
I just got mine, too.
Don't tell her **that**, ew.
I'm off.
Whoa, that prosthetic looks gnarly...
She should see Rabby!
Rabby did her arm! And my dad's foot!
Uh--
You should come to our town!
That's not allowed.
Sure it is, Amos brings people back all the time.
What's your name?

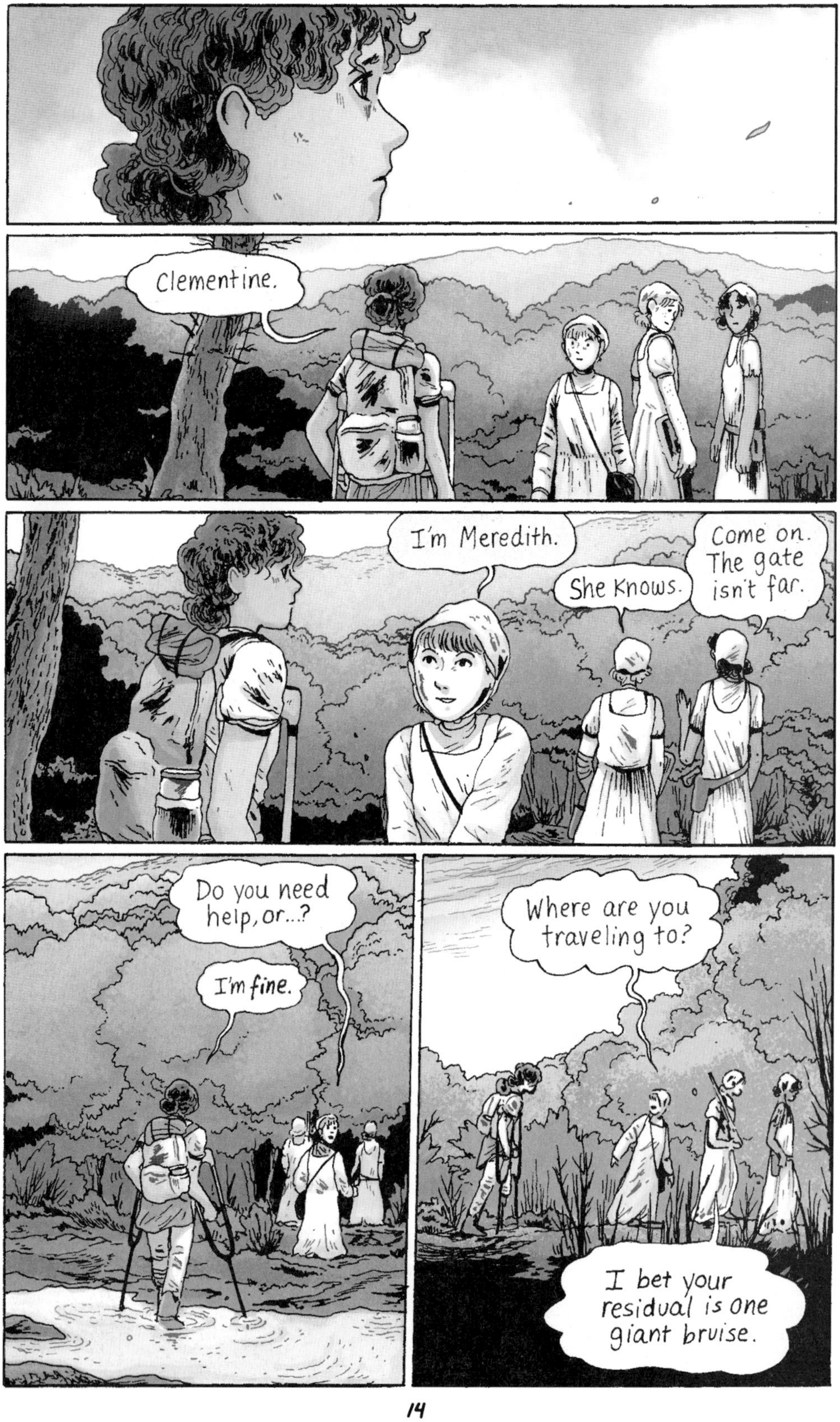
Clementine.
I'm Meredith.
She knows.
Come on. The gate isn't far.
Do you need help, or...?
I'm *fine*.
Where are you traveling to?
I bet your residual is one giant bruise.

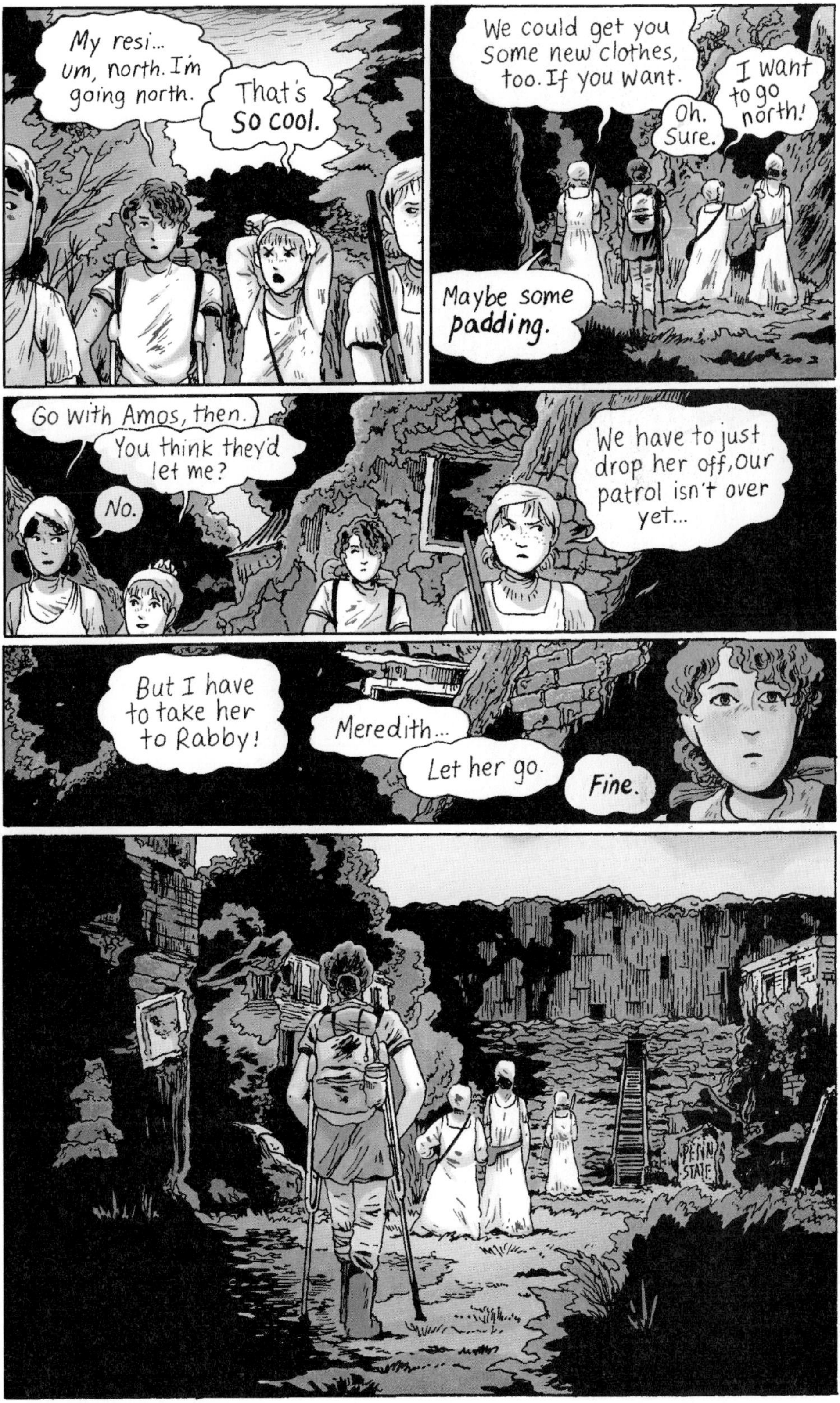
My resi... um, north. I'm going north.
That's So cool.
We could get you some new clothes, too. If you want.
Oh. Sure.
I want to go north!
Maybe some padding.
Go with Amos, then.
You think they'd let me?
No.
We have to just drop her off, our patrol isn't over yet...
But I have to take her to Rabby!
Meredith...
Let her go.
Fine.
PENN STATE

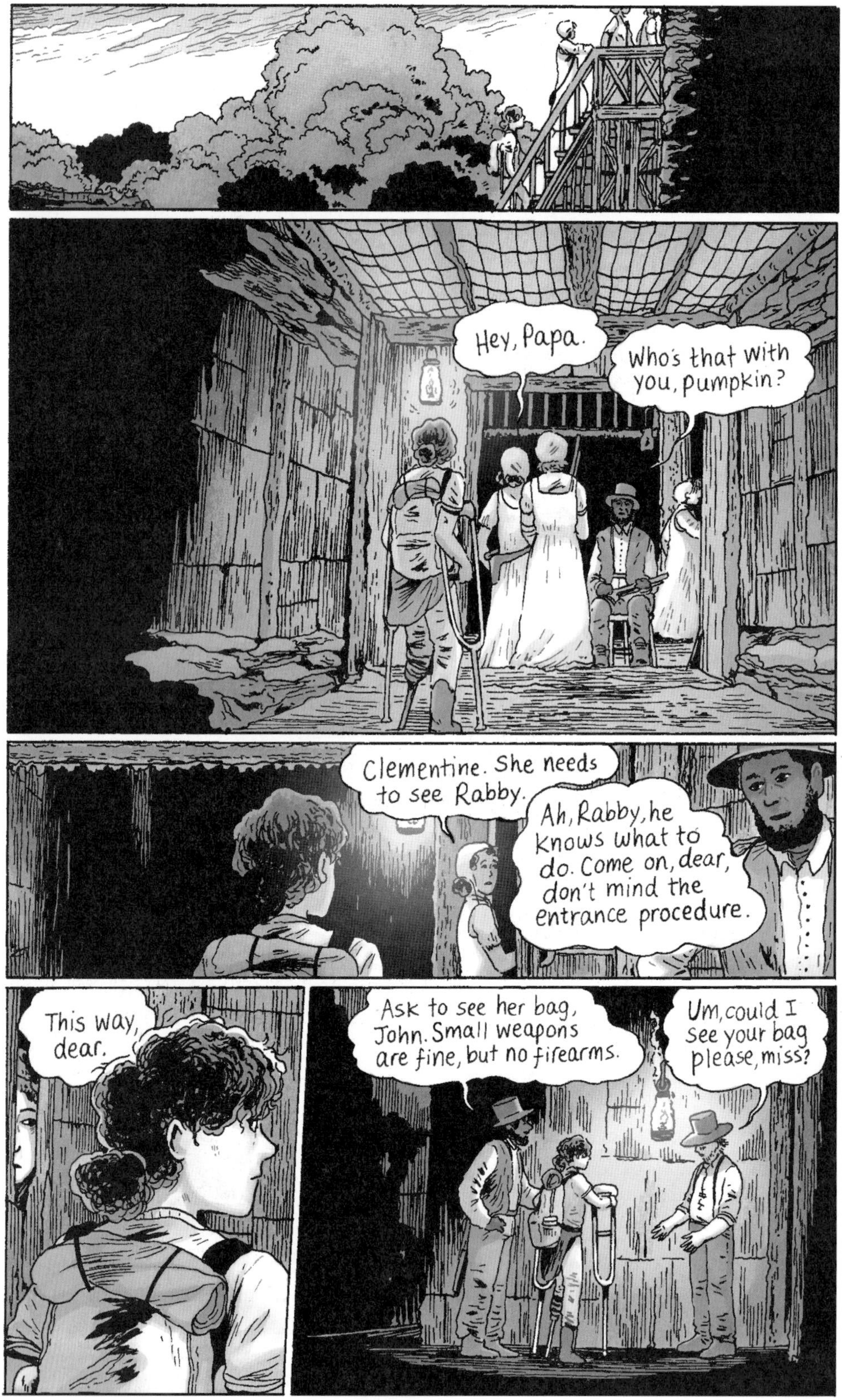
Hey, Papa.
Who's that with you, pumpkin?
Clementine. She needs to see Rabby.
Ah, Rabby, he knows what to do. Come on, dear, don't mind the entrance procedure.
This way, dear.
Ask to see her bag, John. Small weapons are fine, but no firearms.
Um, could I see your bag please, miss?

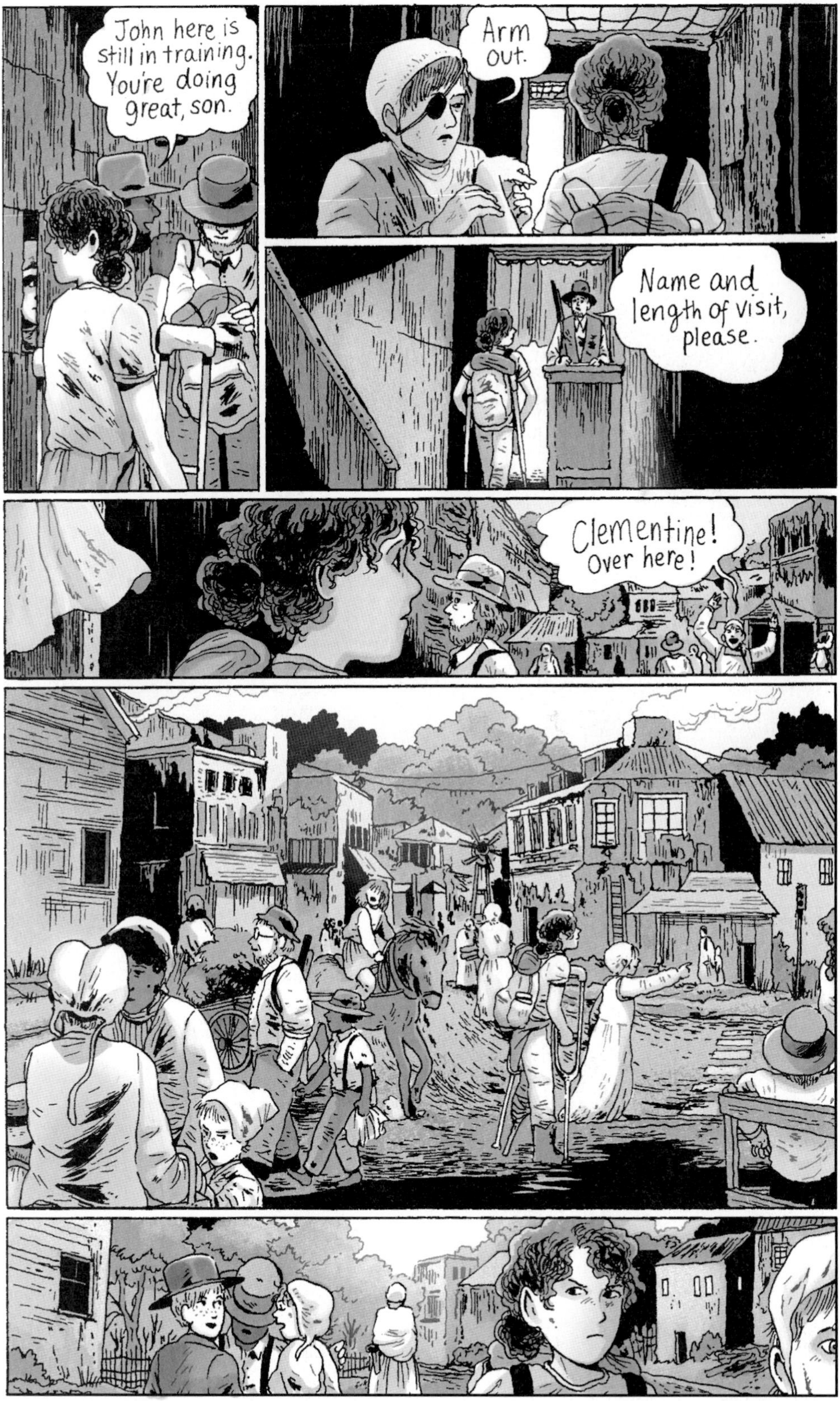
John here is still in training. You're doing great, son.
Arm out.
Name and length of visit, please.
Clementine! Over here!

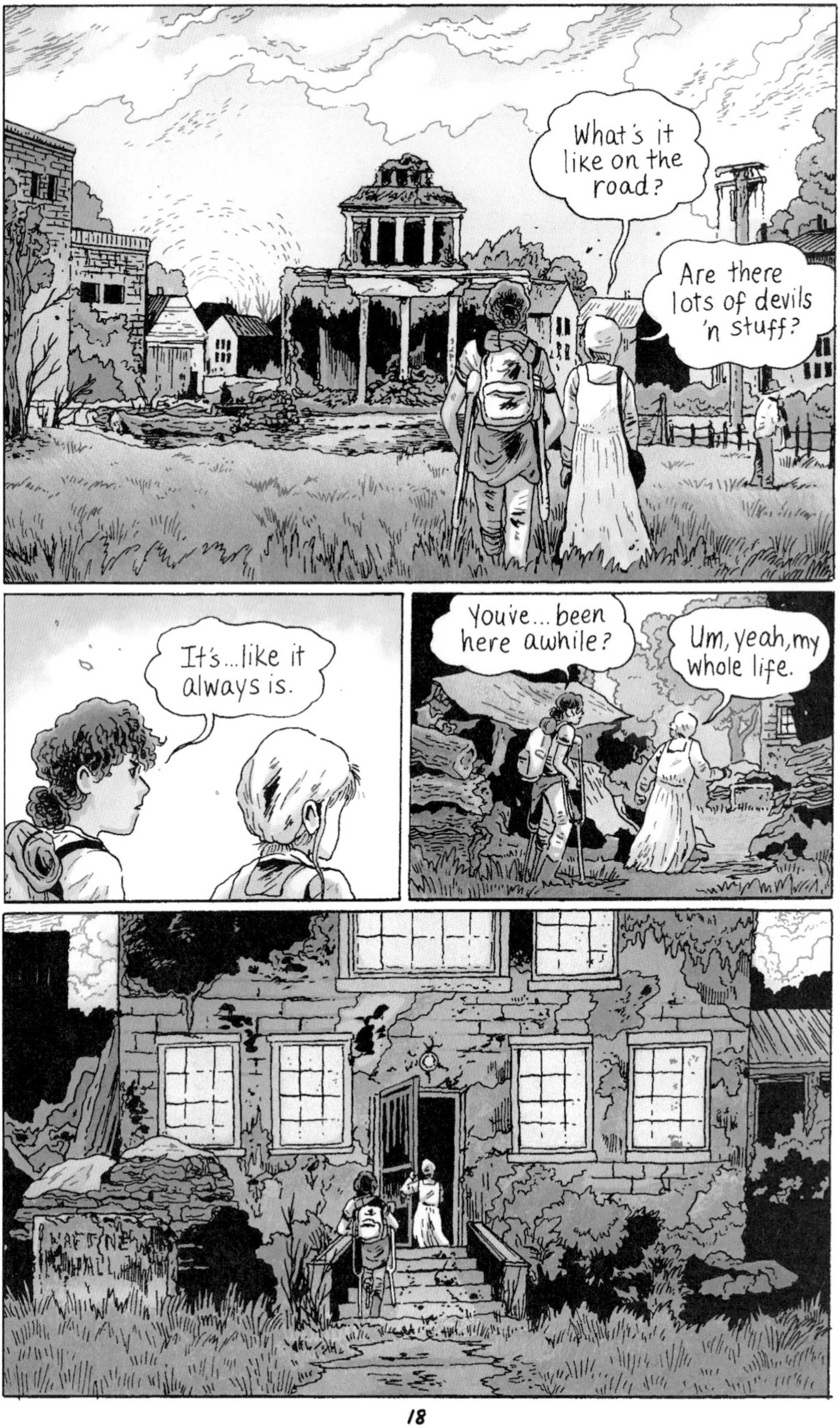
What's it like on the road?
Are there lots of devils 'n stuff?
It's...like it always is.
You've... been here awhile?
Um, yeah, my whole life.

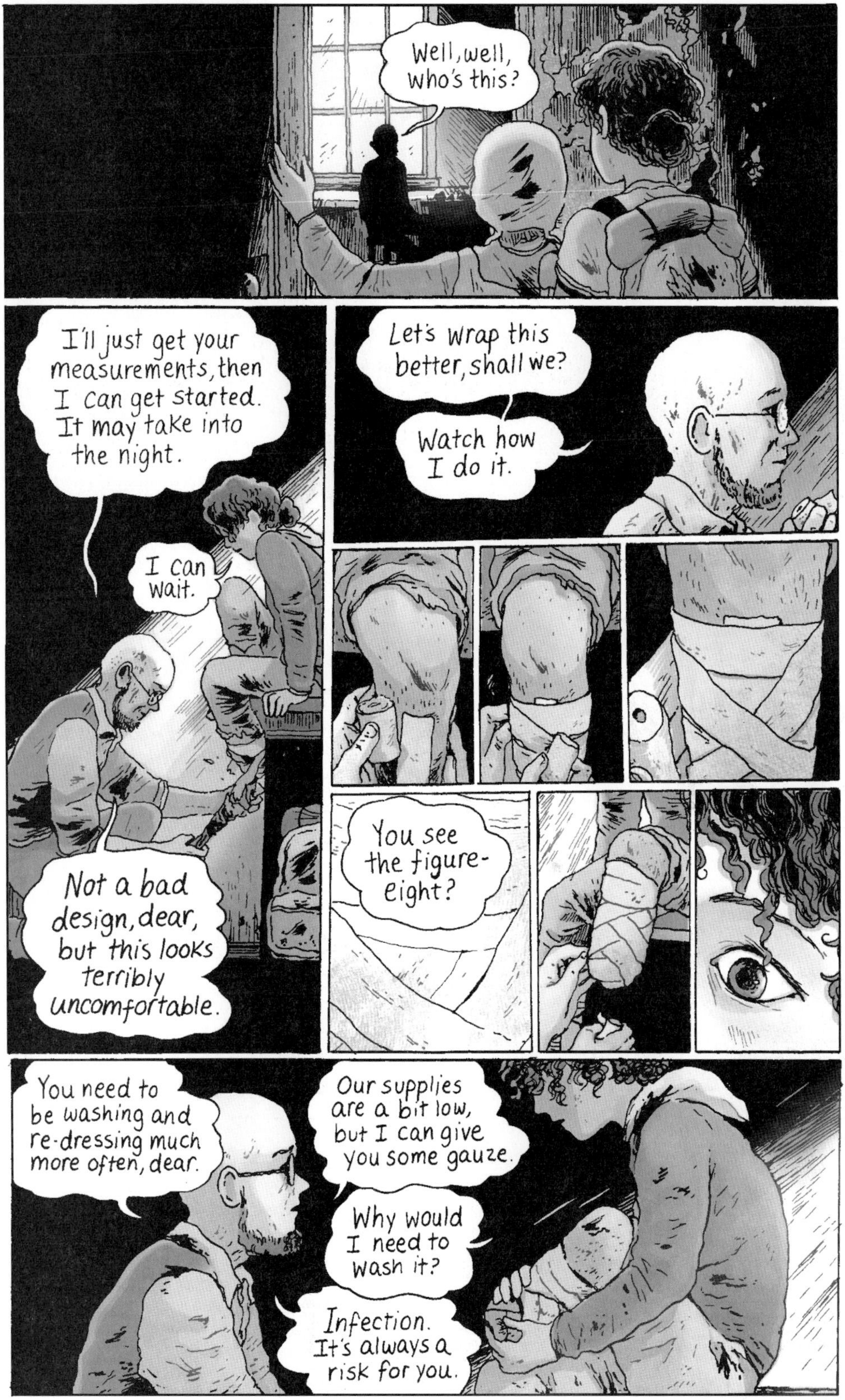
Well, well, who's this?
I'll just get your measurements, then I can get started. It may take into the night.
I can wait.
Not a bad design, dear, but this looks terribly uncomfortable.
Let's wrap this better, shall we?
Watch how I do it.
You see the figure-eight?
You need to be washing and re-dressing much more often, dear.
Our supplies are a bit low, but I can give you some gauze.
Why would I need to wash it?
Infection. It's always a risk for you.

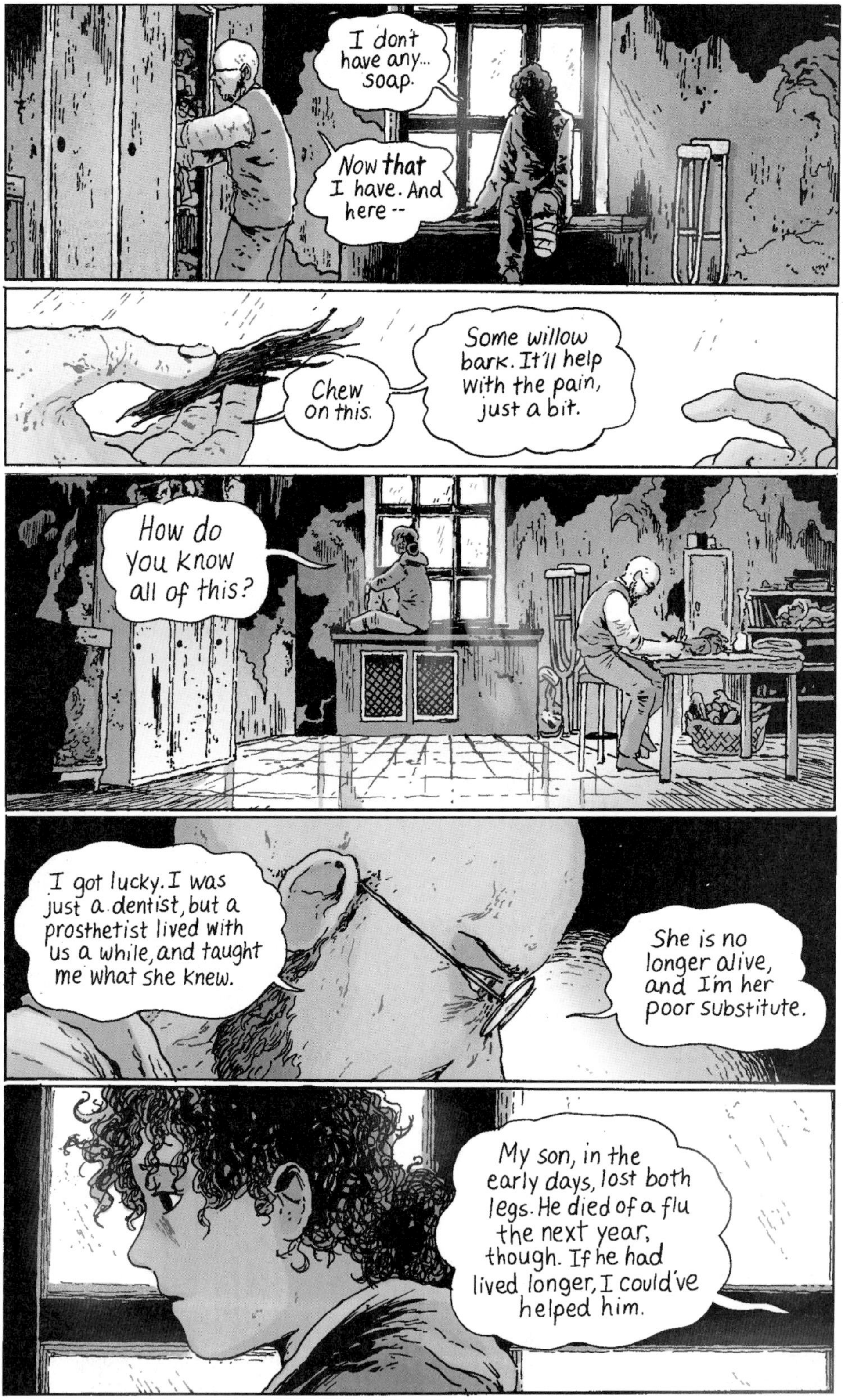

I don't have any... soap.
Now that I have. And here --
Chew on this.
Some willow bark. It'll help with the pain, just a bit.
How do you know all of this?
I got lucky. I was just a dentist, but a prosthetist lived with us a while, and taught me what she knew.
She is no longer alive, and I'm her poor substitute.
My son, in the early days, lost both legs. He died of a flu the next year, though. If he had lived longer, I could've helped him.

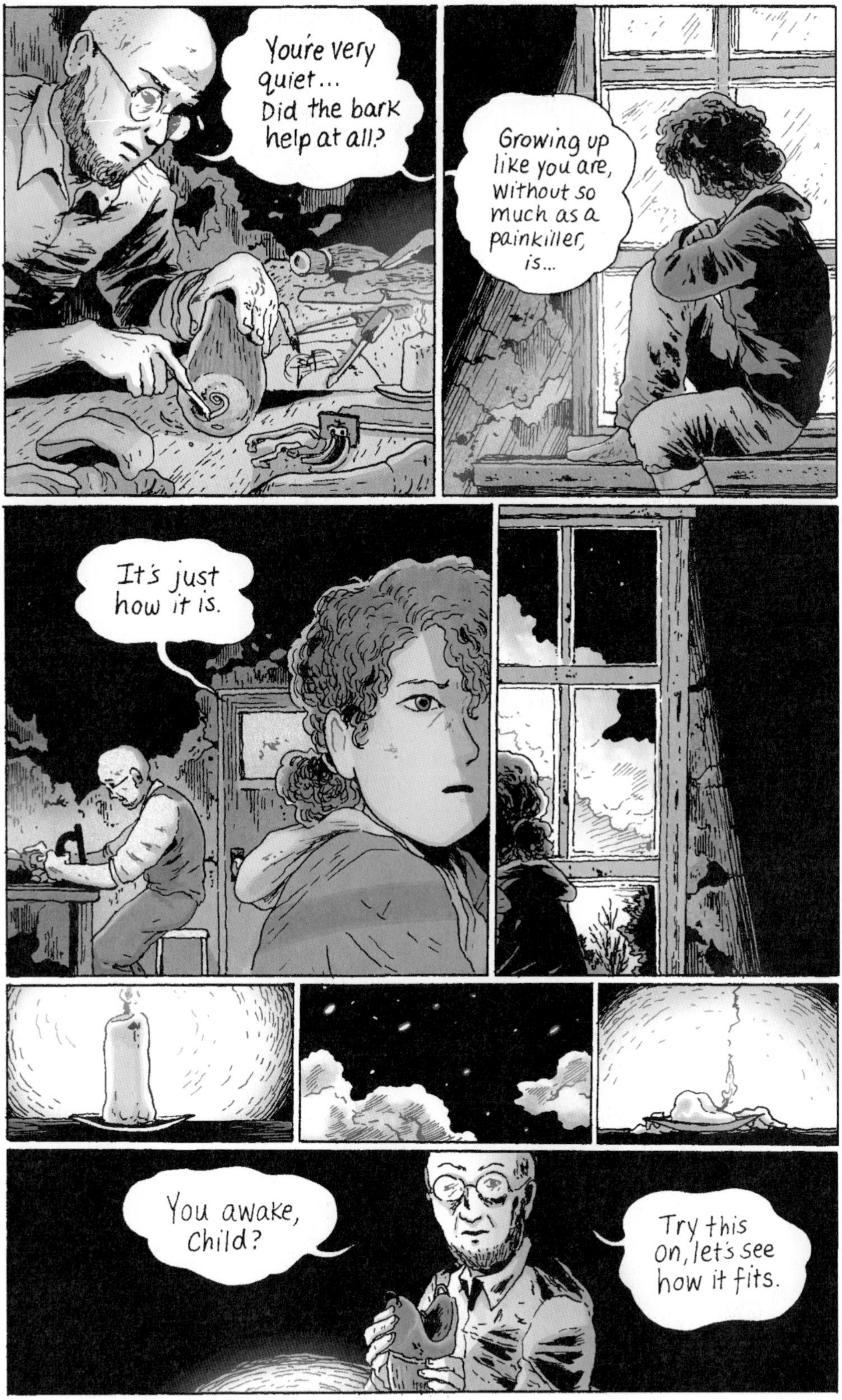
You're very quiet... Did the bark help at all?
Growing up like you are, without so much as a painkiller, is...
It's just how it is.
You awake, Child?
Try this on, let's see how it fits.

Now this socket should keep a good seal for you--

--but I added this belt for extra support.

Roll that over it all, and it would take quite a tug to get it off.

Yes, just like that.

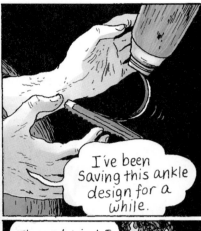

I've been saving this ankle design for a while.

The old kind I made, I've been told, wasn't quite flexible enough.

This one has some bend.

It will take some getting used to.

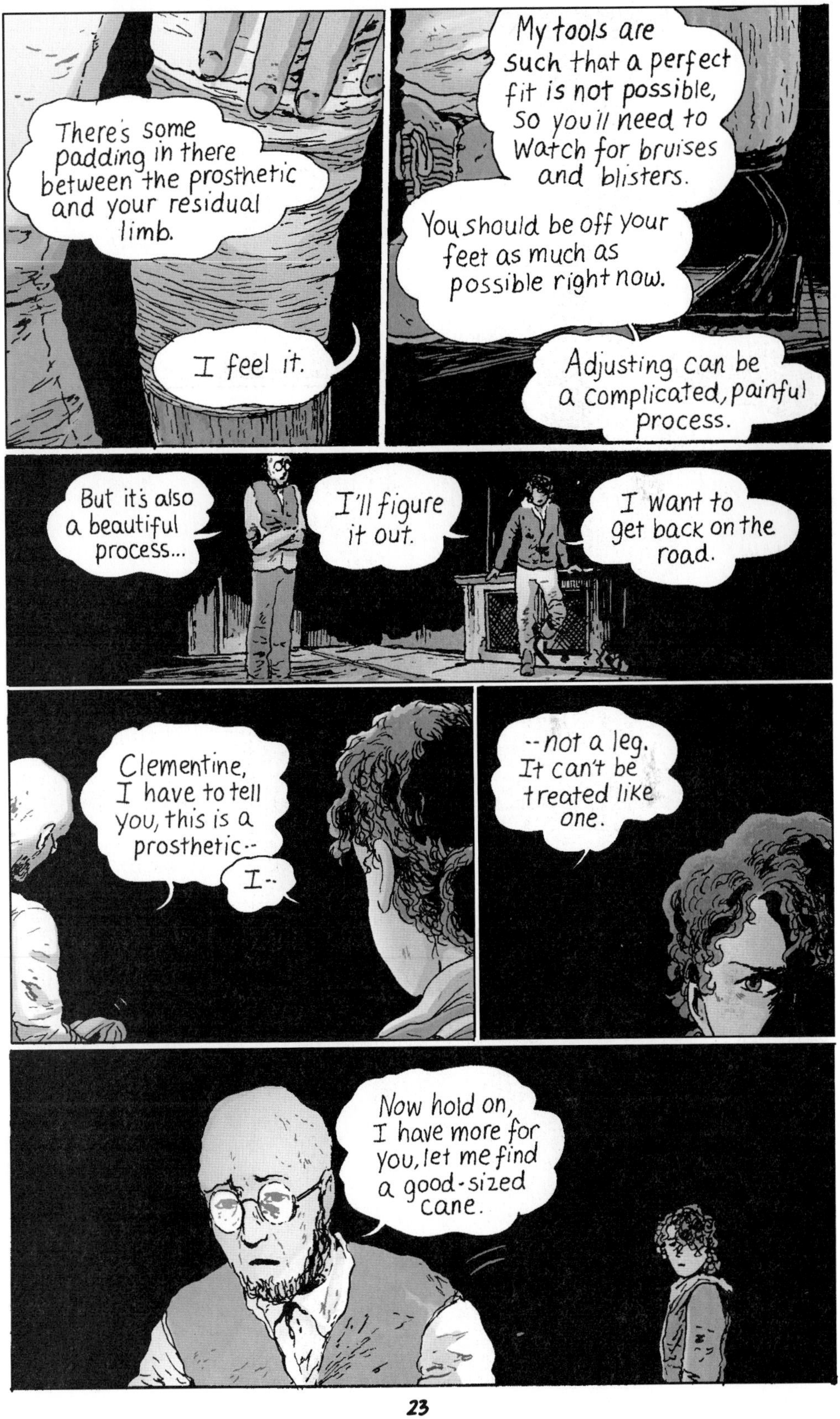
There's some padding in there between the prosthetic and your residual limb.
I feel it.
My tools are such that a perfect fit is not possible, so you'll need to watch for bruises and blisters.
You should be off your feet as much as possible right now.
Adjusting can be a complicated, painful process.
But it's also a beautiful process...
I'll figure it out.
I want to get back on the road.
Clementine, I have to tell you, this is a prosthetic--
I--
--not a leg. It can't be treated like one.
Now hold on, I have more for you, let me find a good-sized cane.

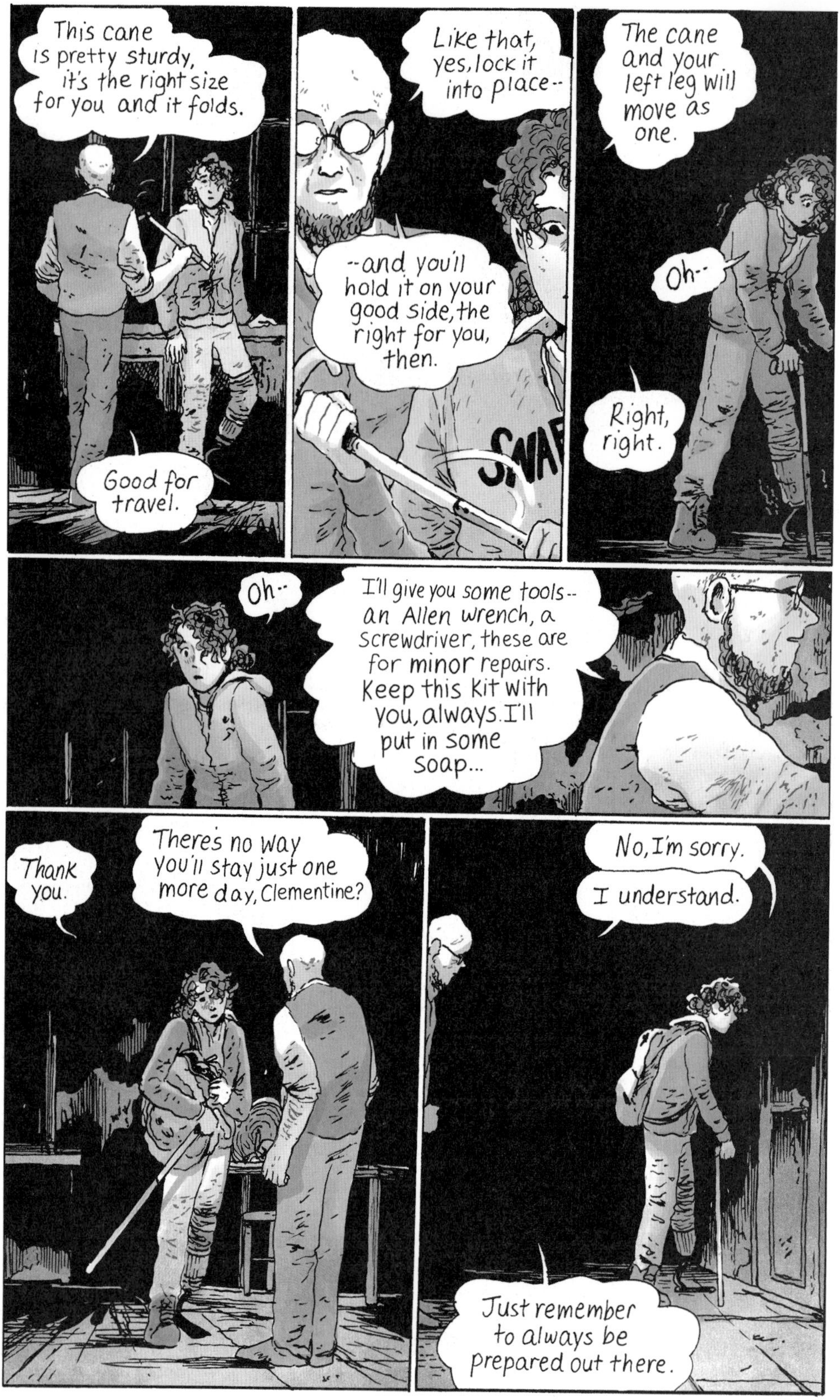
This cane is pretty sturdy, it's the right size for you and it folds.
Good for travel.
Like that, yes, lock it into place--
--and you'll hold it on your good side, the right for you, then.
SNA
The cane and your left leg will move as one.
Oh--
Right, right.
Oh--
I'll give you some tools-- an Allen wrench, a screwdriver, these are for minor repairs. Keep this kit with you, always. I'll put in some soap...
Thank you.
There's no way you'll stay just one more day, Clementine?
No, I'm sorry.
I understand.
Just remember to always be prepared out there.

I've heard that one before.

Come back if you ever need me again.

Do you have any more of that bark?

I put it in your kit, with the tools.

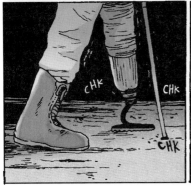

CHK

CHK

CHK

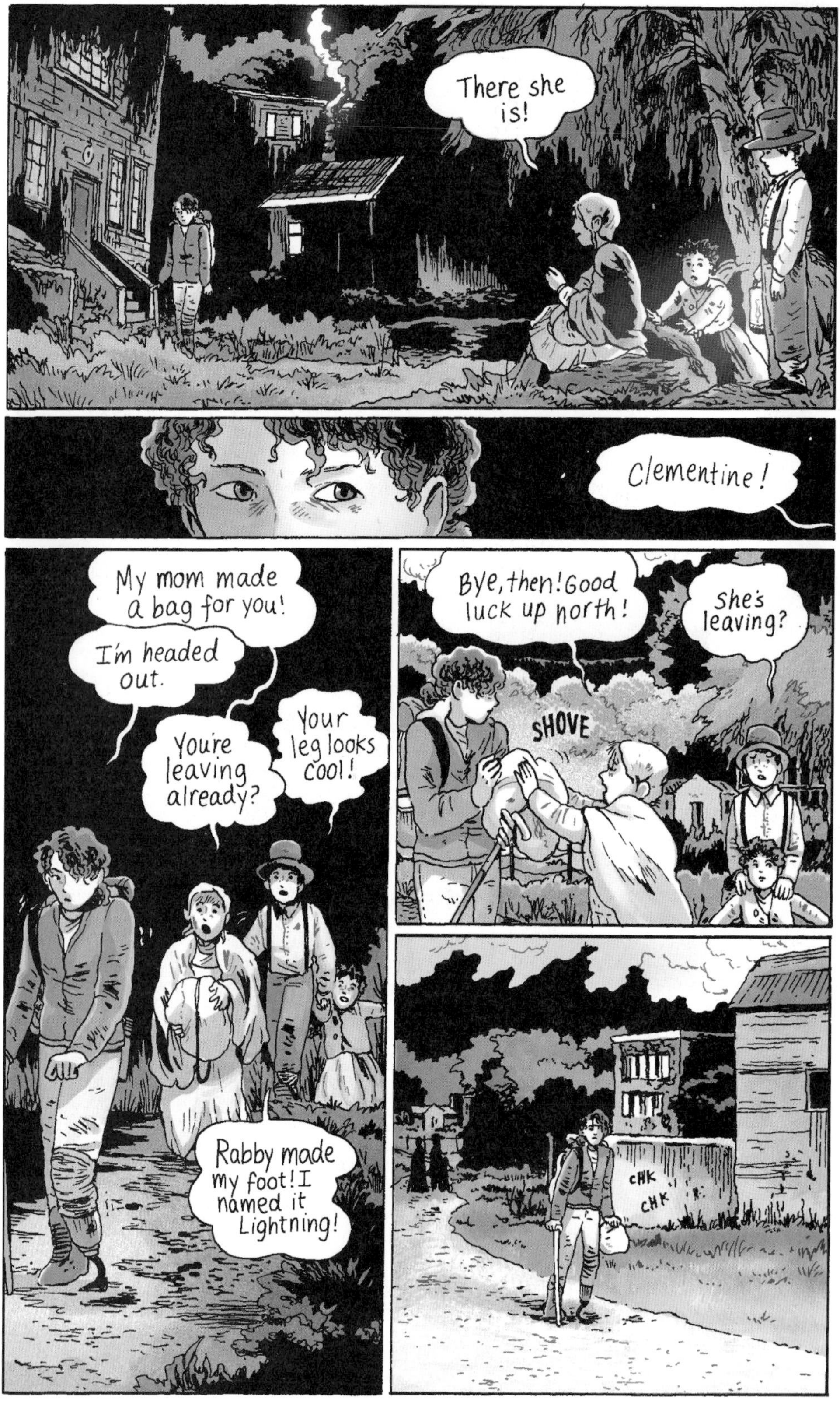
There she is!
Clementine!
My mom made a bag for you!
I'm headed out.
You're leaving already?
Your leg looks cool!
Rabby made my foot! I named it Lightning!
Bye, then! Good luck up north!
She's leaving?
SHOVE
CHK
CHK

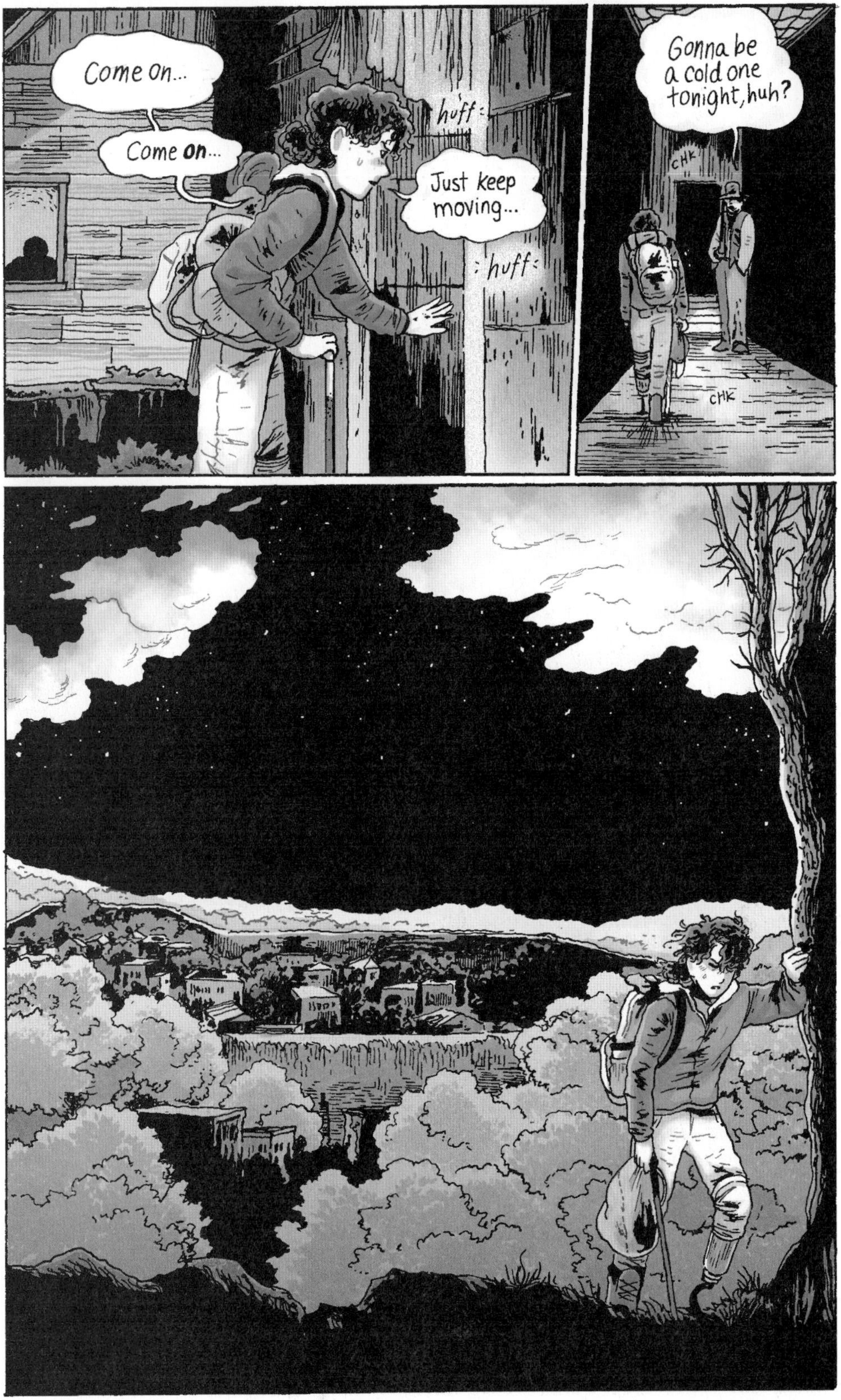
Come on...
Come on...
huff
Just keep moving...
huff
Gonna be a cold one tonight, huh?
CHK
CHK

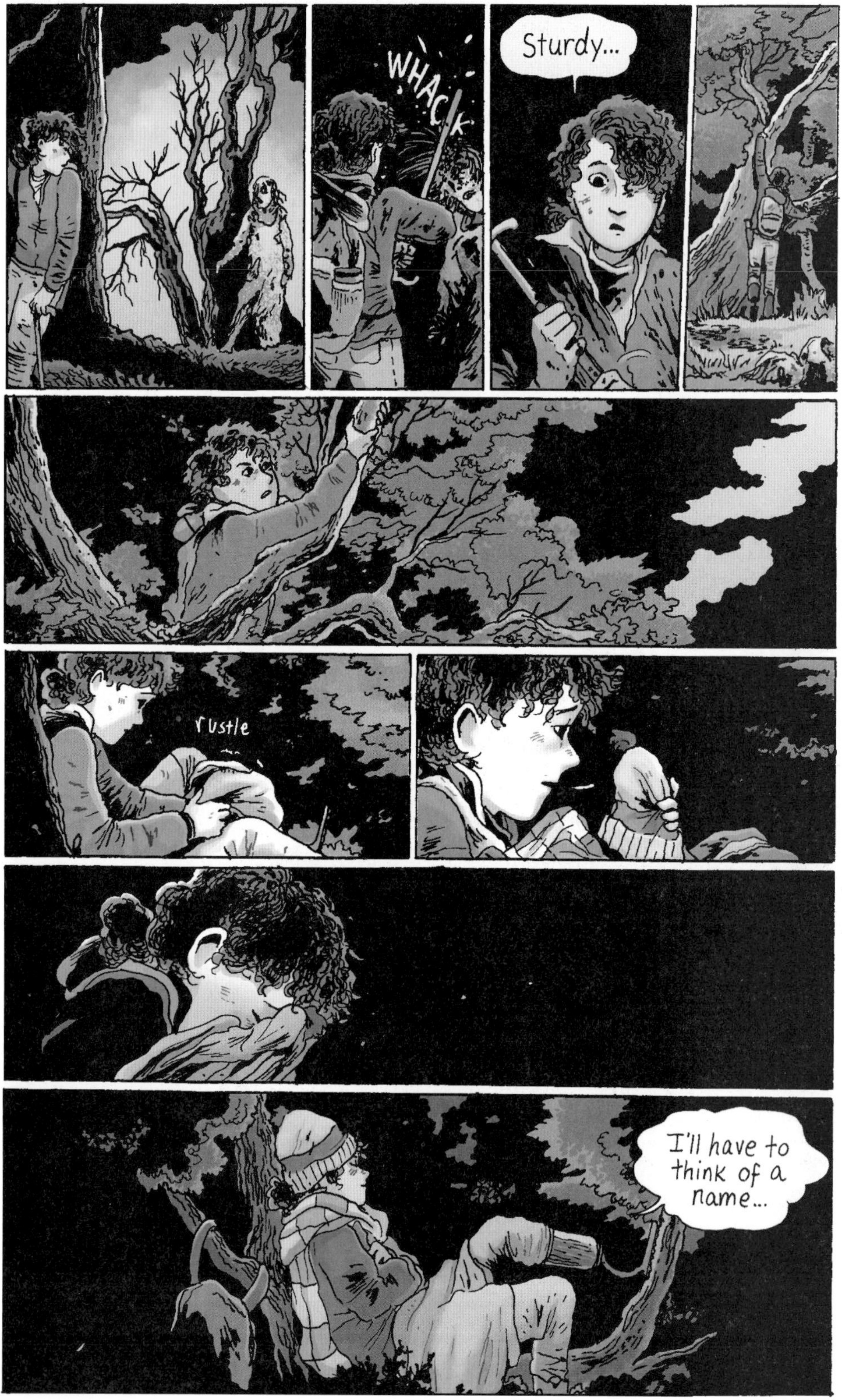
WHACK
Sturdy...
rustle
I'll have to think of a name...

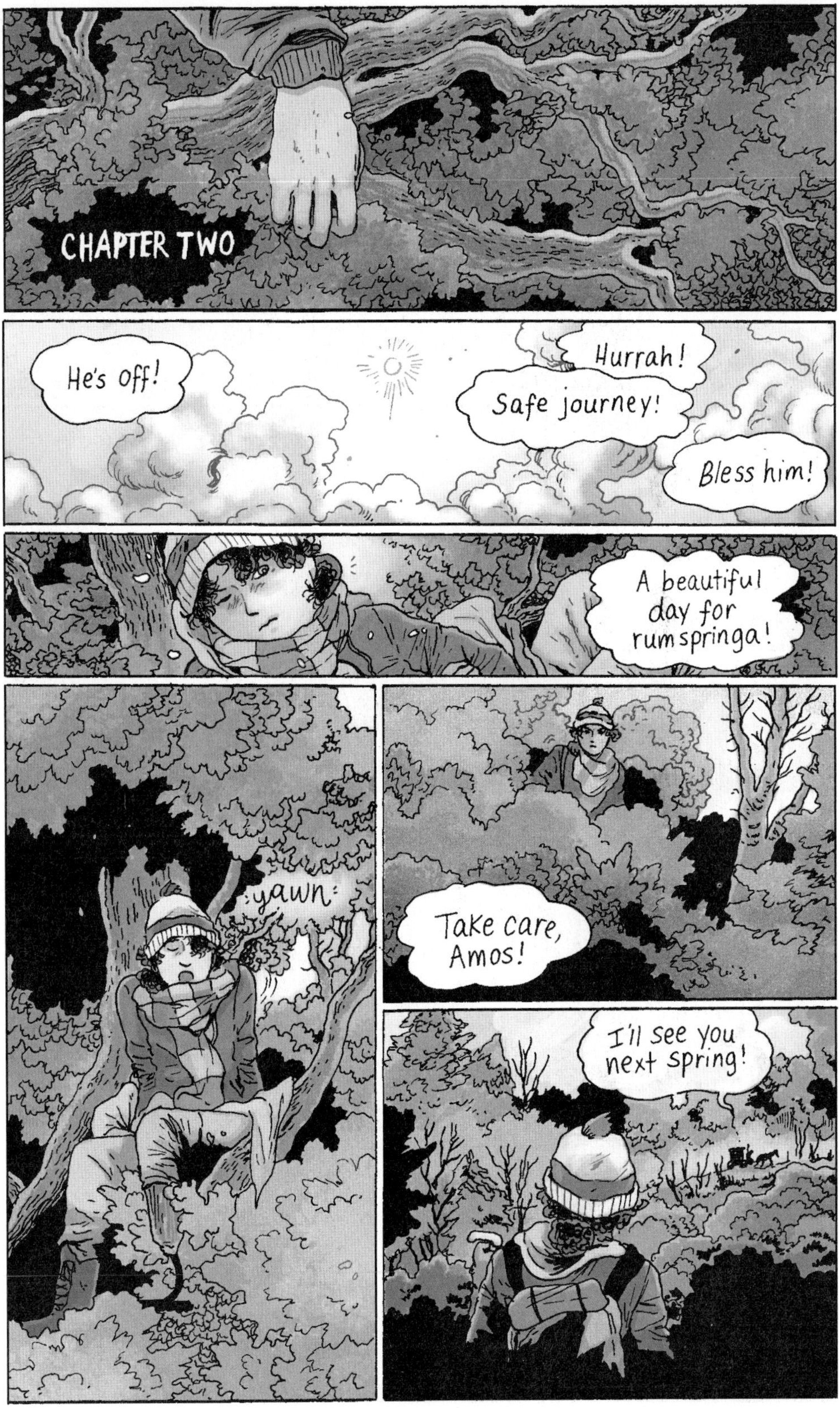
CHAPTER TWO
He's off!
Hurrah!
Safe journey!
Bless him!
A beautiful day for rumspringa!
yawn
Take care, Amos!
I'll see you next spring!

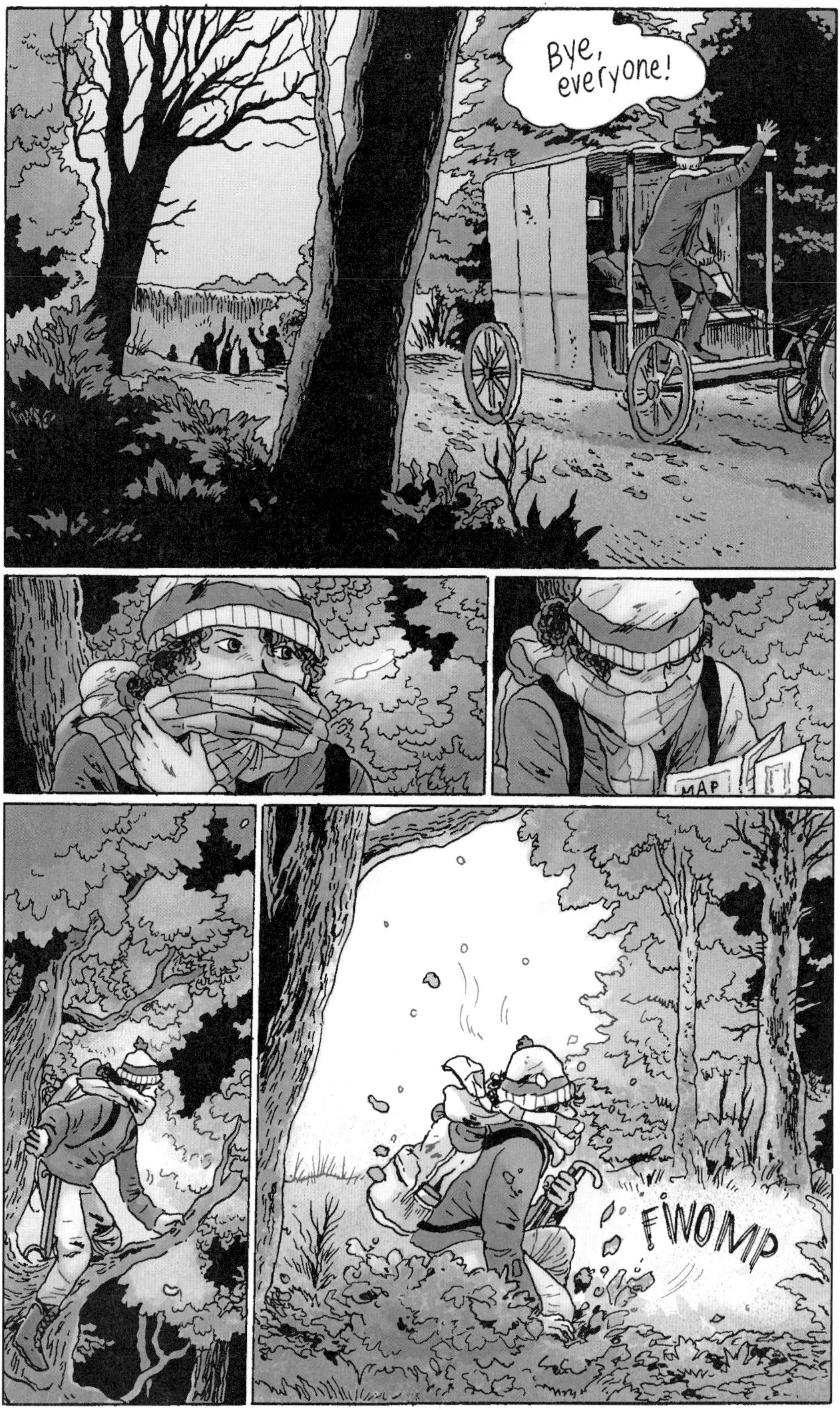
Bye, everyone!
MAP
FWOMP

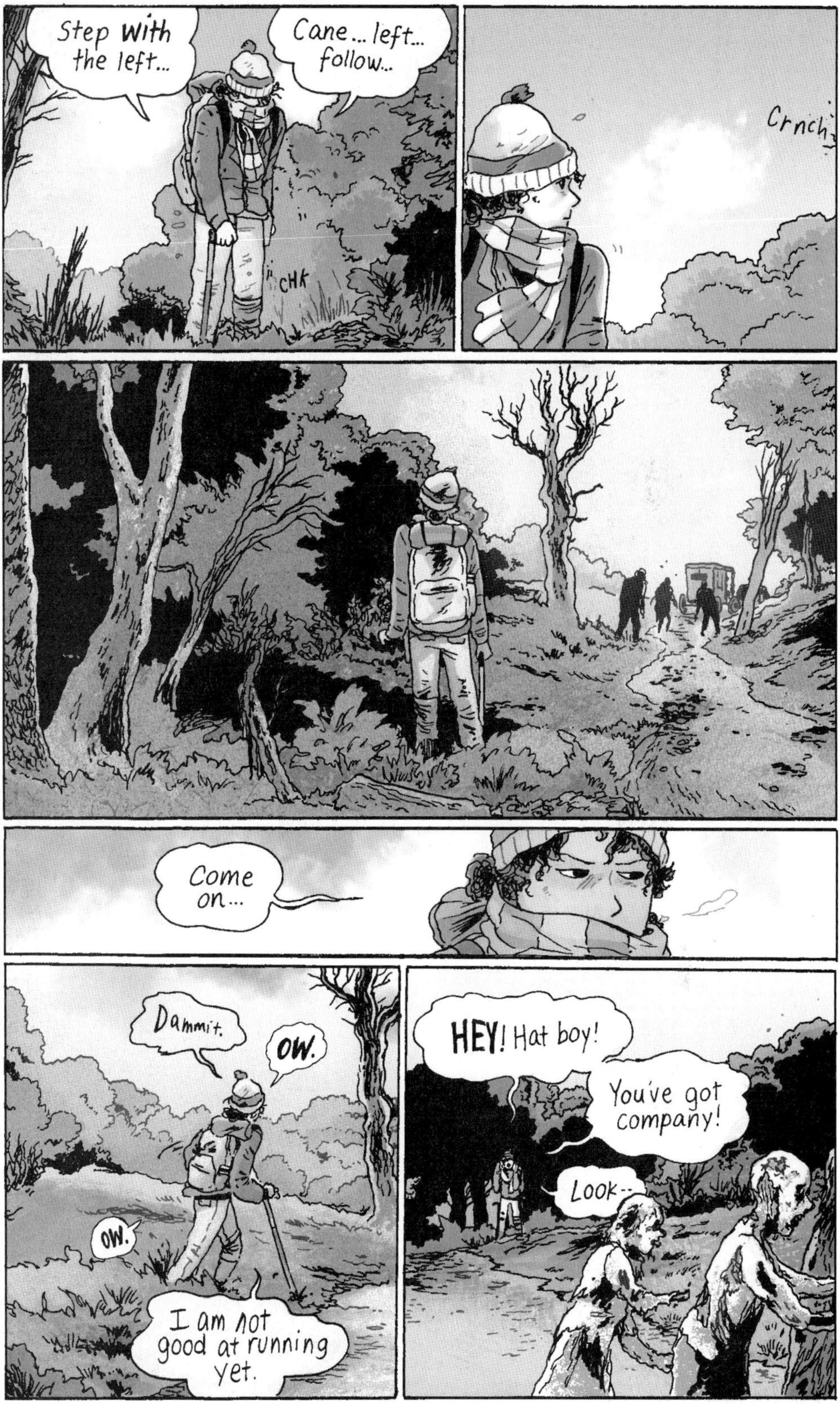

Step with the left...
Cane... left... follow...
CHK
Crnch
Come on...
Dammit.
OW.
OW.
I am not good at running yet.
HEY! Hat boy!
You've got company!
Look--

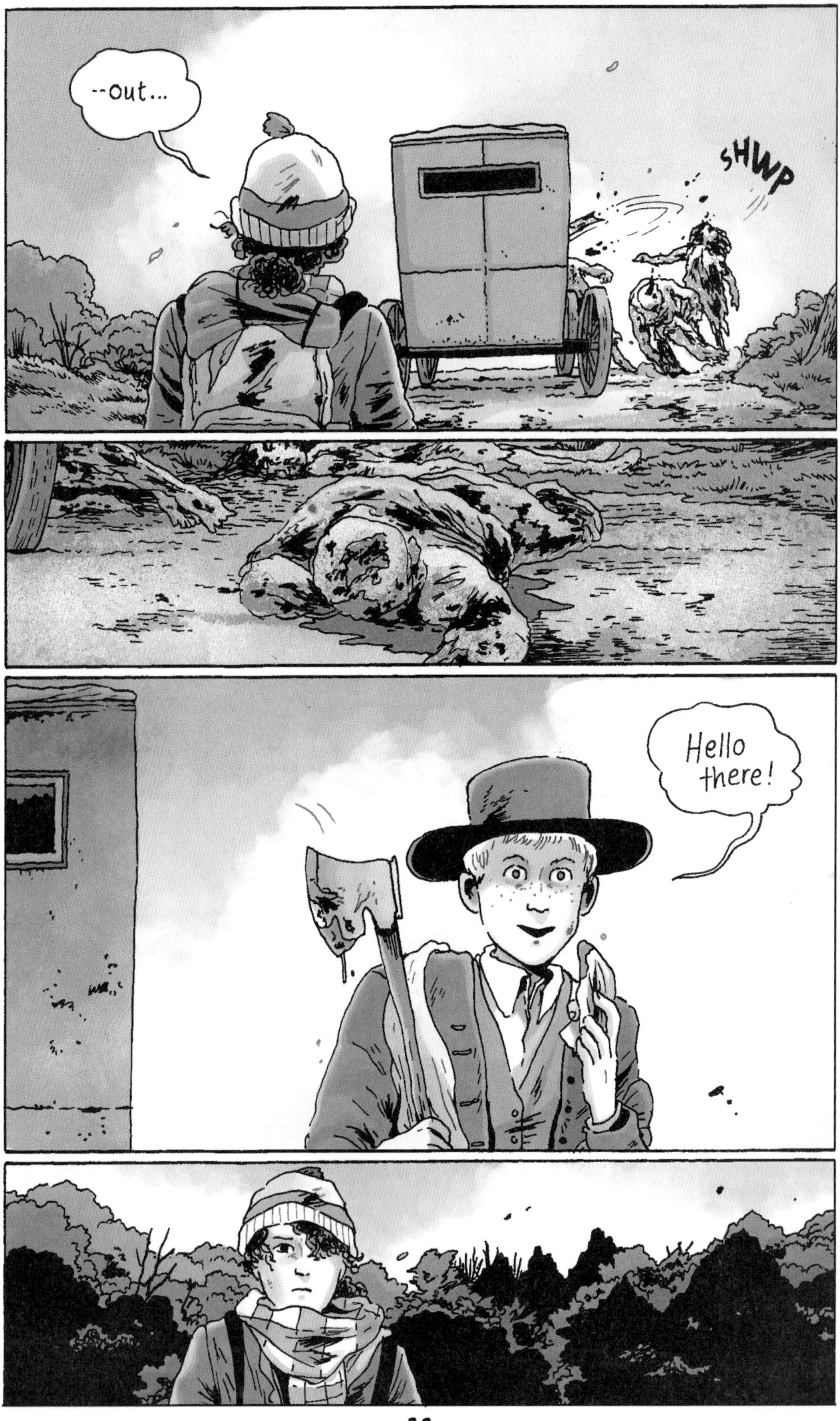
--out...
SHWP
Hello there!

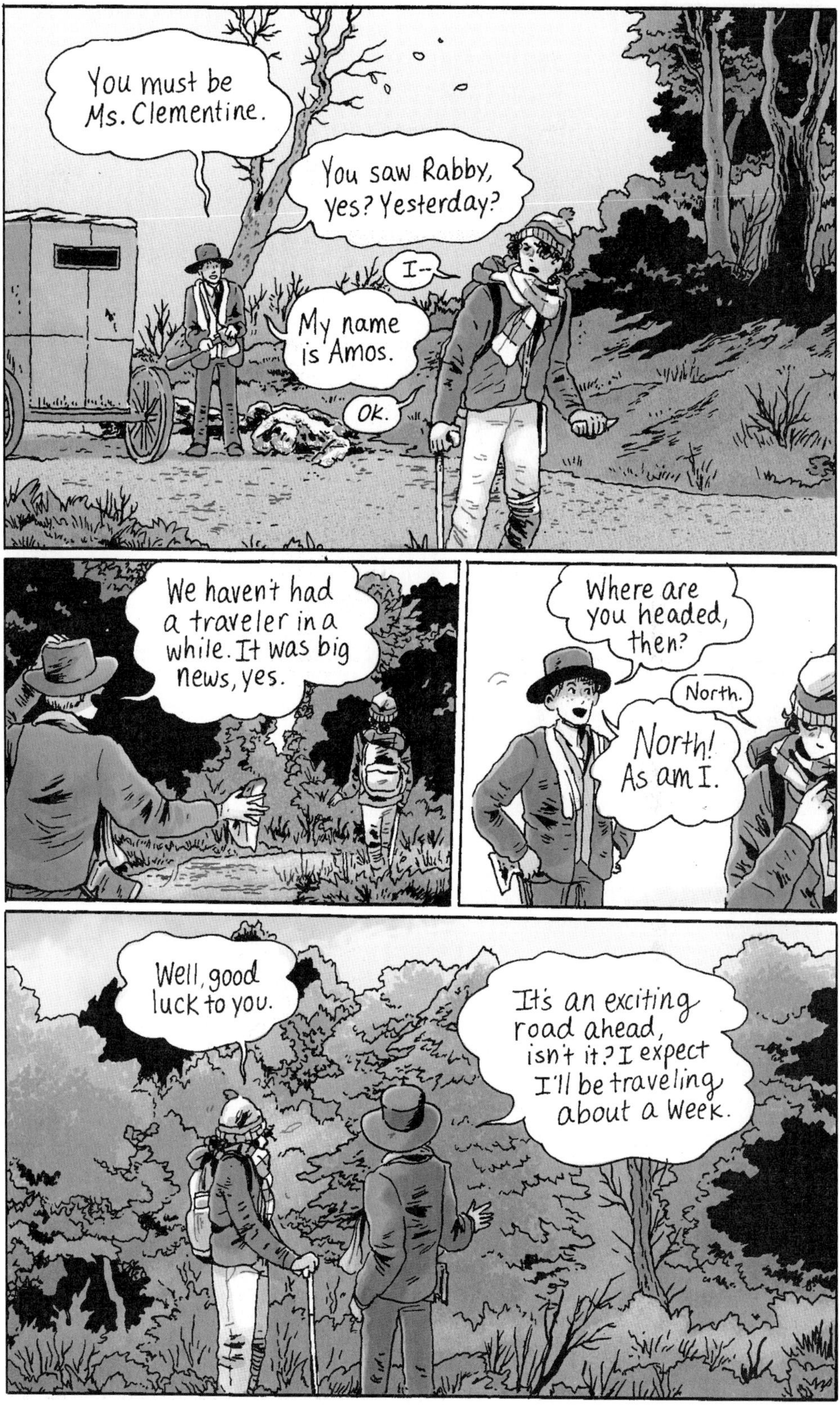
You must be Ms. Clementine.
You saw Rabby, yes? Yesterday?
I--
My name is Amos.
OK.
We haven't had a traveler in a while. It was big news, yes.
Where are you headed, then?
North.
North! As am I.
Well, good luck to you.
It's an exciting road ahead, isn't it? I expect I'll be traveling about a week.

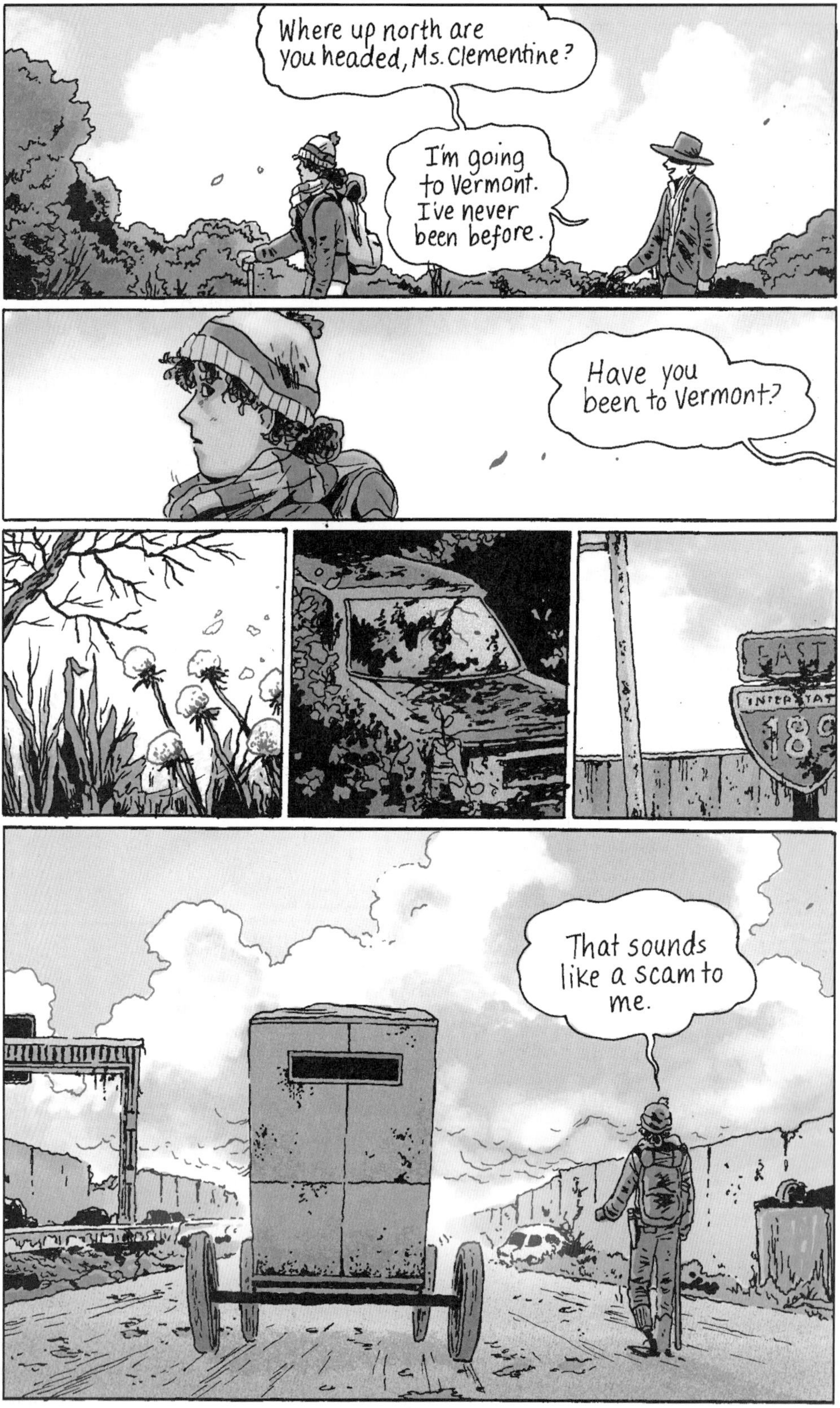
Where up north are you headed, Ms. Clementine?
I'm going to Vermont. I've never been before.
Have you been to Vermont?
EAST
INTERSTATE
189
That sounds like a scam to me.

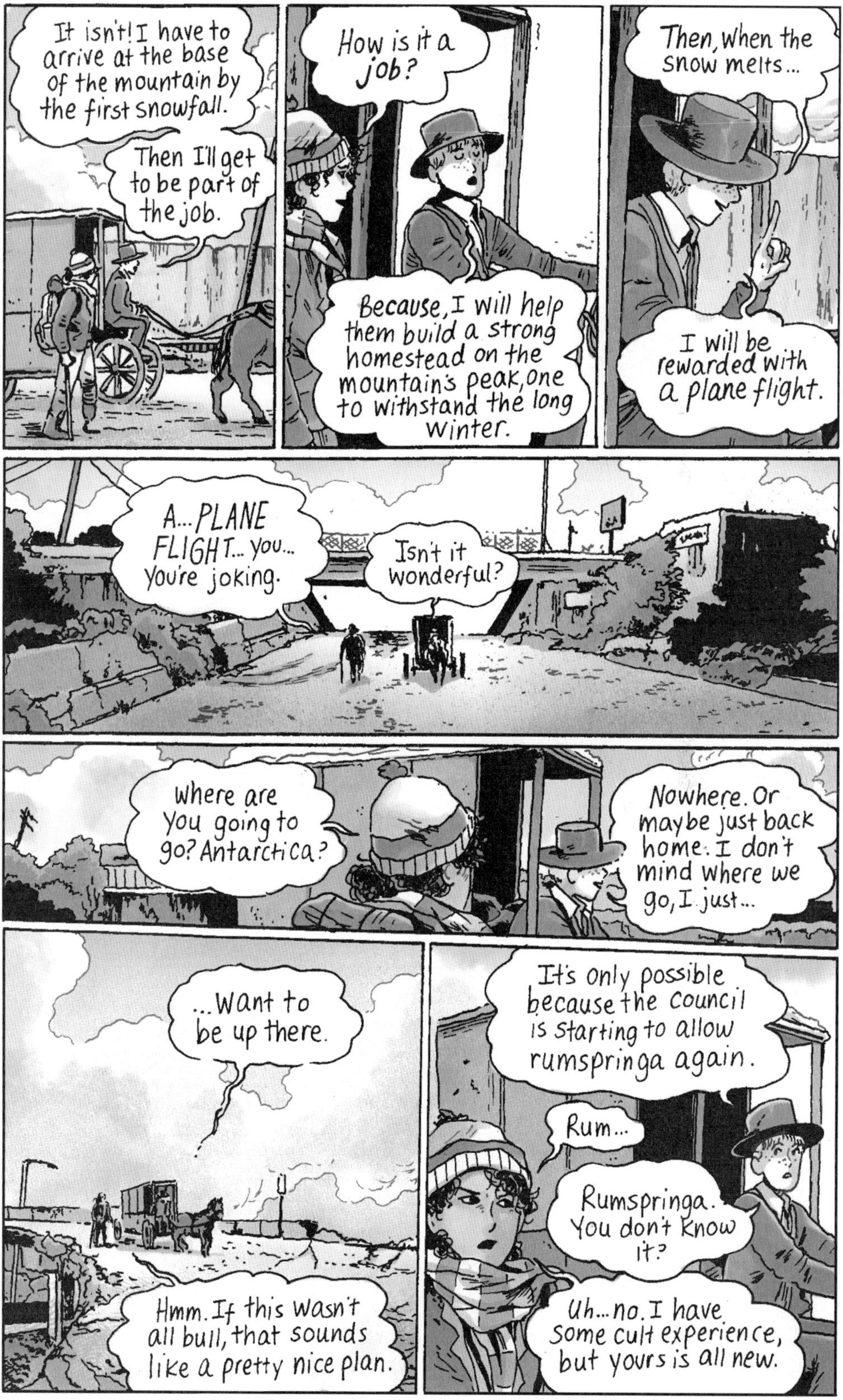
It isn't! I have to arrive at the base of the mountain by the first snowfall.
Then I'll get to be part of the job.
How is it a job?
Because, I will help them build a strong homestead on the mountain's peak, one to withstand the long winter.
Then, when the snow melts...
I will be rewarded with a plane flight.
A... PLANE FLIGHT... you... you're joking.
Isn't it wonderful?
Where are you going to go? Antarctica?
Nowhere. Or maybe just back home. I don't mind where we go, I just...
...want to be up there.
Hmm. If this wasn't all bull, that sounds like a pretty nice plan.
It's only possible because the council is starting to allow rumspringa again.
Rum...
Rumspringa. You don't know it?
Uh... no. I have some cult experience, but yours is all new.

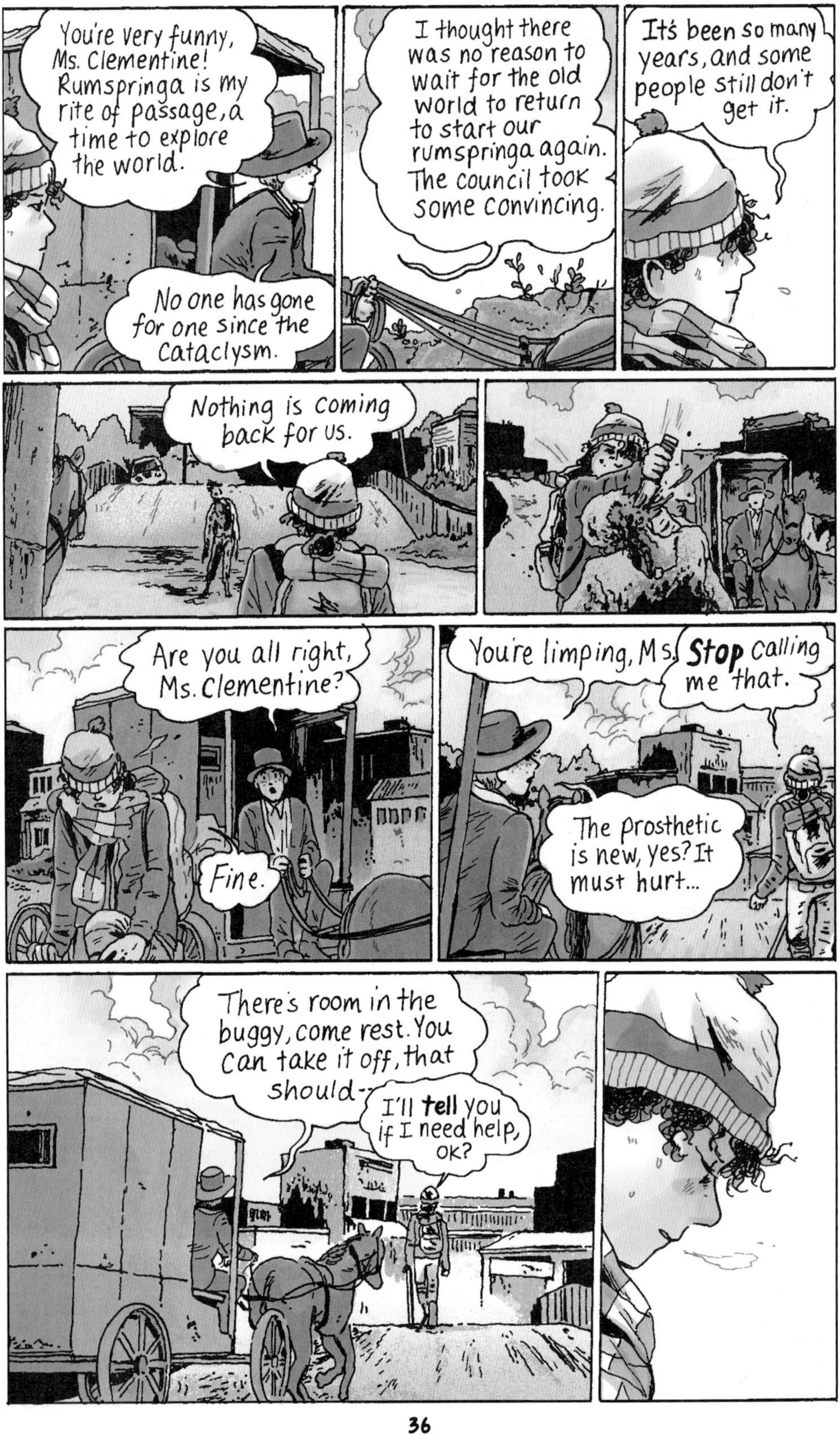
You're very funny, Ms. Clementine! Rumspringa is my rite of passage, a time to explore the world.
No one has gone for one since the Cataclysm.
I thought there was no reason to wait for the old world to return to start our rumspringa again. The council took some convincing.
It's been so many years, and some people still don't get it.
Nothing is coming back for us.
Are you all right, Ms. Clementine?
Fine.
You're limping, Ms.
Stop calling me that.
The prosthetic is new, yes? It must hurt...
There's room in the buggy, come rest. You can take it off, that should--
I'll **tell** you if I need help, ok?

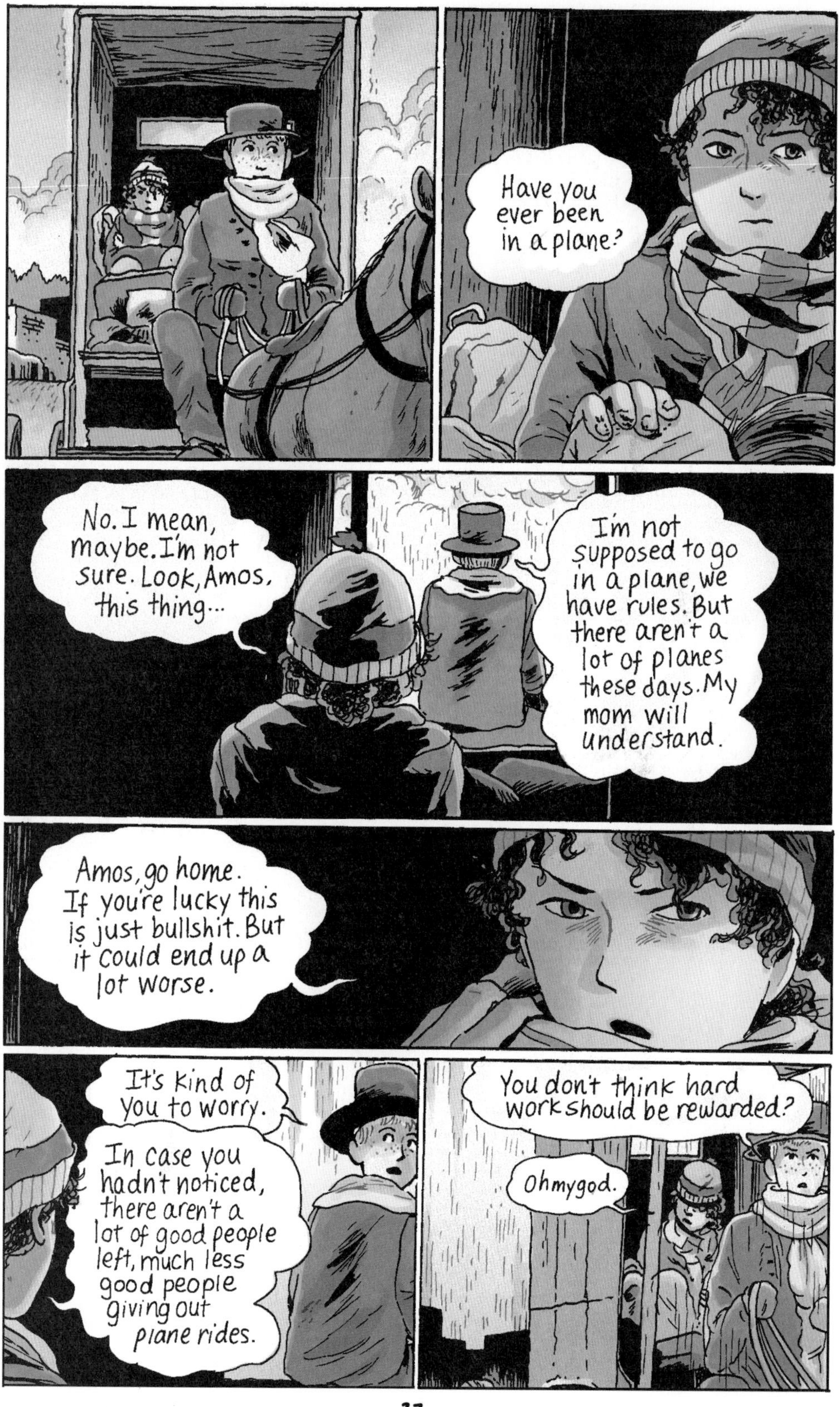
Have you ever been in a plane?
No. I mean, maybe. I'm not sure. Look, Amos, this thing...
I'm not supposed to go in a plane, we have rules. But there aren't a lot of planes these days. My mom will understand.
Amos, go home. If you're lucky this is just bullshit. But it could end up a lot worse.
It's kind of you to worry.
In case you hadn't noticed, there aren't a lot of good people left, much less good people giving out plane rides.
You don't think hard work should be rewarded?
Ohmygod.

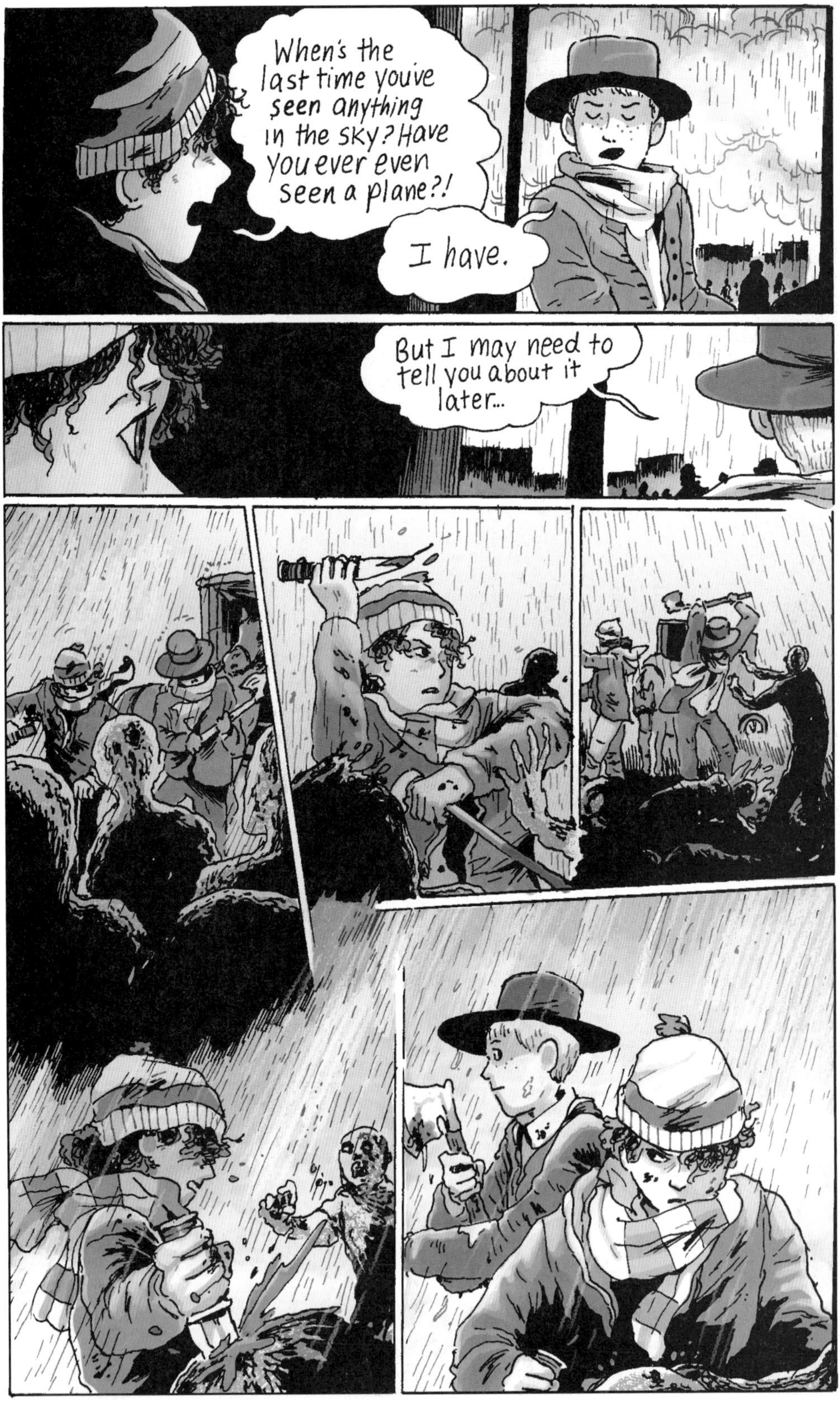
When's the last time you've seen anything in the sky? Have you ever even seen a plane?!
I have.
But I may need to tell you about it later...

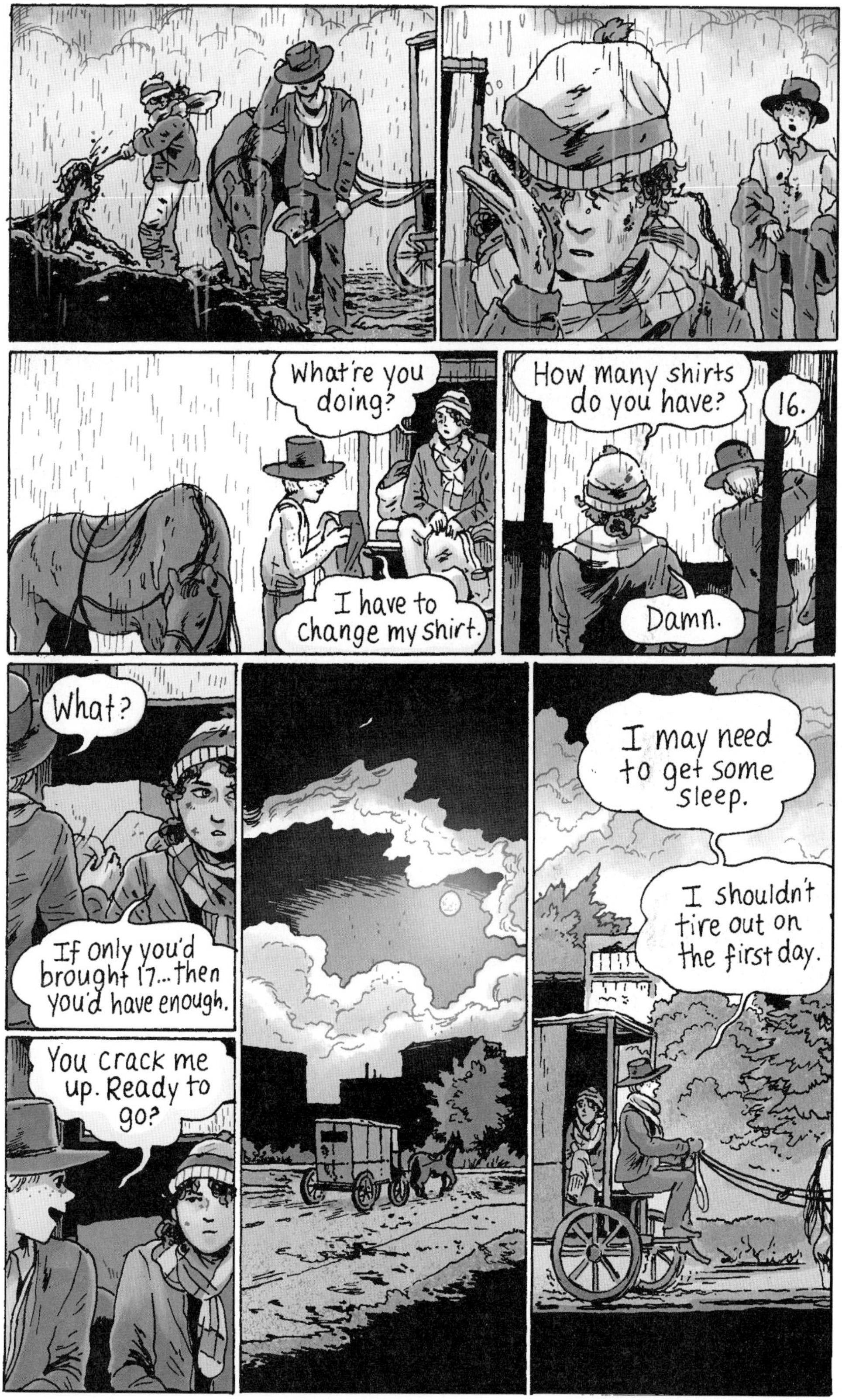
What're you doing?
I have to change my shirt.
How many shirts do you have?
16.
Damn.
What?
If only you'd brought 17... then you'd have enough.
You crack me up. Ready to go?
I may need to get some sleep.
I shouldn't tire out on the first day.

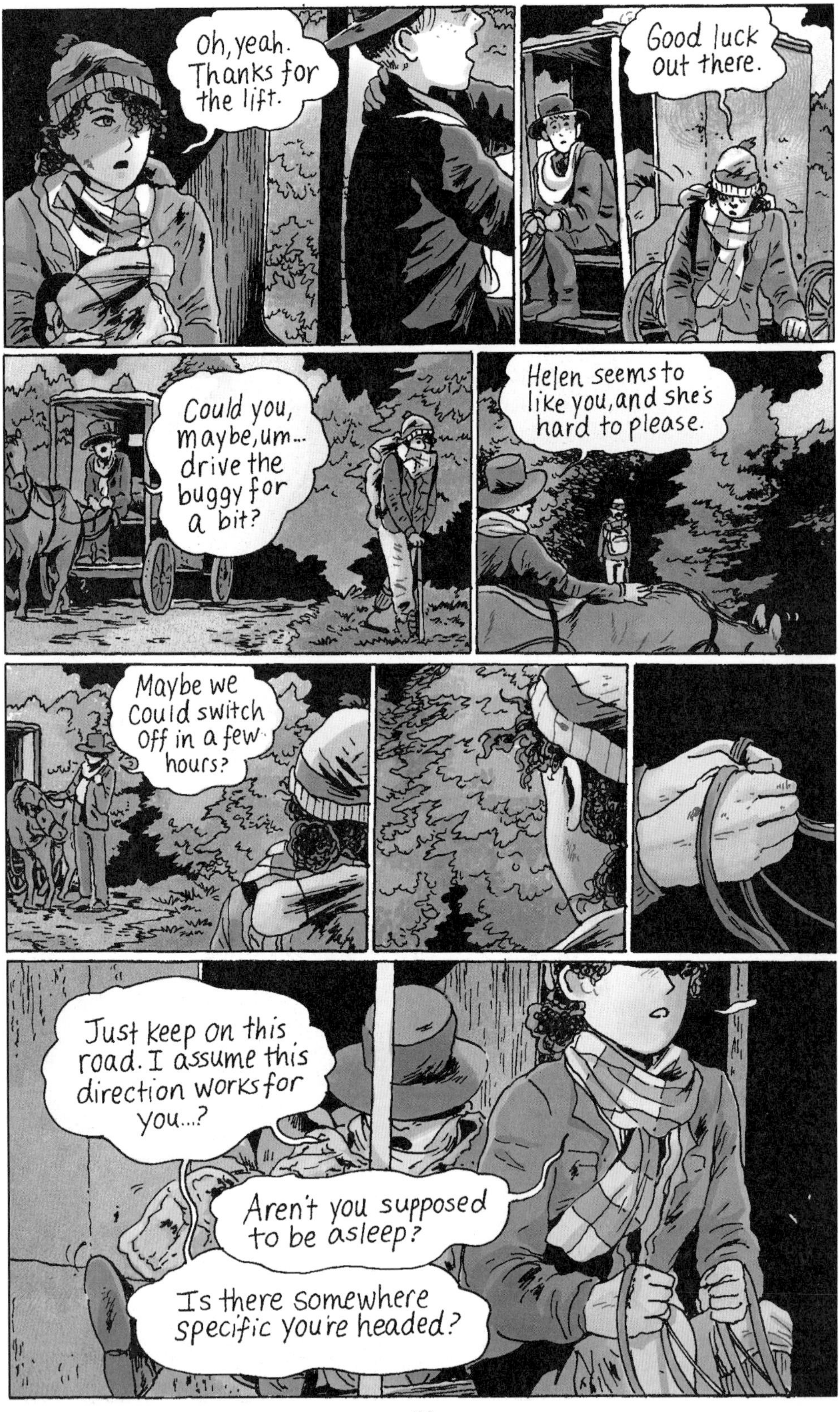
Oh, yeah. Thanks for the lift.
Good luck out there.
Could you, maybe, um... drive the buggy for a bit?
Helen seems to like you, and she's hard to please.
Maybe we could switch off in a few hours?
Just keep on this road. I assume this direction works for you...?
Aren't you supposed to be asleep?
Is there somewhere specific you're headed?

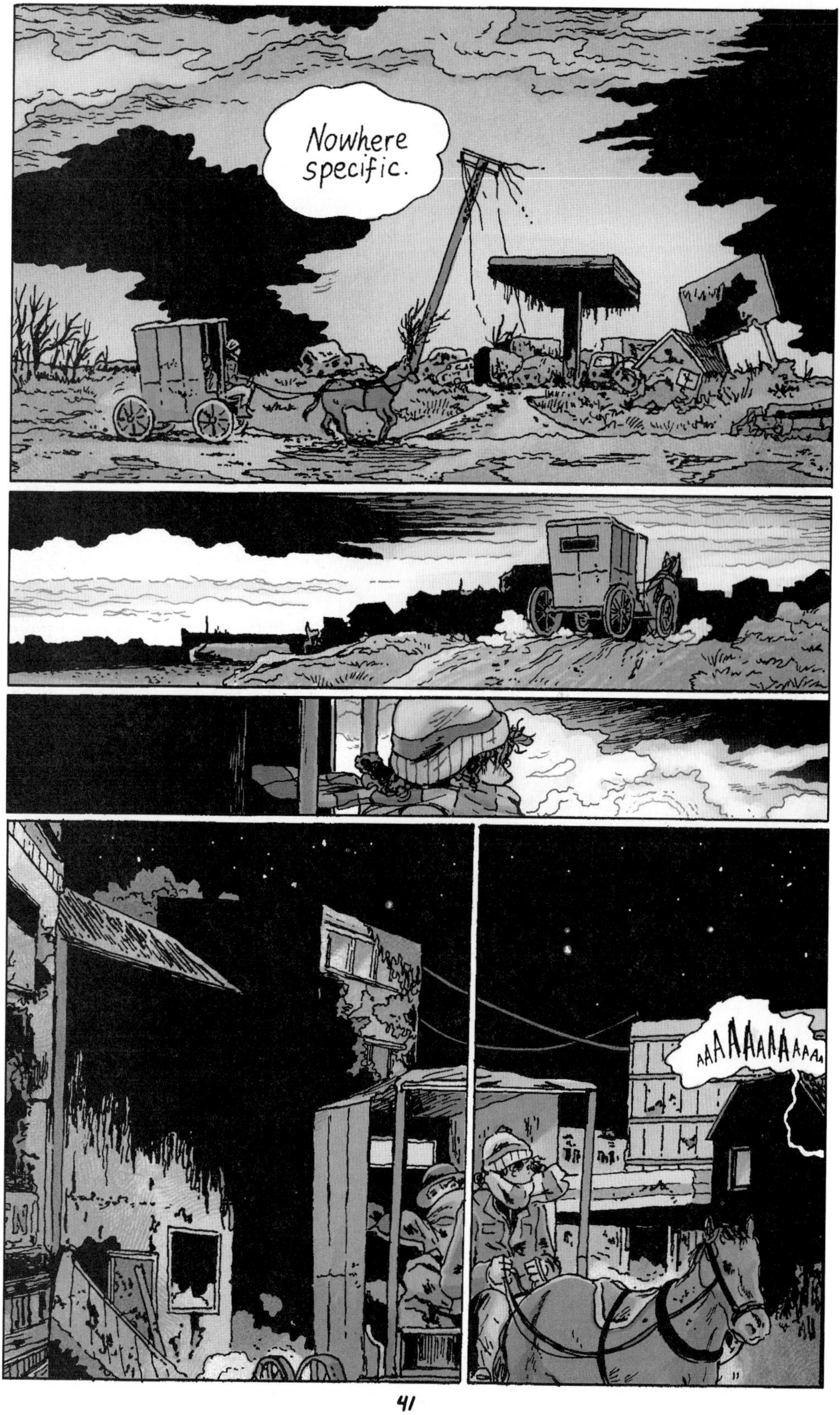
Nowhere specific.
AAAAAAAAAAAA

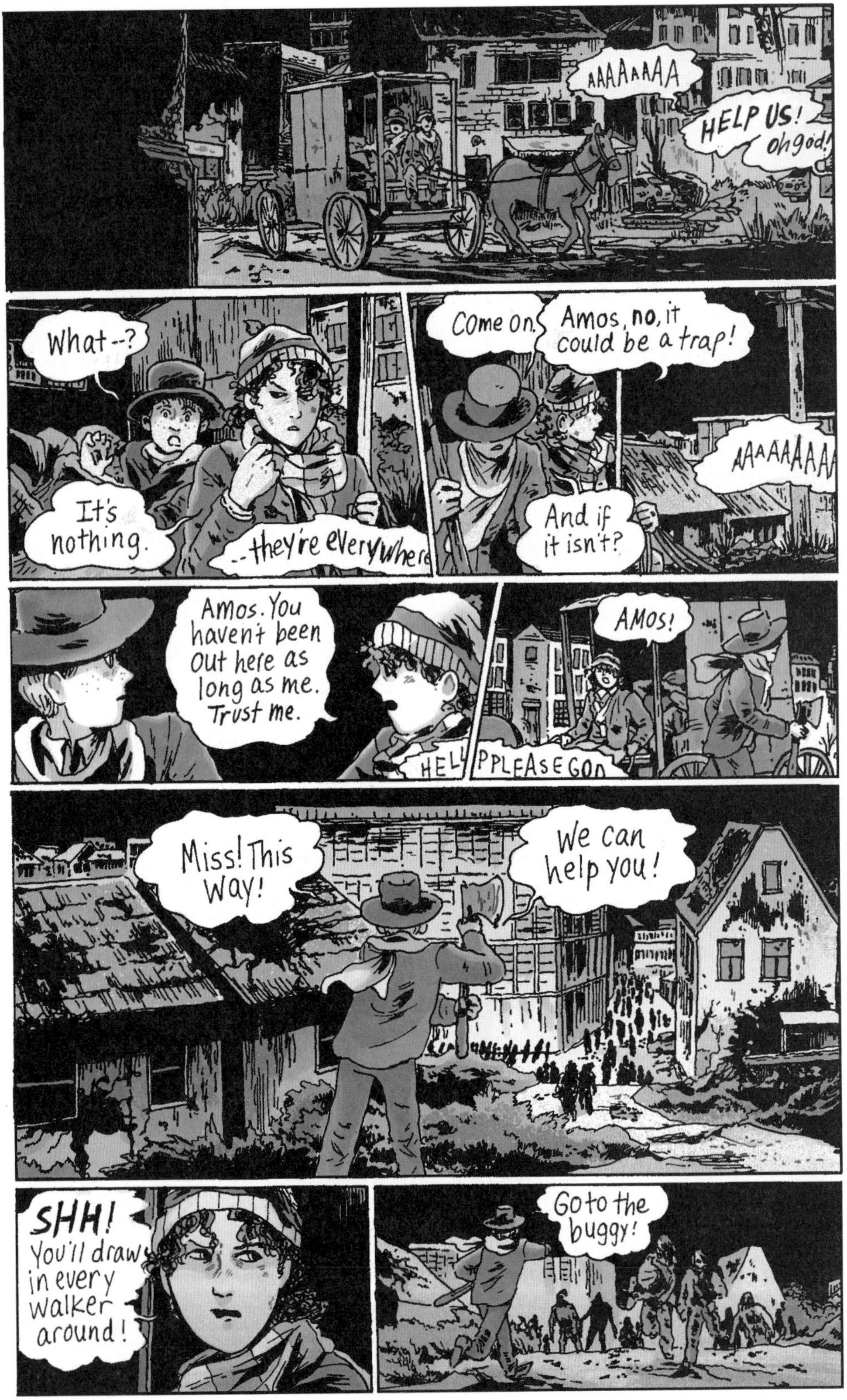
AAAAAAAA
HELP US! ohgod!
What--?
It's nothing.
--they're everywhere
Come on.
Amos, no, it could be a trap!
AAAAAAAA
And if it isn't?
Amos. You haven't been out here as long as me. Trust me.
HEL
AMOS!
PPLEASEGOD
Miss! This Way!
We can help you!
SHH! You'll draw in every walker around!
Go to the buggy!

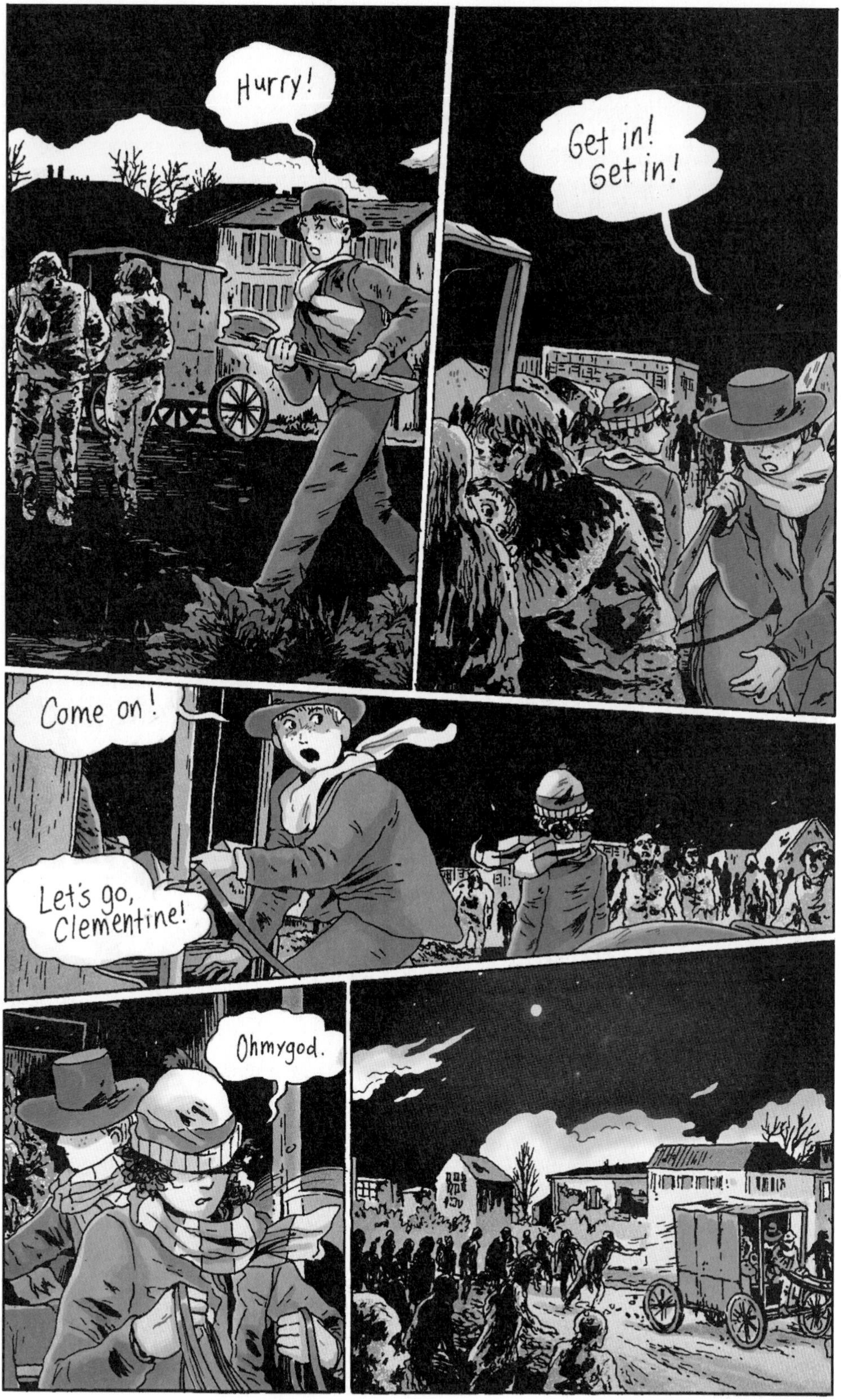
Hurry!
Get in! Get in!
Come on!
Let's go, Clementine!
Ohmygod.

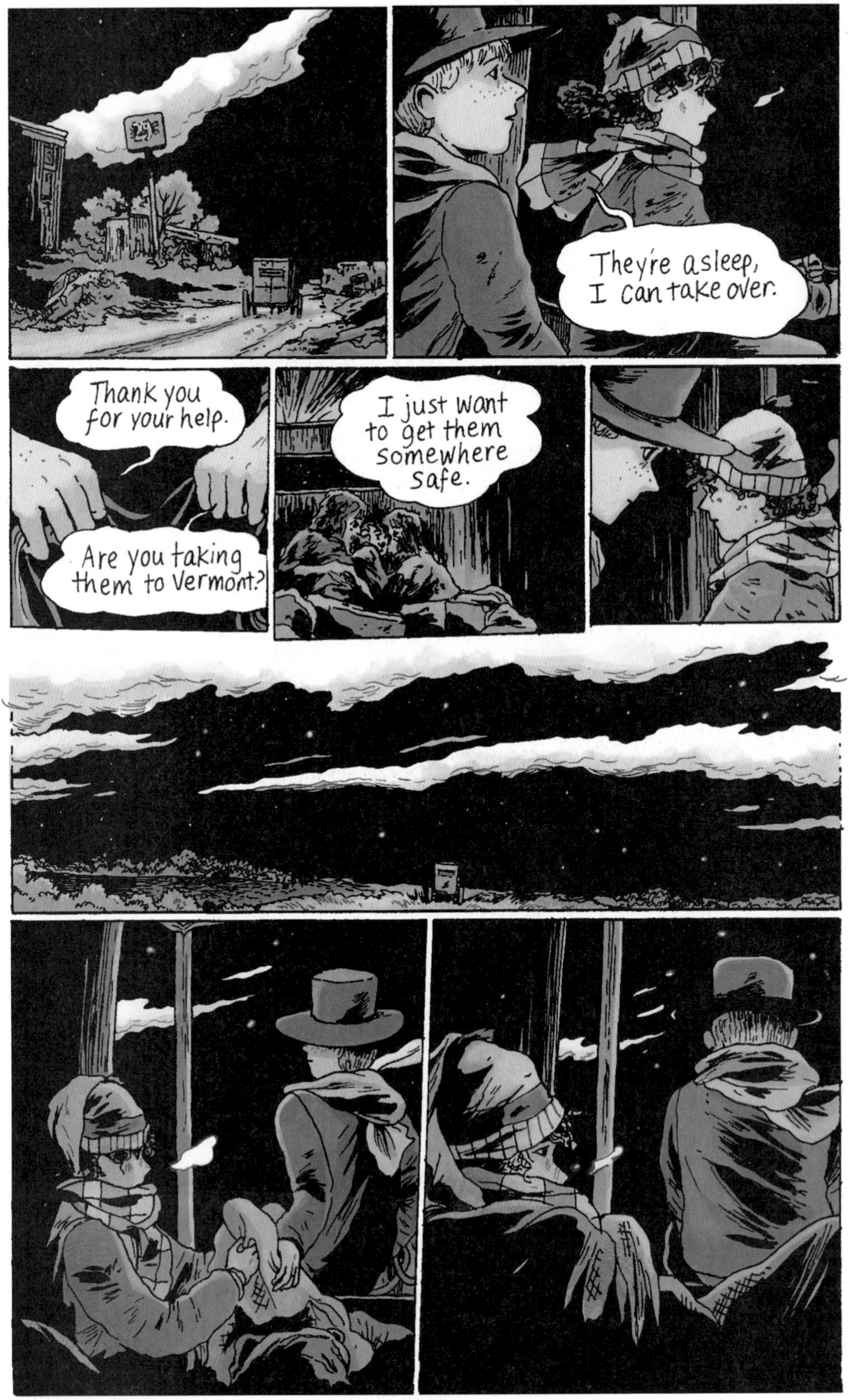
They're asleep, I can take over.
Thank you for your help.
Are you taking them to Vermont?
I just want to get them somewhere safe.

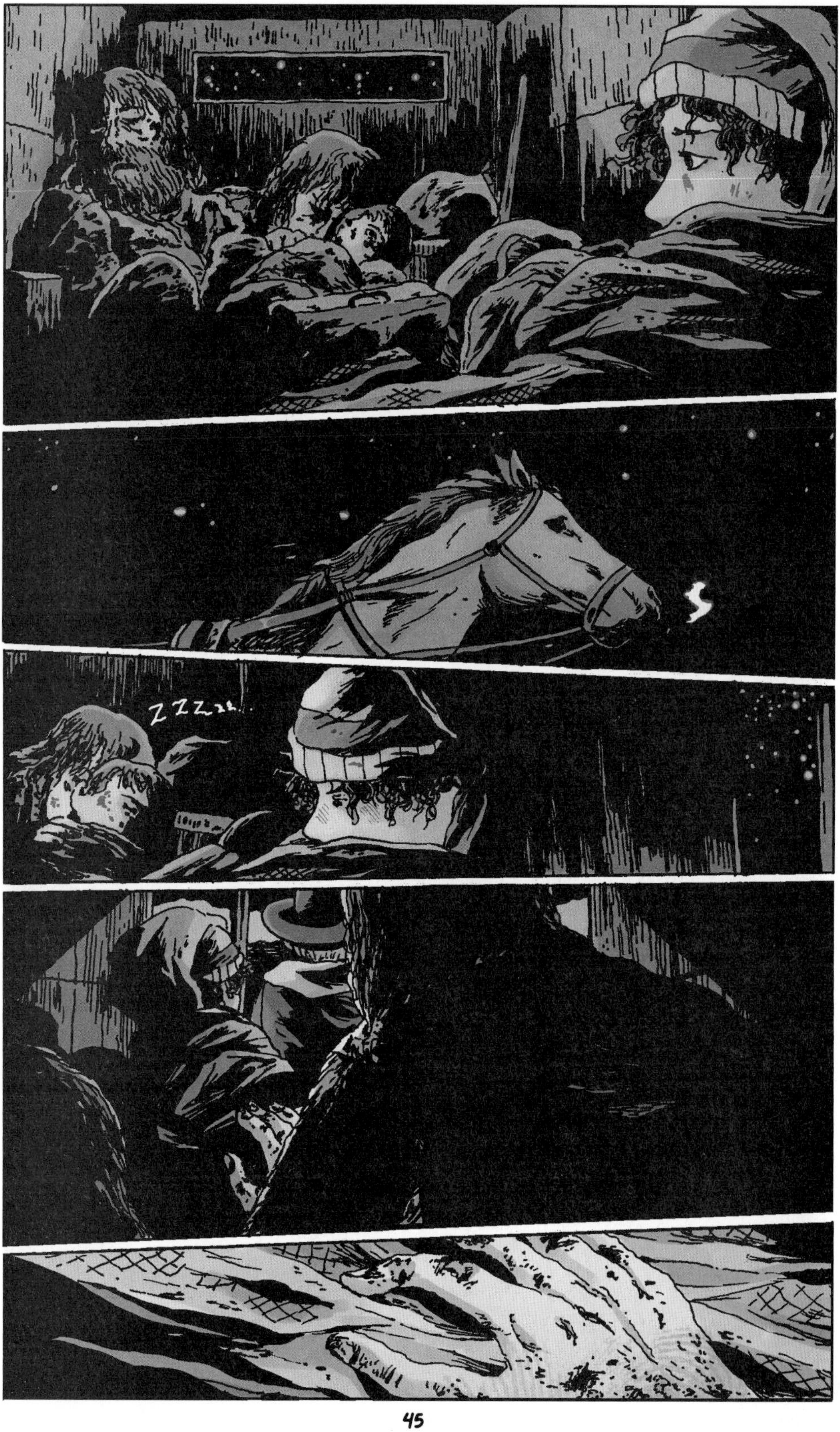
ZZZzzz

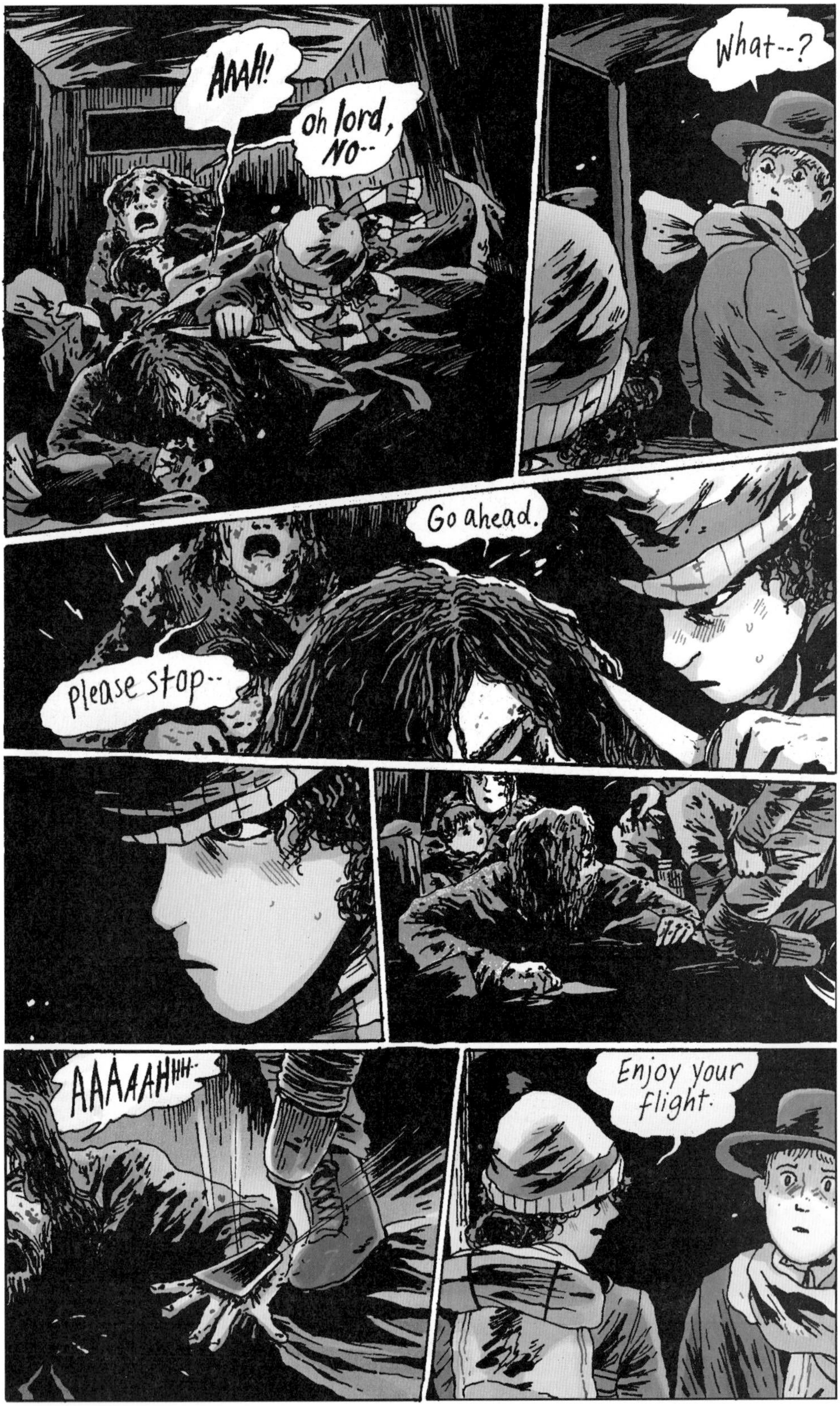
AAAH!
Oh lord, NO--
What--?
Go ahead.
Please stop--
AAAAAHHH--
Enjoy your flight.

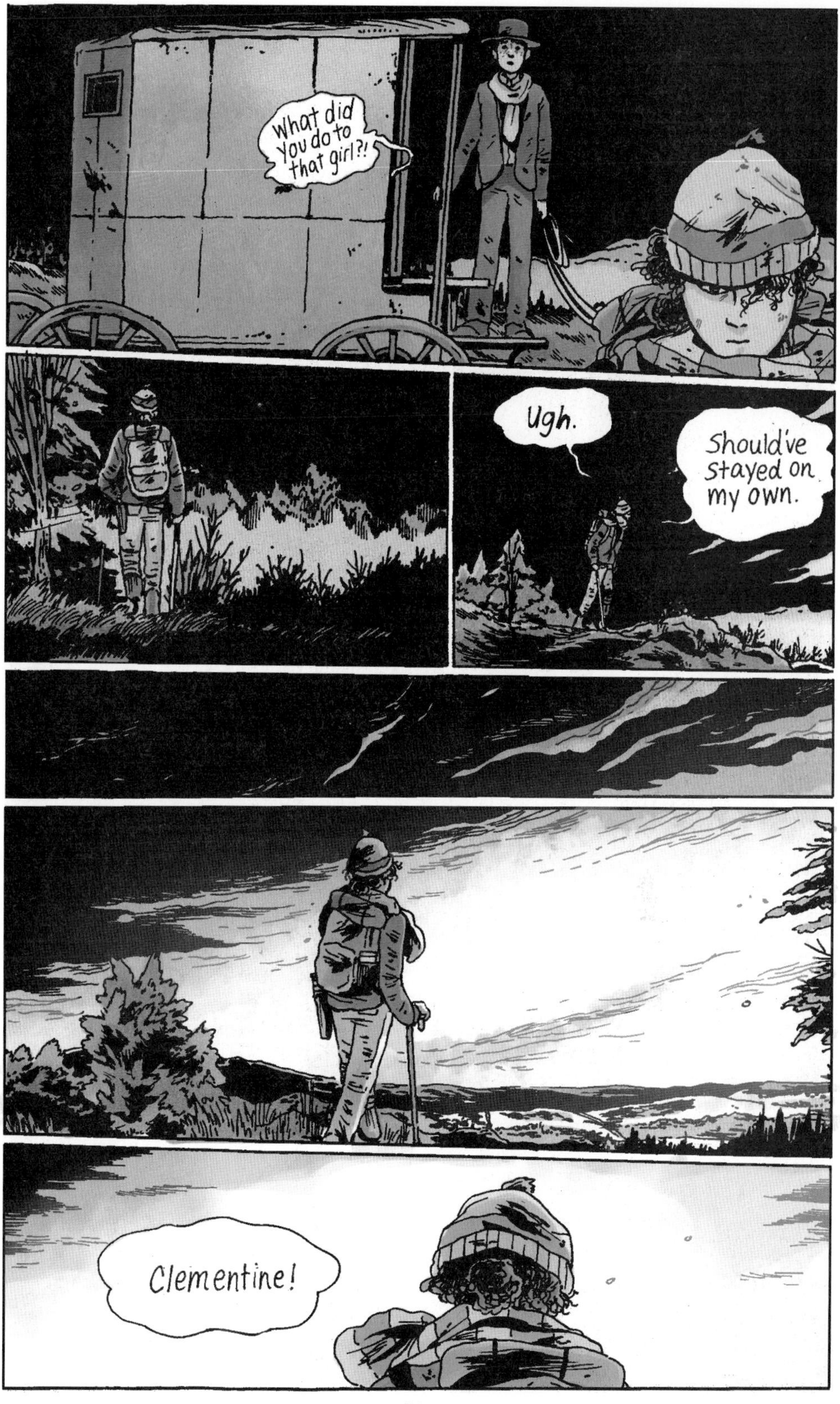
What did you do to that girl?!
Ugh.
Should've stayed on my own.
Clementine!

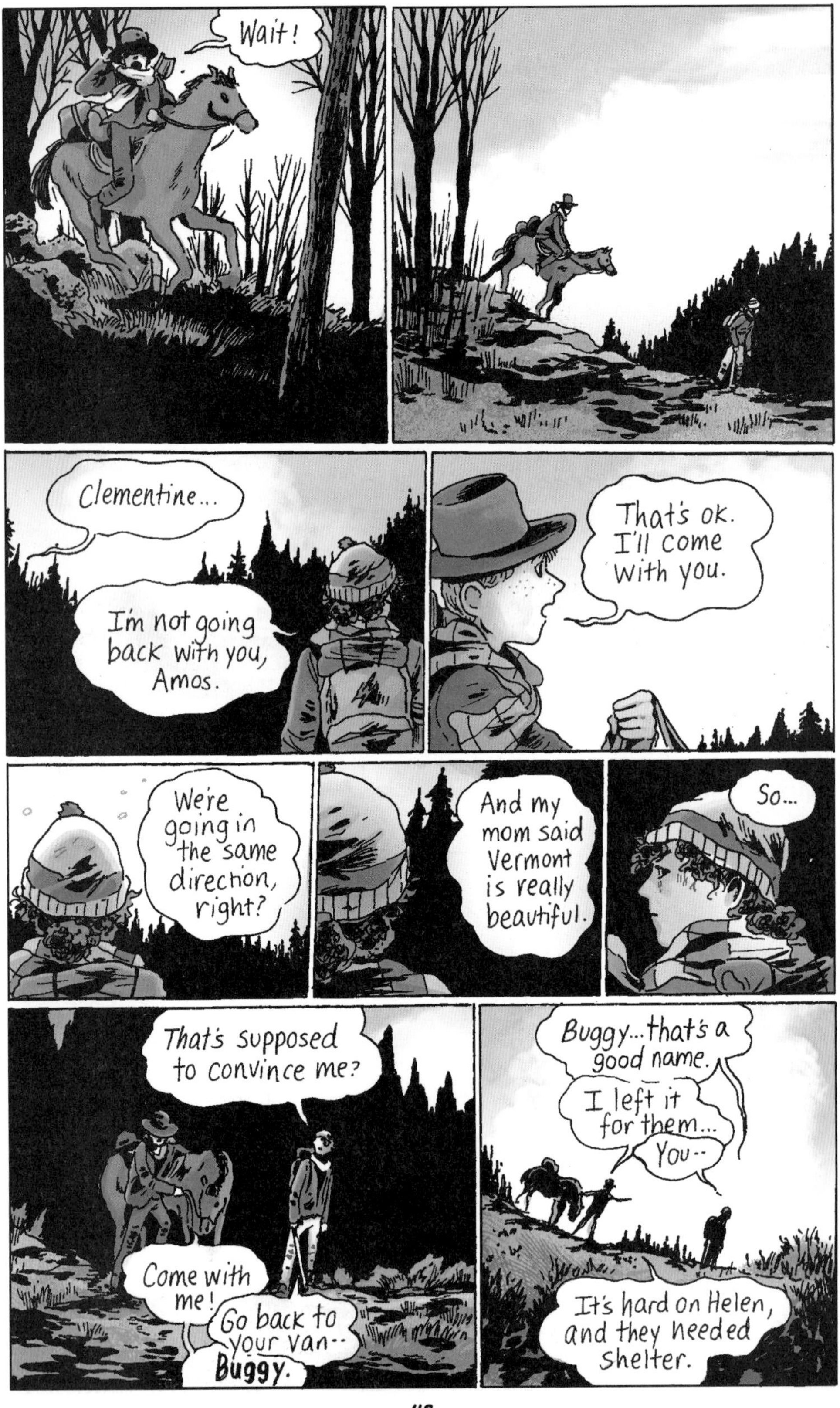
Wait!
Clementine...
I'm not going back with you, Amos.
That's ok. I'll come with you.
We're going in the same direction, right?
And my mom said Vermont is really beautiful.
So...
That's supposed to convince me?
Come with me!
Go back to your van--
Buggy.
Buggy...that's a good name.
I left it for them...
You--
It's hard on Helen, and they needed shelter.

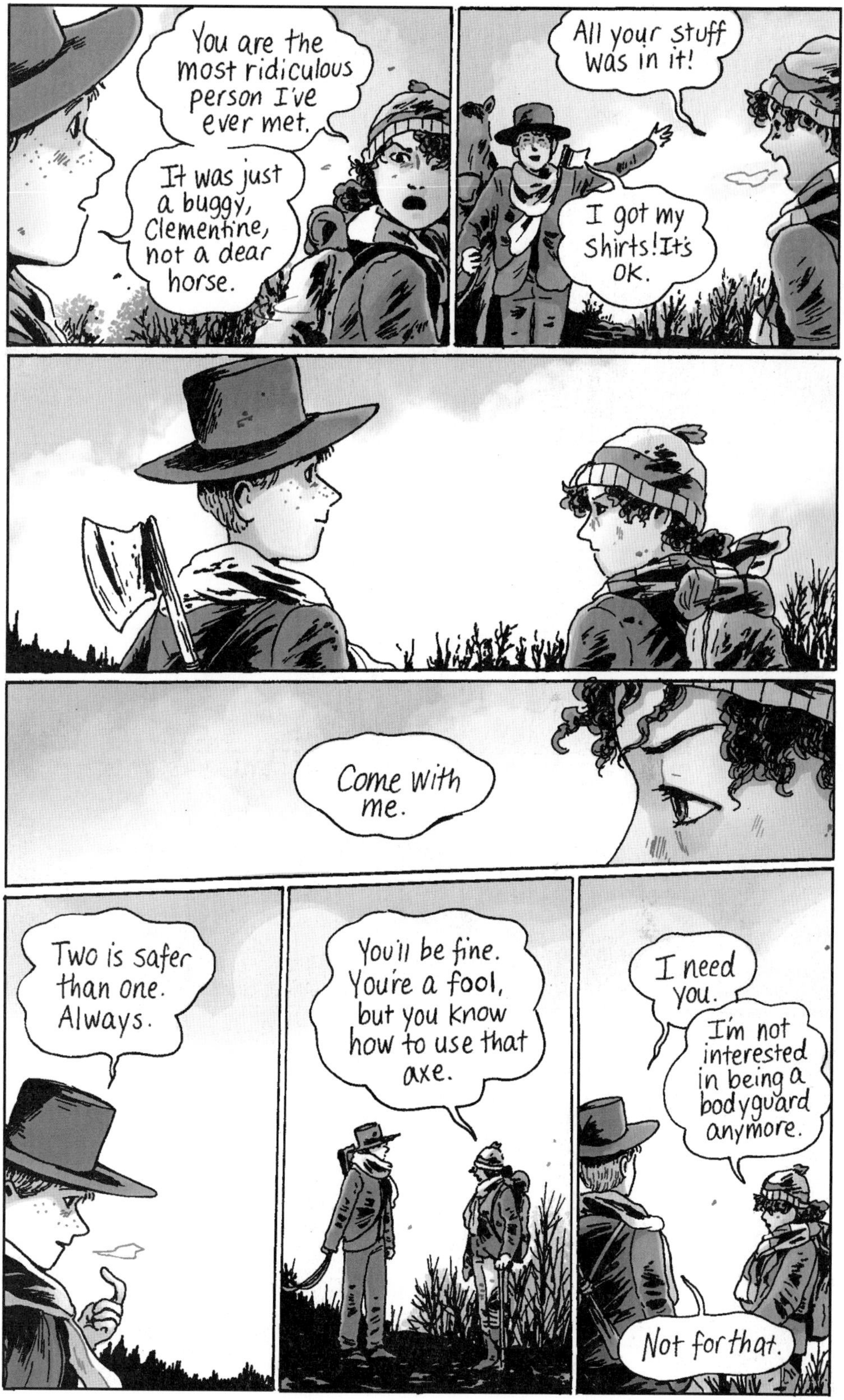
You are the most ridiculous person I've ever met.
It was just a buggy, Clementine, not a dear horse.
All your stuff was in it!
I got my shirts! It's OK.
Come with me.
Two is safer than one. Always.
You'll be fine. You're a fool, but you know how to use that axe.
I need you.
I'm not interested in being a bodyguard anymore.
Not for that.

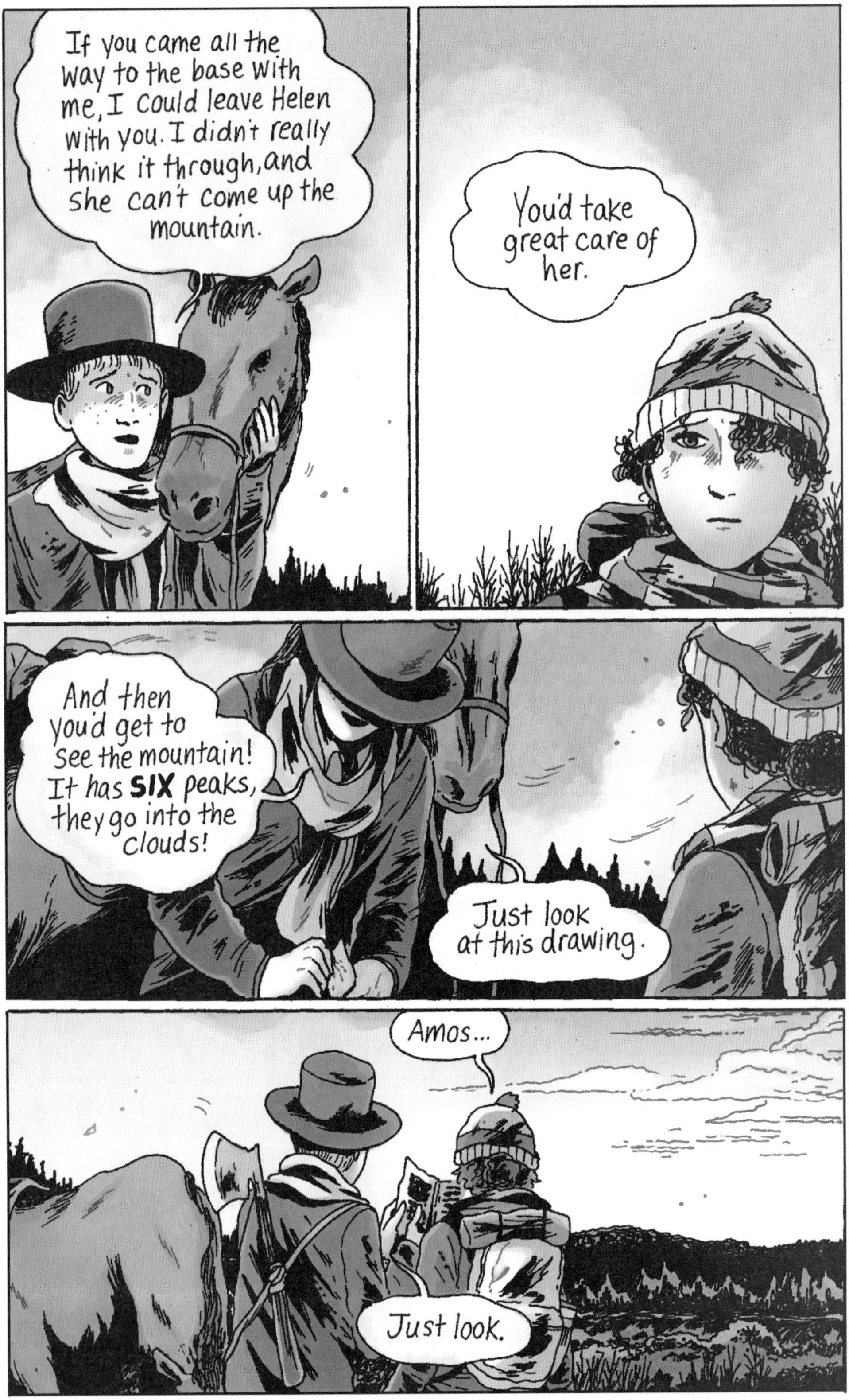
If you came all the way to the base with me, I could leave Helen with you. I didn't really think it through, and she can't come up the mountain.
You'd take great care of her.
And then you'd get to see the mountain! It has **SIX** peaks, they go into the clouds!
Just look at this drawing.
Amos...
Just look.

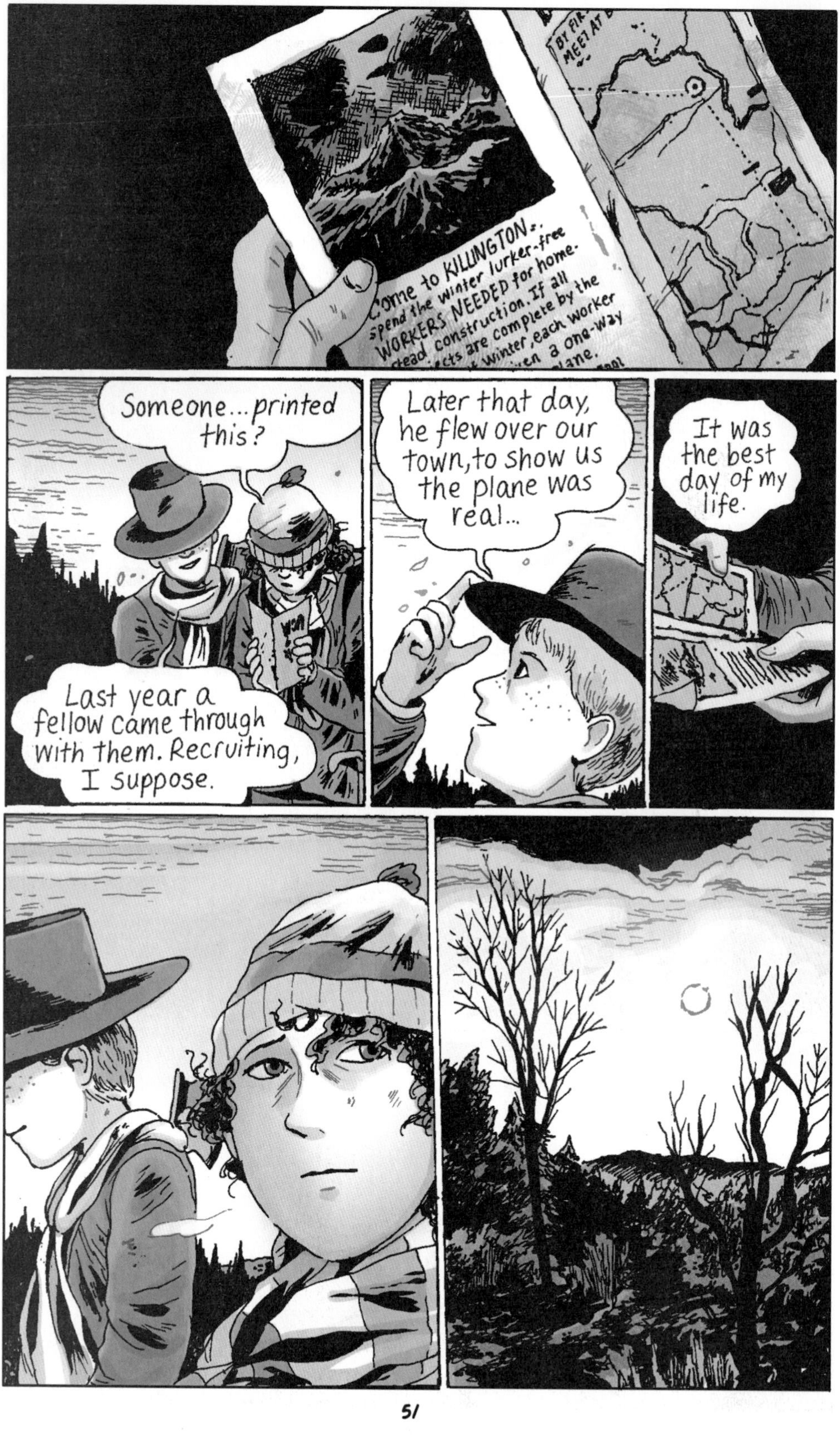
Come to KILLINGTON..
spend the winter lurker-free
WORKERS NEEDED for home-
stead construction. If all
ects are complete by the
winter, each worker
a one-way
plane.
Someone...printed this?
Last year a fellow came through with them. Recruiting, I suppose.
Later that day, he flew over our town, to show us the plane was real...
It was the best day of my life.

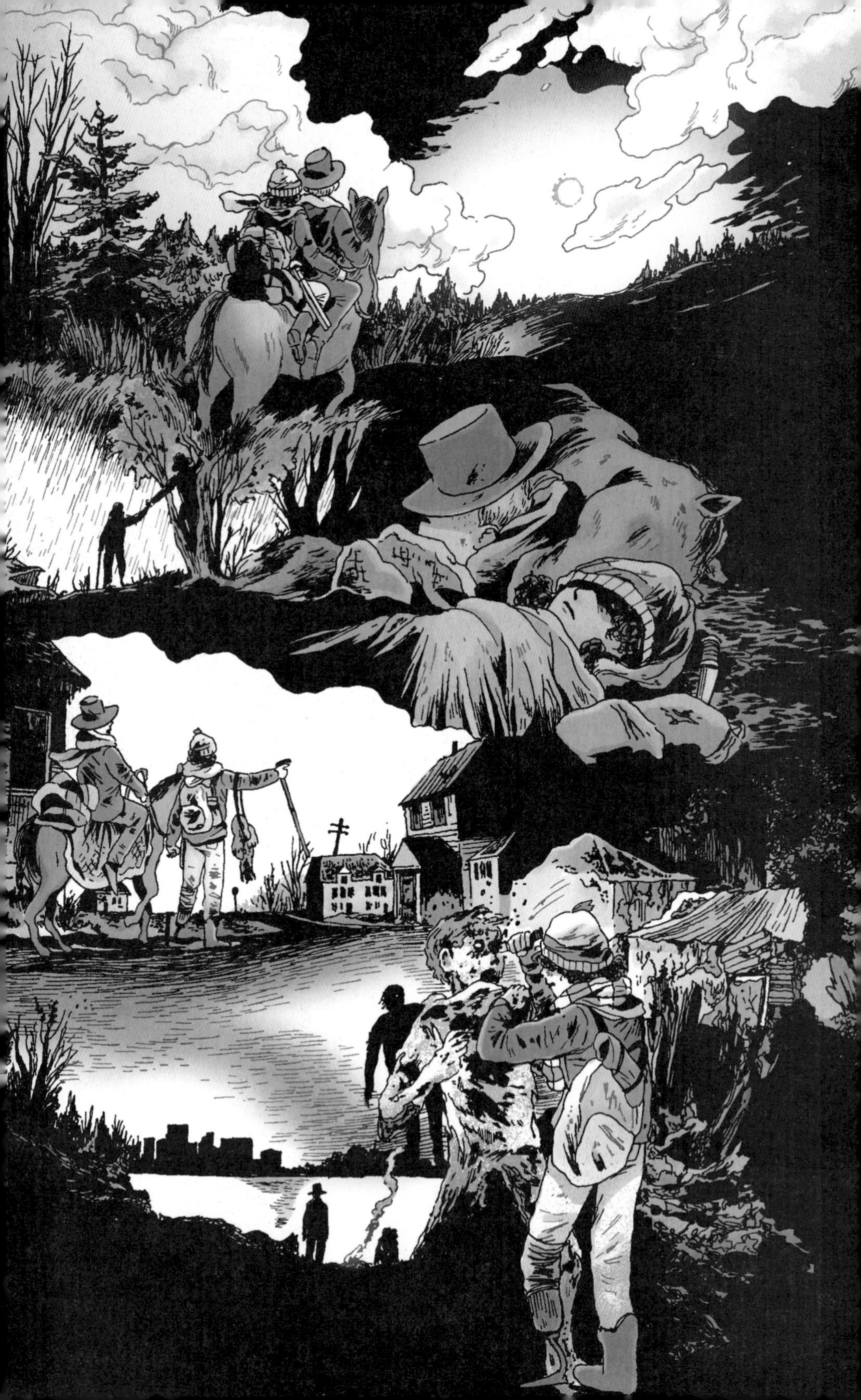

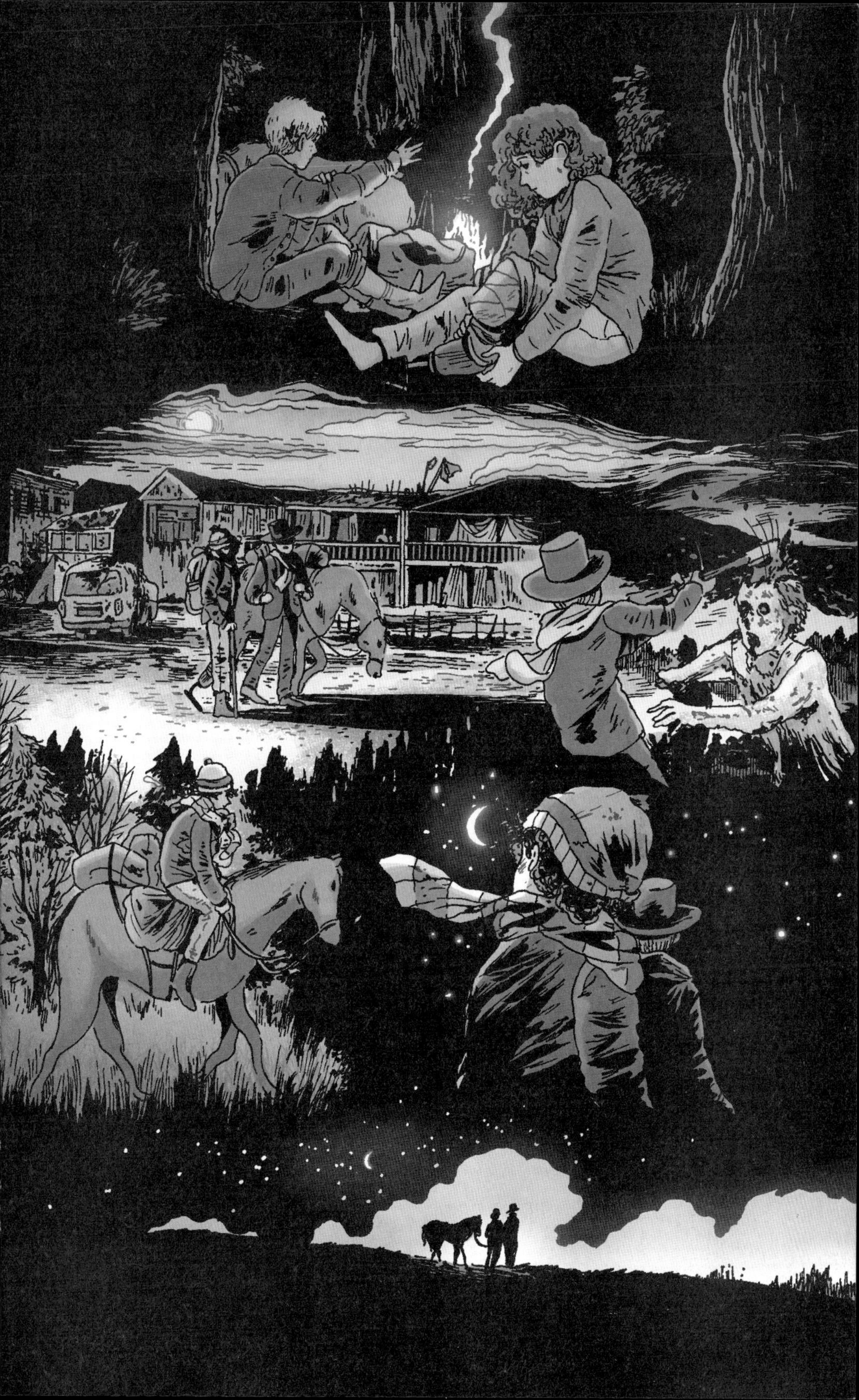

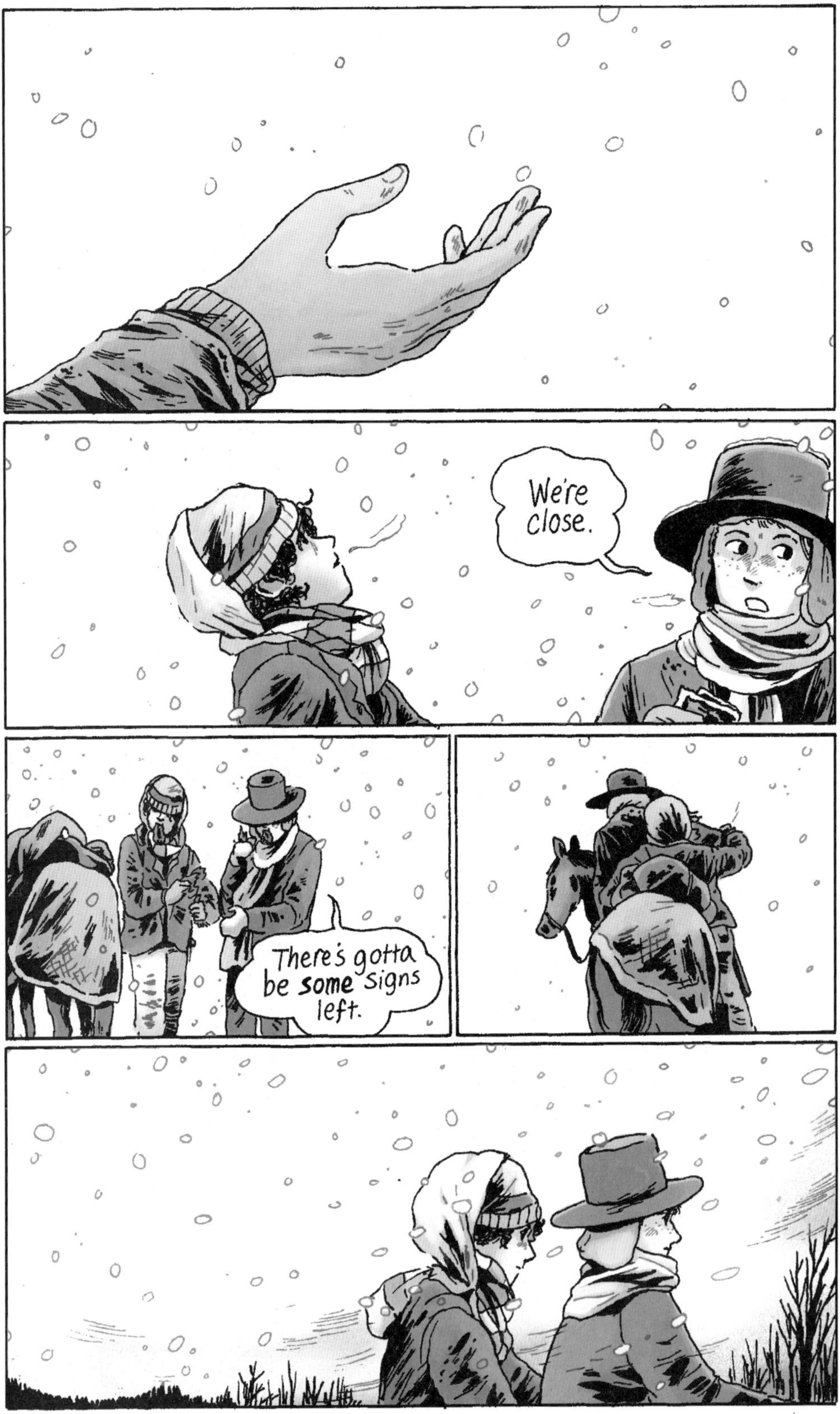
We're close.
There's gotta be **some** signs left.

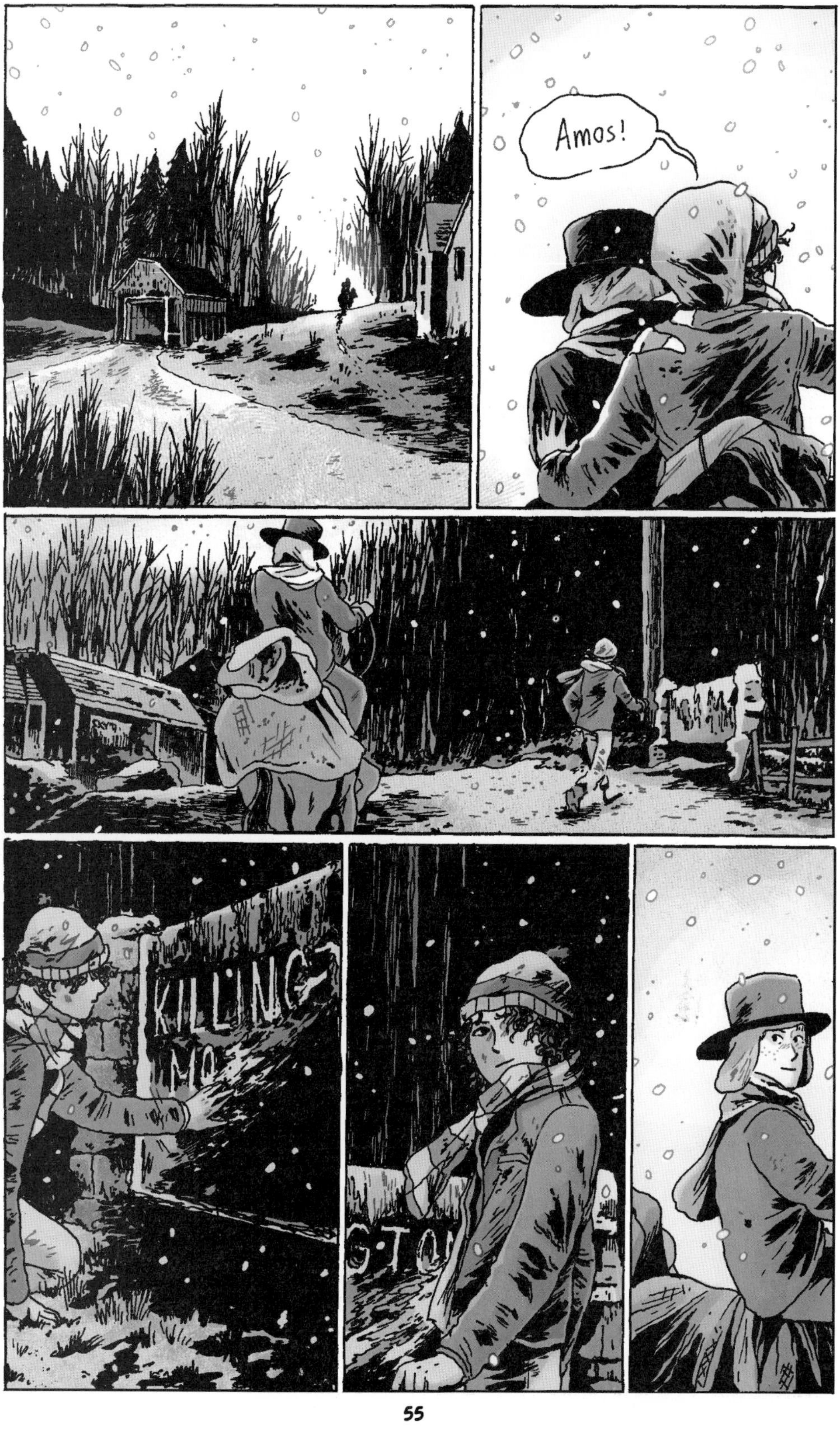
Amos!
KILLING
MO
GTO

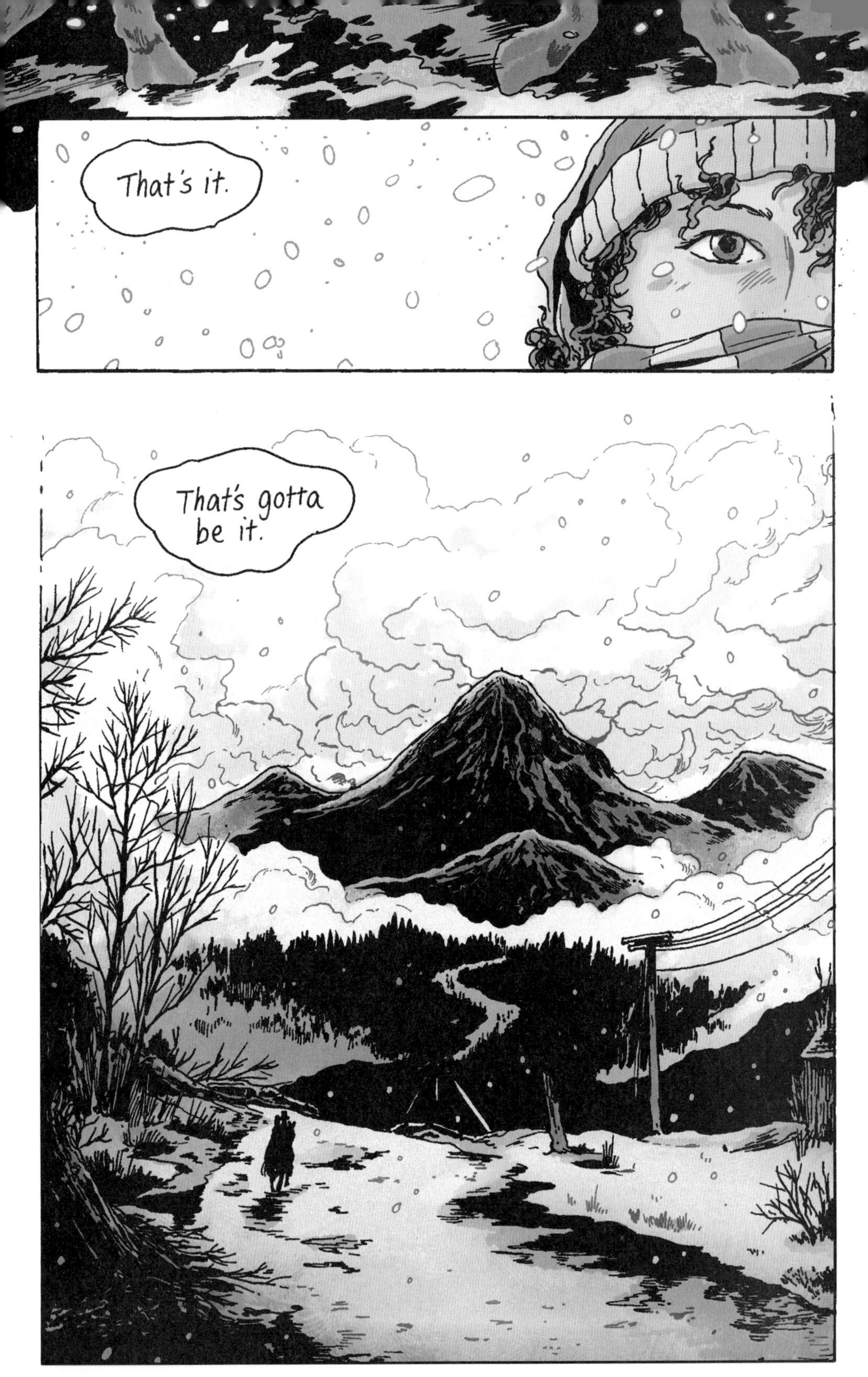

That's it.
That's gotta be it.

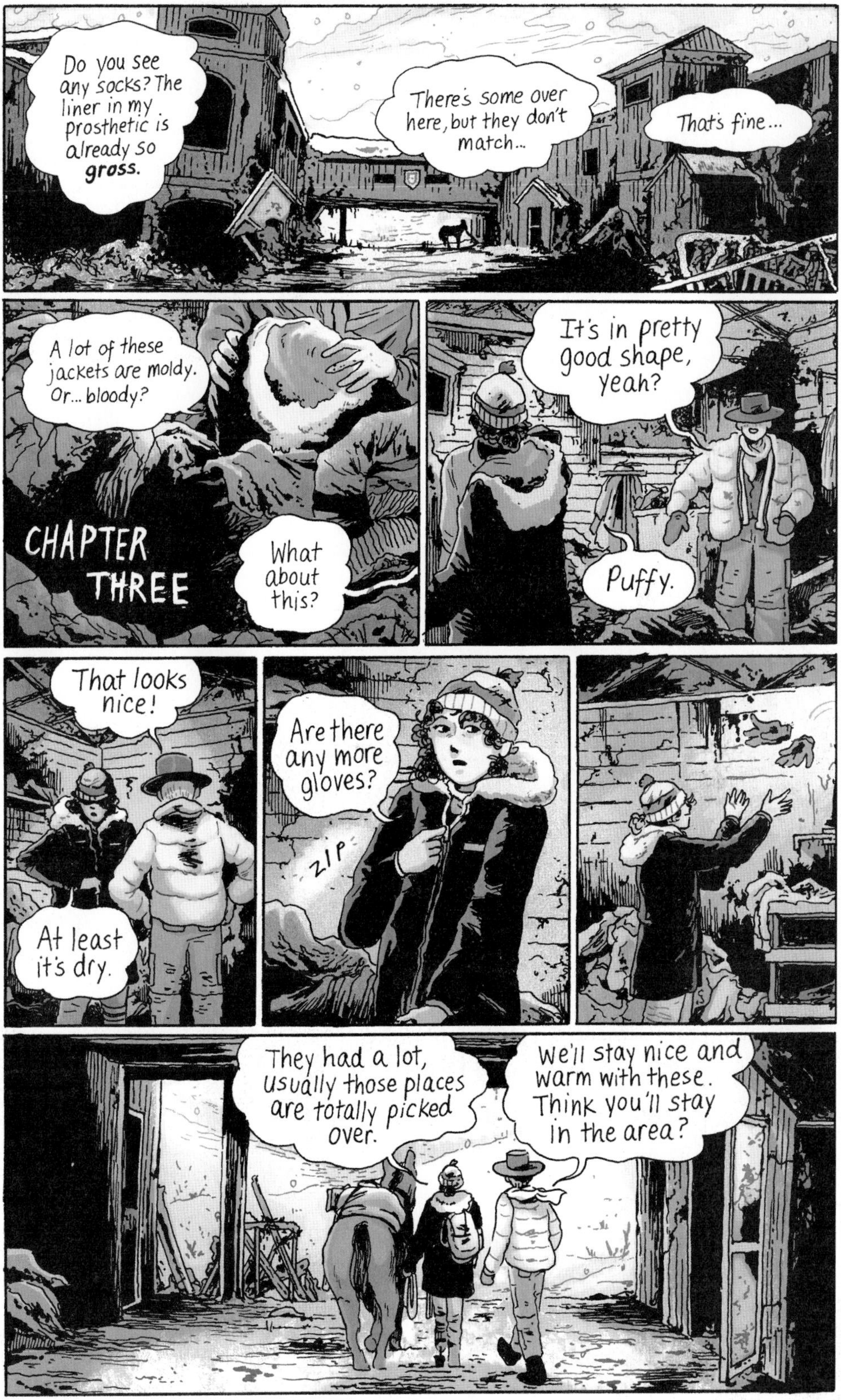
Do you see any socks? The liner in my prosthetic is already so **gross.**
There's some over here, but they don't match...
That's fine...
A lot of these jackets are moldy. Or... bloody?
CHAPTER THREE
What about this?
It's in pretty good shape, yeah?
Puffy.
That looks nice!
At least it's dry.
Are there any more gloves?
ZIP
They had a lot, usually those places are totally picked over.
We'll stay nice and warm with these. Think you'll stay in the area?

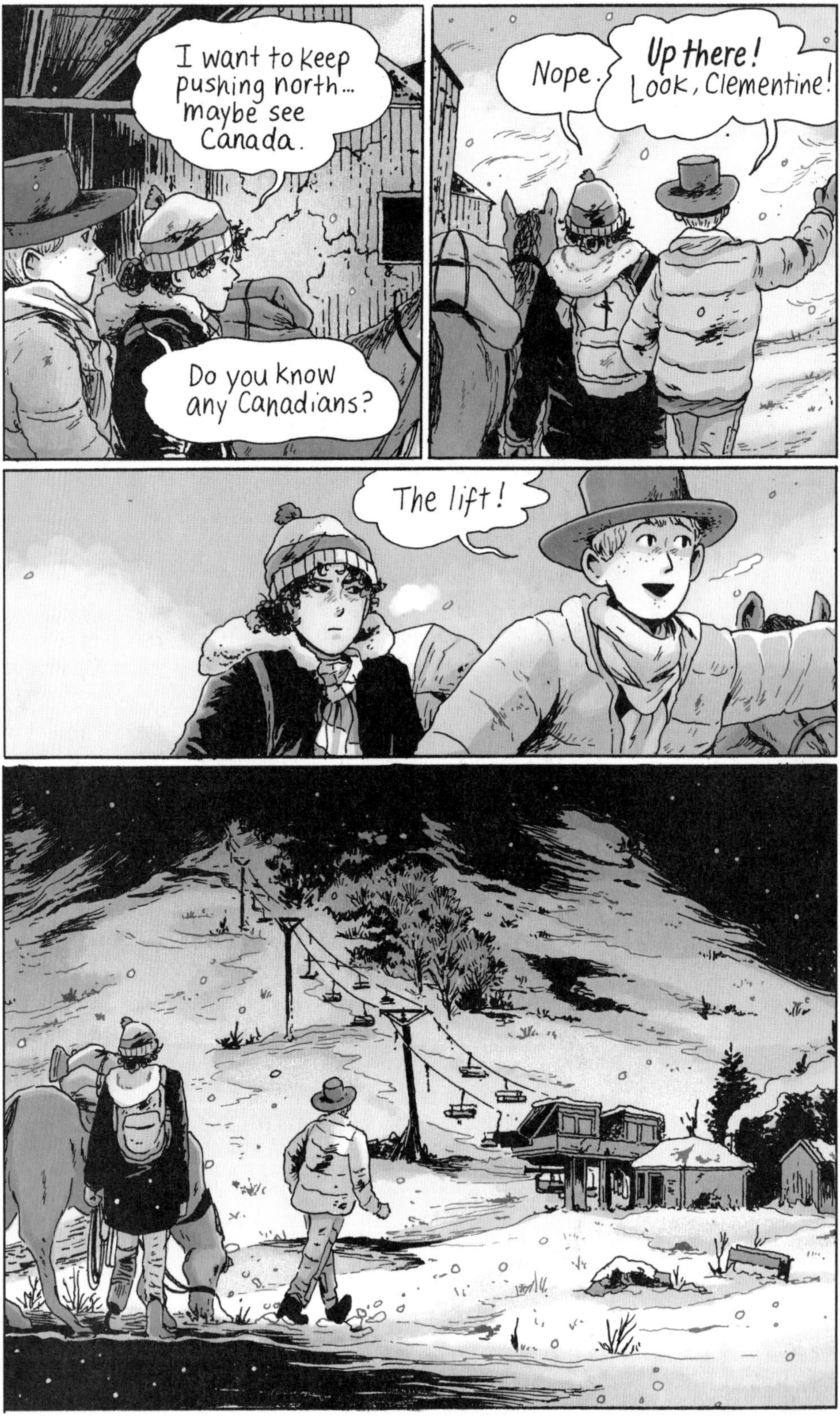
I want to keep pushing north... maybe see Canada.
Do you know any Canadians?
Nope.
Up there! Look, Clementine!
The lift!

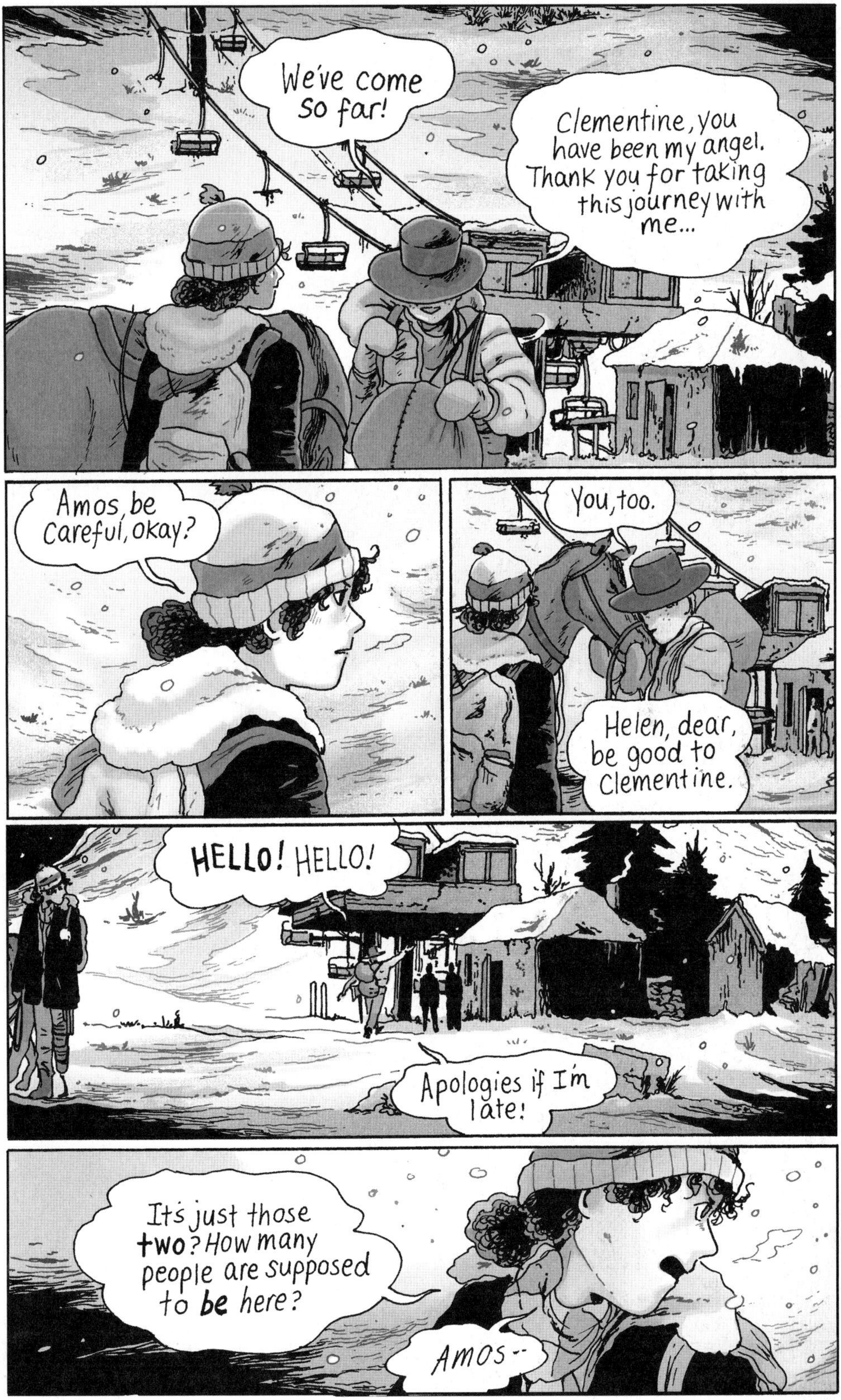
We've come so far!
Clementine, you have been my angel. Thank you for taking this journey with me...
Amos, be careful, okay?
You, too.
Helen, dear, be good to Clementine.
HELLO! HELLO!
Apologies if I'm late!
It's just those **two**? How many people are supposed to **be** here?
Amos--

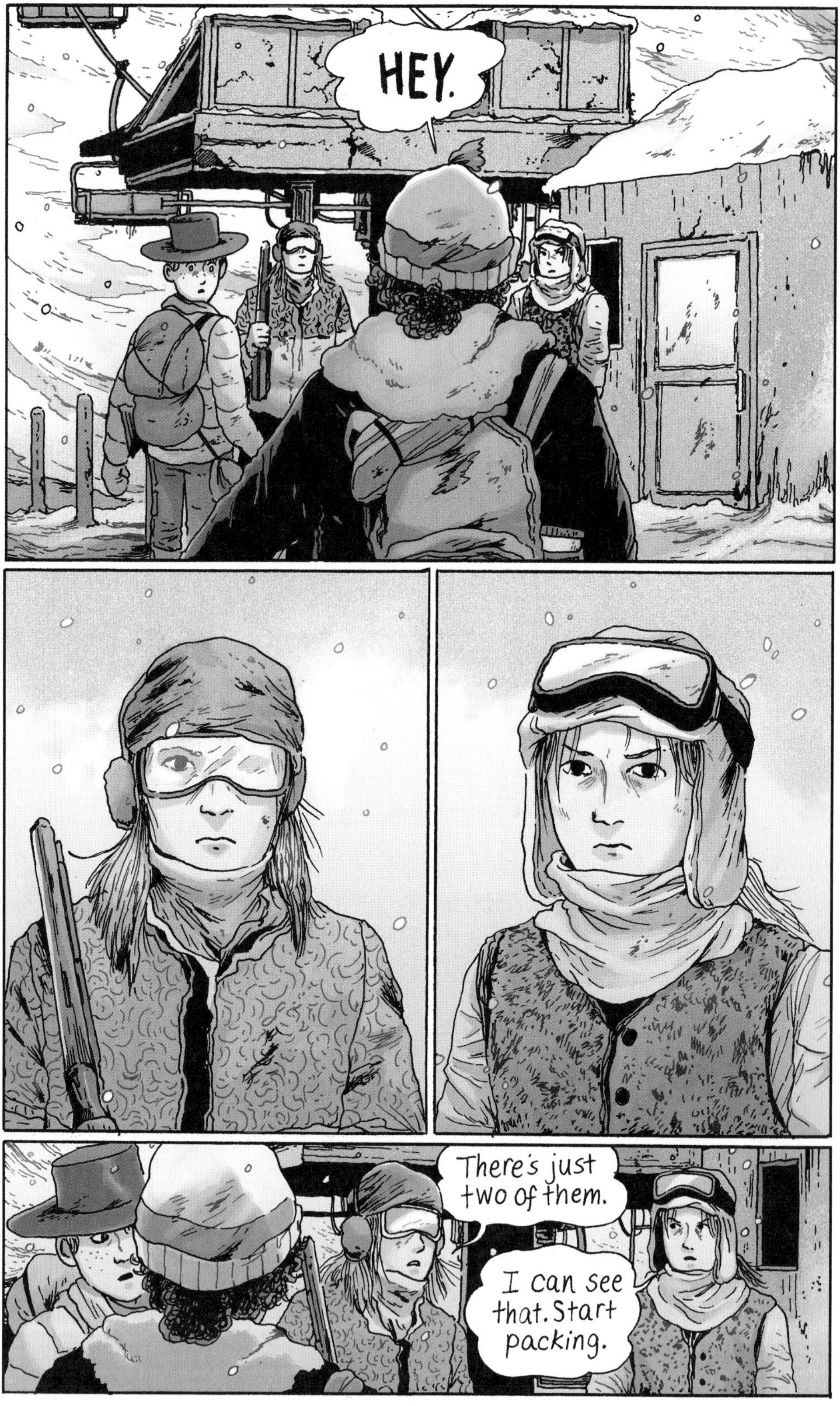
HEY.
There's just two of them.
I can see that. Start packing.

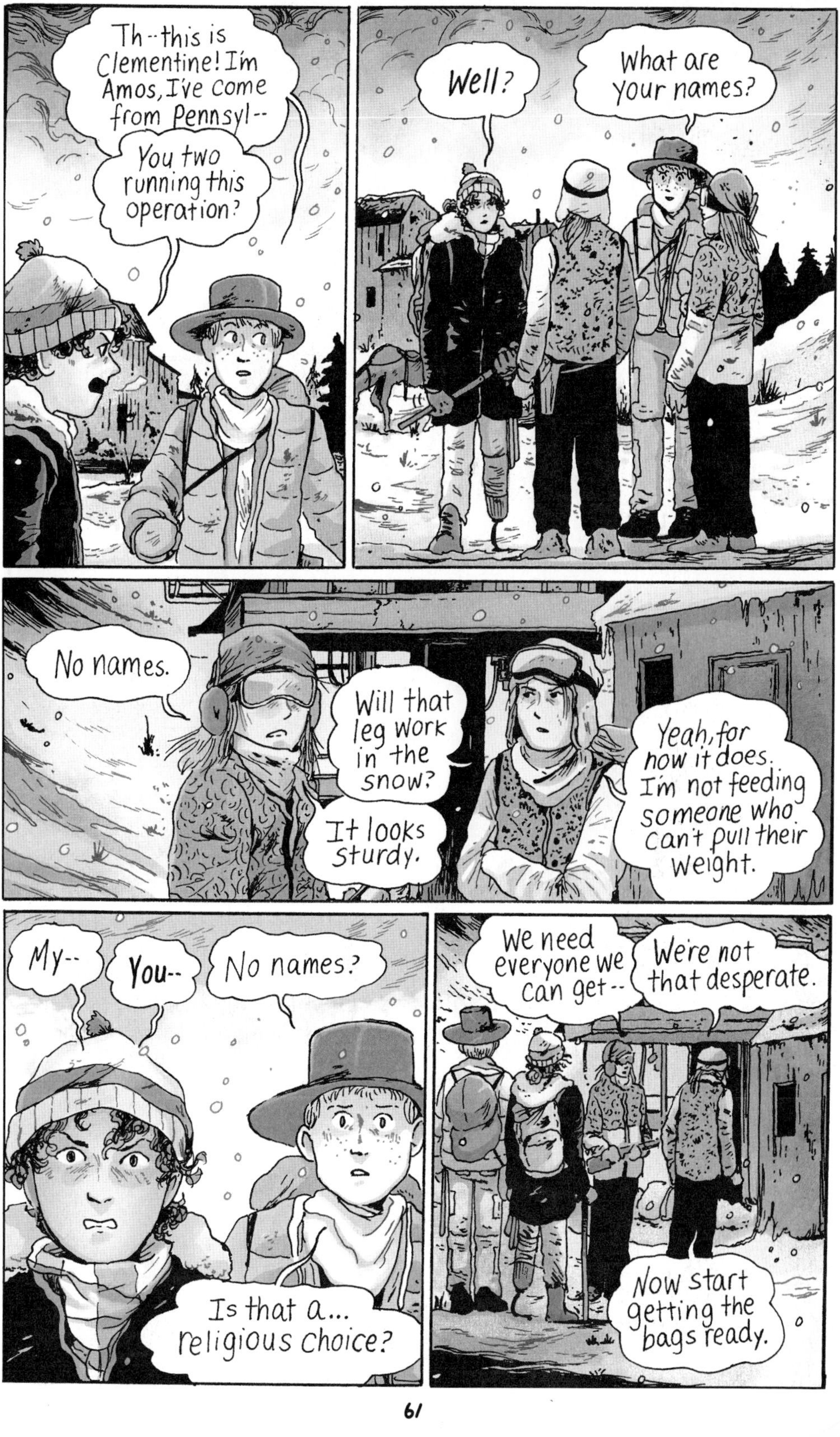
Th--this is Clementine! I'm Amos, I've come from Pennsyl--
You two running this operation?
Well?
What are your names?
No names.
Will that leg work in the snow?
It looks sturdy.
Yeah, for now it does. I'm not feeding someone who can't pull their weight.
My--
You--
No names?
Is that a... religious choice?
We need everyone we can get--
We're not that desperate.
Now start getting the bags ready.

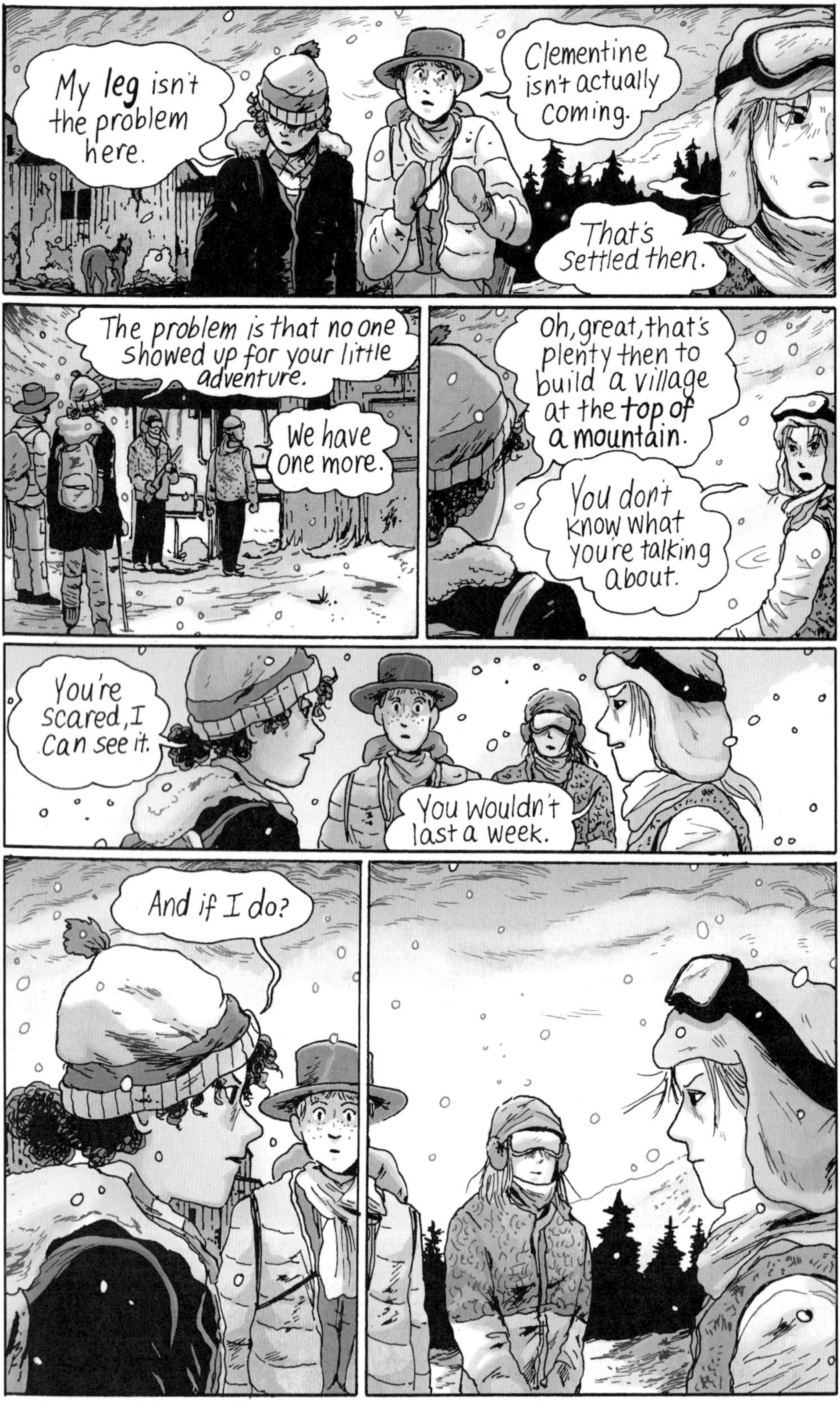

My leg isn't the problem here.
Clementine isn't actually coming.
That's settled then.
The problem is that no one showed up for your little adventure.
We have one more.
Oh, great, that's plenty then to build a village at the top of a mountain.
You don't know what you're talking about.
You're scared, I can see it.
You wouldn't last a week.
And if I do?

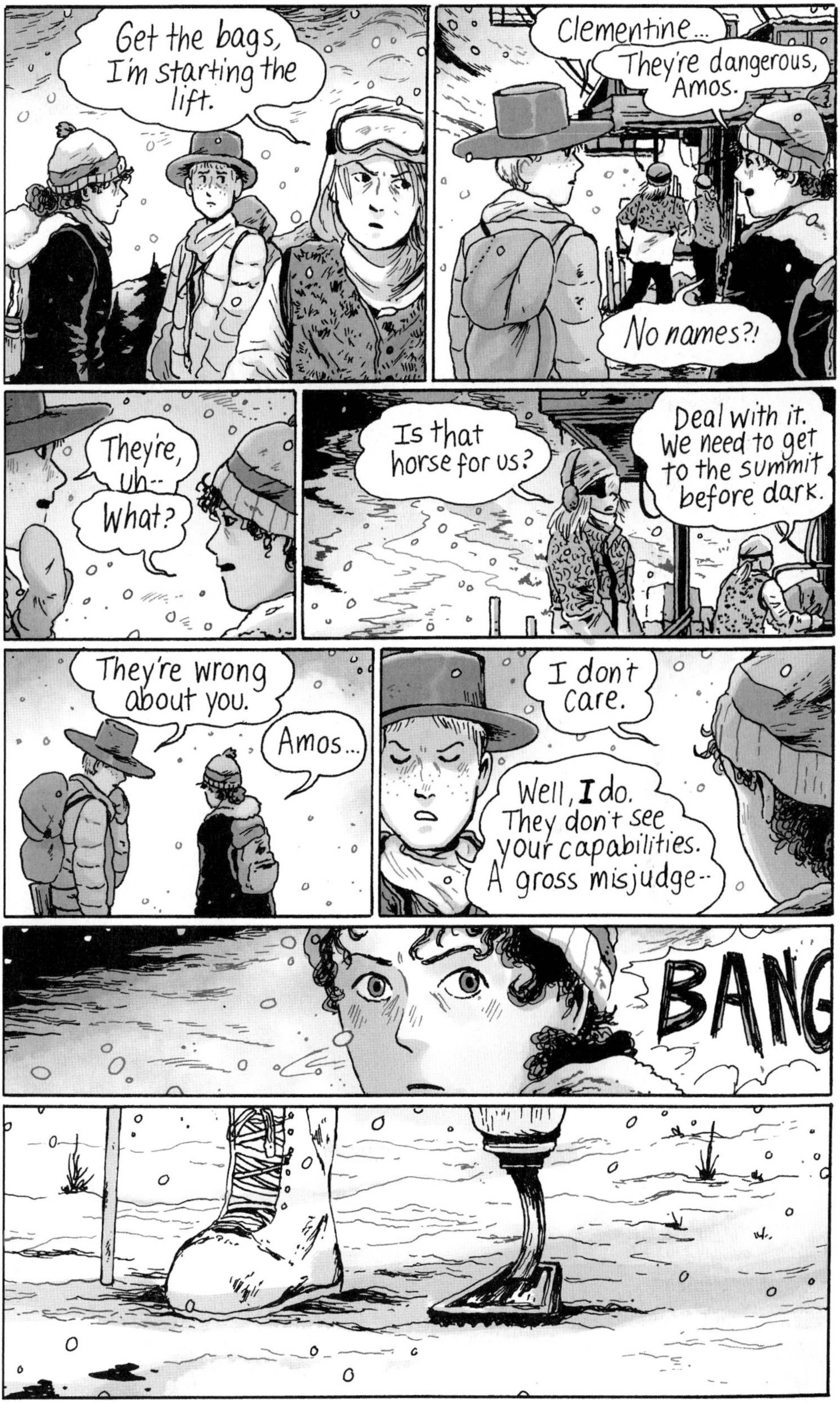
Get the bags, I'm starting the lift.
Clementine...
They're dangerous, Amos.
No names?!
They're, uh--
What?
Is that horse for us?
Deal with it. We need to get to the summit before dark.
They're wrong about you.
Amos...
I don't care.
Well, **I** do. They don't see your capabilities. A gross misjudge--
BANG

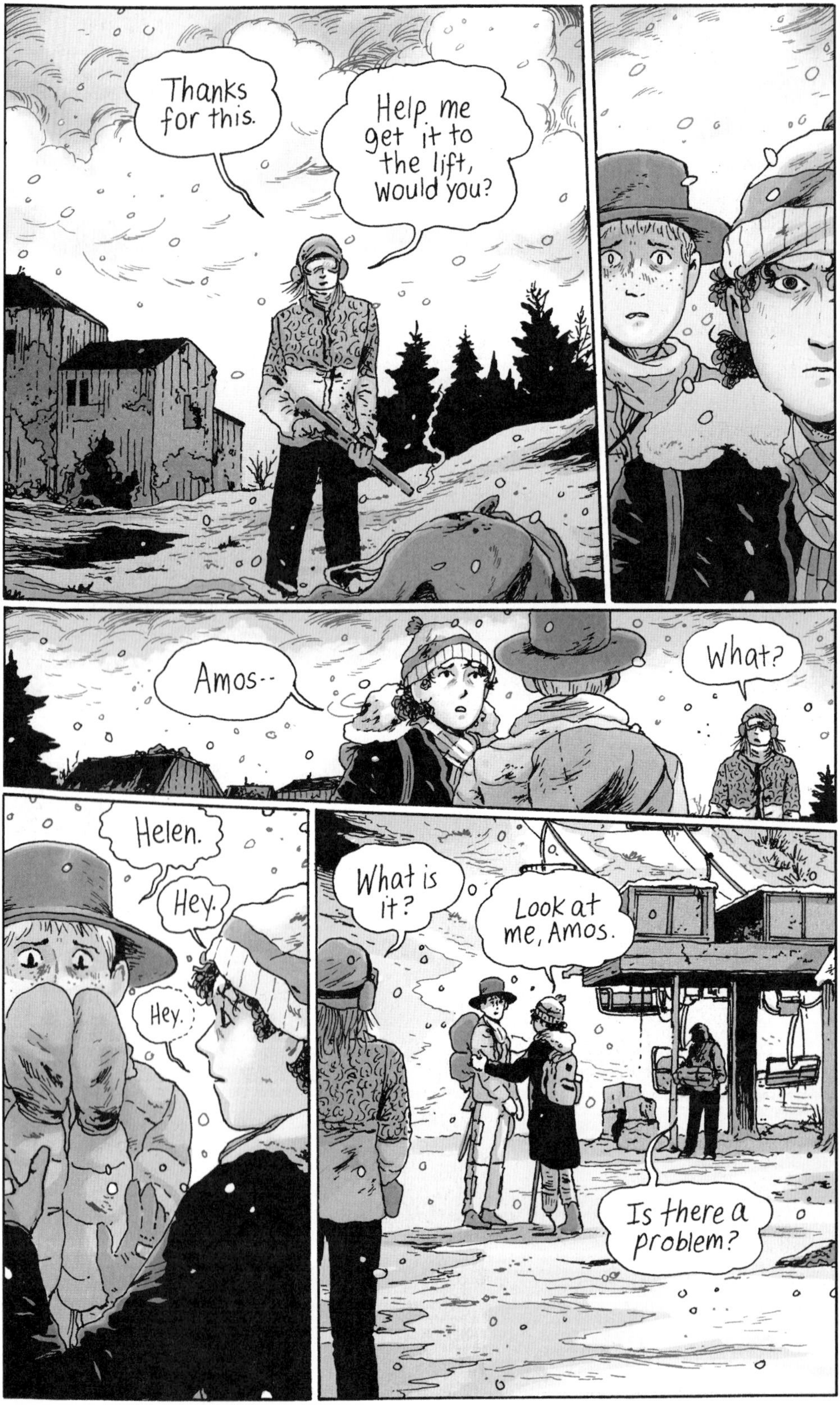
Thanks for this.
Help me get it to the lift, would you?
Amos--
What?
Helen.
Hey.
Hey.
What is it?
Look at me, Amos.
Is there a problem?

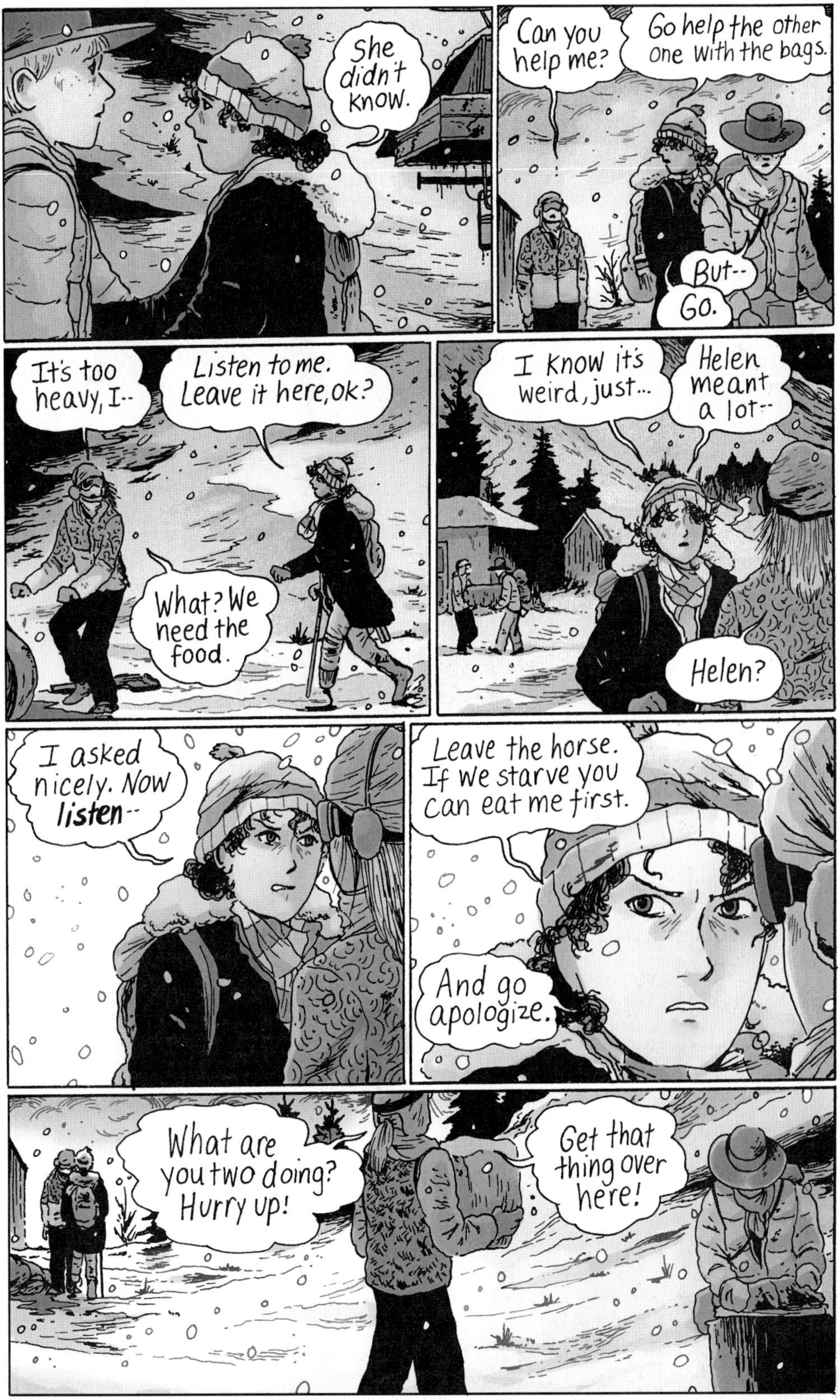
She didn't know.
Can you help me?
Go help the other one with the bags.
But--
Go.
It's too heavy, I--
Listen to me. Leave it here, ok?
What? We need the food.
I know it's weird, just...
Helen meant a lot--
Helen?
I asked nicely. Now **listen**--
Leave the horse. If we starve you can eat me first.
And go apologize.
What are you two doing? Hurry up!
Get that thing over here!

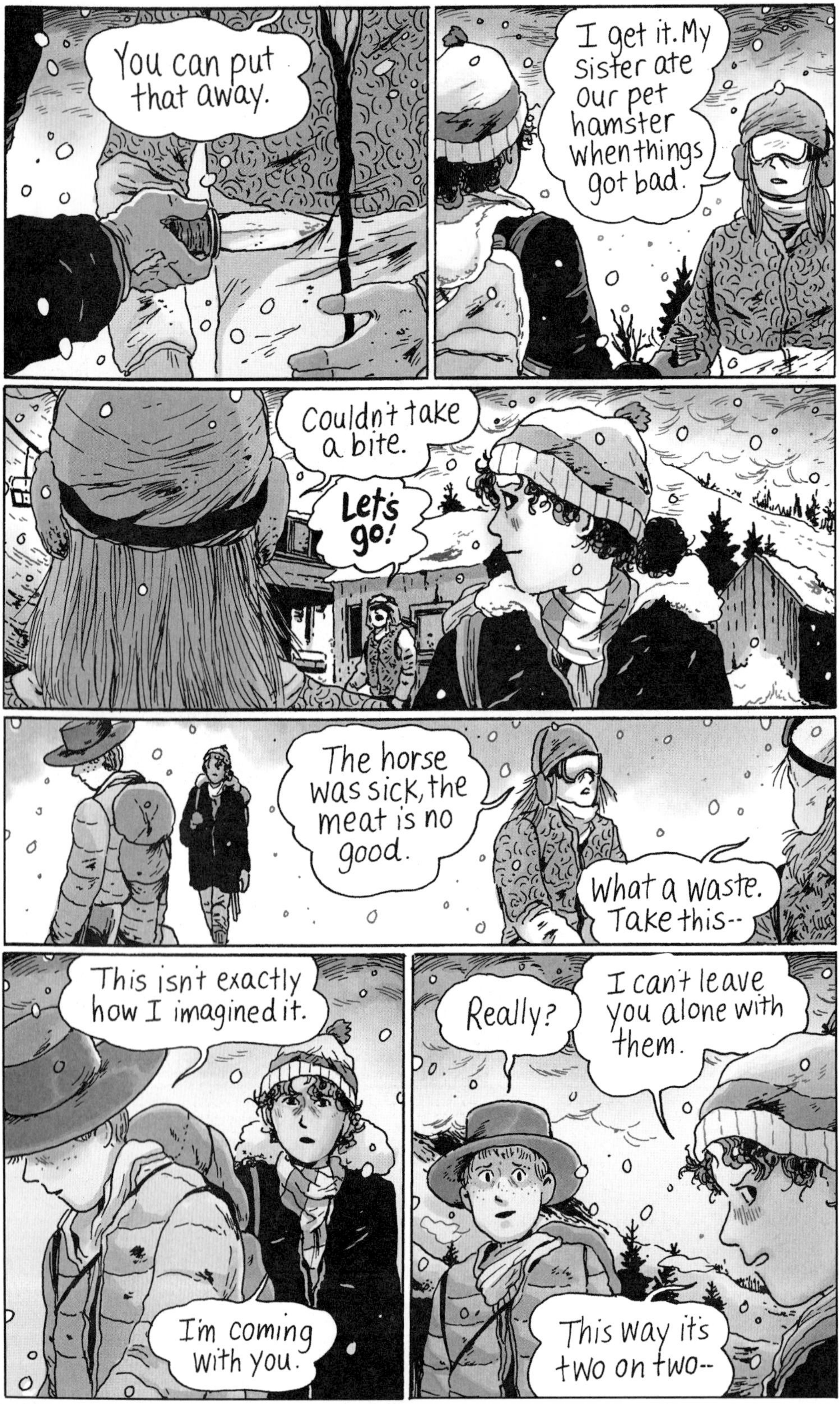
You can put that away.
I get it. My sister ate our pet hamster when things got bad.
Couldn't take a bite.
Let's go!
The horse was sick, the meat is no good.
What a waste. Take this--
This isn't exactly how I imagined it.
I'm coming with you.
Really?
I can't leave you alone with them.
This way it's two on two--

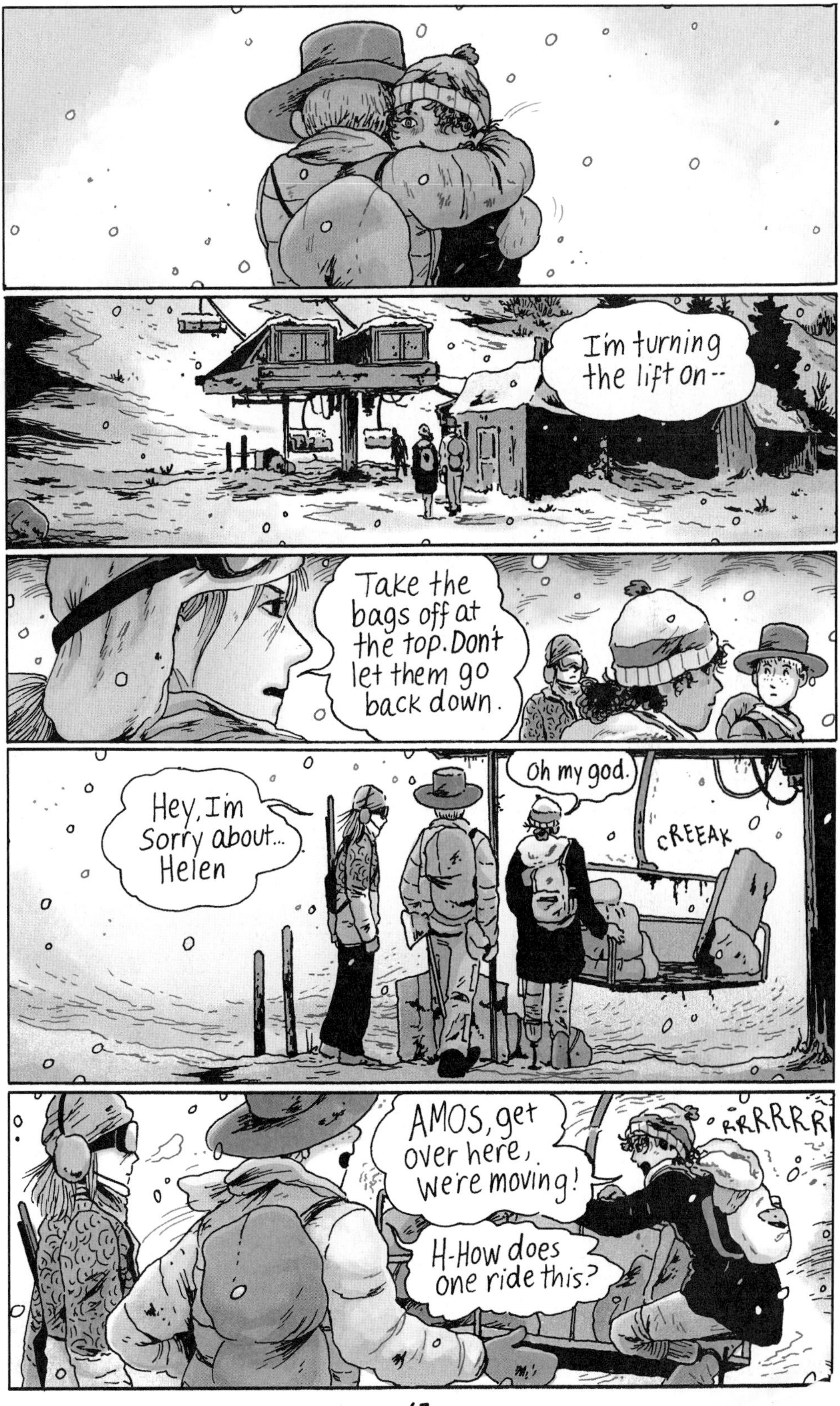
I'm turning the lift on--
Take the bags off at the top. Don't let them go back down.
Hey, I'm Sorry about... Helen
Oh my god.
CREEAK
AMOS, get over here, we're moving!
RRRRRR
H-How does one ride this?

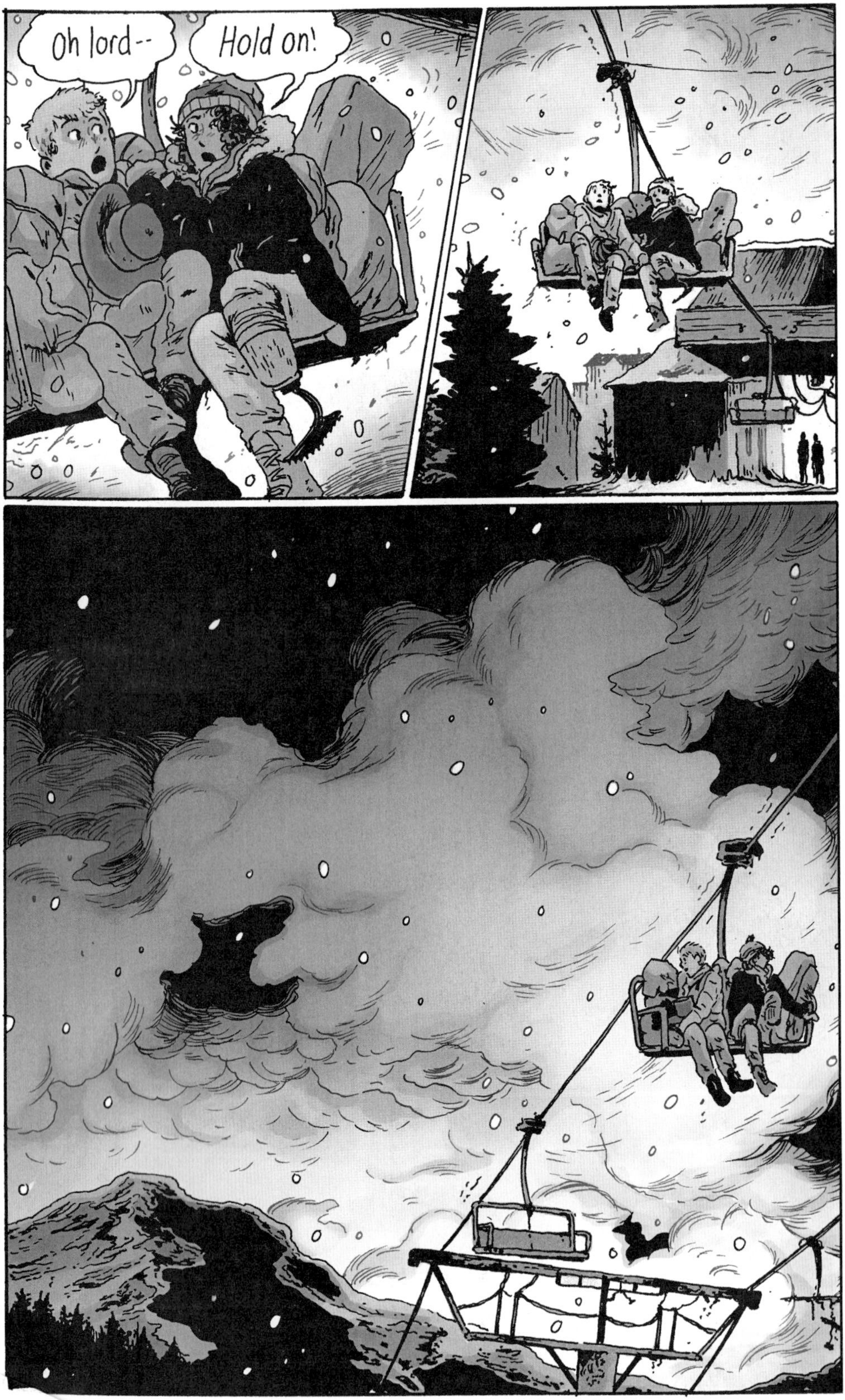
Oh lord--
Hold on!

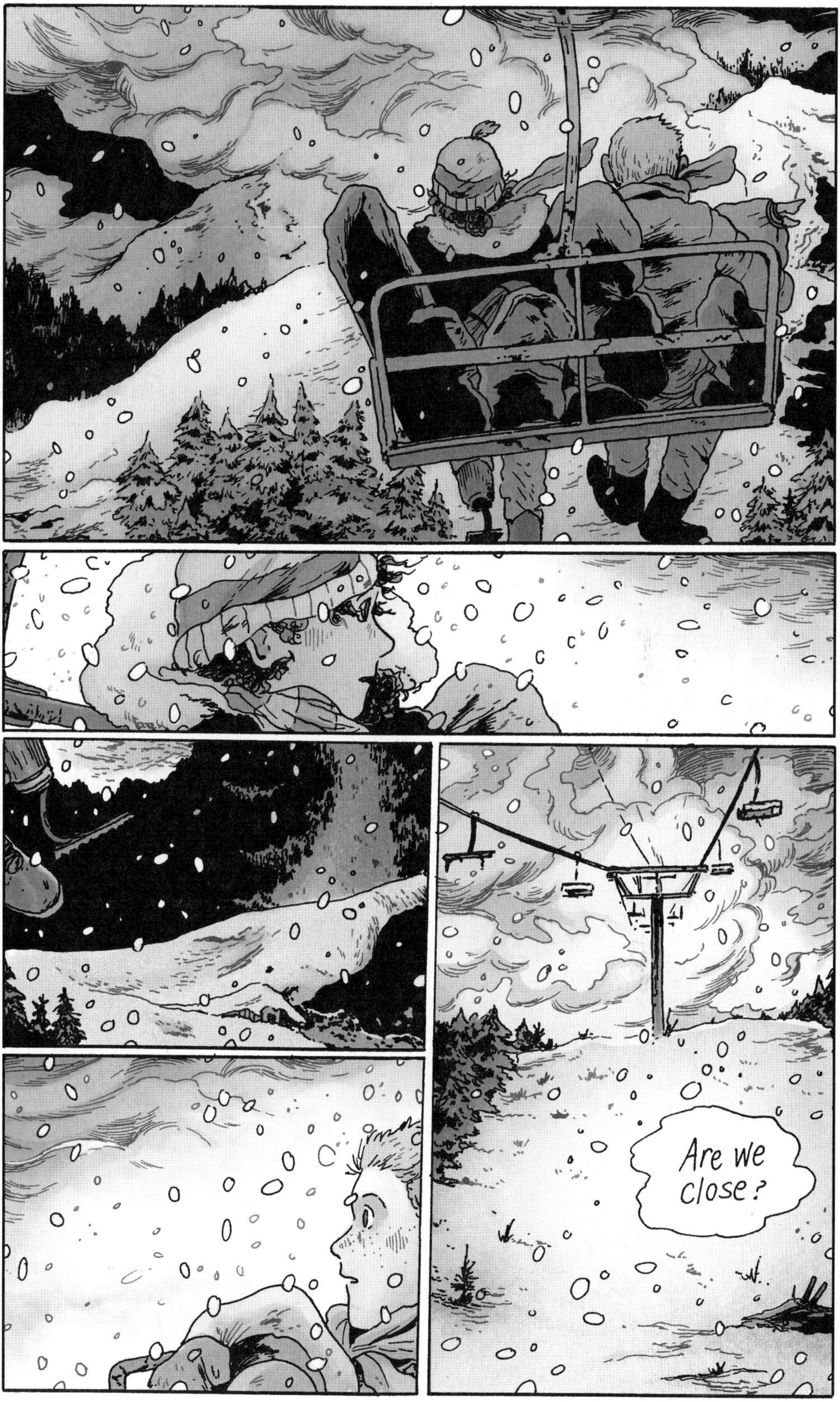
Are we close?

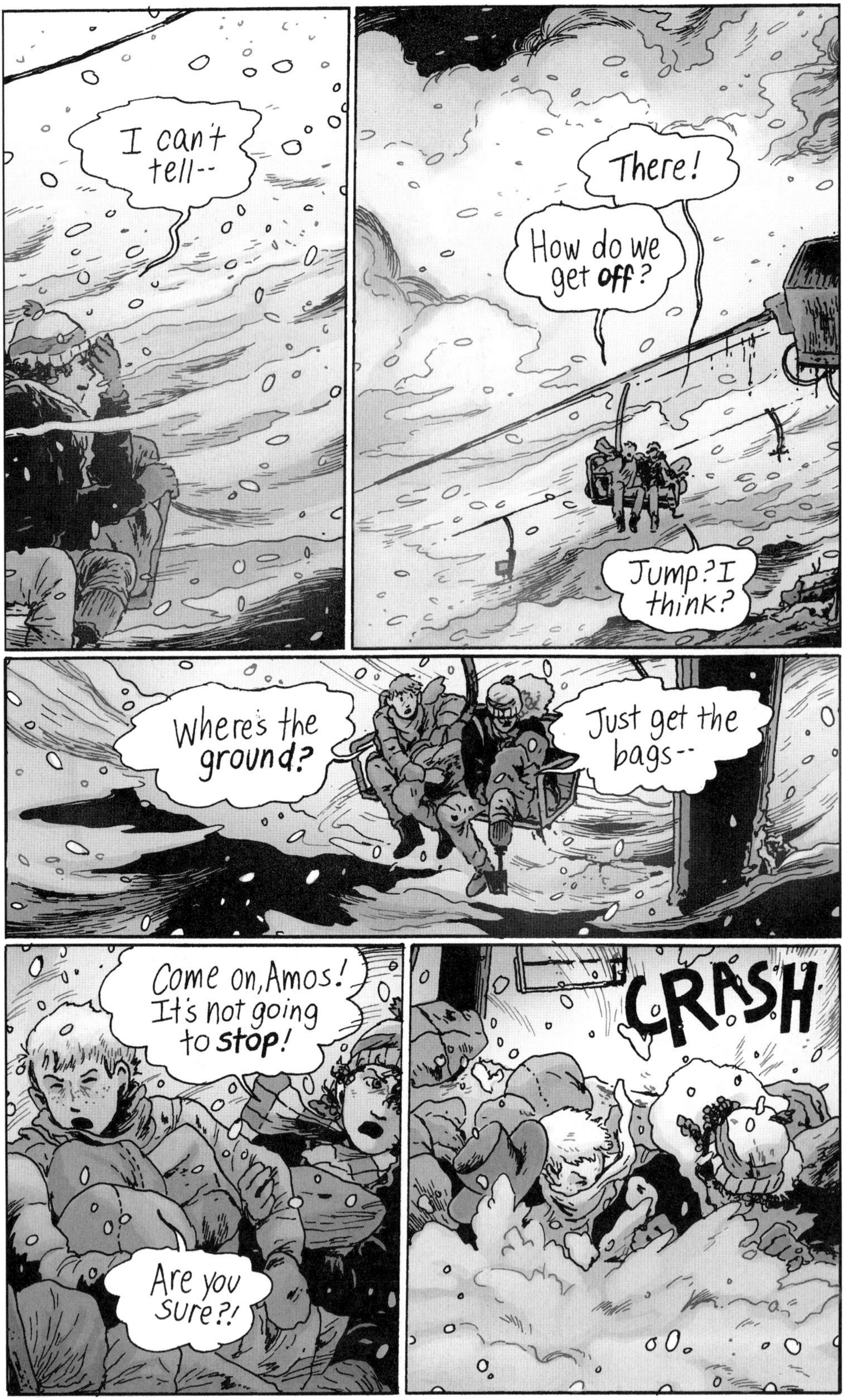
I can't tell--
There!
How do we get off?
Jump? I think?
Where's the ground?
Just get the bags--
Come on, Amos! It's not going to stop!
Are you sure?!
CRASH

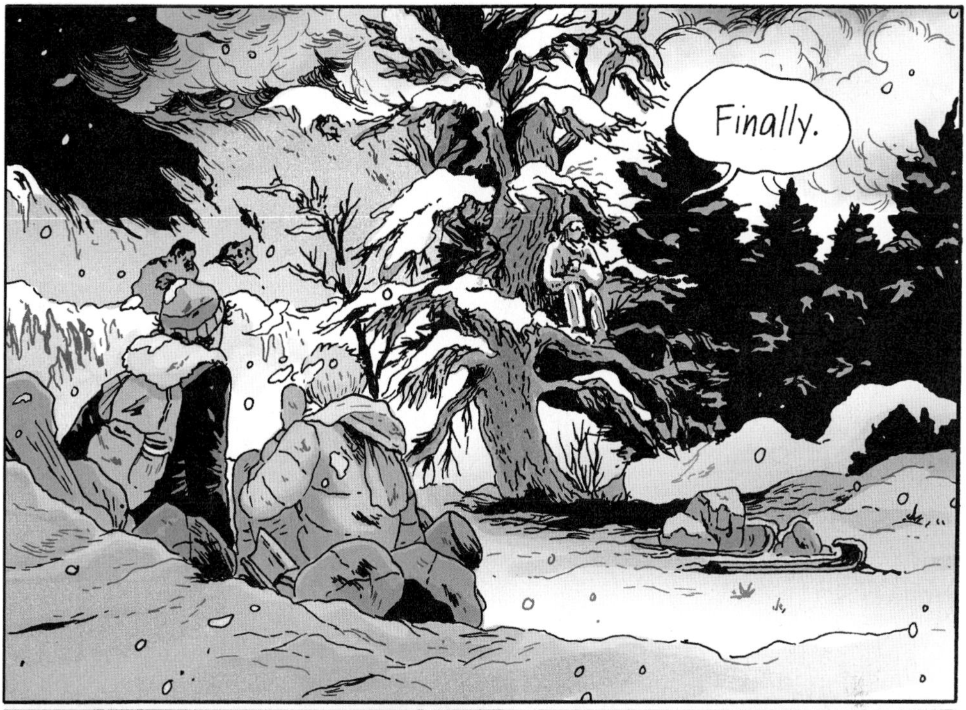
Finally.

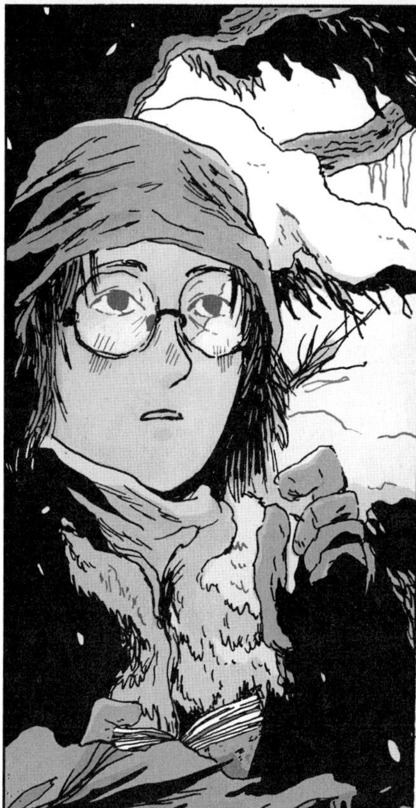

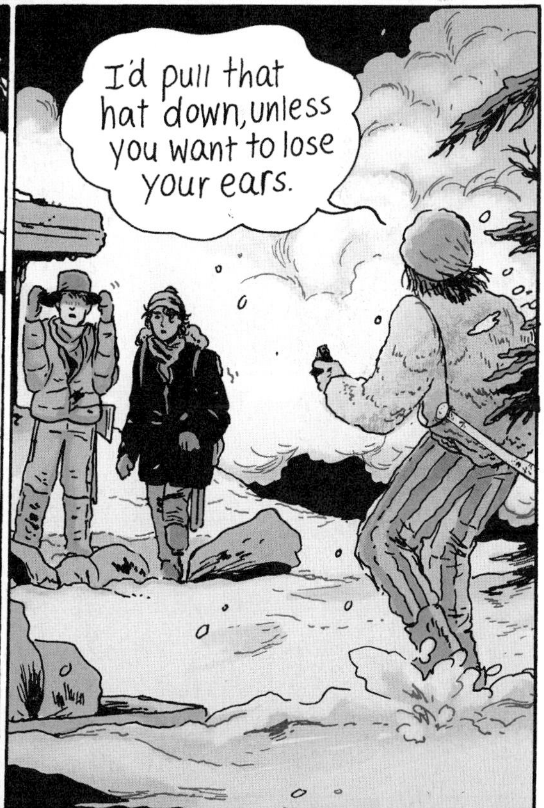
I'd pull that hat down, unless you want to lose your ears.

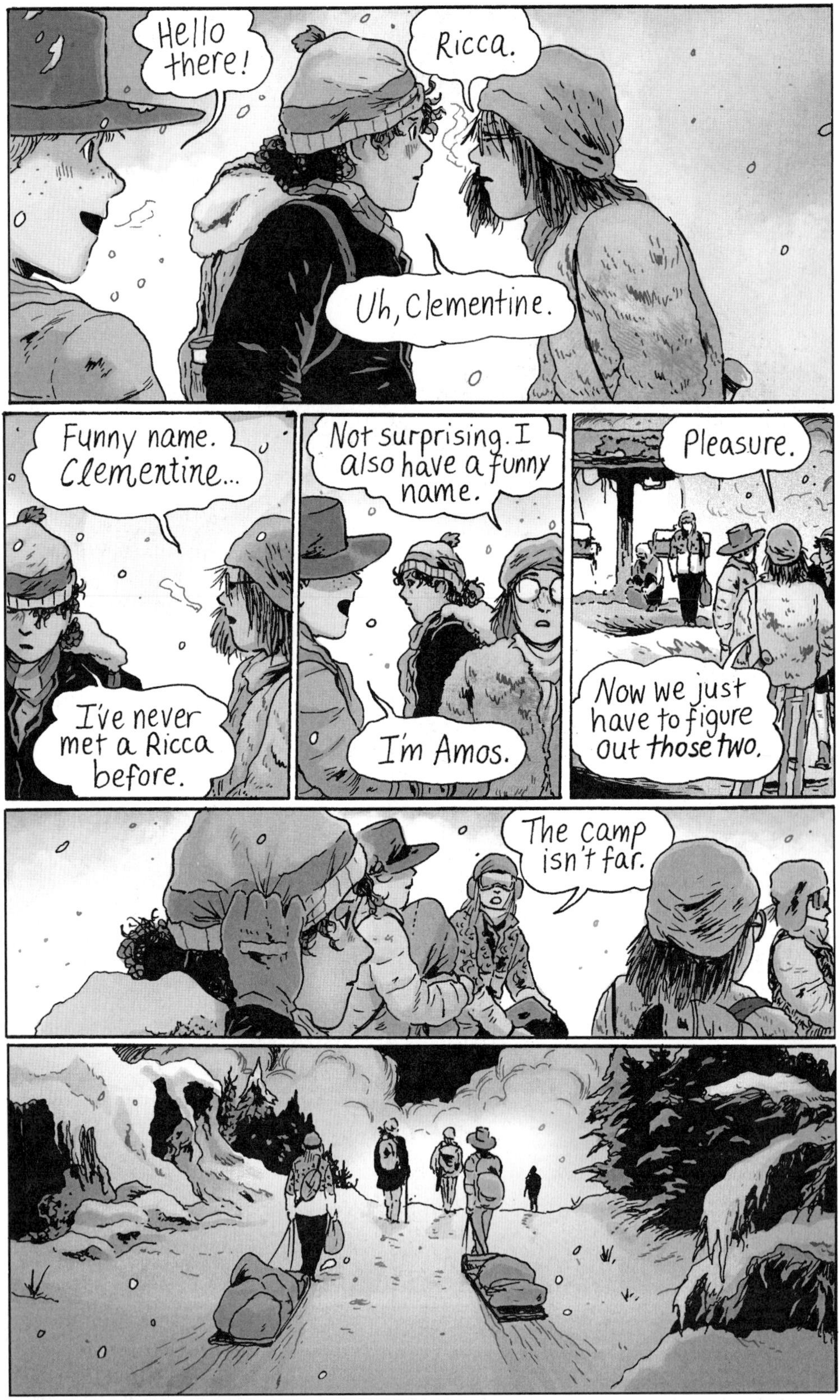
Hello there!
Ricca.
Uh, Clementine.
Funny name. Clementine...
I've never met a Ricca before.
Not surprising. I also have a funny name.
I'm Amos.
Pleasure.
Now we just have to figure out those two.
The camp isn't far.

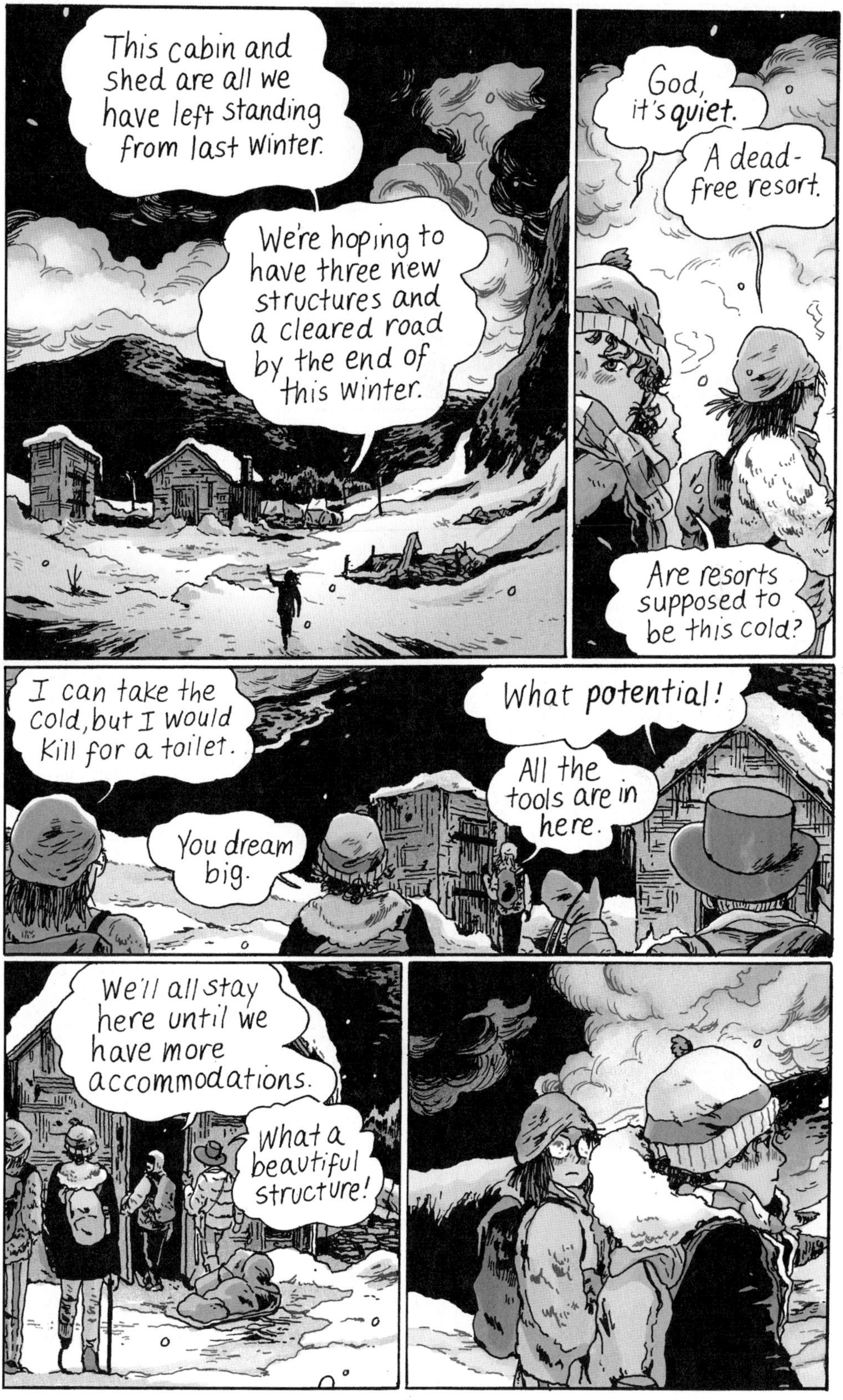
This cabin and shed are all we have left standing from last winter.
We're hoping to have three new structures and a cleared road by the end of this winter.
God, it's quiet.
A dead-free resort.
Are resorts supposed to be this cold?
I can take the cold, but I would kill for a toilet.
You dream big.
What potential!
All the tools are in here.
We'll all stay here until we have more accommodations.
What a beautiful structure!

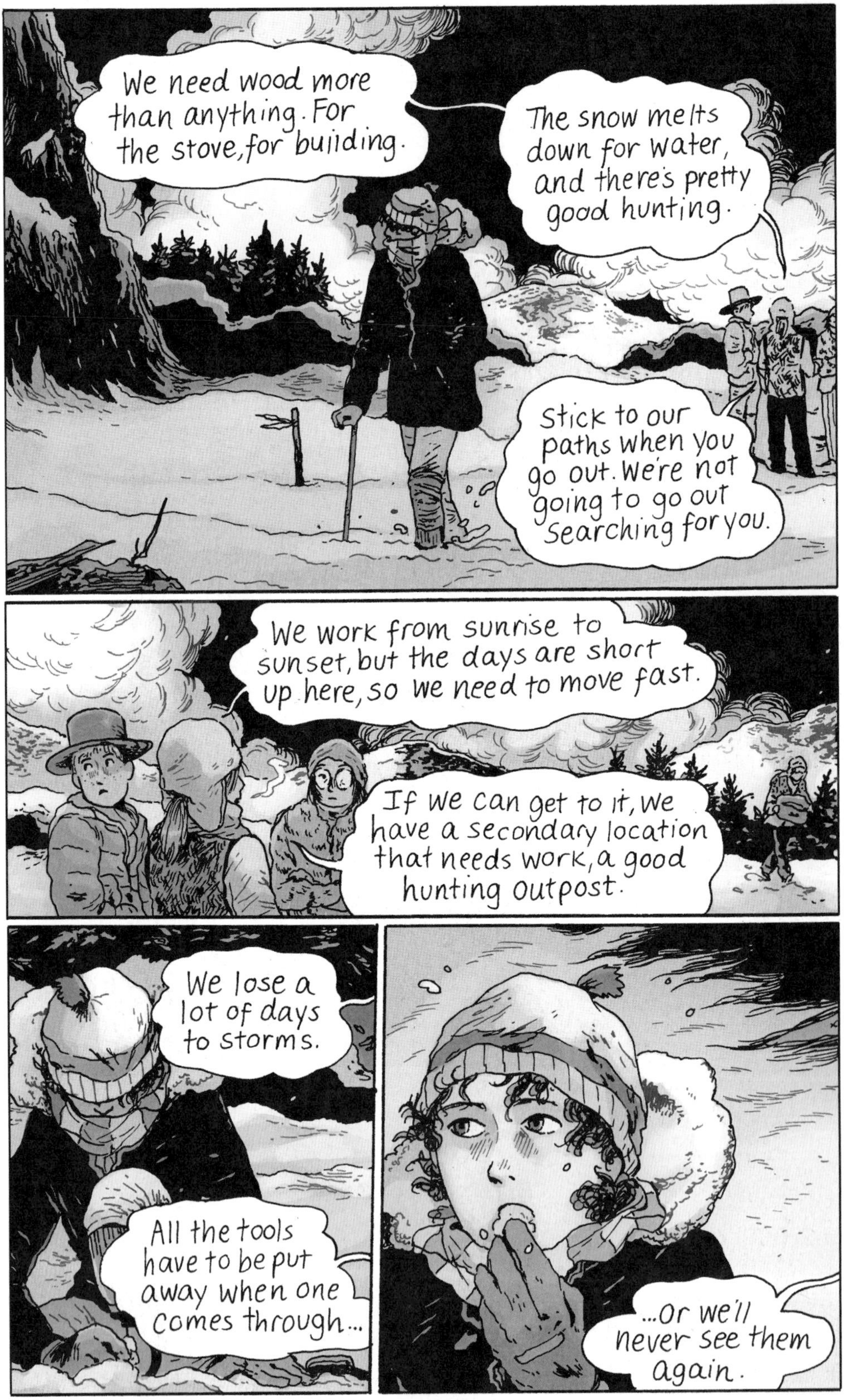
We need wood more than anything. For the stove, for building.
The snow melts down for water, and there's pretty good hunting.
Stick to our paths when you go out. We're not going to go out searching for you.
We work from sunrise to sunset, but the days are short up here, so we need to move fast.
If we can get to it, we have a secondary location that needs work, a good hunting outpost.
We lose a lot of days to storms.
All the tools have to be put away when one comes through...
...or we'll never see them again.

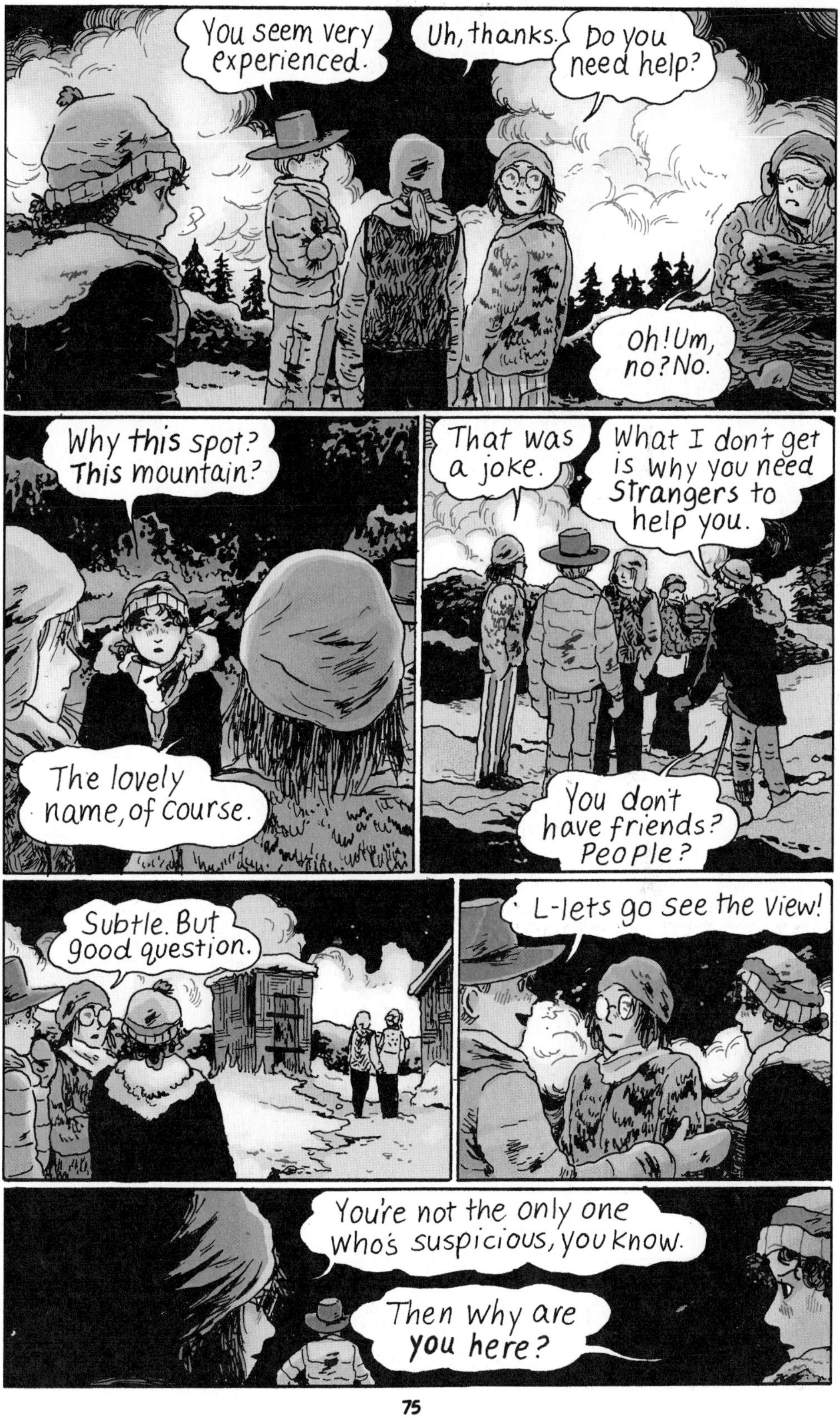
You seem very experienced.
Uh, thanks.
Do you need help?
Oh! Um, no? No.
Why this spot? This mountain?
The lovely name, of course.
That was a joke.
What I don't get is why you need Strangers to help you.
You don't have friends? People?
Subtle. But good question.
L-lets go see the view!
You're not the only one who's suspicious, you know.
Then why are you here?

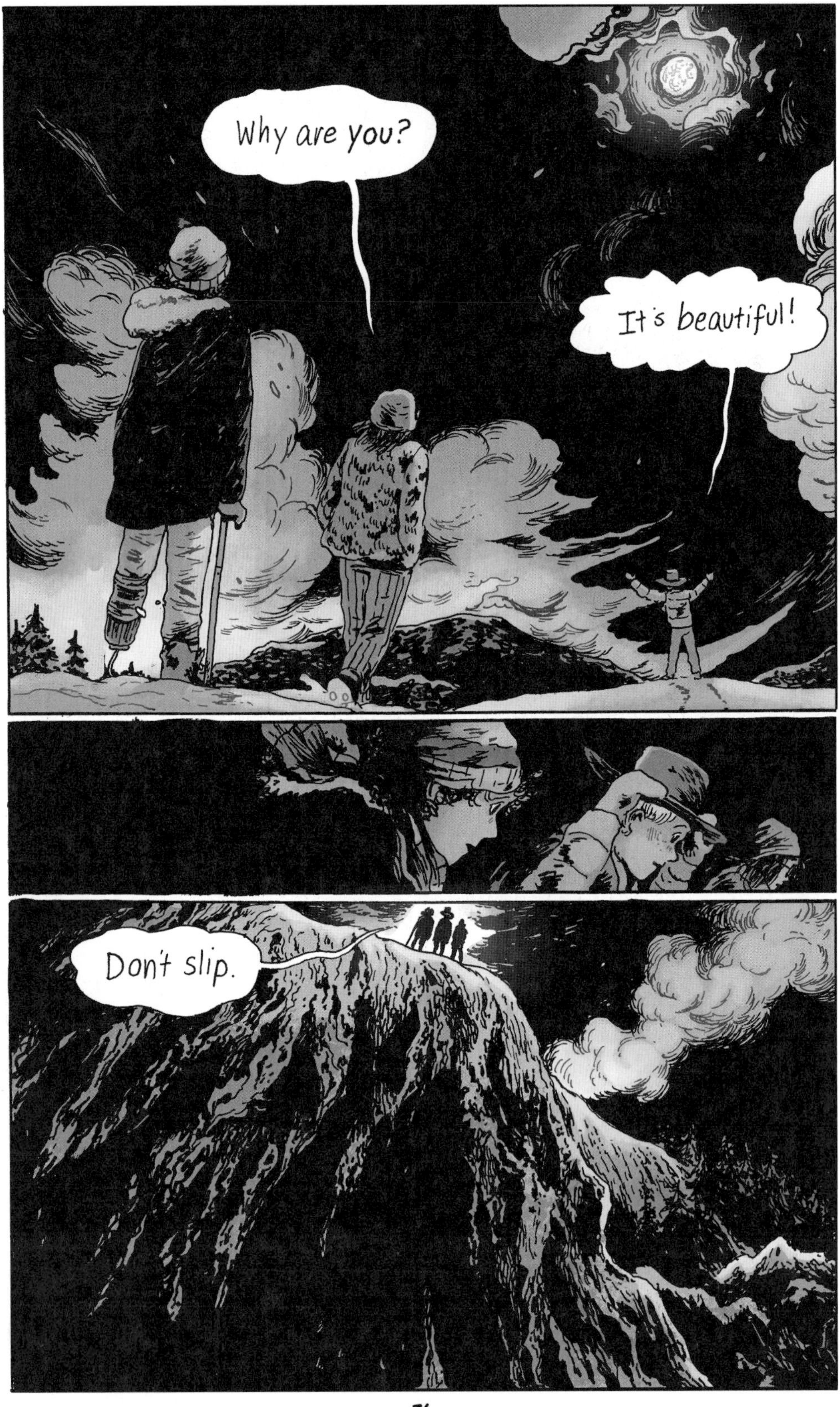
Why are you?
It's beautiful!
Don't slip.

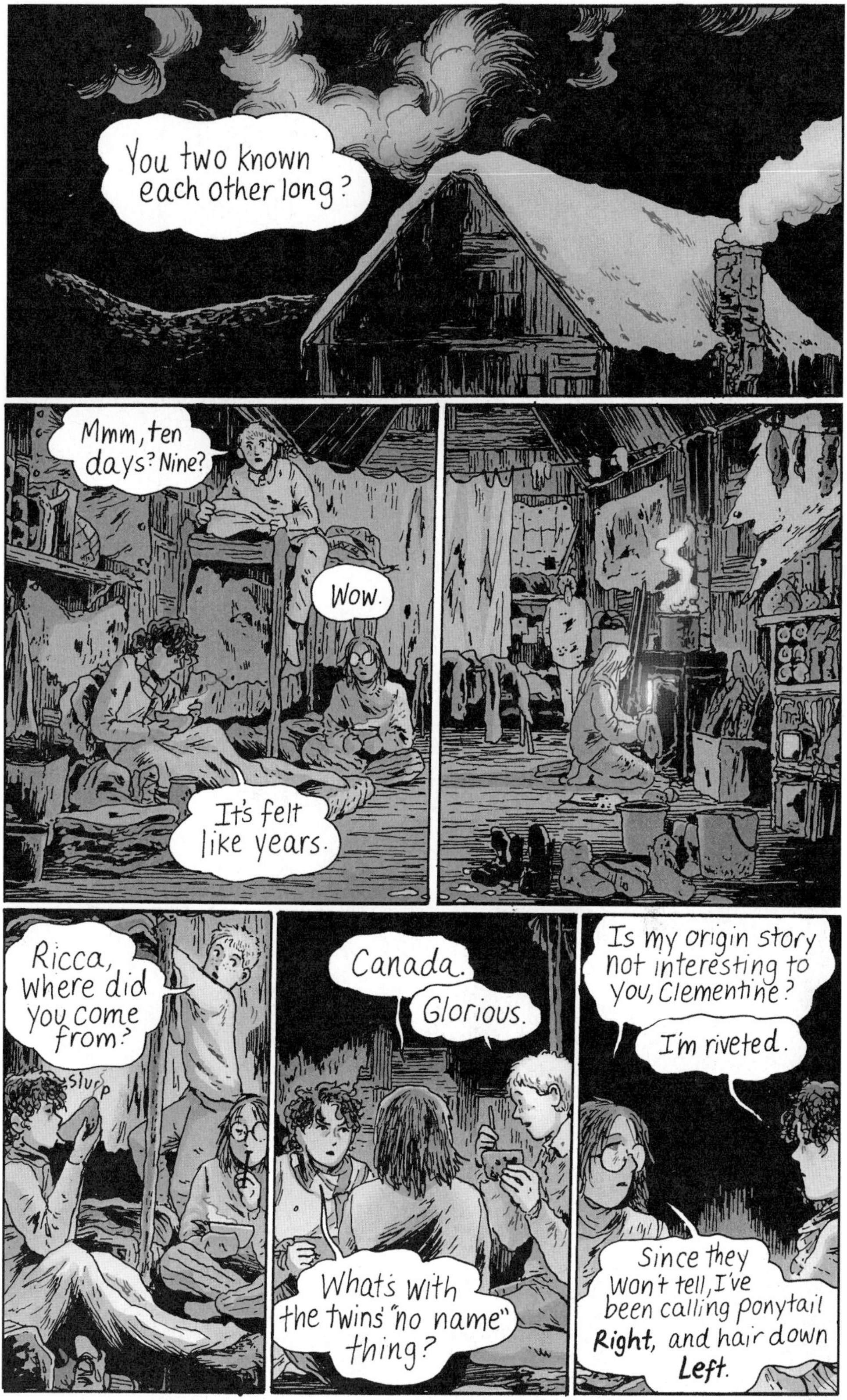
You two known each other long?
Mmm, ten days? Nine?
Wow.
It's felt like years.
Ricca, where did you come from?
slurp
Canada.
Glorious.
What's with the twins' "no name" thing?
Is my origin story not interesting to you, Clementine?
I'm riveted.
Since they won't tell, I've been calling ponytail **Right**, and hair down **Left**.

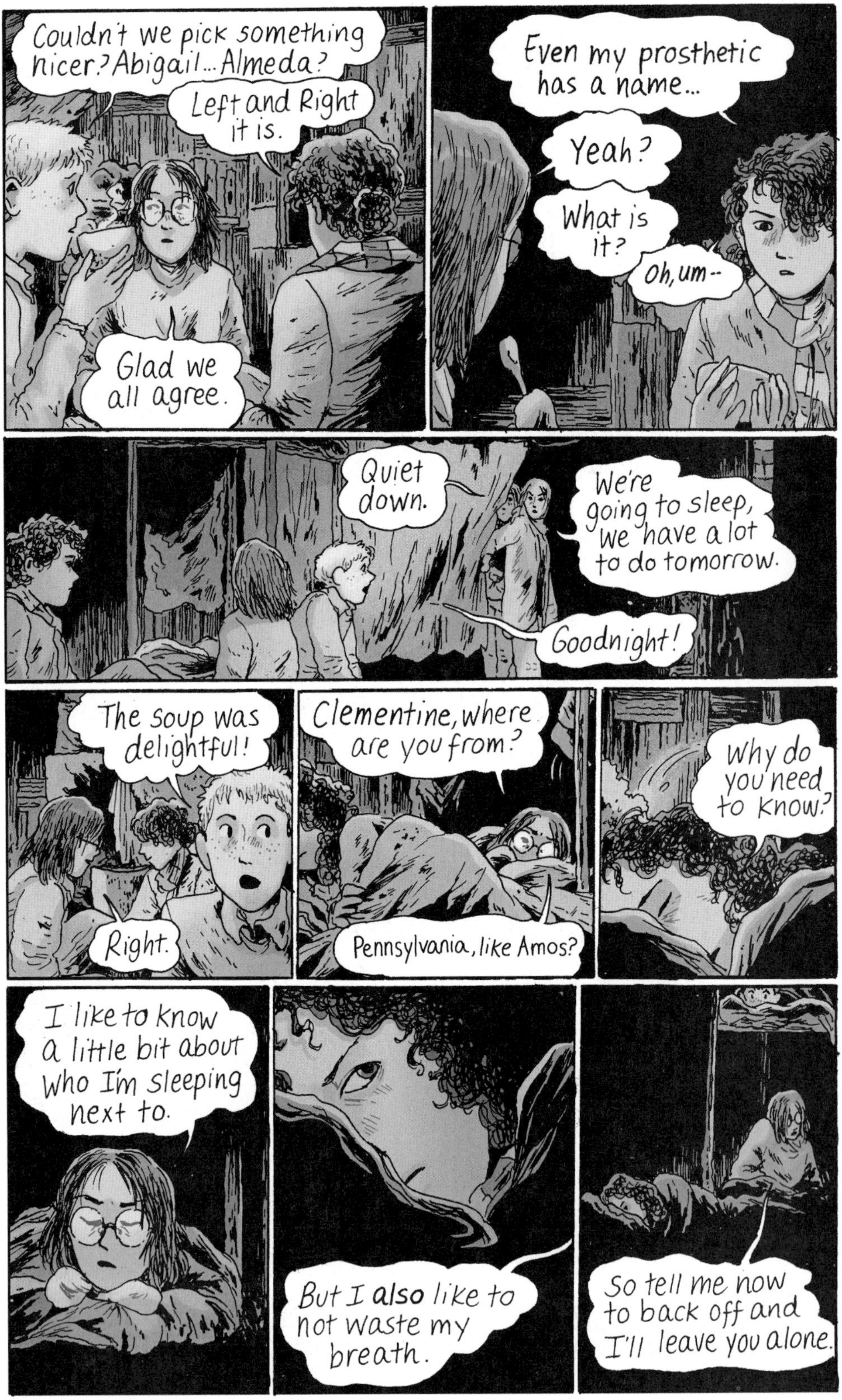
Couldn't we pick something nicer? Abigail... Almeda?
Left and Right it is.
Glad we all agree.
Even my prosthetic has a name...
Yeah?
What is it?
Oh, um--
Quiet down.
We're going to sleep, we have a lot to do tomorrow.
Goodnight!
The soup was delightful!
Right.
Clementine, where are you from?
Pennsylvania, like Amos?
Why do you need to know?
I like to know a little bit about who I'm sleeping next to.
But I also like to not waste my breath.
So tell me now to back off and I'll leave you alone.

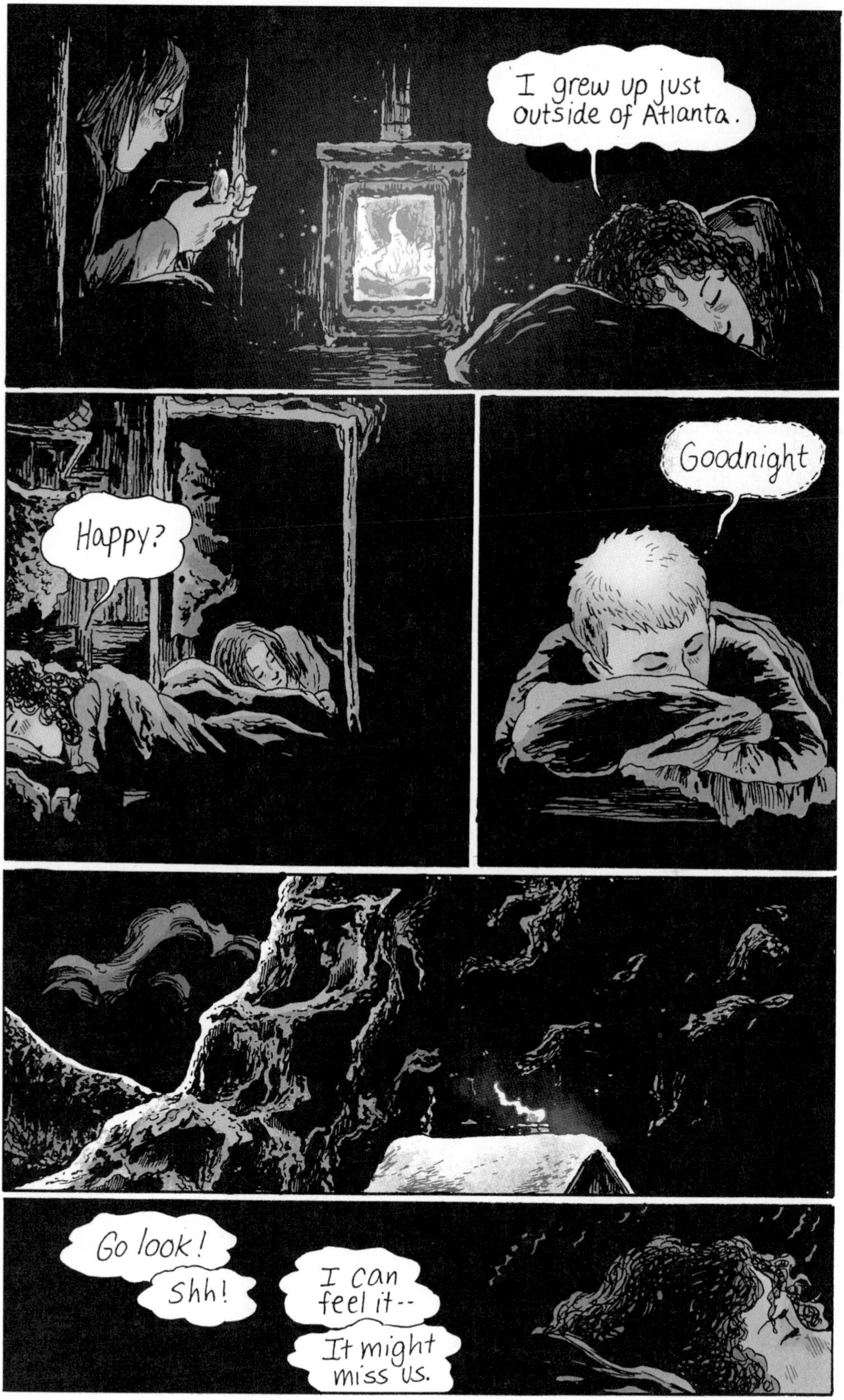
I grew up just outside of Atlanta.
Happy?
Goodnight
Go look!
Shh!
I can feel it--
It might miss us.

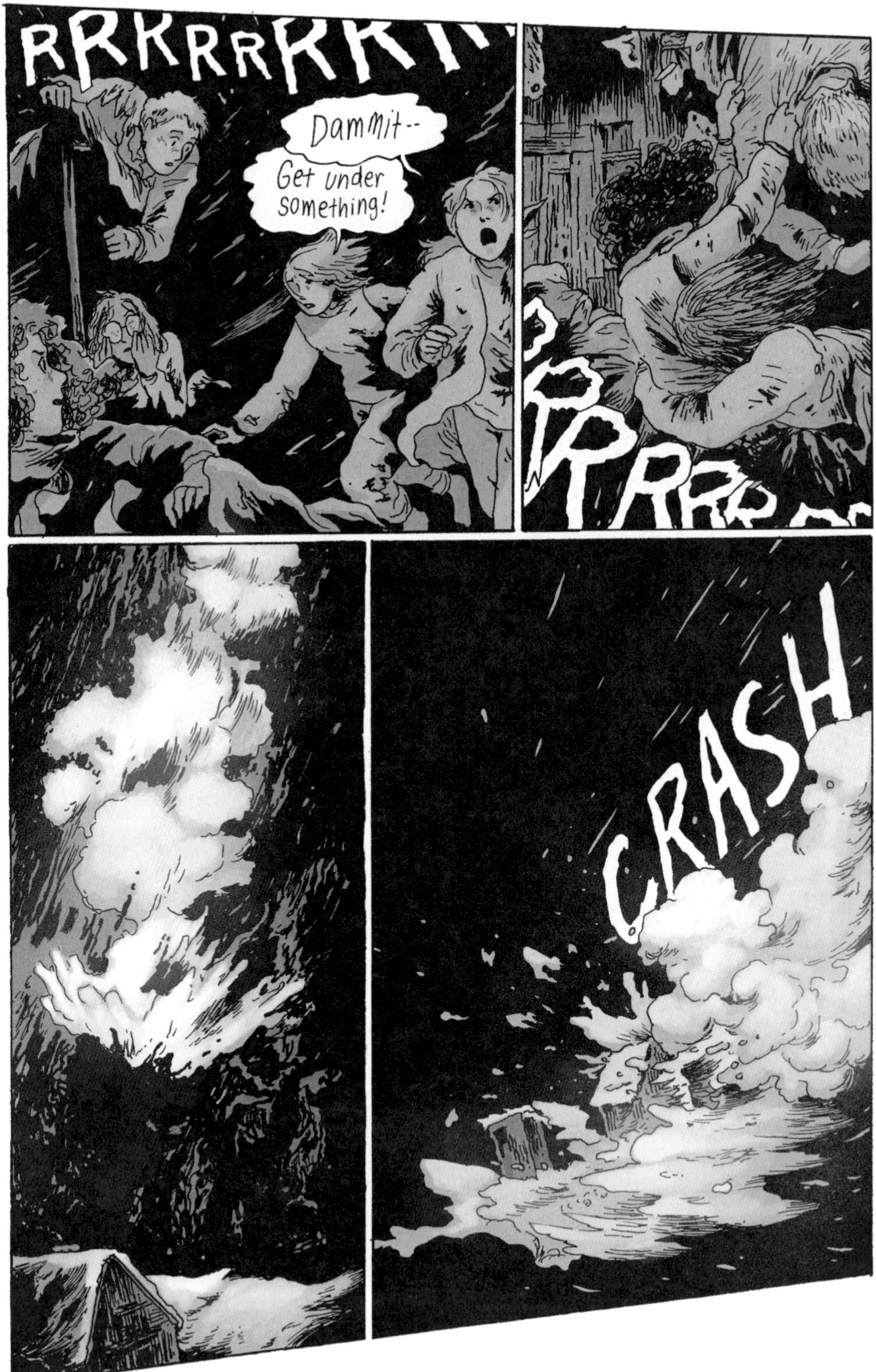
RRKRRRKRR
Dammit--
Get under something!
RRRR
CRASH

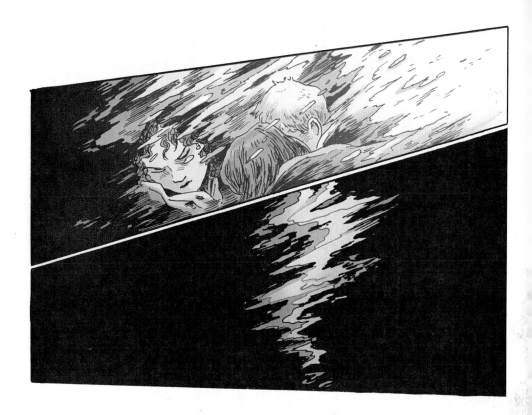

You need to be quiet...

Who is this?

I'm Clementine.

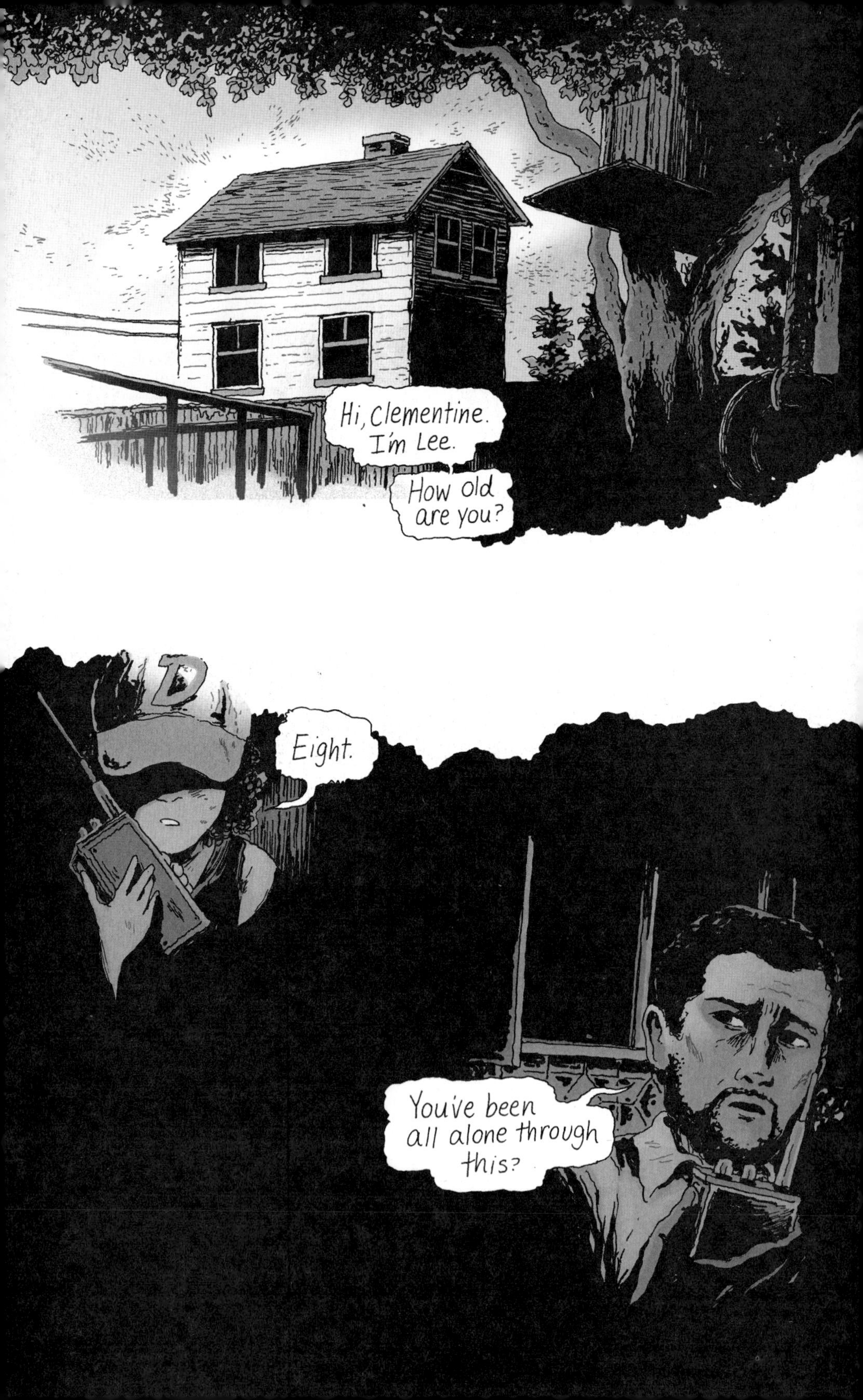
Hi, Clementine. I'm Lee.
How old are you?
Eight.
You've been all alone through this?

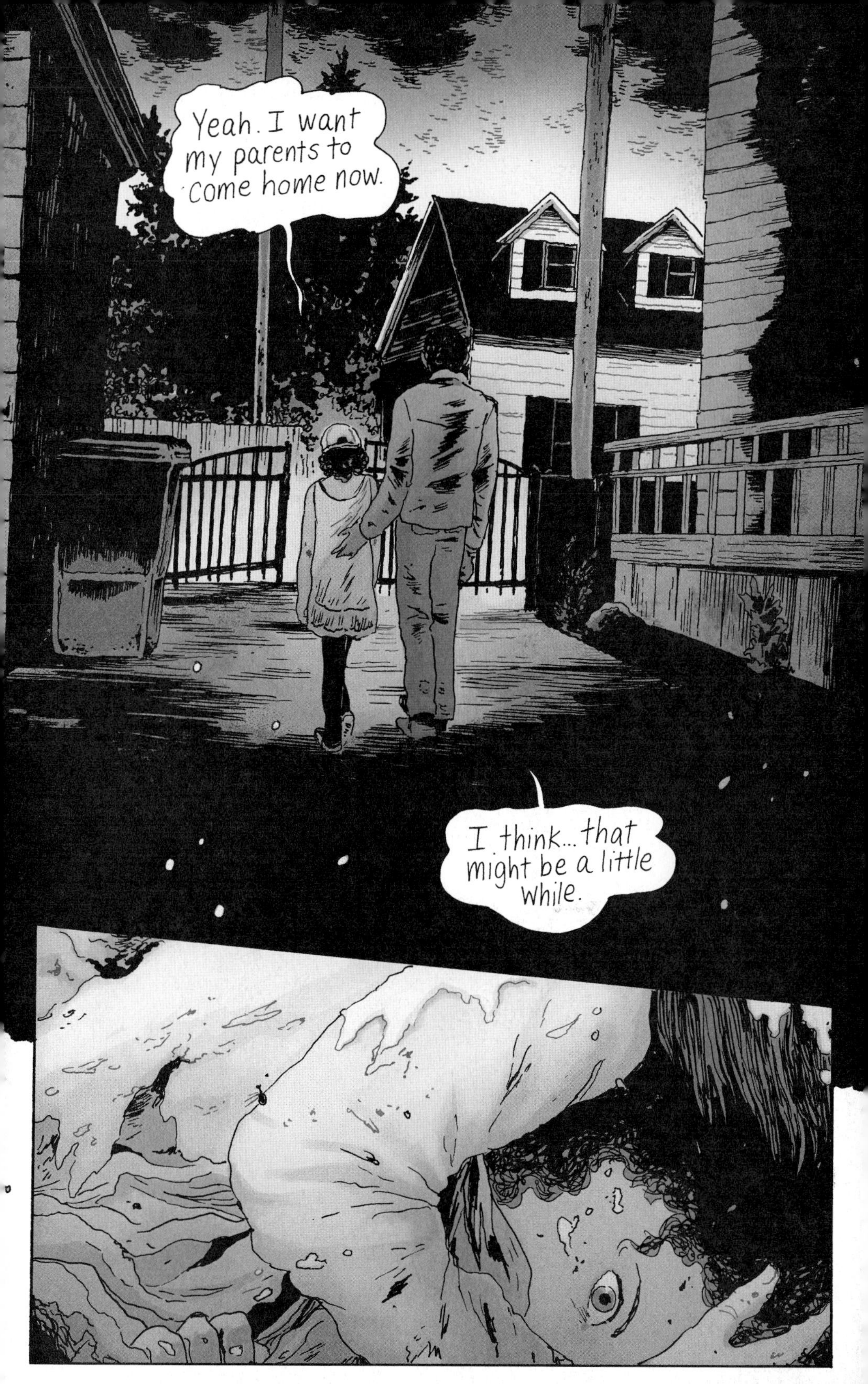
Yeah. I want my parents to come home now.
I think... that might be a little while.

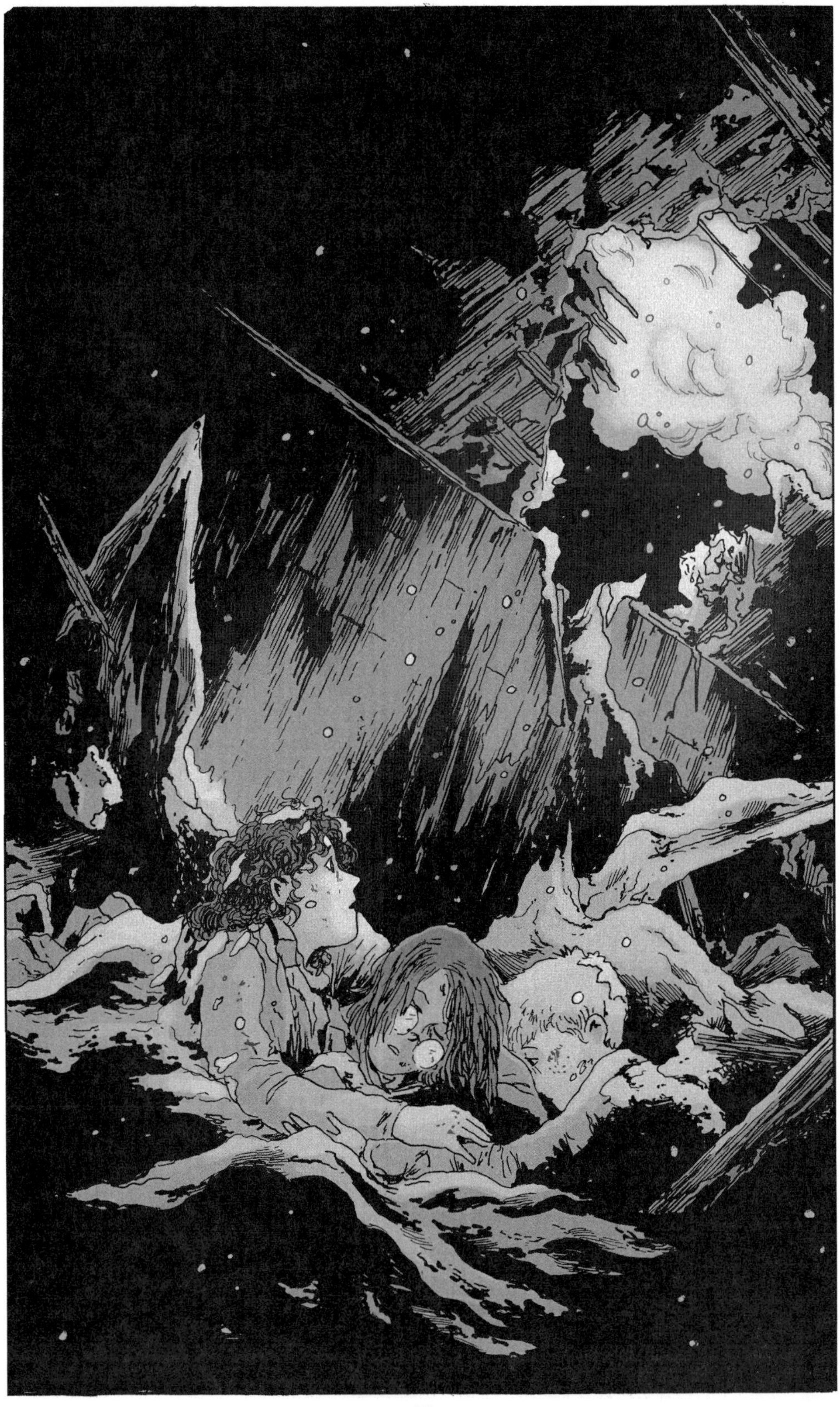

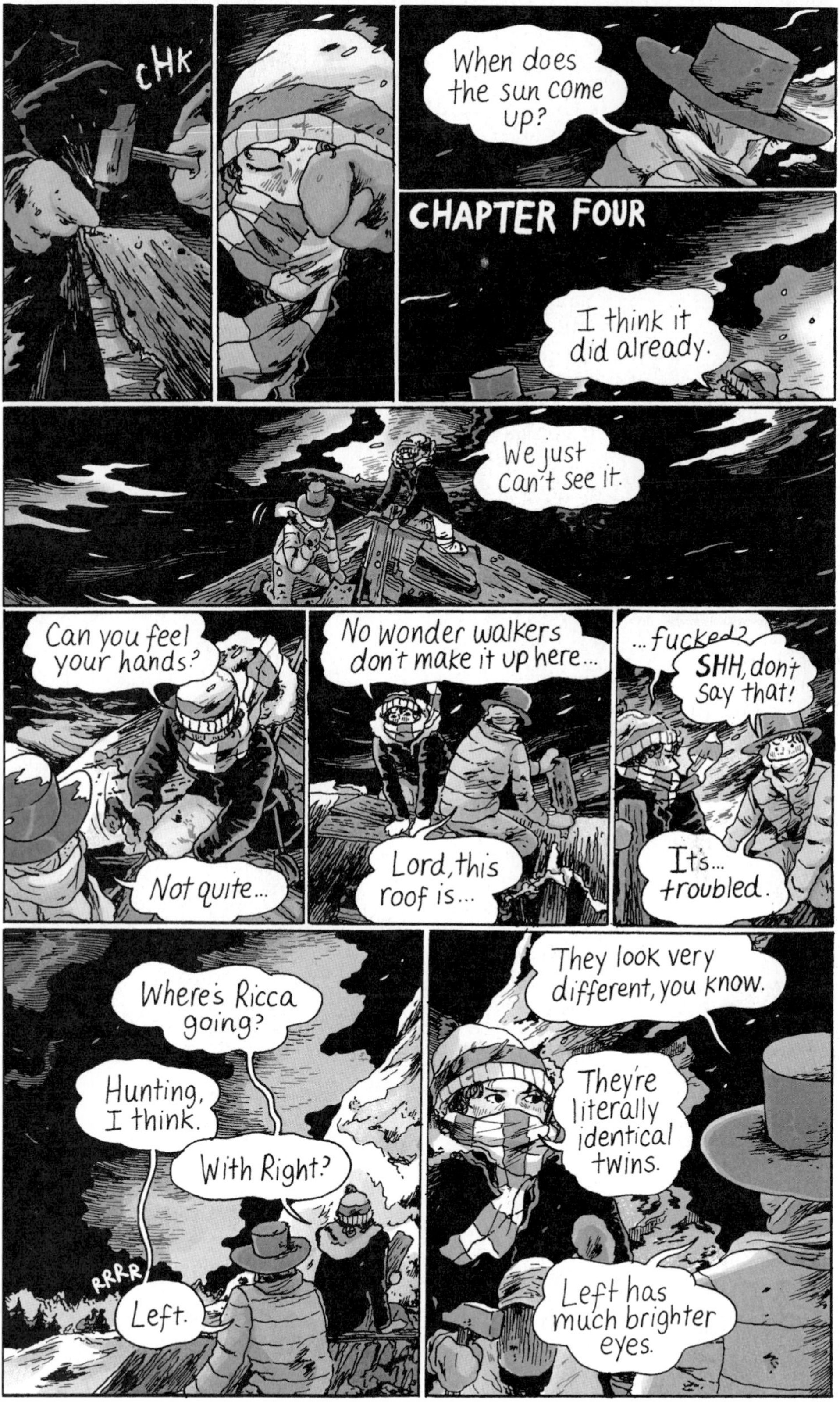
CHK
When does the sun come up?
CHAPTER FOUR
I think it did already.
We just can't see it.
Can you feel your hands?
Not quite...
No wonder walkers don't make it up here...
Lord, this roof is...
...fucked?
SHH, don't say that!
It's... troubled.
Where's Ricca going?
Hunting, I think.
With Right?
RRRR
Left.
They look very different, you know.
They're literally identical twins.
Left has much brighter eyes.

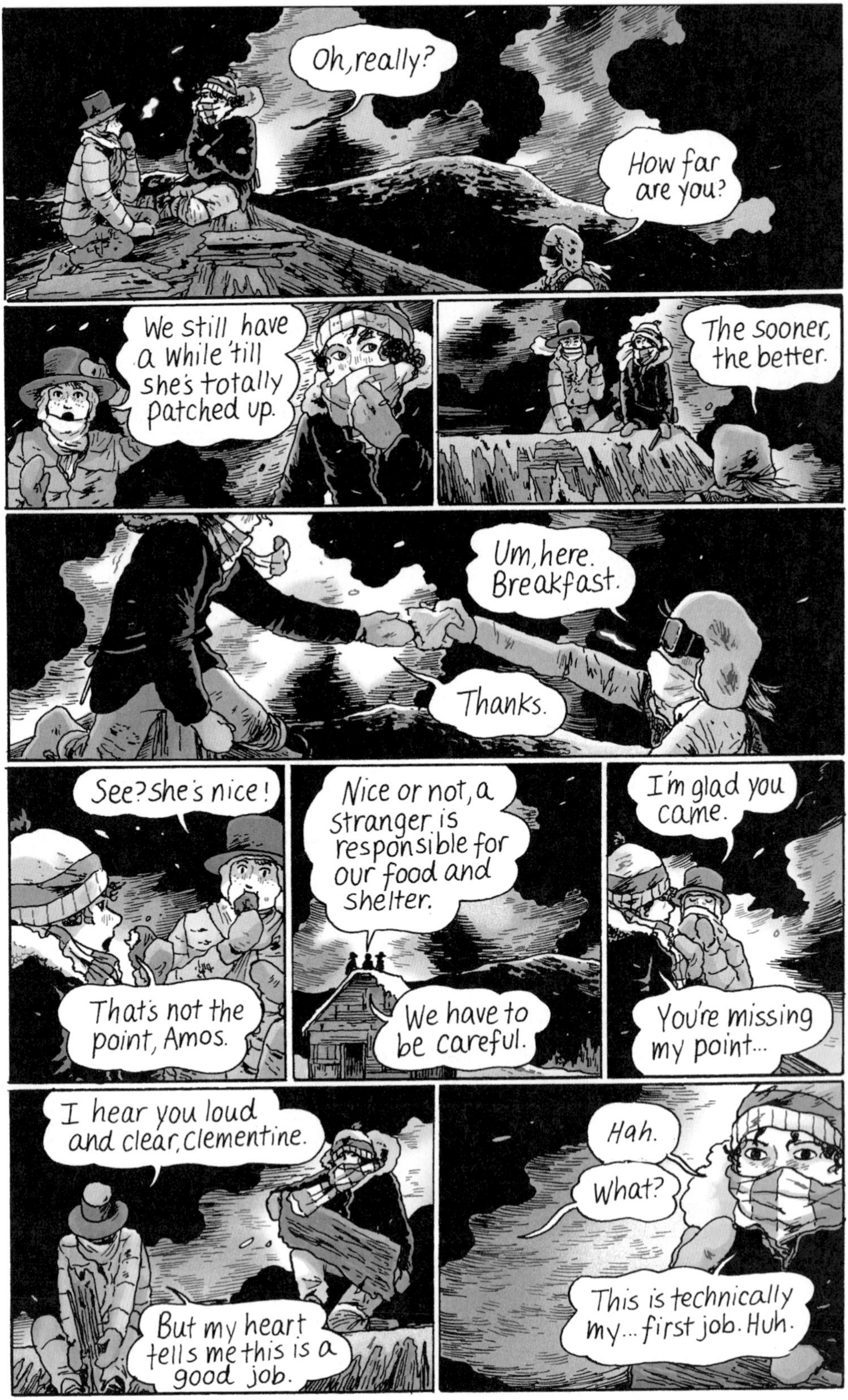
Oh, really?
How far are you?
We still have a while 'till she's totally patched up.
The sooner, the better.
Um, here. Breakfast.
Thanks.
See? She's nice!
That's not the point, Amos.
Nice or not, a stranger is responsible for our food and shelter.
We have to be careful.
I'm glad you came.
You're missing my point...
I hear you loud and clear, Clementine.
But my heart tells me this is a good job.
Hah.
What?
This is technically my... first job. Huh.

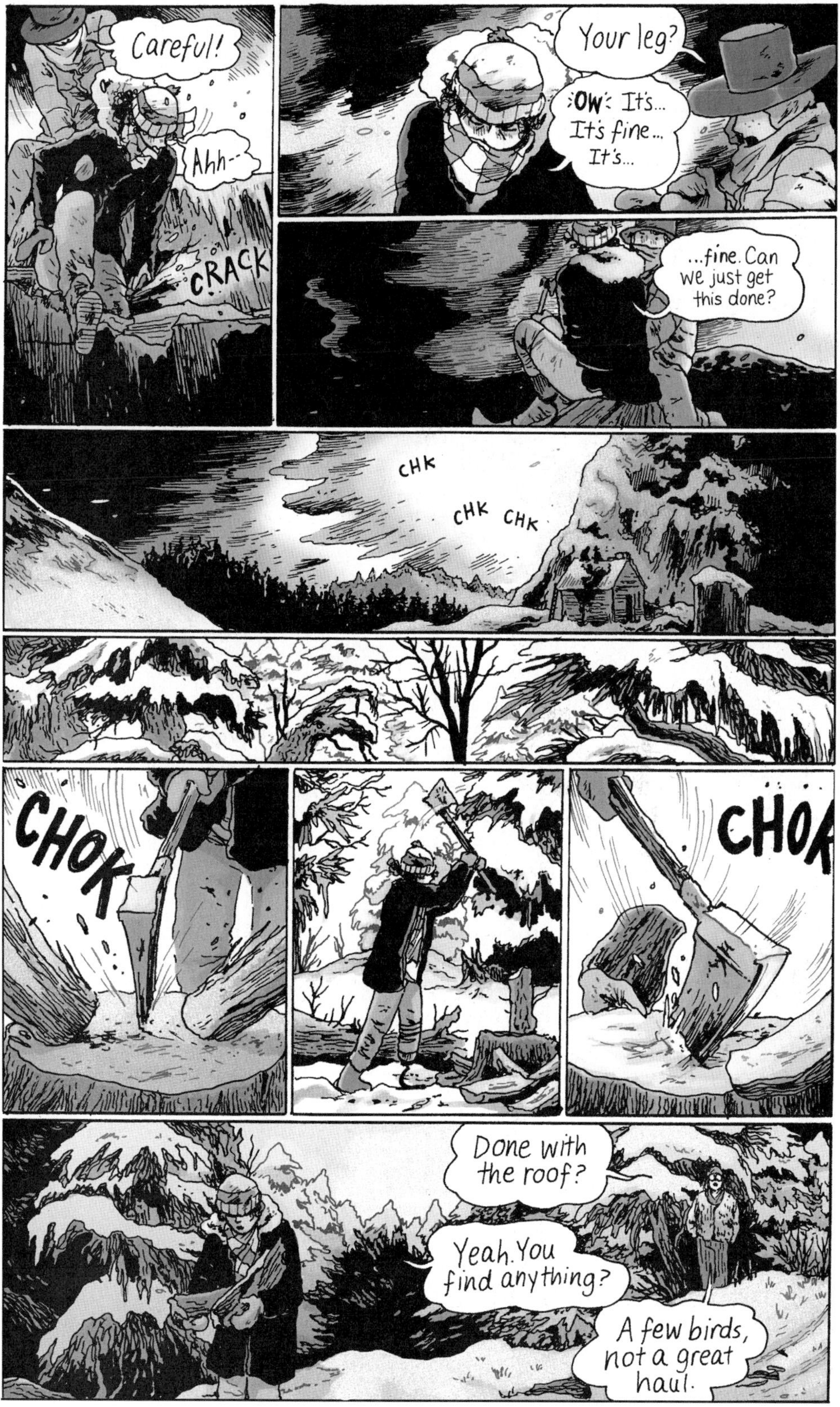
Careful!
Ahh--
CRACK
Your leg?
OW It's... It's fine... It's...
...fine. Can we just get this done?
CHK
CHK CHK
CHOK
CHOK
Done with the roof?
Yeah. You find anything?
A few birds, not a great haul.

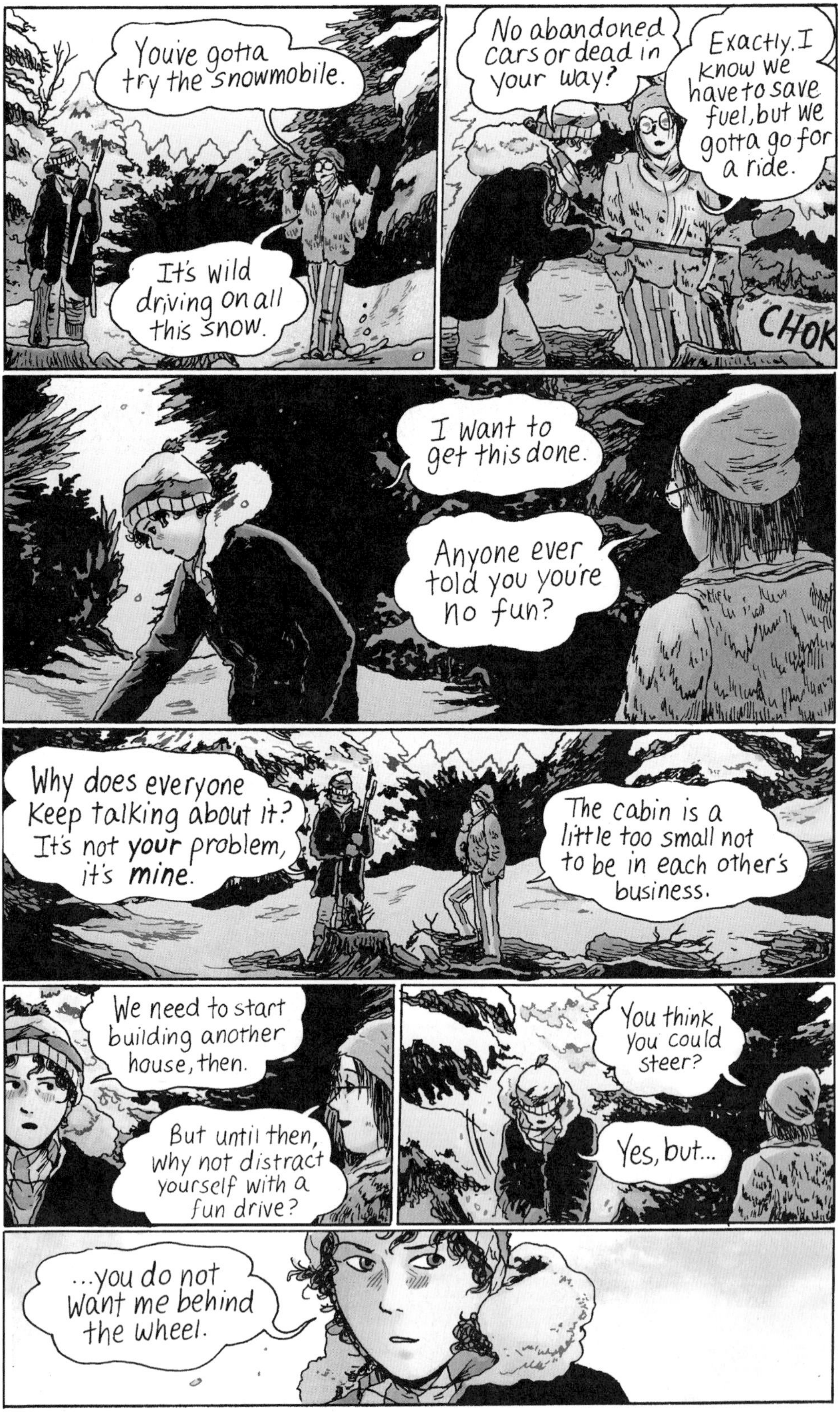

You've gotta try the snowmobile.
It's wild driving on all this snow.
No abandoned cars or dead in your way?
Exactly. I know we have to save fuel, but we gotta go for a ride.
CHOK
I want to get this done.
Anyone ever told you you're no fun?
Why does everyone keep talking about it? It's not **your** problem, it's **mine**.
The cabin is a little too small not to be in each other's business.
We need to start building another house, then.
But until then, why not distract yourself with a fun drive?
You think you could steer?
Yes, but...
...you do not want me behind the wheel.

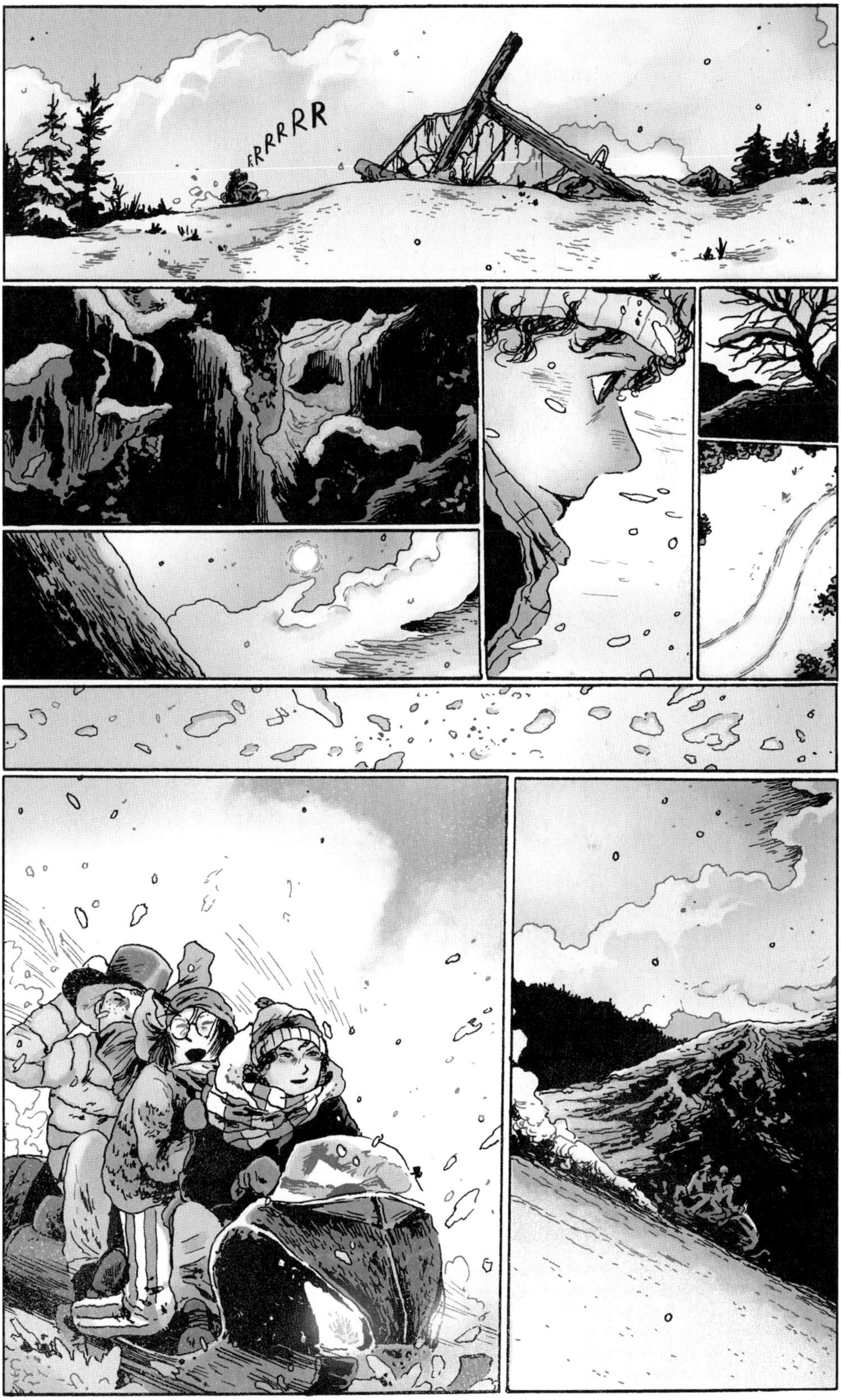
fRRRRRR

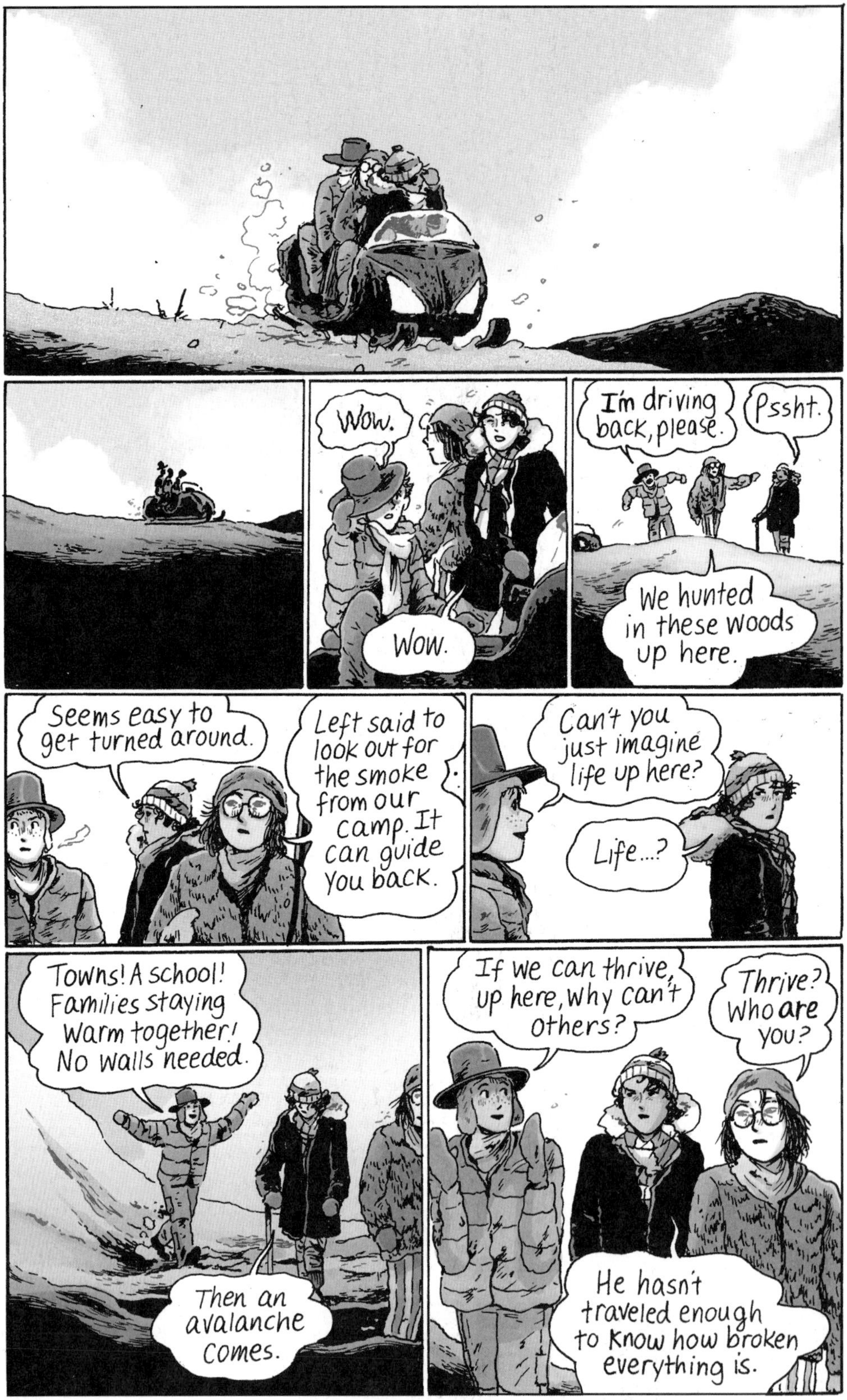
Wow.
Wow.
I'm driving back, please.
Pssht.
We hunted in these woods up here.
Seems easy to get turned around.
Left said to look out for the smoke from our camp. It can guide you back.
Can't you just imagine life up here?
Life...?
Towns! A school! Families staying warm together! No walls needed.
Then an avalanche comes.
If we can thrive, up here, why can't others?
Thrive? Who are you?
He hasn't traveled enough to know how broken everything is.

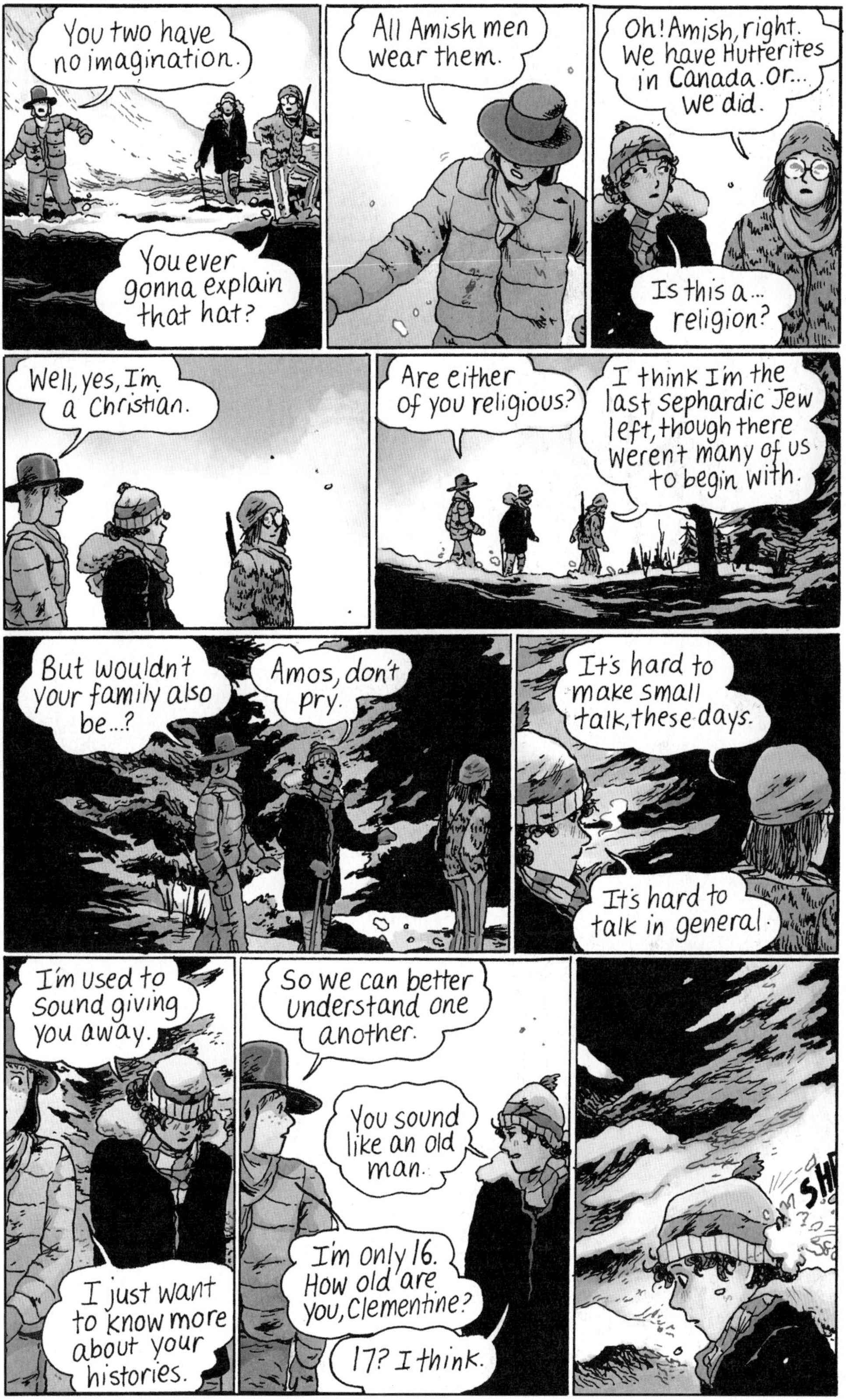
You two have no imagination.
You ever gonna explain that hat?
All Amish men wear them.
Oh! Amish, right. We have Hutterites in Canada. Or... we did.
Is this a... religion?
Well, yes, I'm a Christian.
Are either of you religious?
I think I'm the last sephardic Jew left, though there weren't many of us to begin with.
But wouldn't your family also be...?
Amos, don't pry.
It's hard to make small talk, these days.
It's hard to talk in general.
I'm used to sound giving you away.
I just want to know more about your histories.
So we can better understand one another.
You sound like an old man.
I'm only 16. How old are you, Clementine?
17? I think.

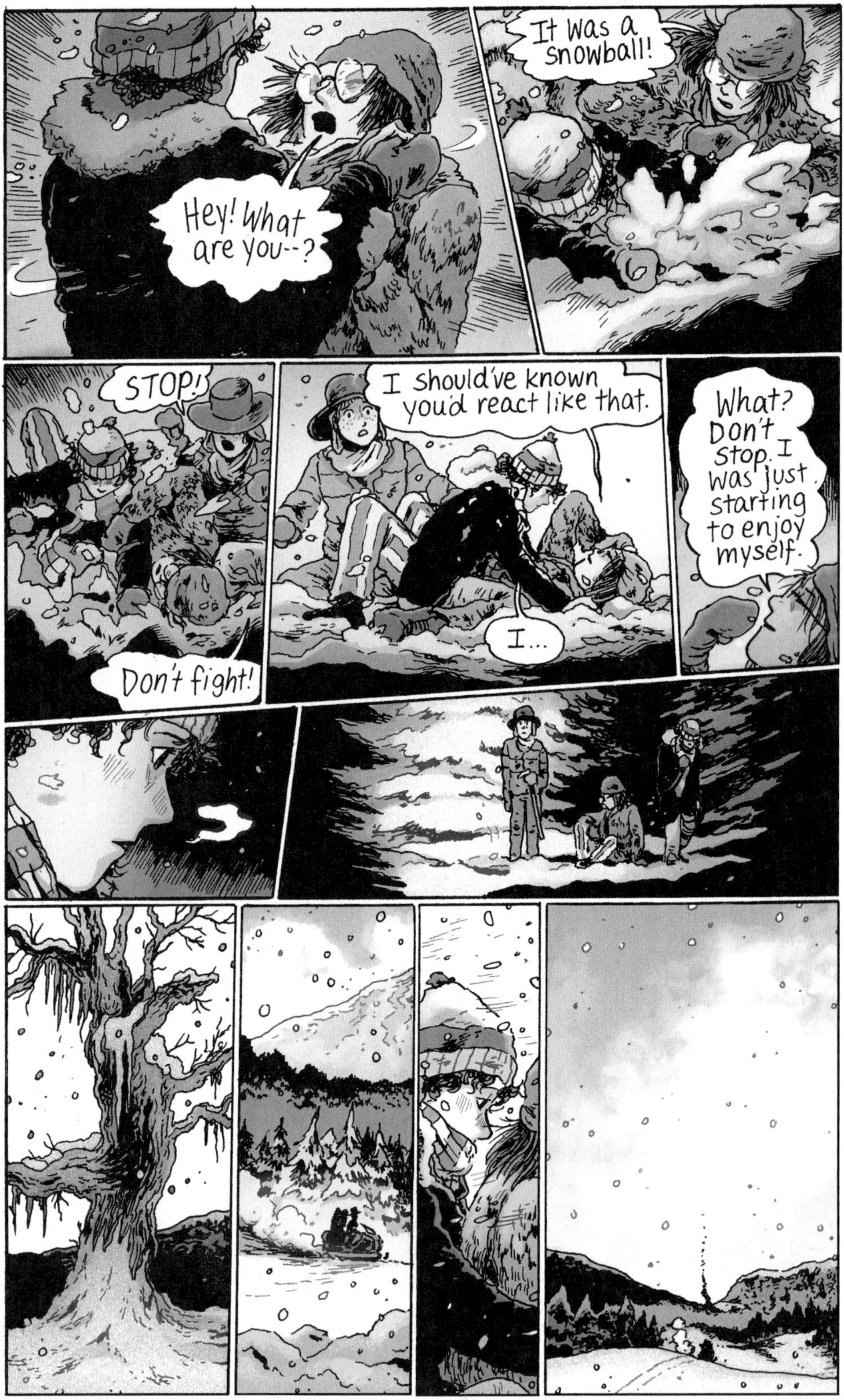
Hey! What are you--?
It was a snowball!
STOP!
Don't fight!
I should've known you'd react like that.
I...
What? Don't stop. I was just starting to enjoy myself.

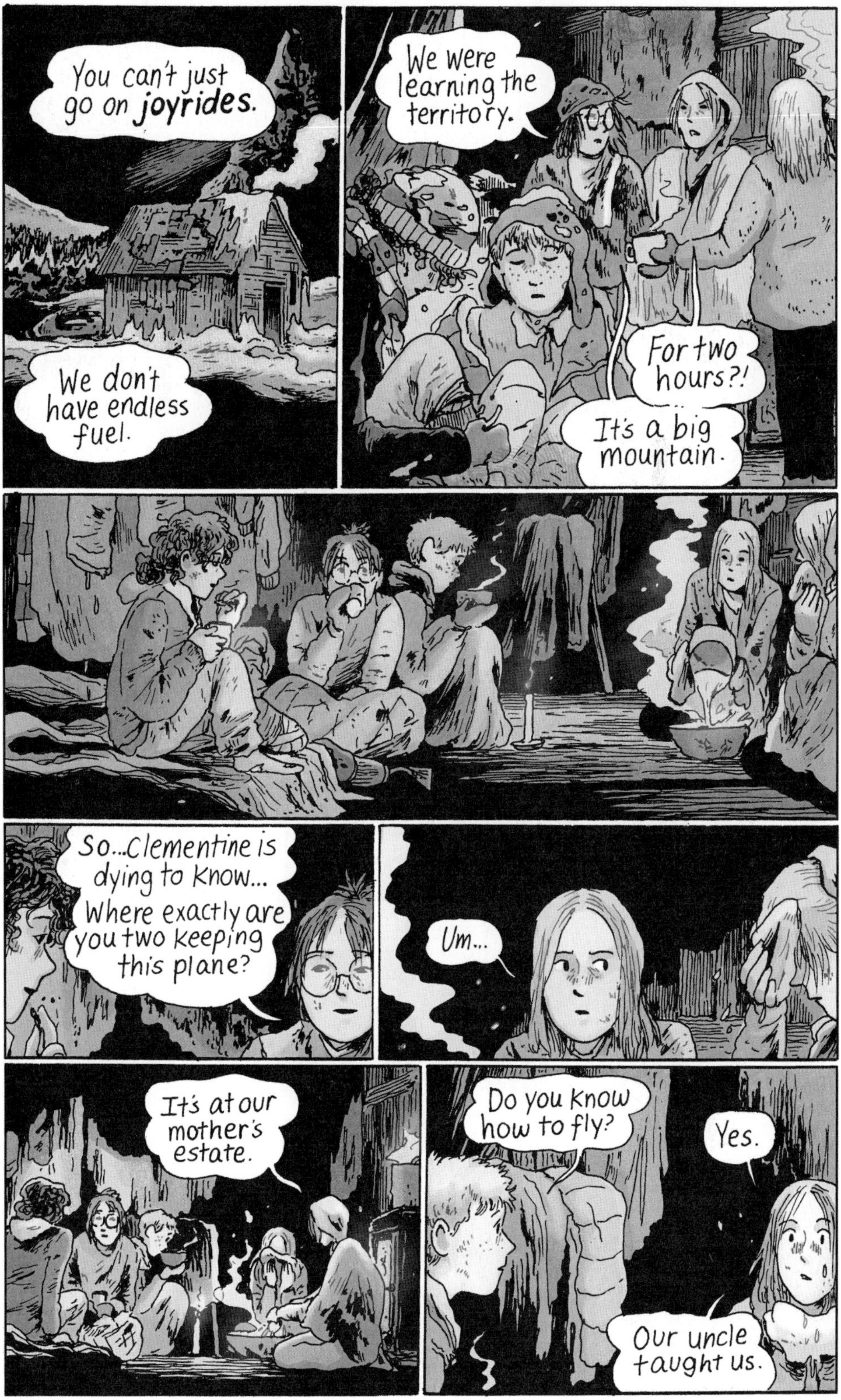
You can't just go on joyrides.
We don't have endless fuel.
We were learning the territory.
For two hours?!
It's a big mountain.
So...Clementine is dying to know... Where exactly are you two keeping this plane?
Um...
It's at our mother's estate.
Do you know how to fly?
Yes.
Our uncle taught us.

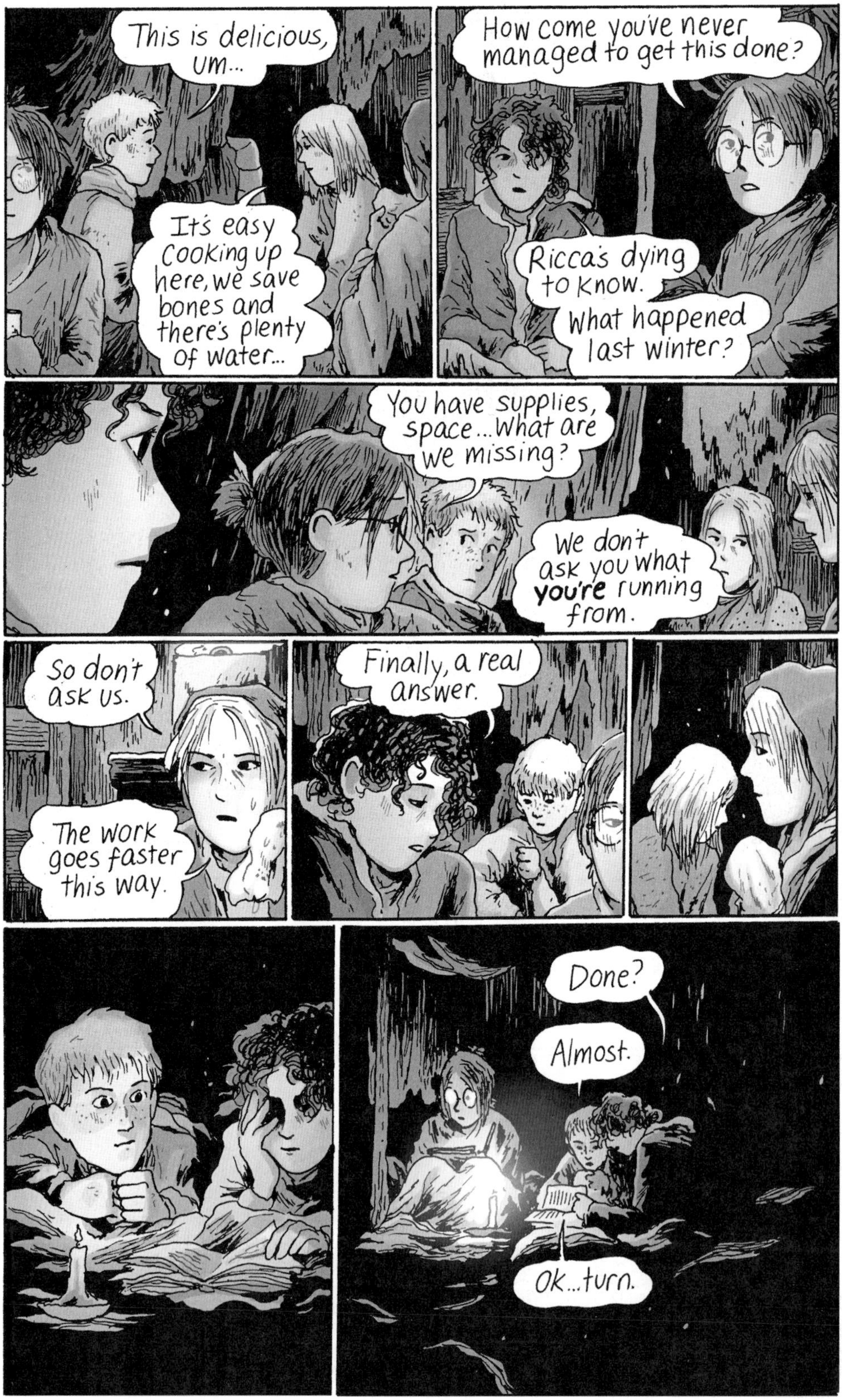
This is delicious, um...
It's easy cooking up here, we save bones and there's plenty of water...
How come you've never managed to get this done?
Ricca's dying to know.
What happened last winter?
You have supplies, space... What are we missing?
We don't ask you what **you're** running from.
So don't ask us.
The work goes faster this way.
Finally, a real answer.
Done?
Almost.
Ok... turn.

Do you know this one?

Another?

Yes, sorry.

I don't mind. Let's see... I...

Impro...ba... No. I don't know.

I·m·p·r·o·b·a·b·l·e.

Oh, lucky, this page didn't fall out.

Improbable: Not likely to be true or happen.

�& reeaaaKKK...

Is it...?

It's ok. It'll hold.

"It was an... impro...bable romance. He was a... co...country...**country** boy and she was a... city girl."

Up there...

Shh.

RICCA.

I'm hungry.

Shut up.

95

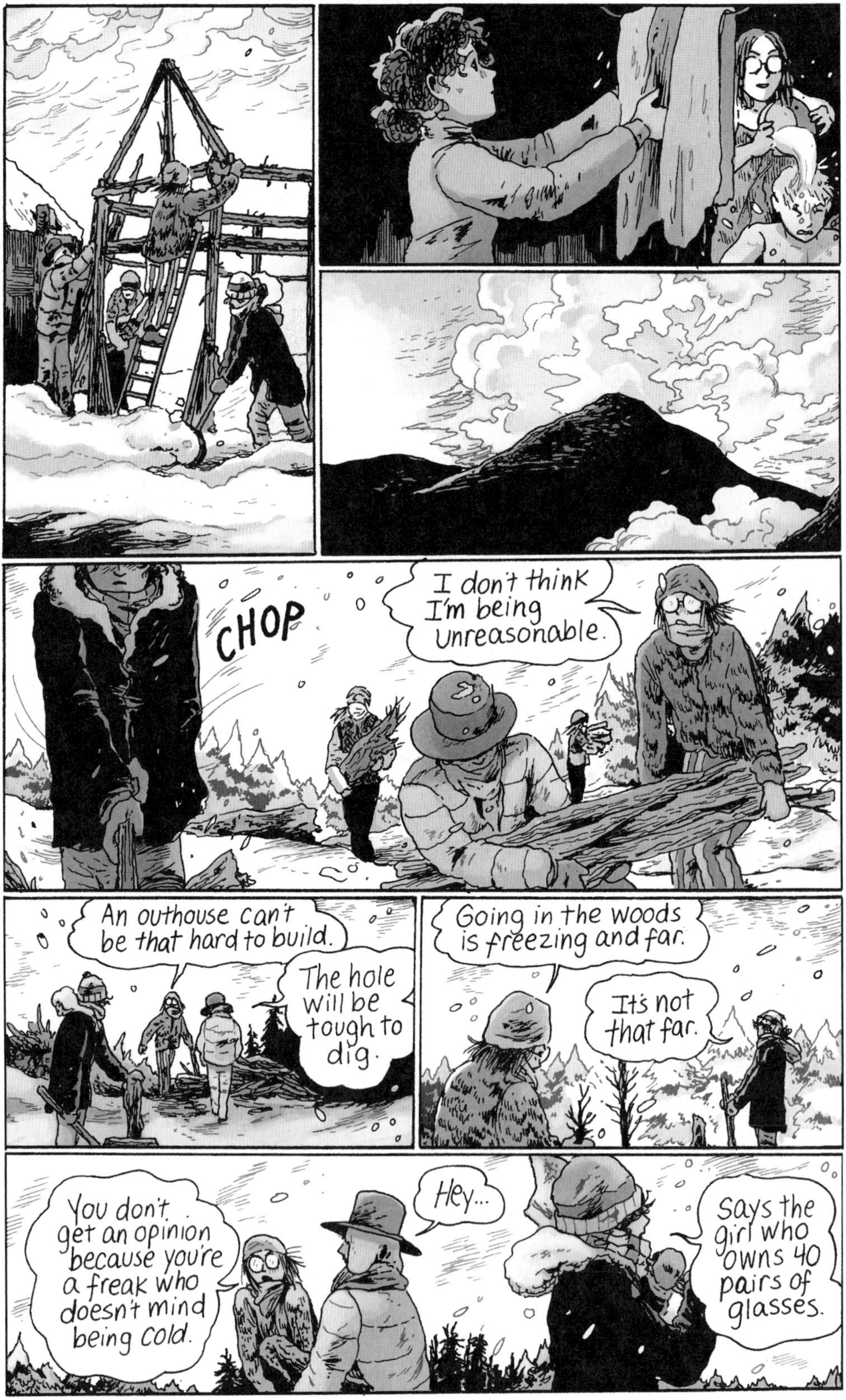
CHOP
I don't think I'm being unreasonable.
An outhouse can't be that hard to build.
The hole will be tough to dig.
Going in the woods is freezing and far.
It's not that far.
You don't get an opinion because you're a freak who doesn't mind being cold.
Hey...
Says the girl who owns 40 pairs of glasses.

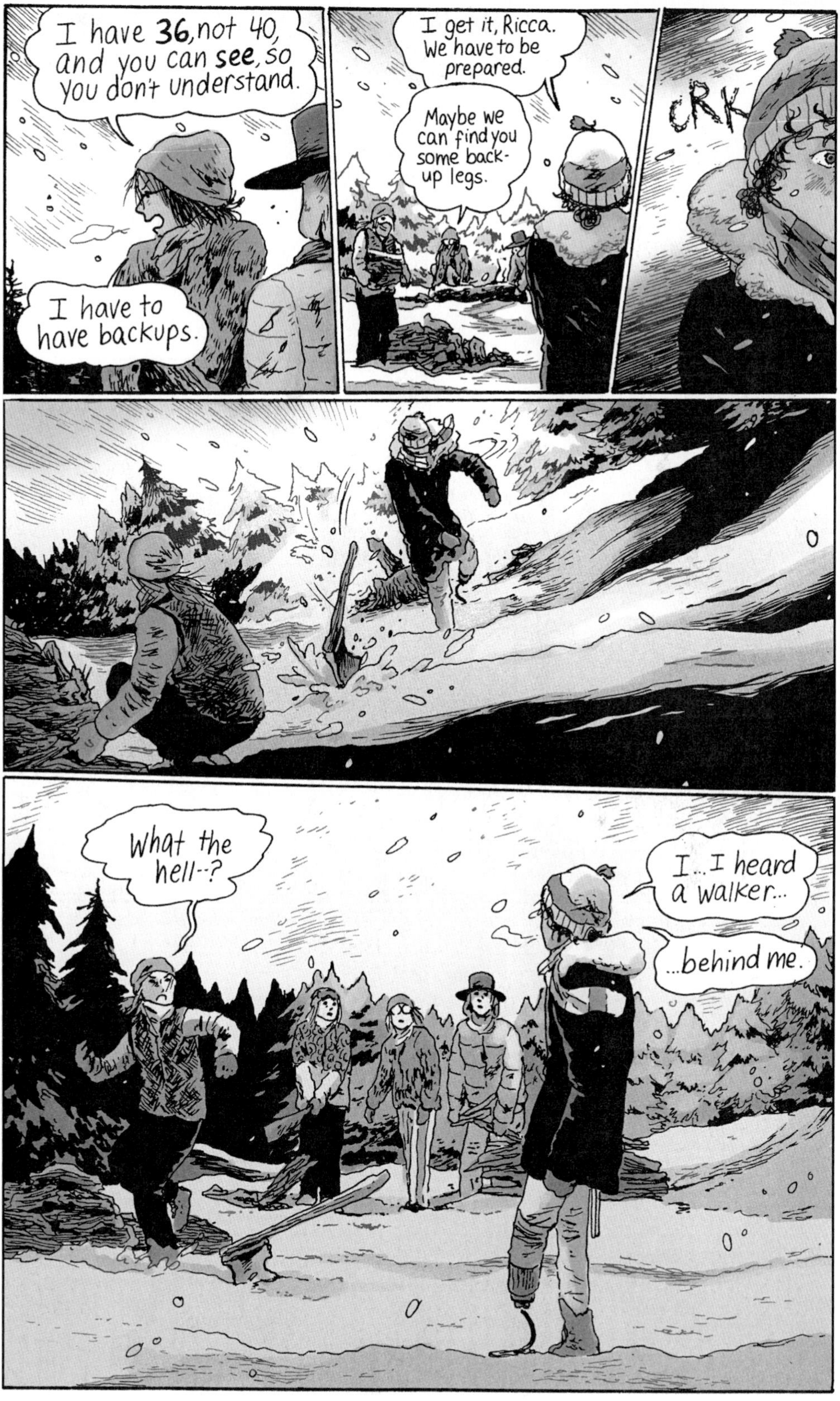
I have 36, not 40, and you can see, so you don't understand.
I have to have backups.
I get it, Ricca. We have to be prepared.
Maybe we can find you some back-up legs.
CRK
What the hell--?
I... I heard a walker...
...behind me.

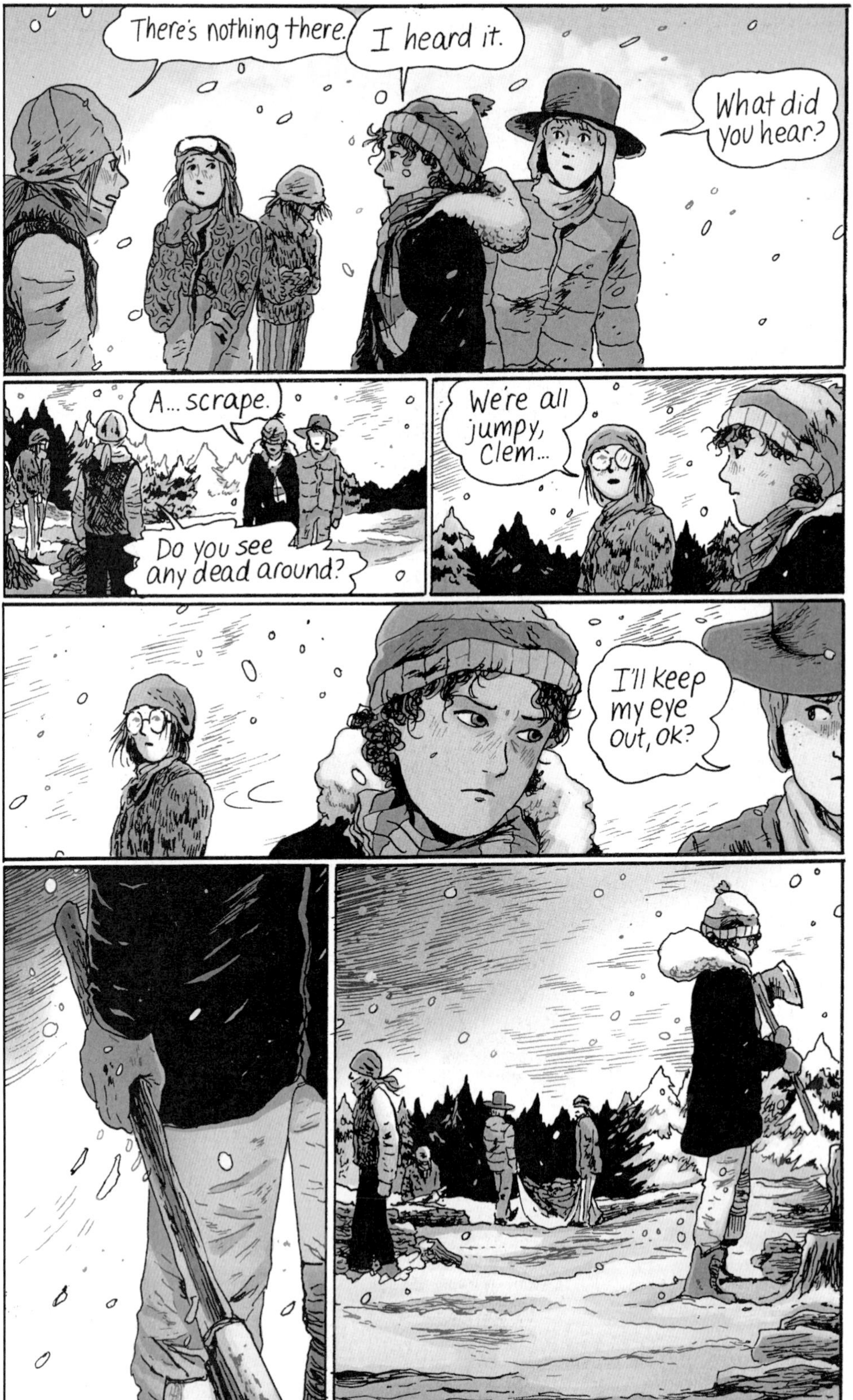
There's nothing there.
I heard it.
What did you hear?
A... scrape.
Do you see any dead around?
We're all jumpy, Clem...
I'll keep my eye out, ok?

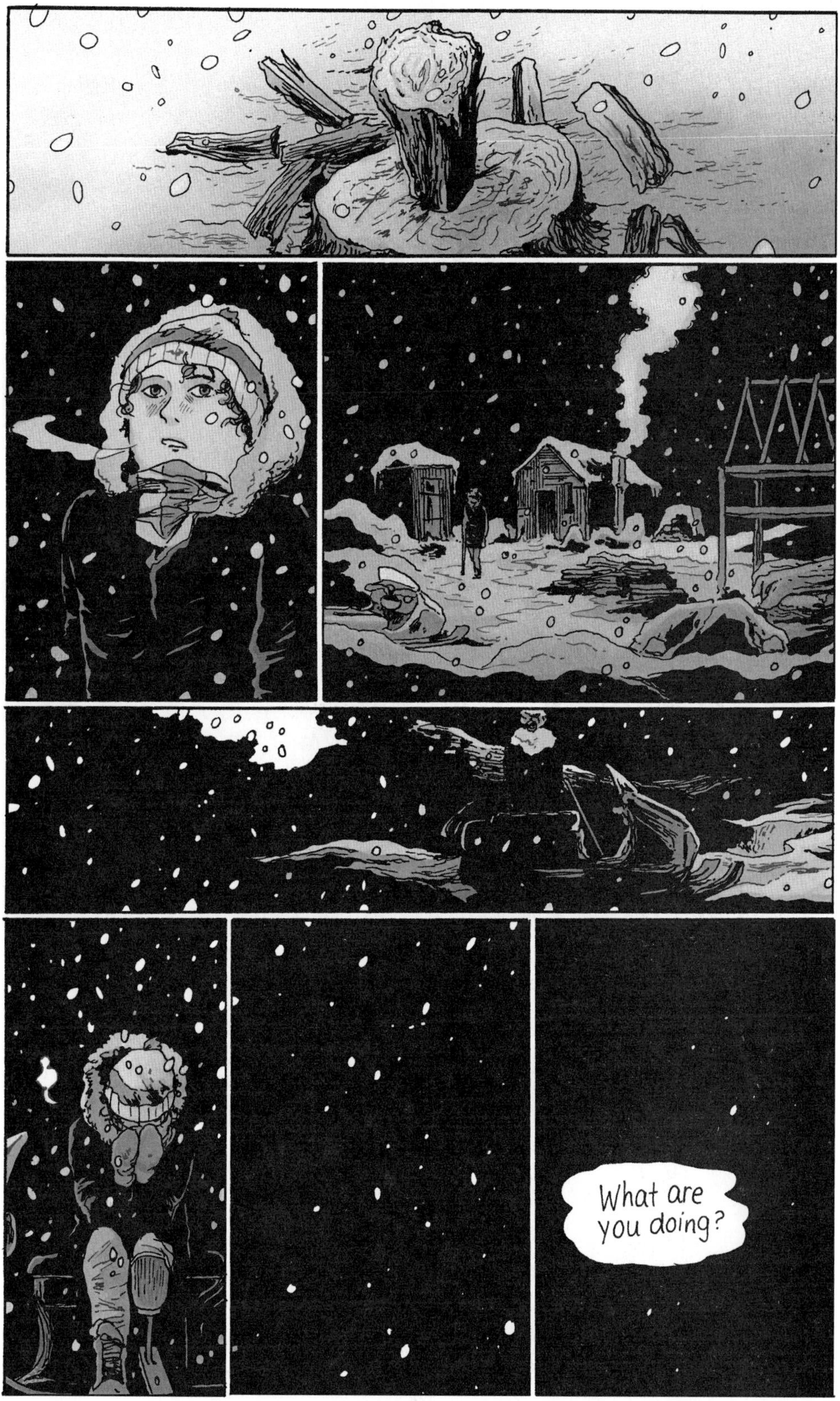
What are you doing?

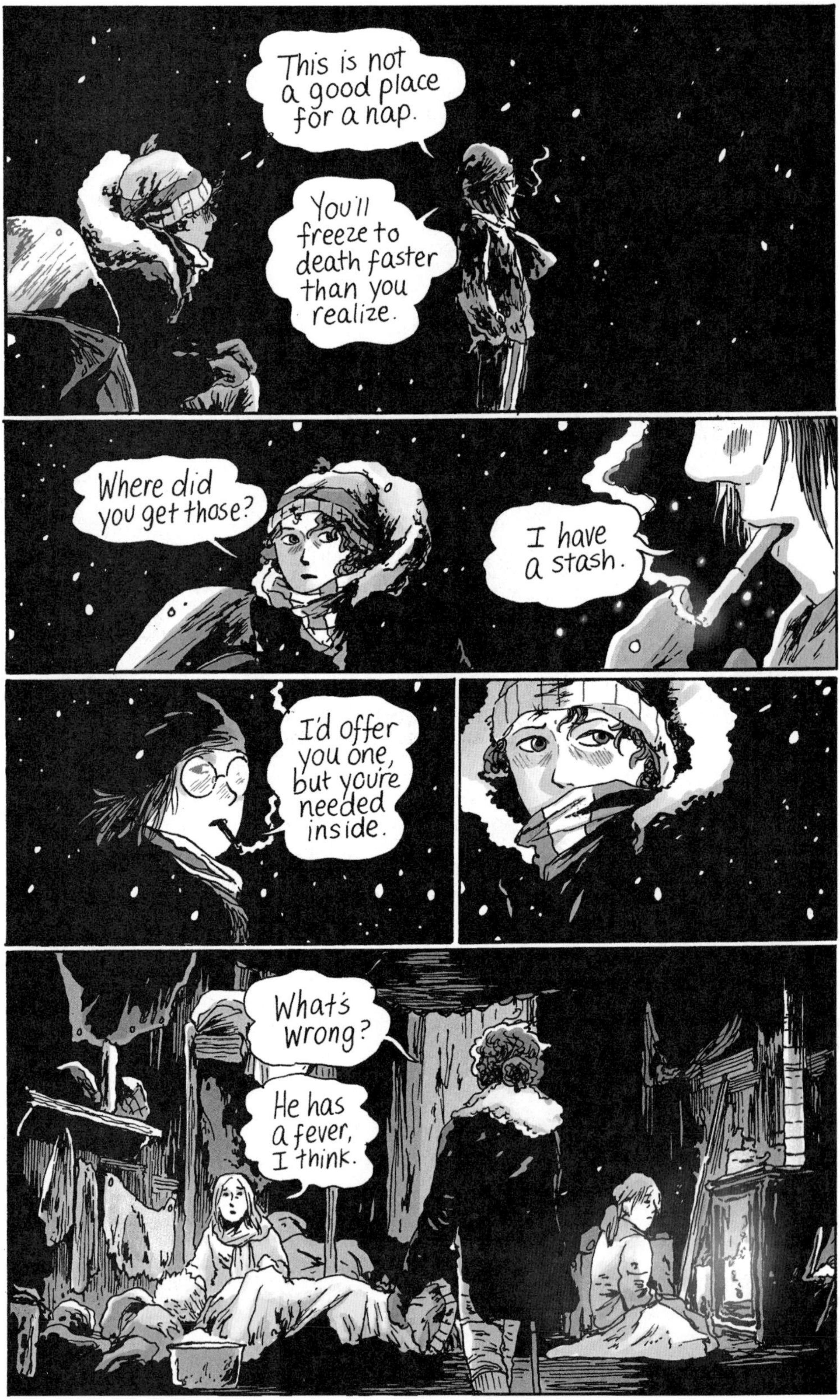
This is not a good place for a nap.
You'll freeze to death faster than you realize.
Where did you get those?
I have a stash.
I'd offer you one, but you're needed inside.
What's wrong?
He has a fever, I think.

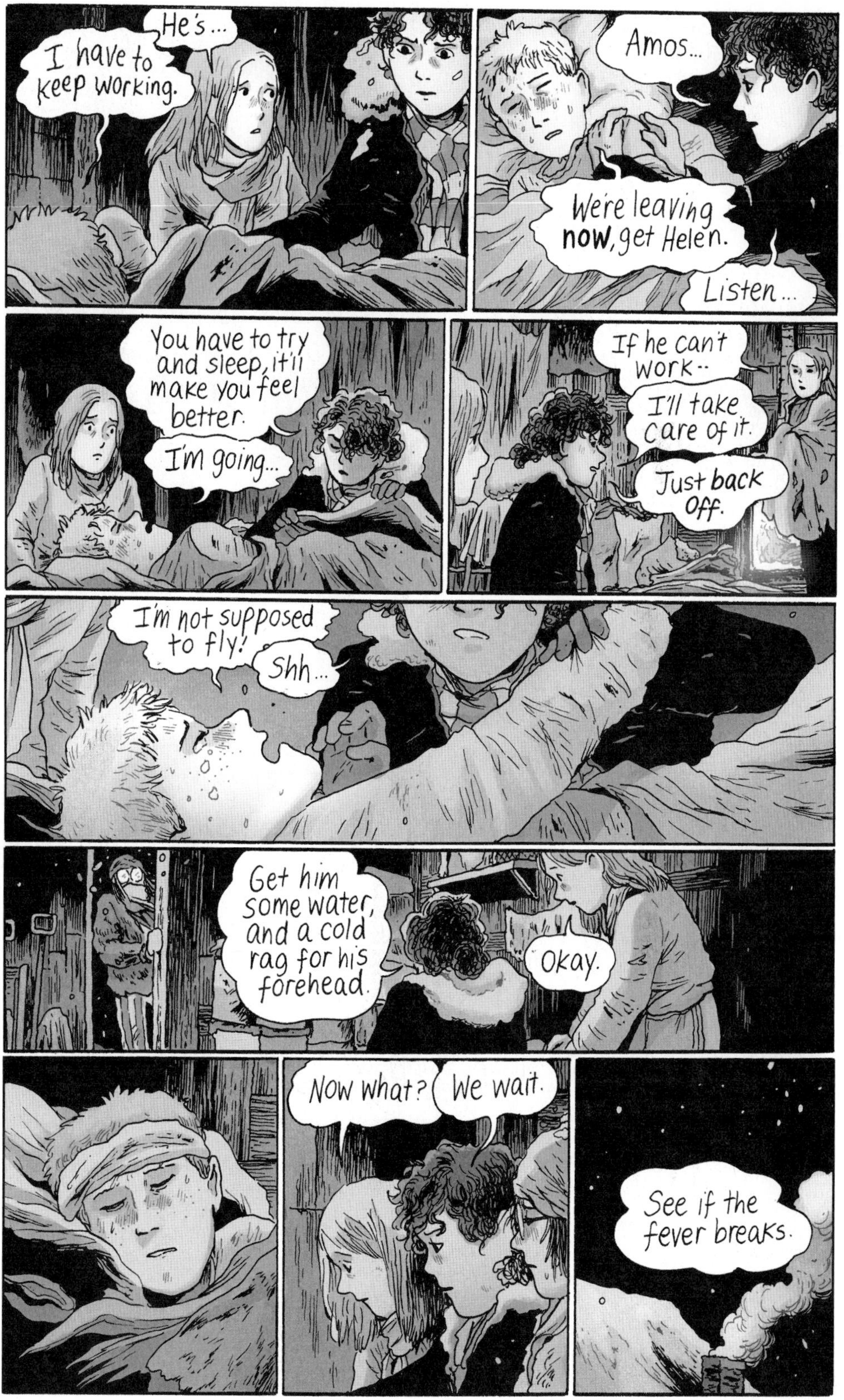
He's...
I have to keep working.
Amos...
We're leaving **now**, get Helen.
Listen...
You have to try and sleep, it'll make you feel better.
I'm going...
If he can't work..
I'll take care of it.
Just **back off**.
I'm not supposed to fly!
Shh...
Get him some water, and a cold rag for his forehead.
Okay.
Now what?
We wait.
See if the fever breaks.

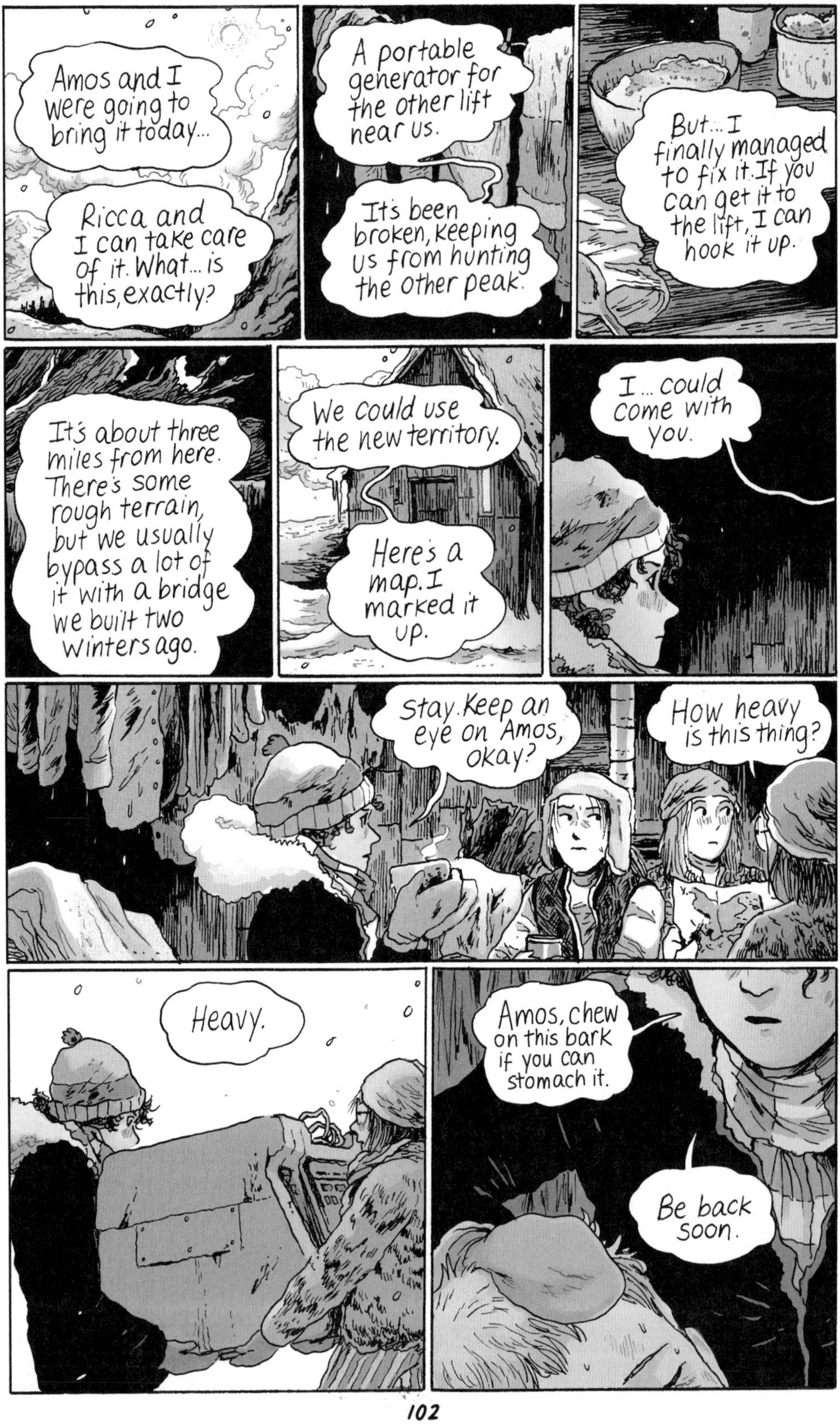
Amos and I were going to bring it today...
Ricca and I can take care of it. What... is this, exactly?
A portable generator for the other lift near us.
It's been broken, keeping us from hunting the other peak.
But... I finally managed to fix it. If you can get it to the lift, I can hook it up.
It's about three miles from here. There's some rough terrain, but we usually bypass a lot of it with a bridge we built two winters ago.
We could use the new territory.
Here's a map. I marked it up.
I... could come with you.
Stay. Keep an eye on Amos, okay?
How heavy is this thing?
Heavy.
Amos, chew on this bark if you can stomach it.
Be back soon.

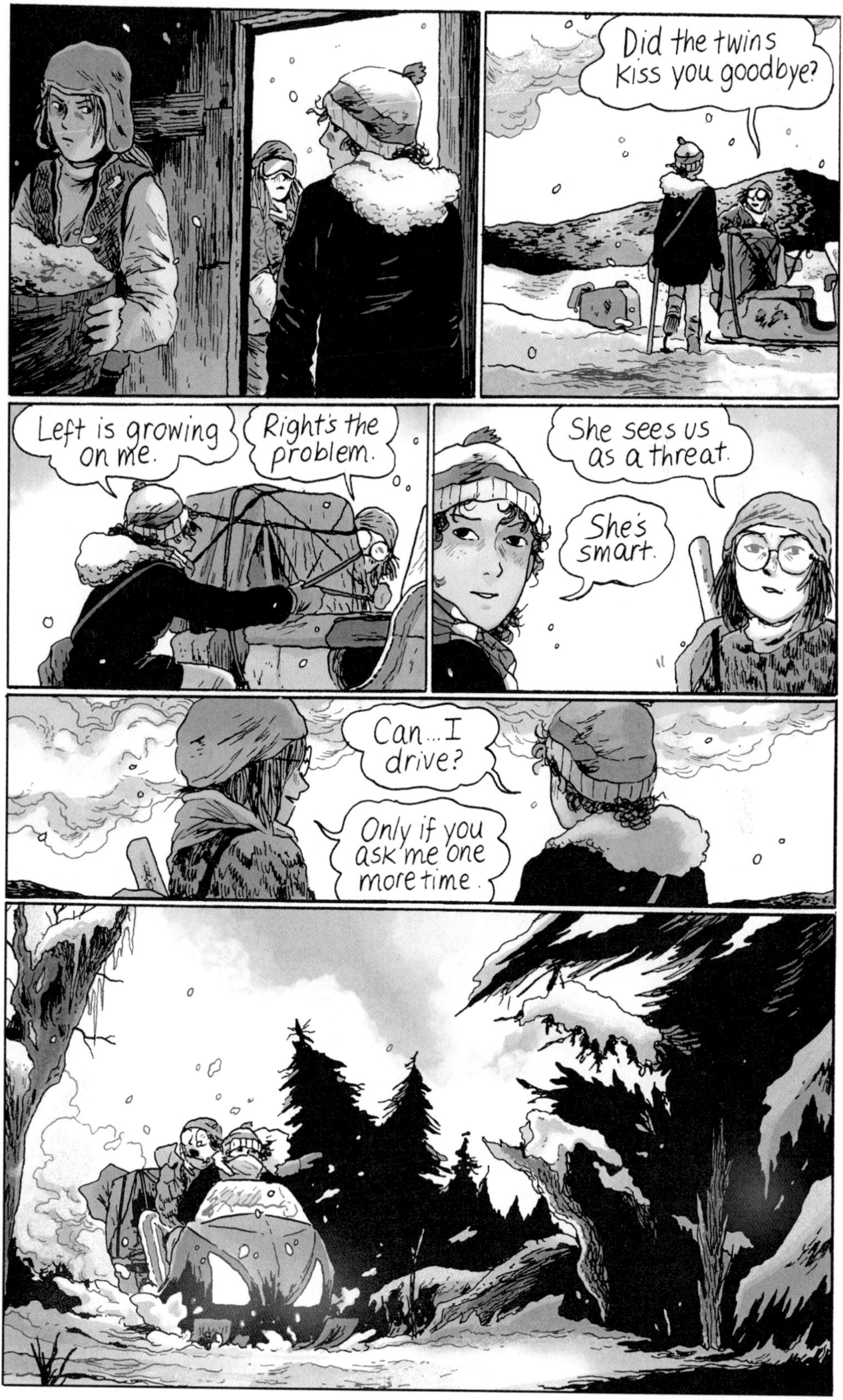
Did the twins kiss you goodbye?
Left is growing on me.
Right's the problem.
She sees us as a threat.
She's smart.
Can... I drive?
Only if you ask me one more time.

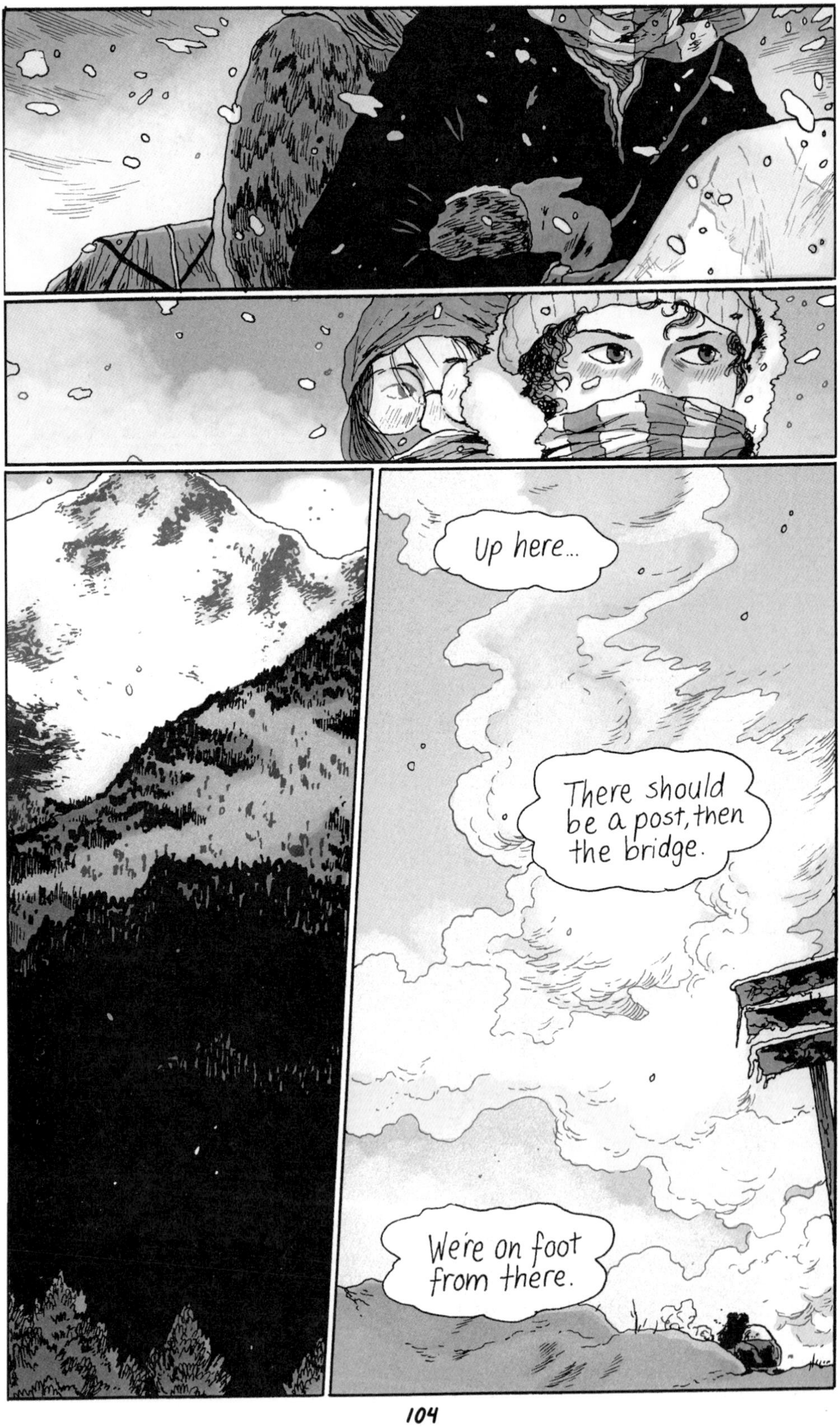
Up here...
There should be a post, then the bridge.
We're on foot from there.

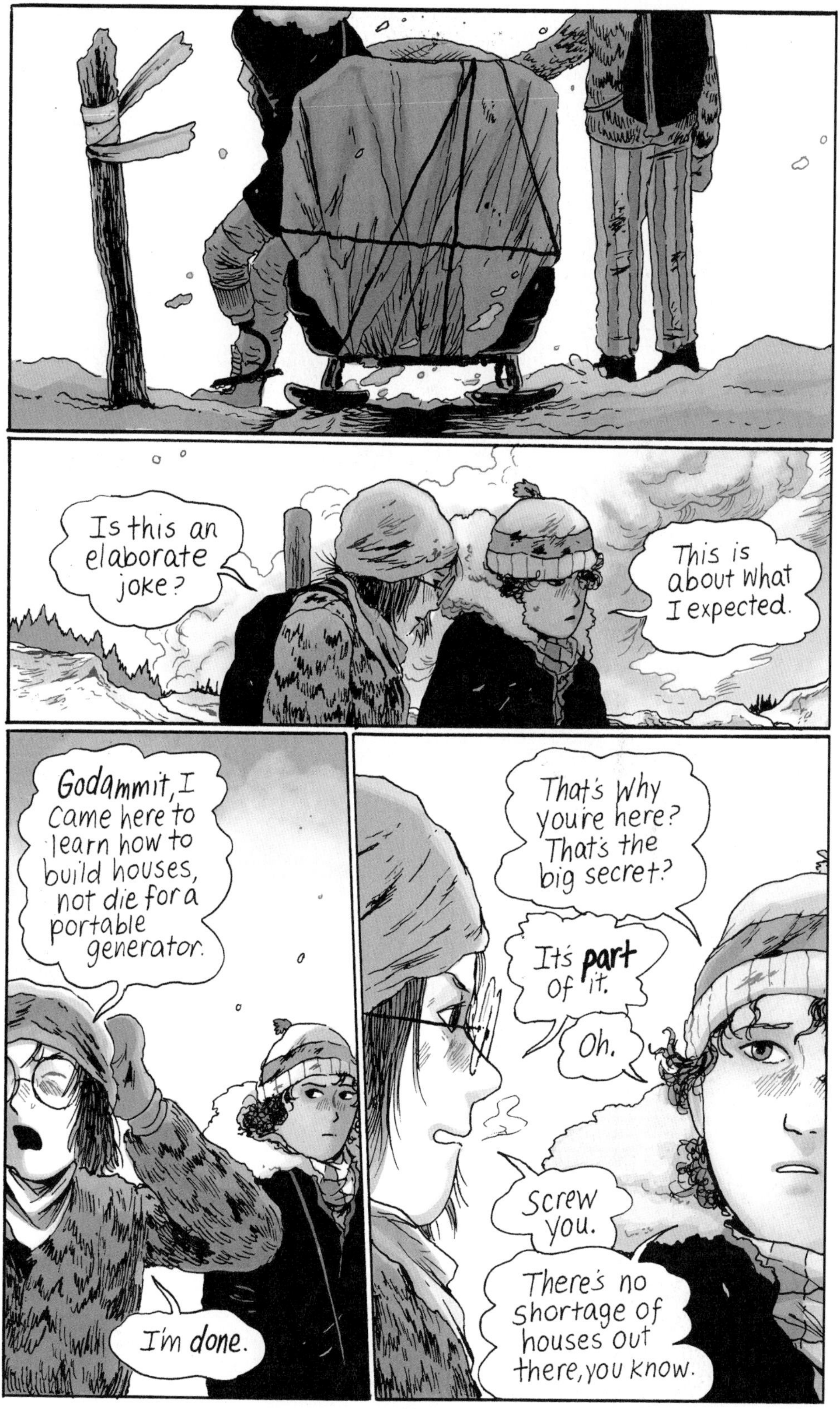
Is this an elaborate joke?
This is about what I expected.
Godammit, I came here to learn how to build houses, not die for a portable generator.
I'm done.
That's why you're here? That's the big secret?
It's part of it.
Oh.
Screw you.
There's no shortage of houses out there, you know.

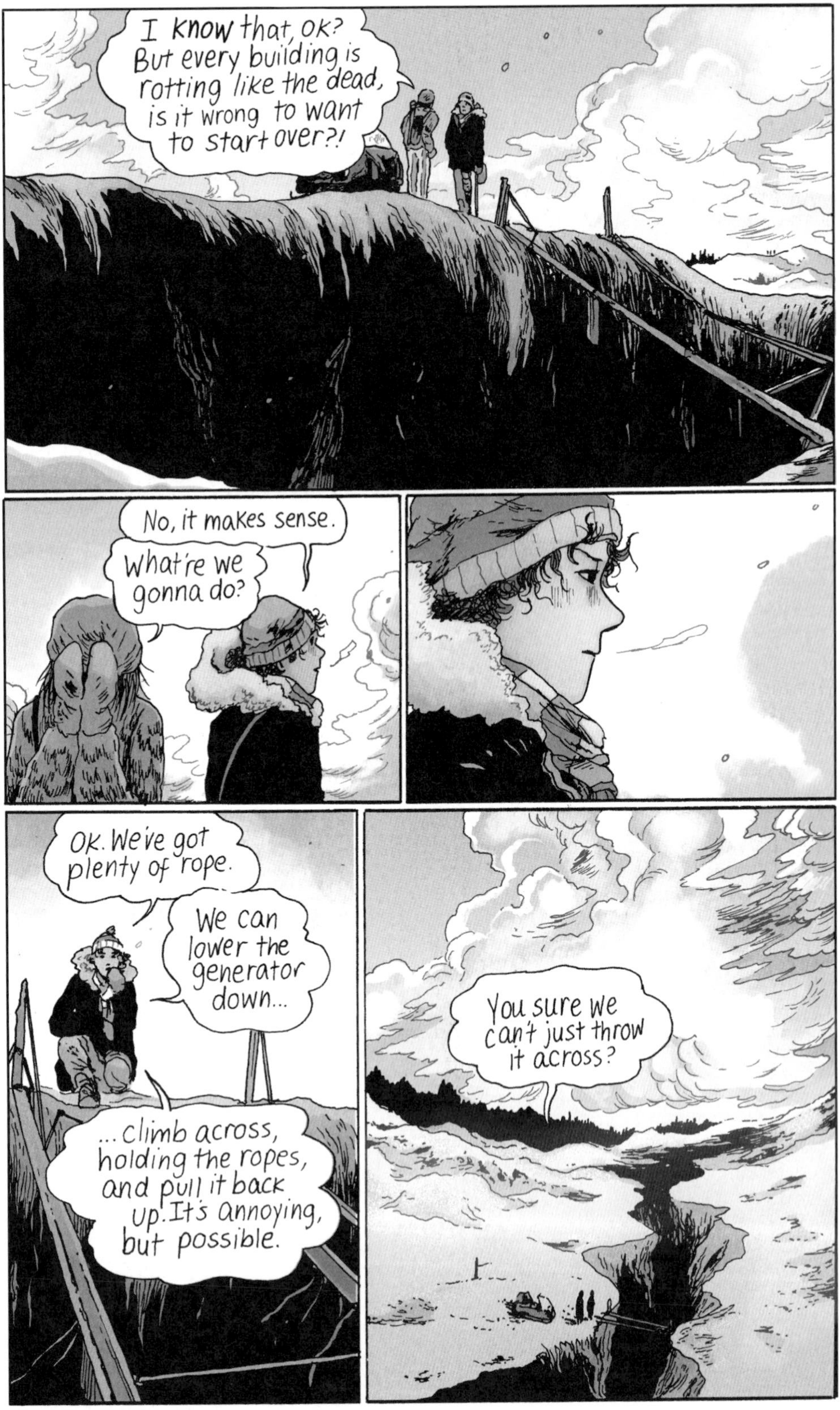

I KNOW that, OK? But every building is rotting like the dead, is it wrong to want to start over?!
No, it makes sense.
What're we gonna do?
OK. We've got plenty of rope.
We can lower the generator down...
...climb across, holding the ropes, and pull it back up. It's annoying, but possible.
You sure we can't just throw it across?

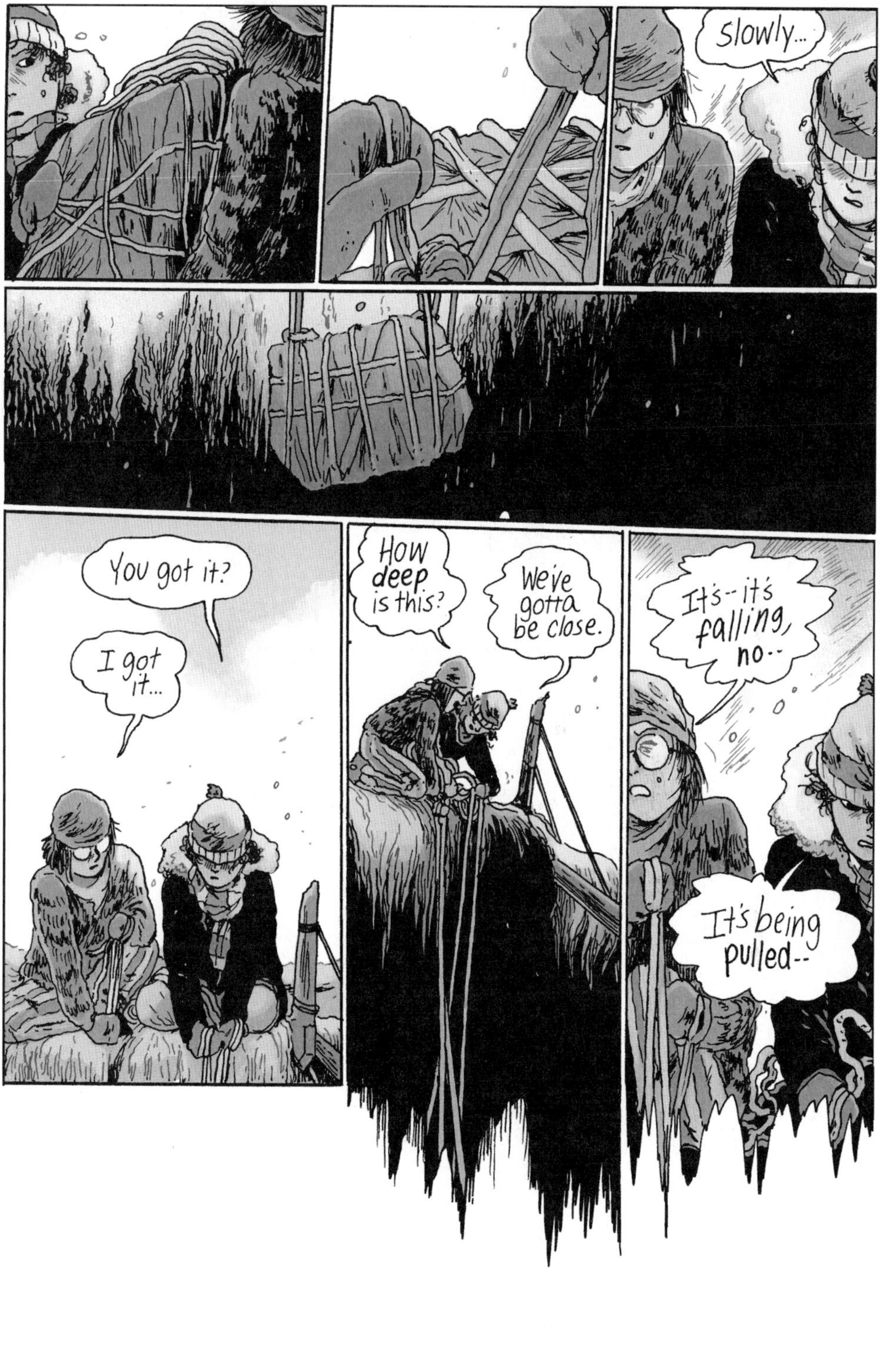
Slowly...
You got it?
I got it...
How deep is this?
We've gotta be close.
It's-- it's falling, no--
It's being pulled--

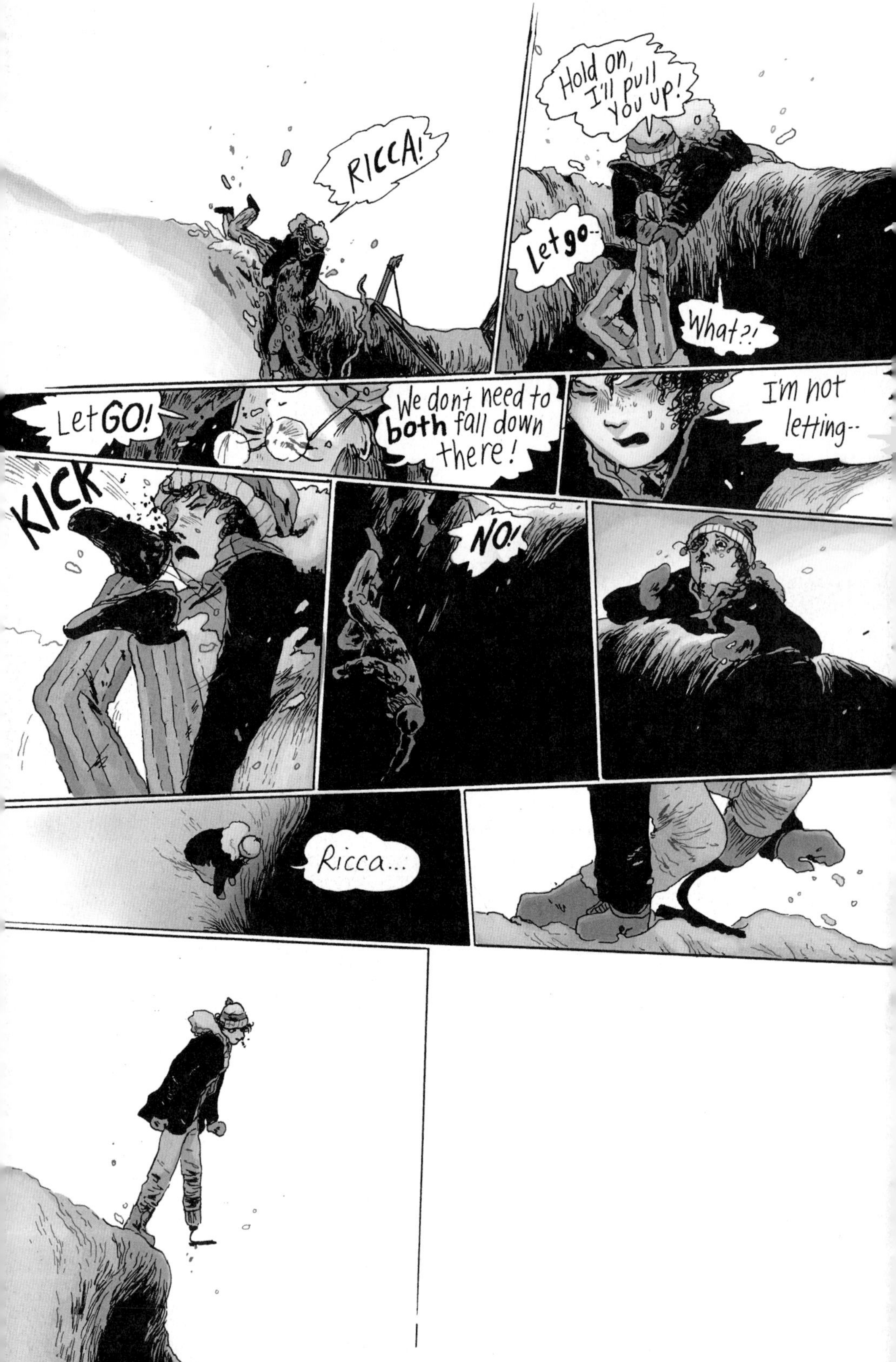
RICCA!
Hold on, I'll pull you up!
Let go--
What?!
Let GO!
We don't need to both fall down there!
I'm not letting--
KICK
NO!
Ricca...

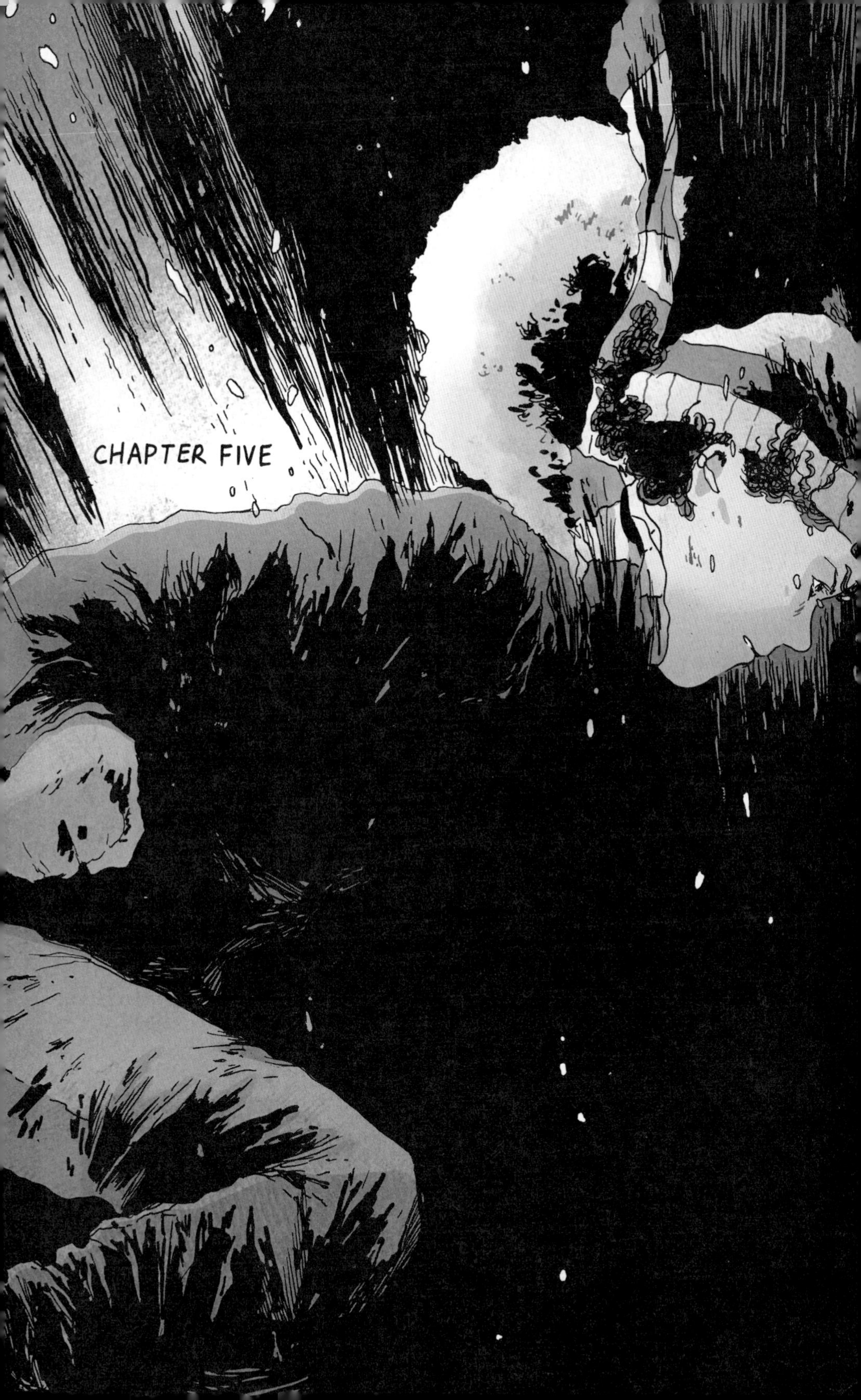
CHAPTER FIVE

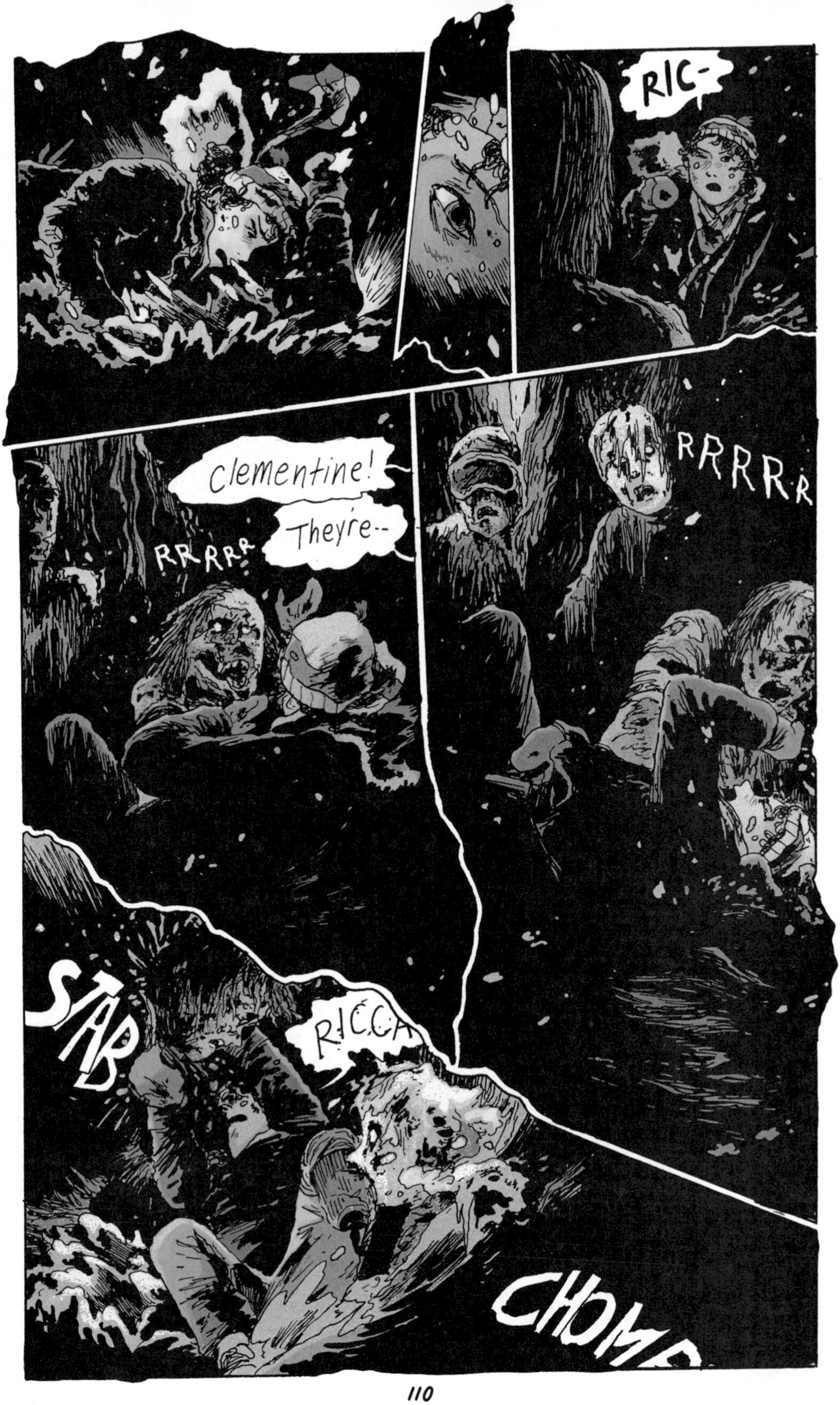
RIC-
Clementine!
Theyre--
RRRRR
RRRRRR
STAB
RICCA
CHOMP

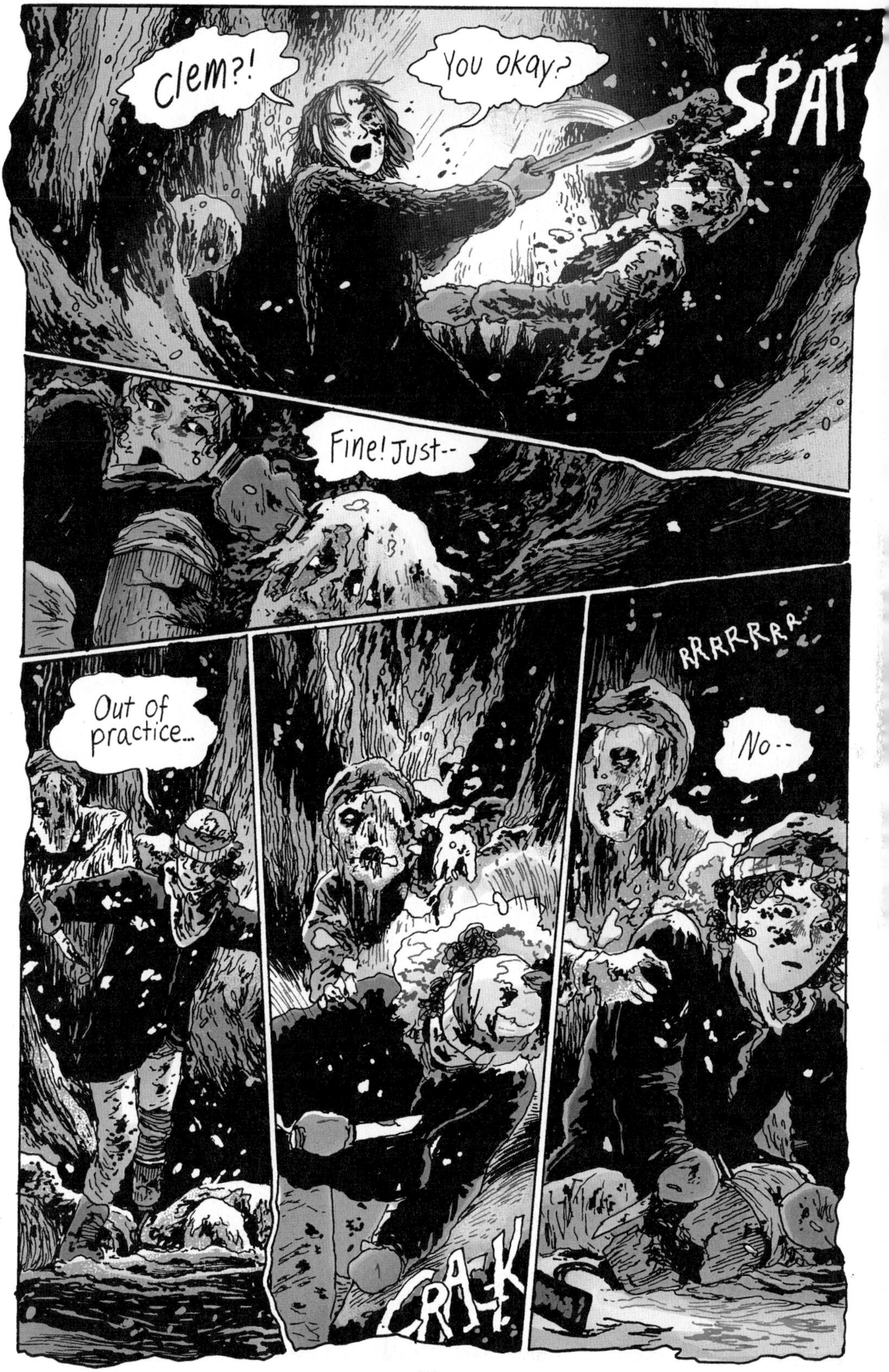
Clem?!
You okay?
SPAT
Fine! Just--
Out of practice...
CRA-K
RRRRRRRR
No--

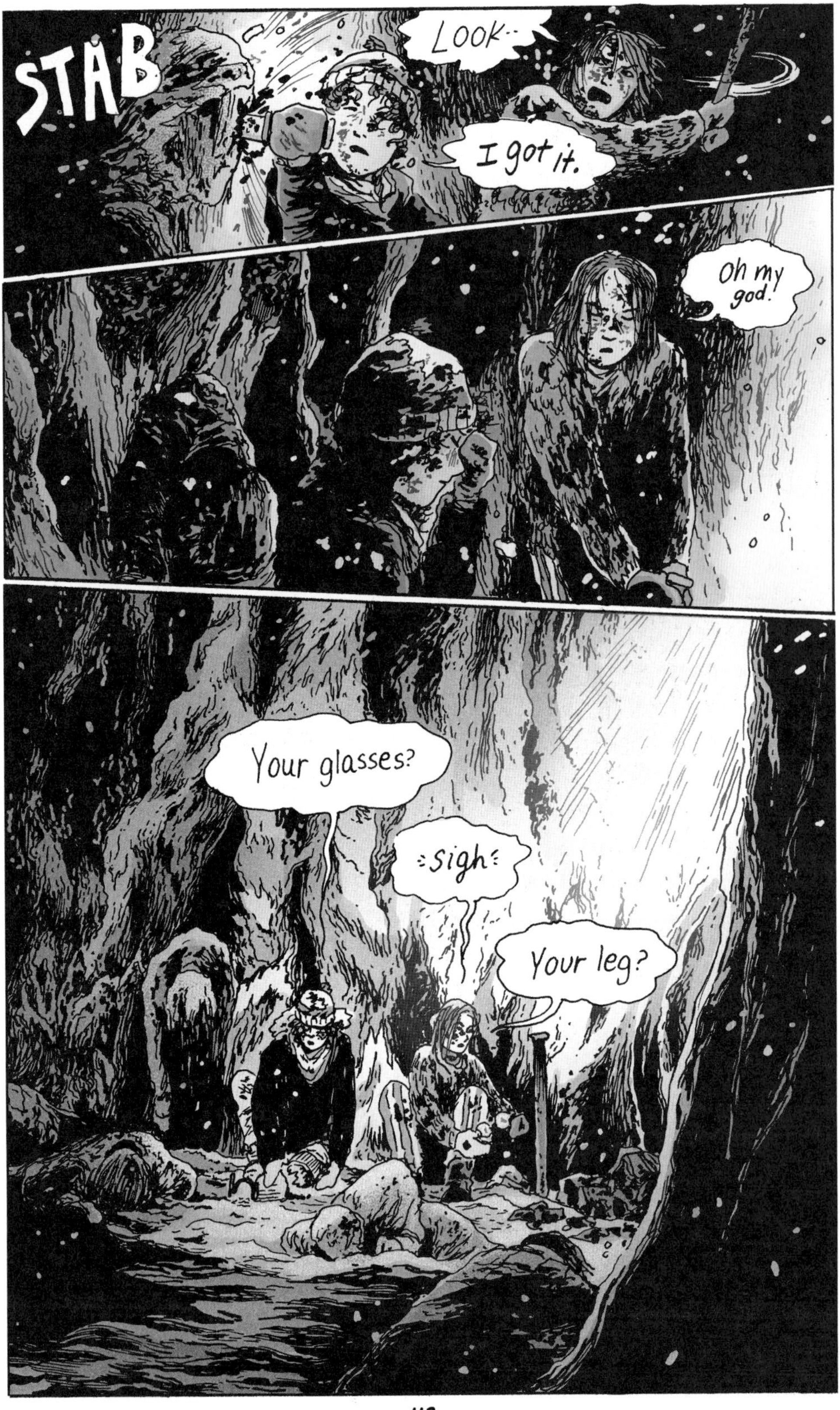
STAB
LOOK
I got it.
Oh my god!
Your glasses?
sigh
Your leg?

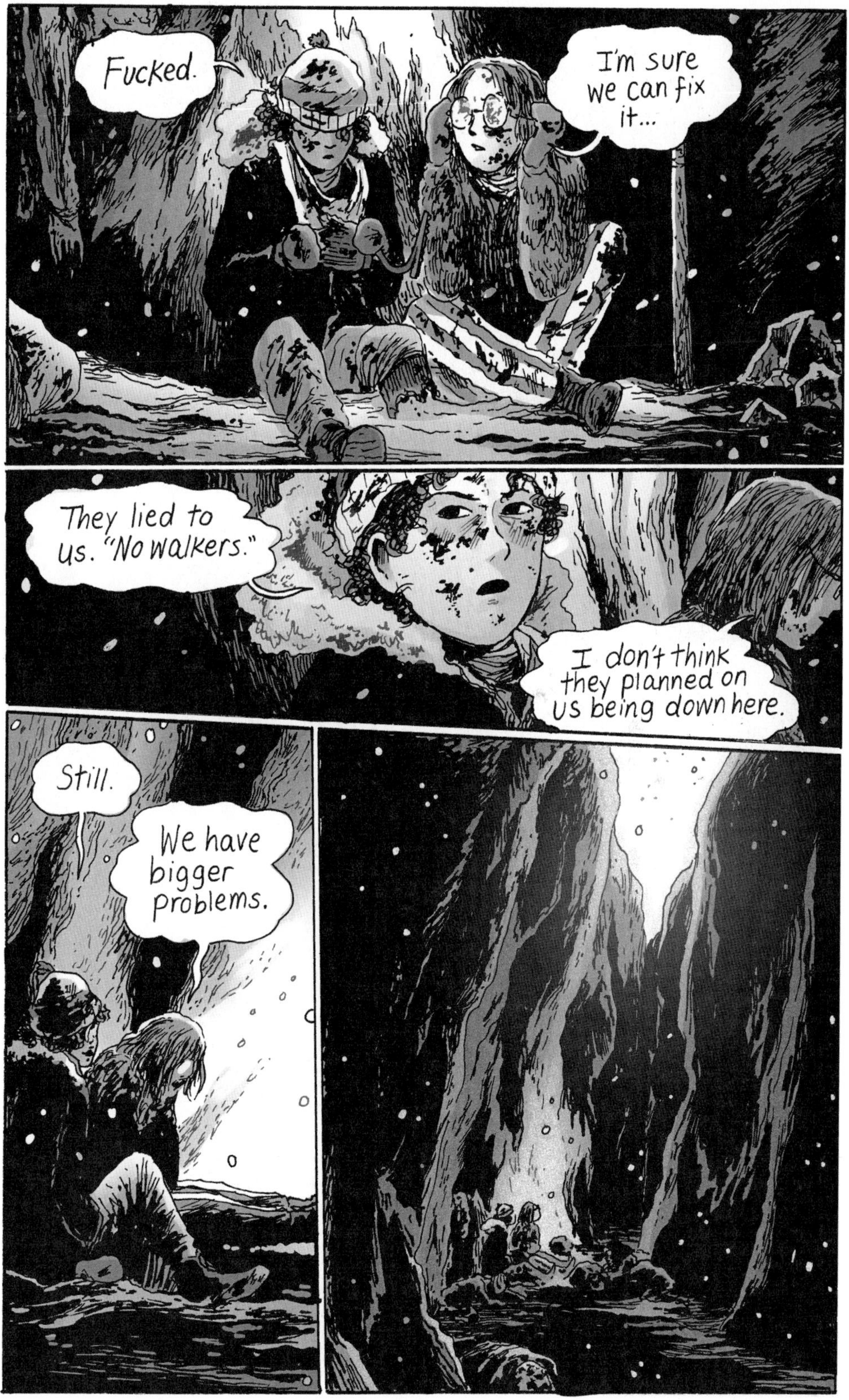
Fucked.
I'm sure we can fix it...
They lied to us. "No walkers."
I don't think they planned on us being down here.
Still.
We have bigger problems.

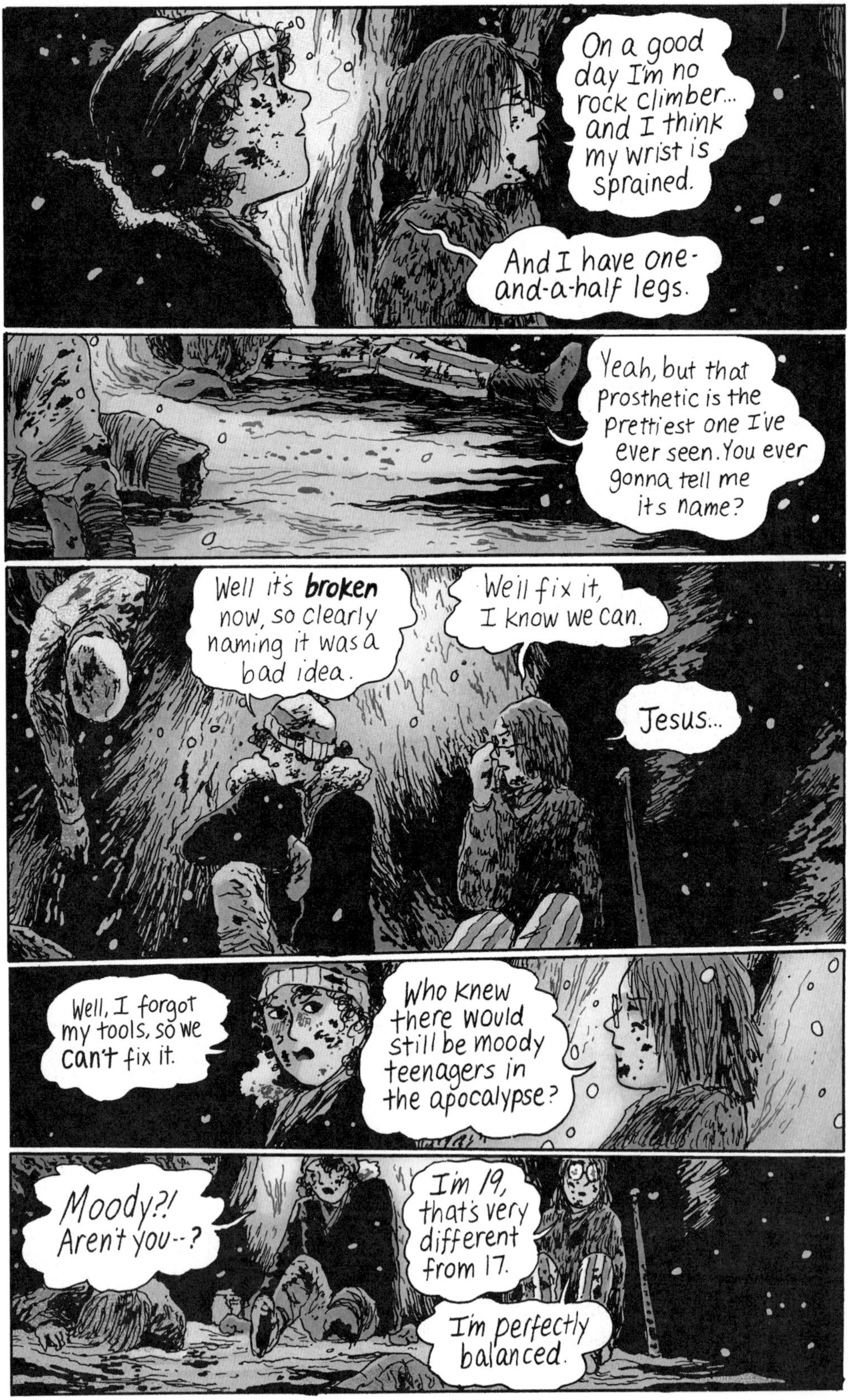
On a good day I'm no rock climber... and I think my wrist is sprained.
And I have one-and-a-half legs.
Yeah, but that prosthetic is the prettiest one I've ever seen. You ever gonna tell me its name?
Well it's **broken** now, so clearly naming it was a bad idea.
We'll fix it, I know we can.
Jesus...
Well, I forgot my tools, so we can't fix it.
Who knew there would still be moody teenagers in the apocalypse?
Moody?! Aren't you--?
I'm 19, that's very different from 17.
I'm perfectly balanced.

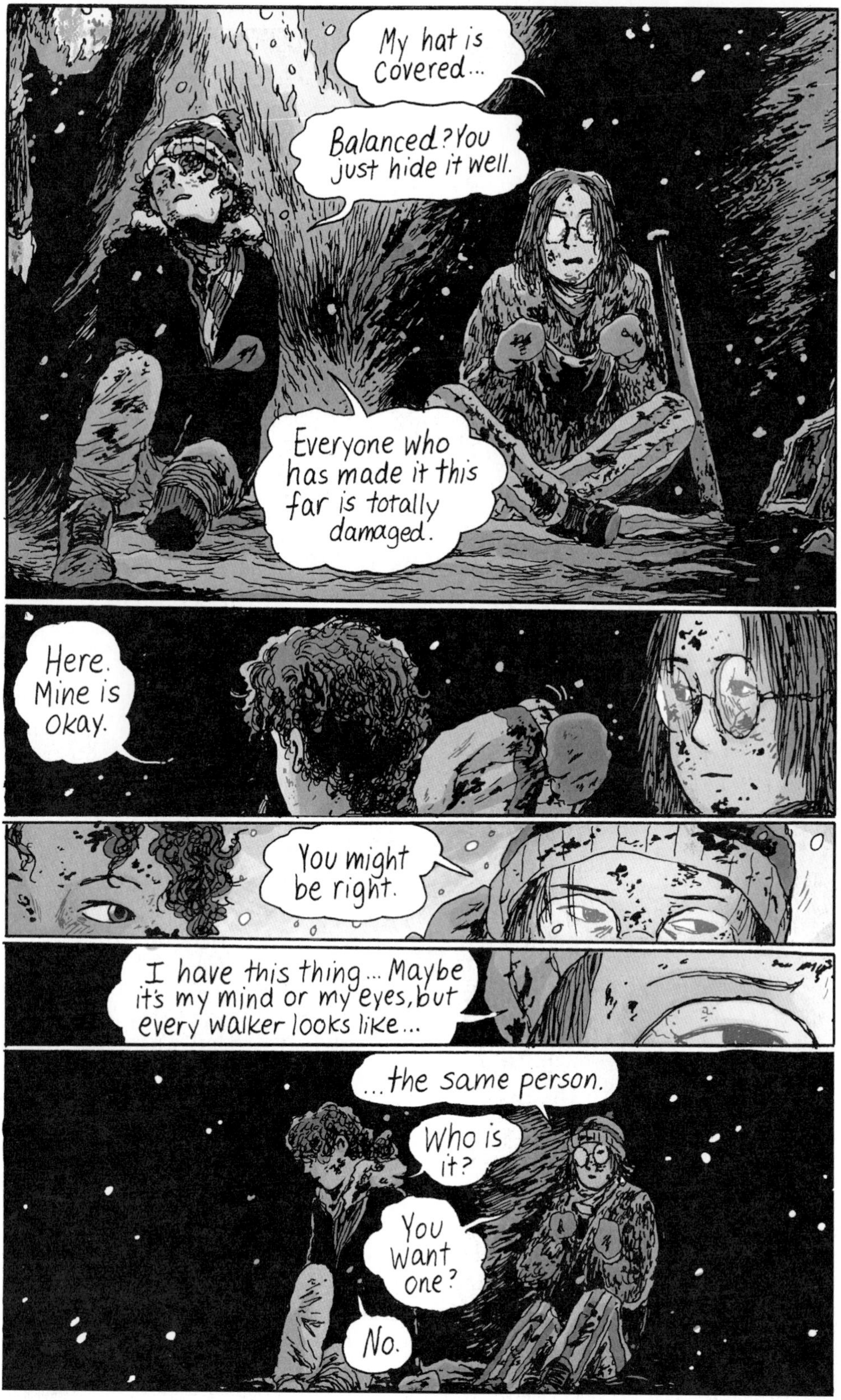
My hat is covered...
Balanced? You just hide it well.
Everyone who has made it this far is totally damaged.
Here. Mine is okay.
You might be right.
I have this thing... Maybe it's my mind or my eyes, but every walker looks like...
...the same person.
Who is it?
You want one?
No.

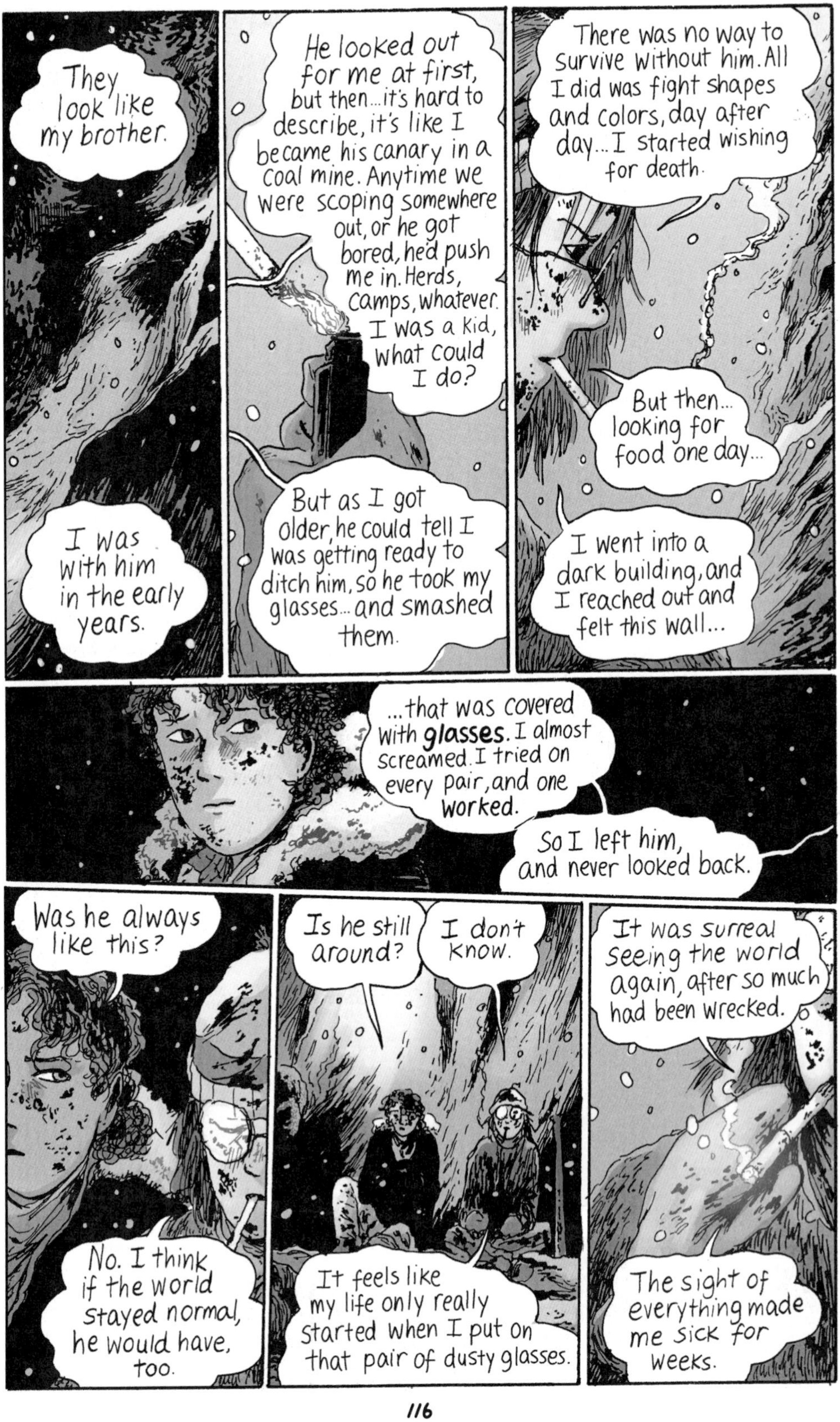
They look like my brother.
I was with him in the early years.
He looked out for me at first, but then...it's hard to describe, it's like I became his canary in a coal mine. Anytime we were scoping somewhere out, or he got bored, he'd push me in. Herds, camps, whatever. I was a kid, what could I do?
But as I got older, he could tell I was getting ready to ditch him, so he took my glasses... and smashed them.
There was no way to survive without him. All I did was fight shapes and colors, day after day... I started wishing for death.
But then... looking for food one day...
I went into a dark building, and I reached out and felt this wall...
...that was covered with glasses. I almost screamed. I tried on every pair, and one worked.
So I left him, and never looked back.
Was he always like this?
No. I think if the world stayed normal, he would have, too.
Is he still around?
I don't know.
It feels like my life only really started when I put on that pair of dusty glasses.
It was surreal seeing the world again, after so much had been wrecked.
The sight of everything made me sick for weeks.

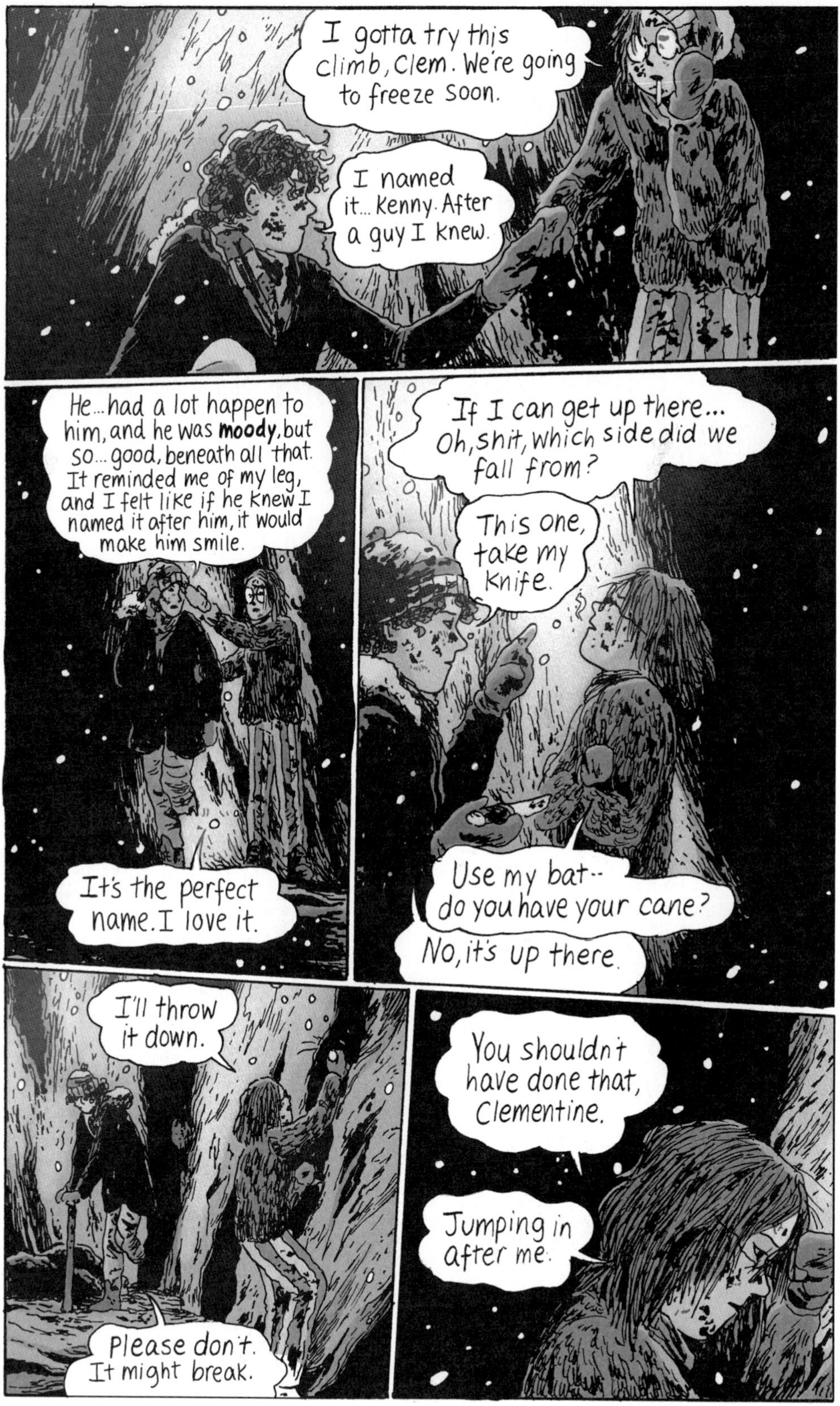
I gotta try this climb, Clem. We're going to freeze soon.
I named it... Kenny. After a guy I knew.
He...had a lot happen to him, and he was **moody**, but so...good, beneath all that. It reminded me of my leg, and I felt like if he knew I named it after him, it would make him smile.
It's the perfect name. I love it.
If I can get up there... Oh, shit, which side did we fall from?
This one, take my knife.
Use my bat-- do you have your cane?
No, it's up there.
I'll throw it down.
Please don't. It might break.
You shouldn't have done that, Clementine.
Jumping in after me.

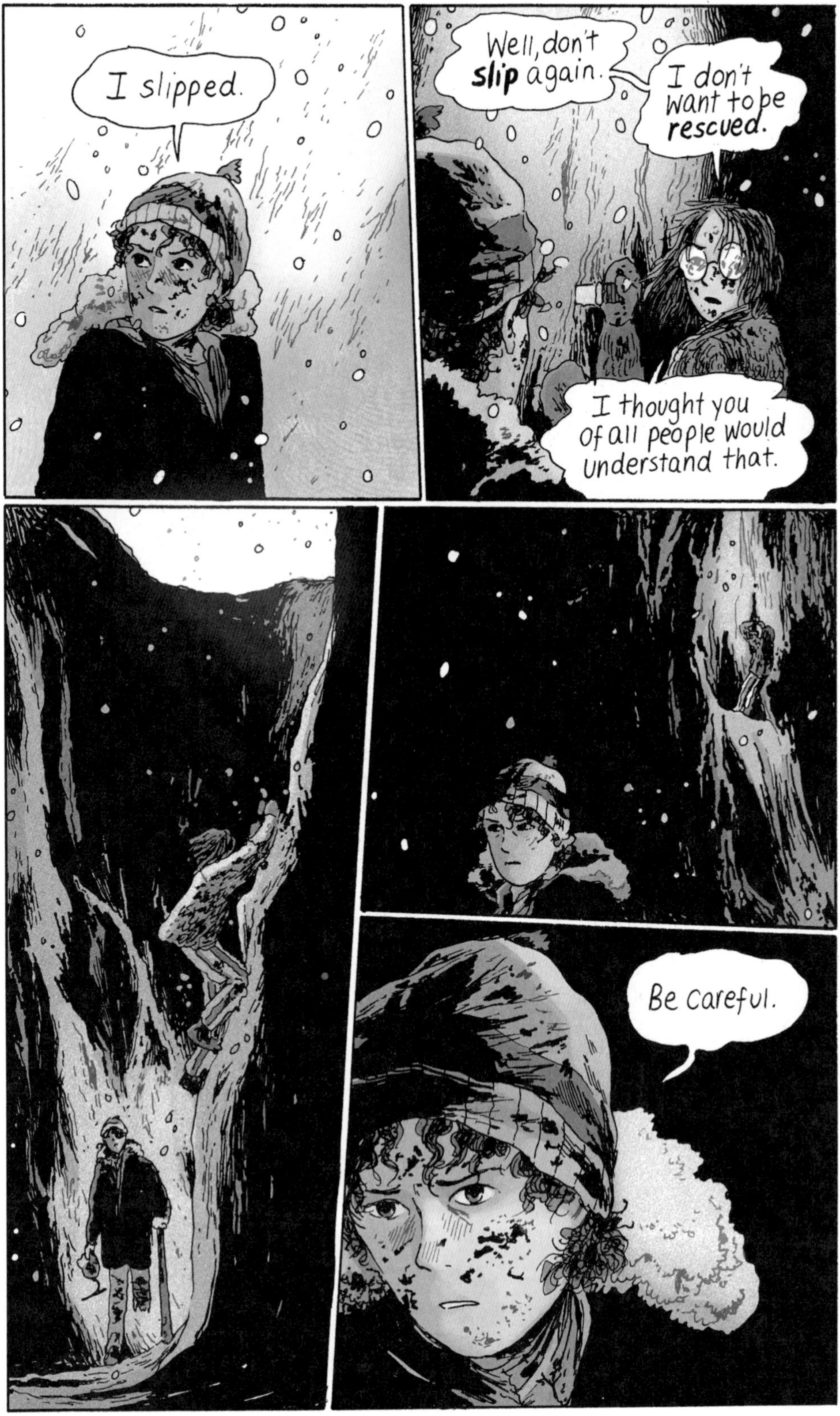
I slipped.
Well, don't **slip** again.
I don't want to be **rescued**.
I thought you of all people would understand that.
Be careful.

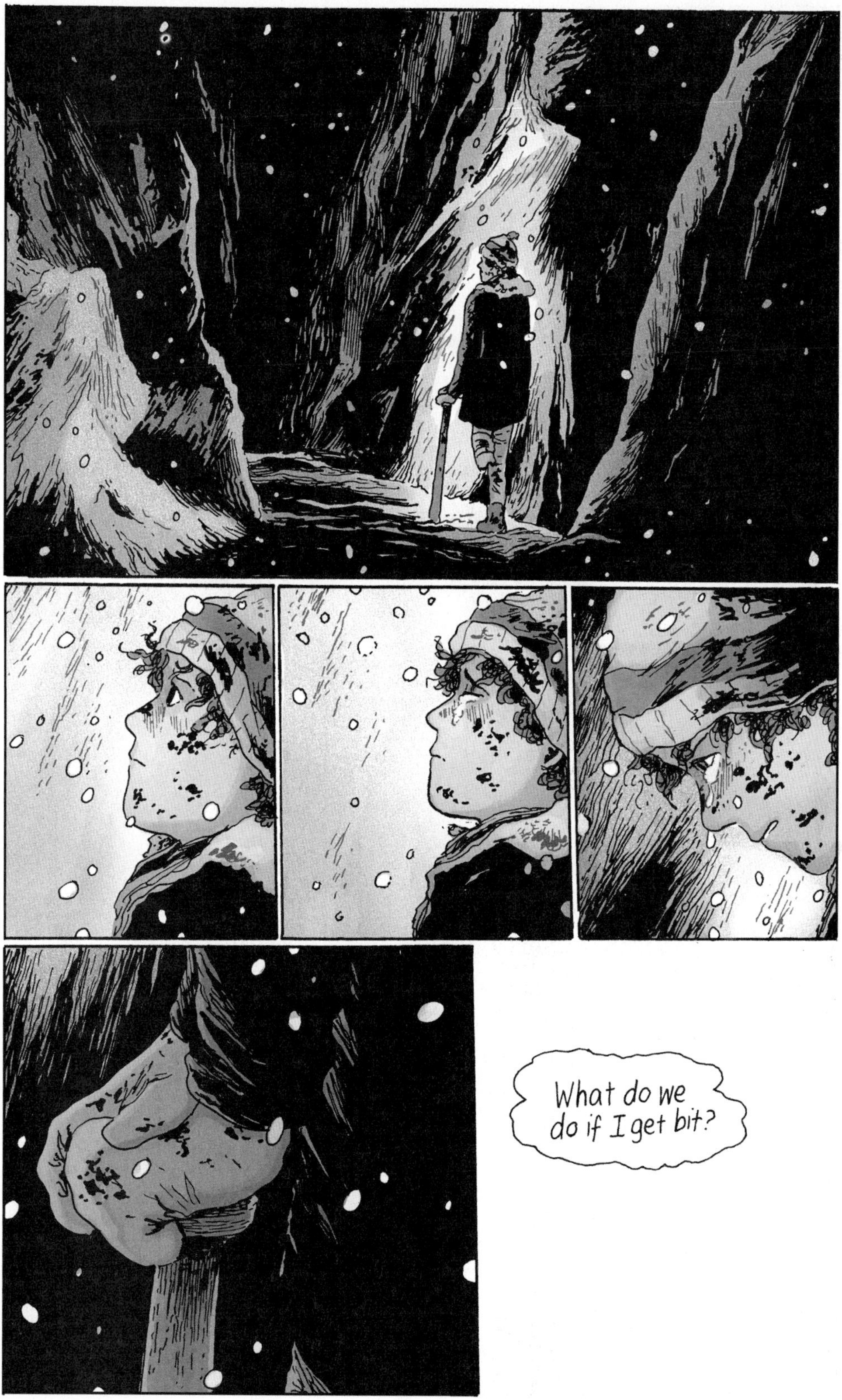
What do we do if I get bit?

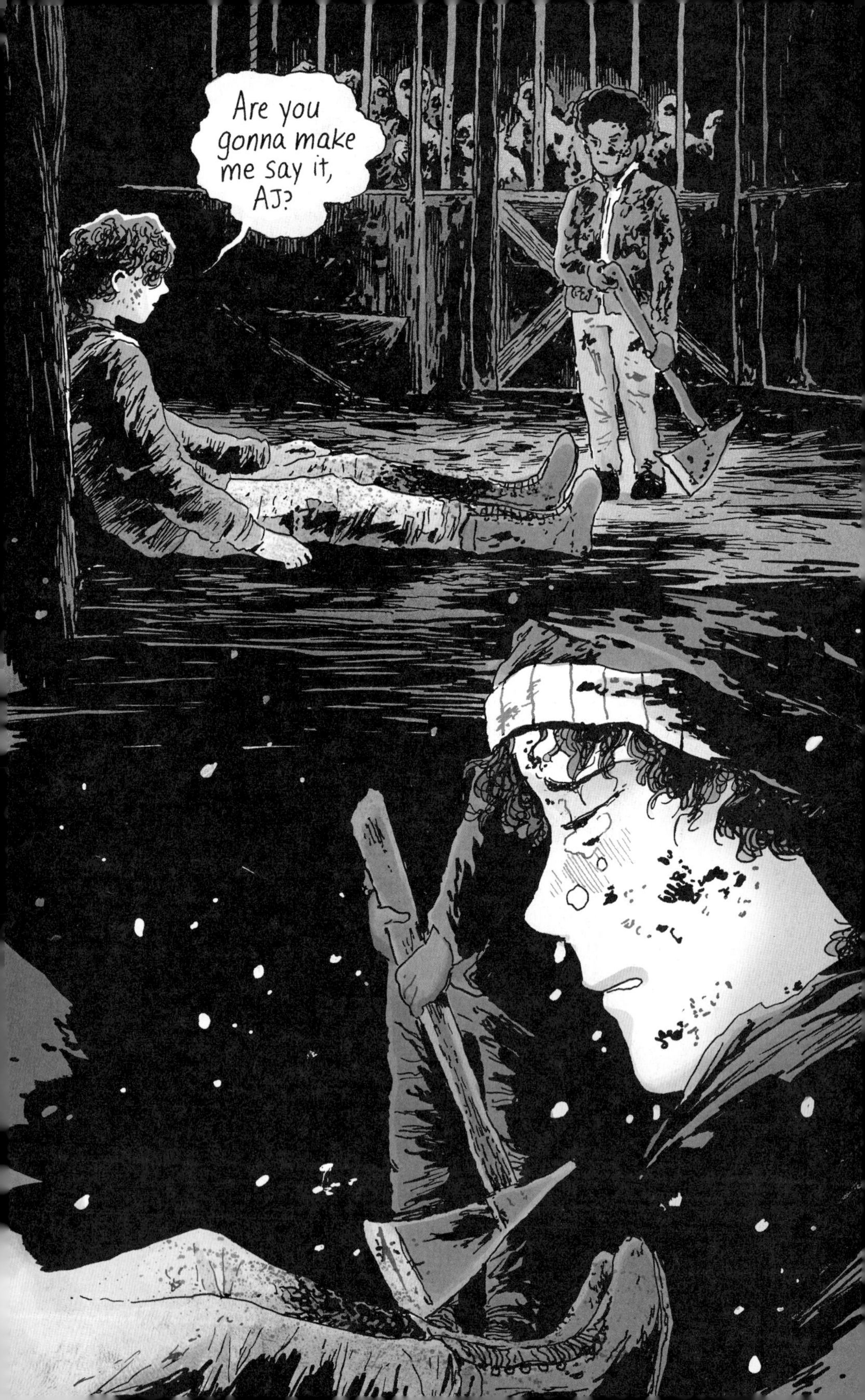
Are you gonna make me say it, AJ?

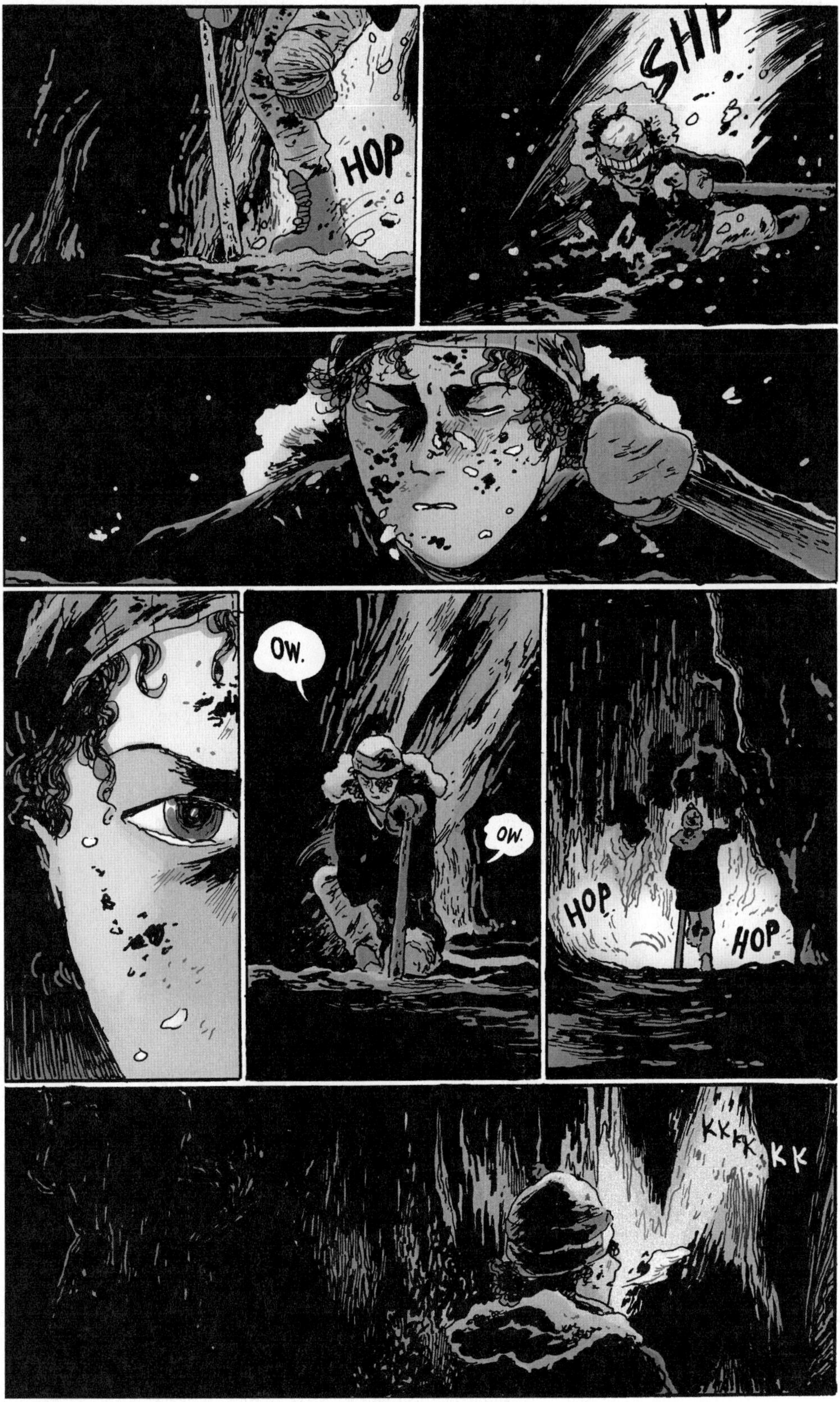
HOP
SHP
OW.
OW.
HOP
HOP
KKKK KK

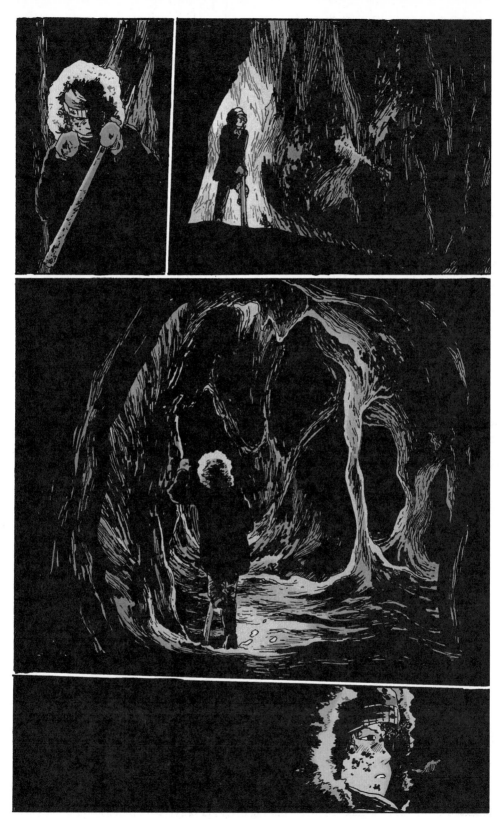

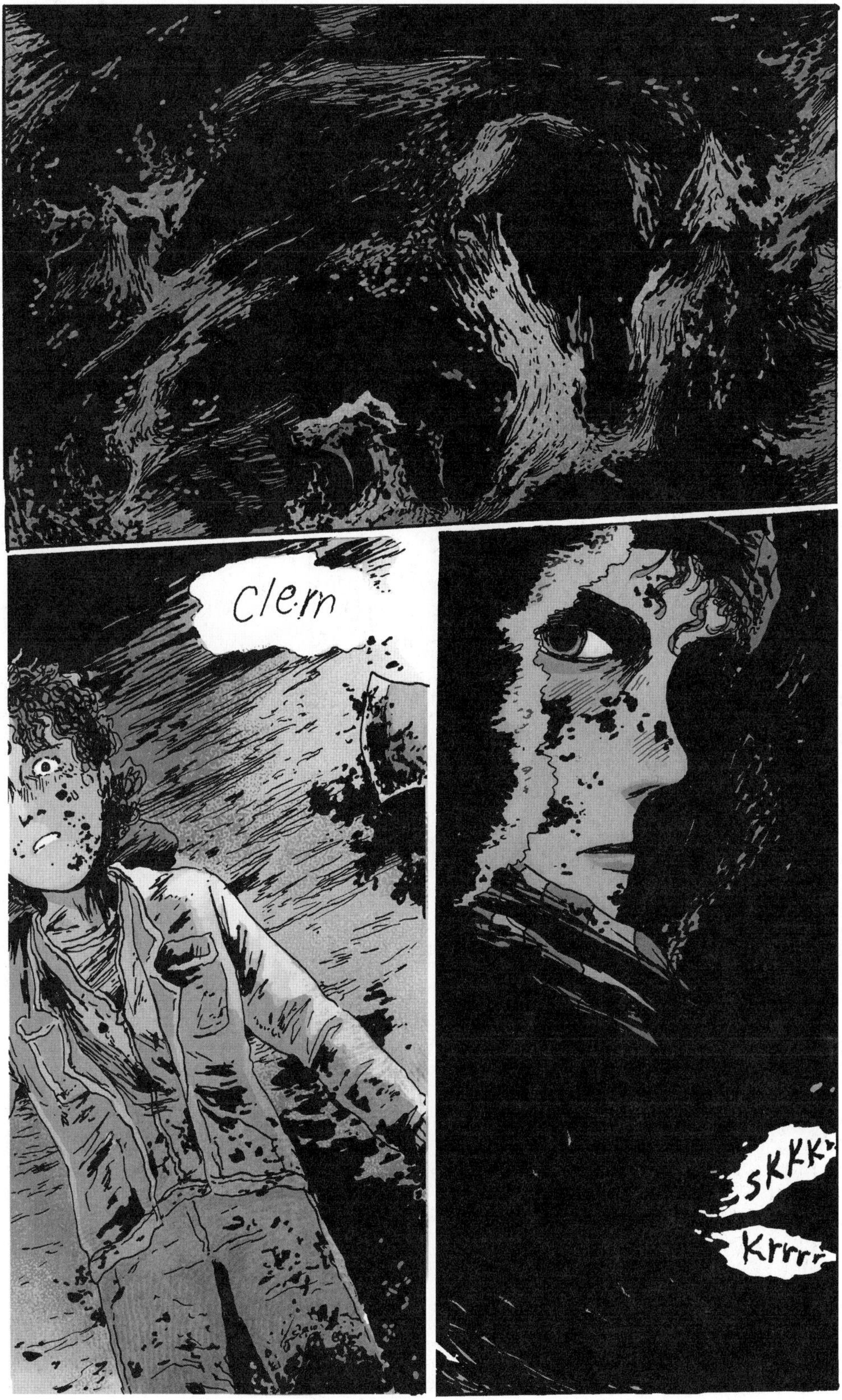
Clem
SKKK
Krrrr

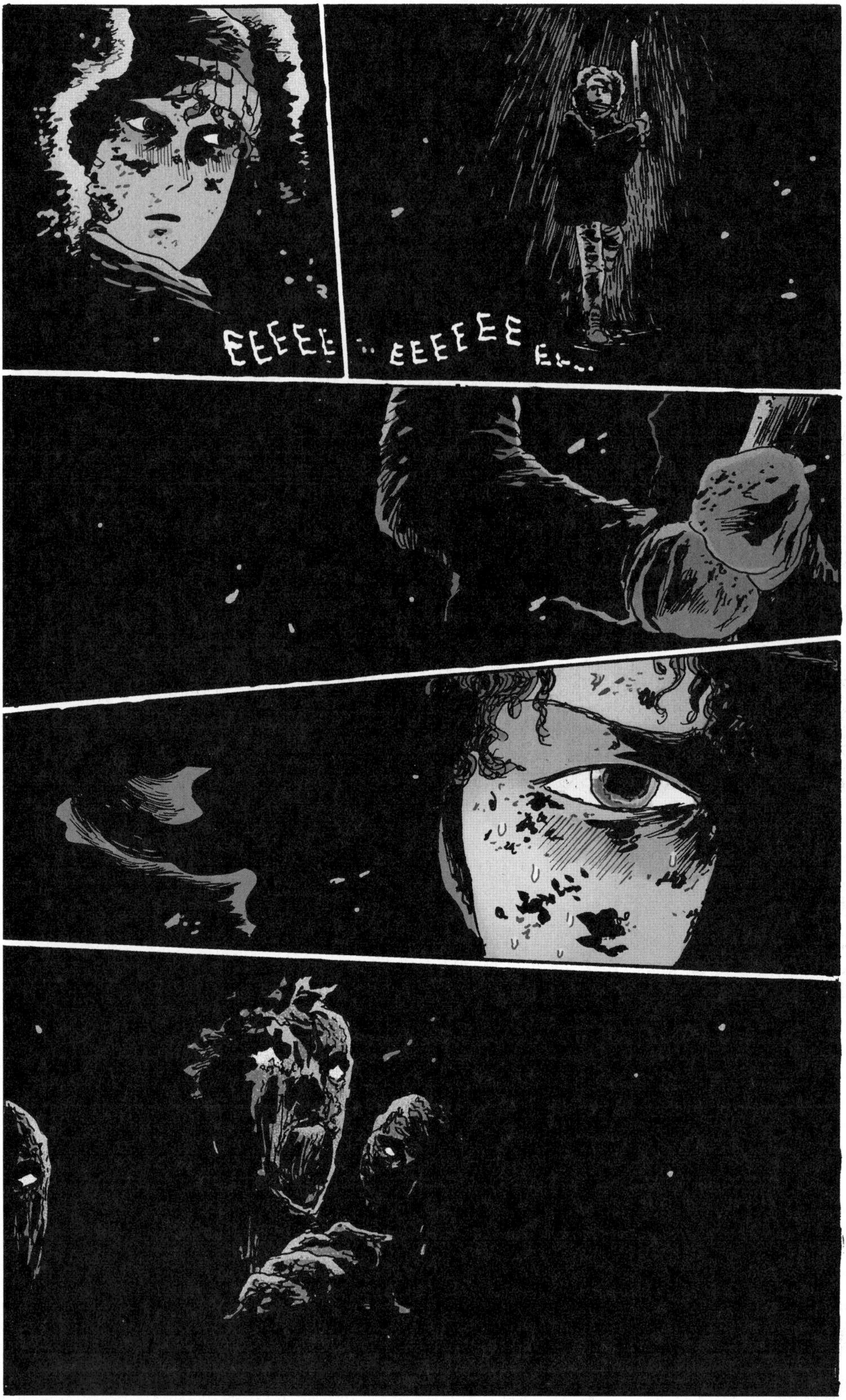
EEEEE
EEEEEE EE...

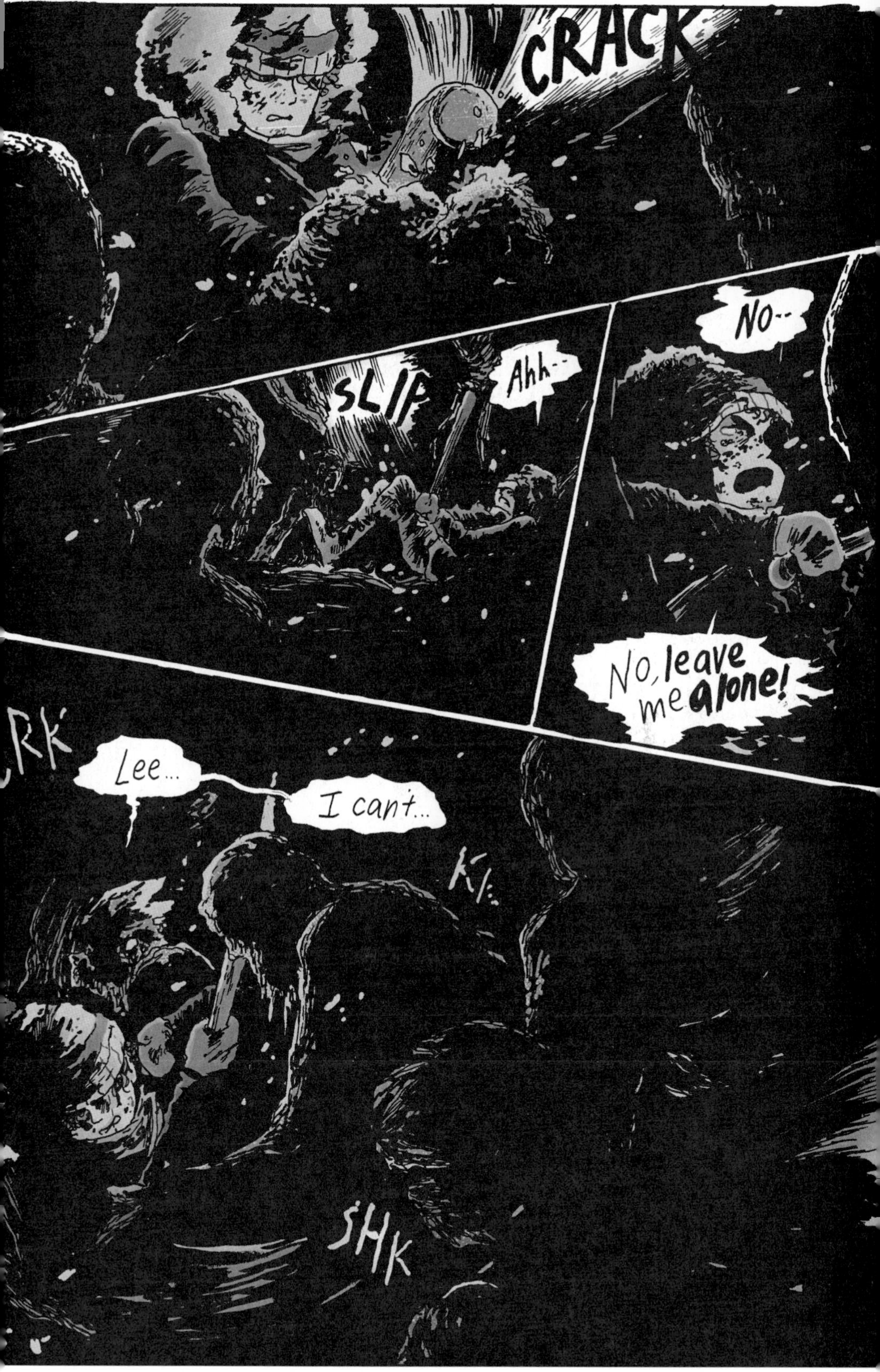
CRACK
SLIP
Ahh--
No--
No, leave me alone!
RK
Lee...
I can't...
K/
SHK

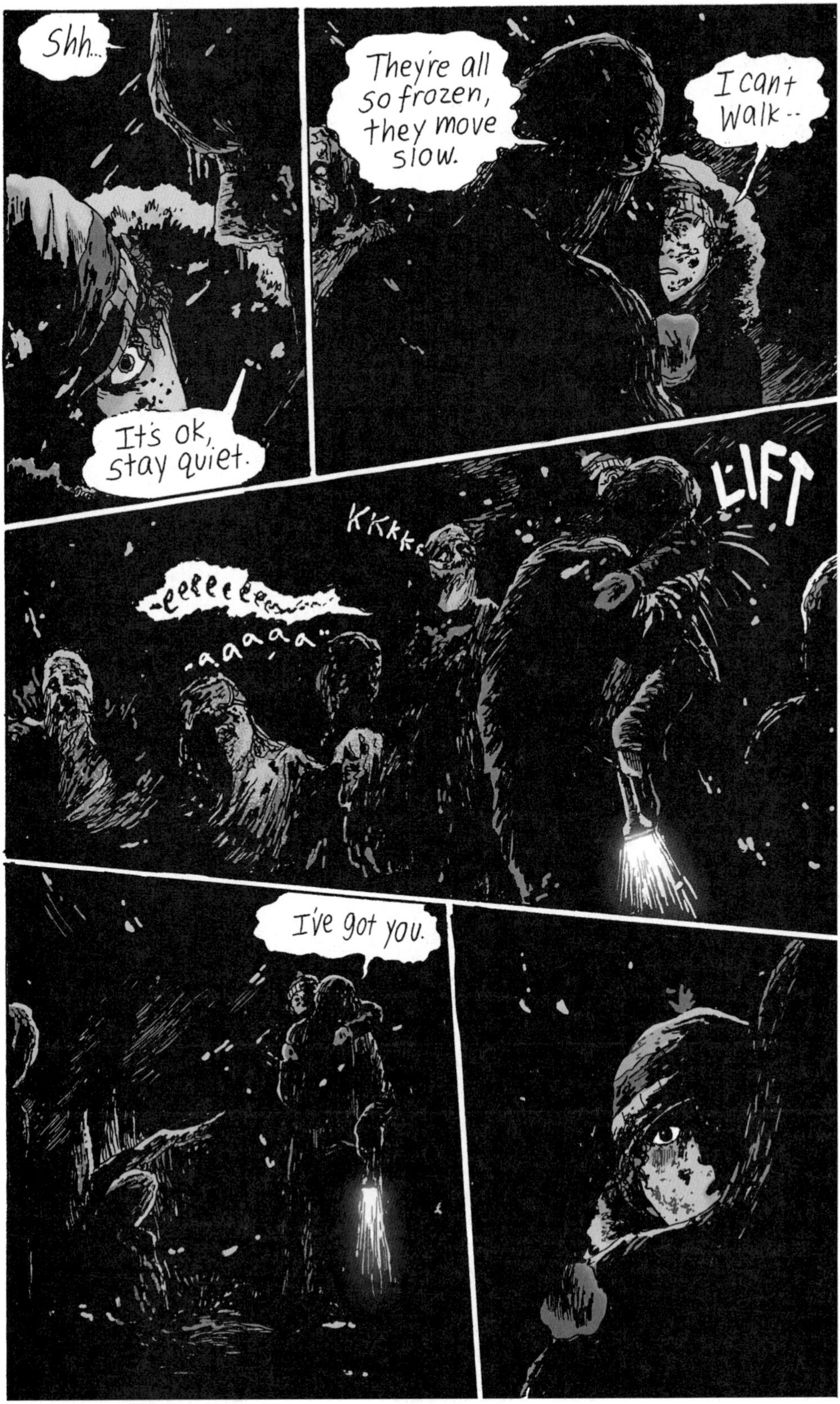
Shh...
It's ok, stay quiet.
They're all so frozen, they move slow.
I can't walk--
KKKKK
-eeeeeee
-aaaaa
LIFT
I've got you.

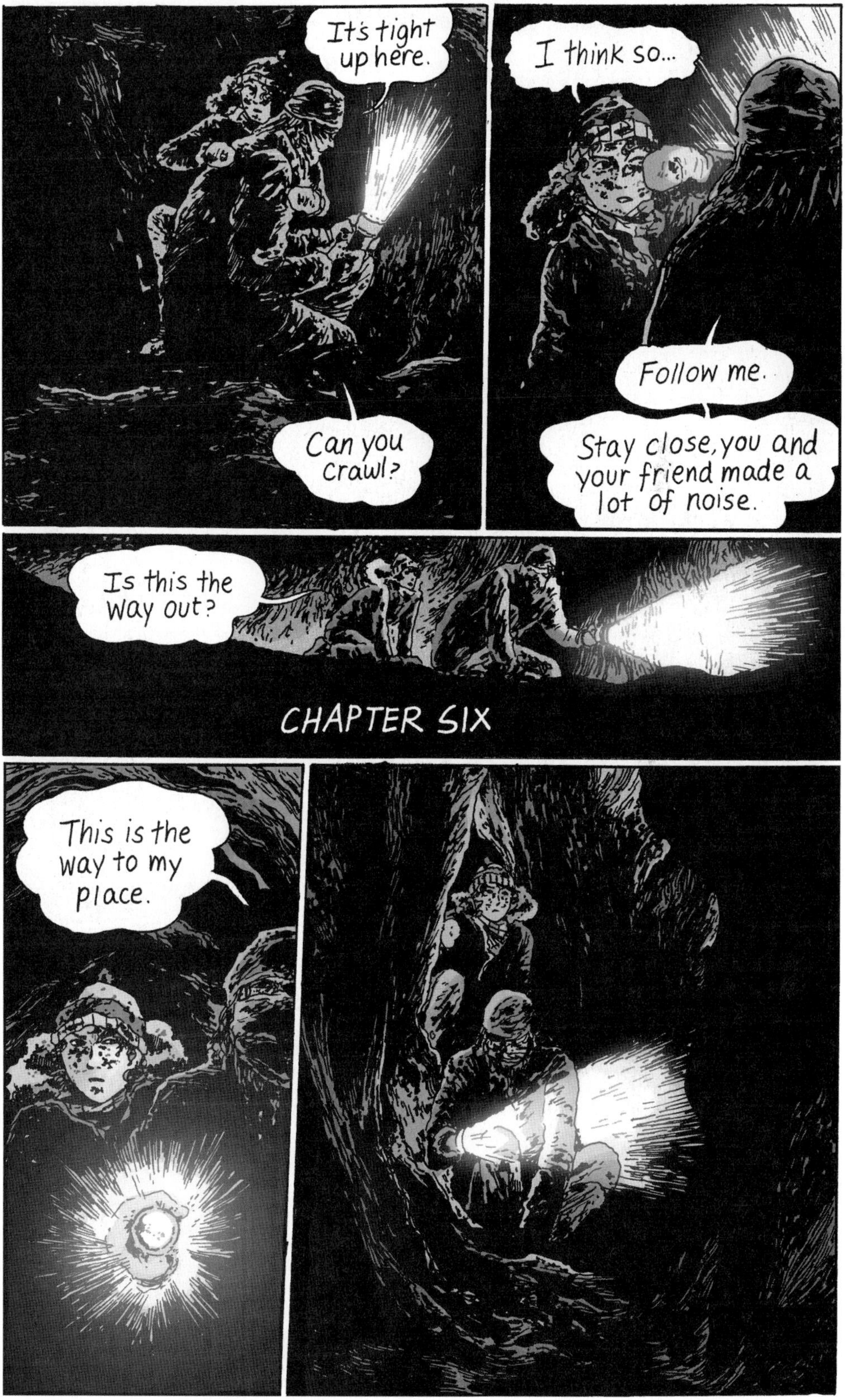
It's tight up here.
Can you crawl?
I think so...
Follow me.
Stay close, you and your friend made a lot of noise.
Is this the way out?
CHAPTER SIX
This is the way to my place.

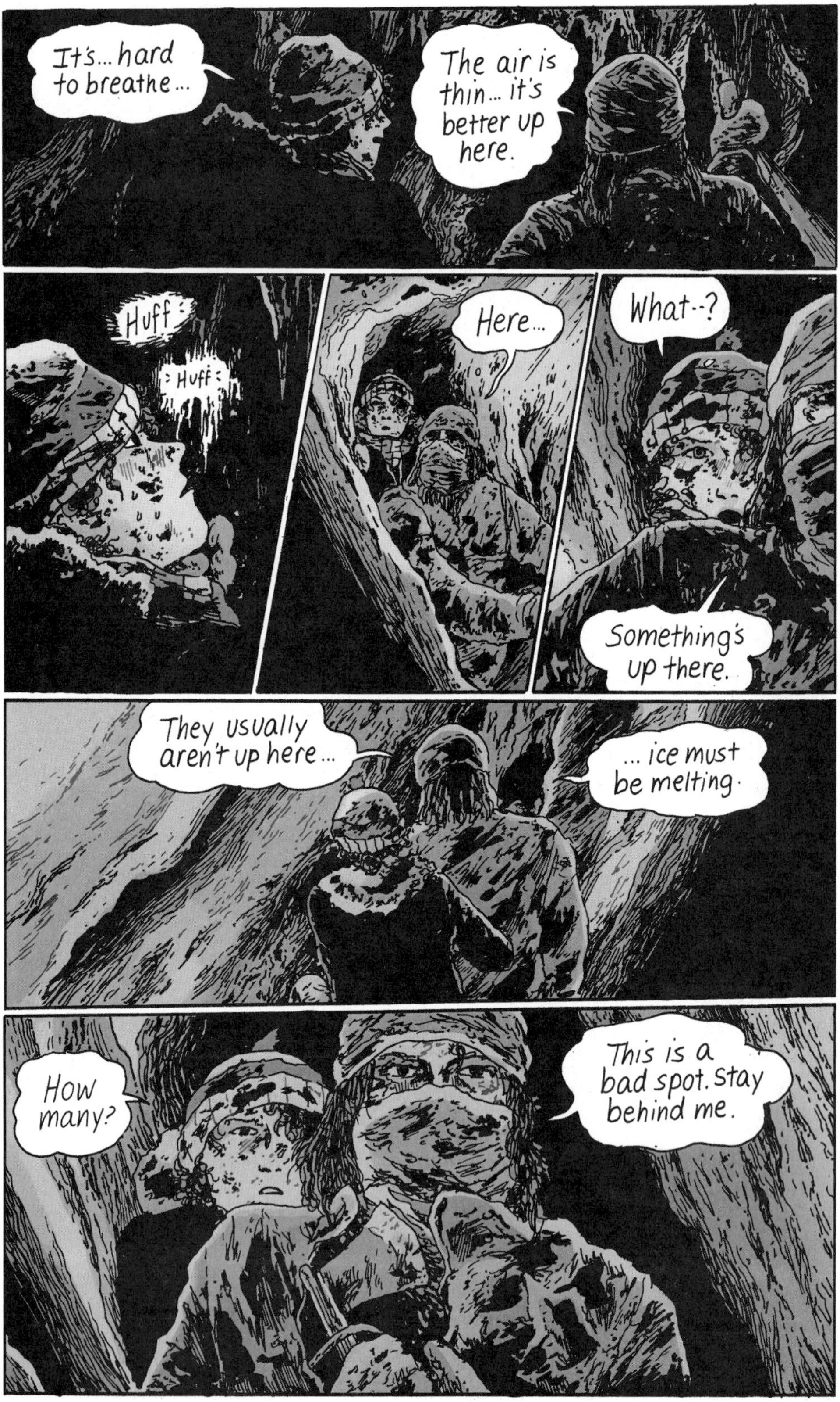
It's... hard to breathe...
The air is thin... it's better up here.
Huff
Huff
Here...
What--?
Something's up there.
They usually aren't up here...
... ice must be melting.
How many?
This is a bad spot. Stay behind me.

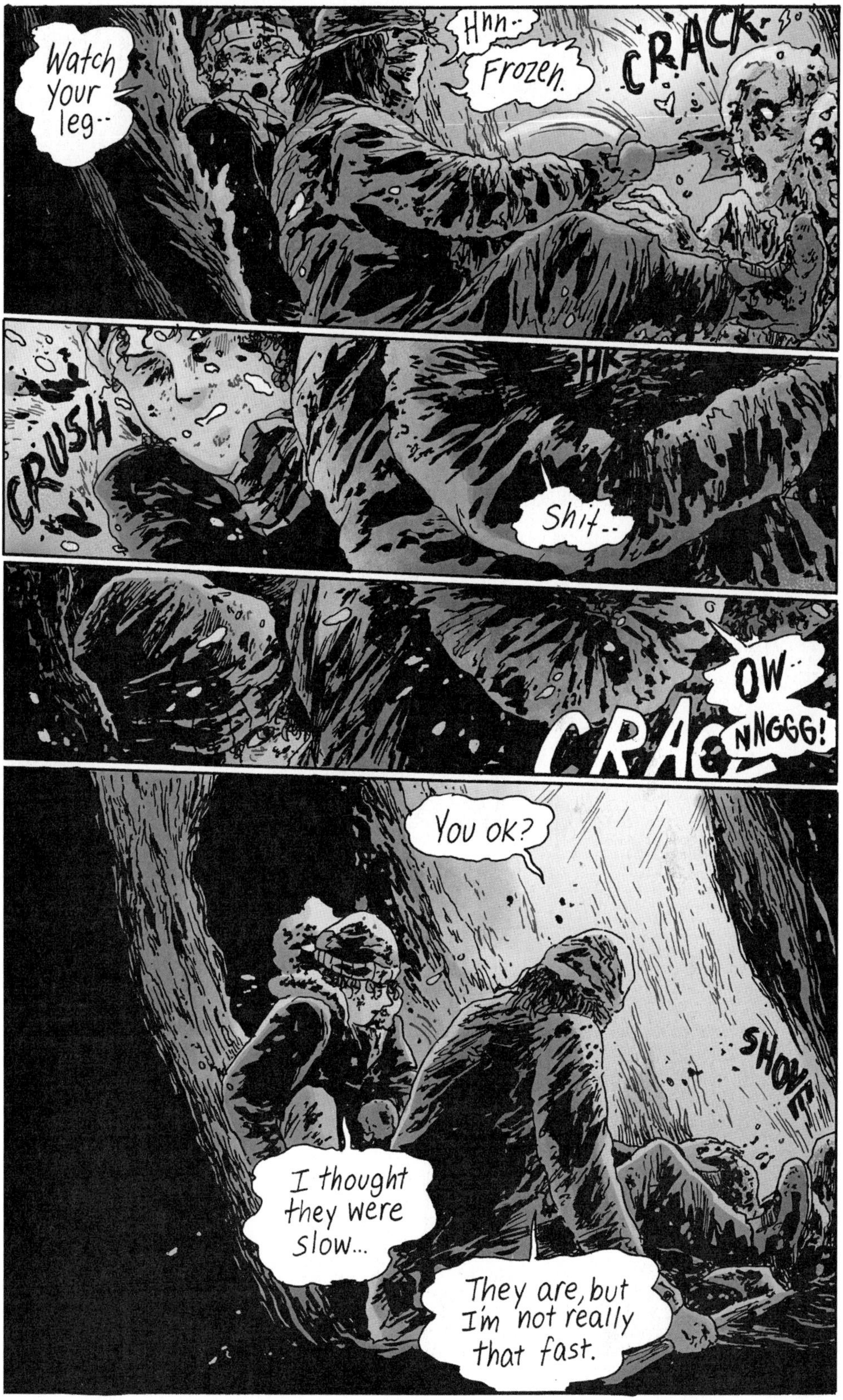
Watch your leg..
Hnn.. Frozen.
CRACK
CRUSH
Shit..
OW..
CRAC
NNGGG!
You ok?
SHOVE
I thought they were slow...
They are, but I'm not really that fast.

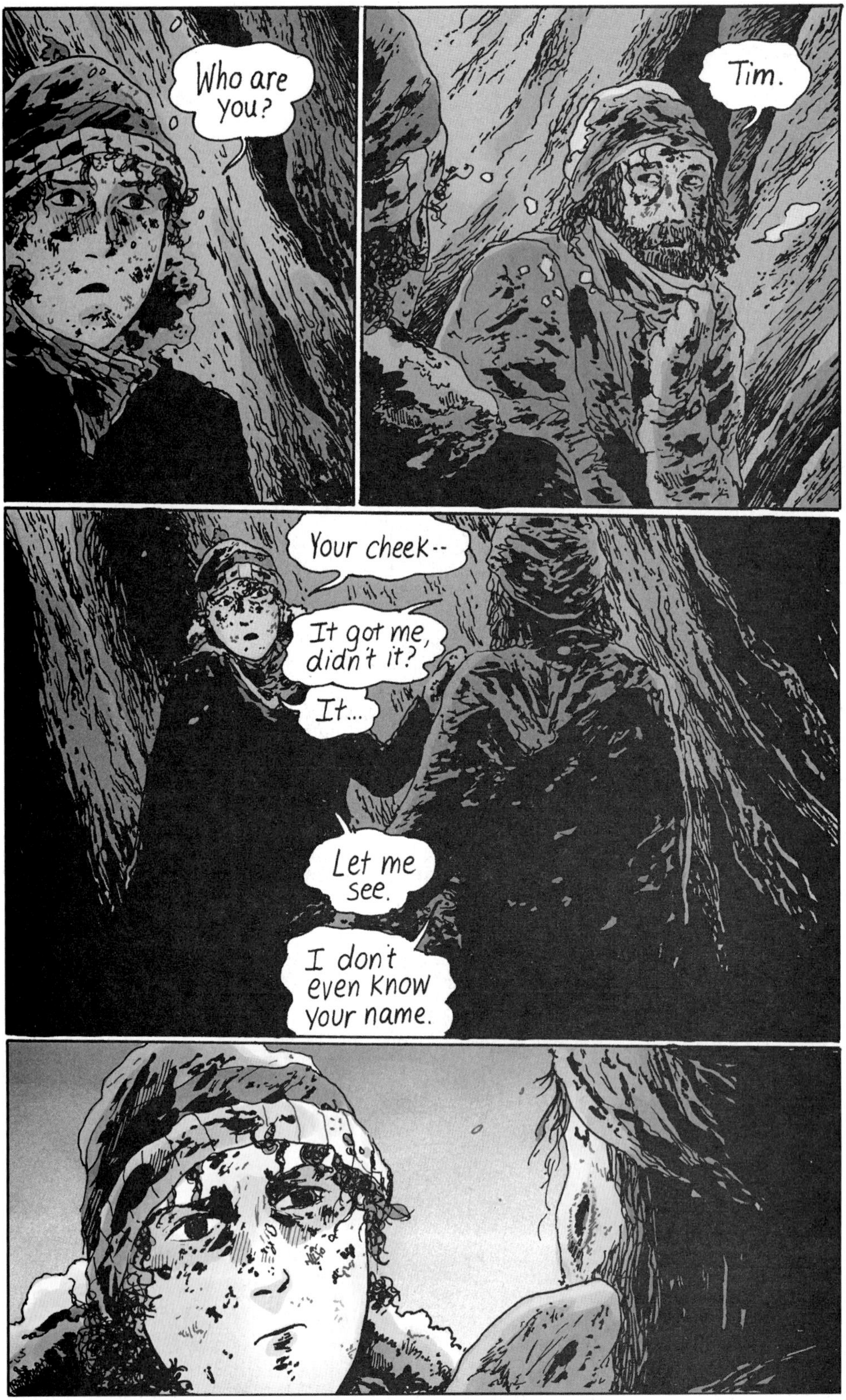
Who are you?
Tim.
Your cheek--
It got me, didn't it?
It...
Let me see.
I don't even know your name.

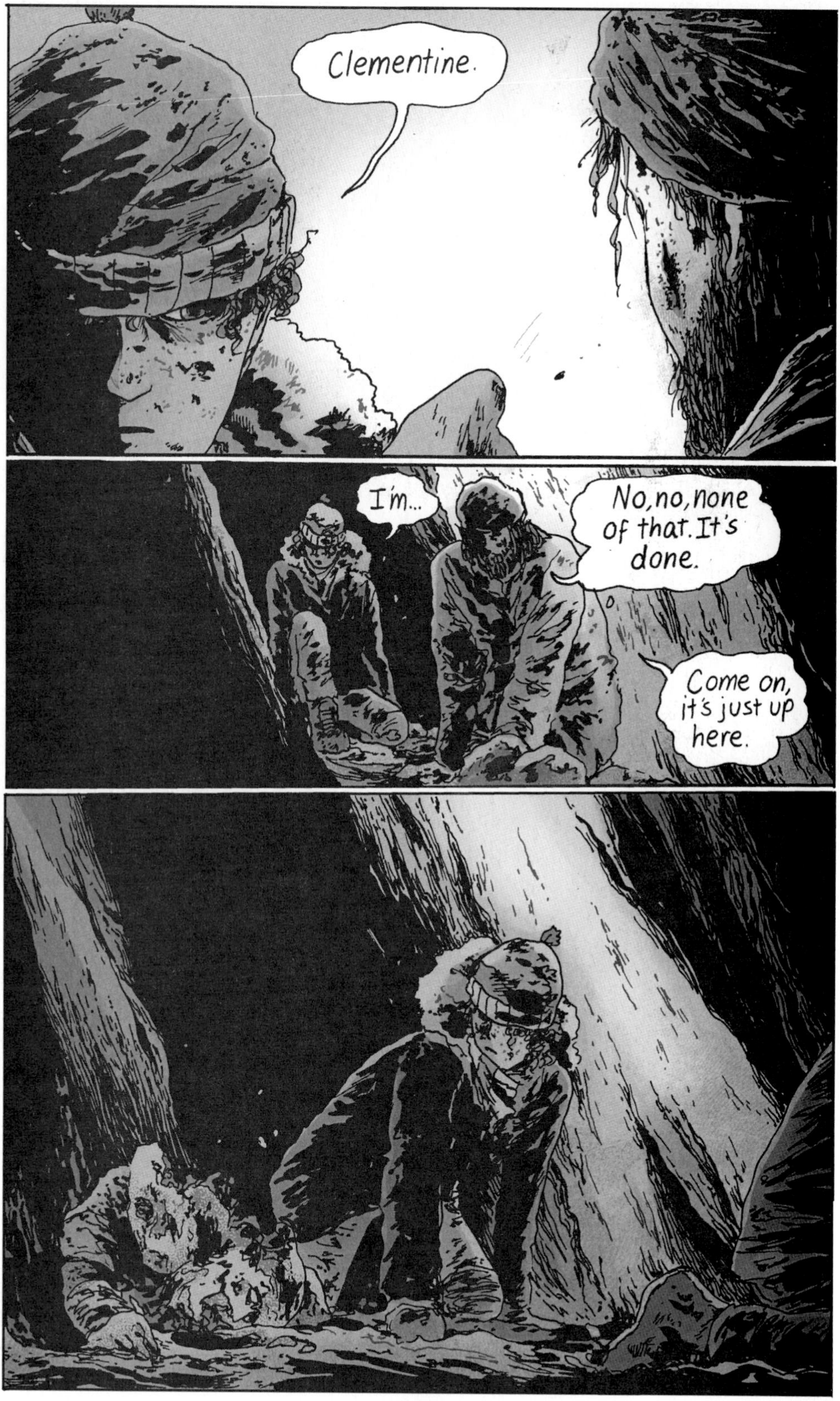
Clementine.
I'm...
No, no, none of that. It's done.
Come on, it's just up here.

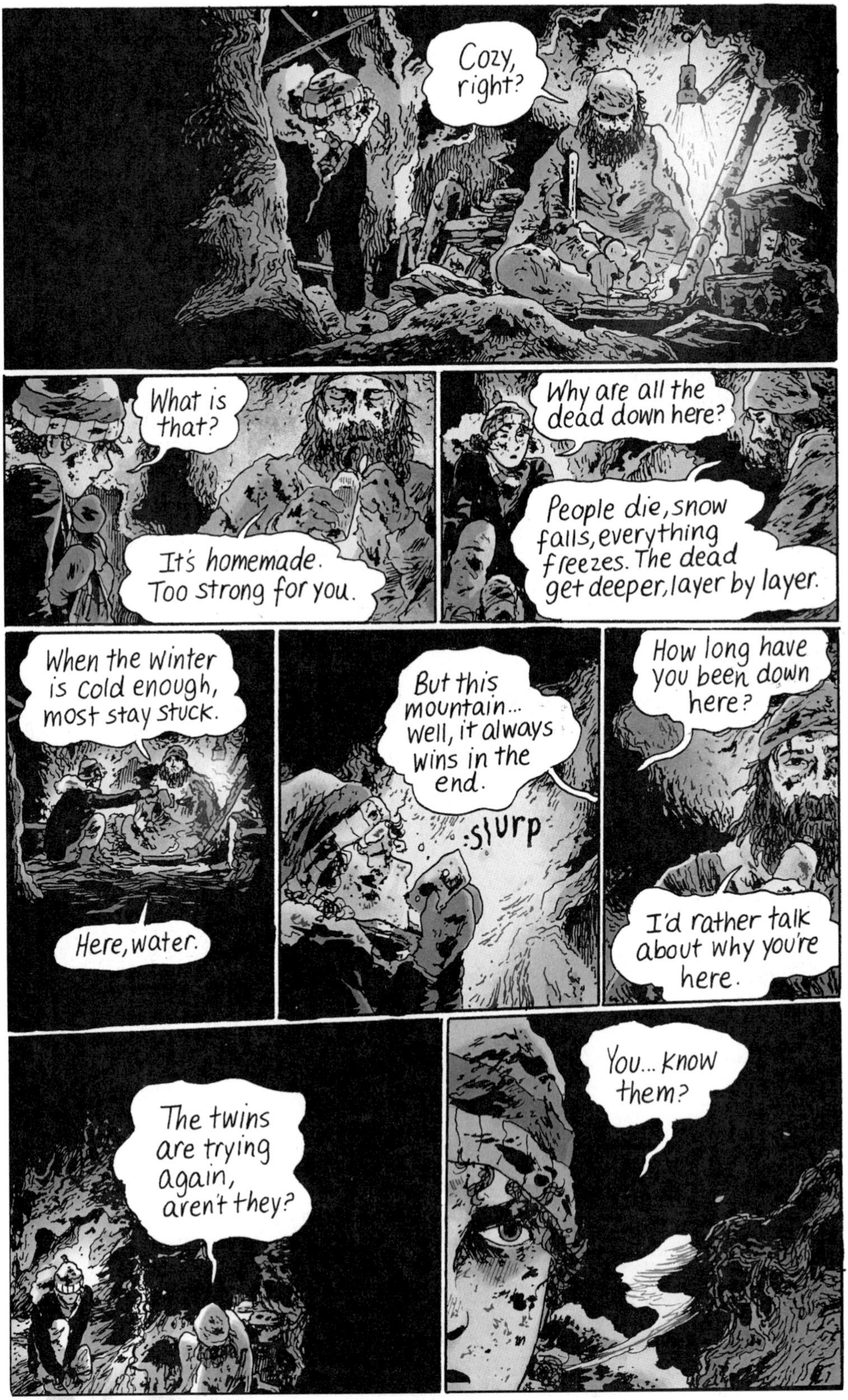
Cozy, right?
What is that?
It's homemade. Too strong for you.
Why are all the dead down here?
People die, snow falls, everything freezes. The dead get deeper, layer by layer.
When the winter is cold enough, most stay stuck.
Here, water.
But this mountain... well, it always wins in the end.
SLURP
How long have you been down here?
I'd rather talk about why you're here.
The twins are trying again, aren't they?
You... know them?

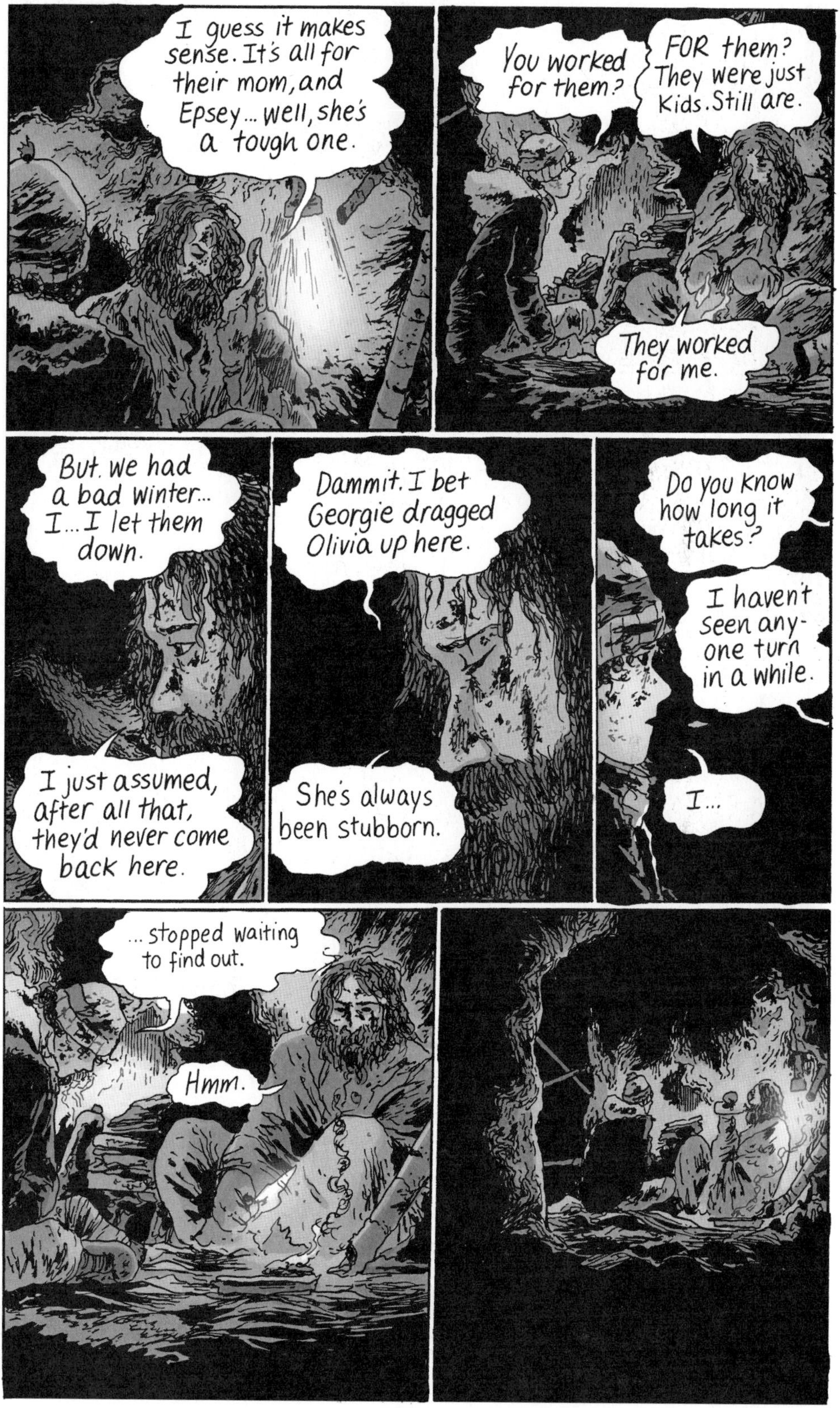
I guess it makes sense. It's all for their mom, and Epsey... well, she's a tough one.
You worked for them?
FOR them? They were just Kids. Still are.
They worked for me.
But. we had a bad winter... I... I let them down.
I just assumed, after all that, they'd never come back here.
Dammit. I bet Georgie dragged Olivia up here.
She's always been stubborn.
Do you know how long it takes?
I haven't seen any-one turn in a while.
I...
... stopped waiting to find out.
Hmm.

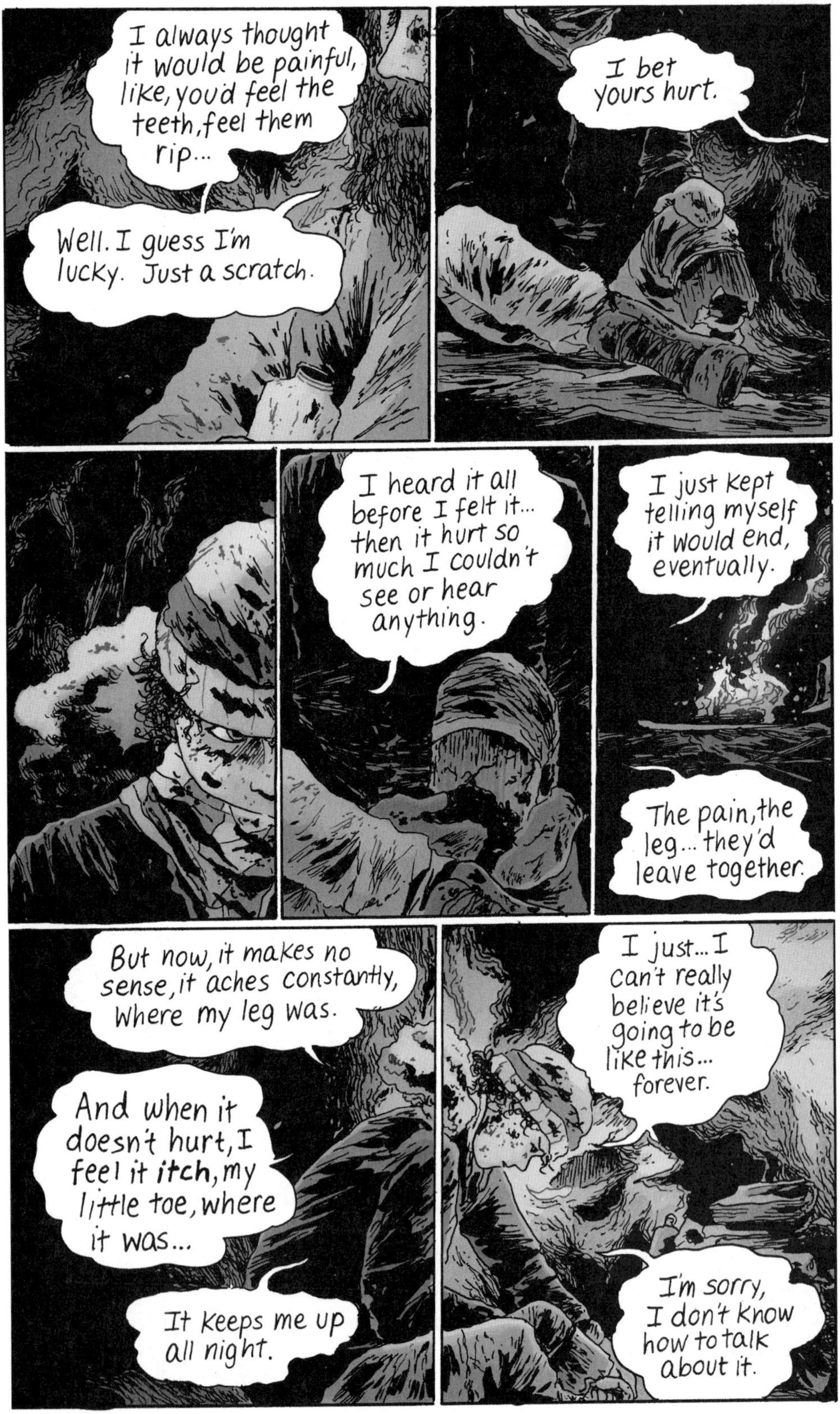
I always thought it would be painful, like, you'd feel the teeth, feel them rip...
Well. I guess I'm lucky. Just a scratch.
I bet yours hurt.
I heard it all before I felt it... then it hurt so much I couldn't see or hear anything.
I just kept telling myself it would end, eventually.
The pain, the leg... they'd leave together.
But now, it makes no sense, it aches constantly, where my leg was.
And when it doesn't hurt, I feel it **itch**, my little toe, where it was...
It keeps me up all night.
I just... I can't really believe it's going to be like this... forever.
I'm sorry, I don't know how to talk about it.

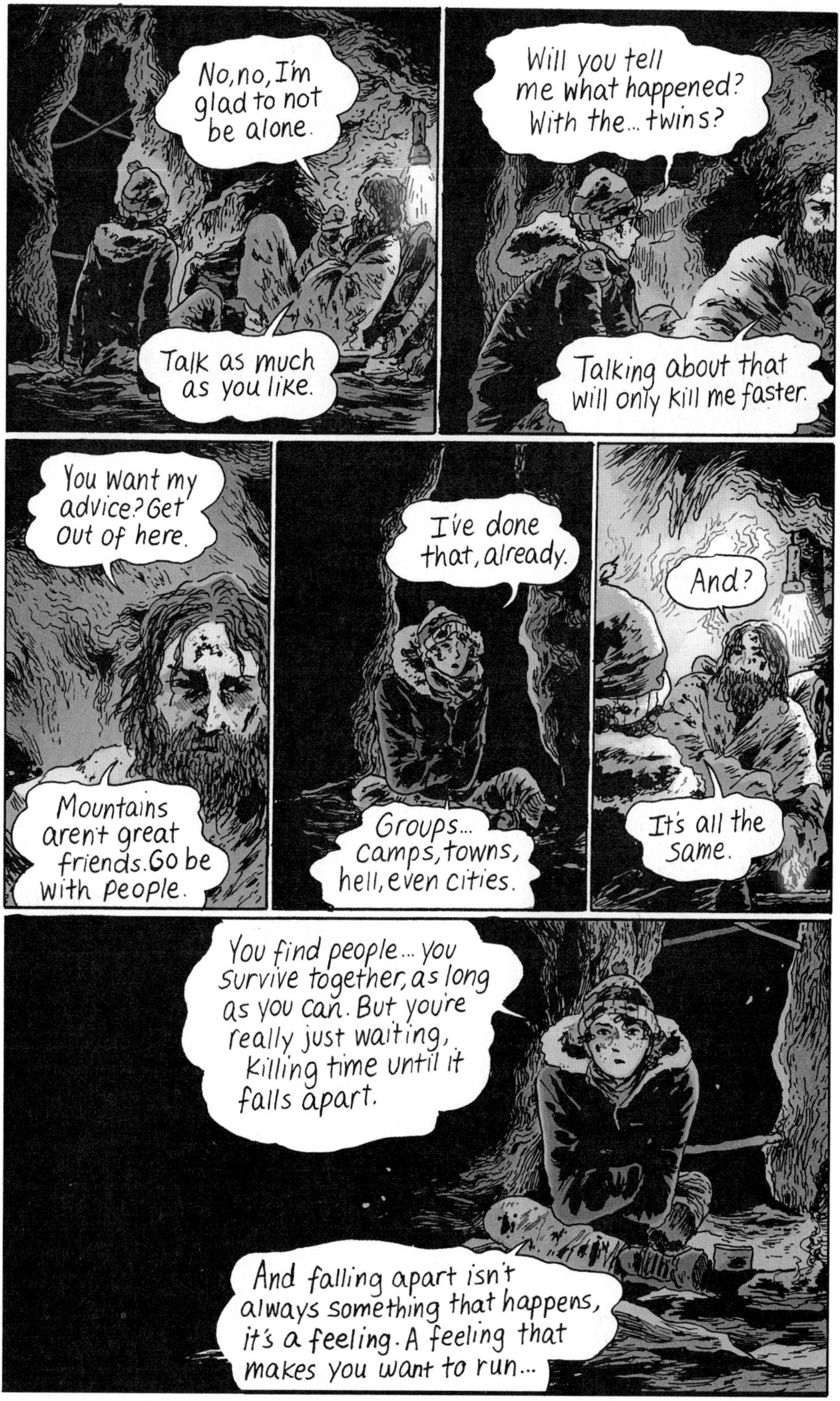
No, no, I'm glad to not be alone.
Talk as much as you like.
Will you tell me what happened? With the... twins?
Talking about that will only kill me faster.
You want my advice? Get out of here.
Mountains aren't great friends. Go be with people.
I've done that, already.
Groups... camps, towns, hell, even cities.
And?
It's all the same.
You find people... you survive together, as long as you can. But you're really just waiting, killing time until it falls apart.
And falling apart isn't always something that happens, it's a feeling. A feeling that makes you want to run...

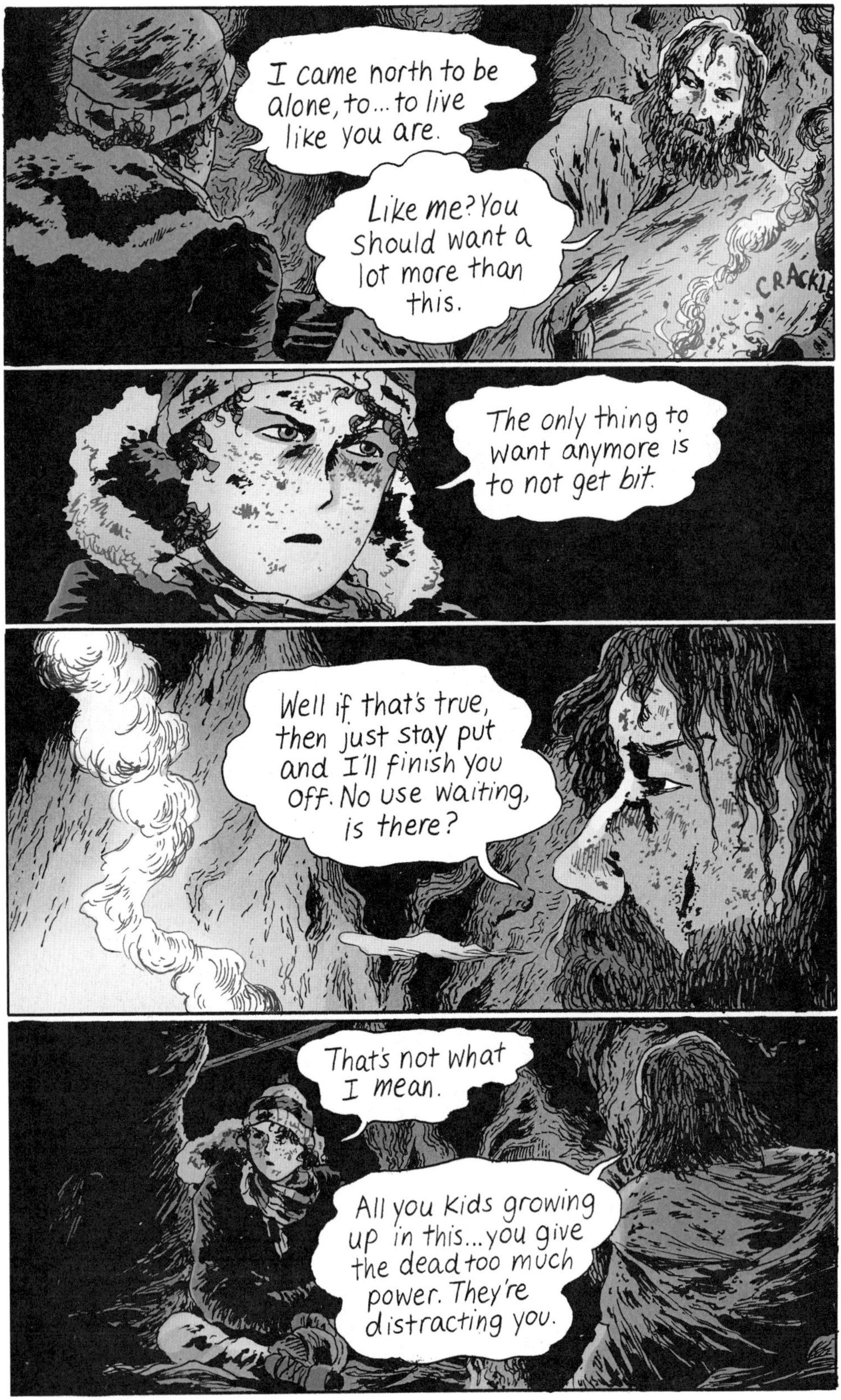
I came north to be alone, to... to live like you are.
Like me? You should want a lot more than this.
CRACKLE
The only thing to want anymore is to not get bit.
Well if that's true, then just stay put and I'll finish you off. No use waiting, is there?
That's not what I mean.
All you kids growing up in this... you give the dead too much power. They're distracting you.

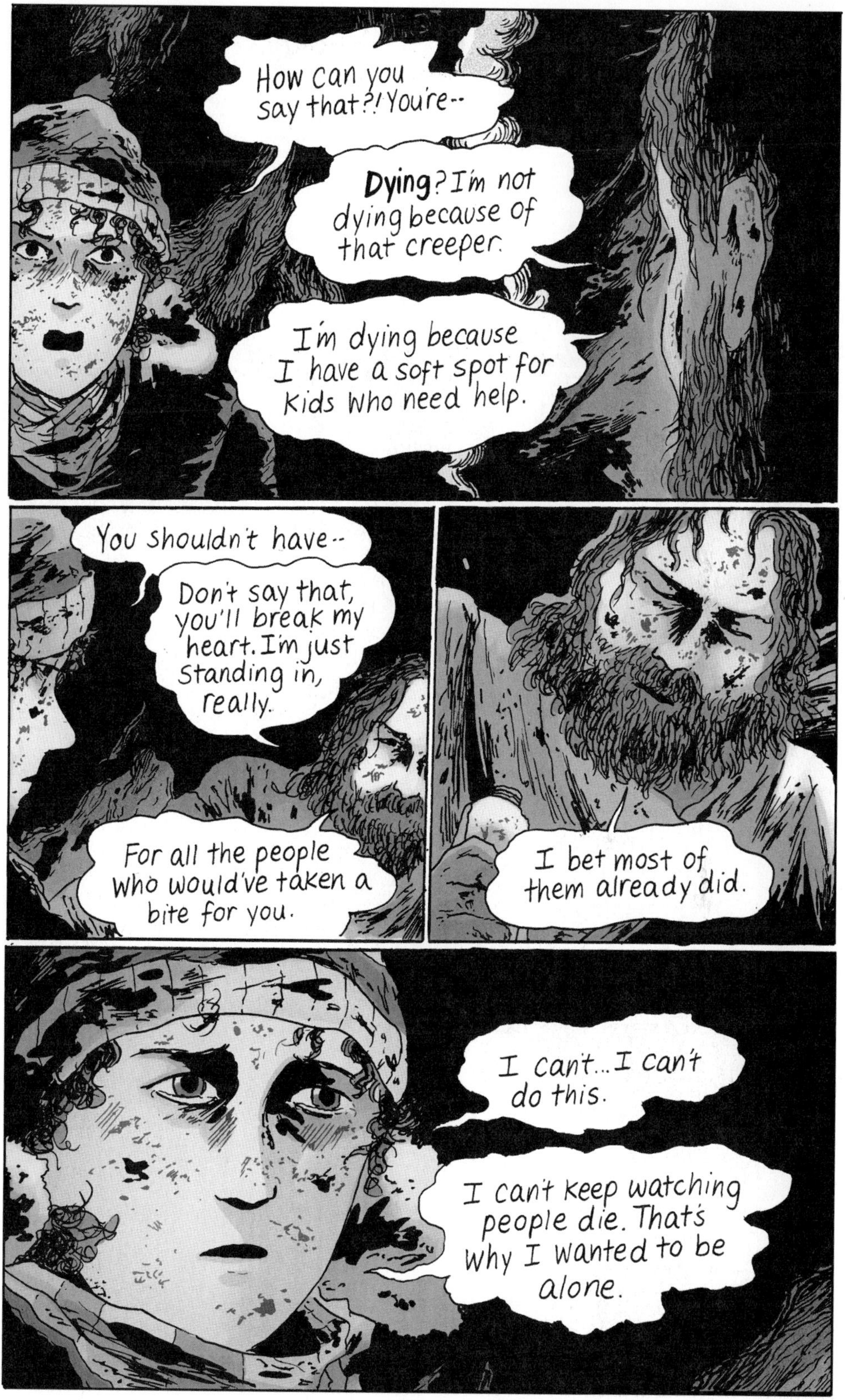
How can you say that?! You're--
Dying? I'm not dying because of that creeper.
I'm dying because I have a soft spot for kids who need help.
You shouldn't have--
Don't say that, you'll break my heart. I'm just standing in, really.
For all the people who would've taken a bite for you.
I bet most of them already did.
I can't... I can't do this.
I can't keep watching people die. That's why I wanted to be alone.

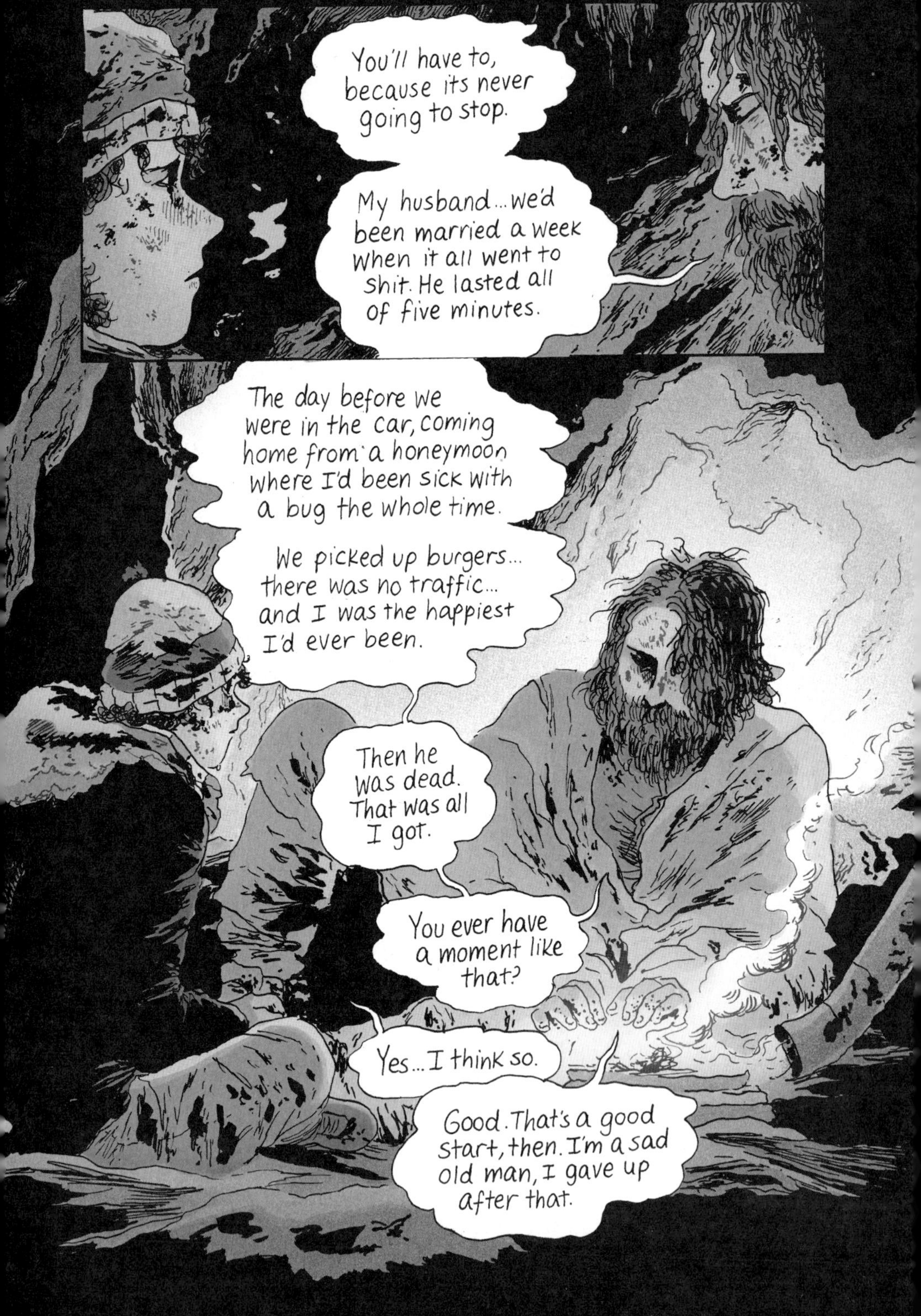
You'll have to, because its never going to stop.
My husband... we'd been married a week when it all went to shit. He lasted all of five minutes.
The day before we were in the car, coming home from a honeymoon where I'd been sick with a bug the whole time.
We picked up burgers... there was no traffic... and I was the happiest I'd ever been.
Then he was dead. That was all I got.
You ever have a moment like that?
Yes... I think so.
Good. That's a good start, then. I'm a sad old man, I gave up after that.

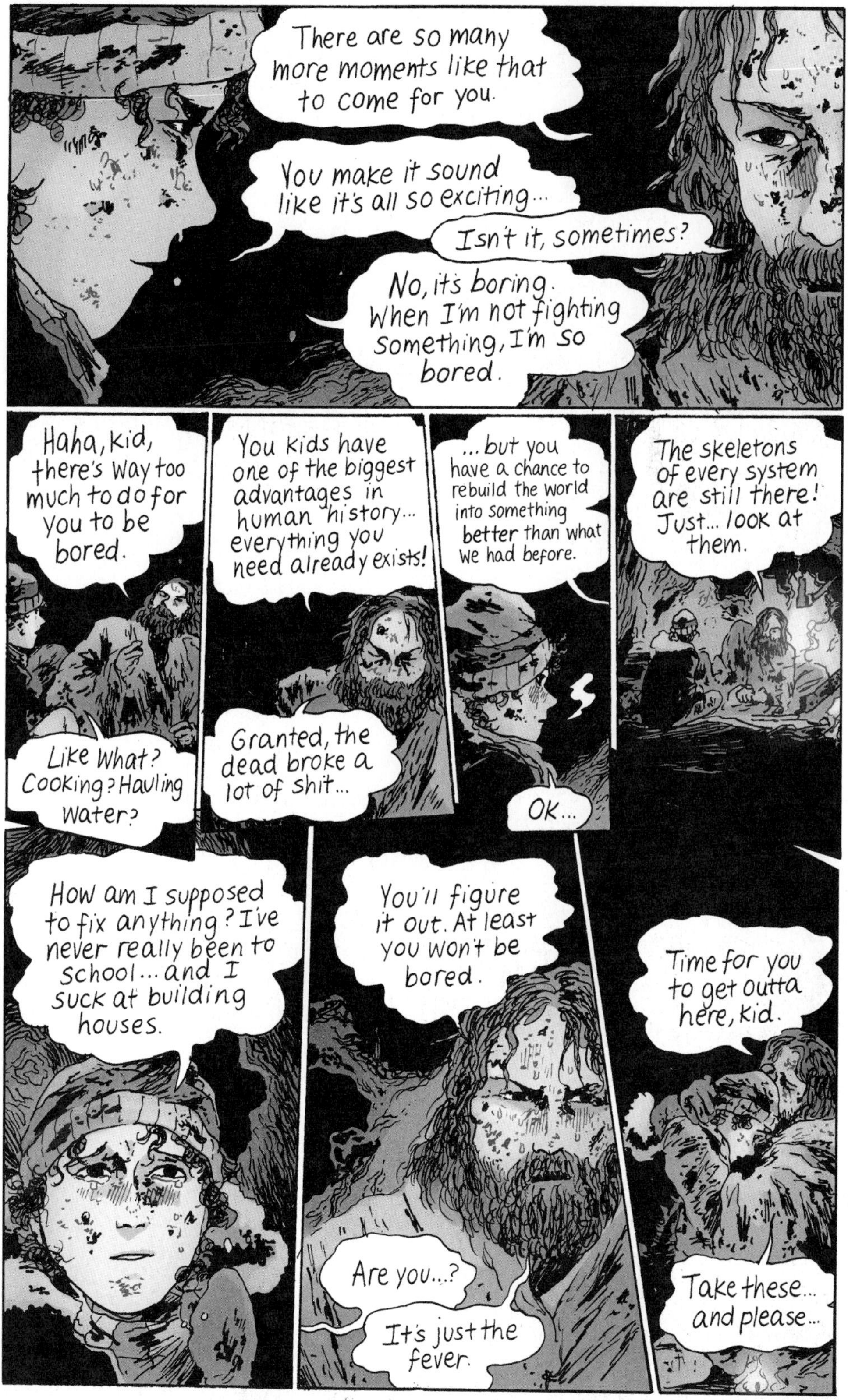
There are so many more moments like that to come for you.
You make it sound like it's all so exciting...
Isn't it, sometimes?
No, it's boring. When I'm not fighting something, I'm so bored.
Haha, kid, there's way too much to do for you to be bored.
Like what? Cooking? Hauling water?
You kids have one of the biggest advantages in human history... everything you need already exists!
Granted, the dead broke a lot of shit...
...but you have a chance to rebuild the world into something better than what we had before.
OK...
The skeletons of every system are still there! Just... look at them.
How am I supposed to fix anything? I've never really been to school... and I suck at building houses.
You'll figure it out. At least you won't be bored.
Are you...?
It's just the fever.
Time for you to get outta here, kid.
Take these... and please...

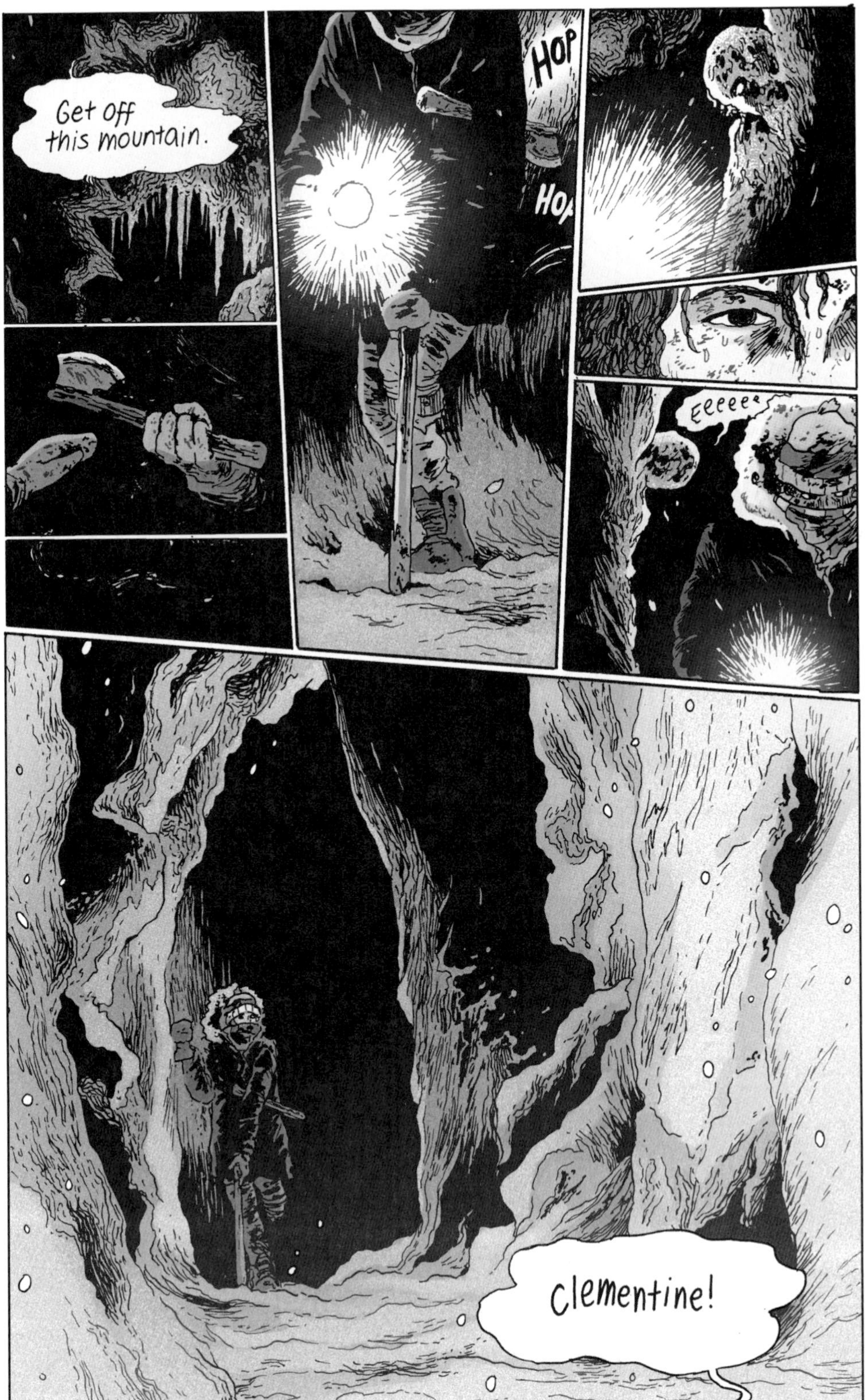
Get off
this mountain.
HOP
HOP
Eeeee
Clementine!

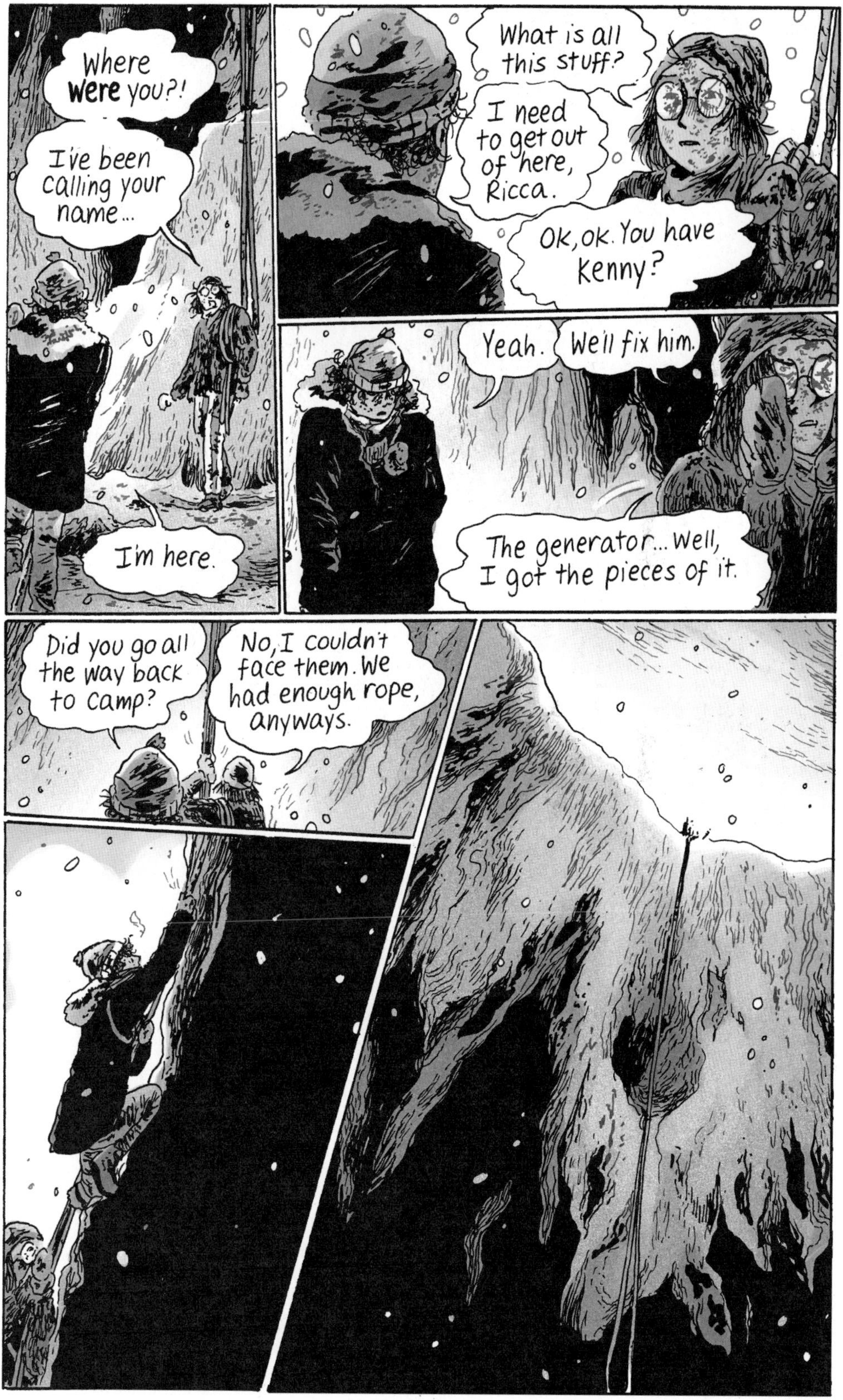
Where were you?!
I've been calling your name...
I'm here.
What is all this stuff?
I need to get out of here, Ricca.
Ok, ok. You have Kenny?
Yeah.
We'll fix him.
The generator... Well, I got the pieces of it.
Did you go all the way back to camp?
No, I couldn't face them. We had enough rope, anyways.

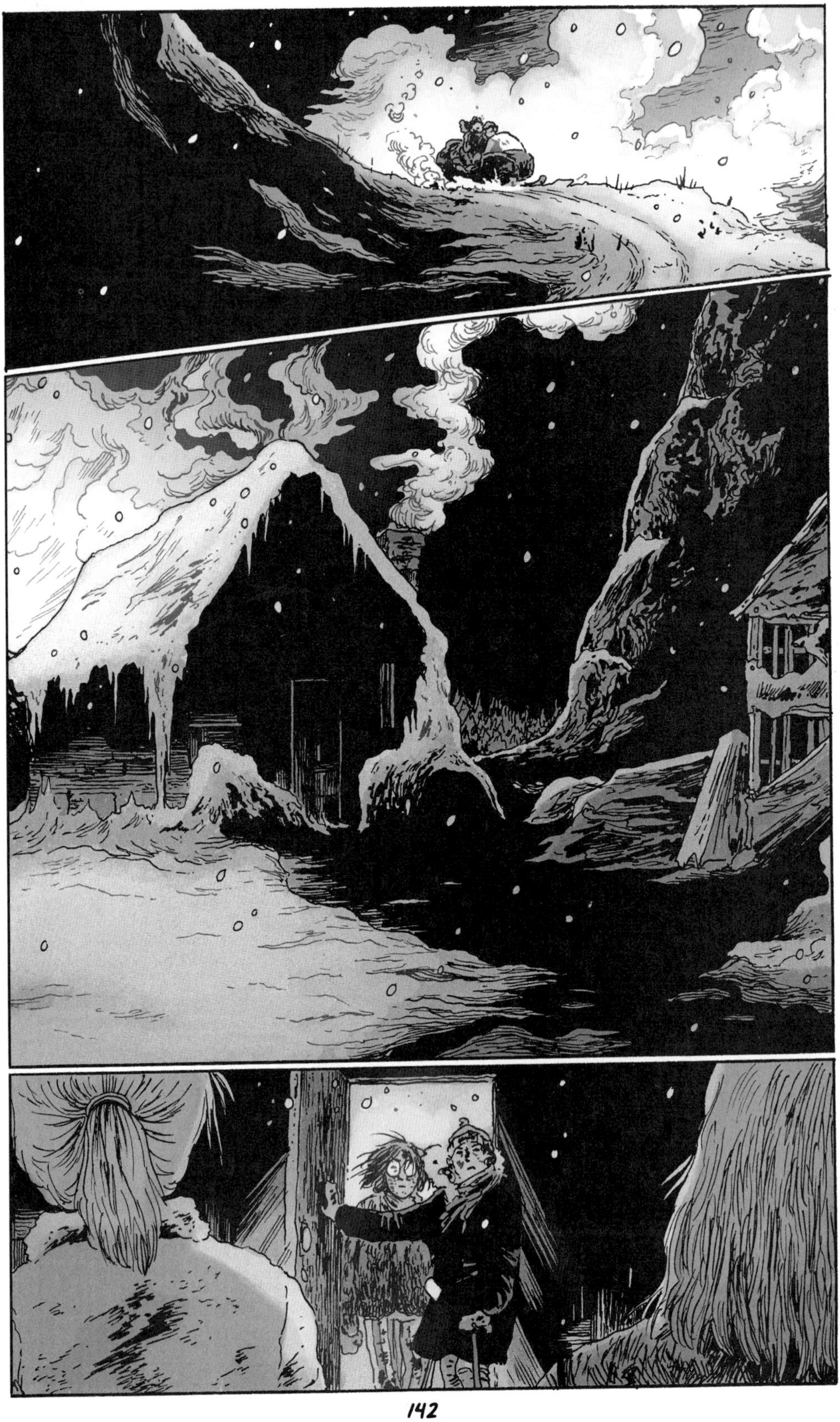

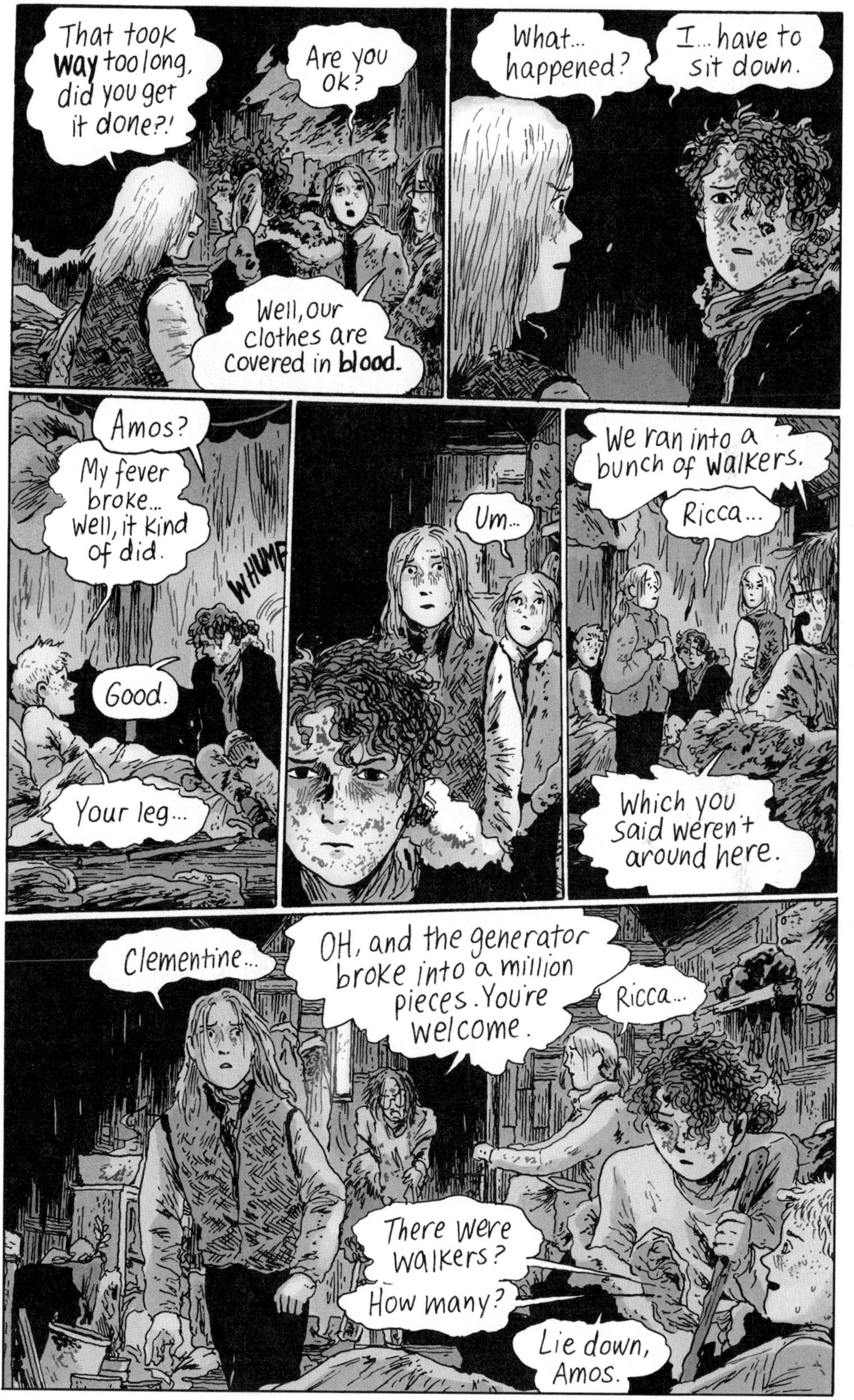
That took **way** too long, did you get it done?!
Are you ok?
Well, our clothes are covered in **blood**.
What... happened?
I... have to sit down.
Amos?
My fever broke... Well, it kind of did.
WHUMP
Good.
Your leg...
Um...
We ran into a bunch of walkers.
Ricca...
Which you said weren't around here.
Clementine...
OH, and the generator broke into a million pieces. You're welcome.
Ricca...
There were walkers?
How many?
Lie down, Amos.

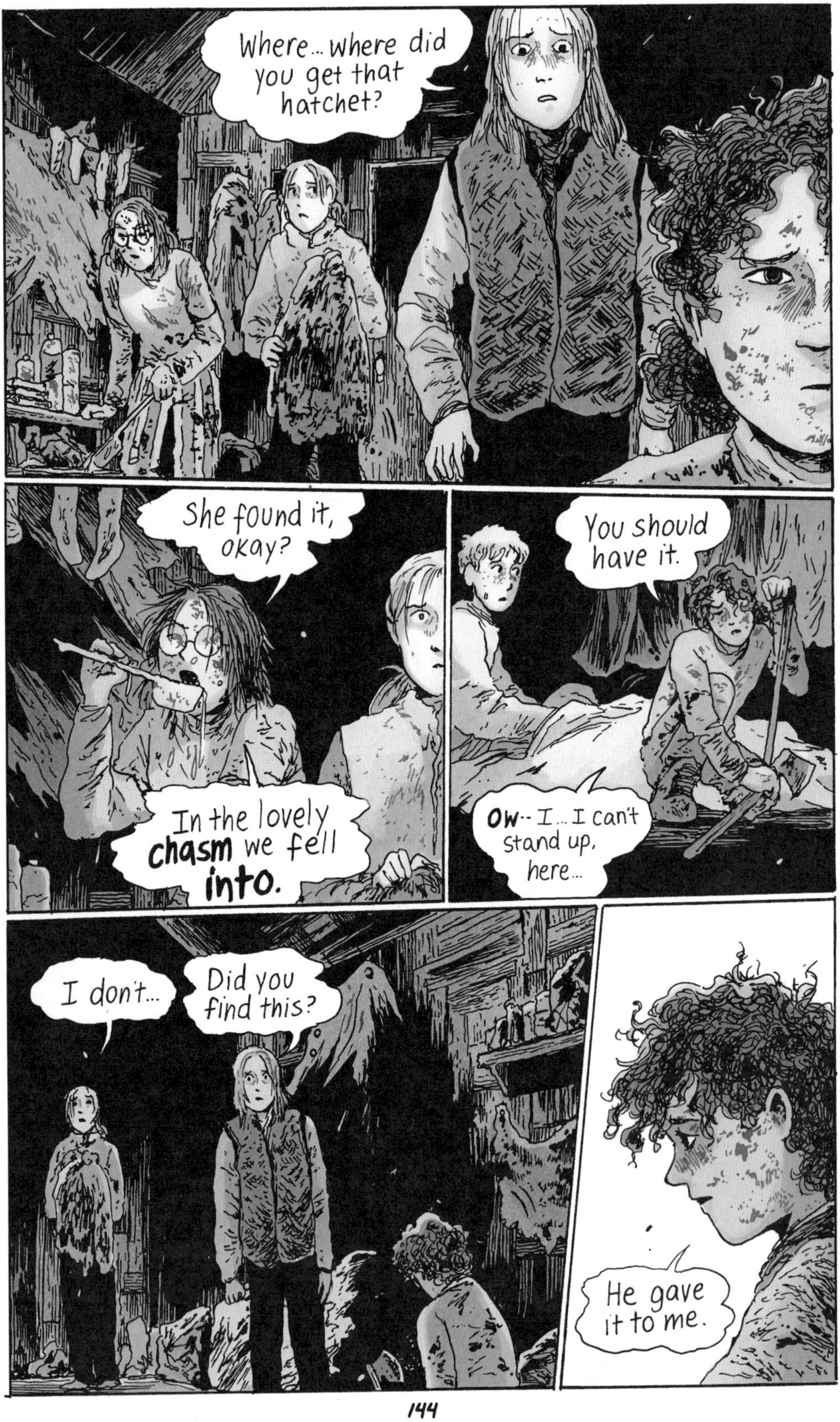
Where... where did you get that hatchet?
She found it, okay?
In the lovely chasm we fell into.
You should have it.
Ow-- I... I can't stand up, here...
I don't...
Did you find this?
He gave it to me.

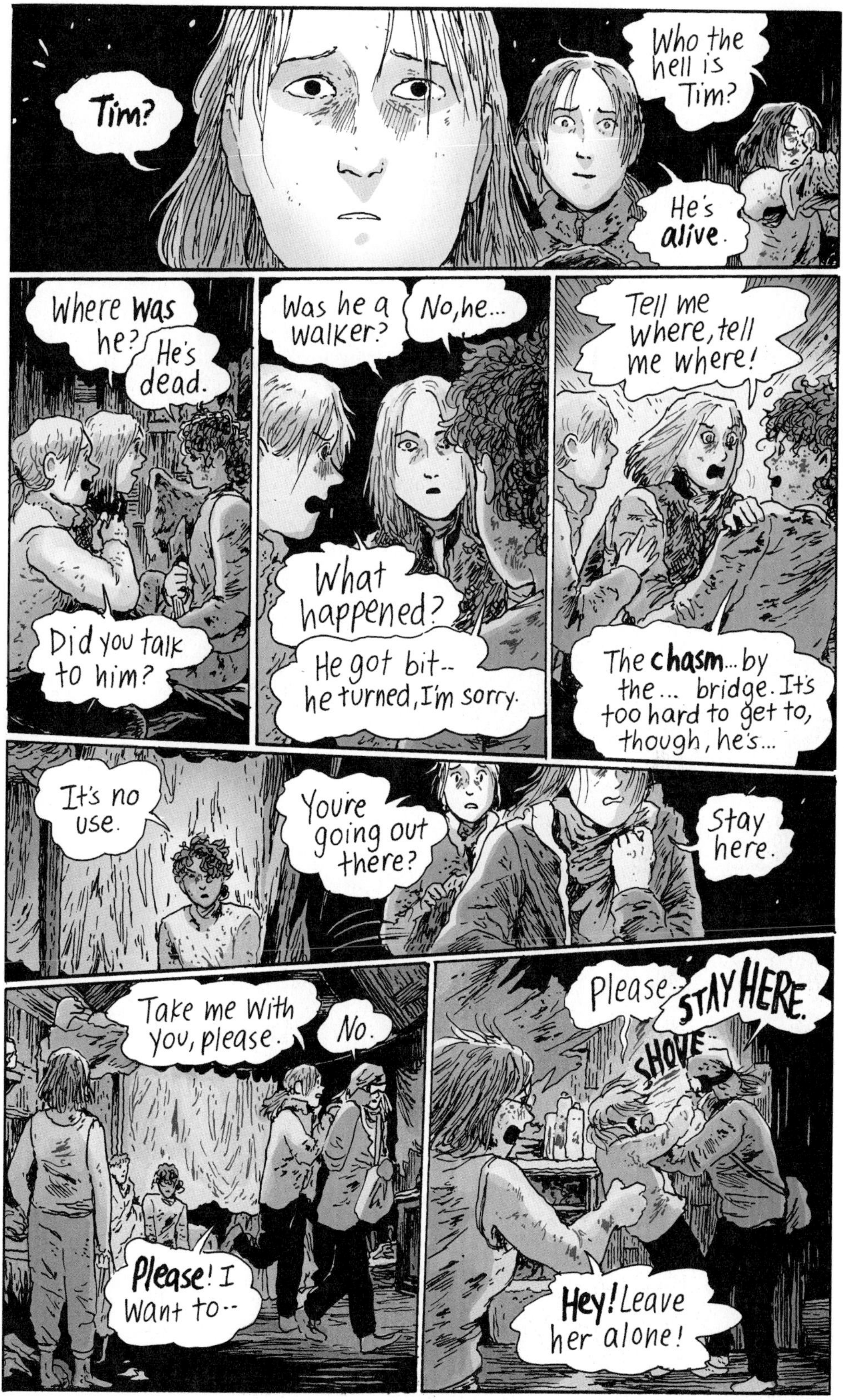
Tim?
Who the hell is Tim?
He's alive.
Where was he?
He's dead.
Did you talk to him?
Was he a walker?
No, he...
What happened?
He got bit-- he turned, I'm sorry.
Tell me where, tell me where!
The chasm... by the... bridge. It's too hard to get to, though, he's...
It's no use.
You're going out there?
Stay here.
Take me with you, please.
No.
Please! I want to--
Please...
STAY HERE.
SHOVE
Hey! Leave her alone!

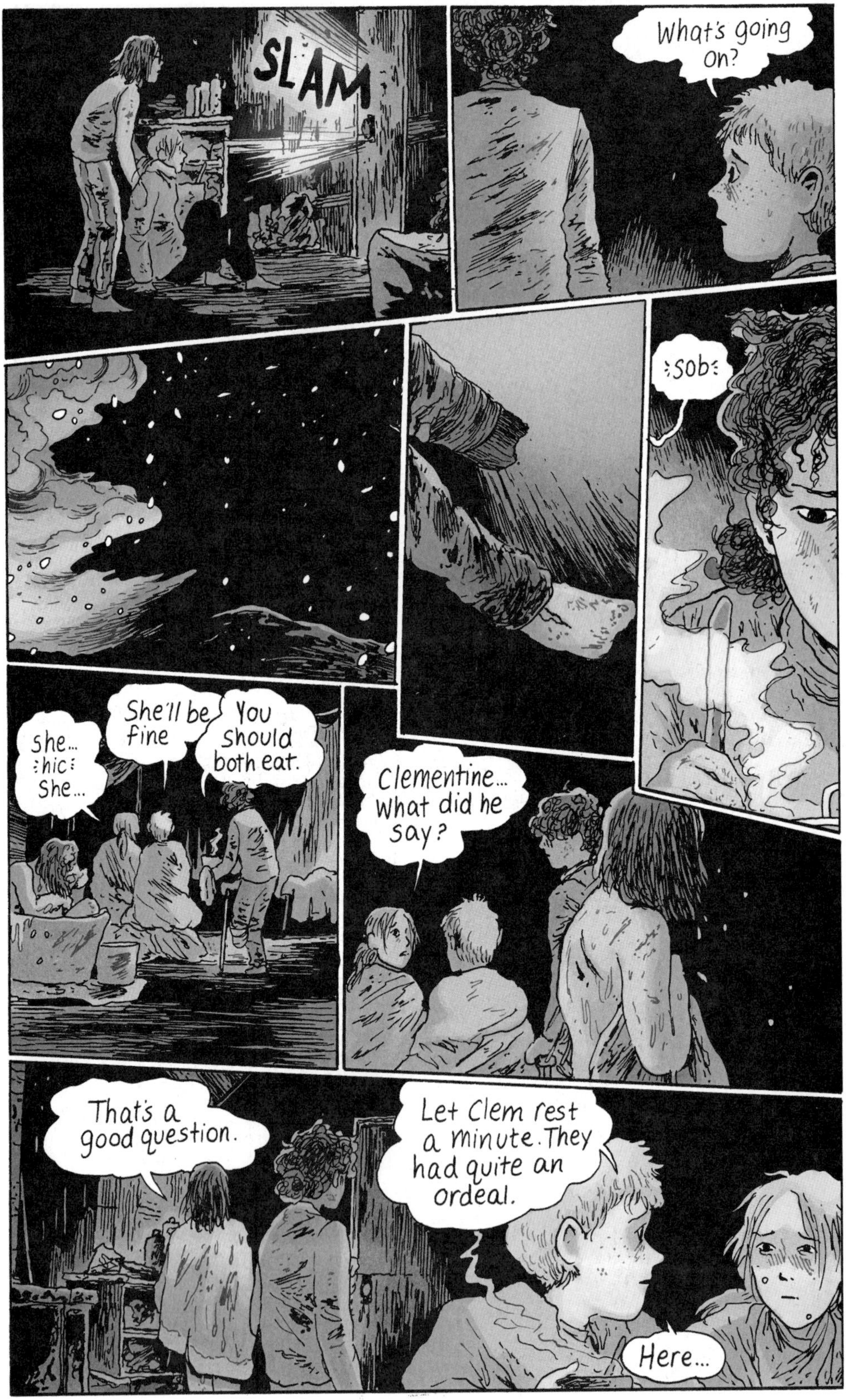
SLAM
What's going on?
:sob:
She... :hic: She...
She'll be fine
You should both eat.
Clementine... What did he say?
That's a good question.
Let Clem rest a minute. They had quite an ordeal.
Here...

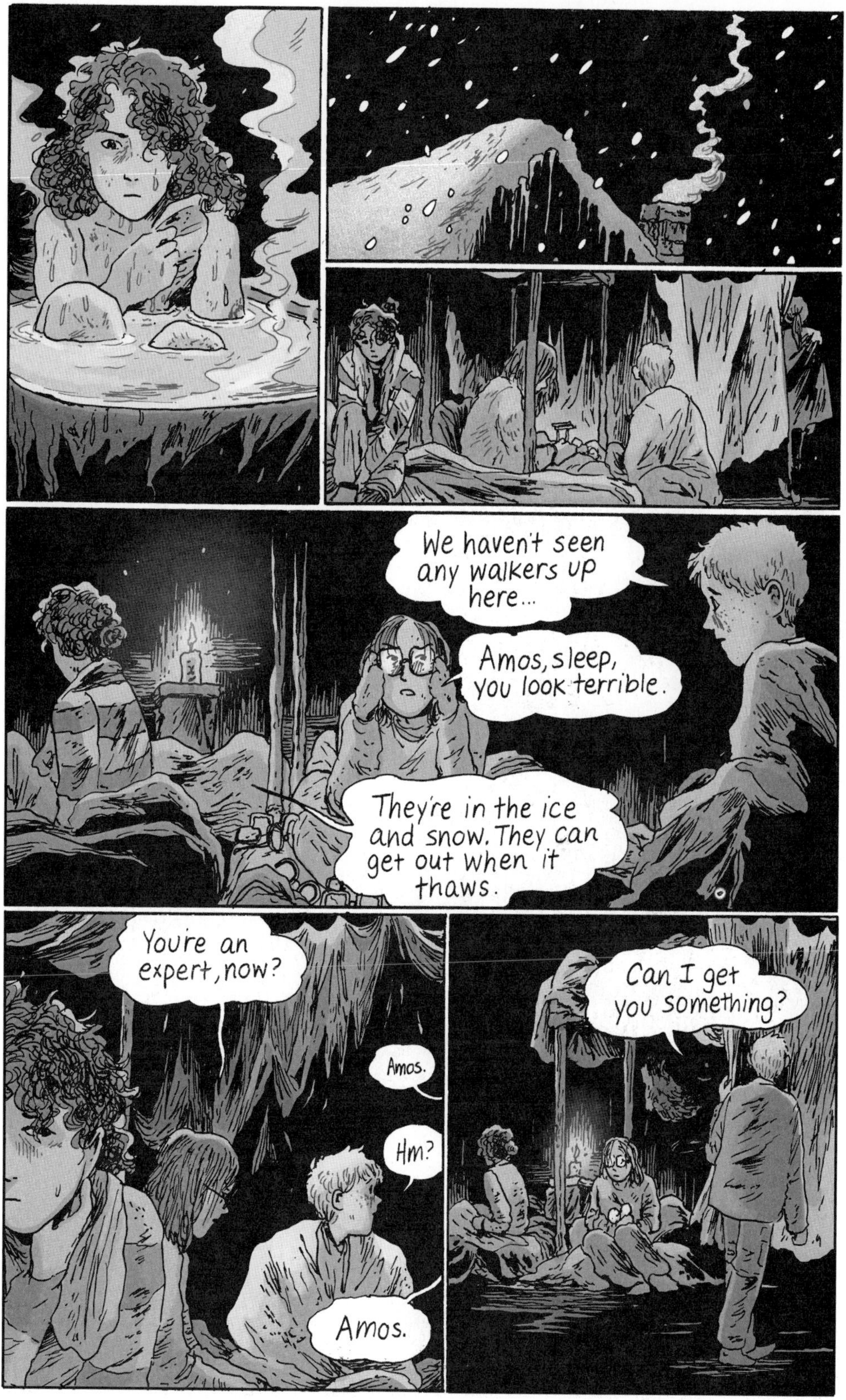

We haven't seen any walkers up here...
Amos, sleep, you look terrible.
They're in the ice and snow. They can get out when it thaws.
You're an expert, now?
Amos.
Hm?
Amos.
Can I get you something?

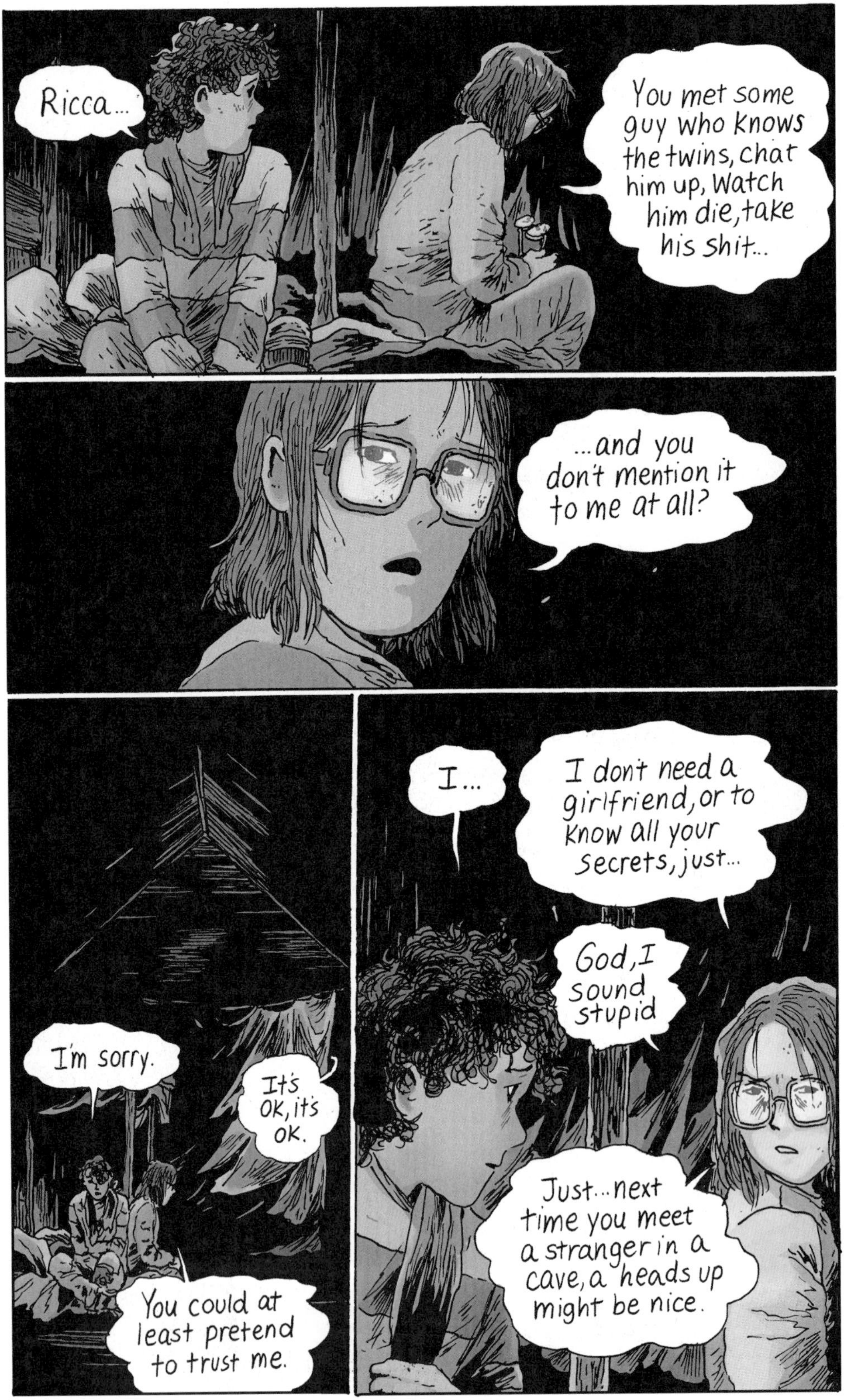
Ricca...
You met some guy who knows the twins, chat him up, watch him die, take his shit...
...and you don't mention it to me at all?
I'm sorry.
It's OK, it's OK.
You could at least pretend to trust me.
I...
I don't need a girlfriend, or to know all your secrets, just...
God, I sound stupid
Just... next time you meet a stranger in a cave, a heads up might be nice.

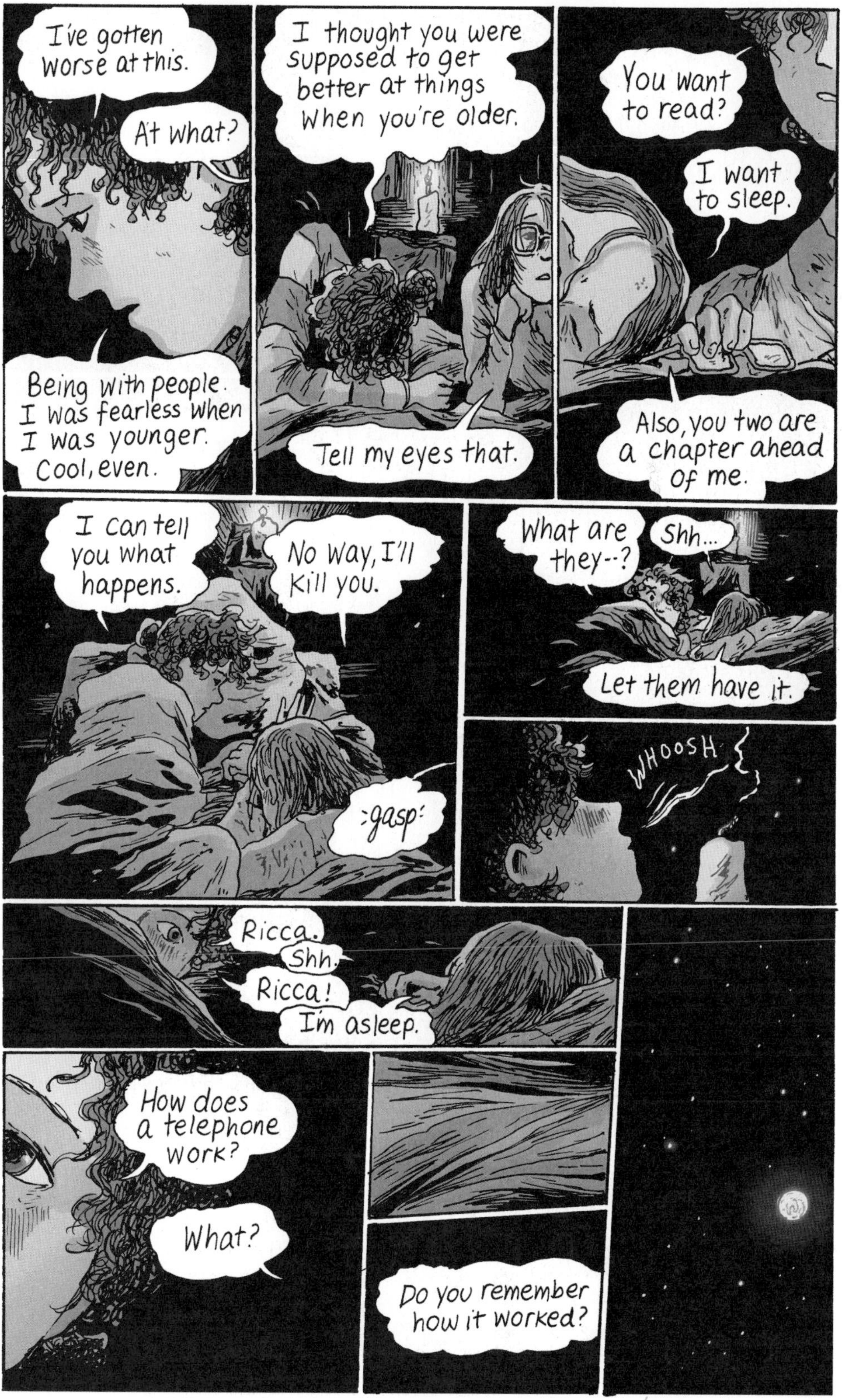
I've gotten worse at this.
At what?
Being with people. I was fearless when I was younger. Cool, even.
I thought you were supposed to get better at things when you're older.
Tell my eyes that.
You want to read?
I want to sleep.
Also, you two are a chapter ahead of me.
I can tell you what happens.
No way, I'll kill you.
gasp
What are they--?
Shh...
Let them have it.
WHOOSH
Ricca.
Shh.
Ricca!
I'm asleep.
How does a telephone work?
What?
Do you remember how it worked?

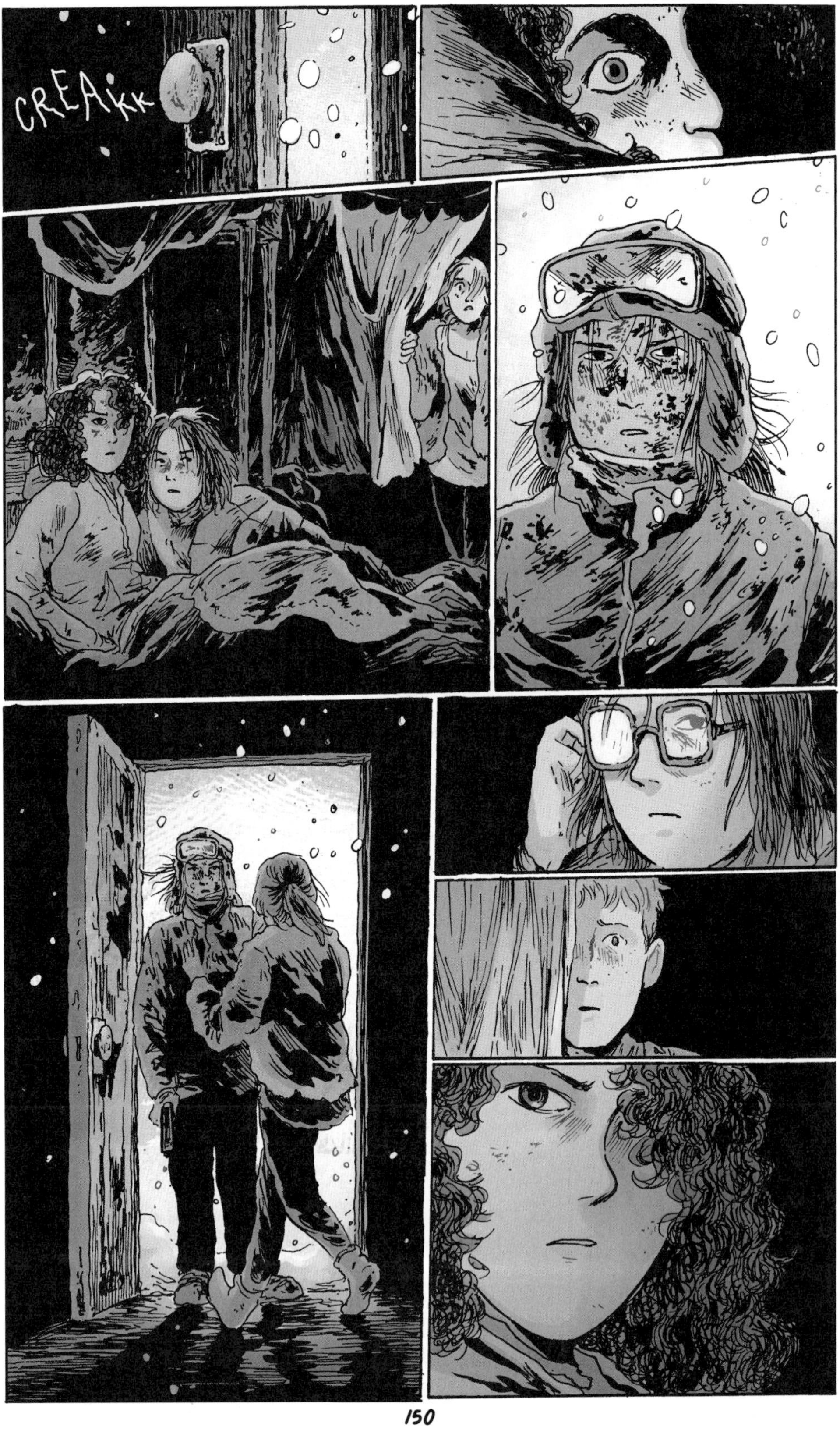
CREAKK

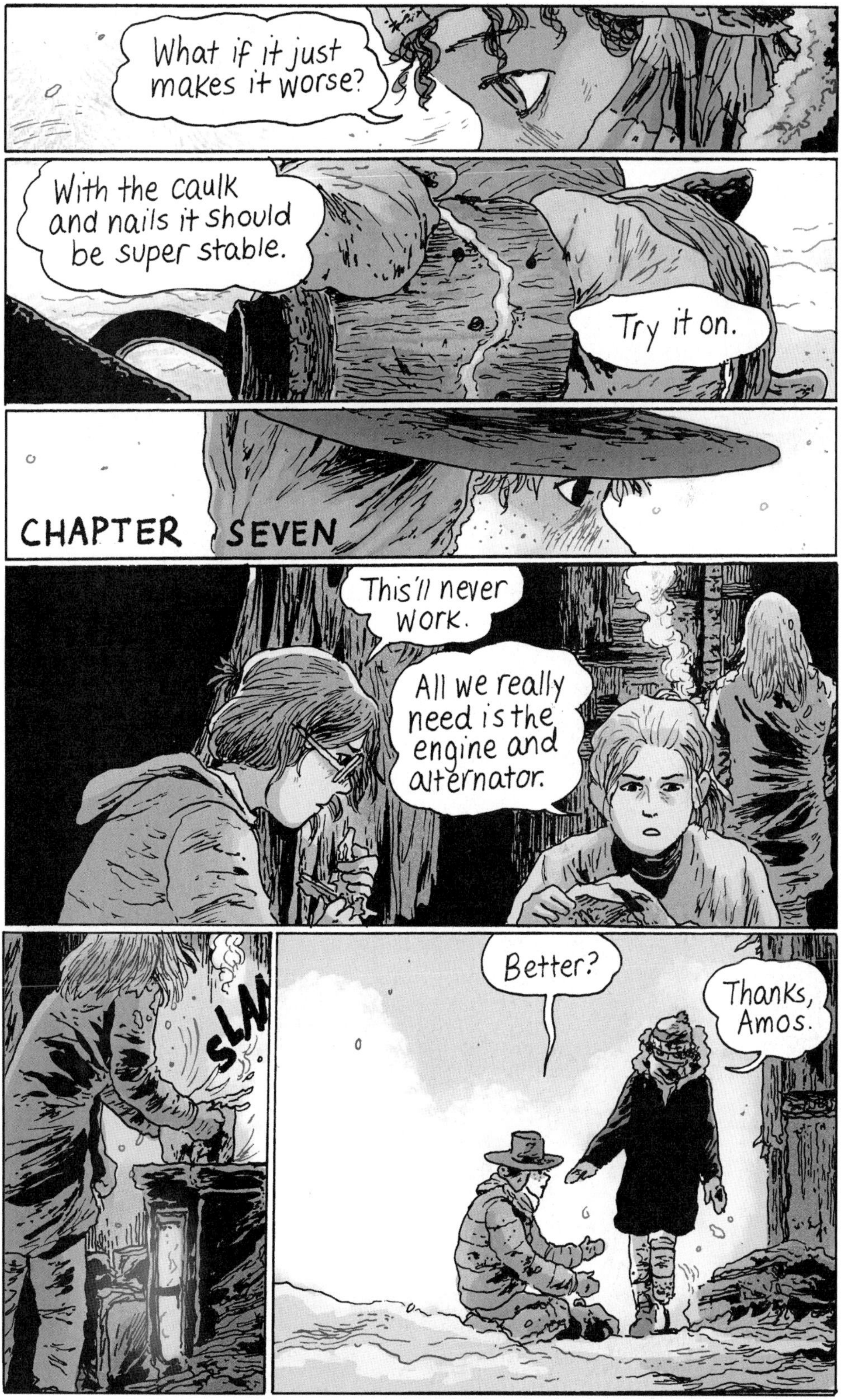
What if it just makes it worse?
With the caulk and nails it should be super stable.
Try it on.
CHAPTER SEVEN
This'll never work.
All we really need is the engine and alternator.
SLAM
Better?
Thanks, Amos.

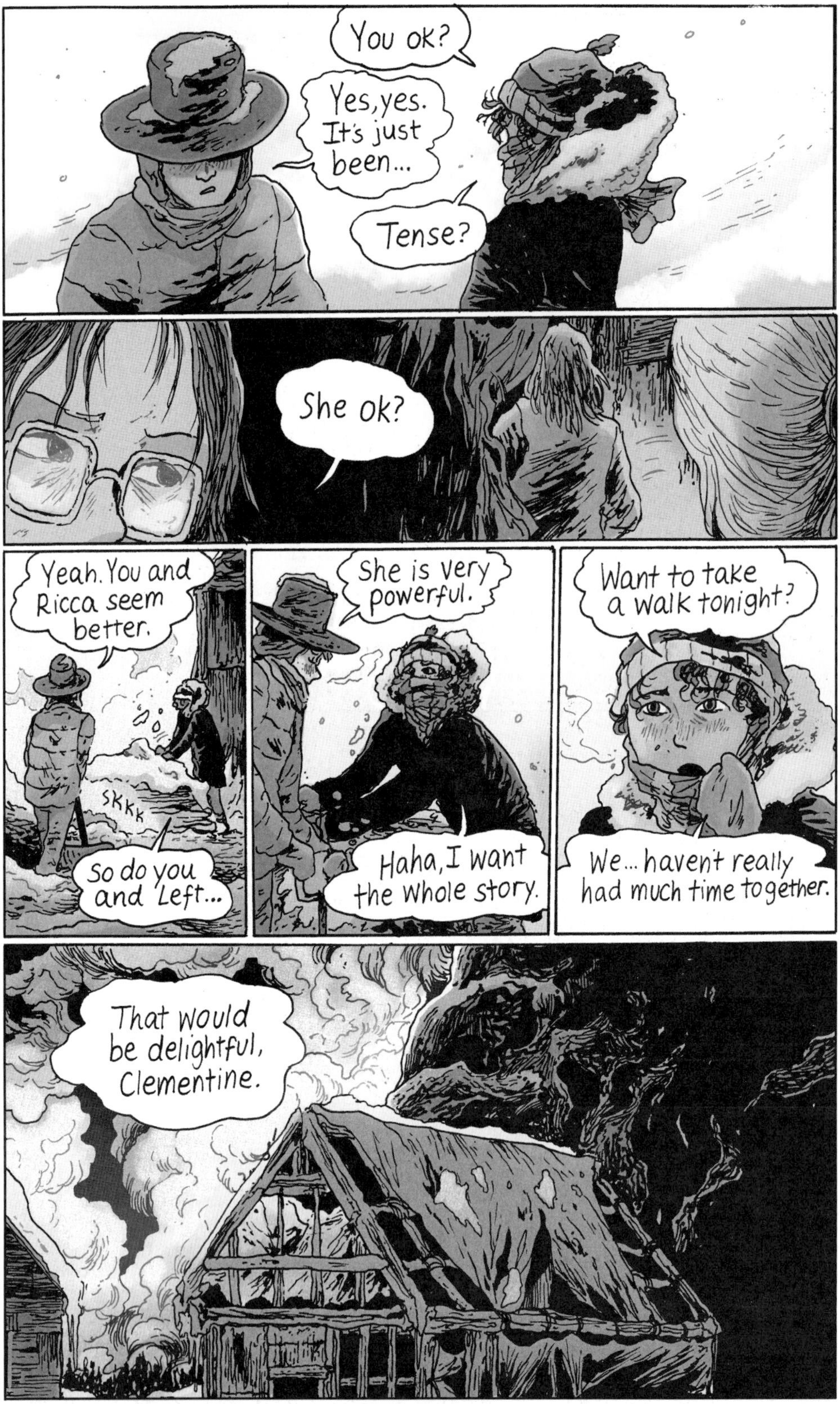
You ok?
Yes, yes. It's just been...
Tense?
She ok?
Yeah. You and Ricca seem better.
SKKK
So do you and Left...
She is very powerful.
Haha, I want the whole story.
Want to take a walk tonight?
We... haven't really had much time together.
That would be delightful, Clementine.

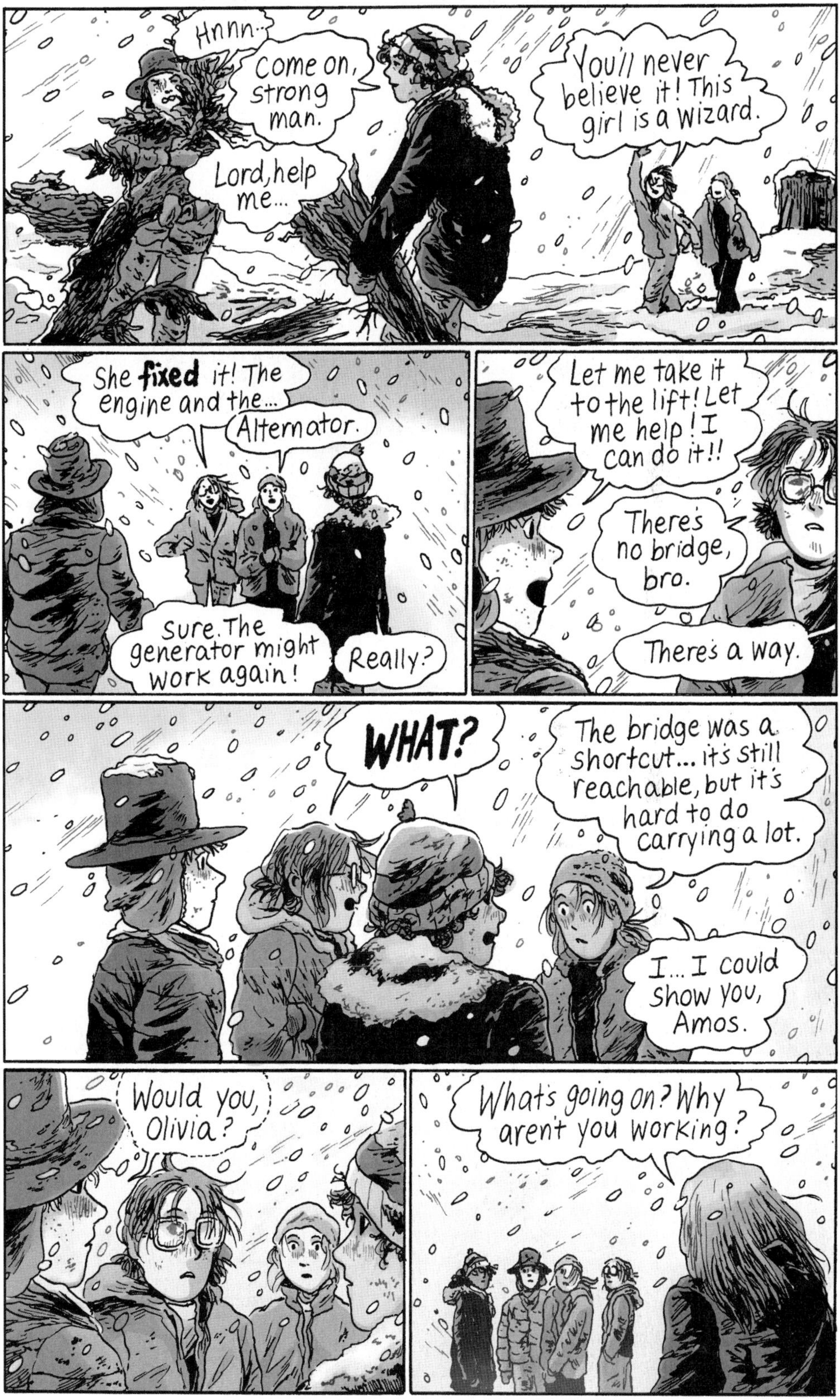
Hnnn..
Come on, strong man.
Lord, help me...
You'll never believe it! This girl is a wizard.
She fixed it! The engine and the...
Alternator.
Sure. The generator might work again!
Really?
Let me take it to the lift! Let me help! I can do it!!
There's no bridge, bro.
There's a way.
WHAT?
The bridge was a shortcut... it's still reachable, but it's hard to do carrying a lot.
I... I could show you, Amos.
Would you, Olivia?
What's going on? Why aren't you working?

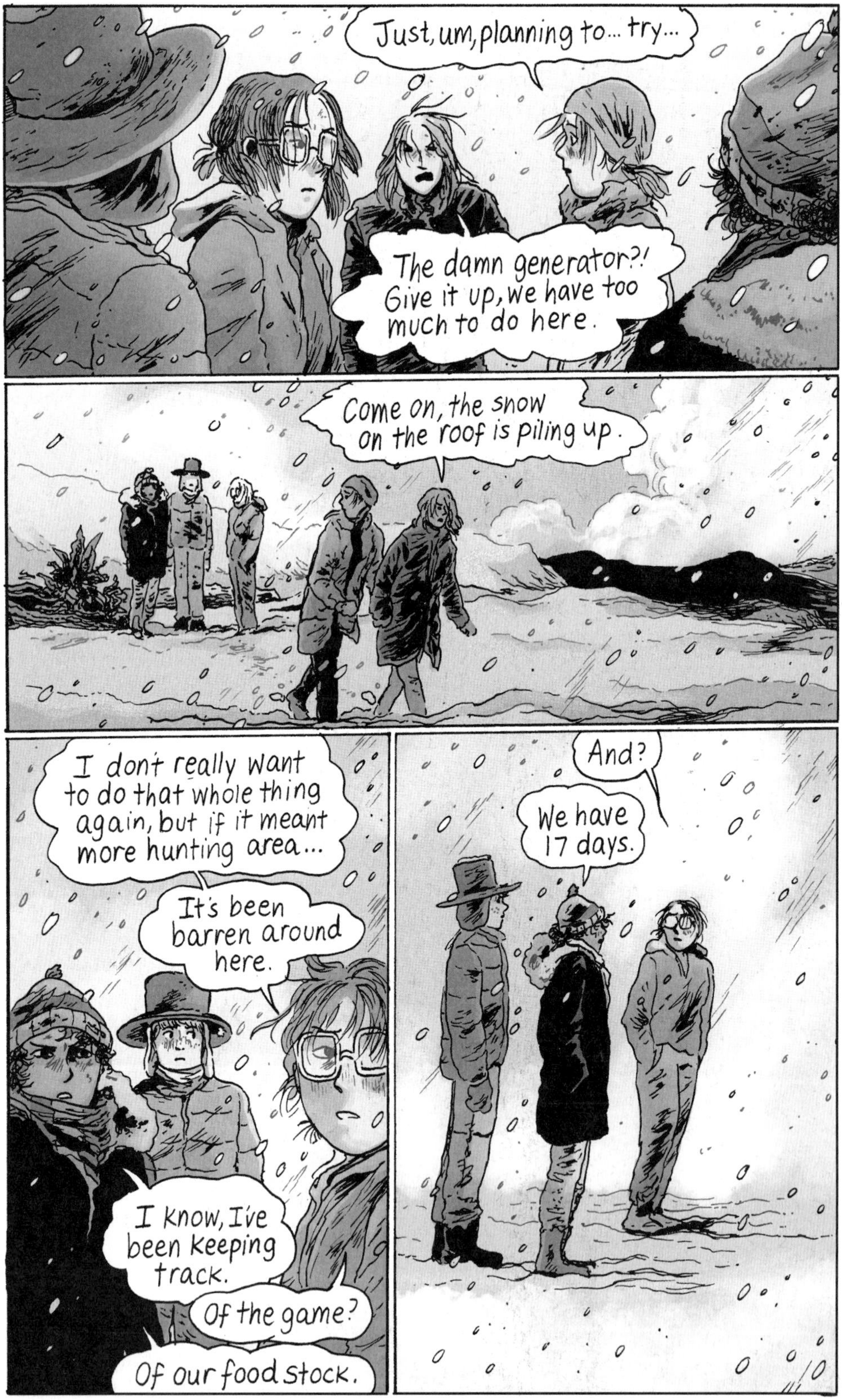
Just, um, planning to... try...
The damn generator?! Give it up, we have too much to do here.
Come on, the snow on the roof is piling up.
I don't really want to do that whole thing again, but if it meant more hunting area...
It's been barren around here.
I know, I've been keeping track.
Of the game?
Of our food stock.
And?
We have 17 days.

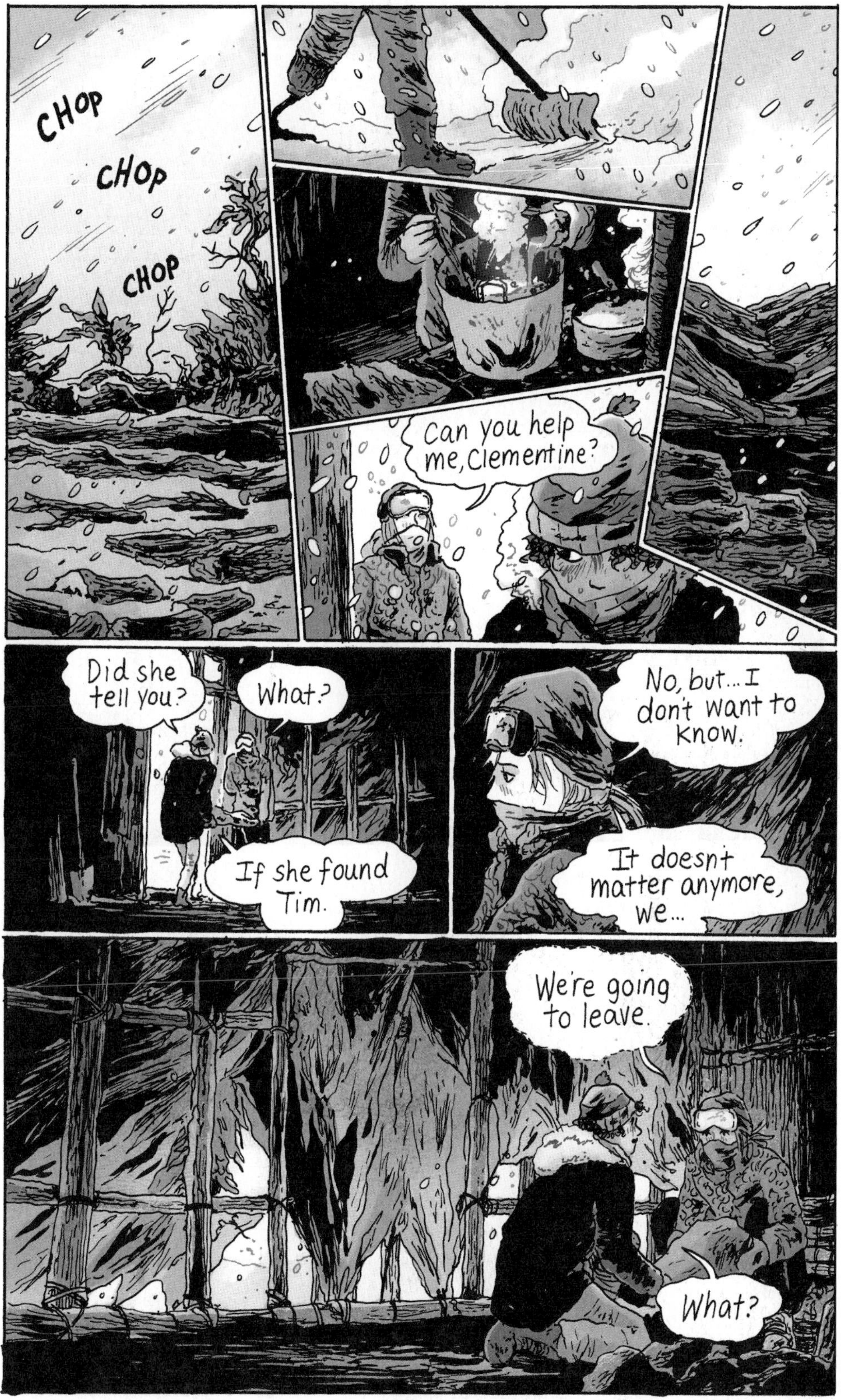
CHOP
CHOP
CHOP
Can you help me, Clementine?
Did she tell you?
What?
If she found Tim.
No, but... I don't want to know.
It doesn't matter anymore, we...
We're going to leave.
What?

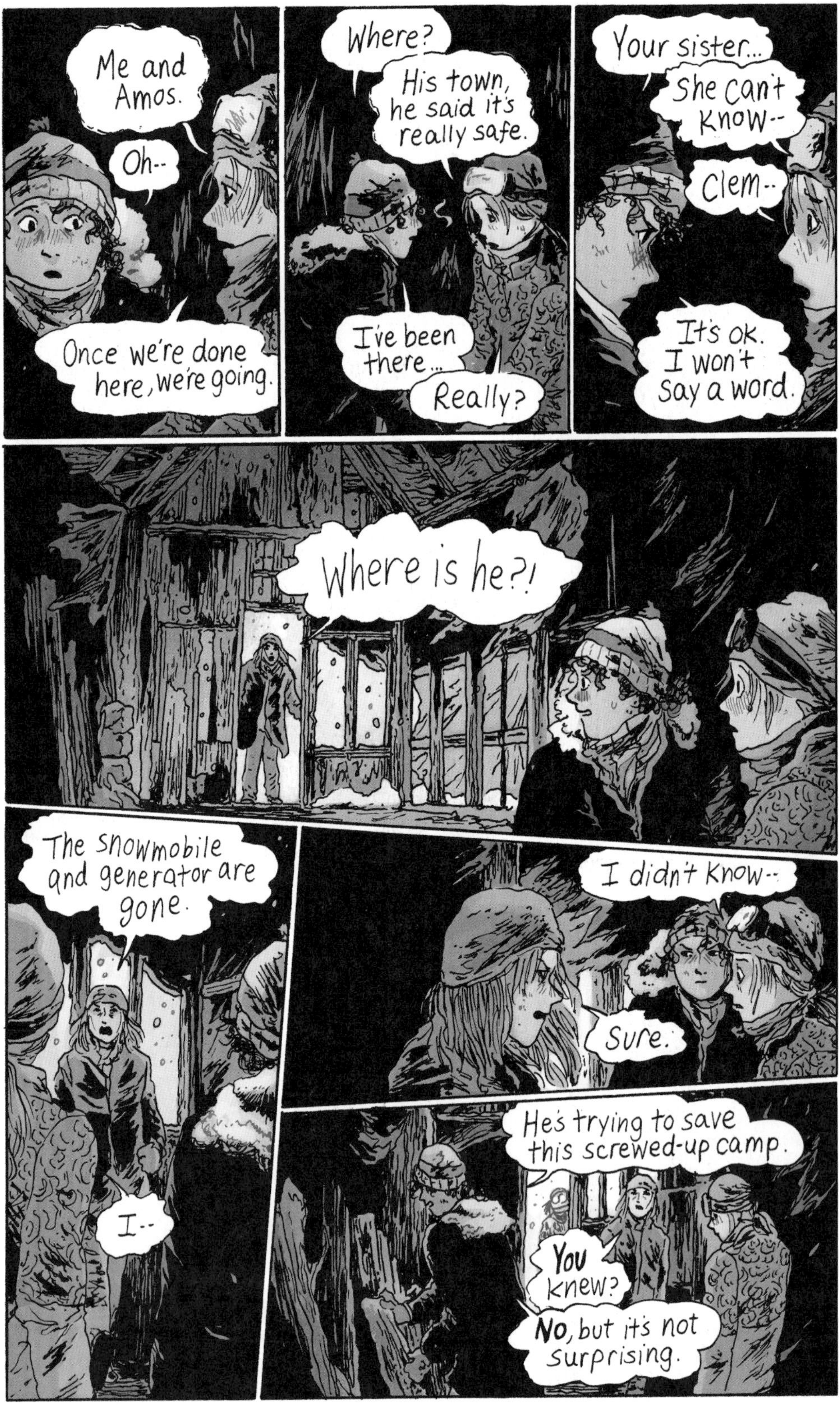
Me and Amos.
Oh--
Once we're done here, we're going.
Where?
His town, he said it's really safe.
I've been there...
Really?
Your sister...
She can't know--
Clem--
It's ok. I won't say a word.
Where is he?!
The snowmobile and generator are gone.
I--
I didn't know--
Sure.
He's trying to save this screwed-up camp.
You knew?
No, but it's not surprising.

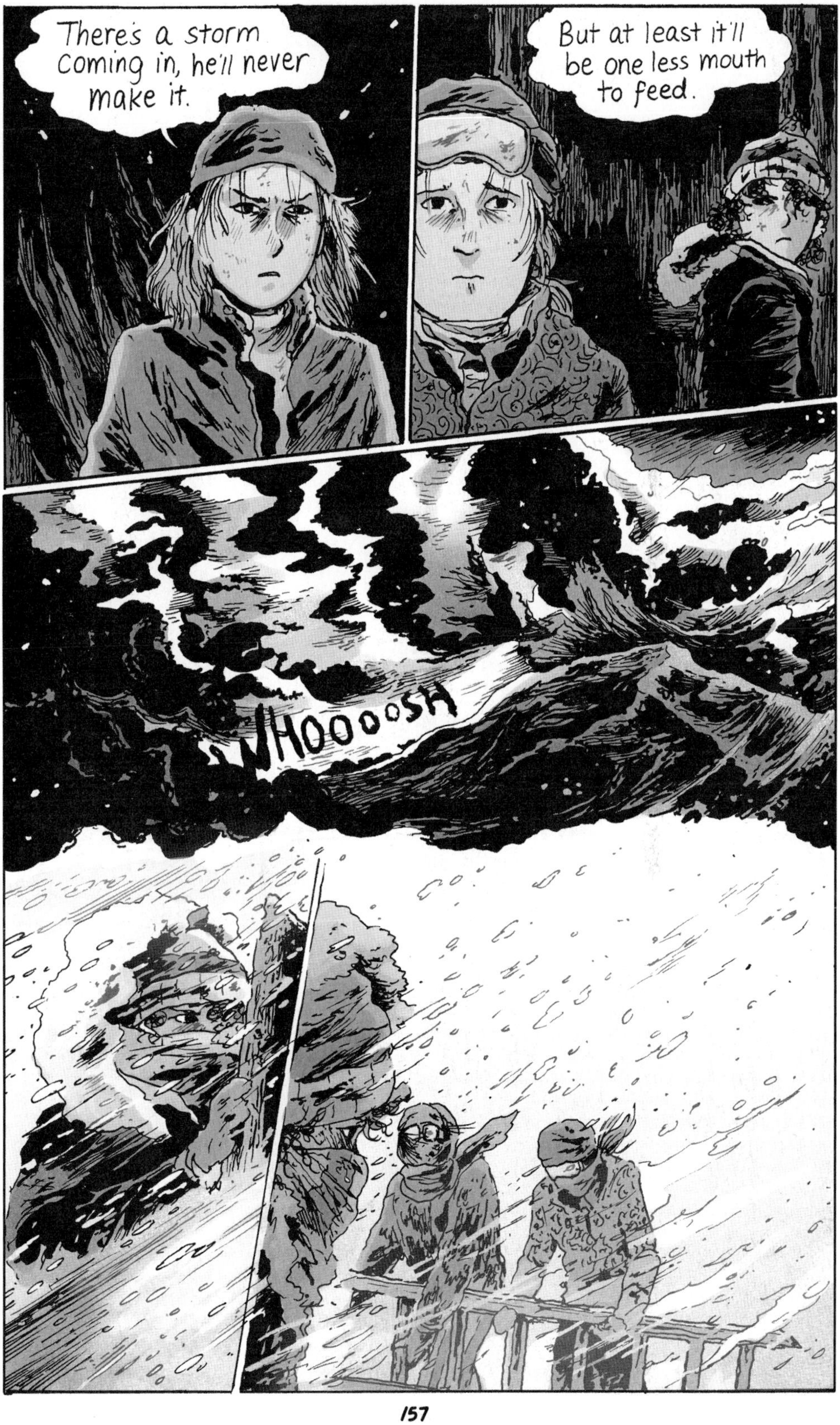
There's a storm coming in, he'll never make it.
But at least it'll be one less mouth to feed.
WHOOOOSH

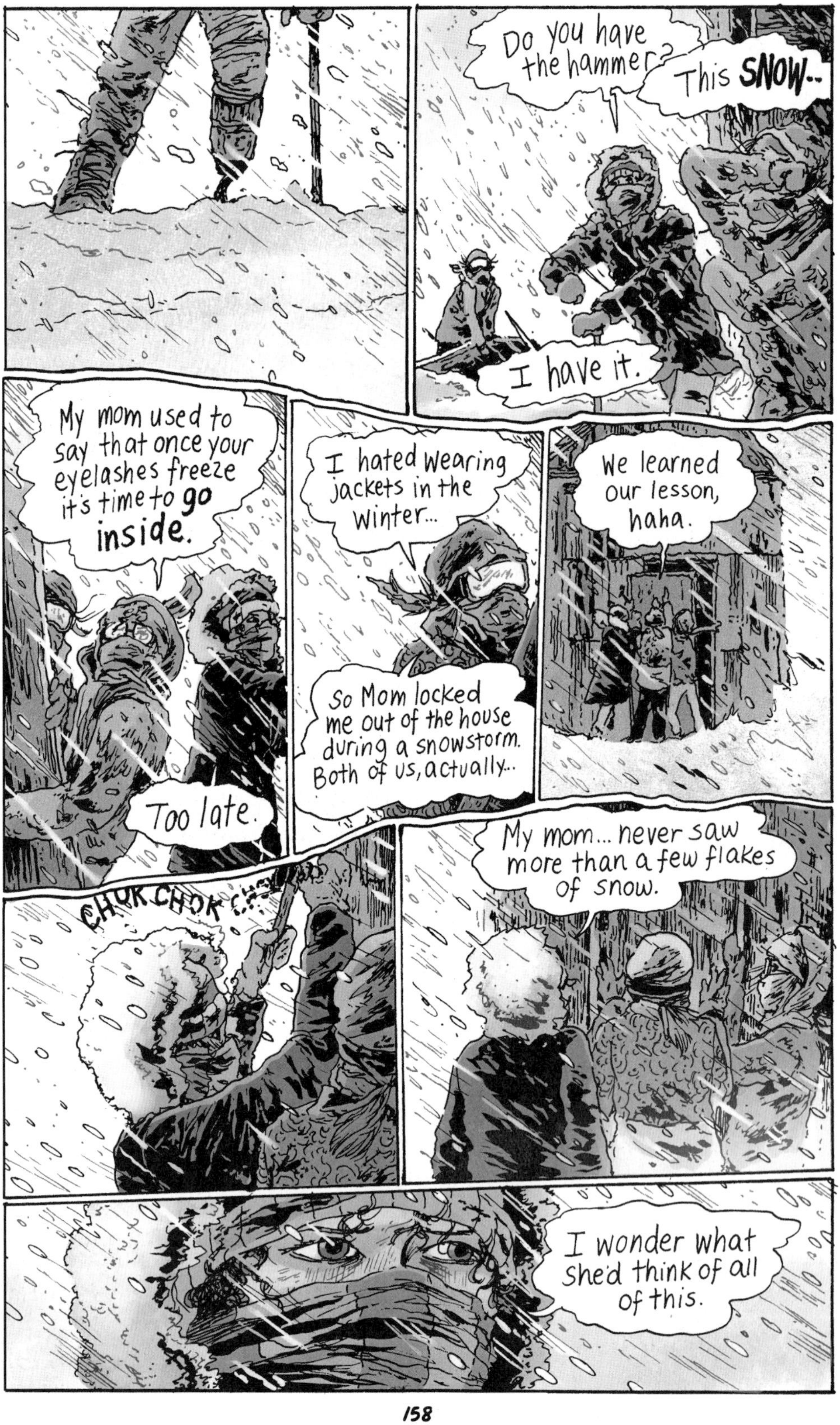
Do you have the hammer?
This SNOW--
I have it.
My mom used to say that once your eyelashes freeze it's time to go inside.
Too late.
I hated wearing jackets in the winter...
So Mom locked me out of the house during a snowstorm. Both of us, actually...
We learned our lesson, haha.
CHOK CHOK
My mom... never saw more than a few flakes of snow.
I wonder what she'd think of all of this.

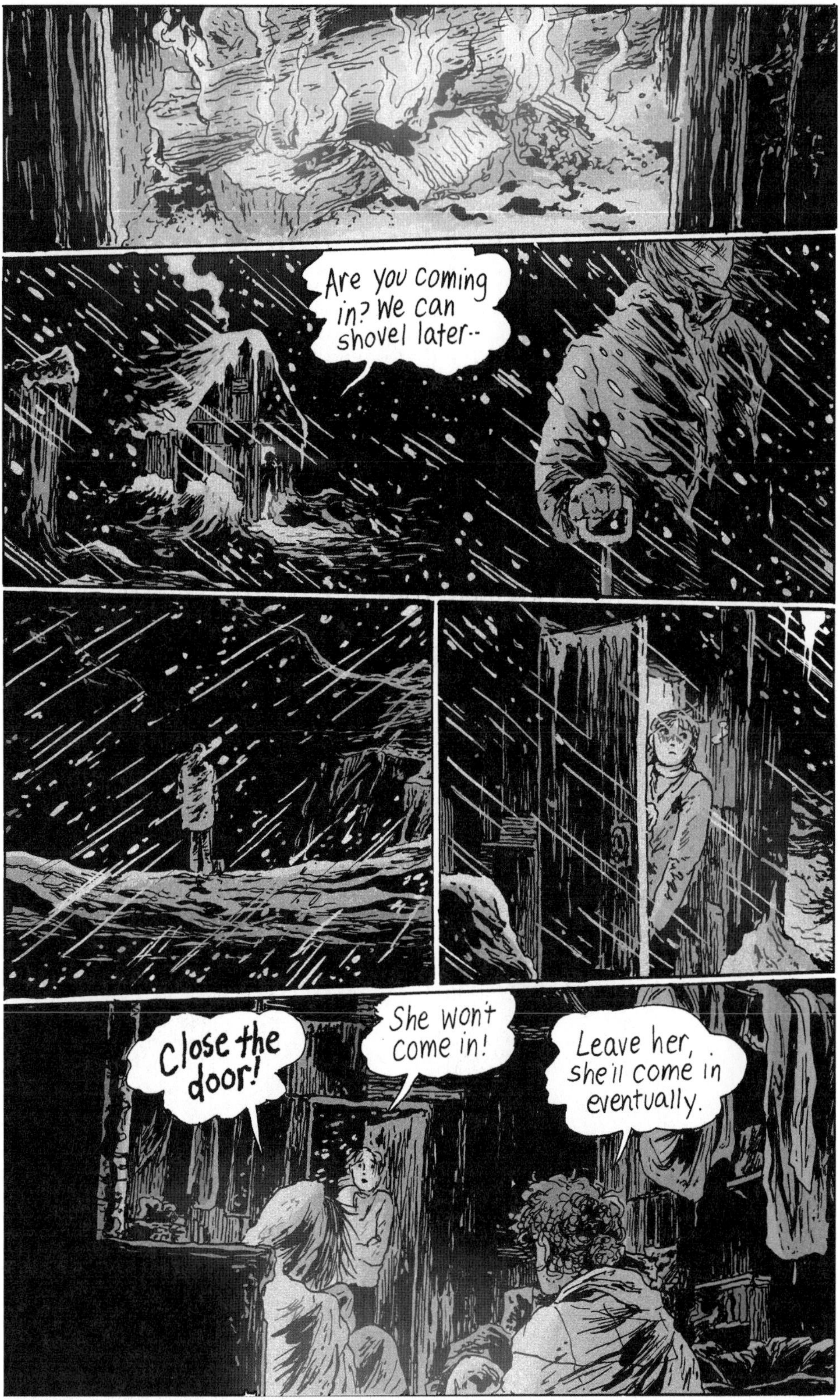
Are you coming in? We can shovel later--
Close the door!
She won't come in!
Leave her, she'll come in eventually.

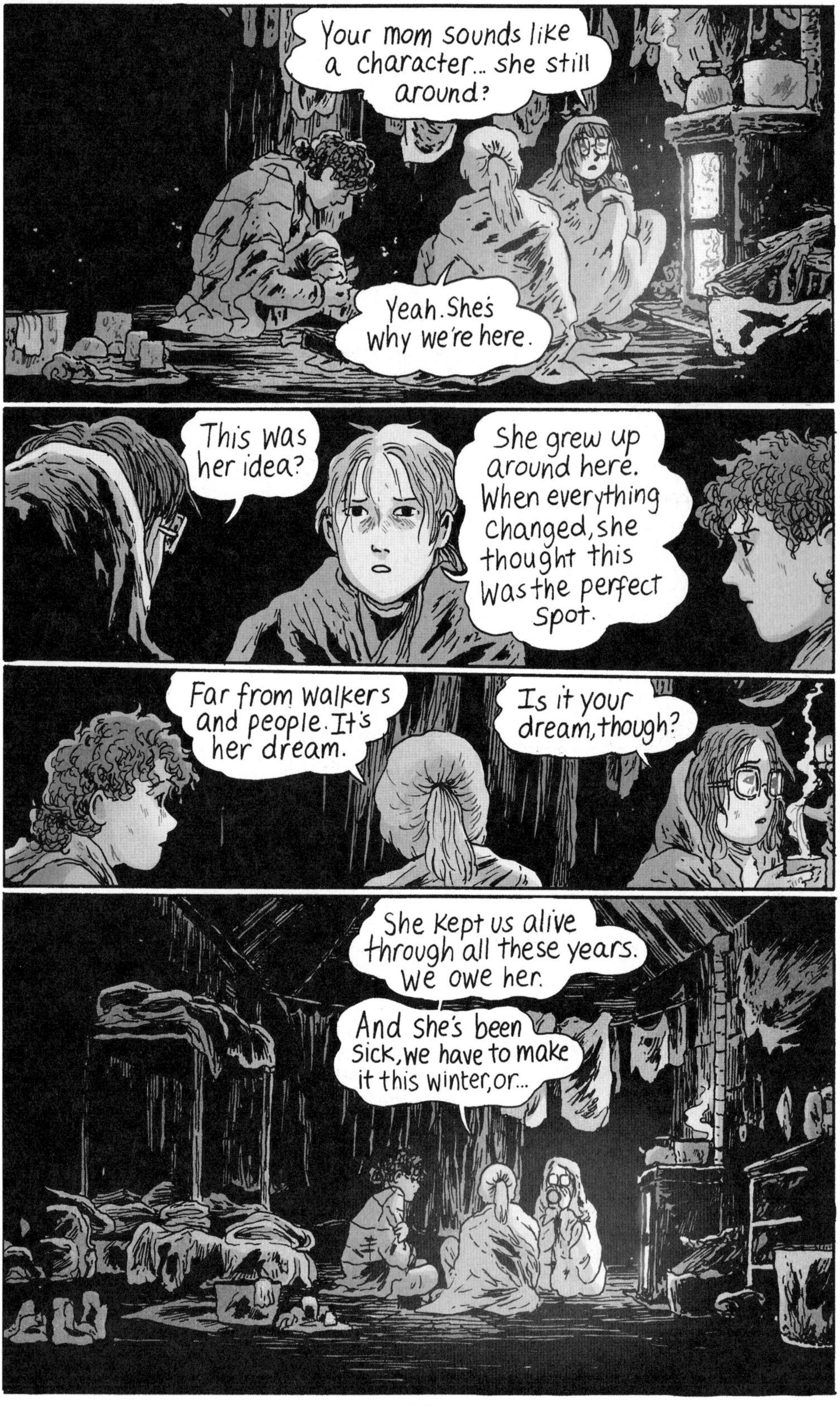
Your mom sounds like a character... she still around?
Yeah. She's why we're here.
This was her idea?
She grew up around here. When everything changed, she thought this was the perfect spot.
Far from walkers and people. It's her dream.
Is it your dream, though?
She kept us alive through all these years. We owe her.
And she's been sick, we have to make it this winter, or...

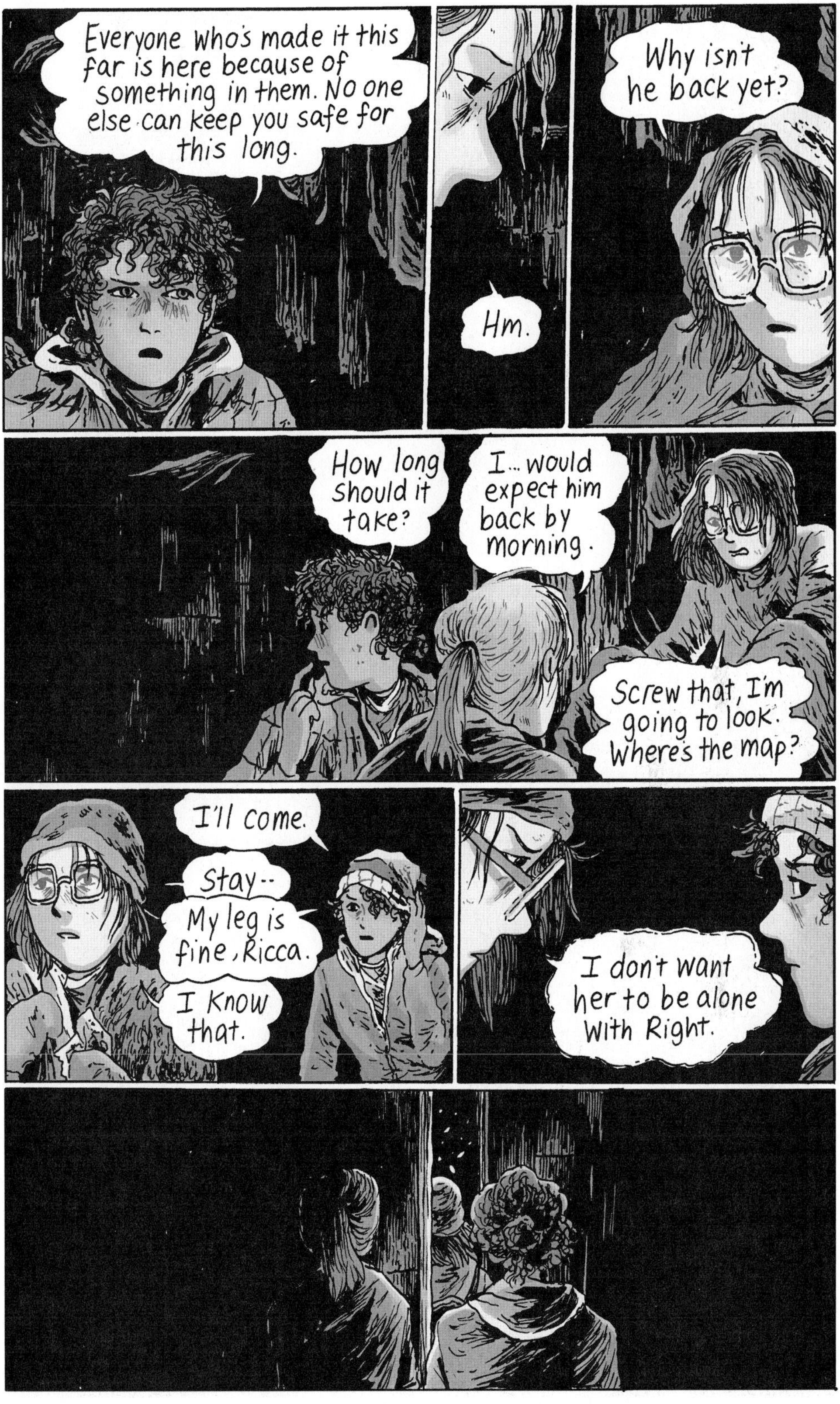
Everyone who's made it this far is here because of something in them. No one else can keep you safe for this long.
Hm.
Why isn't he back yet?
How long should it take?
I... would expect him back by morning.
Screw that, I'm going to look. Where's the map?
I'll come.
Stay--
My leg is fine, Ricca.
I know that.
I don't want her to be alone with Right.

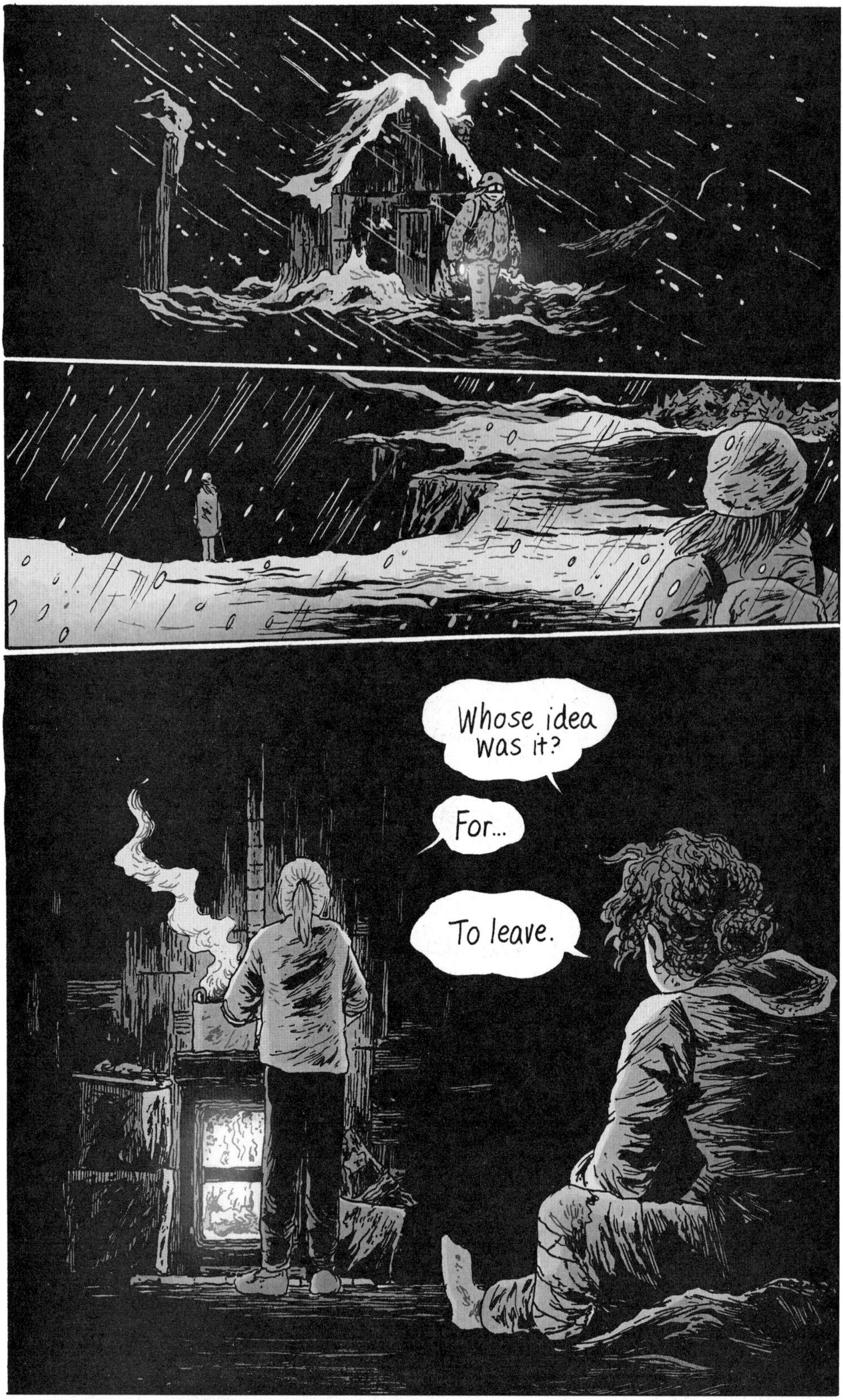
Whose idea was it?
For...
To leave.

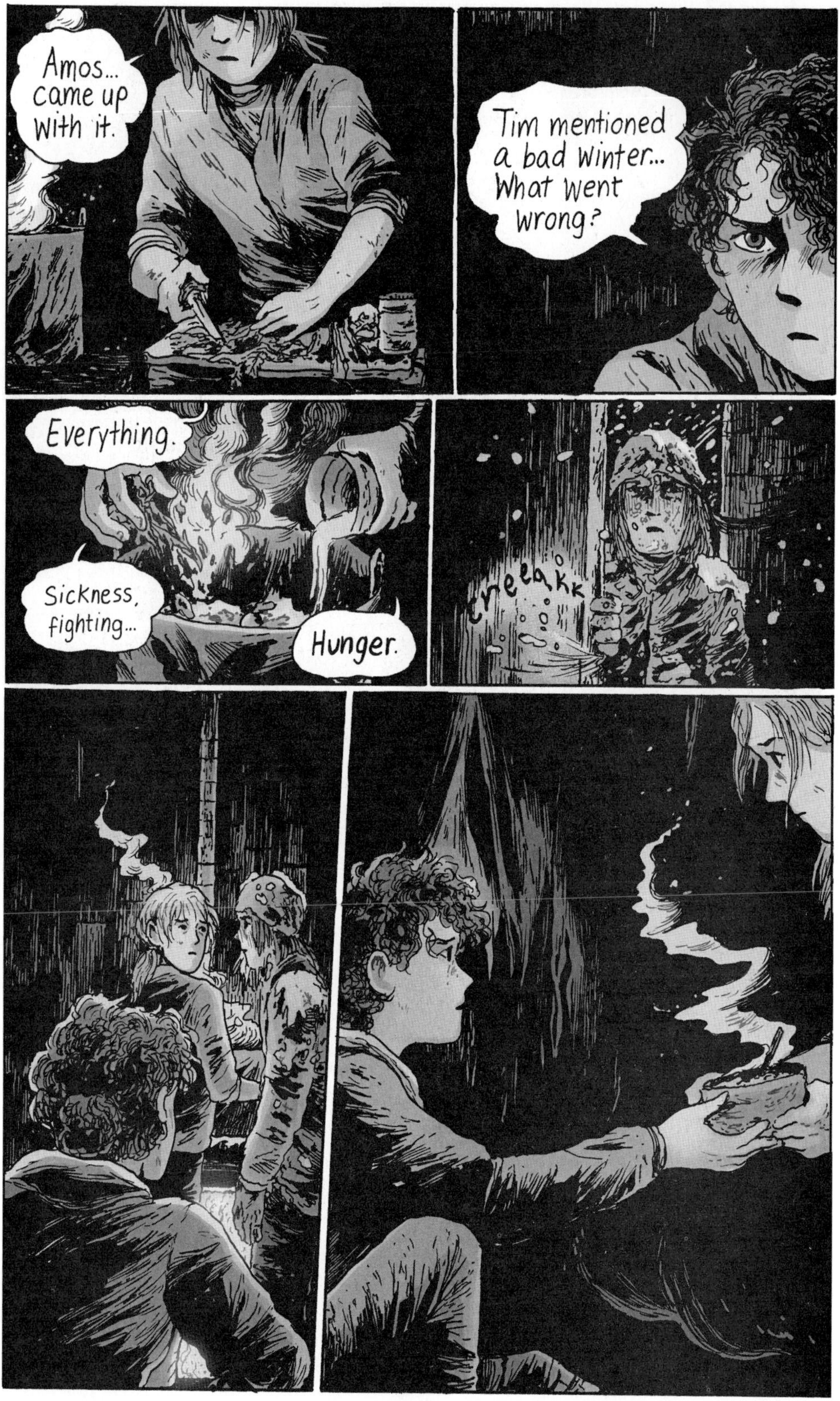
Amos... came up with it.
Tim mentioned a bad Winter... What went wrong?
Everything.
Sickness, fighting...
Hunger.
creeakk

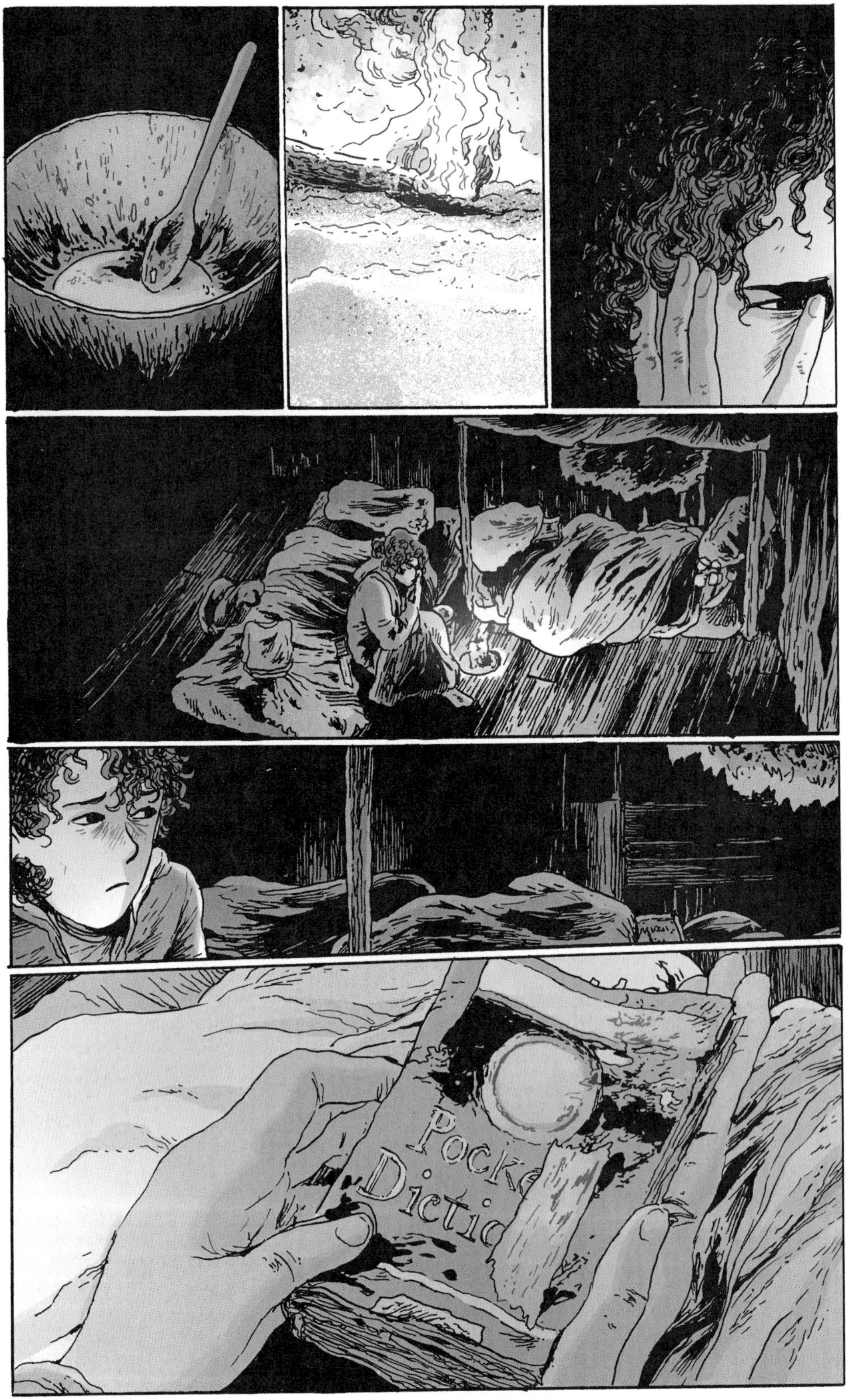
Pocke
Dictic

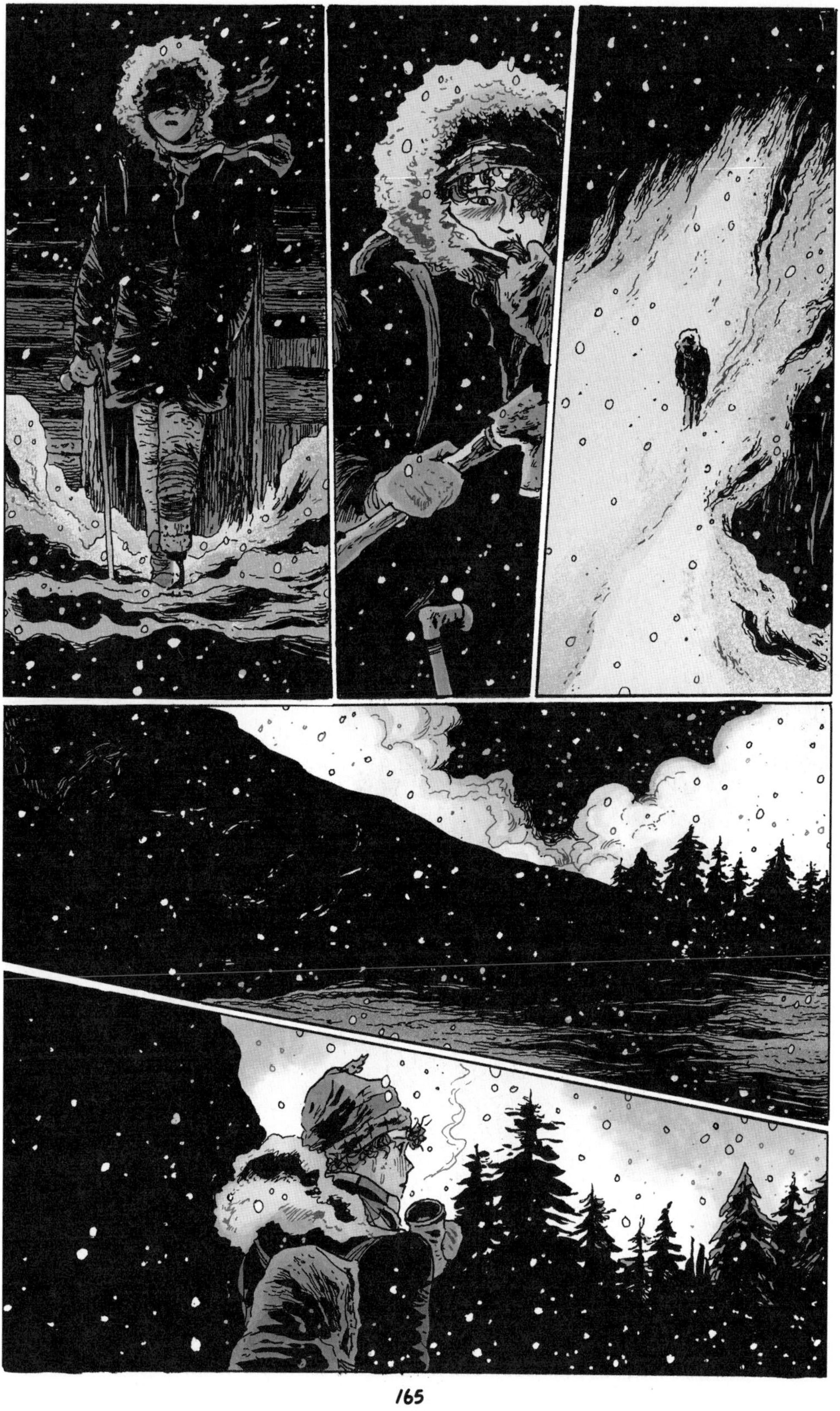

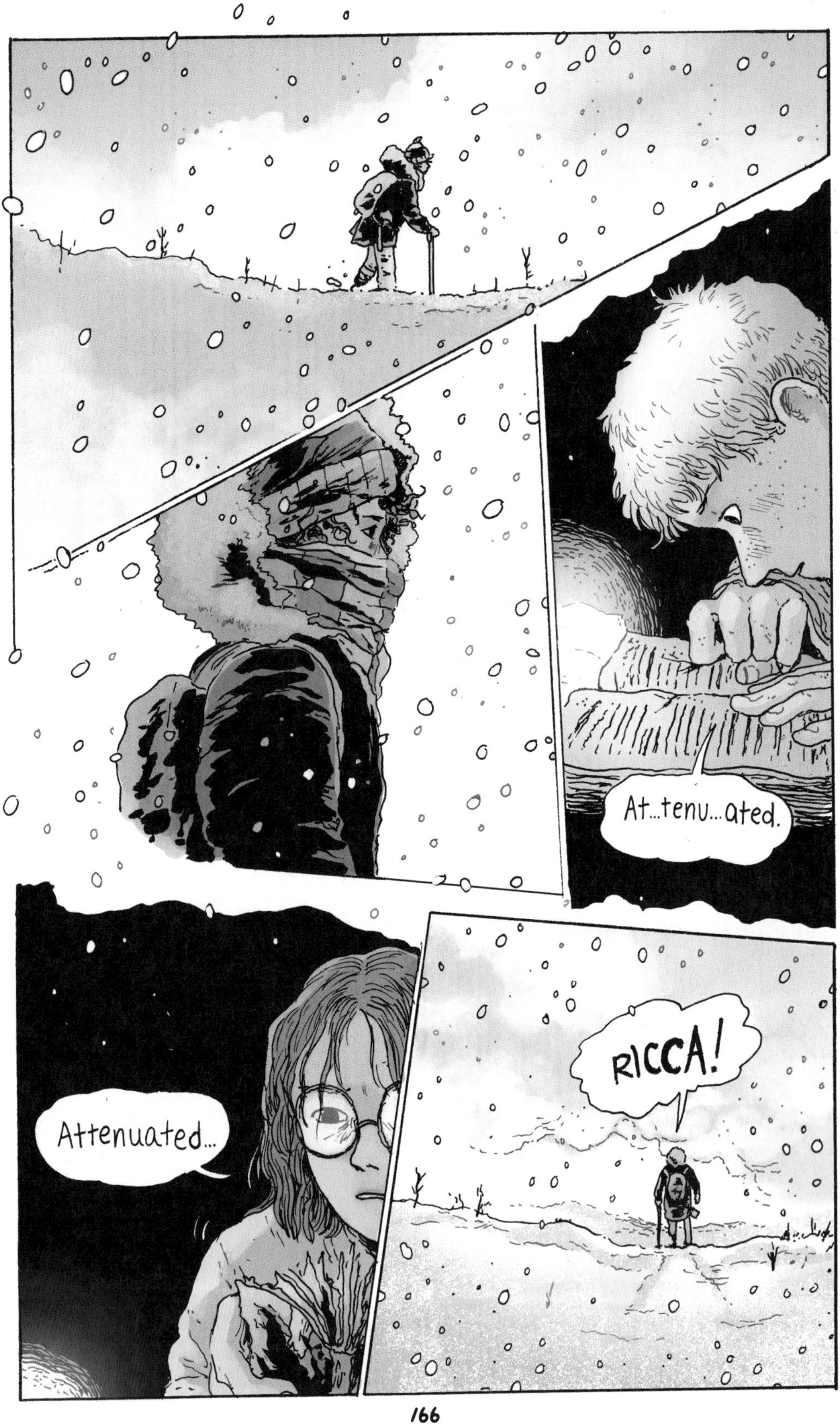
At...tenu...ated.
Attenuated...
RICCA!

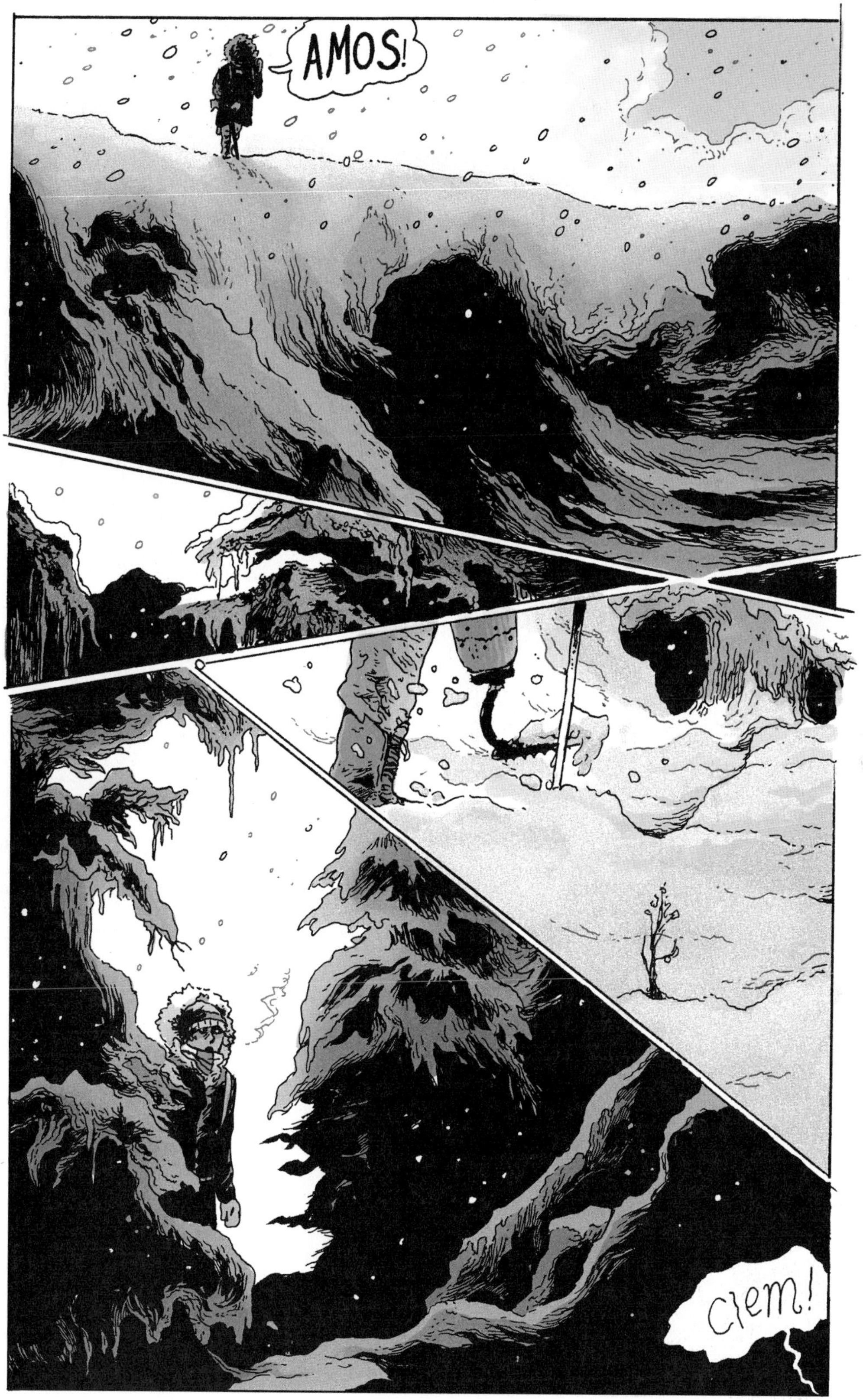
AMOS!
Clem!

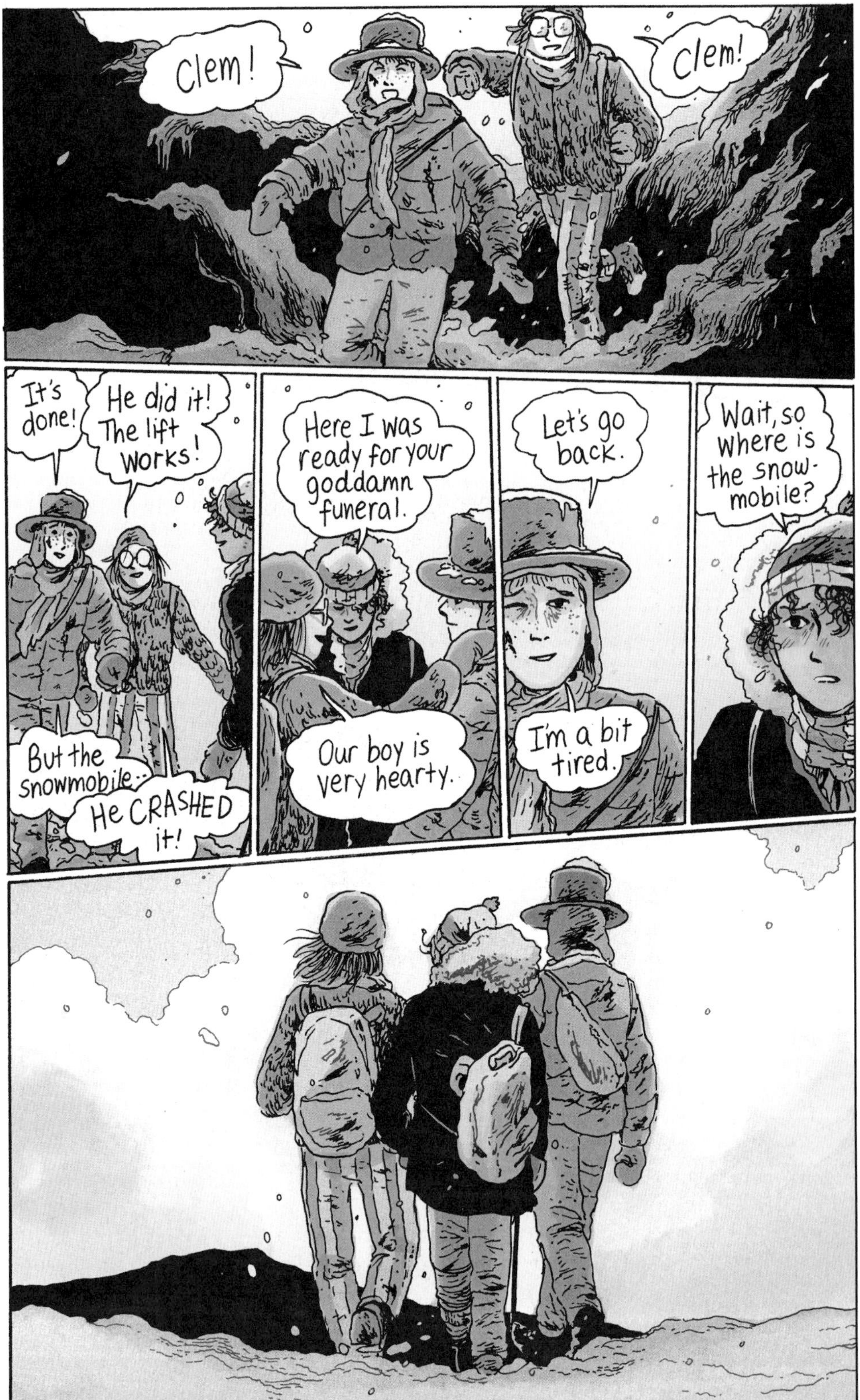

Clem!
Clem!
It's done!
He did it! The lift works!
But the snowmobile...
He CRASHED it!
Here I was ready for your goddamn funeral.
Our boy is very hearty.
Let's go back.
I'm a bit tired.
Wait, so where is the snow-mobile?

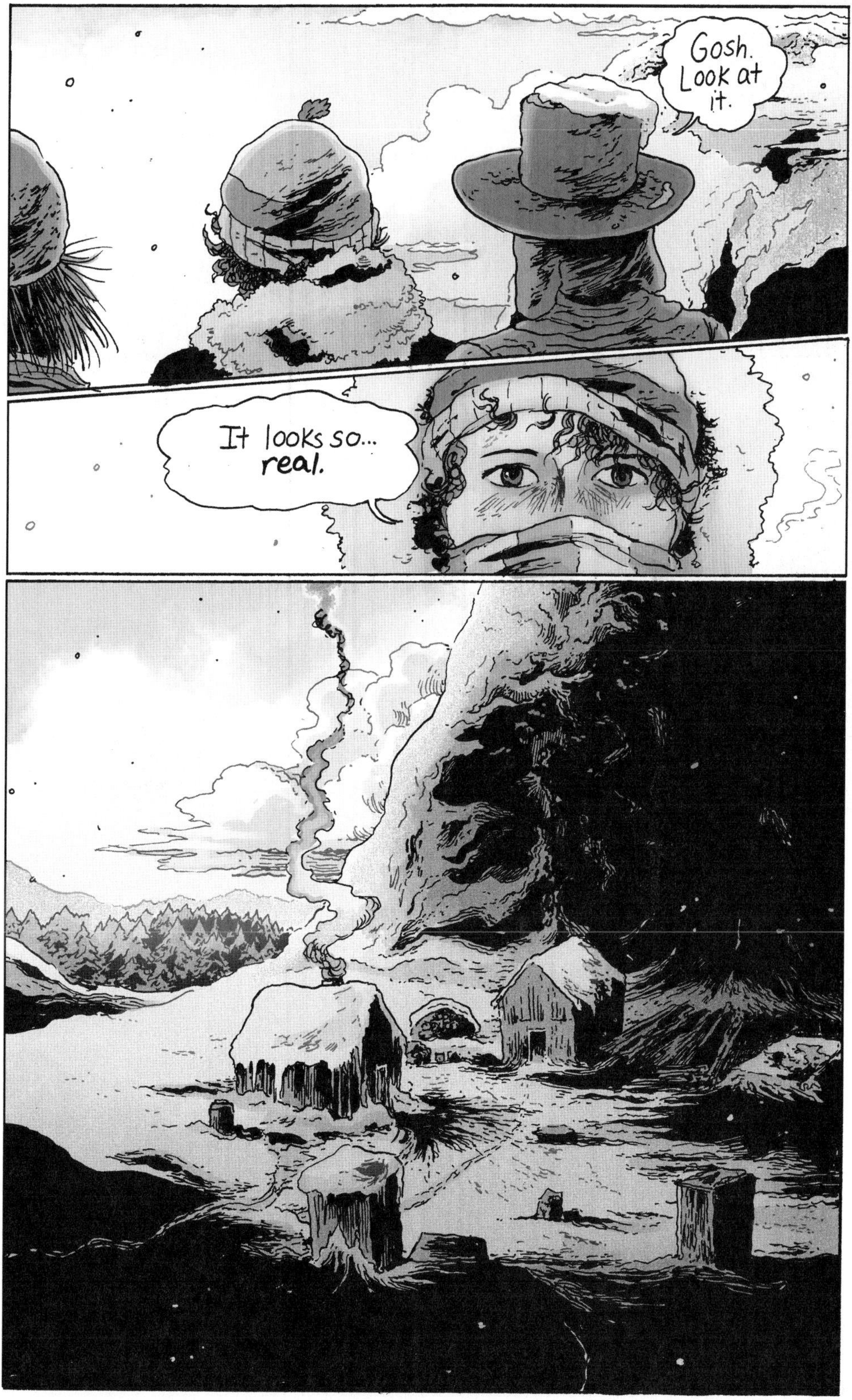
Gosh. Look at it.
It looks so... **real.**

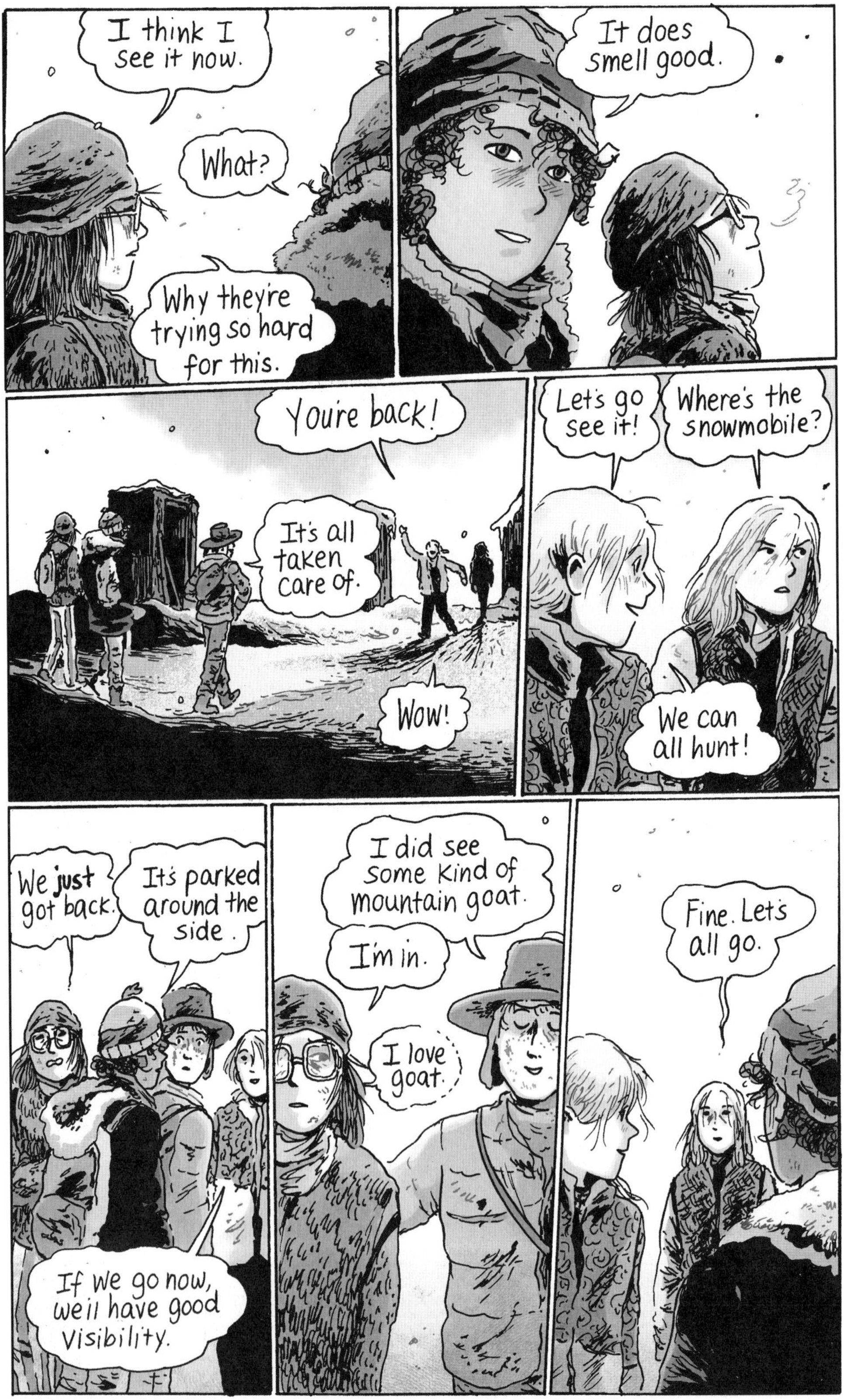
I think I see it now.
What?
Why they're trying so hard for this.
It does smell good.
You're back!
It's all taken care of.
Wow!
Let's go see it!
Where's the snowmobile?
We can all hunt!
We just got back.
It's parked around the side.
If we go now, we'll have good visibility.
I did see some kind of mountain goat.
I'm in.
I love goat.
Fine. Let's all go.

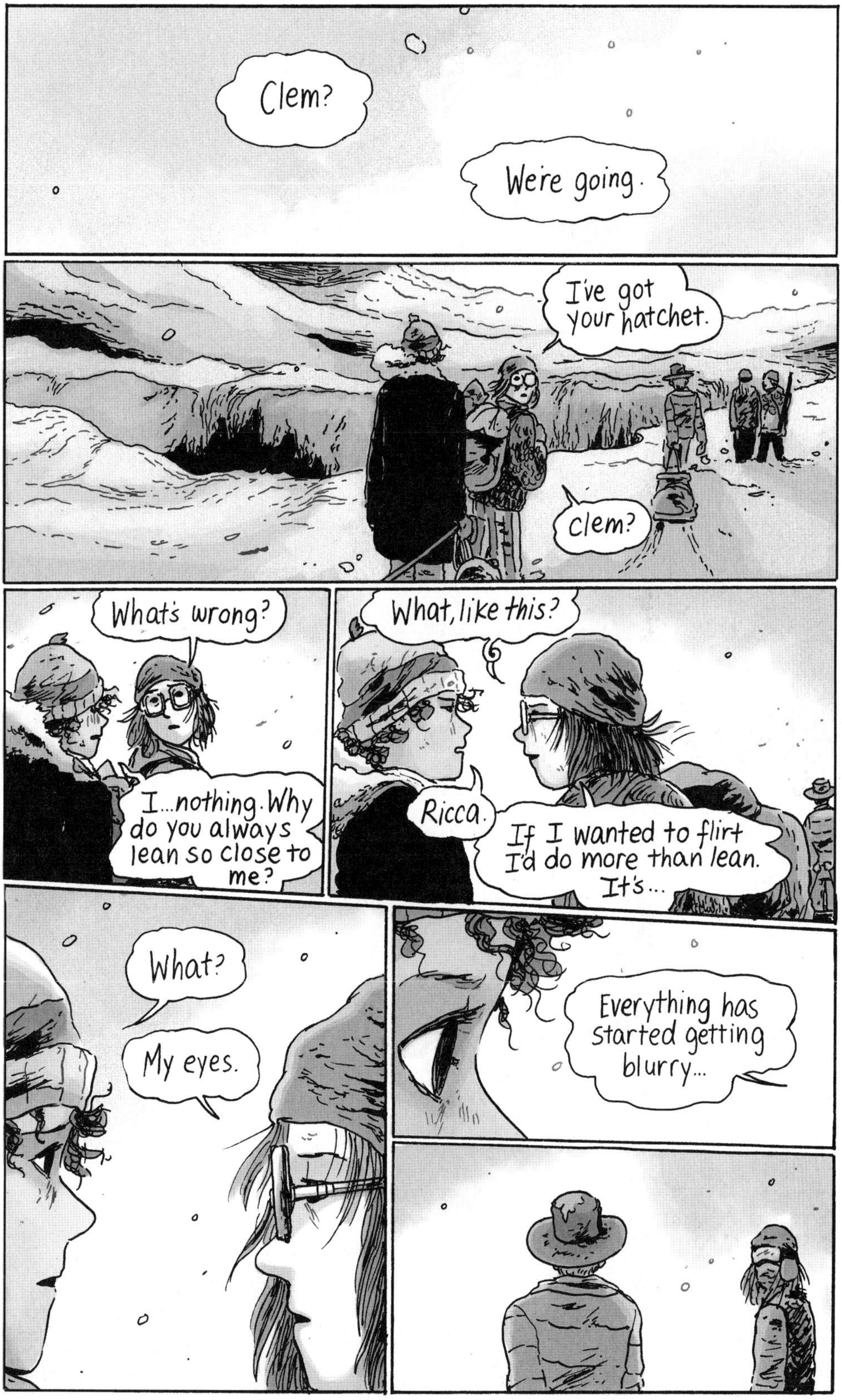
Clem?
We're going.
I've got your hatchet.
Clem?
What's wrong?
I...nothing. Why do you always lean so close to me?
What, like this?
Ricca.
If I wanted to flirt I'd do more than lean. It's...
What?
My eyes.
Everything has started getting blurry...

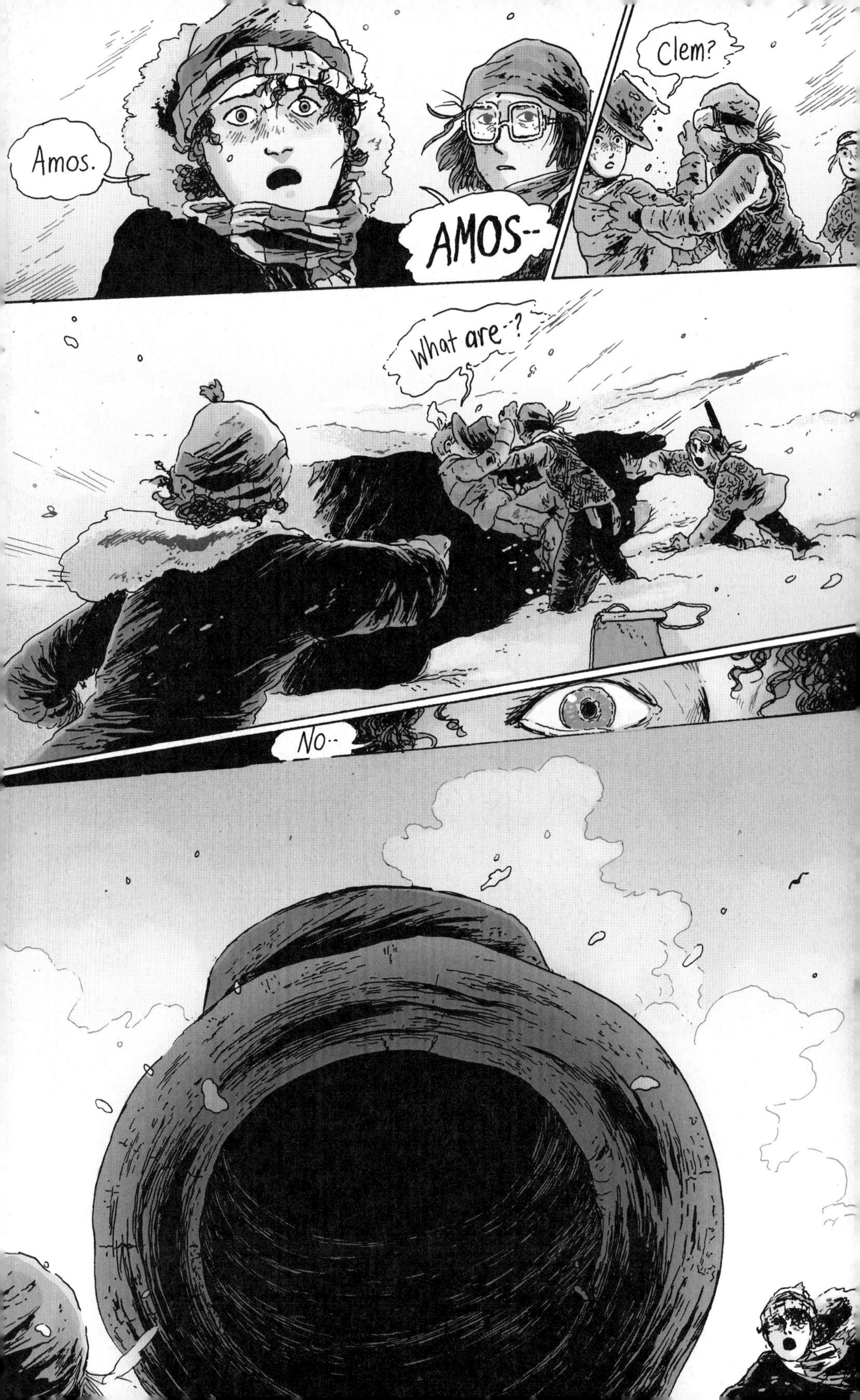
Amos.
AMOS--
Clem?
What are--?
No--

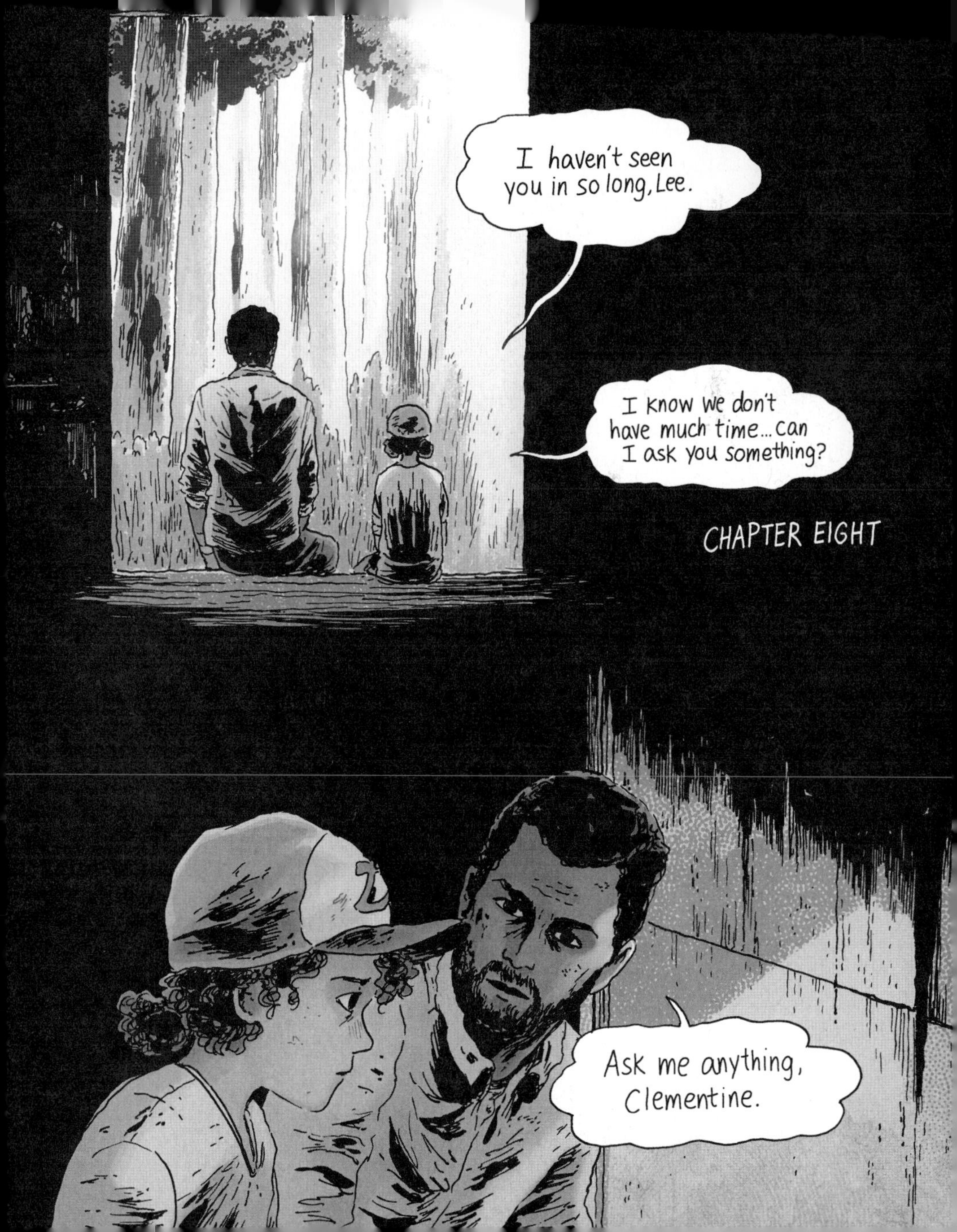
I haven't seen you in so long, Lee.
I know we don't have much time... can I ask you something?
CHAPTER EIGHT
Ask me anything, Clementine.

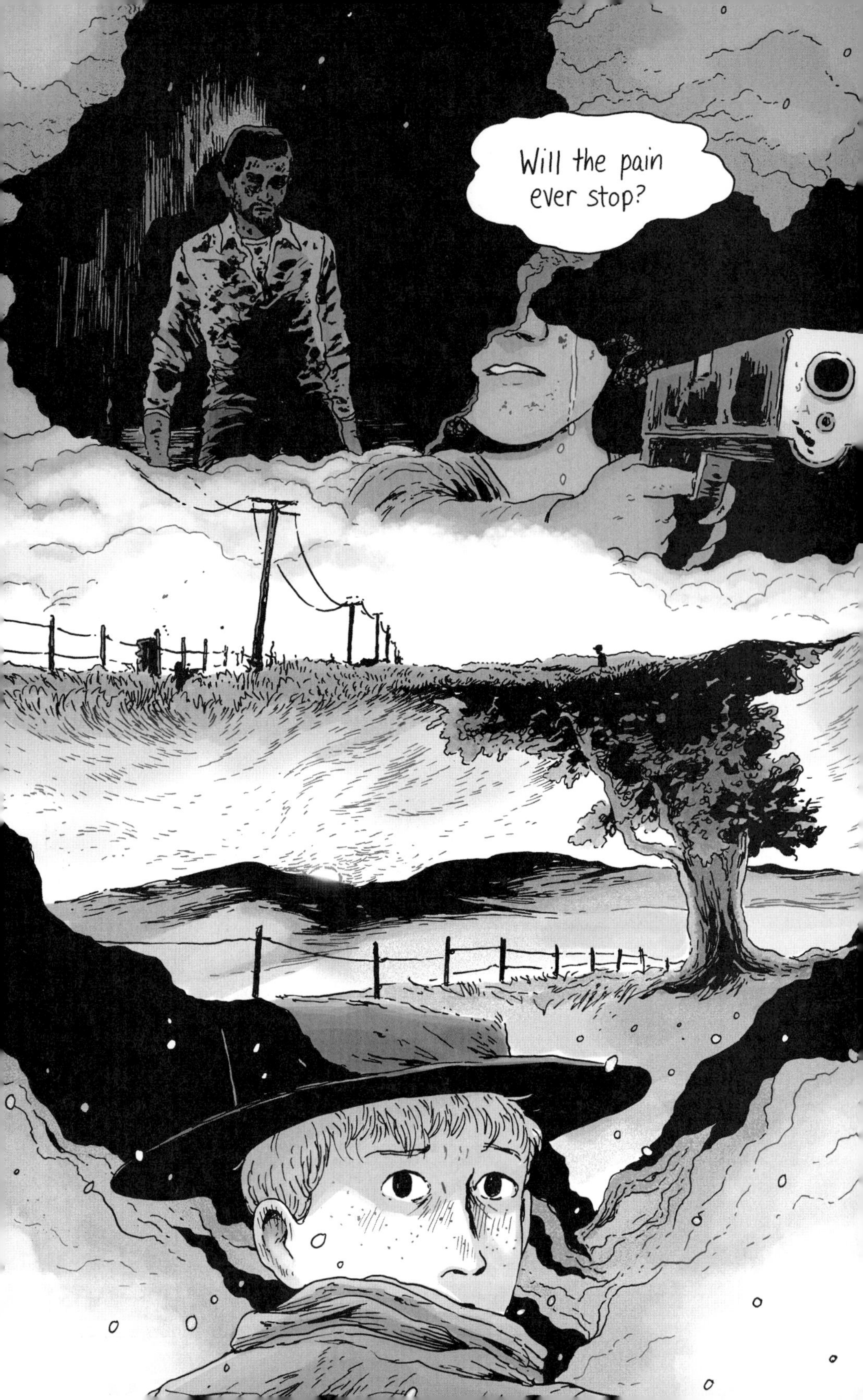
Will the pain ever stop?

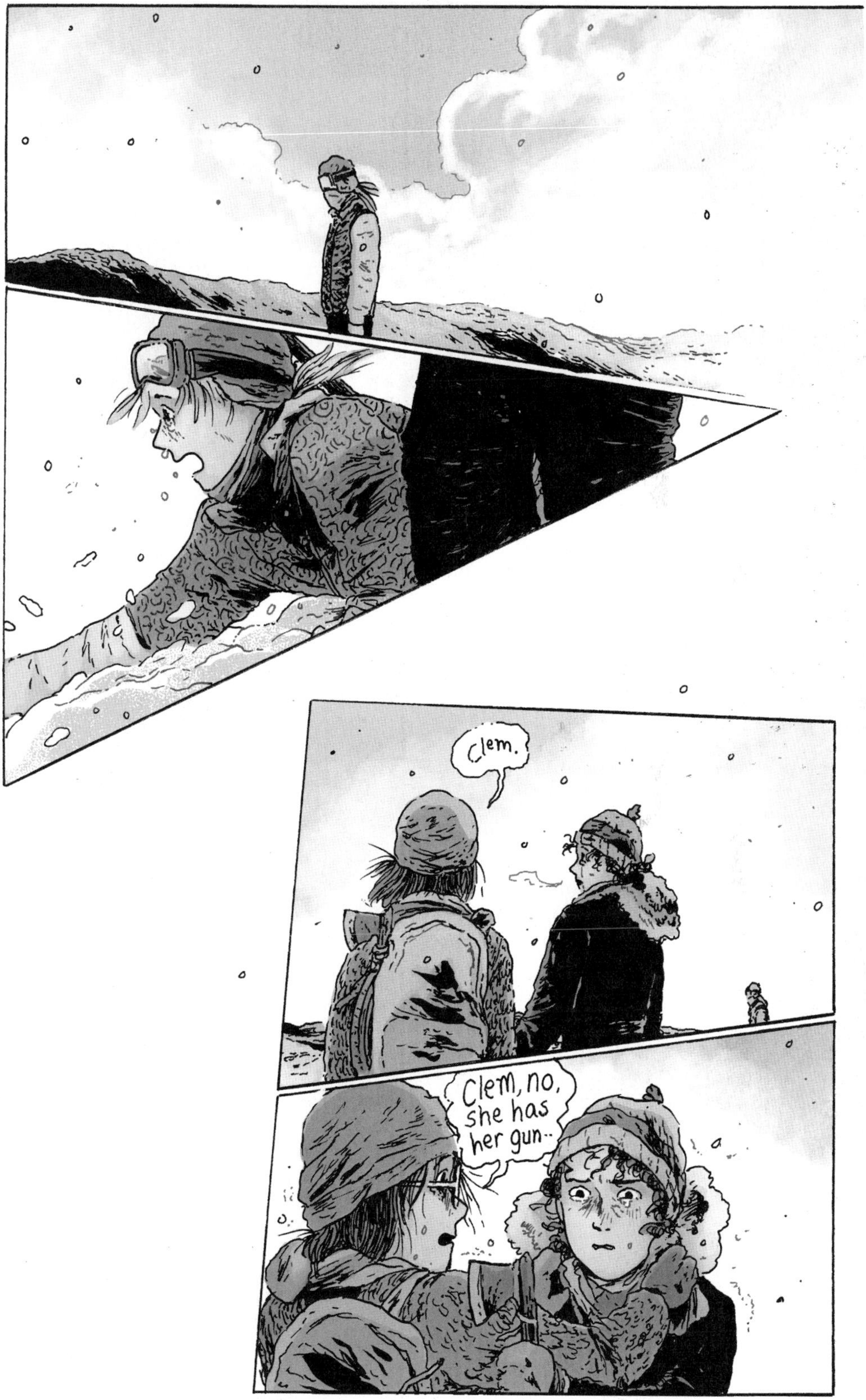
Clem.
Clem, no, she has her gun..

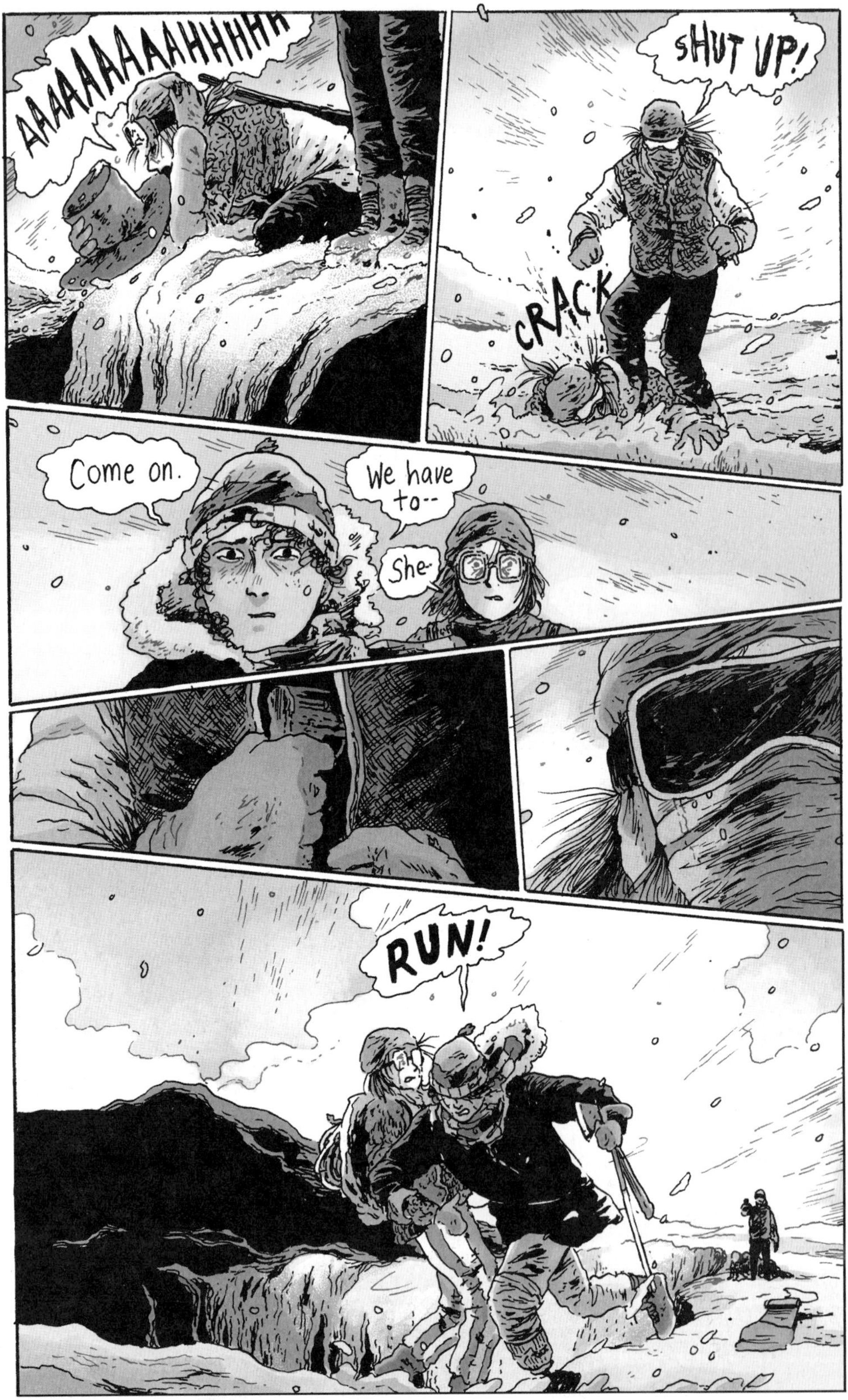
AAAAAAAAAHHHHH
SHUT UP!
CRACK
Come on.
We have to--
She-
RUN!

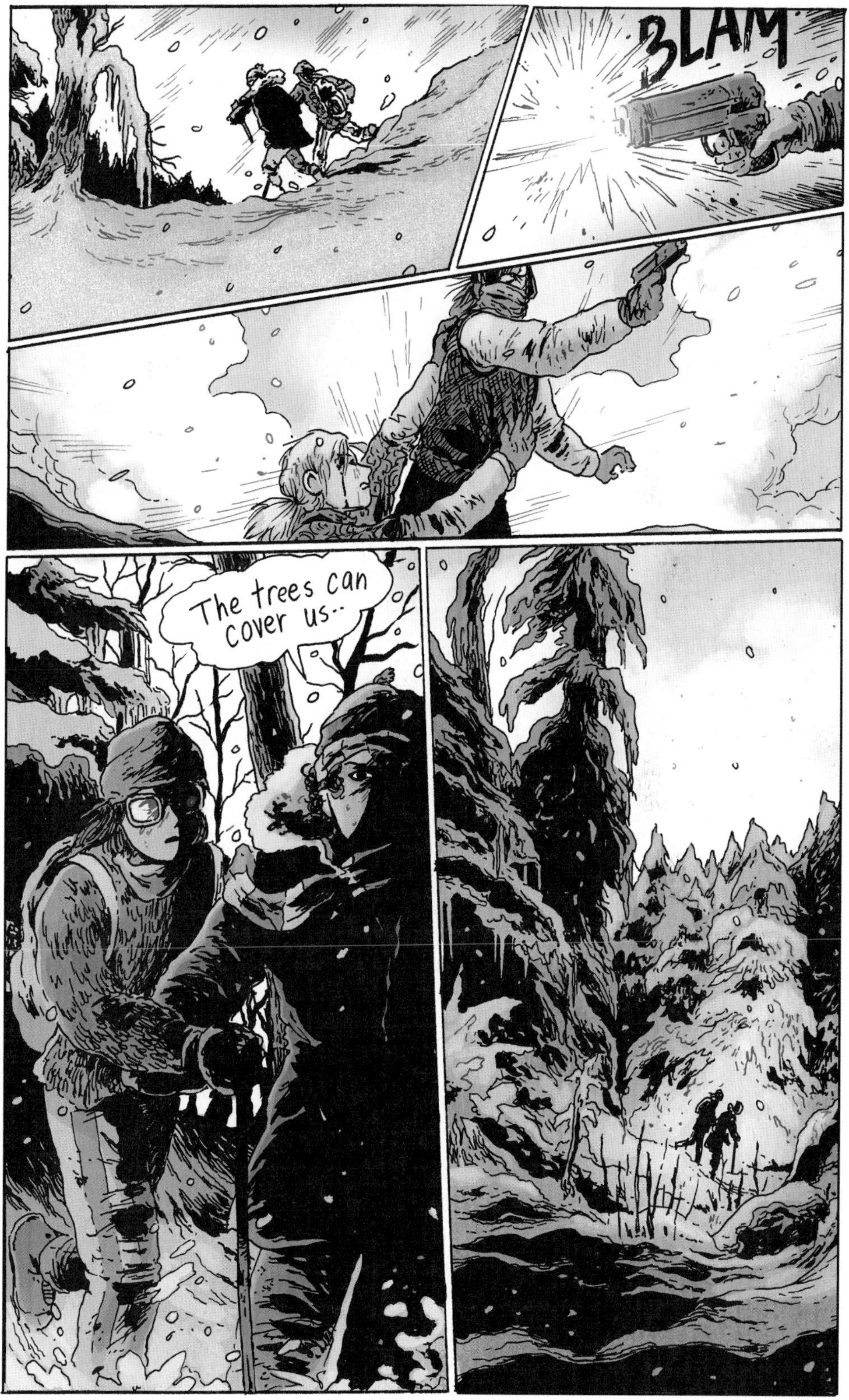
BLAM
The trees can cover us...

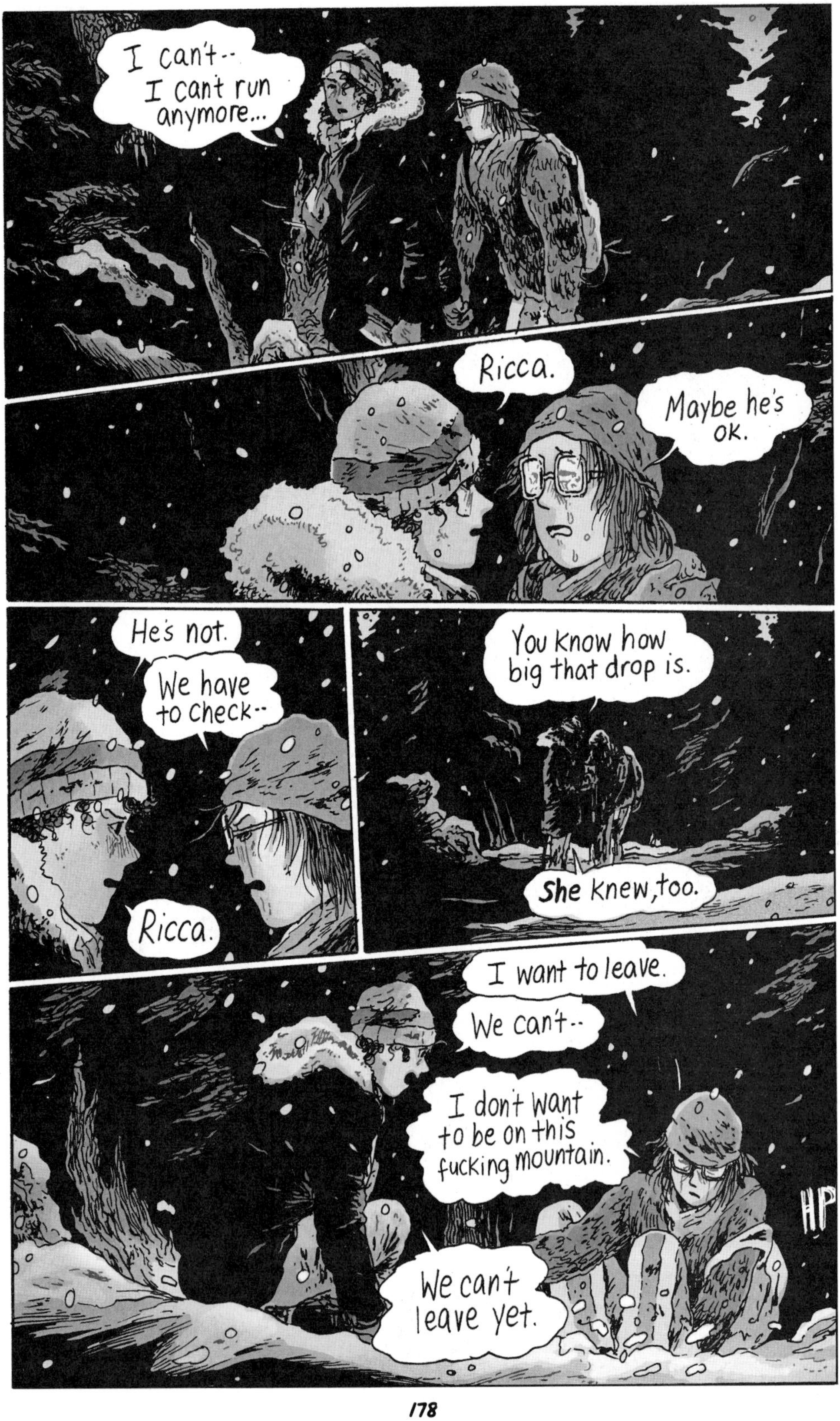
I can't-- I can't run anymore...
Ricca.
Maybe he's ok.
He's not.
We have to check--
Ricca.
You know how big that drop is.
She knew, too.
I want to leave.
We can't--
I don't want to be on this fucking mountain.
We can't leave yet.
HP

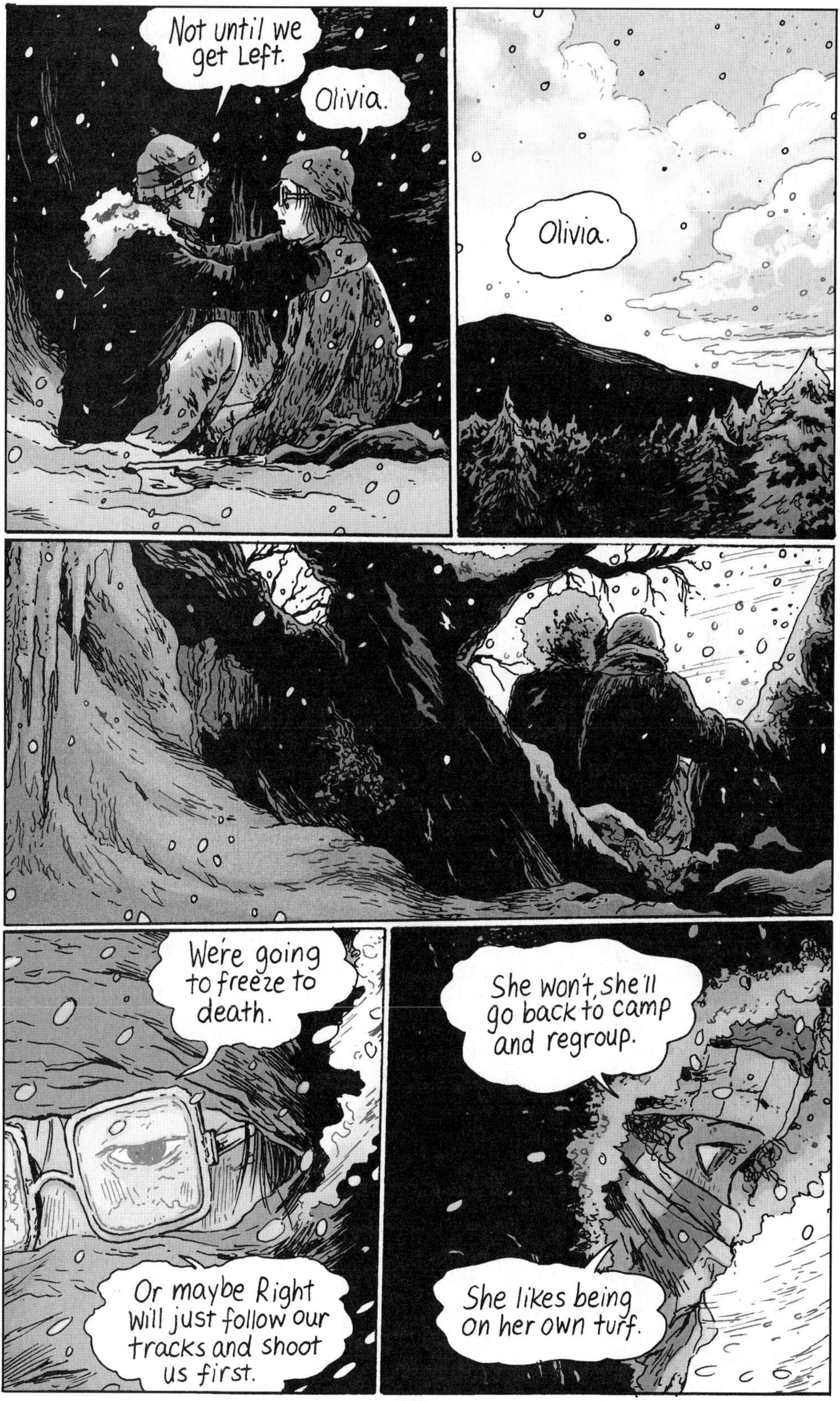
Not until we get Left.
Olivia.
Olivia.
We're going to freeze to death.
Or maybe Right will just follow our tracks and shoot us first.
She won't, she'll go back to camp and regroup.
She likes being on her own turf.

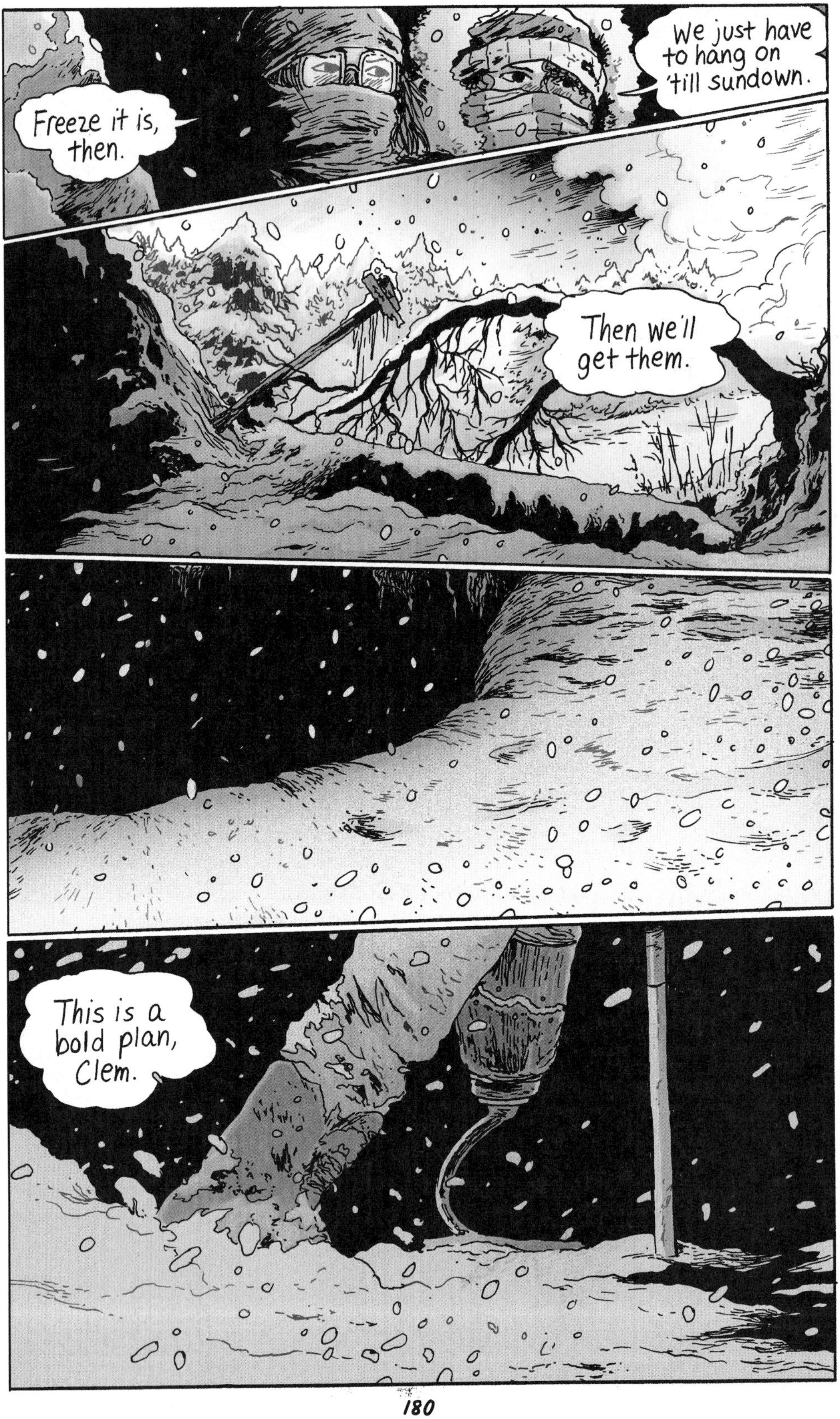
We just have to hang on 'till sundown.
Freeze it is, then.
Then we'll get them.
This is a bold plan, Clem.

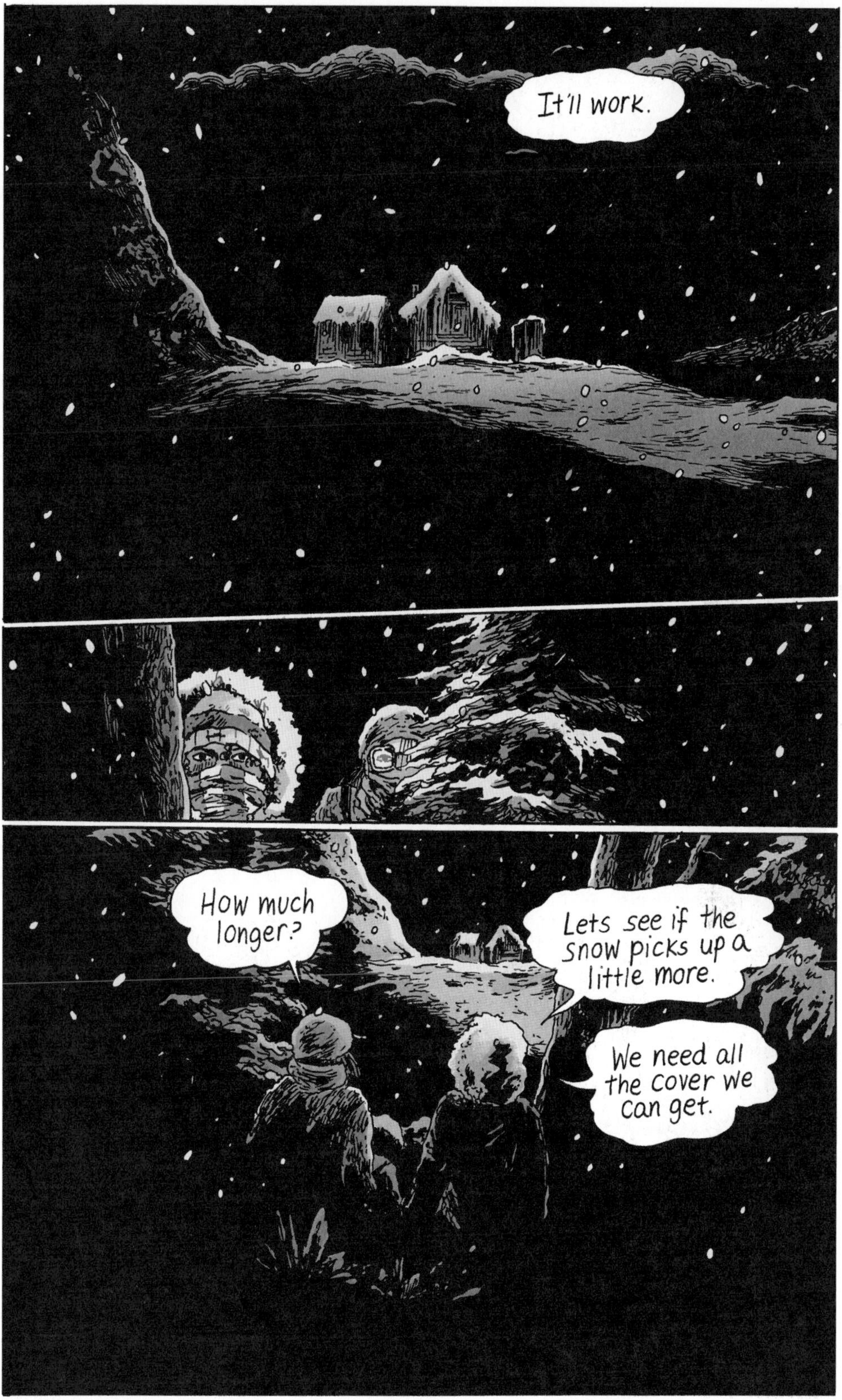
It'll work.
How much longer?
Lets see if the snow picks up a little more.
We need all the cover we can get.

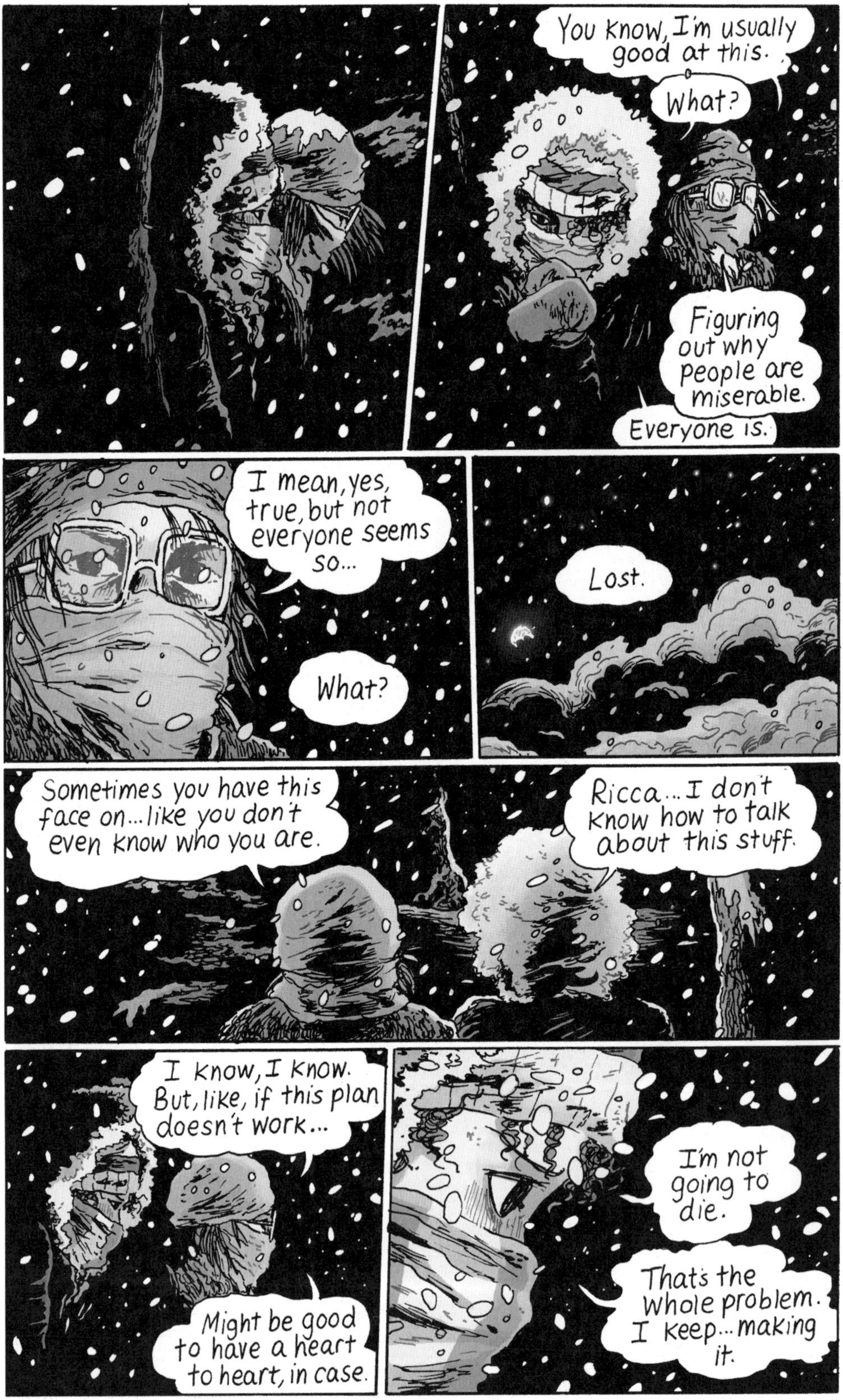

You know, I'm usually good at this.
What?
Figuring out why people are miserable.
Everyone is.
I mean, yes, true, but not everyone seems so...
What?
Lost.
Sometimes you have this face on... like you don't even know who you are.
Ricca... I don't know how to talk about this stuff.
I know, I know. But, like, if this plan doesn't work...
Might be good to have a heart to heart, in case.
I'm not going to die.
That's the whole problem. I keep... making it.

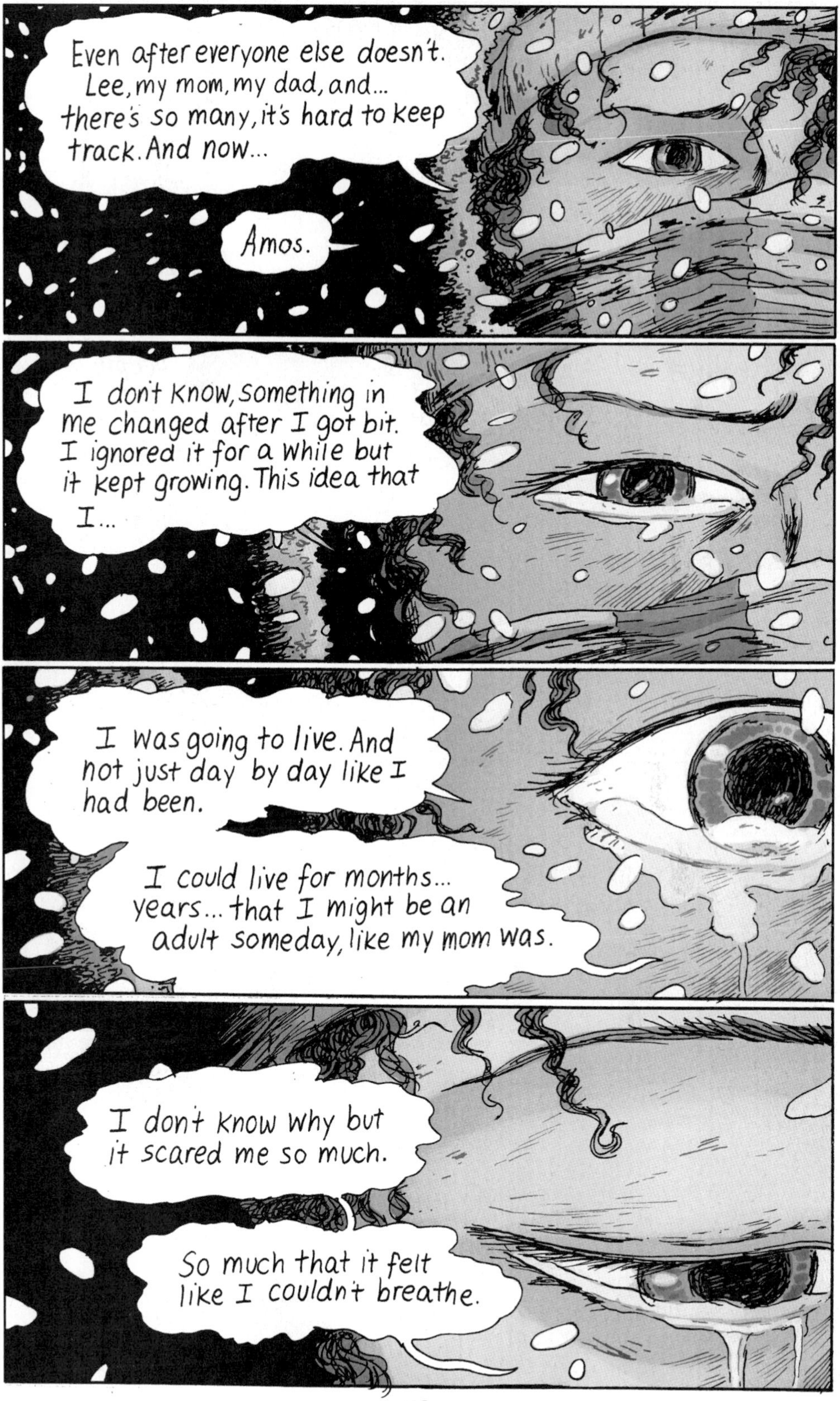
Even after everyone else doesn't. Lee, my mom, my dad, and... there's so many, it's hard to keep track. And now...
Amos.
I don't know, something in me changed after I got bit. I ignored it for a while but it kept growing. This idea that I...
I was going to live. And not just day by day like I had been.
I could live for months... years... that I might be an adult someday, like my mom was.
I don't know why but it scared me so much.
So much that it felt like I couldn't breathe.

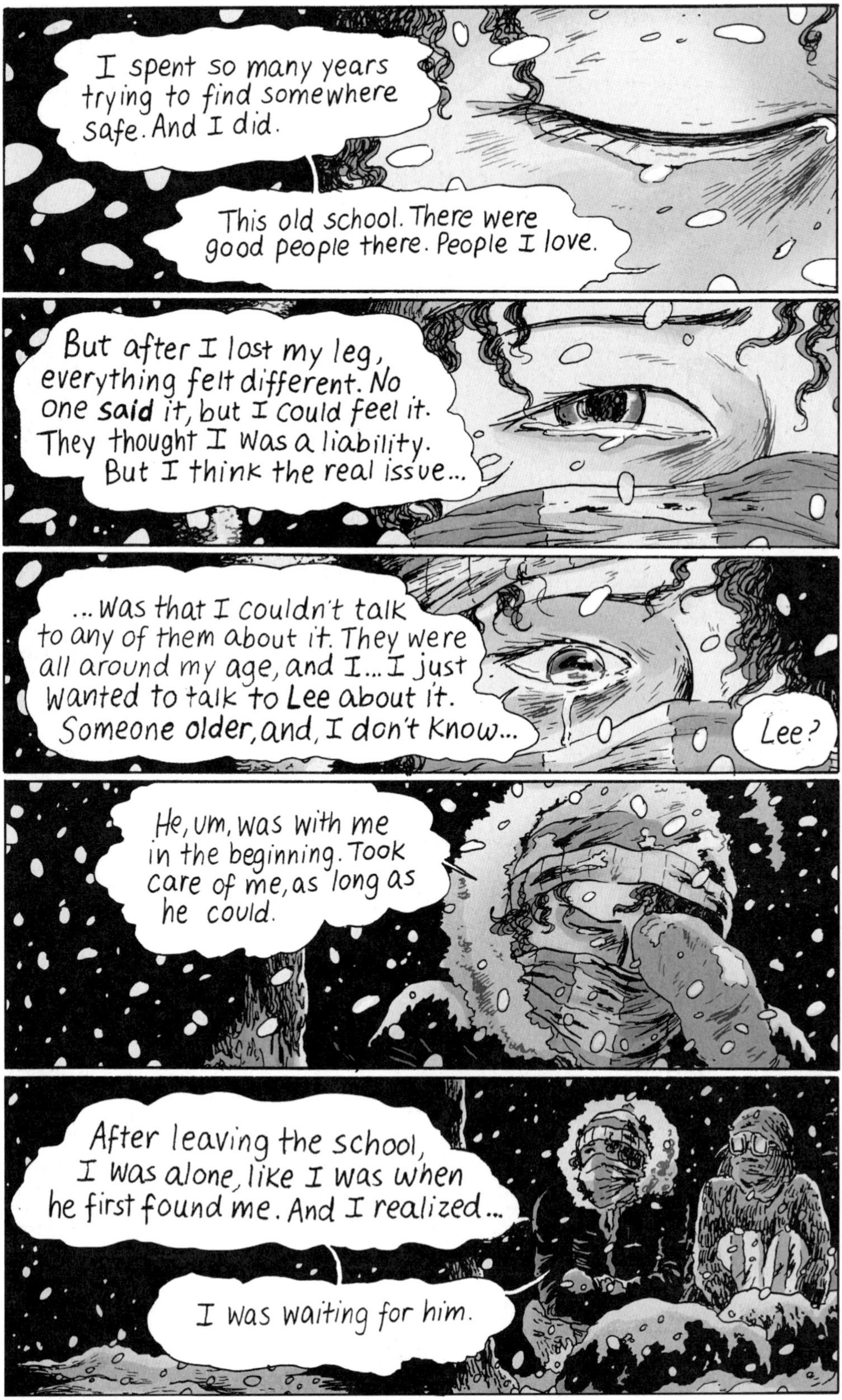
I spent so many years trying to find somewhere safe. And I did.
This old school. There were good people there. People I love.
But after I lost my leg, everything felt different. No one **said** it, but I could feel it. They thought I was a liability. But I think the real issue...
...was that I couldn't talk to any of them about it. They were all around my age, and I... I just wanted to talk to **Lee** about it. Someone **older**, and, I don't know...
Lee?
He, um, was with me in the beginning. Took care of me, as long as he could.
After leaving the school, I was alone, like I was when he first found me. And I realized...
I was waiting for him.

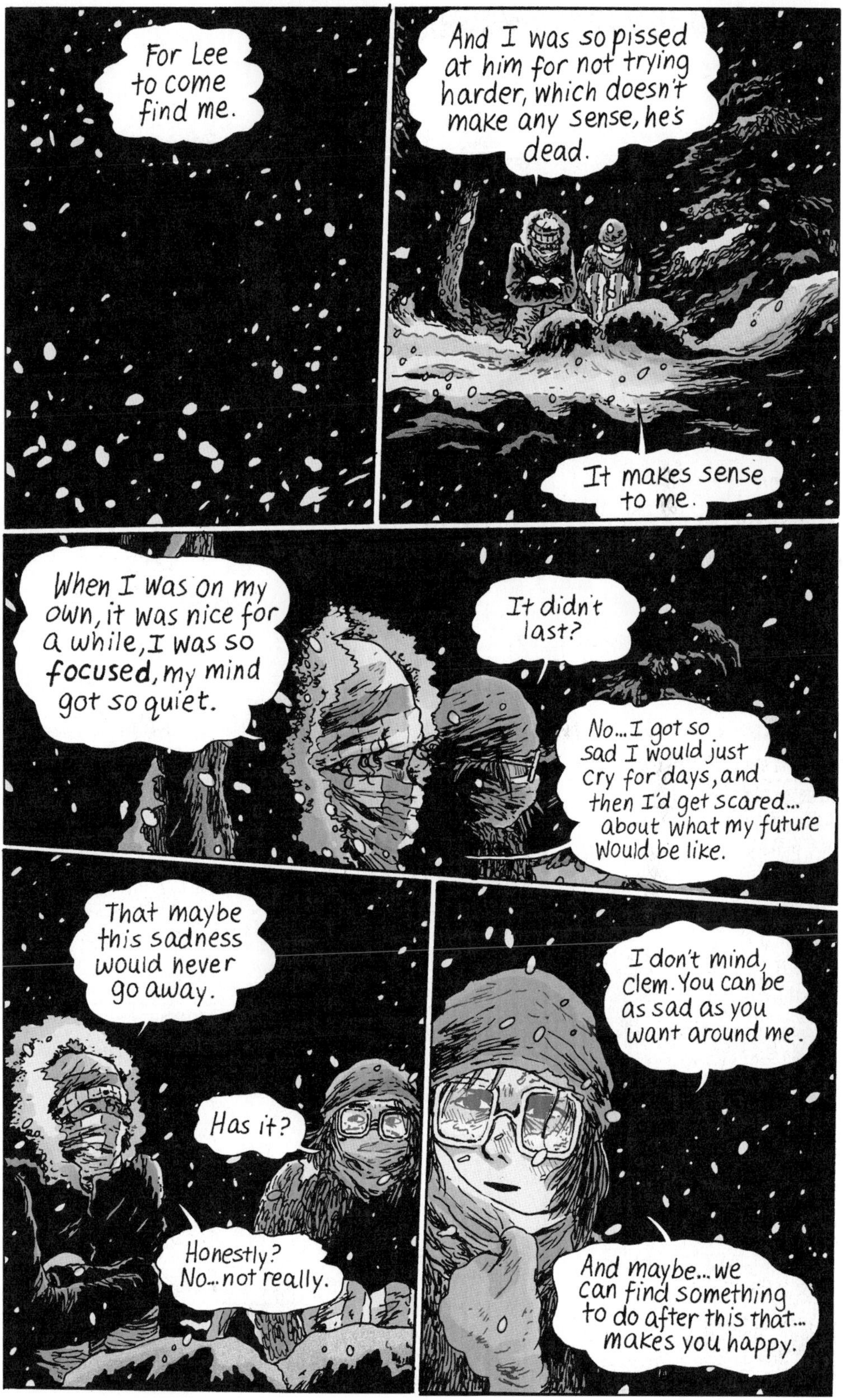
For Lee to come find me.
And I was so pissed at him for not trying harder, which doesn't make any sense, he's dead.
It makes sense to me.
When I was on my own, it was nice for a while, I was so **focused**, my mind got so quiet.
It didn't last?
No... I got so sad I would just cry for days, and then I'd get scared... about what my future would be like.
That maybe this sadness would never go away.
Has it?
Honestly? No... not really.
I don't mind, Clem. You can be as sad as you want around me.
And maybe... we can find something to do after this that... makes you happy.

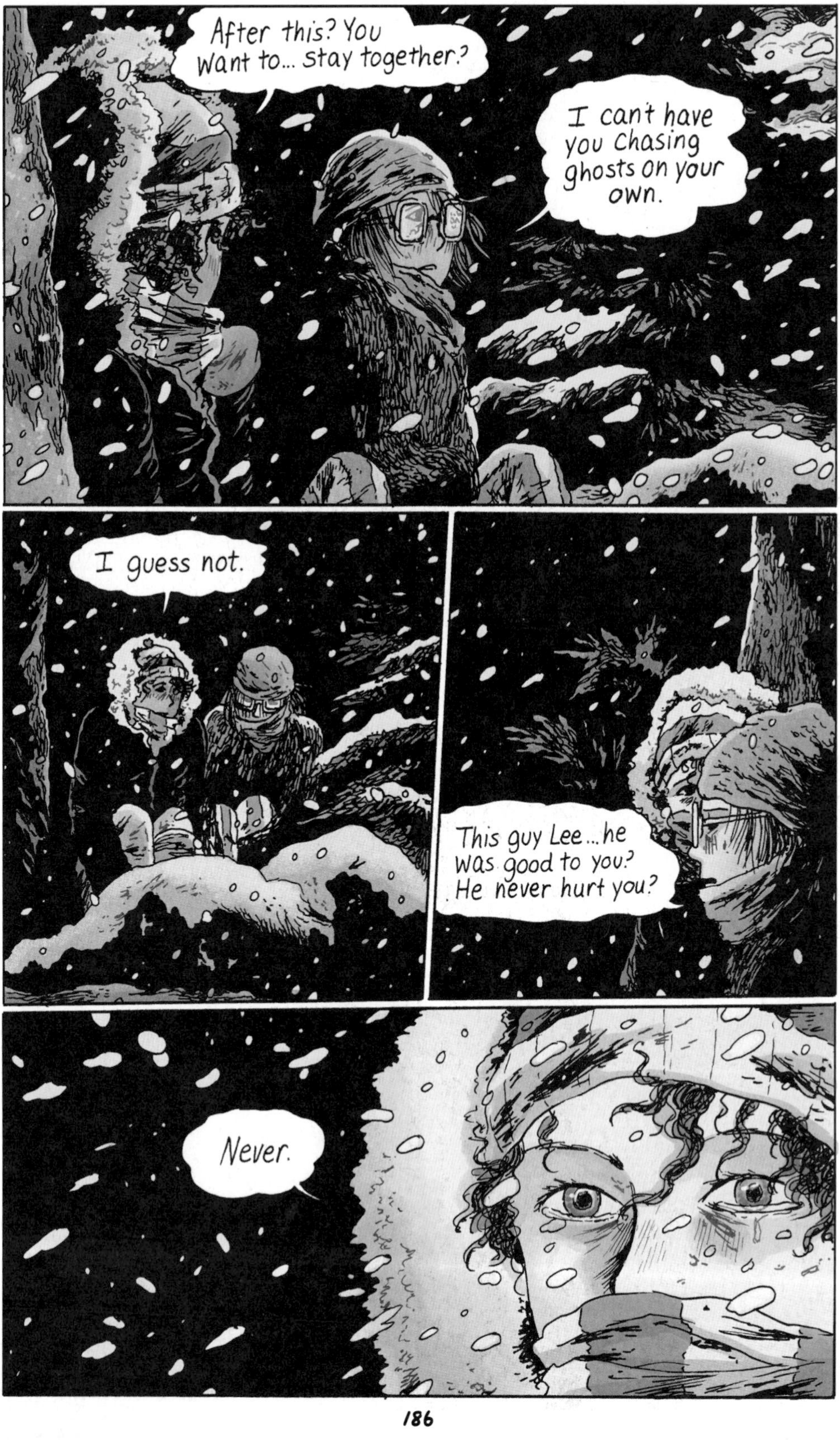
After this? You want to... stay together?
I can't have you chasing ghosts on your own.
I guess not.
This guy Lee... he was good to you? He never hurt you?
Never.

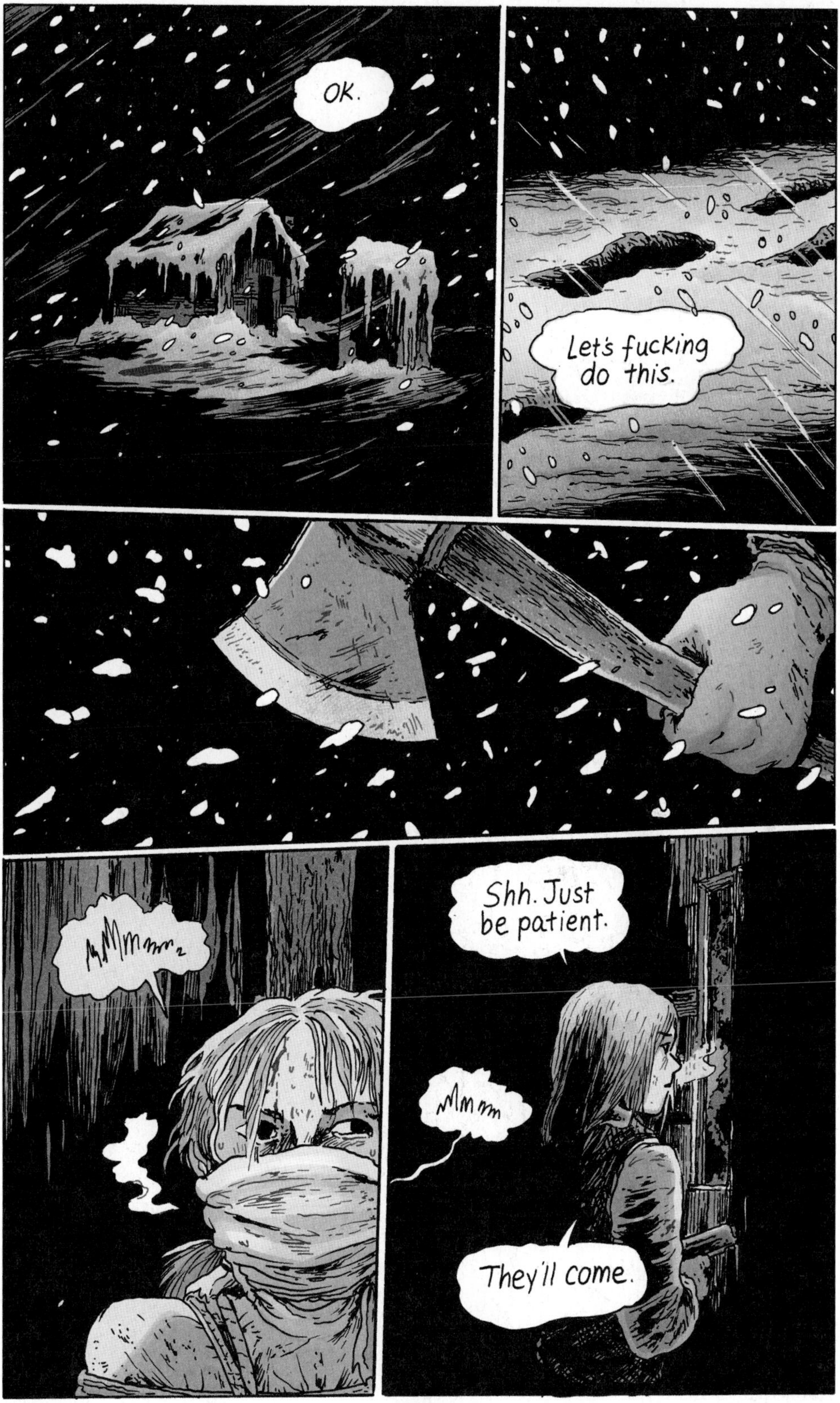
OK.
Let's fucking do this.
MMmmm
Shh. Just be patient.
Mmm
They'll come.

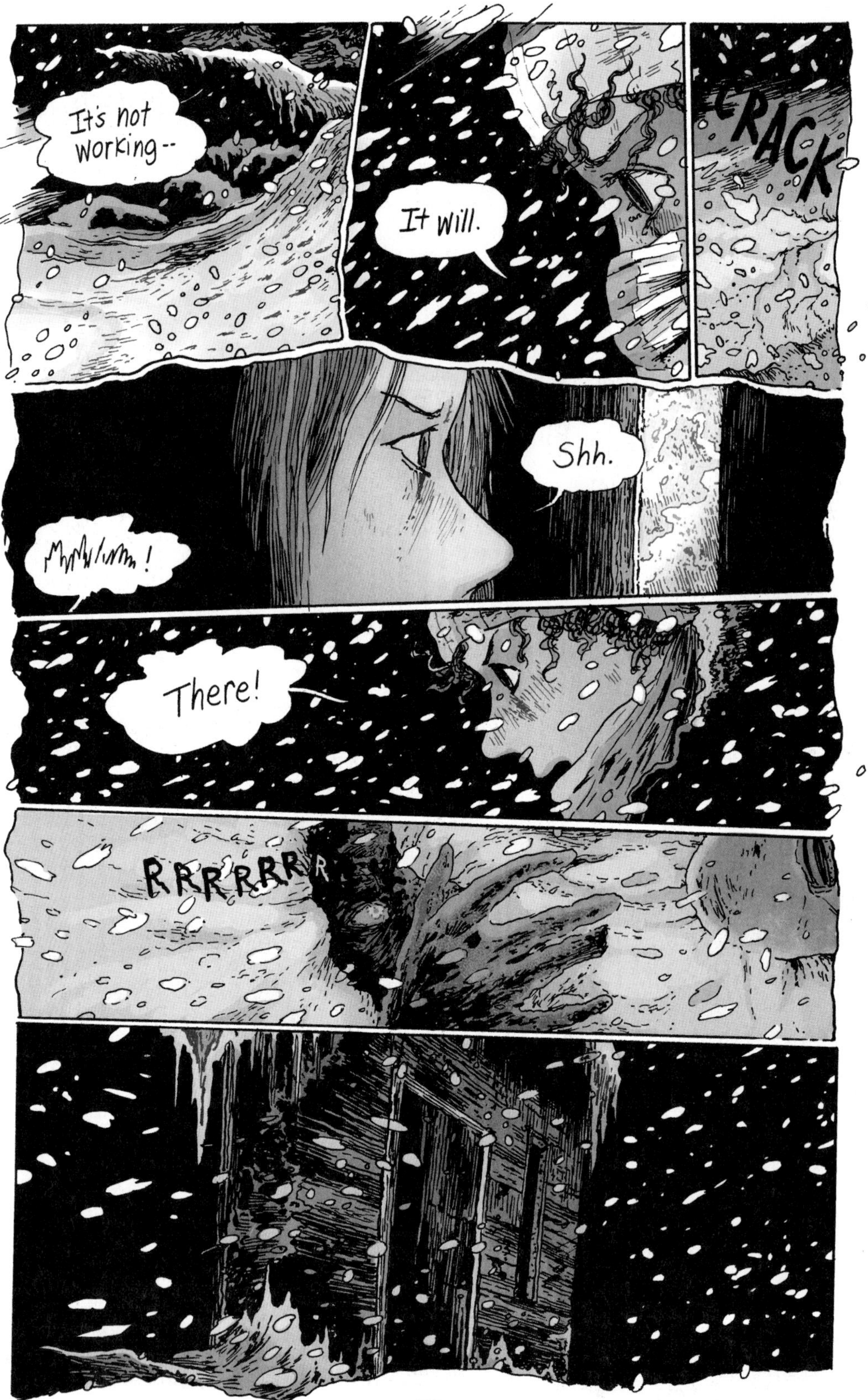
It's not working--
It will.
CRACK
Shh.
Mmm!
There!
RRRRRRR

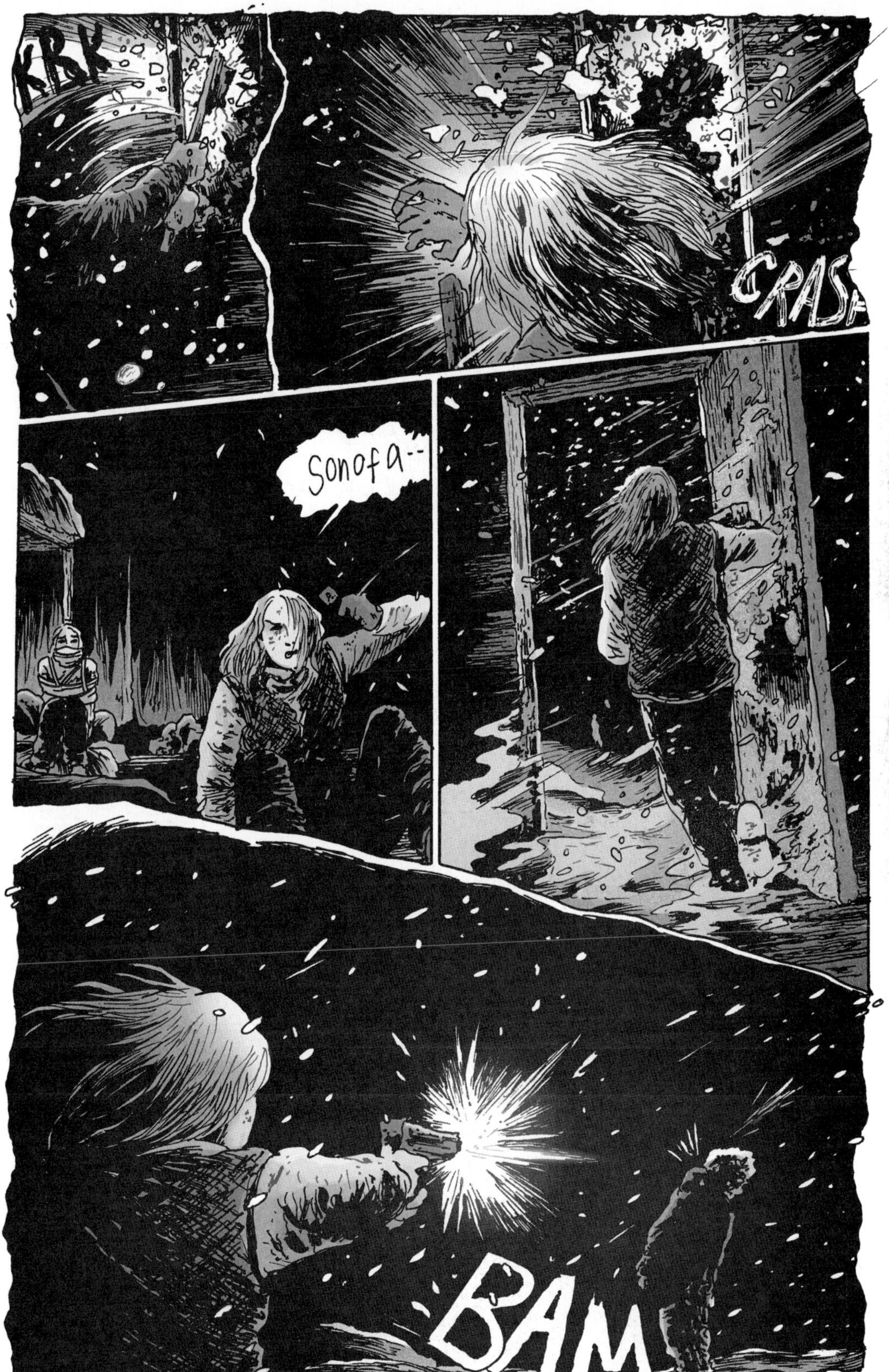
KRAK
CRASH
Sonofa--
BAM

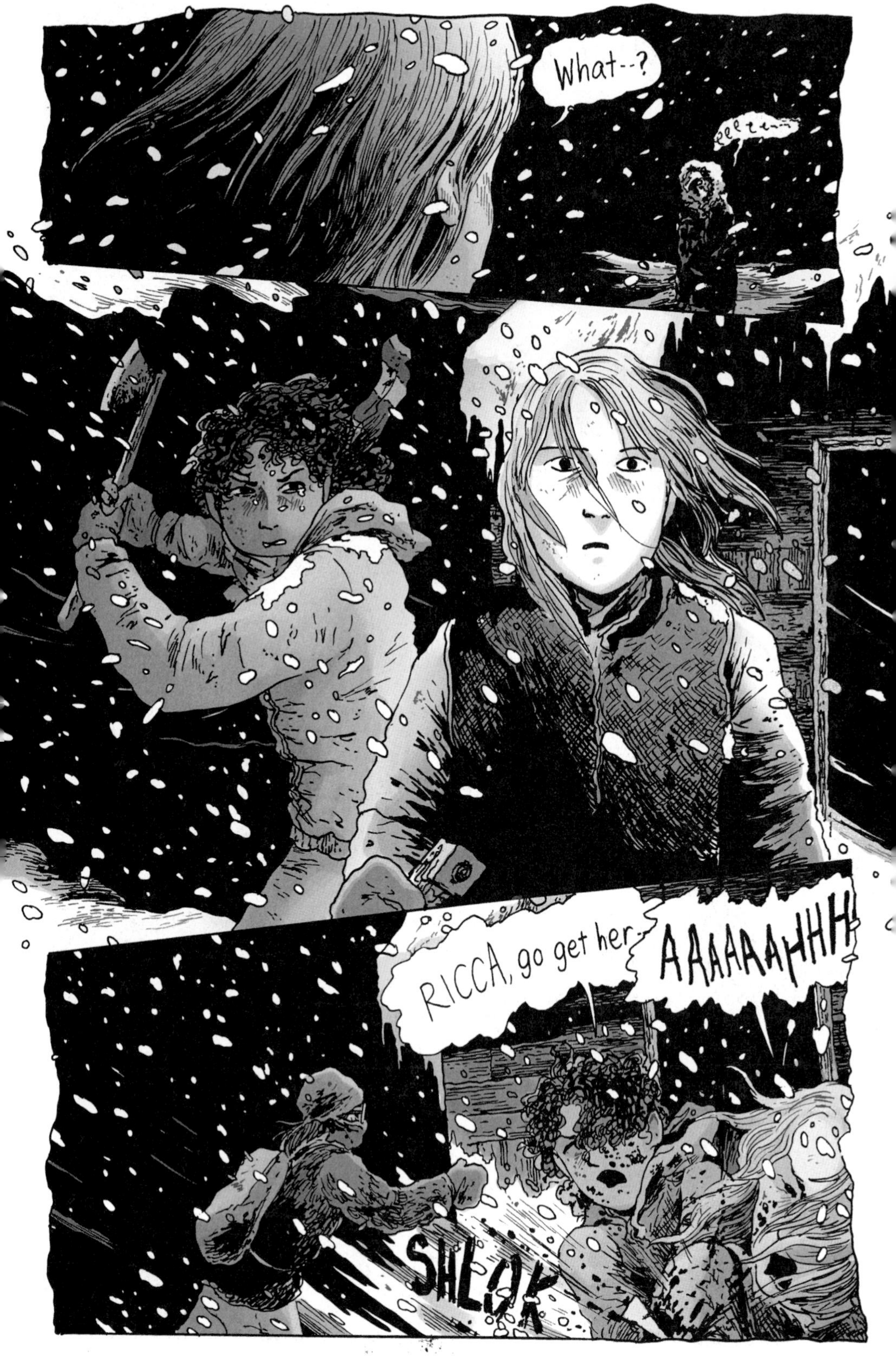
What--?
RICCA, go get her--
AAAAAHHH
SHLOK

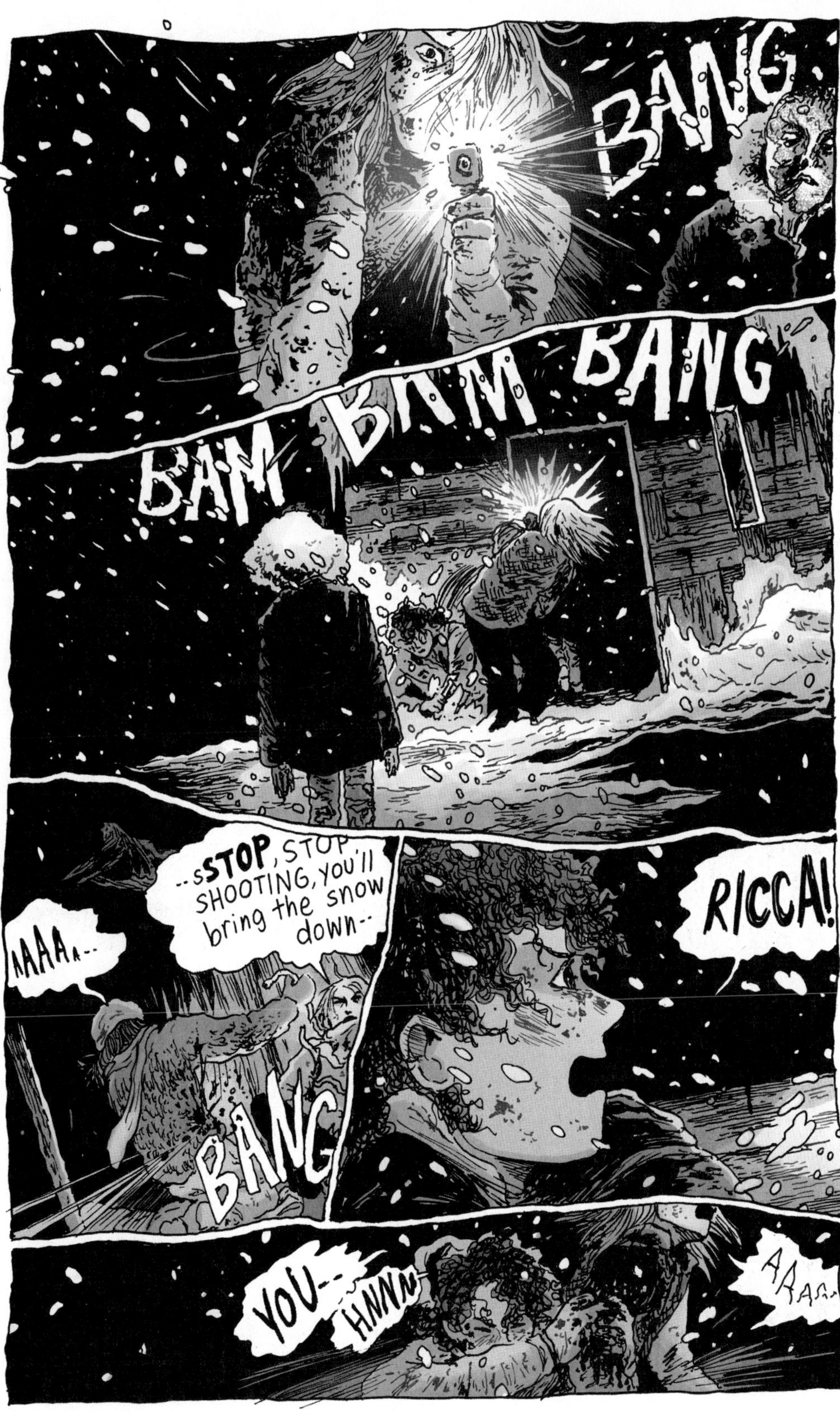
BANG
BAM BRM BANG
--sSTOP, STOP SHOOTING, you'll bring the snow down--
AAAA--
BANG
RICCA!
YOU--
HNNN
AAAA--

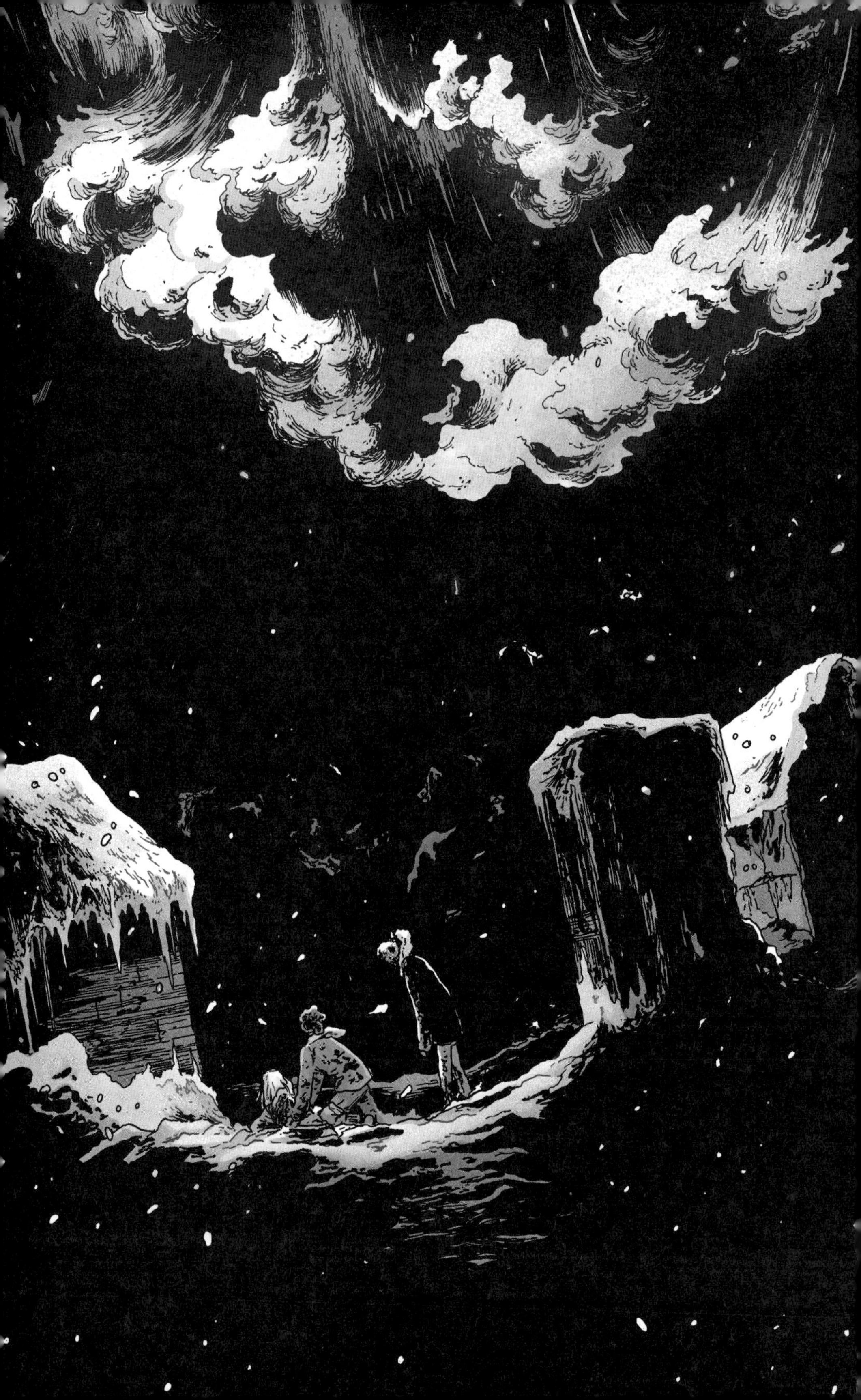

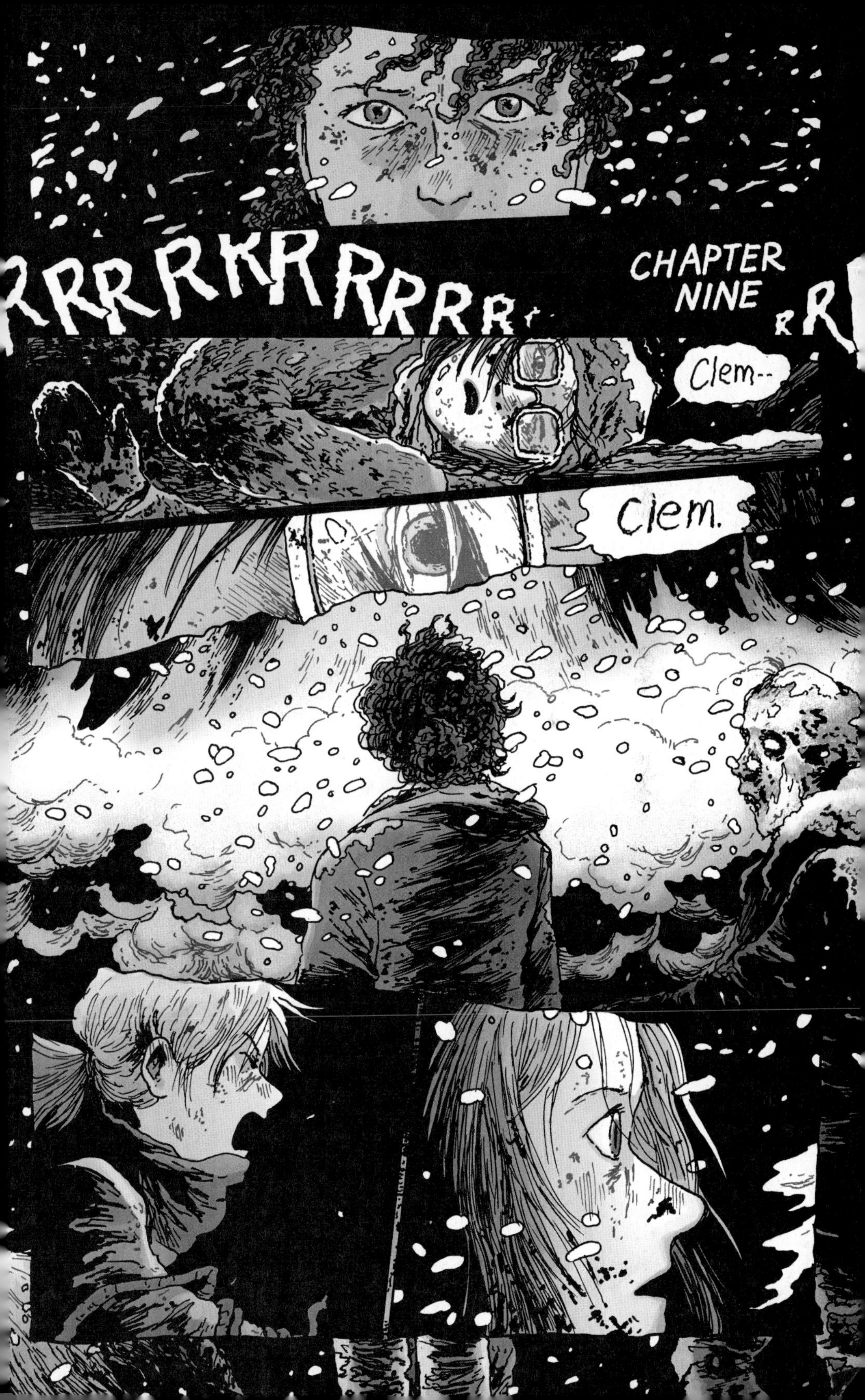
RRRRKRRRRRR
CHAPTER NINE
RR
Clem--
Clem.

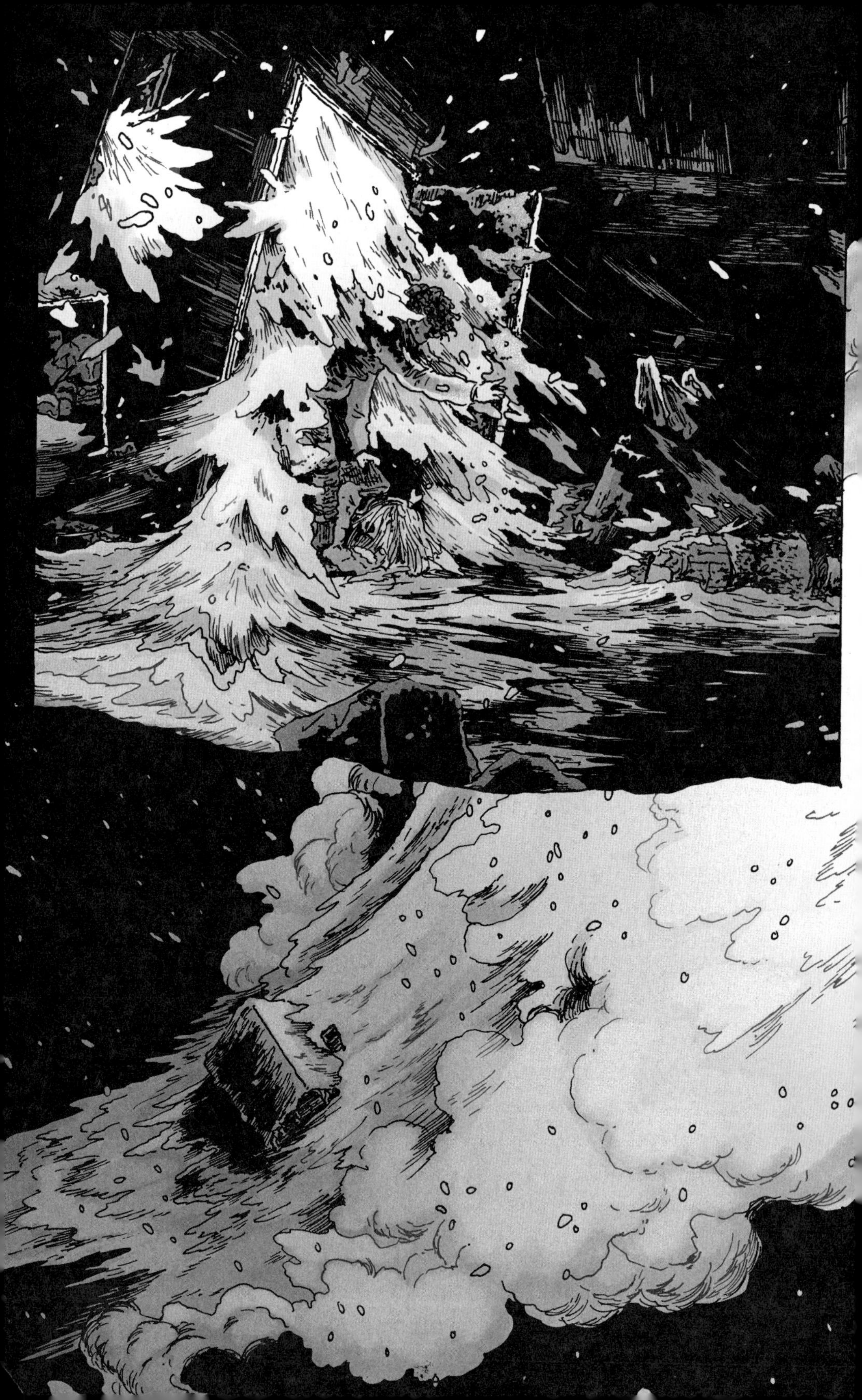

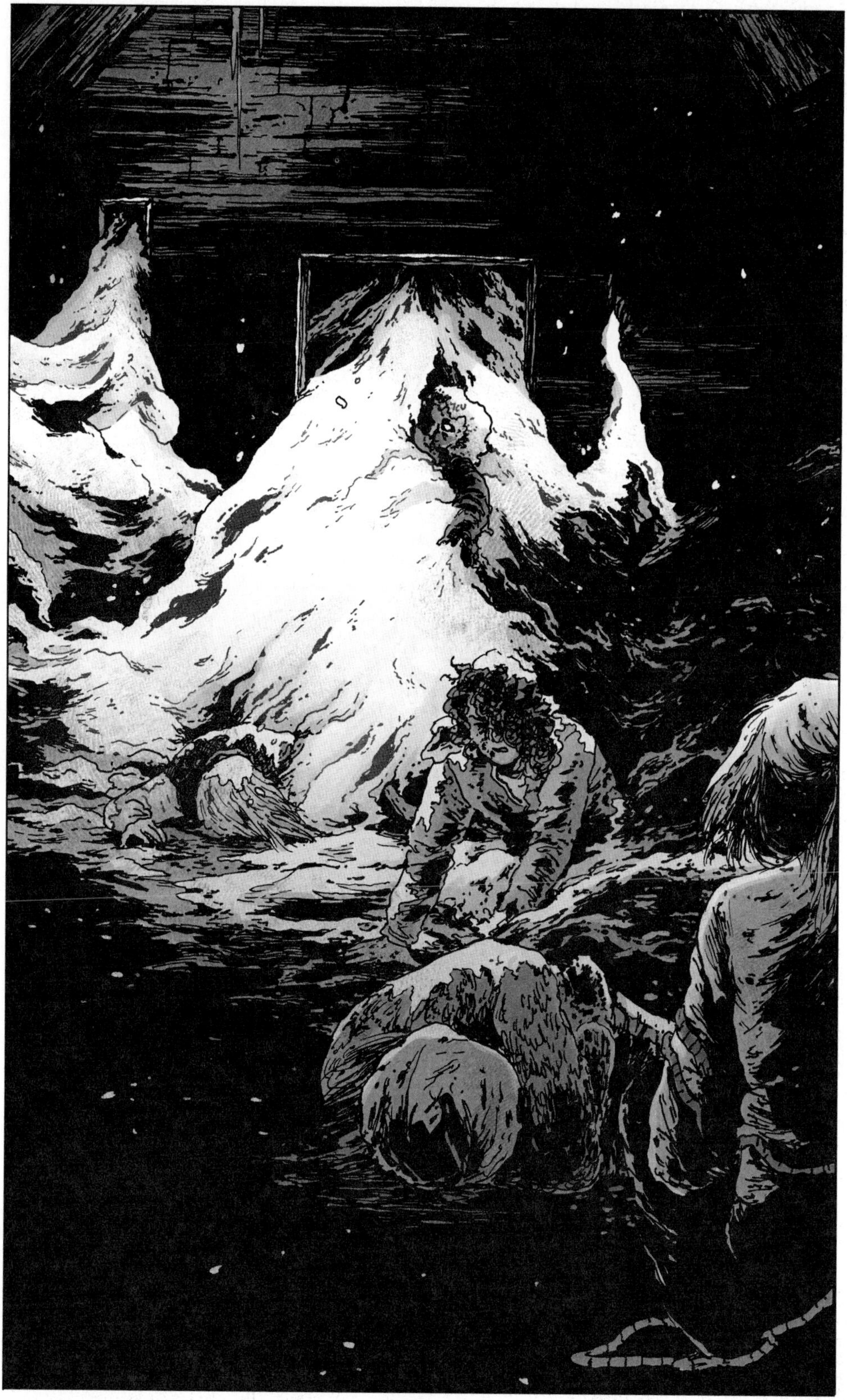

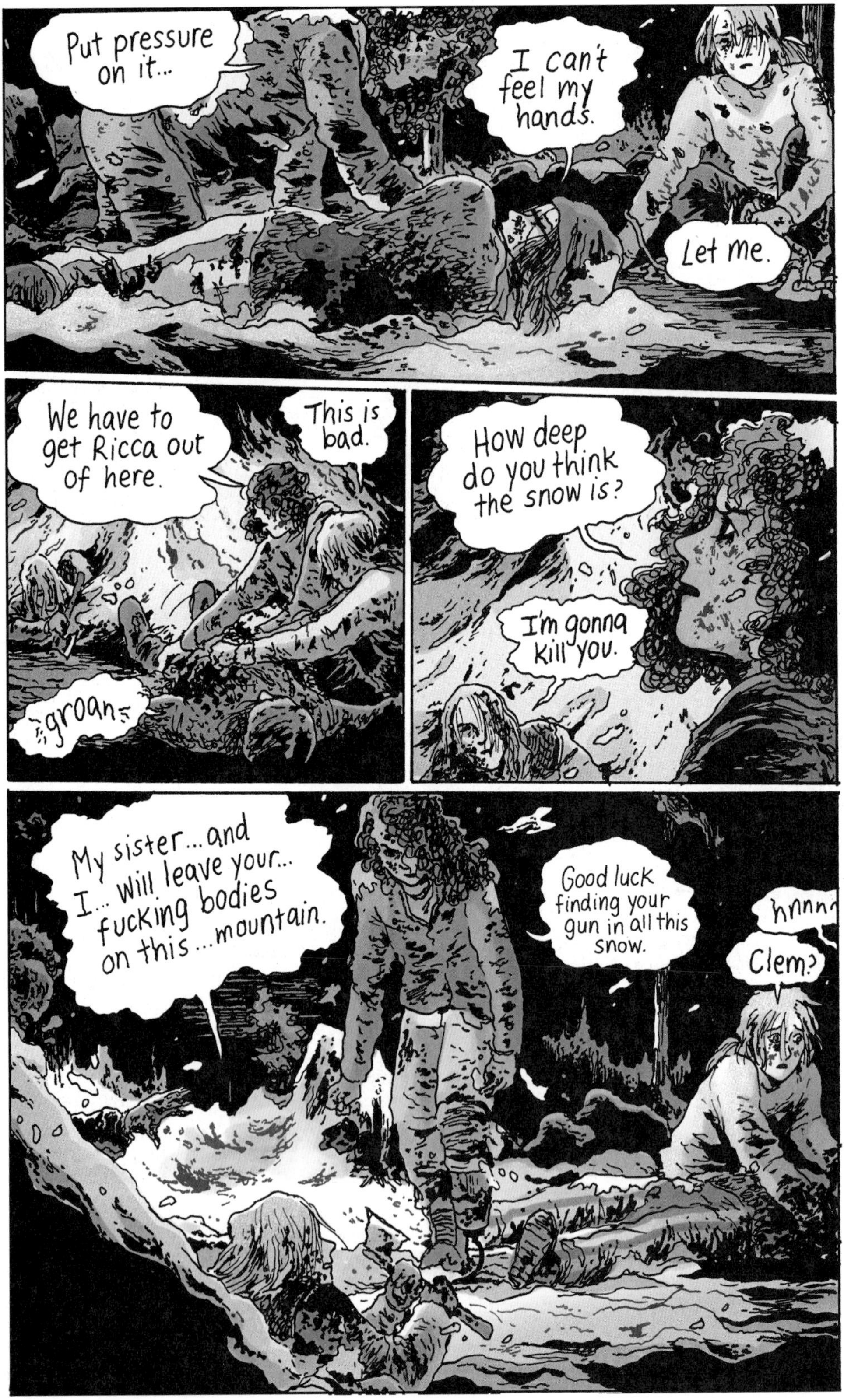
Put pressure on it...
I can't feel my hands.
Let me.
We have to get Ricca out of here.
This is bad.
groan
How deep do you think the snow is?
I'm gonna kill you.
My sister...and I... will leave your... fucking bodies on this...mountain.
Good luck finding your gun in all this snow.
hnnn
Clem?

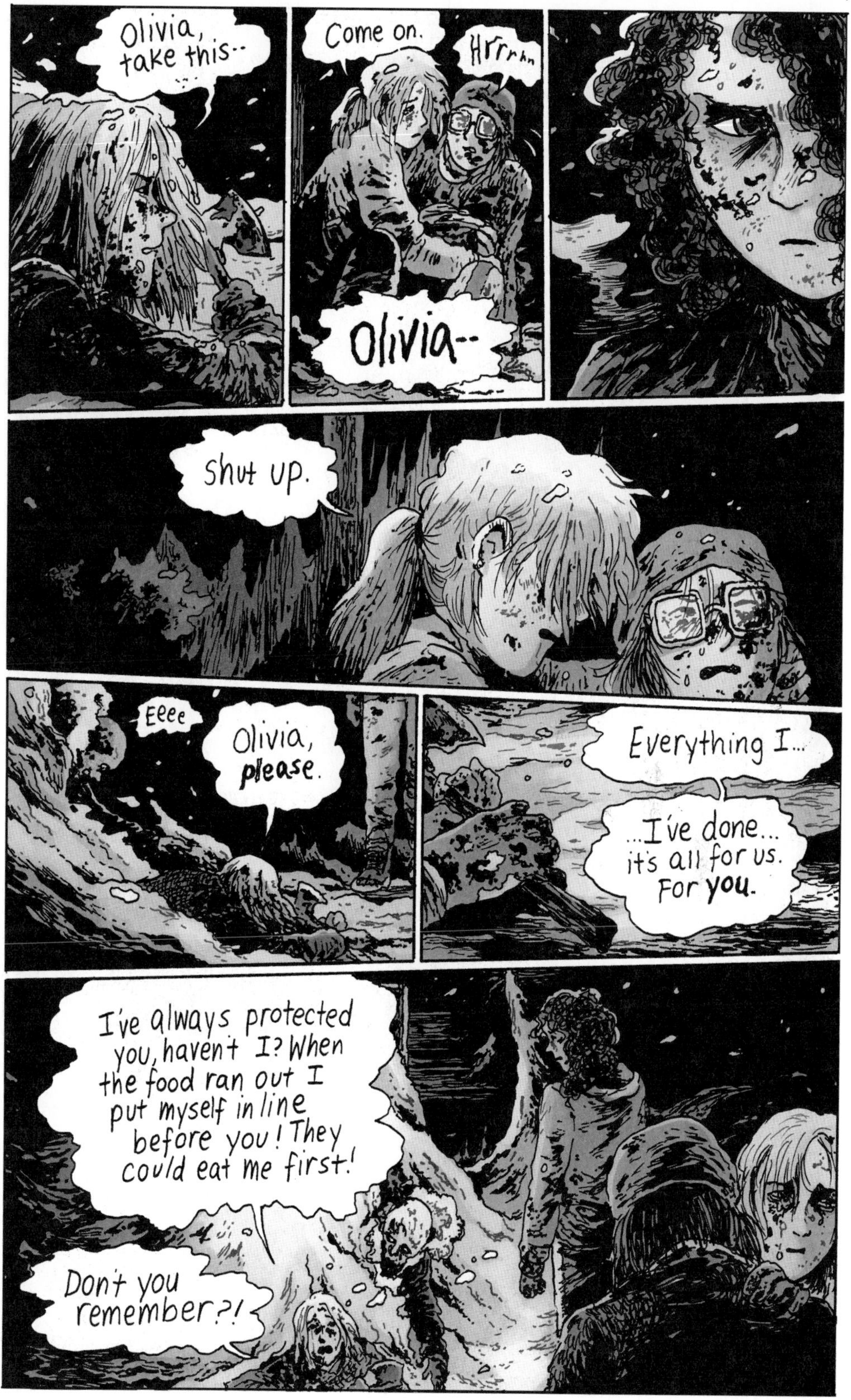
Olivia, take this..
Come on.
Hrrrnn
Olivia--
Shut up.
Eeee
Olivia, please.
Everything I...
...I've done... it's all for us. For you.
I've always protected you, haven't I? When the food ran out I put myself in line before you! They could eat me first!
Don't you remember?!

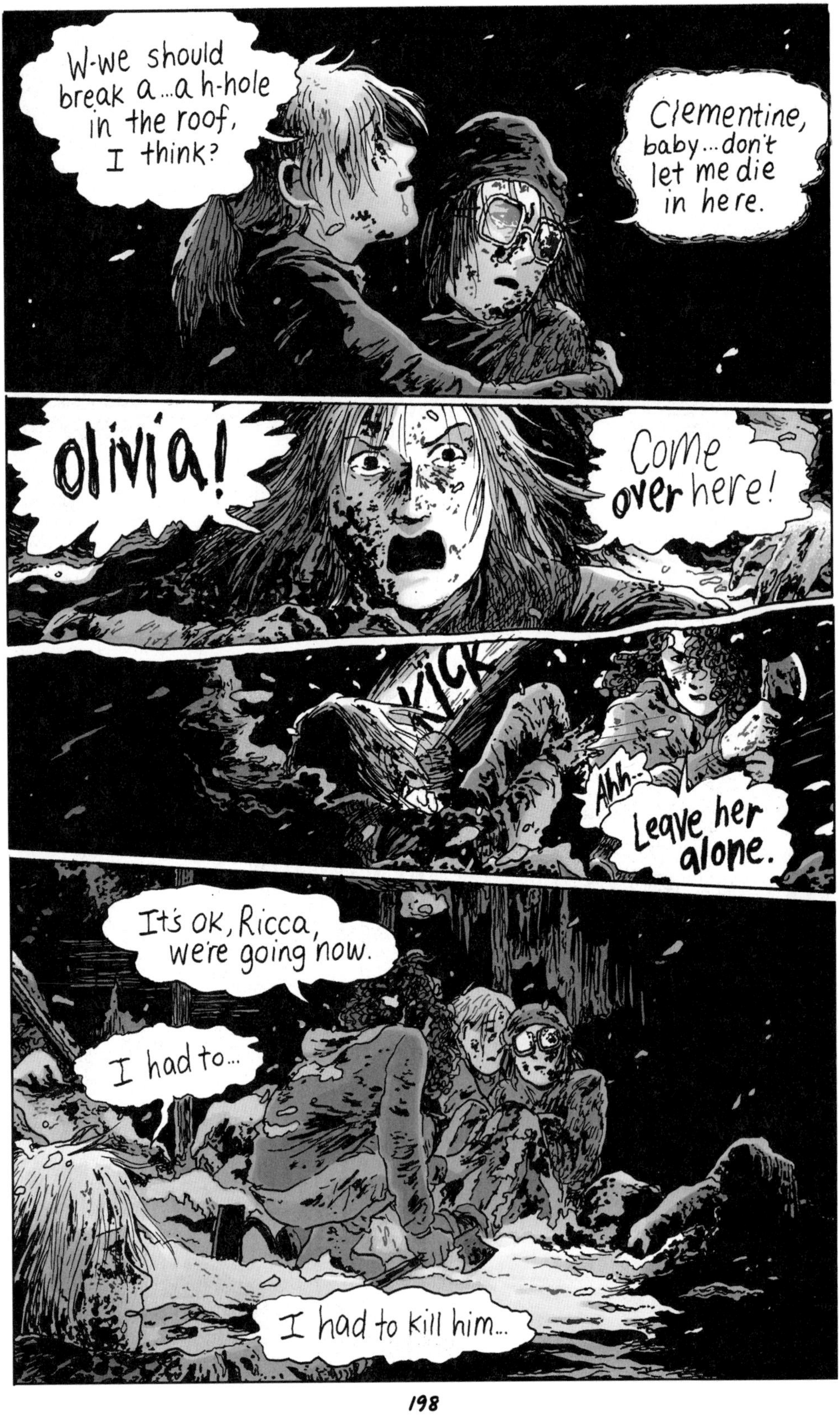
W-we should break a...a h-hole in the roof, I think?
Clementine, baby...don't let me die in here.
Olivia!
Come over here!
KICK
Ahh--
Leave her alone.
It's OK, Ricca, we're going now.
I had to...
I had to kill him...

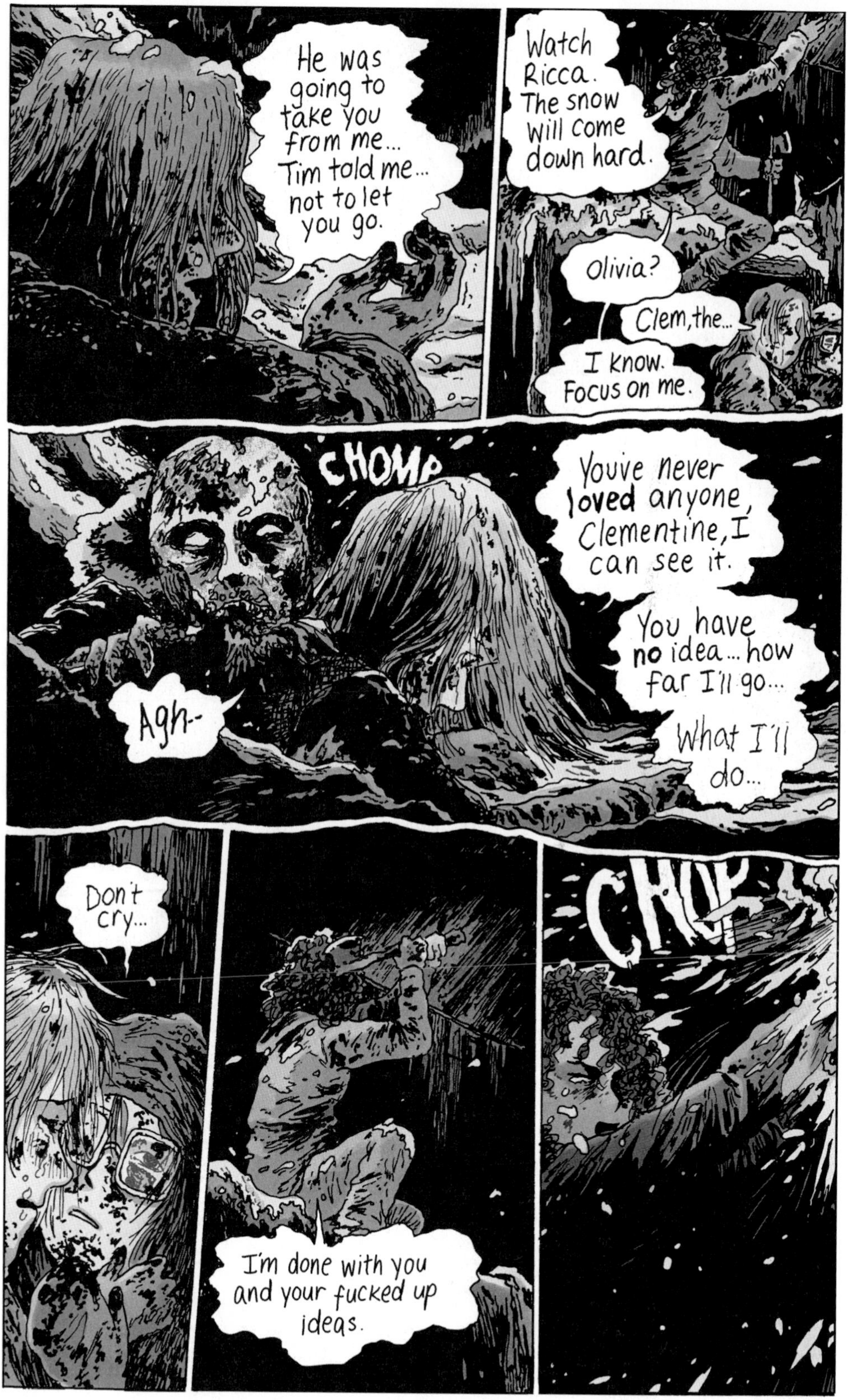
He was going to take you from me... Tim told me... not to let you go.
Watch Ricca. The snow will come down hard.
Olivia?
Clem, the...
I know. Focus on me.
CHOMP
You've never **loved** anyone, Clementine, I can see it.
Agh-
You have **no** idea... how far I'll go...
What I'll do...
Don't cry...
I'm done with you and your fucked up ideas.

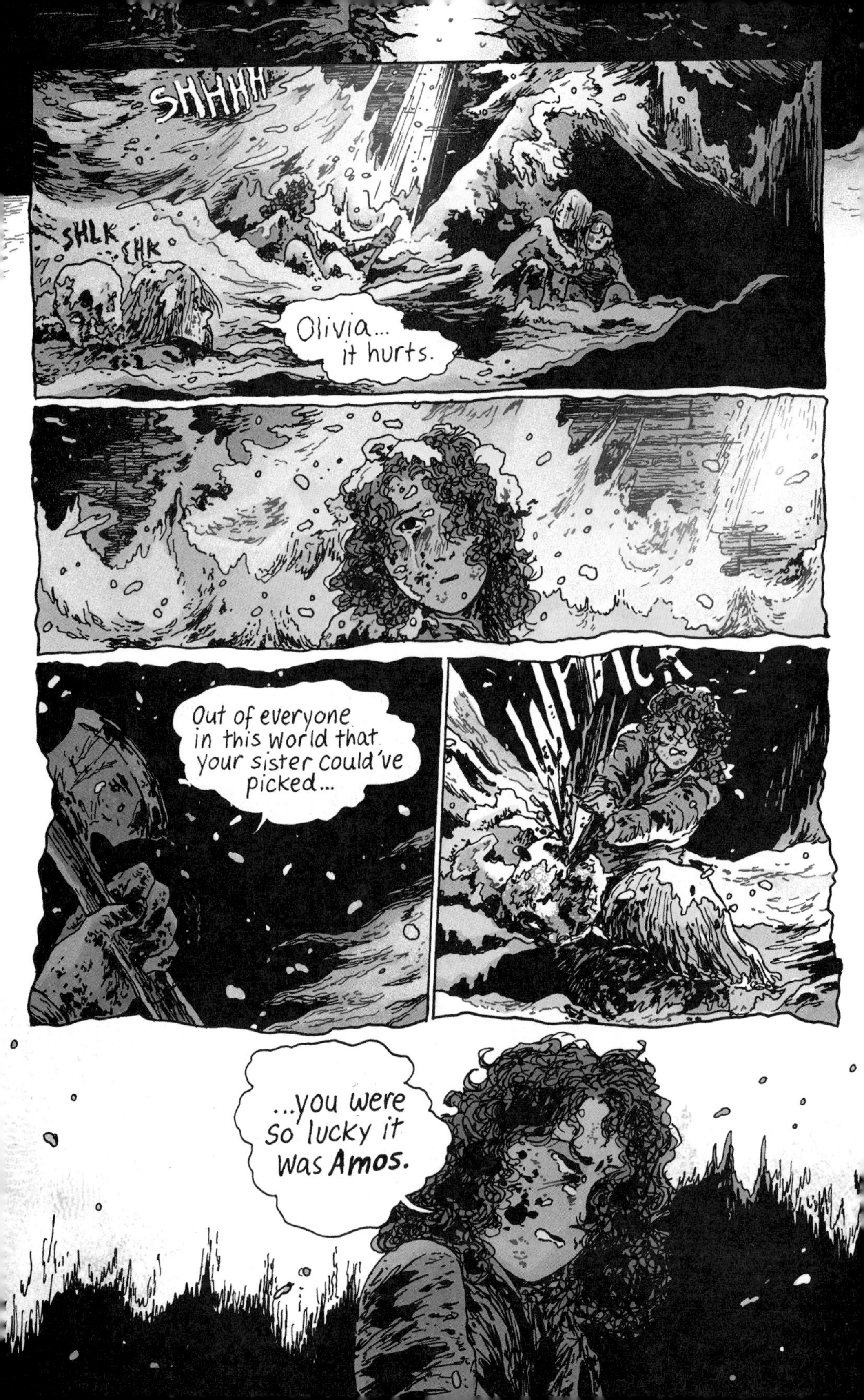
SHHHH
SHLK
CHK
Olivia... it hurts.
Out of everyone in this world that your sister could've picked...
...you were so lucky it was **Amos.**

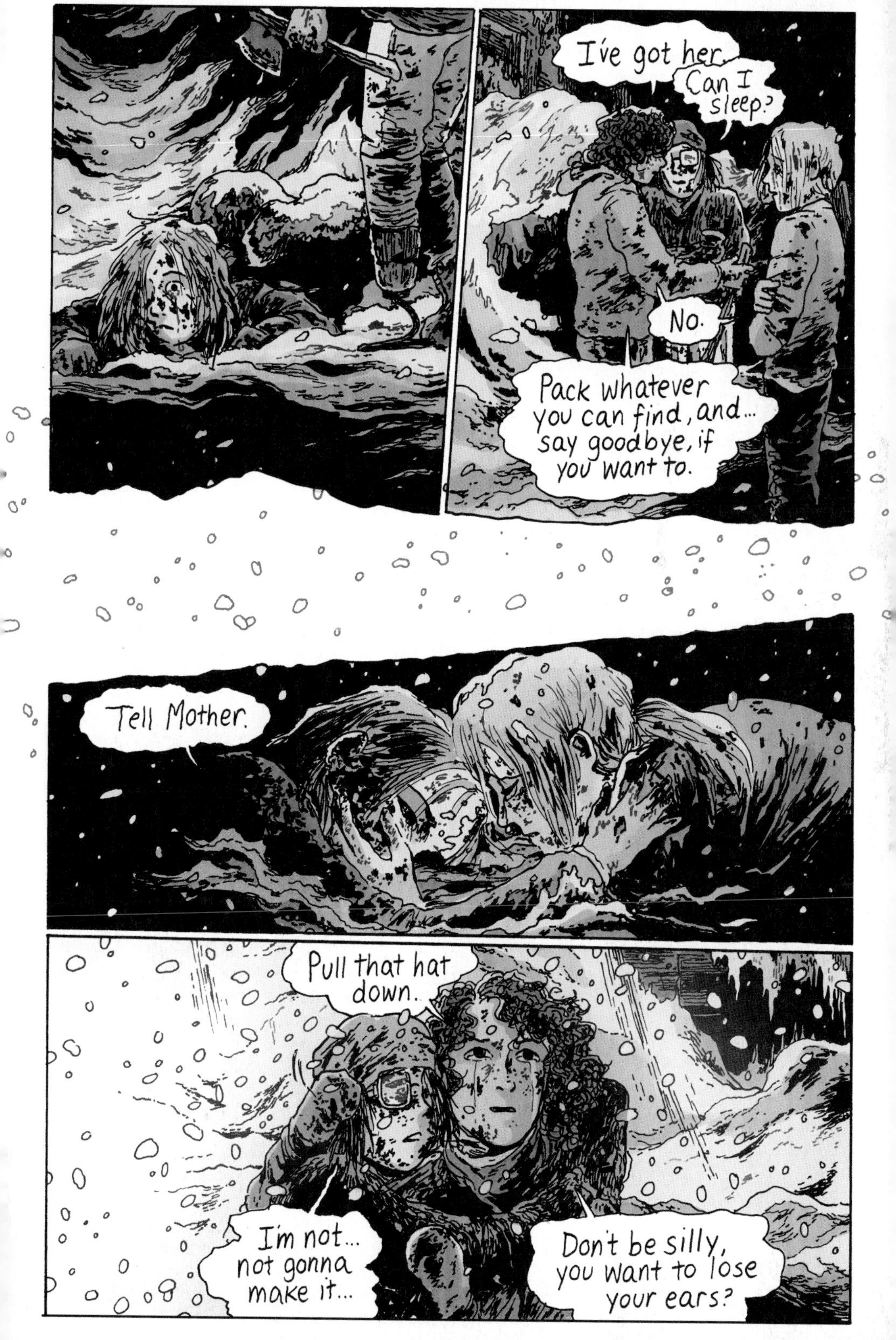
I've got her.
Can I sleep?
No.
Pack whatever you can find, and... say goodbye, if you want to.
Tell Mother.
Pull that hat down.
I'm not... not gonna make it...
Don't be silly, you want to lose your ears?

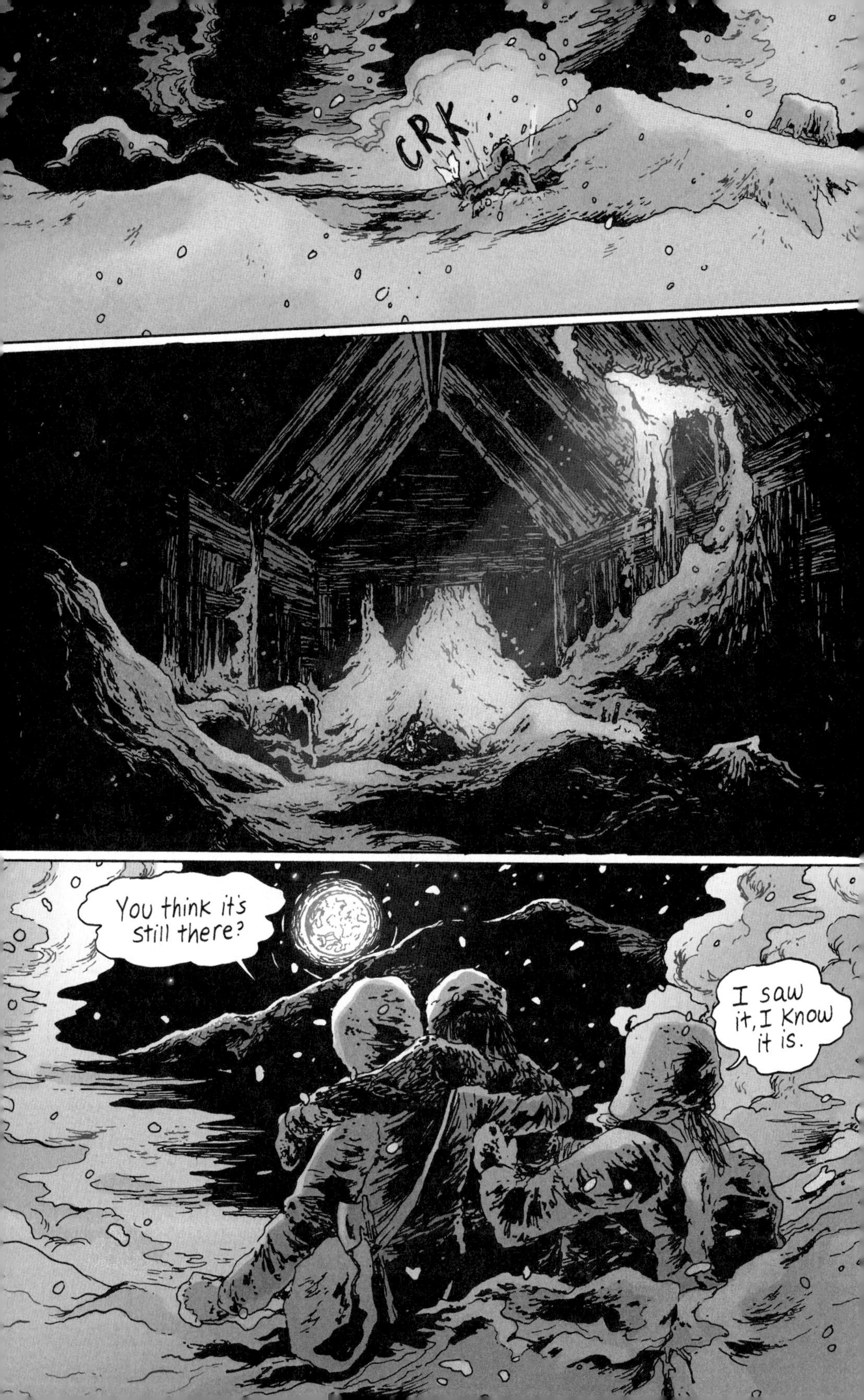
CRK
You think it's still there?
I saw it, I know it is.

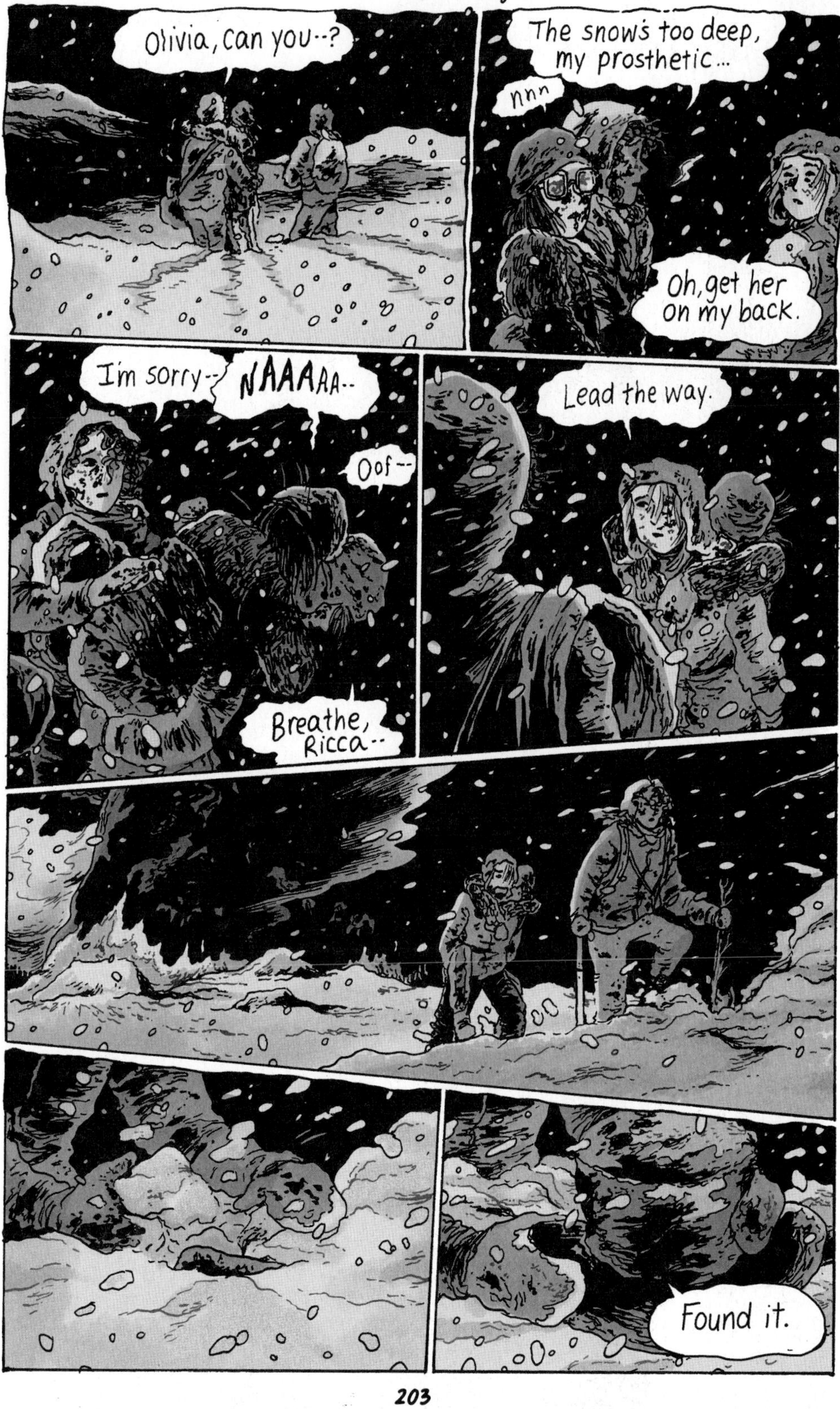
Olivia, can you--?
The snow's too deep, my prosthetic...
nnn
Oh, get her on my back.
I'm sorry--
NAAAAA--
Oof--
Breathe, Ricca--
Lead the way.
Found it.

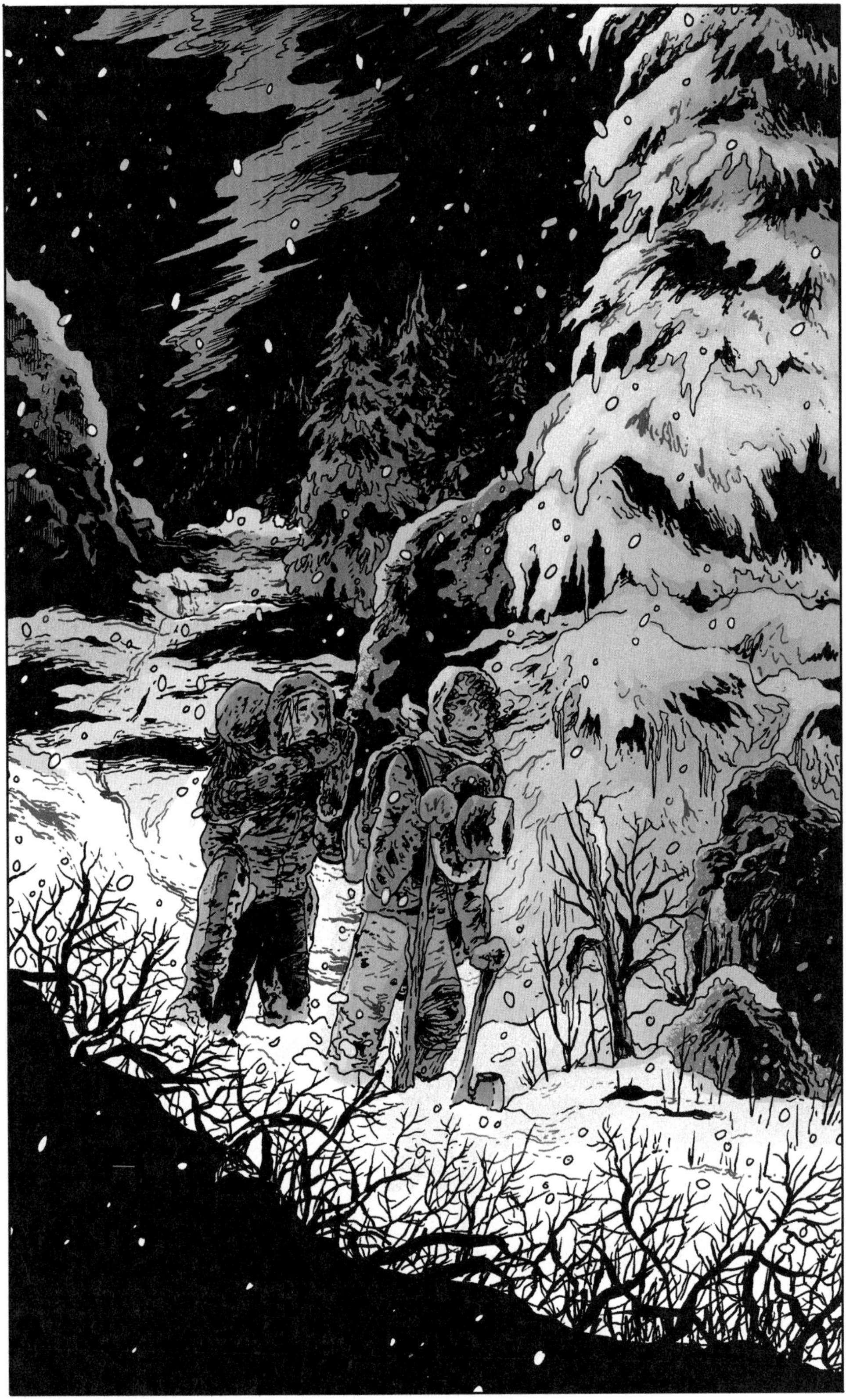

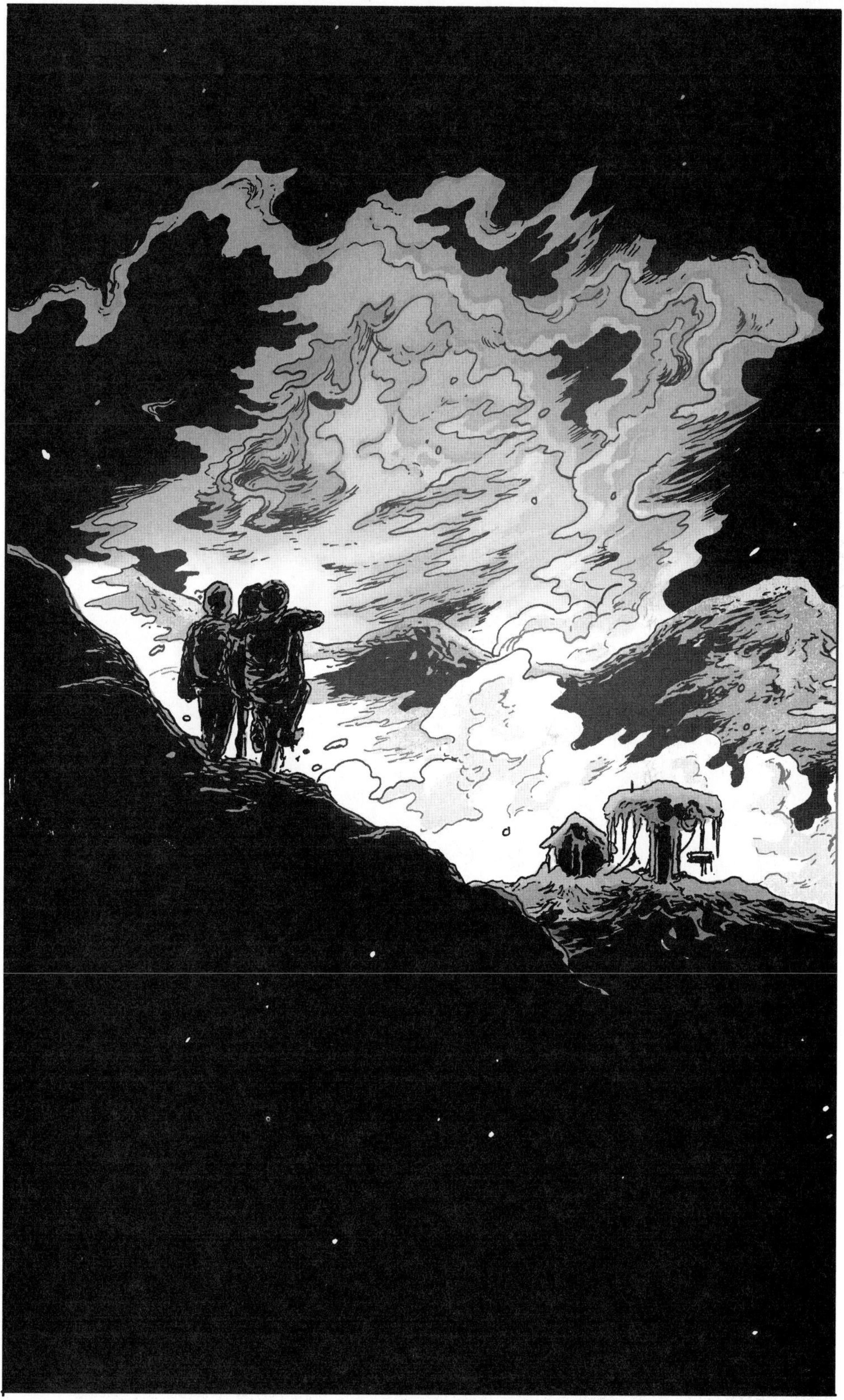

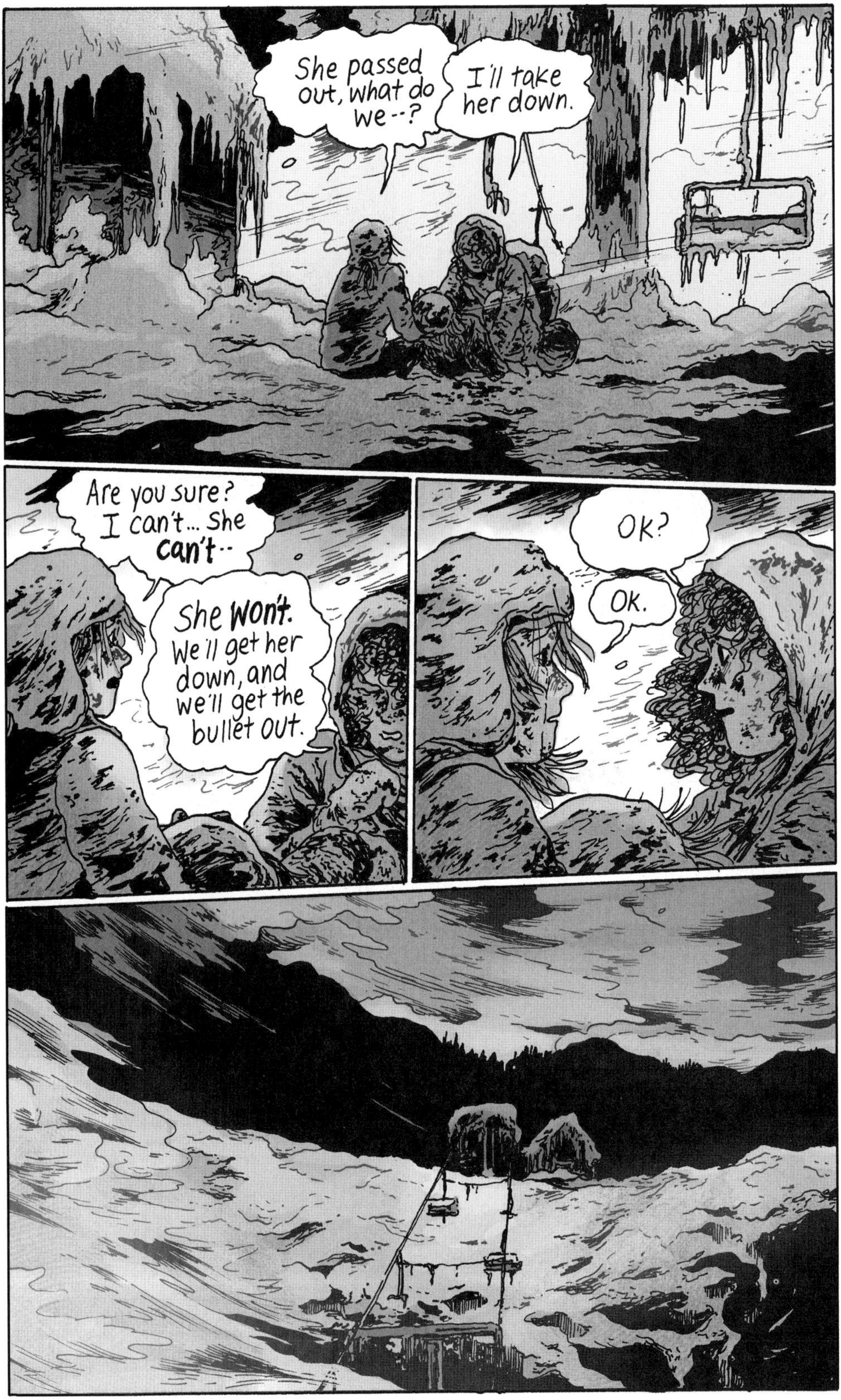
She passed out, what do we--?
I'll take her down.
Are you sure? I can't... She can't--
She won't. We'll get her down, and we'll get the bullet out.
OK?
Ok.

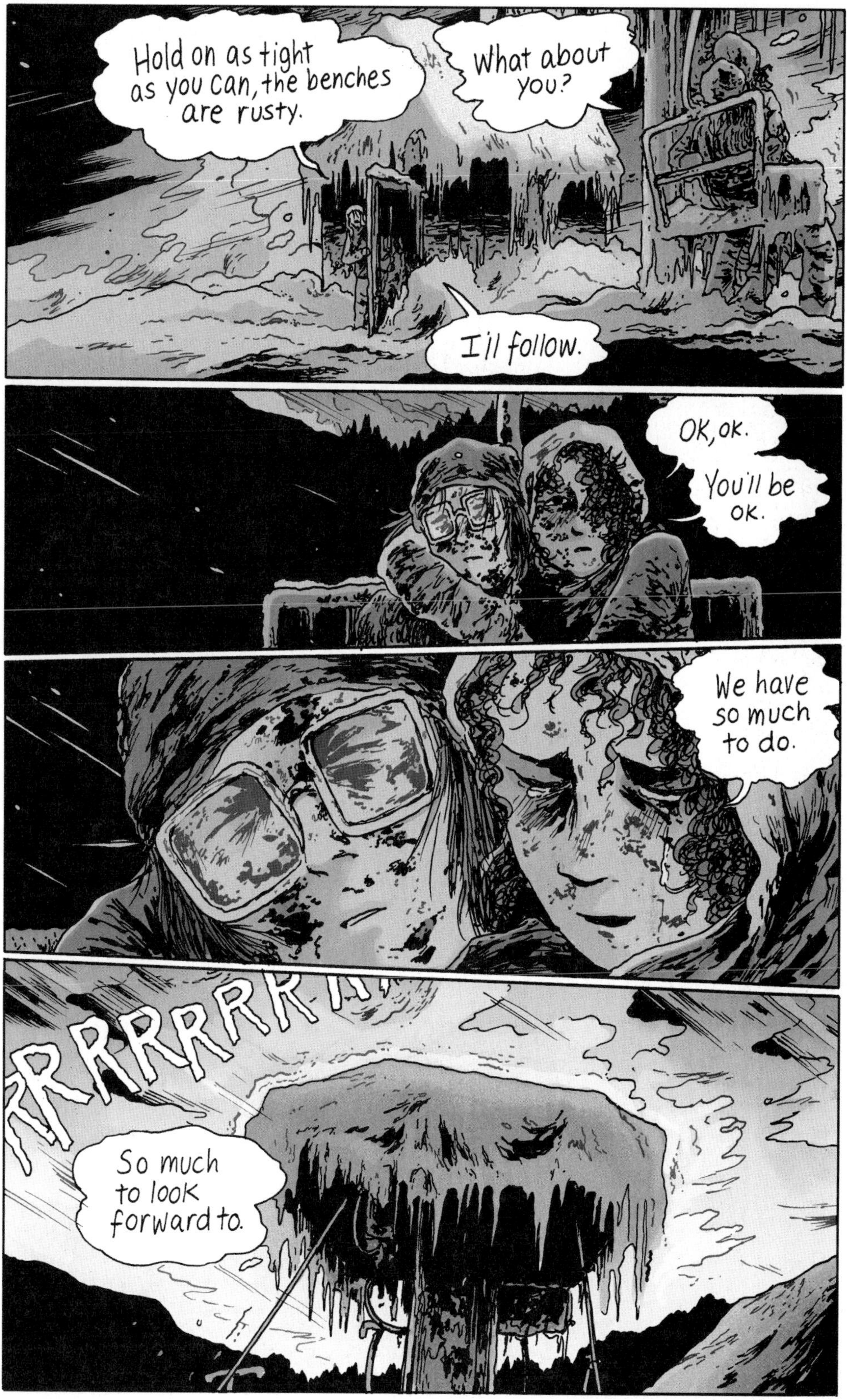

Hold on as tight as you can, the benches are rusty.
What about you?
I'll follow.
OK, ok.
You'll be ok.
We have so much to do.
RRRRRRR
So much to look forward to.

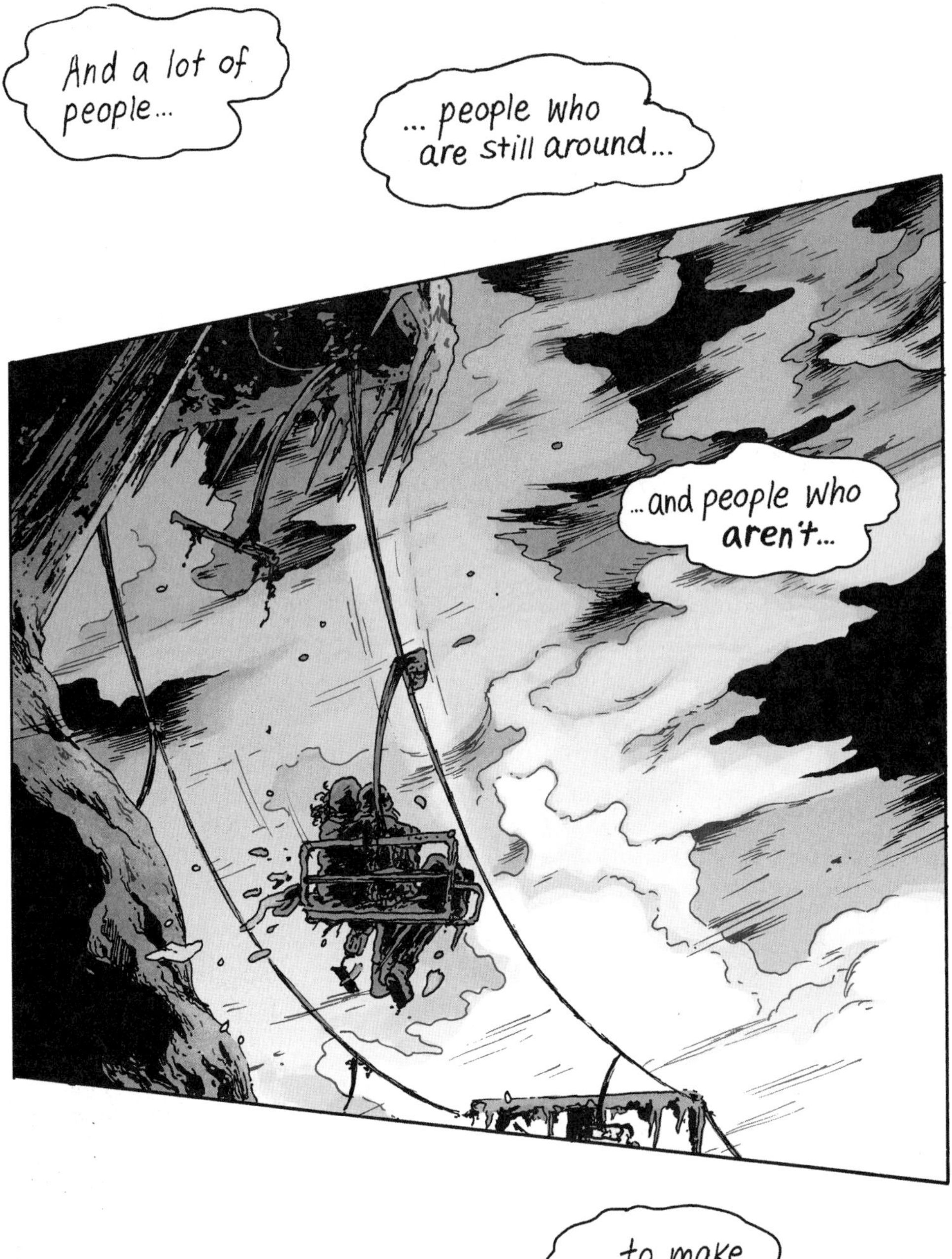
And a lot of people...
... people who are still around...
...and people who **aren't**...
... to make proud.

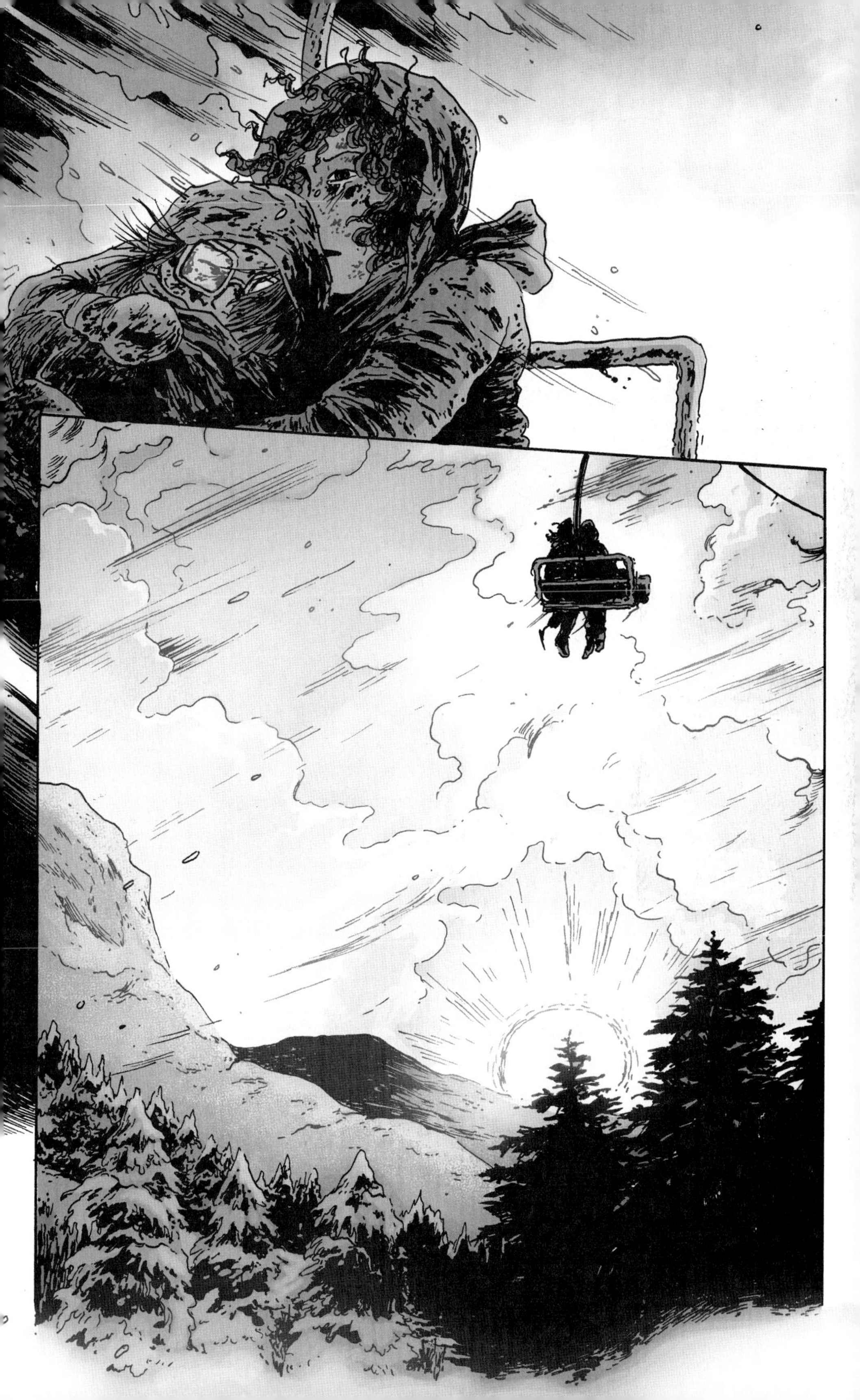

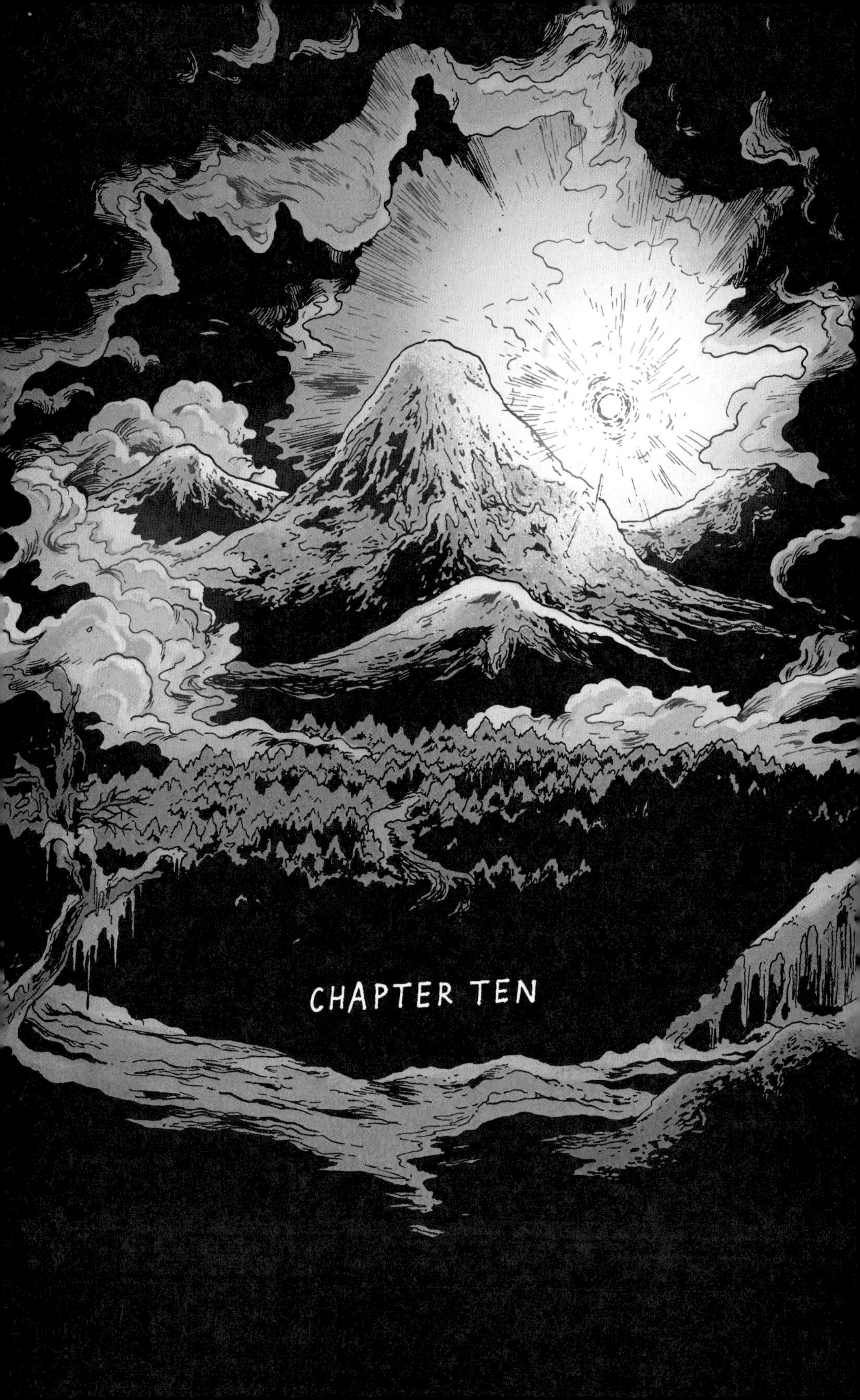
CHAPTER TEN

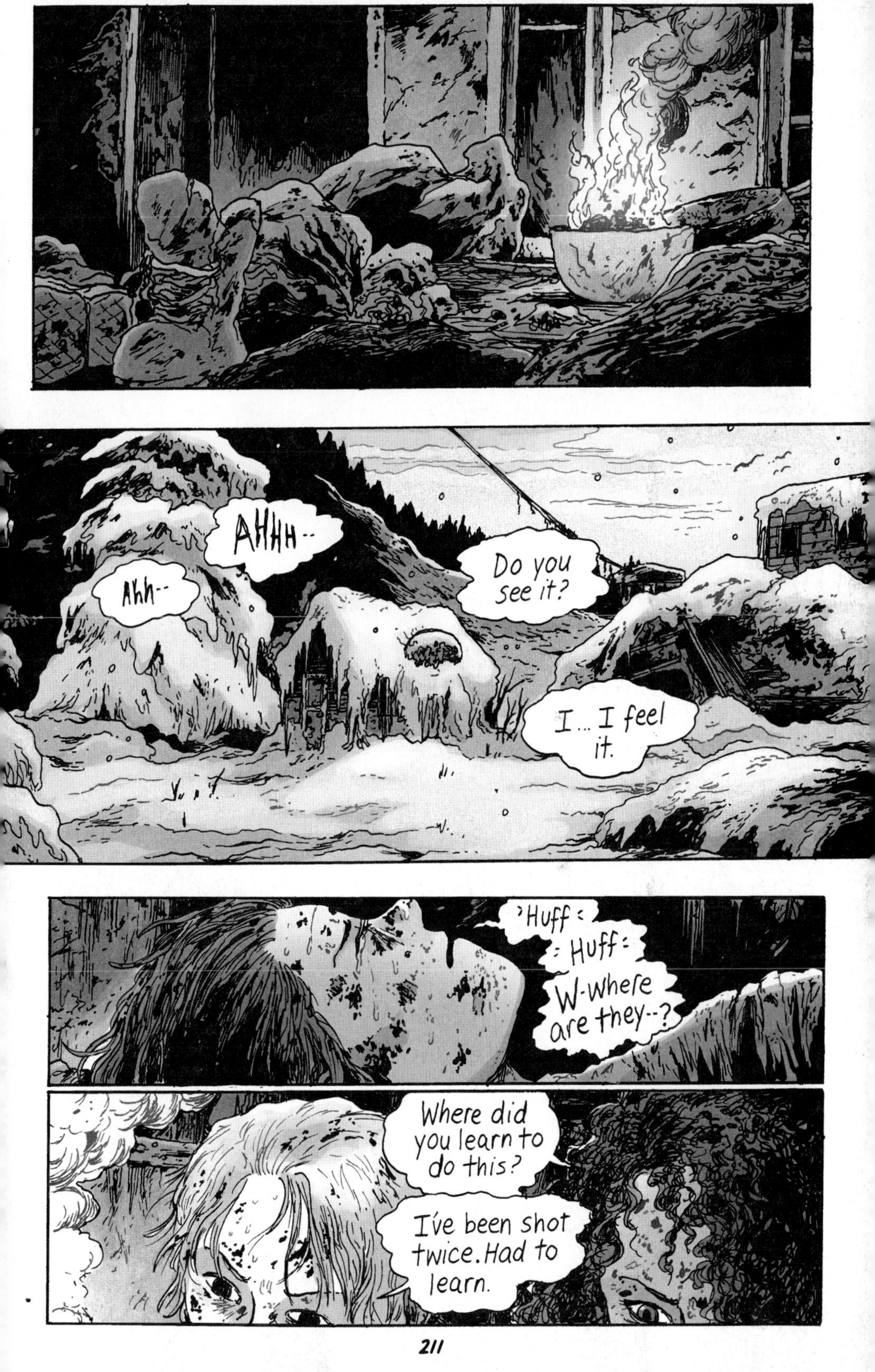
AHHH--
Ahh--
Do you see it?
I... I feel it.
Huff
Huff
W-where are they--?
Where did you learn to do this?
I've been shot twice. Had to learn.

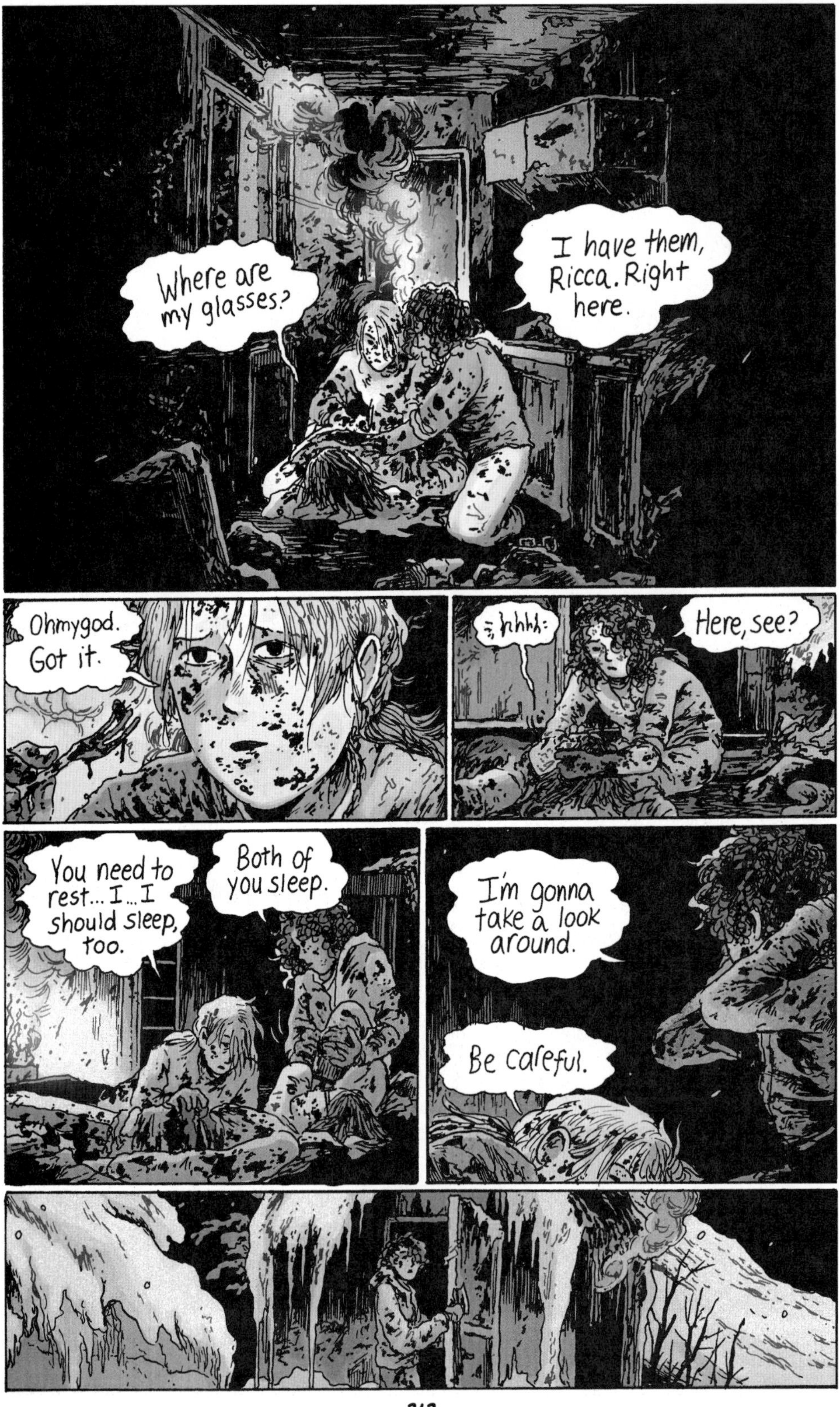
Where are my glasses?
I have them, Ricca. Right here.
Ohmygod. Got it.
Hhhh
Here, see?
You need to rest... I... I should sleep, too.
Both of you sleep.
I'm gonna take a look around.
Be careful.

KILLING
WEeeee
What--?
Weeee

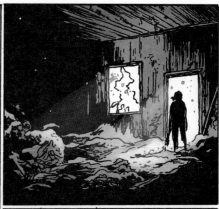

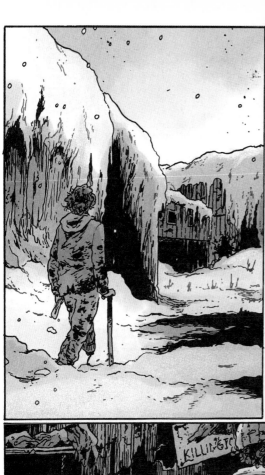

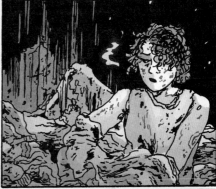

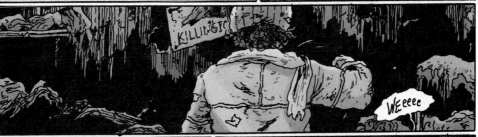

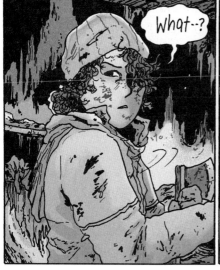

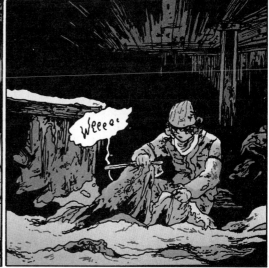

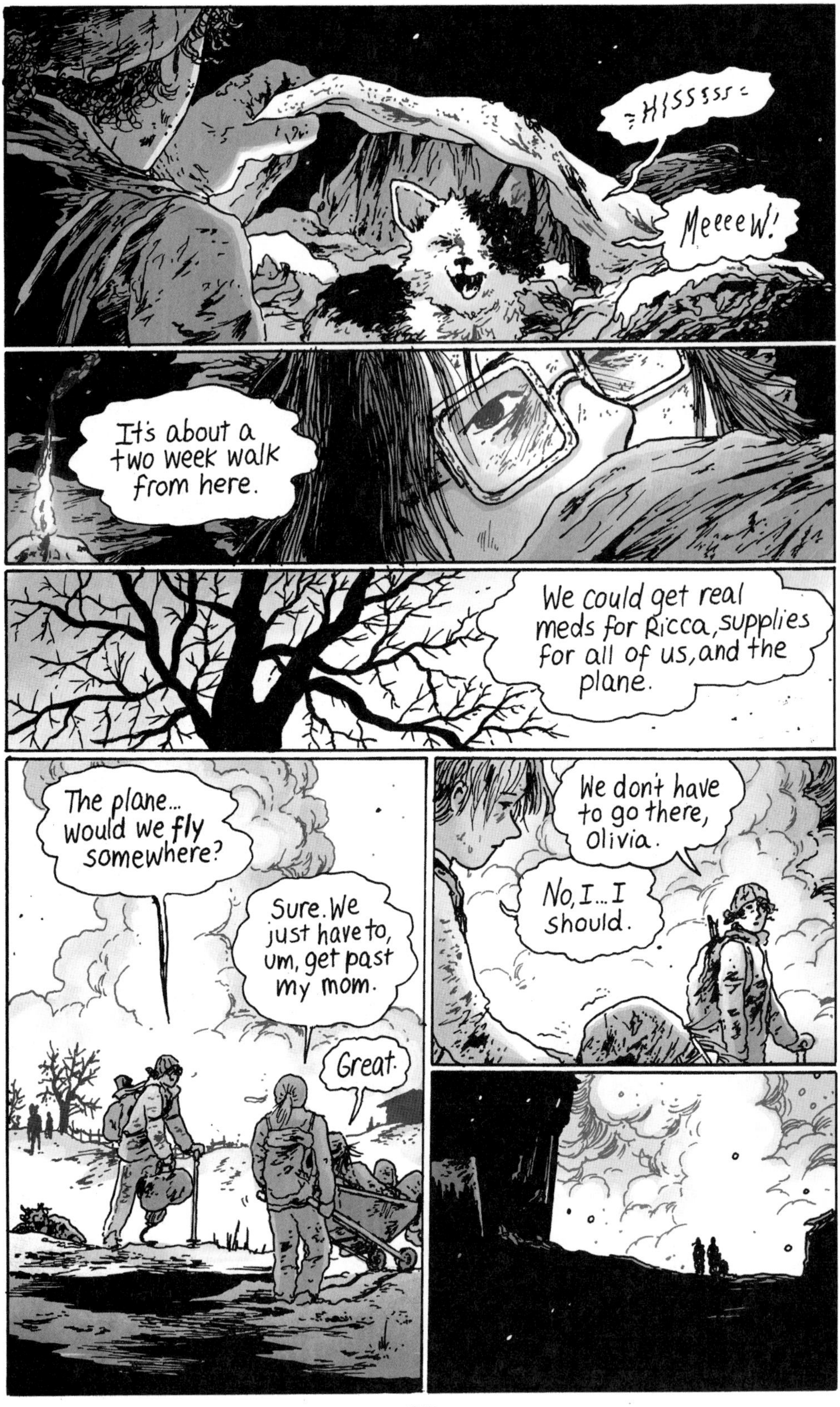
HISSSSS
MeeeeW!
It's about a two week walk from here.
We could get real meds for Ricca, supplies for all of us, and the plane.
The plane... would we fly somewhere?
Sure. We just have to, um, get past my mom.
Great.
We don't have to go there, Olivia.
No, I... I should.

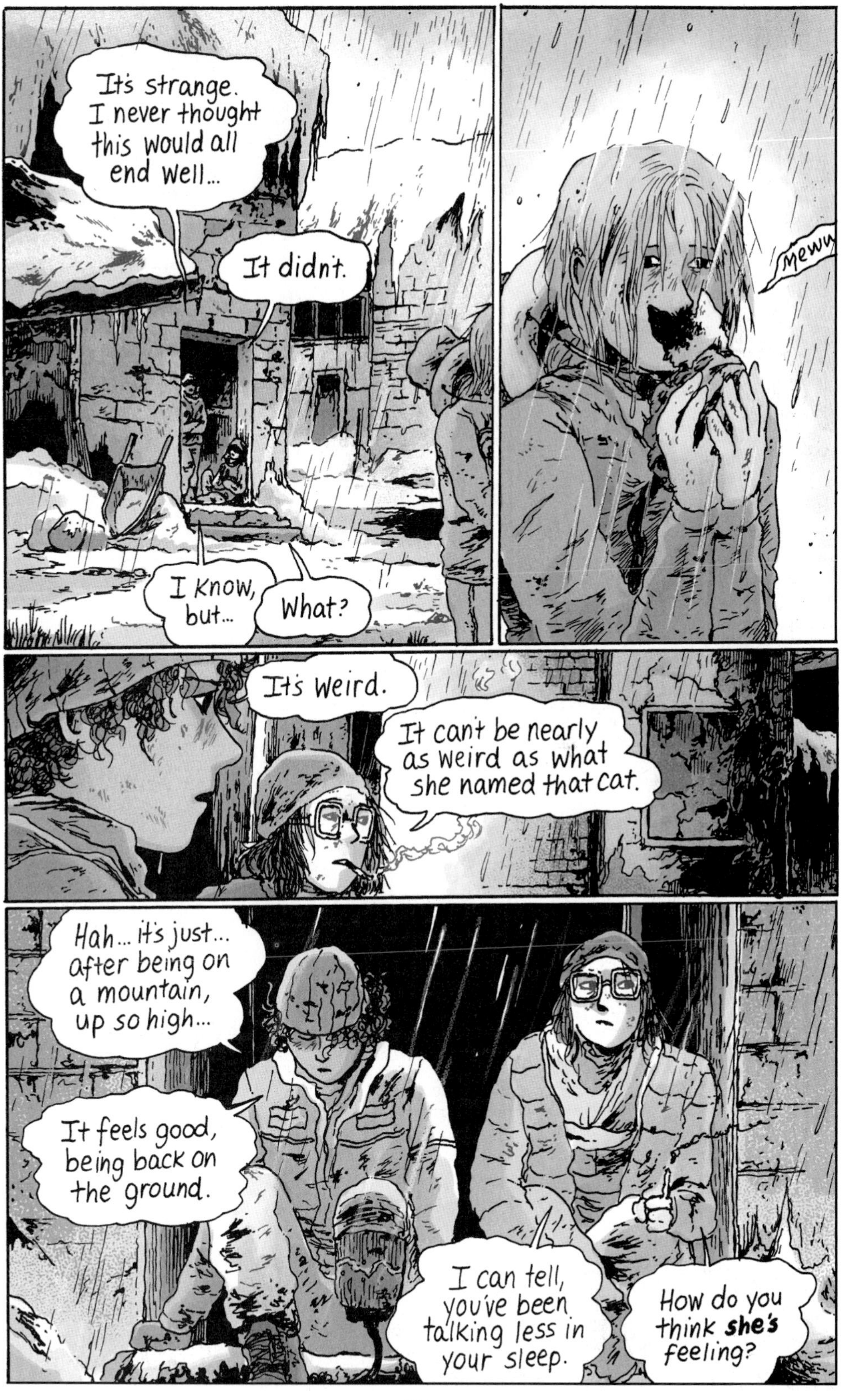

It's strange. I never thought this would all end well...
It didn't.
I know, but...
What?
Meww
It's weird.
It can't be nearly as weird as what she named that cat.
Hah... it's just... after being on a mountain, up so high...
It feels good, being back on the ground.
I can tell, you've been talking less in your sleep.
How do you think **she's** feeling?

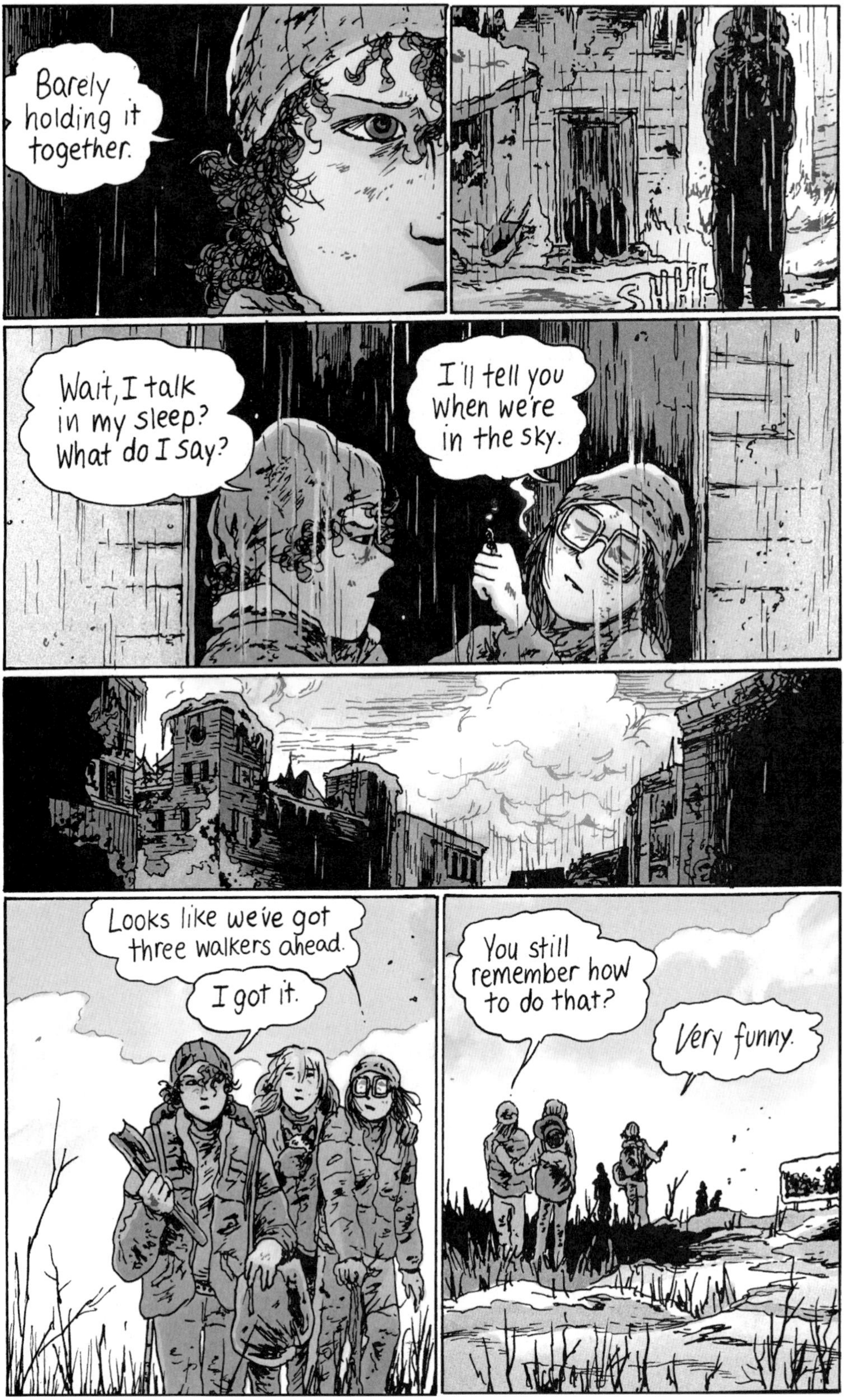
Barely holding it together.
SHHH
Wait, I talk in my sleep? What do I say?
I'll tell you when we're in the sky.
Looks like we've got three walkers ahead.
I got it.
You still remember how to do that?
Very funny.

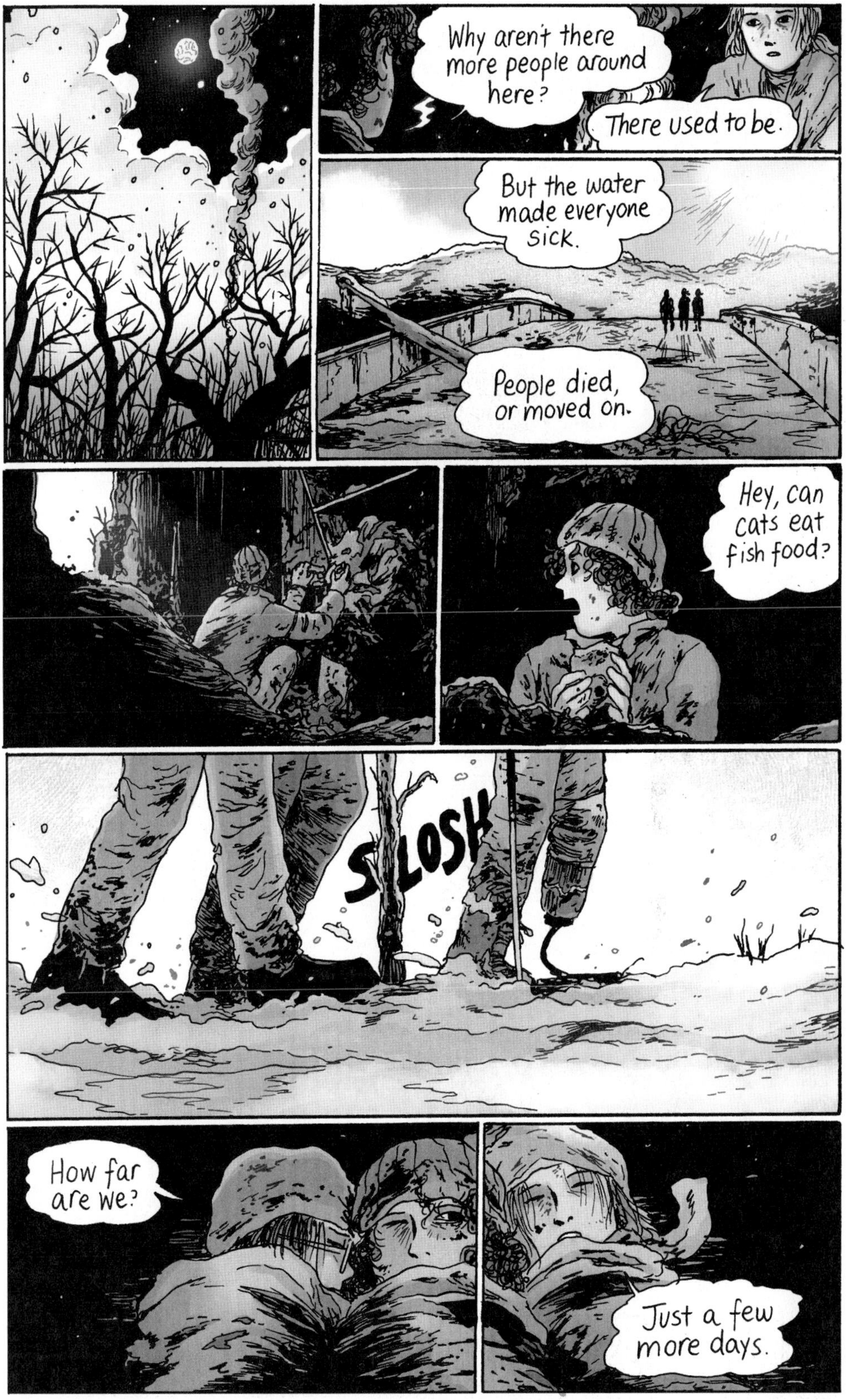
Why aren't there more people around here?
There used to be.
But the water made everyone sick.
People died, or moved on.
Hey, can cats eat fish food?
SLOSH
How far are we?
Just a few more days.

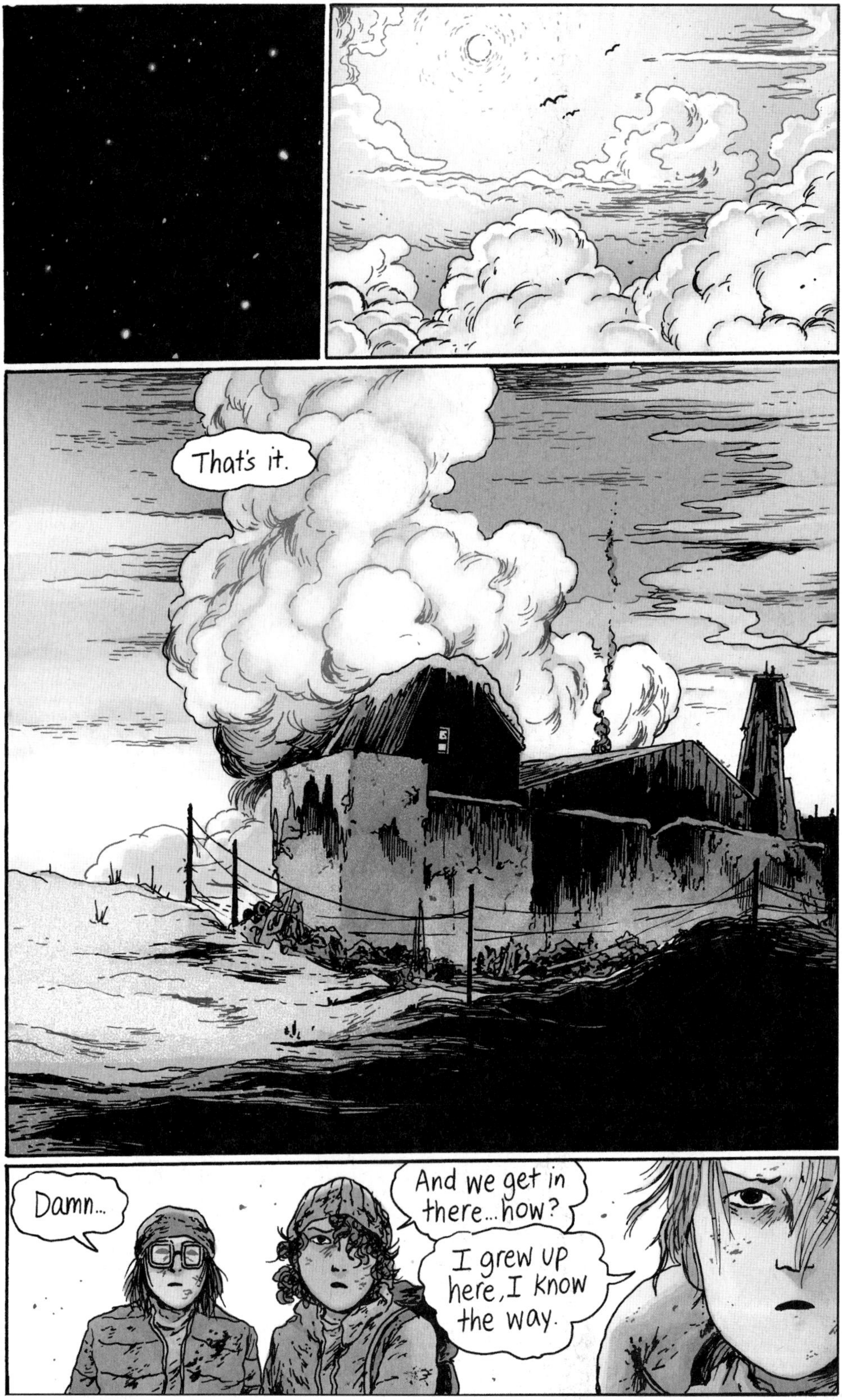
That's it.
Damn...
And we get in there... how?
I grew up here, I know the way.

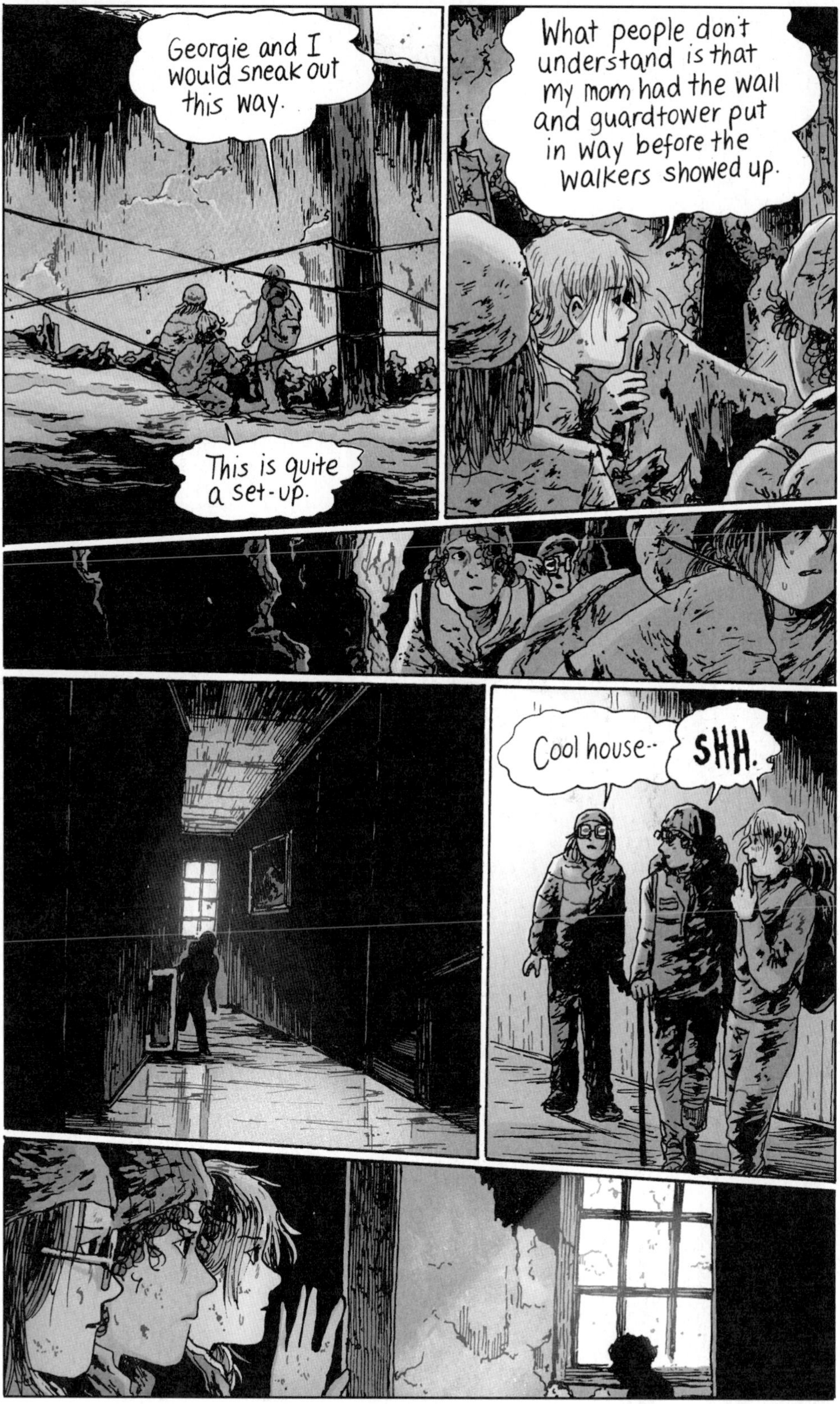
Georgie and I would sneak out this way.
This is quite a set-up.
What people don't understand is that my mom had the wall and guardtower put in way before the walkers showed up.
Cool house--
SHH.

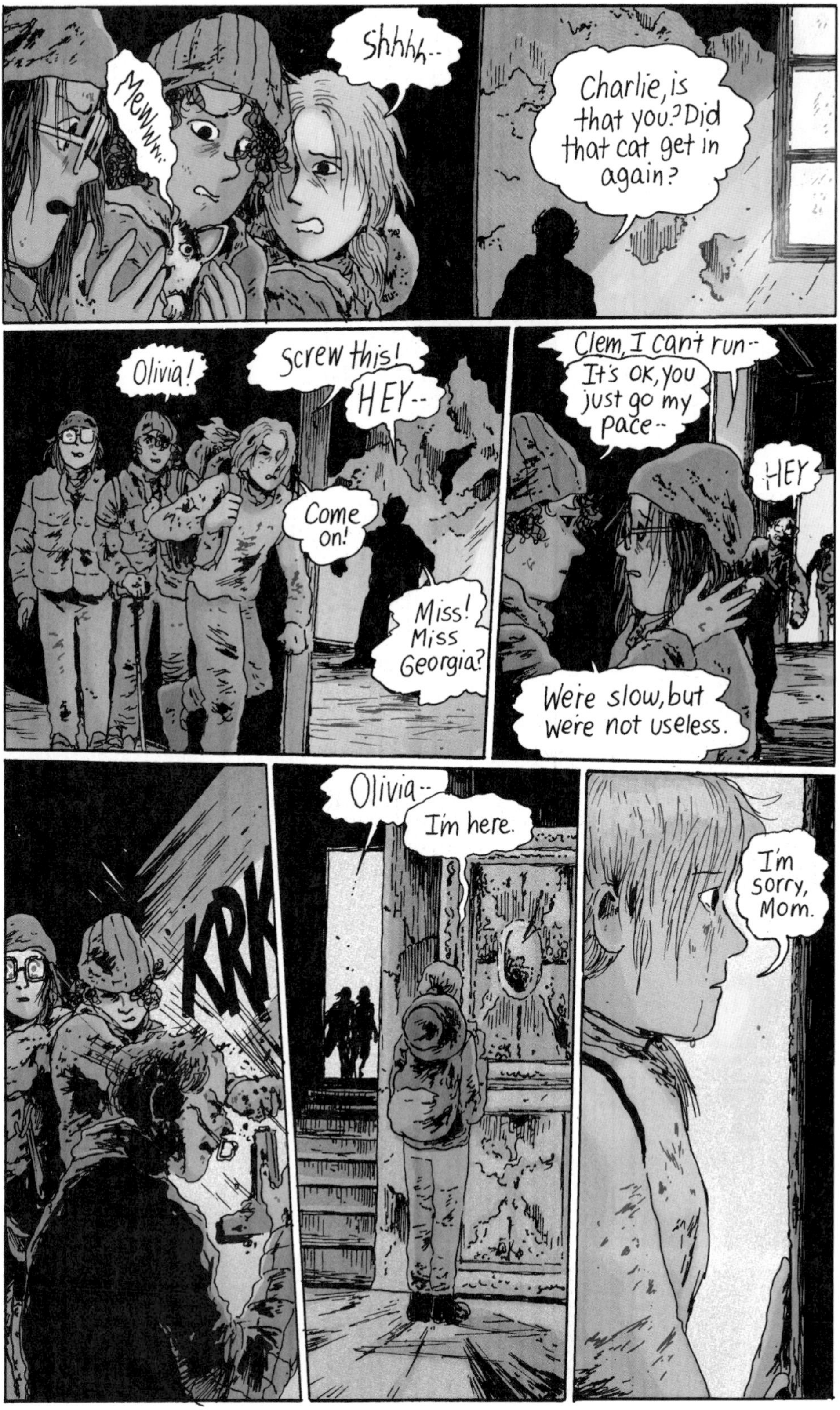
Mewww..
Shhhh--
Charlie, is that you? Did that cat get in again?
Olivia!
Screw this!
HEY--
Come on!
Miss! Miss Georgia?
Clem, I can't run--
It's OK, you just go my pace--
HEY
We're slow, but we're not useless.
KRK
Olivia--
I'm here.
I'm sorry, Mom.

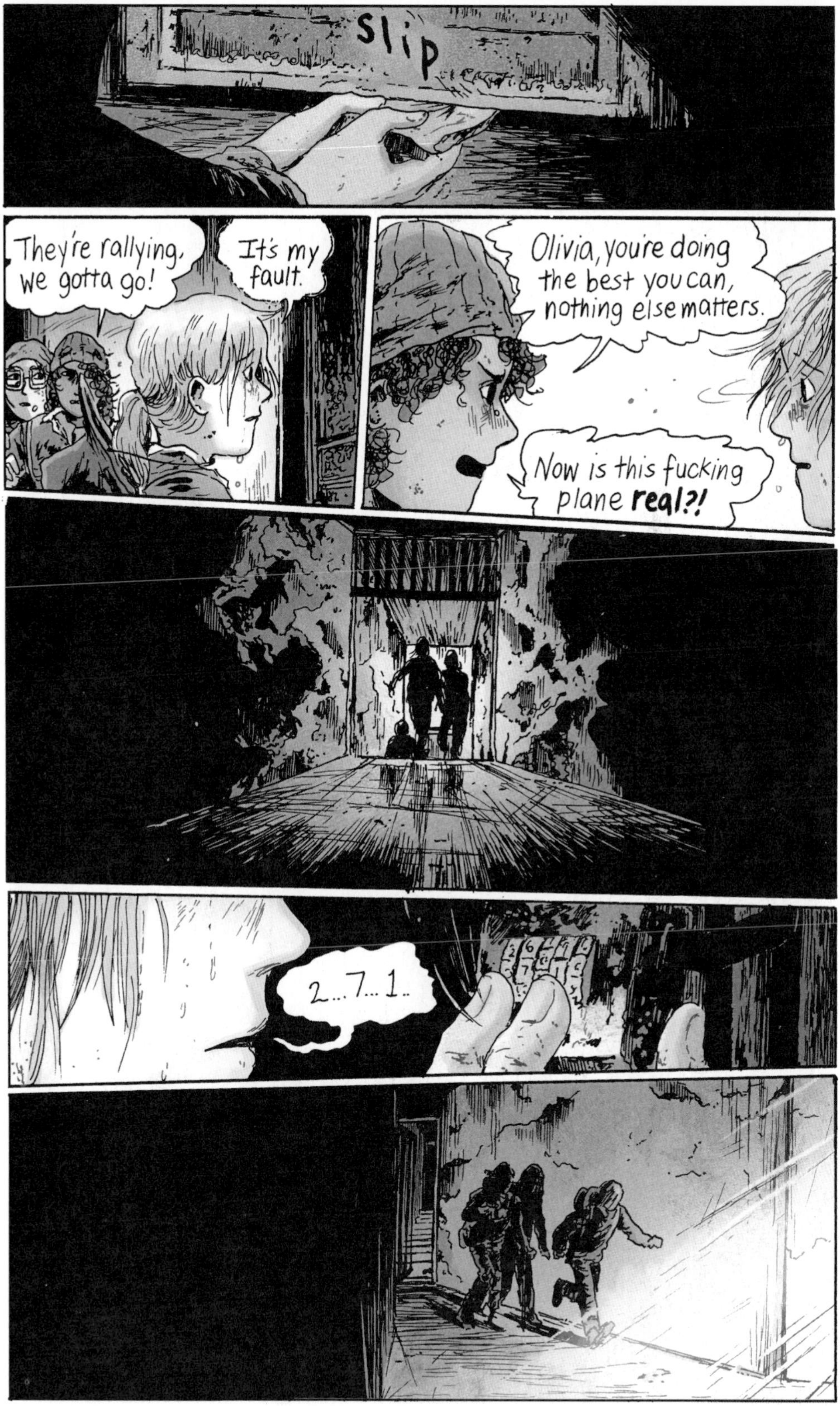

Slip
They're rallying, we gotta go!
It's my fault.
Olivia, you're doing the best you can, nothing else matters.
Now is this fucking plane **real?!**
2... 7... 1..

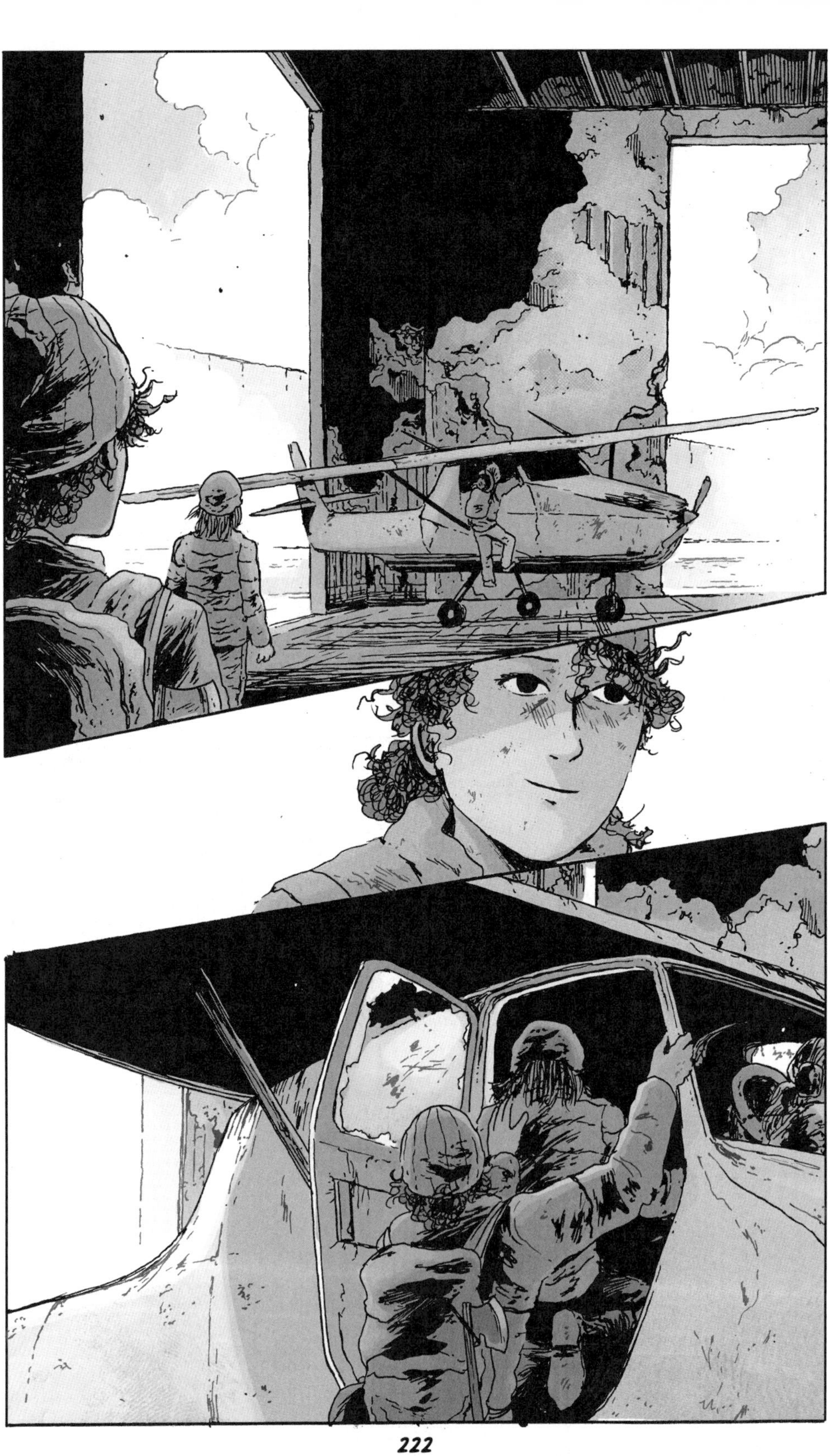

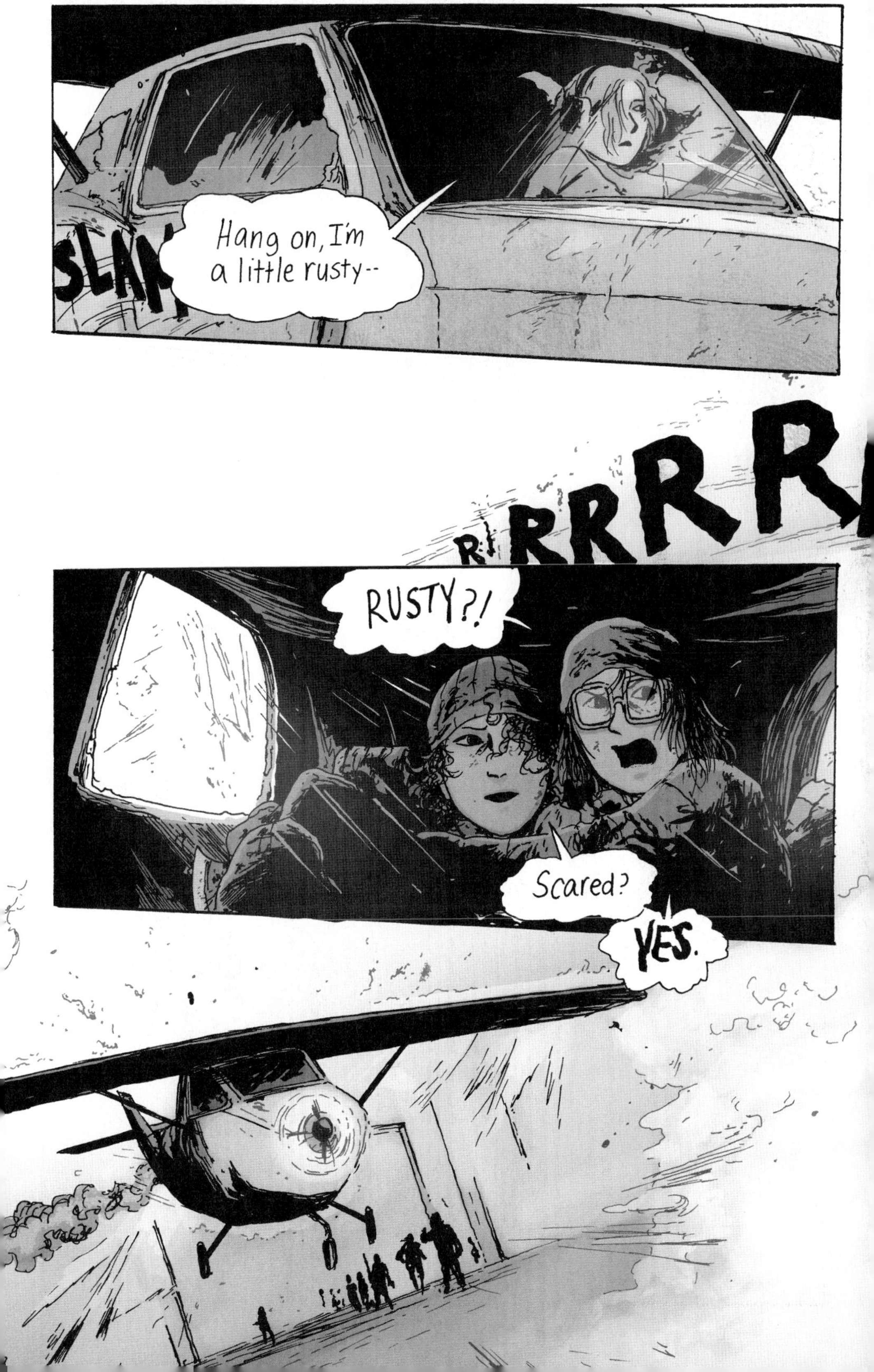
SLAM
Hang on, I'm a little rusty--
RRRRR
RUSTY?!
Scared?
YES.

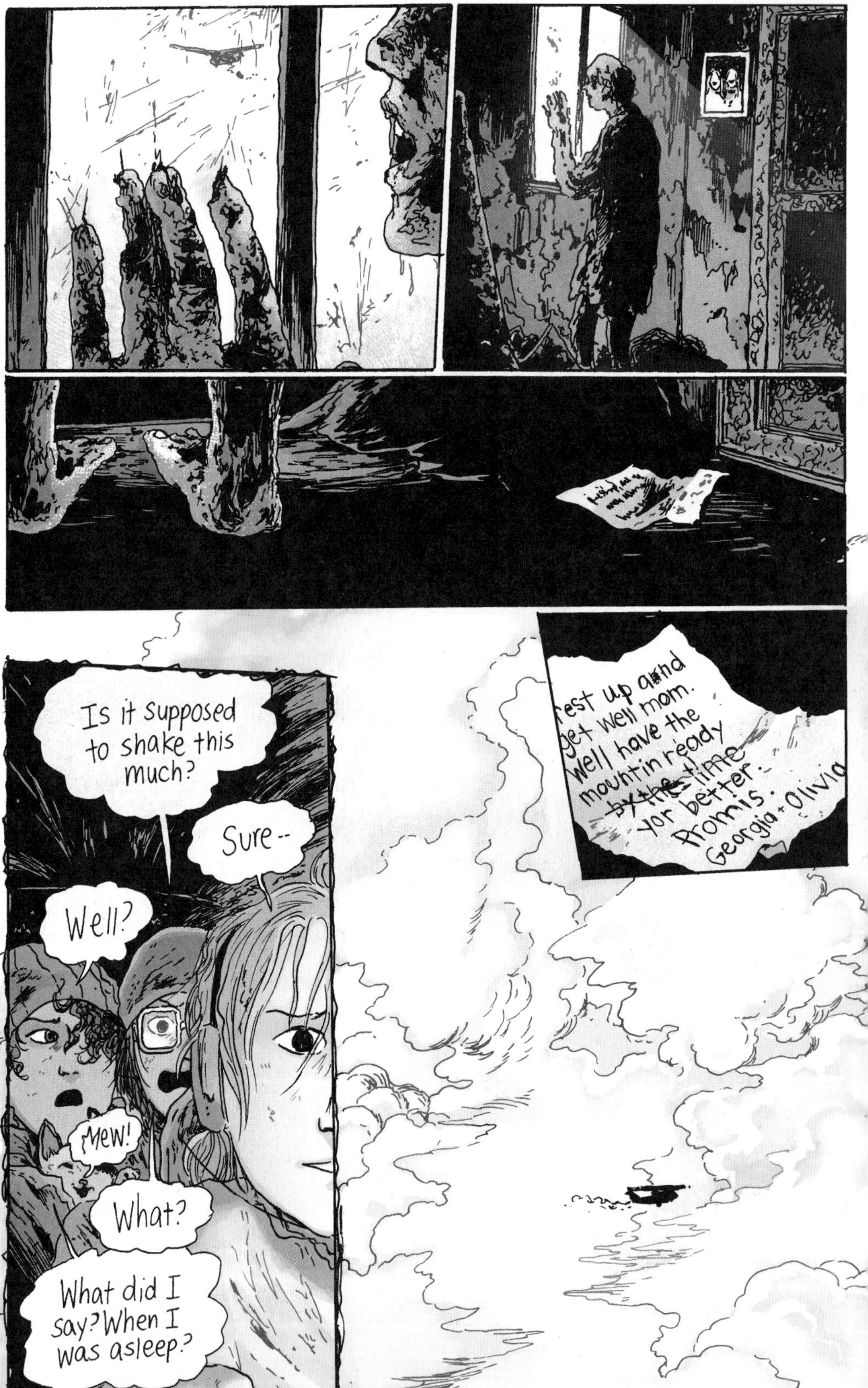
rest up and
get well mom.
Well have the
mountin ready
by the time
yor better.
Promis.
Georgia + Olivia
Is it supposed to shake this much?
Sure--
Well?
Mew!
What?
What did I say? When I was asleep?

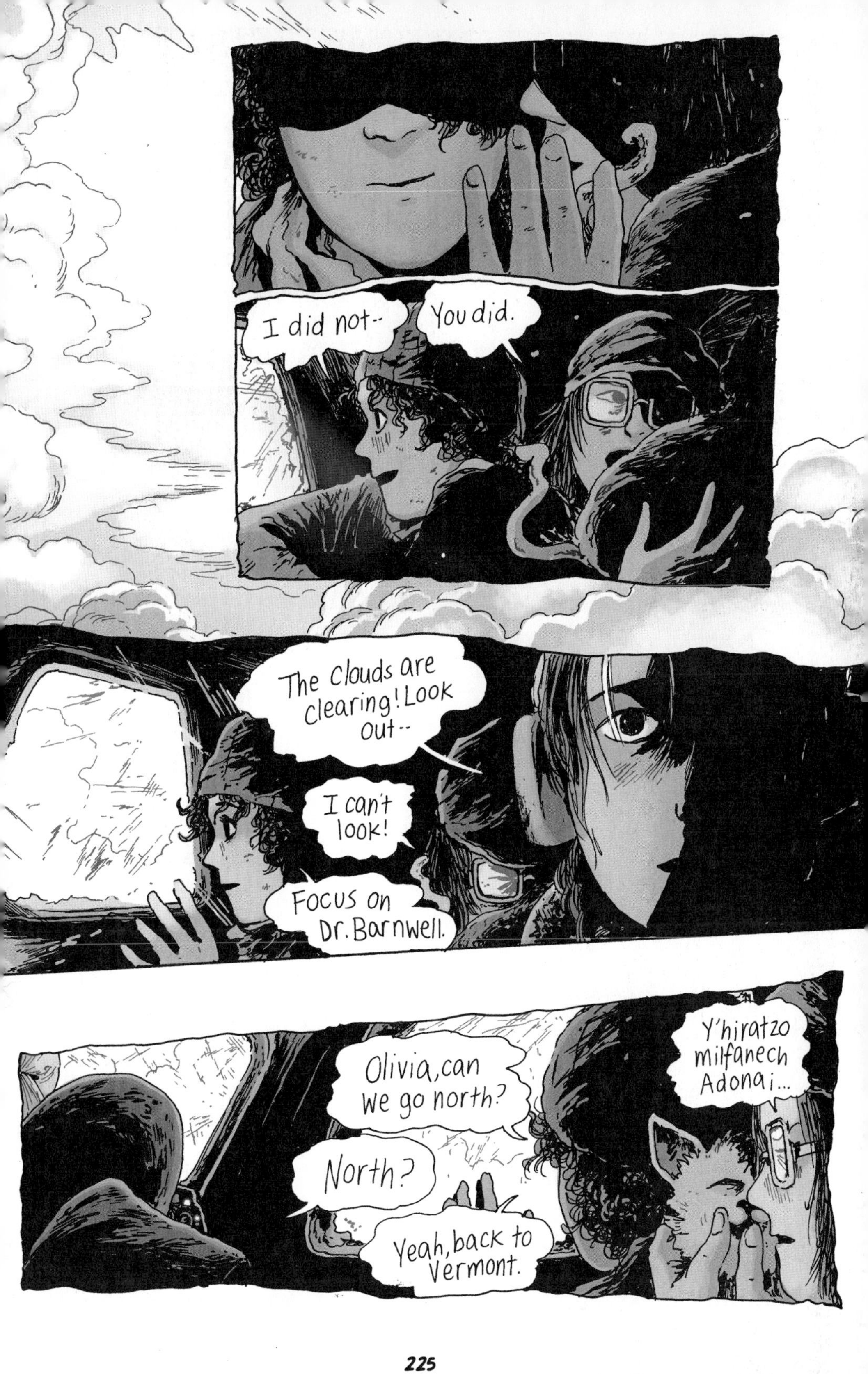
I did not--
You did.
The Clouds are clearing! Look out--
I can't look!
Focus on Dr. Barnwell.
Olivia, can we go north?
Y'hiratzo milfanech Adonai...
North?
Yeah, back to Vermont.

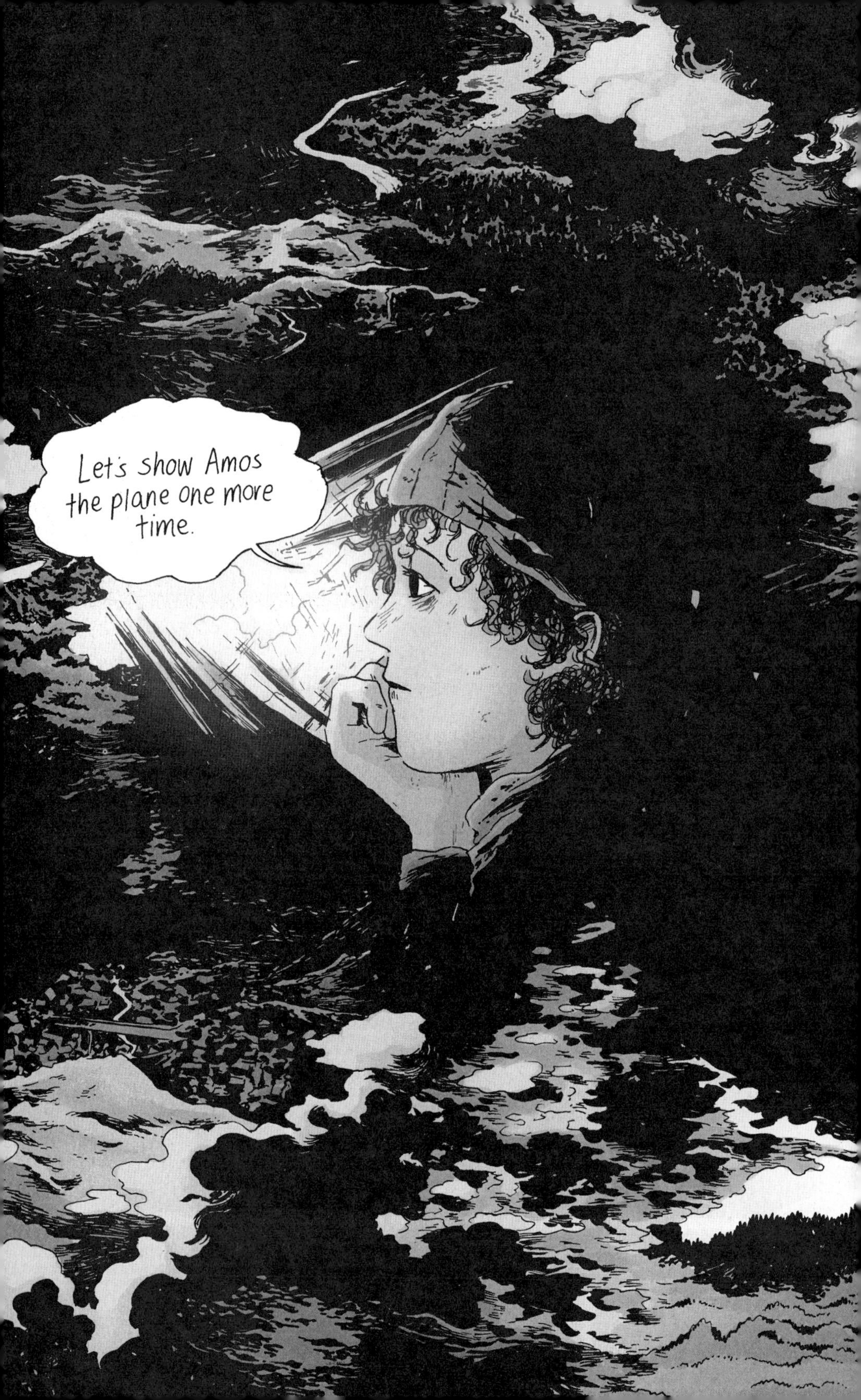
Let's show Amos the plane one more time.

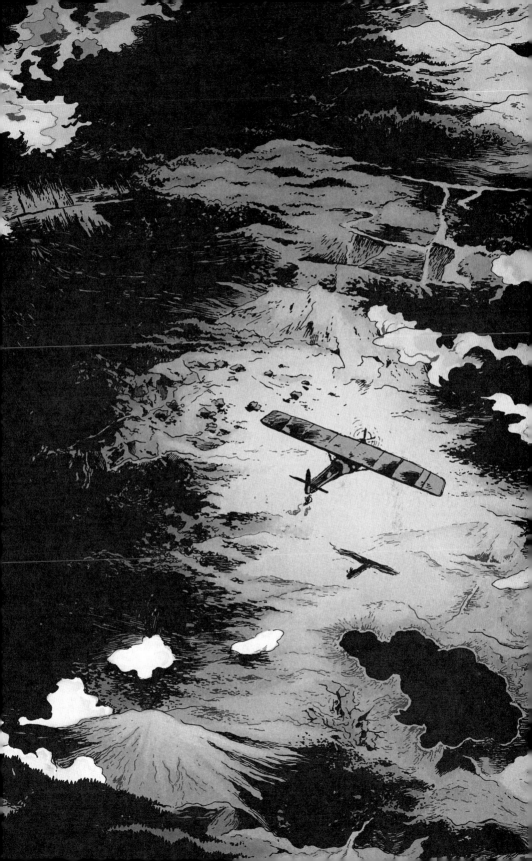

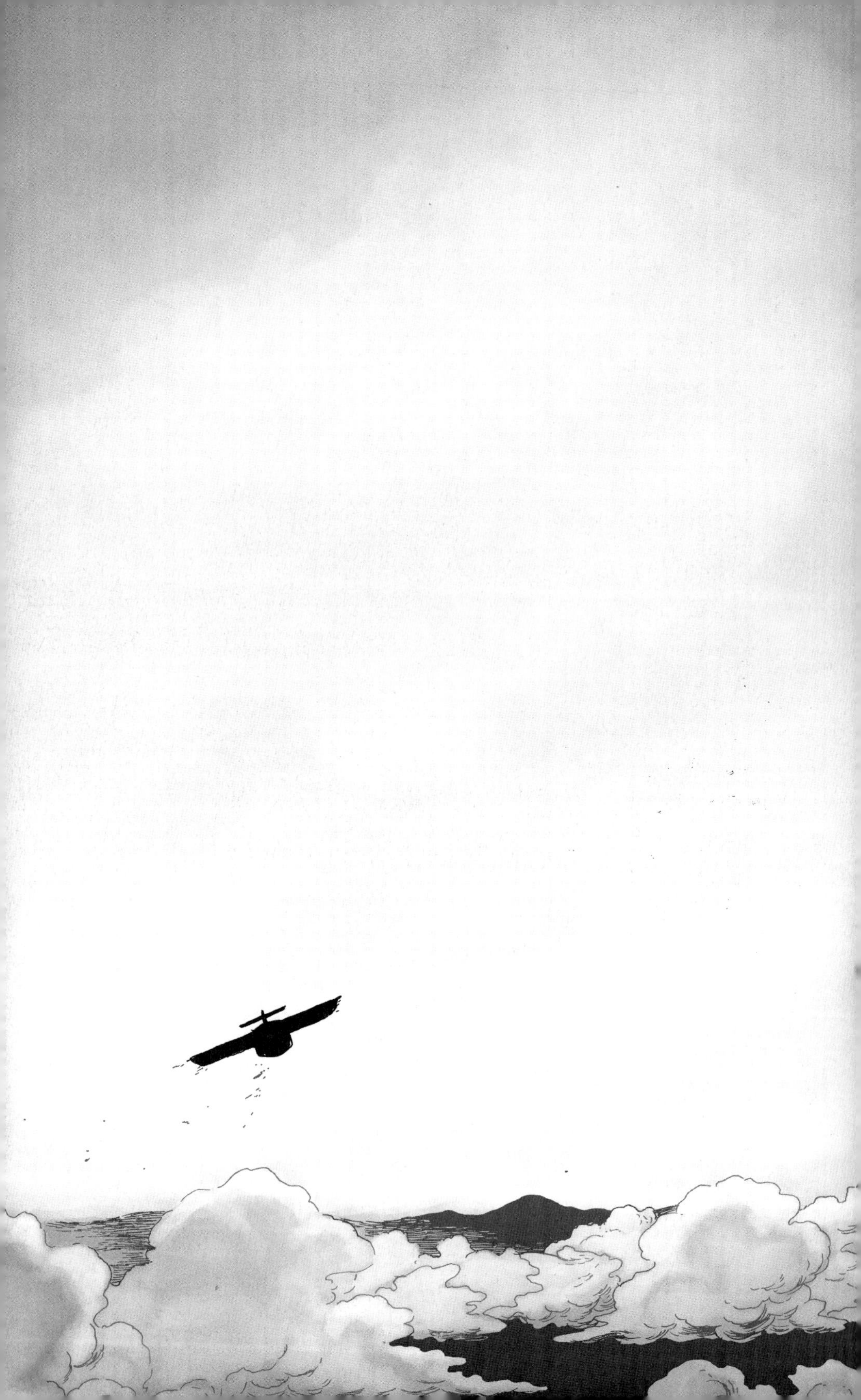

TO BE CONTINUED
IN BOOK TWO

rest up and
get well mom.
well have the
mountin ready
by the time
yor better.
Promis.
Georgia + Olivia

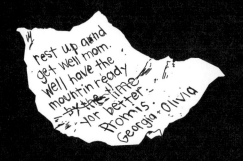

clementine

Ricca

Amos

Olivia   Georgia

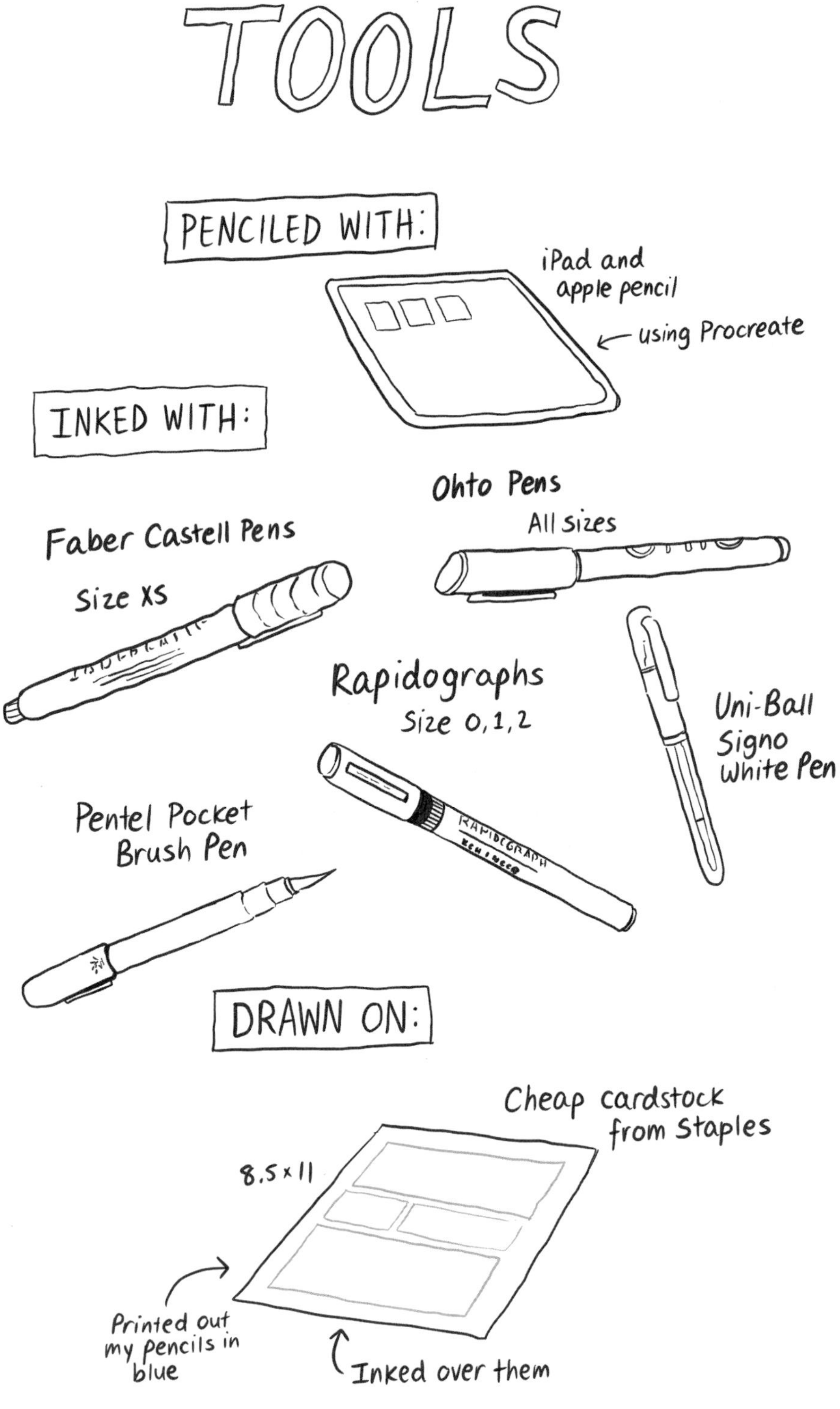
TOOLS
PENCILED WITH:
iPad and apple pencil
using Procreate
INKED WITH:
Ohto Pens
All sizes
Faber Castell Pens
Size XS
Rapidographs
Size 0,1,2
Uni-Ball Signo White Pen
Pentel Pocket Brush Pen
RAPIDOGRAPH
DRAWN ON:
Cheap cardstock from Staples
8.5 x 11
Printed out my pencils in blue
Inked over them

Acknowledgements

Clementine book 1 would not have been possible without the endless help and support of everyone at Skybound. Huge thank you to my editor Alex Antone for all his hard work and understanding, Carina Taylor for her beautiful design work, Arune Singh for his help getting Clementine out there, and Shawn Kittelsen, Sean Mackiewicz, and Robert Kirkman for their continual guidance. Thank you Sean Vanaman, Jake Rodkin, and everyone else who brought Clementine to life.

Thank you to Cliff Rathburn for truly making this book sing with his gray tones.

Enormous thank you to Jennifer Kretchmer, Jo Beckwith, and Eman Rimawi for their help and insight into what life would really be like for Clementine.

Thank you to my agent Seth Fishman, as always, for keeping me employed and supported. Thank you to everyone at the Center for Cartoon Studies for continuing to inspire me with all your beautiful work.

Thank you to my pals Dave, Mel, Jarad, Robyn, Wei, and my new sisters Georgia, Olivia, and Sarah. All of you give me a place to land when I need one.

Thank you to my family for always asking, "Is the book done?" because you all know I can do it.

And finally, thank you to my beautiful wife Emma, for being the best partner and cheerleader I could've ever asked for.

I'll see you all again in the acknowledgements for books 2 and 3.

Tillie Walden is a cartoonist and
illustrator from Austin, TX. She is the
creator of a number of graphic novels,
including the Hugo Award nominee **On
a Sunbeam** and Eisner Award winning
Are You Listening? She is a graduate
of the Center for Cartoon Studies, where
she now teaches. She currently lives in
Vermont with her wife and two cats.

CLEMENTINE: BOOK ONE
Tillie Walden: *Writer, Artist, Letterer*
Cliff Rathburn: *Grey Tones*
Alex Antone: *Editor*
Carina Taylor: *Logo + Book Design*
Andres Juarez: *Production*
The Walking Dead created by Robert Kirkman

SKYBOUND ENTERTAINMENT
Robert Kirkman: *Chairman*
David Alpert: *CEO*
Sean Mackiewicz: *SVP, Publisher*
Shawn Kirkham: *SVP, Business Development*
Brian Huntington: *VP, Online Content*
Andres Juarez: *Art Director*
Arune Singh: *Director of Brand, Editorial*
Shannon Meehan: *Public Relations Manager*

Alex Antone: *Senior Editor*
Jon Moisan: *Editor*
Amanda LaFranco: *Editor*
Jillian Crab: *Graphic Designer*
Morgan Perry: *Brand Manager, Editorial*
Dan Petersen: *Sr. Director, Operations & Events*
Foreign Rights & Licensing Inquiries: contact@skybound.com
SKYBOUND.COM

IMAGE COMICS, INC.
Todd McFarlane: *President*
Jim Valentino: *Vice President*
Marc Silvestri: *Chief Executive Officer*
Erik Larsen: *Chief Financial Officer*
Robert Kirkman: *Chief Operating Officer*
Eric Stephenson: *Publisher / Chief Creative Officer*
Nicole Lapalme: *Controller*
Leanna Caunter: *Accounting Analyst*
Sue Korpela: *Accounting & HR Manager*
Marla Eizik: *Talent Liaison*
Dirk Wood: *Director of International Sales & Licensing*
Alex Cox: *Director of Direct Market Sales*
Chloe Ramos: *Book Market & Library Sales Manager*

Emilio Bautista: *Digital Sales Coordinator*
Jon Schlaffman: *Specialty Sales Coordinator*
Kat Salazar: *Director of PR & Marketing*
Drew Fitzgerald: *Marketing Content Associate*
Heather Doornink: *Production Director*
Drew Gill: *Art Director*
Hilary DiLoreto: *Print Manager*
Tricia Ramos: *Traffic Manager*
Melissa Gifford: *Content Manager*
Erika Schnatz: *Senior Production Artist*
Ryan Brewer: *Production Artist*
Deanna Phelps: *Production Artist*
IMAGECOMICS.COM

nd dreamy. This book feels like a mash up between He
Guillermo Del Toro with its heart, mystery, and adven

-TILLIE WALDEN
(*Spinning*, *On A Sunbeam*, CLEMENTINE)

MAIRGHREAD SCOTT   PABLO TUNICA

AVAILABLE OCTOBER 2022

RE NEW WORLDS
et | SkyboundComet.com

**SKYBO
COM**

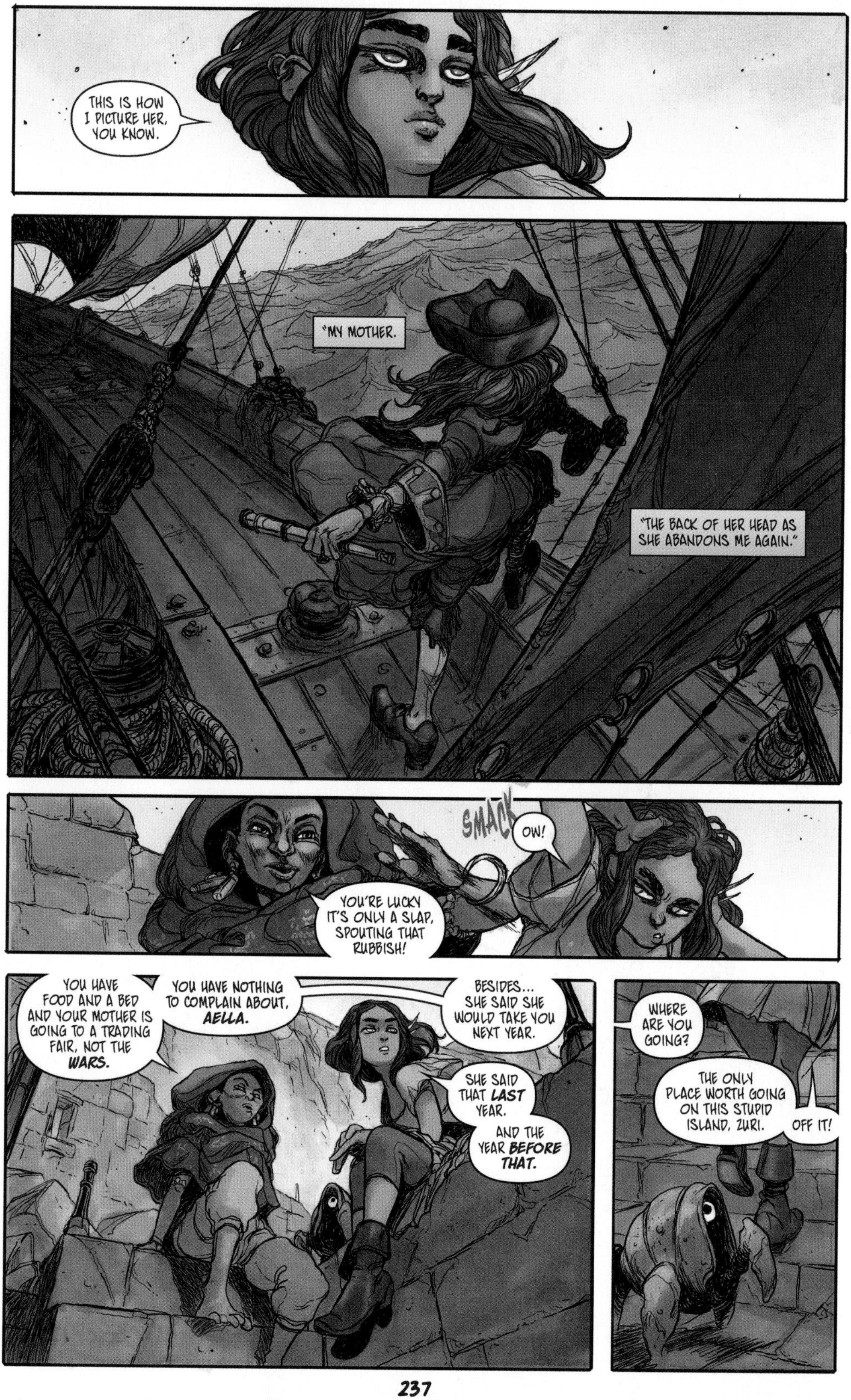
THIS IS HOW I PICTURE HER, YOU KNOW.
"MY MOTHER.
"THE BACK OF HER HEAD AS SHE ABANDONS ME AGAIN."
SMACK
OW!
YOU'RE LUCKY IT'S ONLY A SLAP, SPOUTING THAT RUBBISH!
YOU HAVE FOOD AND A BED AND YOUR MOTHER IS GOING TO A TRADING FAIR, NOT THE WARS.
YOU HAVE NOTHING TO COMPLAIN ABOUT, AELLA.
BESIDES... SHE SAID SHE WOULD TAKE YOU NEXT YEAR.
SHE SAID THAT LAST YEAR.
AND THE YEAR BEFORE THAT.
WHERE ARE YOU GOING?
THE ONLY PLACE WORTH GOING ON THIS STUPID ISLAND, ZURI.
OFF IT!

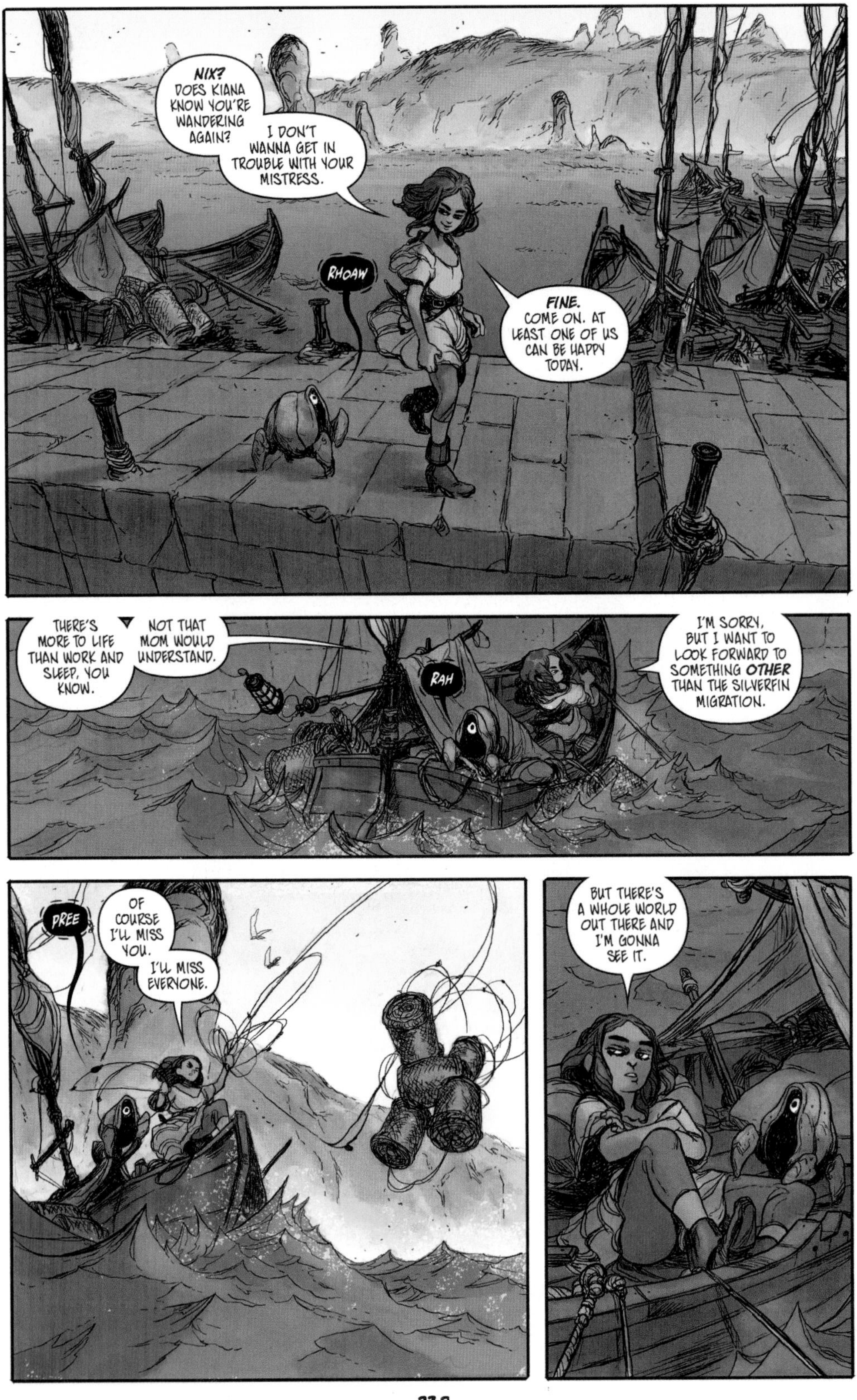
NIX? DOES KIANA KNOW YOU'RE WANDERING AGAIN?
I DON'T WANNA GET IN TROUBLE WITH YOUR MISTRESS.
RHOAW
FINE. COME ON. AT LEAST ONE OF US CAN BE HAPPY TODAY.
THERE'S MORE TO LIFE THAN WORK AND SLEEP, YOU KNOW.
NOT THAT MOM WOULD UNDERSTAND.
RAH
I'M SORRY, BUT I WANT TO LOOK FORWARD TO SOMETHING OTHER THAN THE SILVERFIN MIGRATION.
PREE
OF COURSE I'LL MISS YOU.
I'LL MISS EVERYONE.
BUT THERE'S A WHOLE WORLD OUT THERE AND I'M GONNA SEE IT.

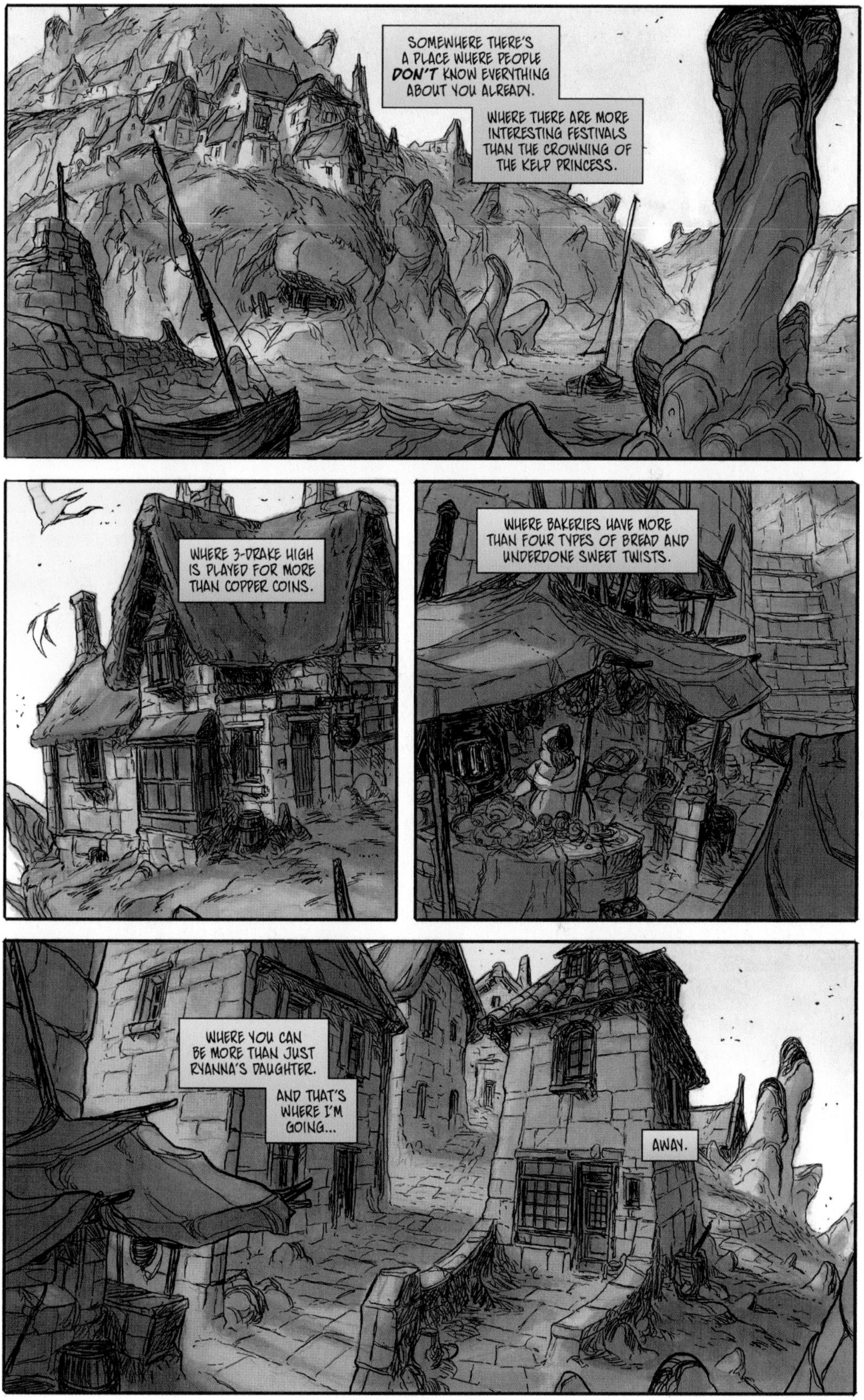
SOMEWHERE THERE'S A PLACE WHERE PEOPLE **DON'T** KNOW EVERYTHING ABOUT YOU ALREADY.
WHERE THERE ARE MORE INTERESTING FESTIVALS THAN THE CROWNING OF THE KELP PRINCESS.
WHERE 3-DRAKE HIGH IS PLAYED FOR MORE THAN COPPER COINS.
WHERE BAKERIES HAVE MORE THAN FOUR TYPES OF BREAD AND UNDERDONE SWEET TWISTS.
WHERE YOU CAN BE MORE THAN JUST RYANNA'S DAUGHTER.
AND THAT'S WHERE I'M GOING...
AWAY.

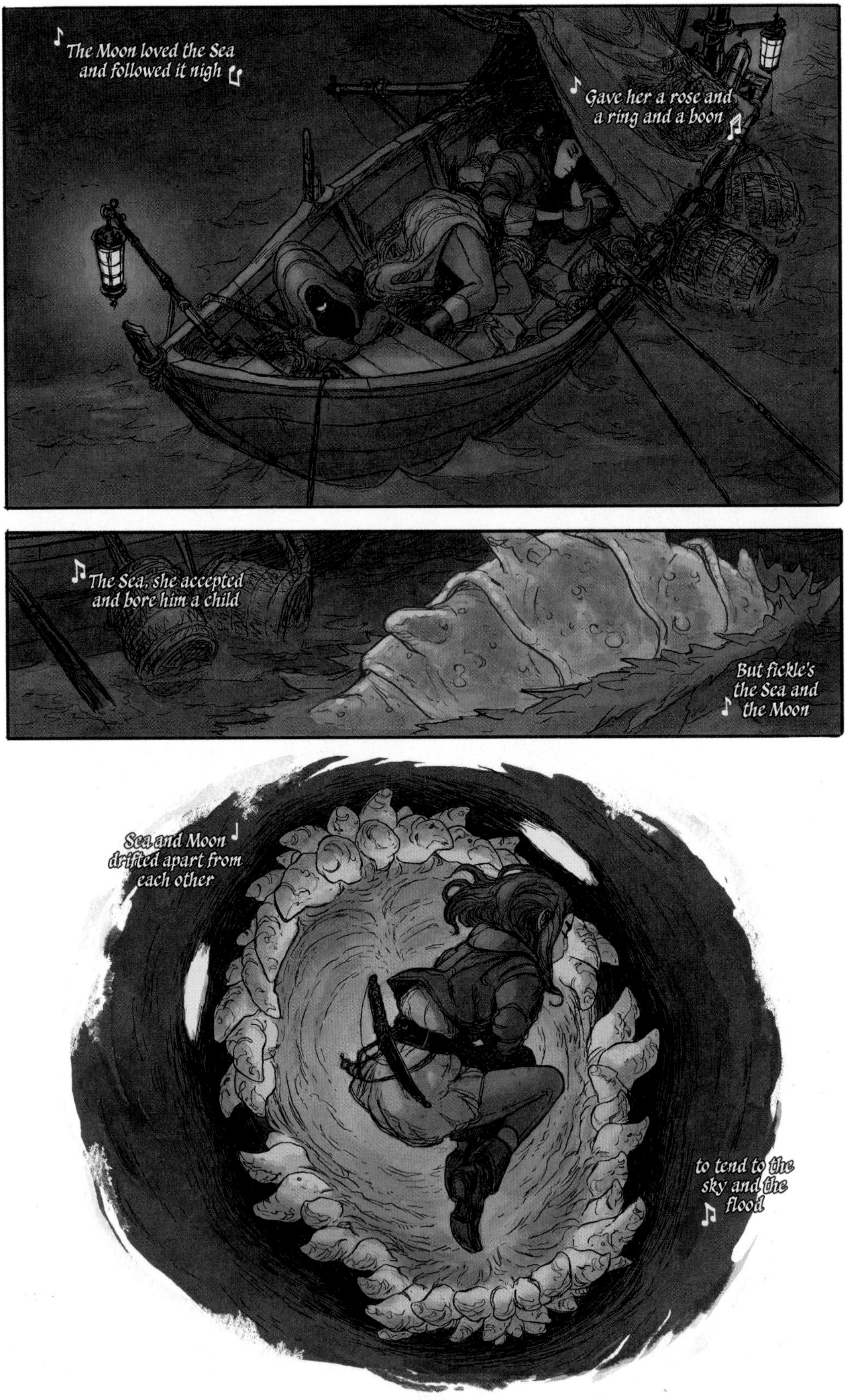
The Moon loved the Sea
and followed it nigh
Gave her a rose and
a ring and a boon
The Sea, she accepted
and bore him a child
But fickle's
the Sea and
the Moon
Sea and Moon
drifted apart from
each other
to tend to the
sky and the
flood

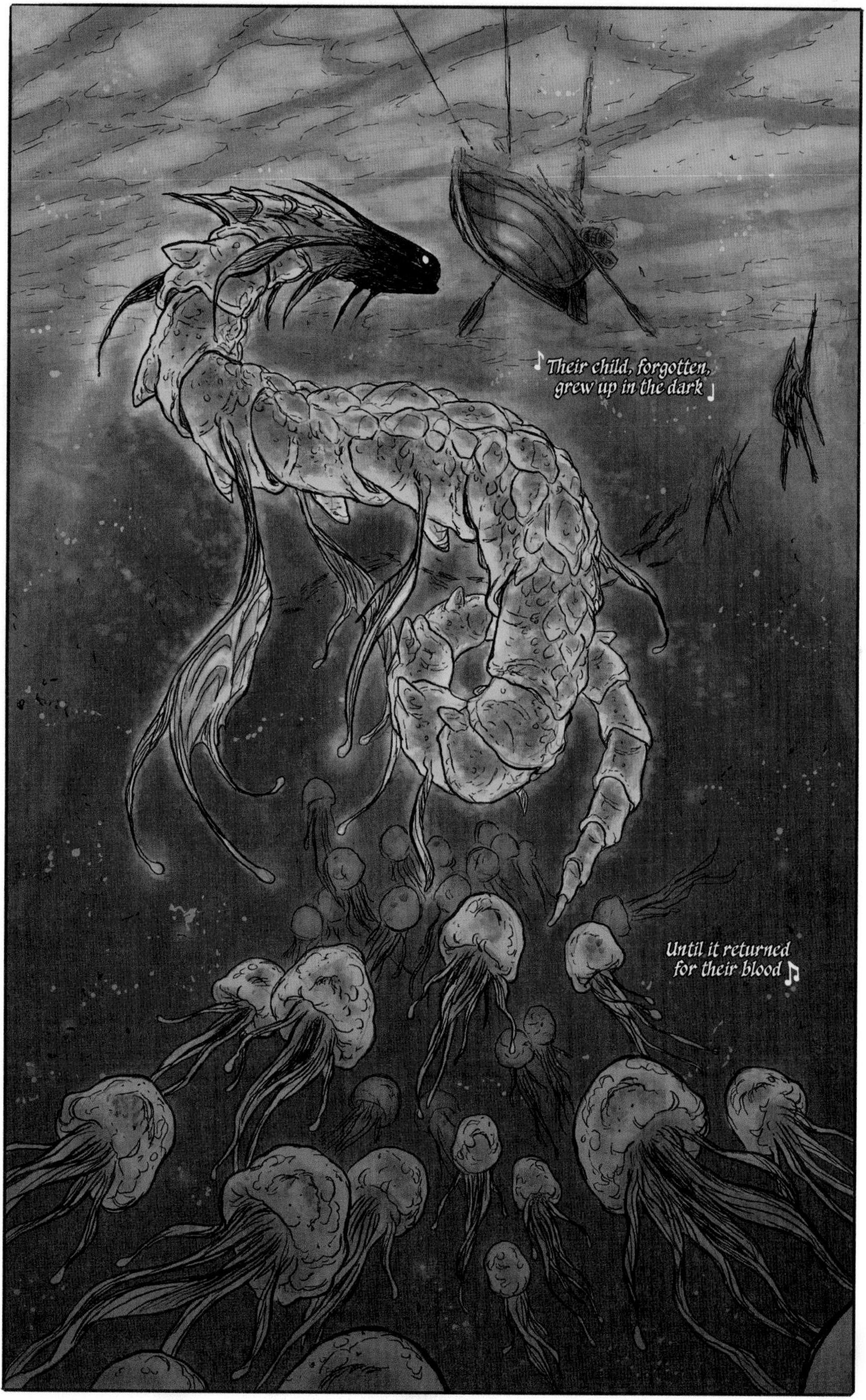
♪ Their child, forgotten, grew up in the dark ♩
Until it returned for their blood ♫

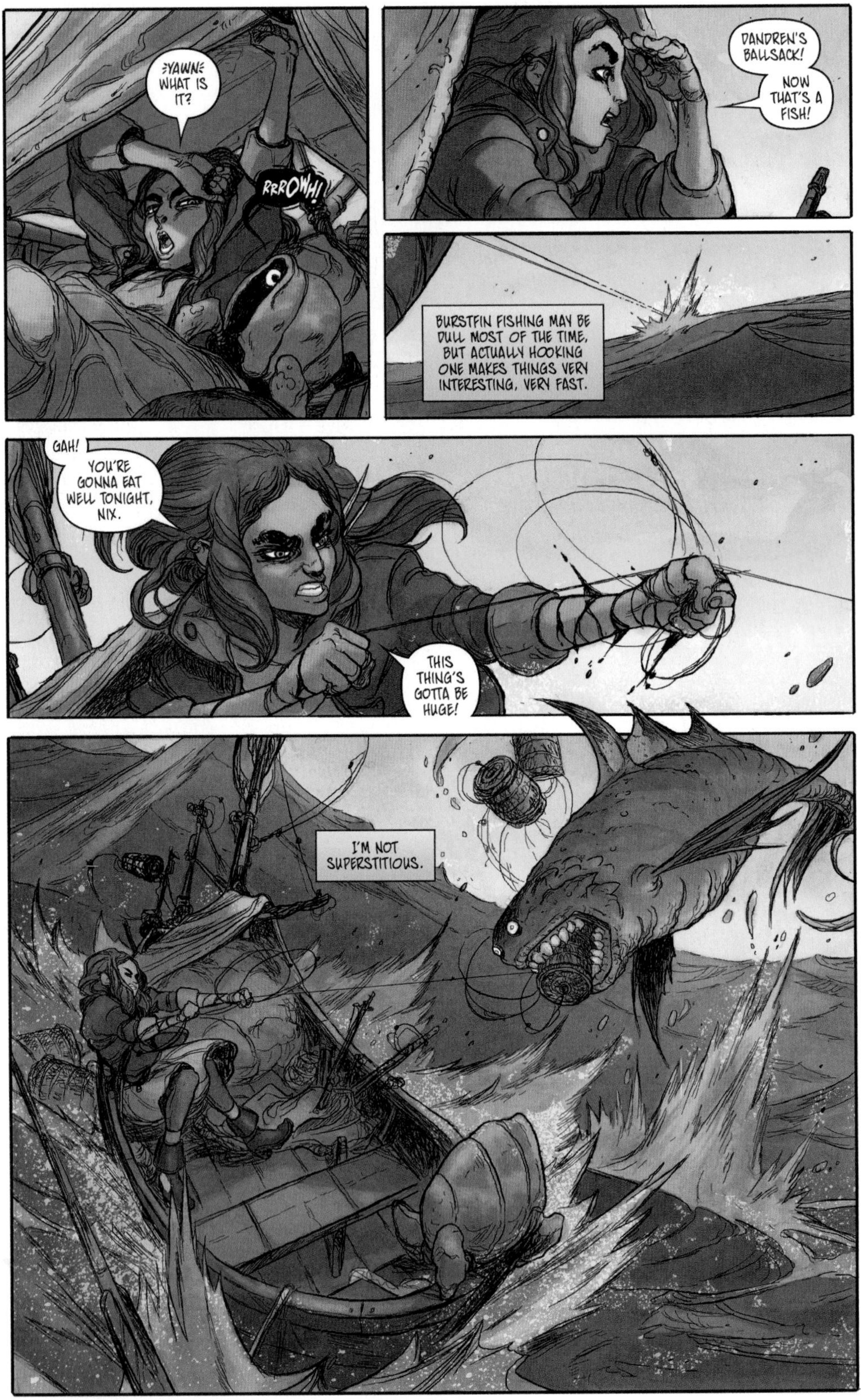

=YAWN= WHAT IS IT?
RRROWH!
DANDREN'S BALLSACK!
NOW THAT'S A FISH!
BURSTFIN FISHING MAY BE DULL MOST OF THE TIME, BUT ACTUALLY HOOKING ONE MAKES THINGS VERY INTERESTING, VERY FAST.
GAH!
YOU'RE GONNA EAT WELL TONIGHT, NIX.
THIS THING'S GOTTA BE HUGE!
I'M NOT SUPERSTITIOUS.

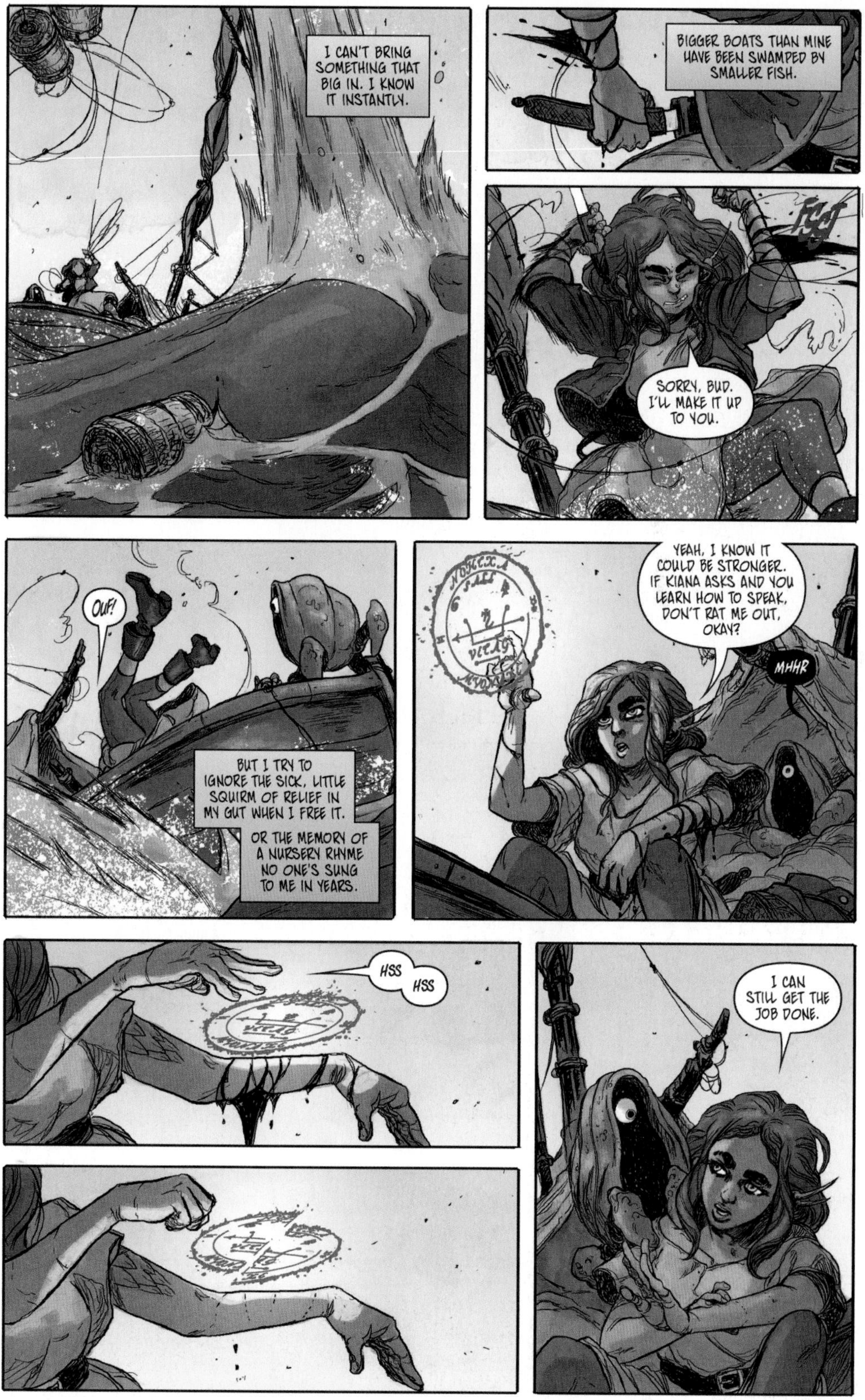
I CAN'T BRING SOMETHING THAT BIG IN. I KNOW IT INSTANTLY.
BIGGER BOATS THAN MINE HAVE BEEN SWAMPED BY SMALLER FISH.
SORRY, BUD. I'LL MAKE IT UP TO YOU.
OUF!
BUT I TRY TO IGNORE THE SICK, LITTLE SQUIRM OF RELIEF IN MY GUT WHEN I FREE IT.
OR THE MEMORY OF A NURSERY RHYME NO ONE'S SUNG TO ME IN YEARS.
YEAH, I KNOW IT COULD BE STRONGER. IF KIANA ASKS AND YOU LEARN HOW TO SPEAK, DON'T RAT ME OUT, OKAY?
MHHR
HSS
HSS
I CAN STILL GET THE JOB DONE.

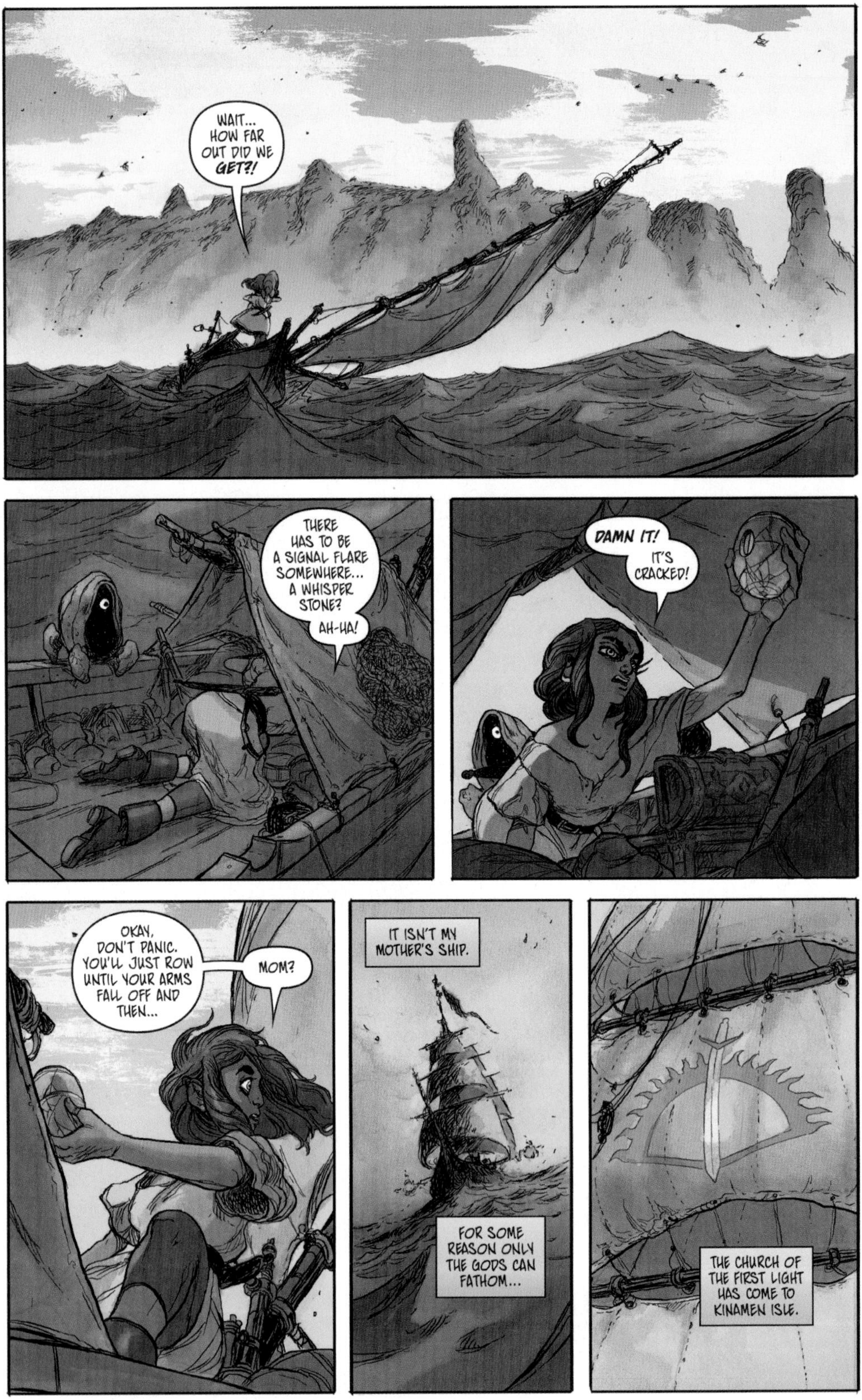
WAIT... HOW FAR OUT DID WE GET?!
THERE HAS TO BE A SIGNAL FLARE SOMEWHERE... A WHISPER STONE?
AH-HA!
DAMN IT!
IT'S CRACKED!
OKAY, DON'T PANIC. YOU'LL JUST ROW UNTIL YOUR ARMS FALL OFF AND THEN...
MOM?
IT ISN'T MY MOTHER'S SHIP.
FOR SOME REASON ONLY THE GODS CAN FATHOM...
THE CHURCH OF THE FIRST LIGHT HAS COME TO KINAMEN ISLE.

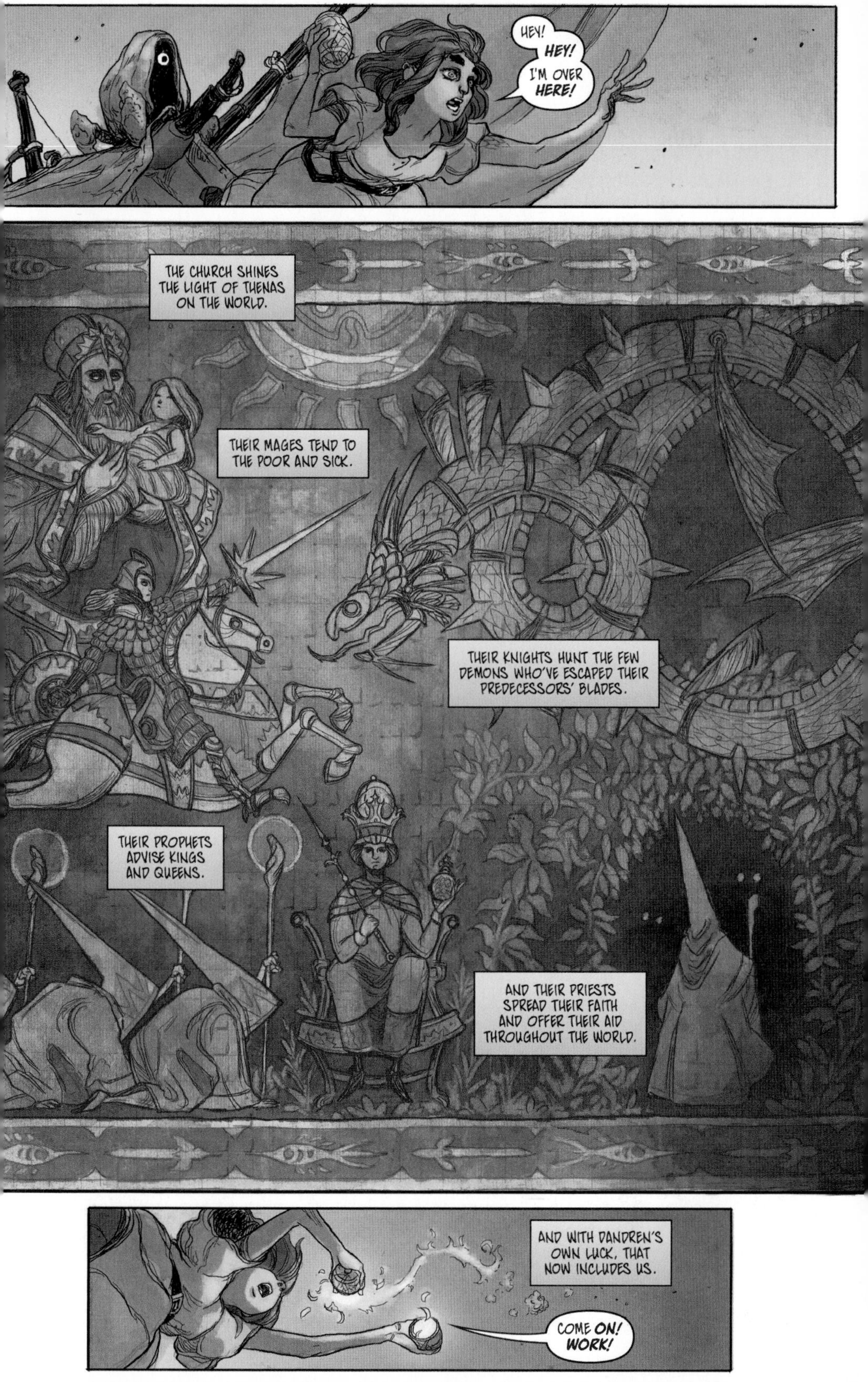
HEY!
HEY!
I'M OVER HERE!
THE CHURCH SHINES THE LIGHT OF THENAS ON THE WORLD.
THEIR MAGES TEND TO THE POOR AND SICK.
THEIR KNIGHTS HUNT THE FEW DEMONS WHO'VE ESCAPED THEIR PREDECESSORS' BLADES.
THEIR PROPHETS ADVISE KINGS AND QUEENS.
AND THEIR PRIESTS SPREAD THEIR FAITH AND OFFER THEIR AID THROUGHOUT THE WORLD.
AND WITH DANDREN'S OWN LUCK, THAT NOW INCLUDES US.
COME ON! WORK!

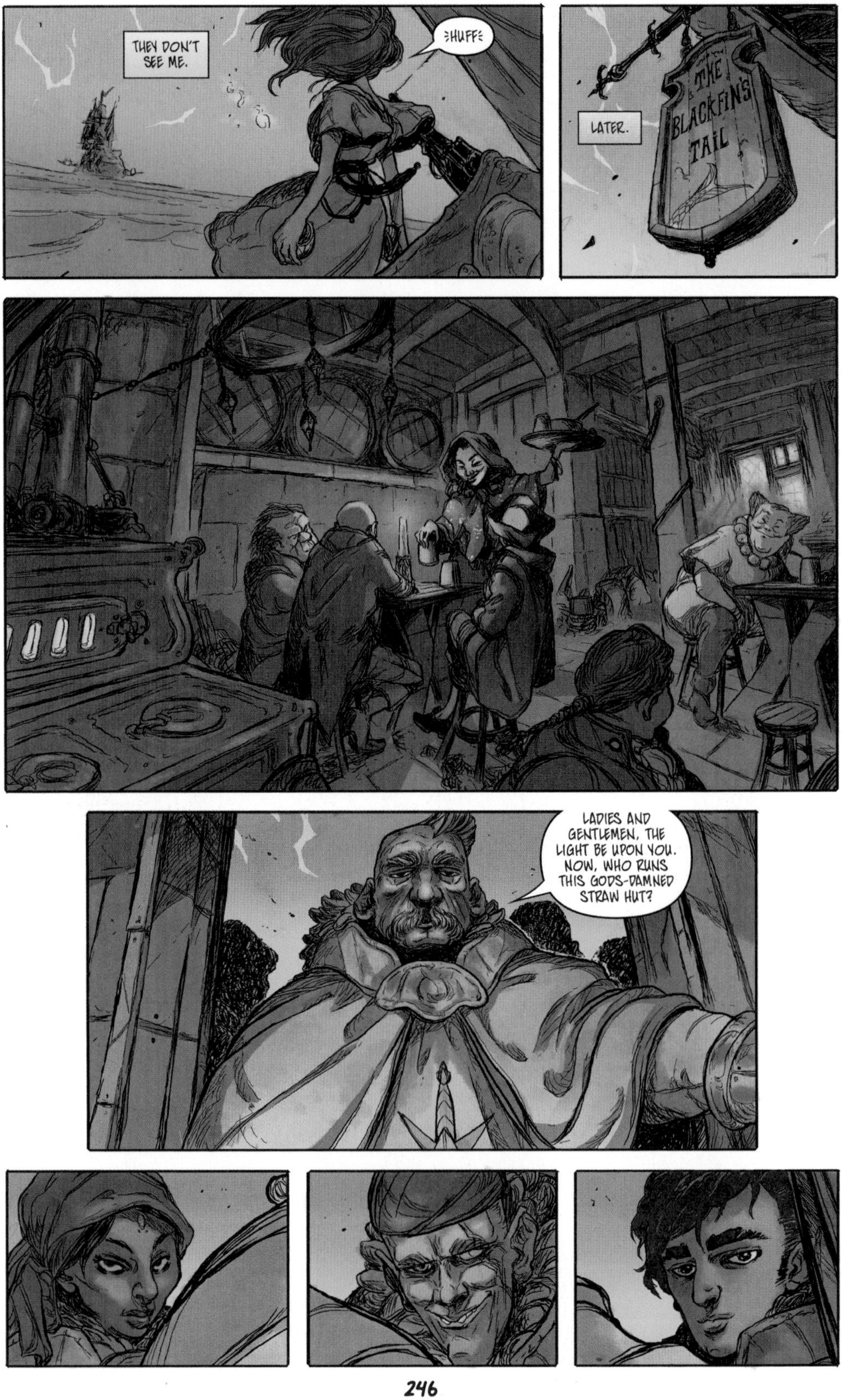
THEY DON'T SEE ME.
HUFF
LATER.
THE BLACKFIN'S TAIL
LADIES AND GENTLEMEN, THE LIGHT BE UPON YOU. NOW, WHO RUNS THIS GODS-DAMNED STRAW HUT?

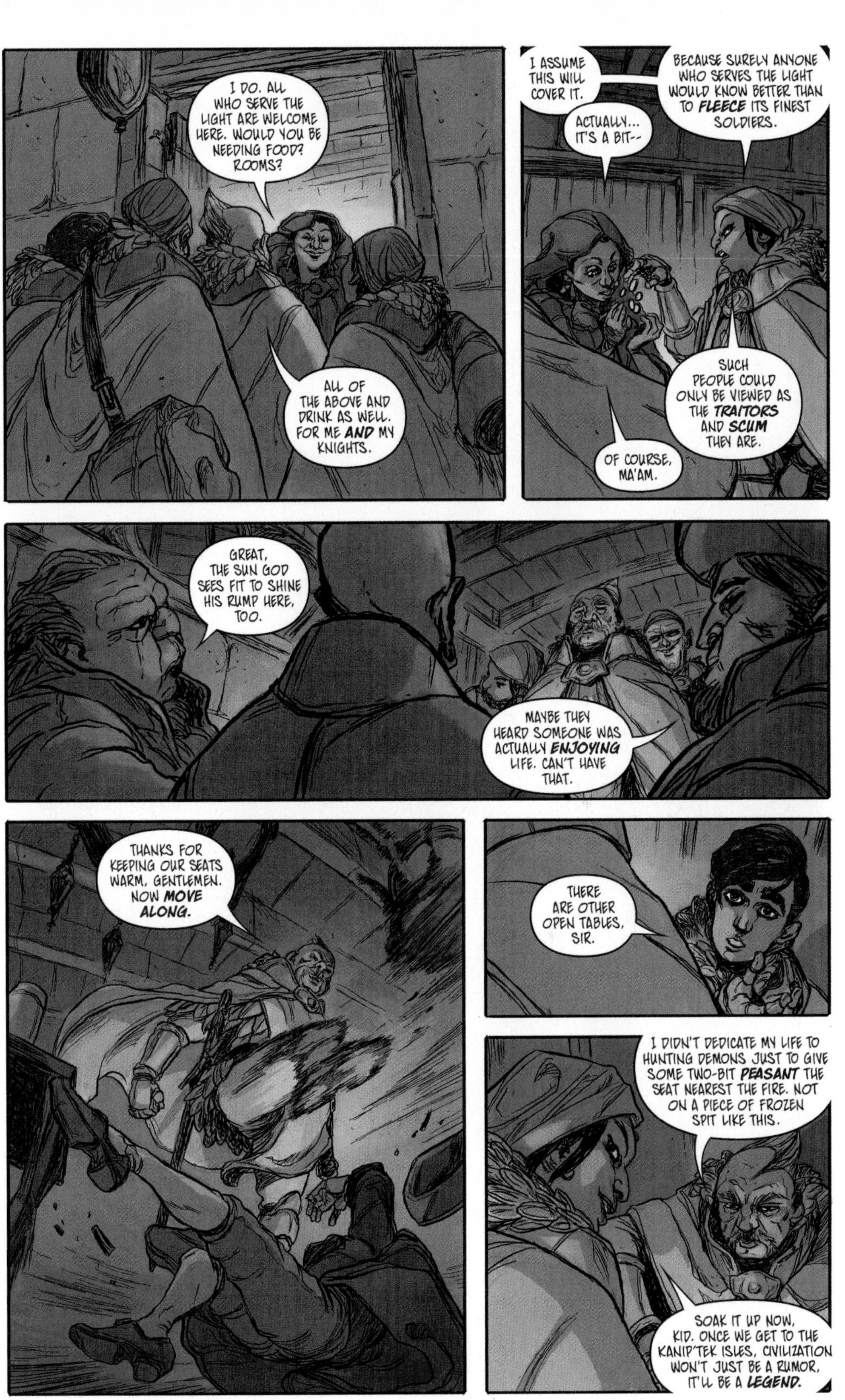
I DO. ALL WHO SERVE THE LIGHT ARE WELCOME HERE. WOULD YOU BE NEEDING FOOD? ROOMS?
ALL OF THE ABOVE AND DRINK AS WELL. FOR ME AND MY KNIGHTS.
I ASSUME THIS WILL COVER IT.
ACTUALLY... IT'S A BIT--
BECAUSE SURELY ANYONE WHO SERVES THE LIGHT WOULD KNOW BETTER THAN TO FLEECE ITS FINEST SOLDIERS.
SUCH PEOPLE COULD ONLY BE VIEWED AS THE TRAITORS AND SCUM THEY ARE.
OF COURSE, MA'AM.
GREAT, THE SUN GOD SEES FIT TO SHINE HIS RUMP HERE, TOO.
MAYBE THEY HEARD SOMEONE WAS ACTUALLY ENJOYING LIFE. CAN'T HAVE THAT.
THANKS FOR KEEPING OUR SEATS WARM, GENTLEMEN. NOW MOVE ALONG.
THERE ARE OTHER OPEN TABLES, SIR.
I DIDN'T DEDICATE MY LIFE TO HUNTING DEMONS JUST TO GIVE SOME TWO-BIT PEASANT THE SEAT NEAREST THE FIRE. NOT ON A PIECE OF FROZEN SPIT LIKE THIS.
SOAK IT UP NOW, KID. ONCE WE GET TO THE KANIP'TEK ISLES, CIVILIZATION WON'T JUST BE A RUMOR, IT'LL BE A LEGEND.

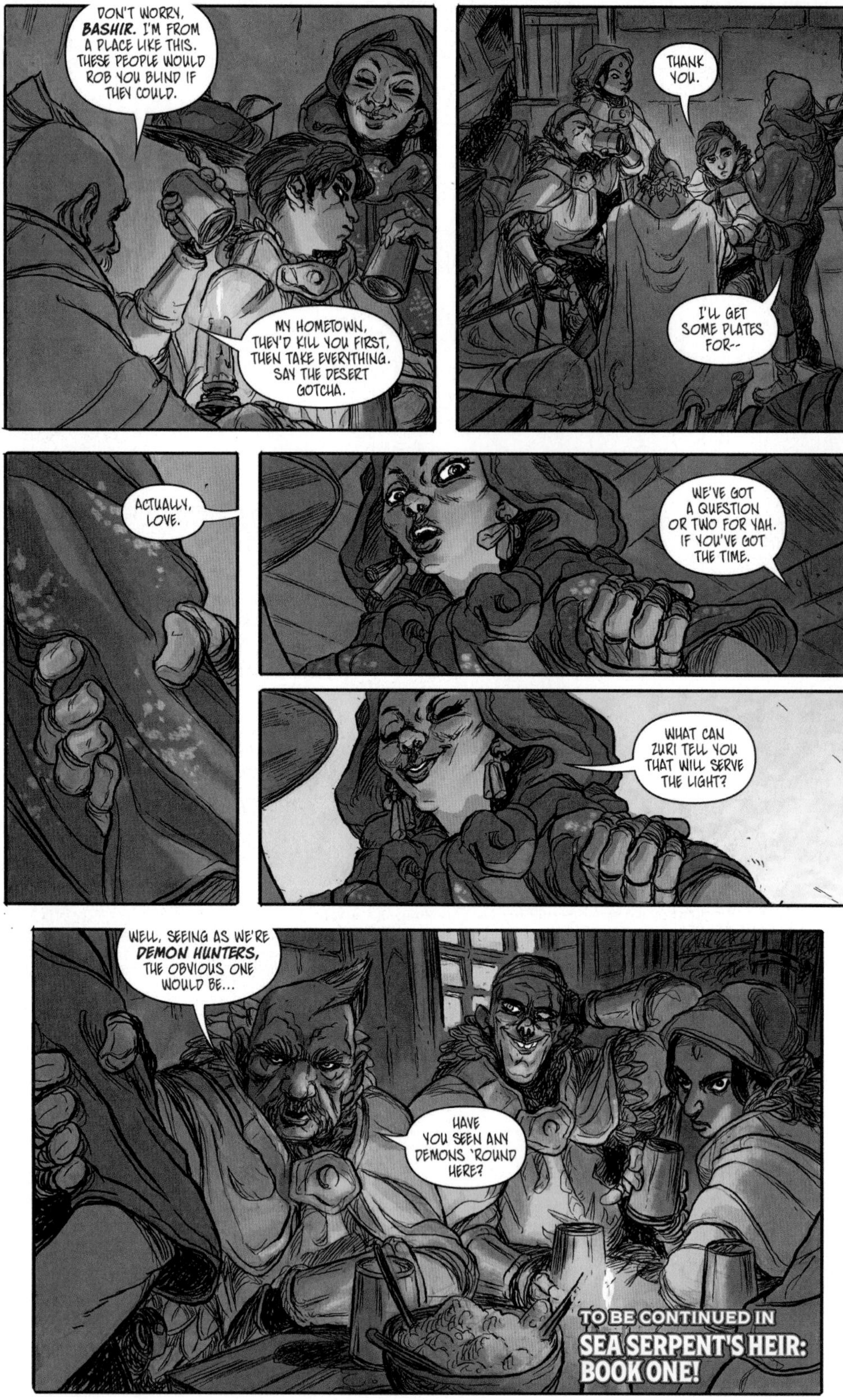
DON'T WORRY, BASHIR. I'M FROM A PLACE LIKE THIS. THESE PEOPLE WOULD ROB YOU BLIND IF THEY COULD.
MY HOMETOWN, THEY'D KILL YOU FIRST, THEN TAKE EVERYTHING. SAY THE DESERT GOTCHA.
THANK YOU.
I'LL GET SOME PLATES FOR--
ACTUALLY, LOVE.
WE'VE GOT A QUESTION OR TWO FOR YAH. IF YOU'VE GOT THE TIME.
WHAT CAN ZURI TELL YOU THAT WILL SERVE THE LIGHT?
WELL, SEEING AS WE'RE DEMON HUNTERS, THE OBVIOUS ONE WOULD BE...
HAVE YOU SEEN ANY DEMONS 'ROUND HERE?
TO BE CONTINUED IN
SEA SERPENT'S HEIR: BOOK ONE!

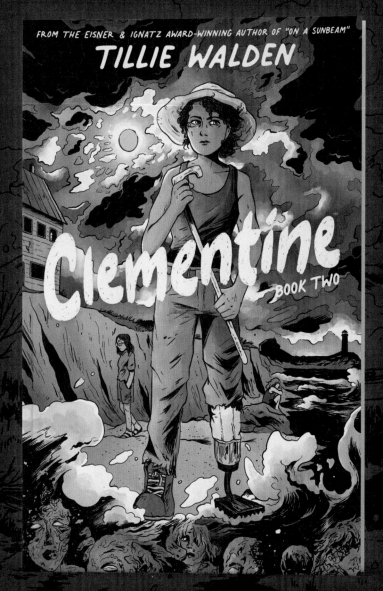

EXPLORE NEW WORLDS

For Young Adult & Middle Grade Readers in SKYBOUND COMET

**Activate your heart.
Be an Everyday Hero!**

IRMA KNIIVILA   TRI VUONG

ON SALE SEPTEMBER 2022!
ISBN: 978-1-5343-2130-4 • $12.99

**What if you were
destined to destroy
the world?**

MAIRGHREAD SCOTT   PABLO TUNICA

ON SALE OCTOBER 2022!
ISBN: 978-1-5343-2129-8 • $14.99

**Tiny heroes,
epic adventures!**

SCURRY
MAC SMITH

ON SALE FEBRUARY 2023!
ISBN: 978-1-5343-2436-7 • $14.99

**Welcome to the smallest
town in the universe.**

SEAN KELLEY
McKEEVER
ALEXANDRE
TEFENGKI

ON SALE APRIL 2023!
ISBN: 978-1-5343-2437-4 • $17.99

**Will you make
the pact?**

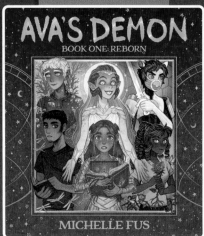

MICHELLE FUS

ON SALE MAY 2023!
ISBN: 978-1-5343-2438-1 • $17.99

SKYBOUND
COMET

Visit **SkyboundComet.com** for more information,
previews, teaching guides and more!

Image